PRAISE FOR W. MICHAEL GEAR
AND *THE ATHENA FACTOR*

"In *The Athena Factor*, Michael Gear has transformed America's obsession with Hollywood beauty into an epic thriller of transcendent terror. I thought the world would come to an end with comet strikes, mushroom clouds, and apocalyptic plagues. I never dreamed we'd overwhelm the earth with J-Lo look-alikes and George Clooney clones."
—Jack Anderson, Pulitzer Prize-winning journalist

"With a Crichton-like mix of scientific intrigue and pulse-pounding suspense, the Gears deliver a fascinating exploration of the frontiers of science."
—*Booklist* on *Raising Abel*

"Gear writes superbly rolling prose with flair, confidence, wit, an ear for sounds, and an eye for details. . . . And he has another gift: the ability to teach his readers as he entertains them."
—*Rocky Mountain News* on *The Morning River*

"Extraordinary . . . Colorfully integrates authentic archaeological and anthropological details with a captivating story replete with romance, intrigue, mayhem, and a nail-biting climax."
—*Library Journal* on *People of the Owl*

"Gripping plot, lots of action, well-developed characters, and a wealth of authentic historical facts."
—*Booklist* on *People of the Masks*

"Simple prose brightened by atmospheric detail sweeps this fluid, suspenseful mix of anthropological research and character-driven mystery to a solid, satisfying resolution."
—*Publishers Weekly* on *People of the Mist*

W9-CLC-486

The
Athena
Factor

W. MICHAEL GEAR

FORGE®

A TOM DOHERTY ASSOCIATES BOOK
NEW YORK

This is a work of fiction. All the characters and events portrayed in this book are either products of the author's imagination or are used fictitiously.

THE ATHENA FACTOR

Copyright © 2005 by W. Michael Gear

A Forge Book
Published by Tom Doherty Associates, LLC
175 Fifth Avenue
New York, NY 10010

www.tor.com

Forge® is a registered trademark of Tom Doherty Associates, LLC.

ISBN 0-765-35023-8
EAN 978-0-765-35023-7

First edition: July 2005
First mass market edition: July 2006

Printed in the United States of America

0 9 8 7 6 5 4 3 2 1

To
Jim and "Tuck" Mills
in hopes that
the joy of the hunt
forever fills your hearts.

ACKNOWLEDGMENTS

The Athena Factor was written with the help and encouragement of John Meyer, Jr., vice president of sales and the international training division at Heckler & Koch in Sterling, Virginia. John graciously allowed us to participate in the elite HK Executive Protection course. Additional appreciation is extended to Patsy Drew-Rios, Forrest "Skip" Carroll, Bob Schneider, Tom Taylor, and the 9-02 Executive Training class; thank you all for indulging an amateur among professionals. If *The Athena Factor* succeeds, it is due to your intense and comprehensive training.

A novel isn't created in a vacuum. Half of this work is Kathleen O'Neal Gear's. Bob Gleason added his input while Eric Raab shepherded the novel to completion. To our copy editor, Deanna Hoak, go the highest praises and appreciation. Deanna catches my goofs. Finally, thanks to Linda Quinton, Elena Stokes, Kathleen Fogarty, Brian Heller, and David Moench for their dedication to the story.

The
Athena
Factor

PROLOGUE

That morning, Gregor McEwan was faced with two of his greatest hatreds: He hated to rush. He hated hangovers even more. A bottle of orange juice, followed by a breakfast of rashers, toast and jam, and cheddar-laced eggs had taken neither the edge off his quaking nerves nor the quiver out of his rebellious stomach. They had, however, dulled the sour taste of undigested red ale that still cloyed the back of his tongue.

Nothing would cut the headache but time.

The clock showed half seven, and given the thick fog hanging beyond the window, his normal forty-five-minute commute to the lab would be doubled.

Gregor stopped in the hallway, where he donned his wool coat and looked at the plaque hung there for all to see.

TO GREGOR A. McEWAN
OUR BRIGHTEST STAR
FOR OUTSTANDING LEADERSHIP
Q-GEN LABORATORIES

Beside it was a framed glossy photo showing Gregor wearing a tweed jacket, narrow dark blue tie, and pressed trousers. For once his sandy hair had been combed, and the blaze of superiority in his dark brown eyes had been fairly won. Gregor liked his face—smooth-shaven, with a handsome combination of angles over a strong chin. At the podium beside him stood Q-Gen's president, Calvin Fowler. Fowler was handing Gregor a check along with the plaque. They were smiling at the camera, plaque in one hand, the check in the other. Gregor thought they looked like the sort of self-congratulatory politicians who concocted flawed Middle Eastern peace accords.

Gregor, a Ph.D. two years out of Cambridge, had just turned twenty-nine, and already he had become the most successful team leader at Q-Gen.

Not that he wasn't without faults. He had serious failings when it came to both women and full-bodied ales. As had been the case last night when Beatrice stood him up at the Chop and Ale. Spurned by one, he had overindulged in the other.

Which was why he was miserable, hungover, and late to work. Not that it actually mattered in the grand scheme of things. He had no peers at Q-Gen when it came to coaxing zygotes to begin that initial stage of division that led to a viable embryo. He rarely put in less than a sixty-hour week. So even if he was a wee bit late on occasion, nothing would be said by his superiors.

Gregor didn't mind that his colleagues called him a prick. Given his recent successes in nuclear DNA extraction while maintaining cytoplasmic integrity, he could find work in any laboratory in the world. At that very moment he and his team were drafting a seminal paper for publication in the prestigious journal *Nature* that would revolutionize the biotech world the way Wilmut and Campbell had done with Dolly.

The key was in avoiding cellular disturbance as the large mass of nuclear DNA was extracted and replaced. The more the organelles—the working structures inside the cell—were disturbed, the less likely the chance for success.

Dolly, it turned out, had been a miracle. Given the techniques of the time, her creation had been the equivalent of brain surgery accomplished with a stone ax. Gregor and his Q-Gen team were taking the manipulation of reproductive science in totally new directions.

Assuming his head didn't split from the damned hangover and kill him first.

"The price of greatness," he told his reflection. Then winked at himself, just for good luck. He reached down for his briefcase where it sat by his rubber boots and plucked his wool cap from its peg before opening the door.

The morning smelled cool and damp. Thick gray fog softened the lines of his hedgerow and the trellised gate that let out onto the road. He turned right, following the stepping stones embedded in his uncut grass to his old green Jaguar. Skid marks in the gravel marked where the car had slewed to a stop mere inches from a cock-up.

Gregor winced, glancing suspiciously at the body. Water beaded and trickled in round droplets from the waxed surface, but no dents or scrapes marred the sleek metal.

It appeared he hadn't hit anything on the way home. Thank God for that! He'd been lucky again.

"Have to stop that shit," he muttered as he walked up to the driver's door and fished his keys from his pocket. He lifted the lever, surprised to find it locked.

He never locked the car here, so far out in the country. Using his fingers he slicked the dampness from the glass to see the lock was down. He squinted at his key fob. Pressing the right button, the locks clicked up.

"Bloody hell." He squinted against the pain in his head and a sudden queasiness that tightened around his breakfast and made his mouth water. He pressed his eyes closed, willing the sickness away.

When he finally opened them, two men had stepped up to take positions on either side of him. It was as if they had just popped out of the fog.

He jumped, startled, whirling about and stammering, "Who're you? Damn! Gave me a start, you did."

"Dr. McEwan," the man to his right said with an accented voice. "We are sorry to bother you."

Gregor peered past the lowered brim of the man's dew-silvered wool cap, seeing intense black eyes and a thin hooked nose above a severe mouth. He looked Arab or Persian. His right hand was balled in the coat's large pocket.

The companion had a thickset body with powerful shoulders and a similar, if broader, face atop a hard jaw. They both wore long waxed-cloth jackets over denim pants. Heavy hiking boots, dark with dew, impressed patterns into the gravel. "Right, right." Gregor recovered, one hand to his heart. "Look, I'm running bloody late. Whatever it is, can it wait until later? My number's in the book. Ring me up or leave a message on the machine."

"We hate to bother," the first man said, stepping close. His hand slipped free of the pocket. Gregor blinked, his mind stumbling over the reality of the sleek black pistol pointed at his navel.

"Shit!" Was that a real gun? "Look, I don't know what this is about, but if I did something last night, I bloody well apologize. I'll make it square, whatever it was. Honest, you don't have to go to extremes, right?"

"You will come with us." The second man's voice had a harsh raspy quality.

"It is not what you have done," the first rejoined. "It is what you *will* do. Hold still. This will hurt only a little."

From the corner of his eye, he caught the second man's quick movement. Arms, strong as steel bands, tightened around him. His briefcase gave a hollow thunk as it fell to the gravel.

"I . . ." Gregor never finished. The first man stepped close, the pistol jamming into Gregor's stomach. For an instant their eyes held—remorseless inevitability behind the Arab's. The man's other hand rose. Gregor caught a glimpse of the needle: a filament on the syringe. Then a sharp sting was followed by a cool rush into the side of his neck.

Gregor opened his mouth to scream, but the pistol speared hard under his solar plexus.

Dear God! What's happening to me? This couldn't be happening! Not to him! He was a scientist, for God's sake! It wasn't possible. It just wasn't. . . .

His last memory was of those hard black eyes dropping away into eternity.

WOODLAND, CALIFORNIA

The black minute hand pointed at the ten, and the thick hour hand had crept way past the eleven. Nancy Hartlee arched her back as she studied the clock. The lab was cluttered with tubes and tube racks, rows of micropipettes, several microscopes, different sizes of centrifuges and electrophoresis gel trays with wires running to the power supplies, two transilluminators, a PCR machine, and a big hood next to the autoclave. It all looked stark under the white fluorescent light.

Nancy had passed her twenty-seventh birthday two days ago and had missed the celebration. Something about being unable to fit it into her twenty-hour days. When at work she kept her shoulder-length brown hair pulled back in a ponytail. Green eyes and a delicate nose didn't quite balance the strong jaw and sharp cheeks. She wasn't homely, just different. Oddly, men thought her attractive, mostly because of the poise and the natural grace with which she carried herself. Swimming had been her passion during her high school years; she had the state championship medals on her wall to prove it.

She'd been in the lab for sixteen intense hours. No wonder her whole body ached, and she couldn't think straight. Stretching didn't seem to help the cramps in her back. Twelve hours ago, she'd seen the clock hands in the same position—but that had been just before she, Mark, and Jim had walked down the hall, out to the parking lot, and bought warm burritos from the canteen van.

"Hey," Nancy called as she returned her attention to the micrographs on the light table. "What's the verdict?"

Jim poked his head around the lab door and replied, "We're there! Mark just placed the last tray in the incubator. As far as we can tell, everything's okay." He grinned. "Cool, huh?"

"Great. Button up and get the hell out of here. If you hurry, you can still make it before midnight." She gave him a meaningful nod. "*Just* before midnight."

She rubbed her tired eyes and walked back to her little cubicle of an office. The light's white glow ate right through her into her brain. She closed her eyes for a moment's respite. When she blinked them open again, the world was maddeningly just the way she'd left it.

She slid into her chair, rolled in front of the computer, and began tapping in her notes. Seventeen of their twenty specimens were positive and ready for implantation. The oocytes had been interrupted at the second meiosis, the point where the maternal chromosomes were duplicated and separated. In that state her team had incised the cellular wall with their latest generation nanoscalpel and carefully removed the nuclear DNA through a process called enucleation.

Nanotechnology was their prize. Nancy had always believed that many of the problems in reliably cloning mammals lay in the manner in which nuclear DNA was removed and reinserted into the host oocyte. Their nanoscalpel sliced through the plasma membrane, the vitelline space, and the zona pellucida instead of punching through them with all the finesse of a blunt-nosed bullet the way the older pipettes did.

Then nuclear DNA from a donor—for ethical reasons Nancy had used her own—had been inserted. The cytoplasm, the liquid soup of cellular function, was comprehensively monitored for minute changes in chemistry. Rumor had it that Q-Gen was way ahead of her team when it came to that. Let them be. She had the nanoscalpel.

Nancy recorded the last of her observations as Mark called, "Good night. See you . . . when?"

"Take tomorrow off. Sleep. Rest. Recharge your batteries."

"Cool! Good night."

She turned back to the screen and frowned. They had been sure that the key to a viable clone lay in the cytoplasm and the orientation of the inserted nuclear DNA. Cellular trauma and disruption to the organelles, especially the endoplasmic reticulum, had to be minimized; the nuclear DNA had to be placed in just the right position to ensure the embryo's correct development.

Finishing her notes, she smiled up at the picture over her desk. There, a bright-eyed baby chimp lay cuddled in its mother's arms. Her first triumph.

Nancy saved her work, backed it up, and put the computer into sleep mode before she found her purse and walked to the door. Flipping off the lights, she locked up, set the security system, and yawned as she tottered down the hall. The fifteen-minute drive to her apartment was going to feel interminable.

Nevertheless, as she stepped out into the cool California night, she experienced a sense of exhilaration. If they had seventeen of twenty viable embryos, they had beaten the odds. She was already composing the article for *Science* in her head.

Three vehicles were left in the lot. The security guy's Ford pickup was off in the corner, and an unfamiliar Excursion gleamed in the spot beside her battered Toyota. Had someone gotten a new SUV? And such a monster, at that?

Her tired mind dismissed it as she walked between the vehicles and bent to insert her key into the lock.

The soft click of a door behind her was the only warning. It came much too late.

ECHUNGA FARMS, NEAR ADELAIDE, SOUTH AUSTRALIA

Brian Everly kicked manure from his rubber overshoes and climbed the cement steps to the farm office. Echunga Farms Ltd. had a large complex of paddocks and hay barns with a tool shed and mechanical building for the storage of tractors and loaders.

Brian's four-door Holden sedan was parked on the other side of the fence next to a hay wagon. He could see heat waves on the bonnet as the faded brown paint baked in the hot sun.

He opened the office door, slipped off his overshoes, and stepped inside.

Clairice Higgins sat at the desk. She looked up and arched an inquisitive eyebrow. She was in her forties, gray-haired, with a round face used to smiling. Too many years in the Aussie sun had faded her blue eyes and taken its toll on her wrinkling skin.

Brian smiled. "All three of the lambs are doing well. No signs of any abnormality at all. The vet just left with blood and urine specimens to run at university, but I think they're doing brilliantly."

"And the celebrities?" she asked.

Brian turned slightly so he could look out the window at the "wolf" building. This wasn't a real wolf, but the once-extinct marsupial wolf, *Thylacinus cynocephalus,* a predator native to Australia before the arrival of the Europeans. Brian liked to say "once-extinct" because now two immature females were exploring the hay out in the wolf building. The third, a little male, had just begun peeking out of Bertha's pouch. Bertha was a matronly, if somewhat foul-tempered, giant red kangaroo. Her uteri had been host to "Beth" the first wolf, and then "Gina" and "Max" in sequence.

Clairice didn't jest when she called them celebrities. ABC, BBC, and a slew of American, French, and Japanese media had paraded through the farm when Beth was first born.

Echunga Farms had been host to the first successful resurrection of an extinct species. Brian, working in a postdoctoral position, had succeeded where so many had failed. Not just once, but with three different embryos created from three different museum-derived donor specimens. He was waiting for the patent to be registered before he authored his first refereed paper on the methodology.

"Max is a terror," Brian replied. "I'm afraid if he bites Bertha one more time, she's going to boot him right through the wall."

"So the vet says they're healthy?" Clairice lifted an eyebrow. "I've got to phone in to the ABC in Melbourne, you know. They want weekly reports. A bit of Aussie pride, right? We *were* the first."

Brian sobered. "I wish they wouldn't be so bloody sure of themselves. It is a first. I keep reminding people of that. They have forgotten that we only got three successes out of four hundred and six attempts. So much can still go wrong. It's like being in the red center, right? We don't know where we're at, or if there's even water at the end of the road. It's damned easy to get lost when you're a trailblazer."

Clairice reached for her glasses, rubbed them on her blue cotton skirt, and slipped them on. "All I need to say is that they are still alive and healthy. One day at a time."

"Right. I'm out of here. I have a meeting this afternoon at the agricultural station. Martin wants to go over some figures, and then it's off to the solicitor."

"Price of success. Drive carefully," Clairice added as she returned her attention to the papers on her desk.

Brian walked through the office and out the front door. He followed the cement walk to his Holden and slipped into the driver's seat. The vinyl on the dash was cracked, the steering wheel warm under his hands. The car smelled old and dusty in the hot air.

The engine ground, squealed, and roared to life when Brian turned the key. He grasped the shift lever with his left hand, slipping it into reverse. Once he backed around the hay wagon he followed the road out. At the security gate, the guard waved while the chain-link gate rumbled open.

Brian turned onto the blacktop and ran through the gears. Someday soon, when the paperwork was done and his process licensed, he'd have enough for a nice car. Maybe a Lexus or top-line Toyota.

Winding along the banks of Echunga Creek, he passed manicured farms alternating with virgin patches of eucalyptus trees. He slowed, downshifting as he approached the intersection. A man was standing beside the stop sign where the road T'd at Mt. Bold Reservoir. To Brian's surprise, he waved, and stepped over as the Holden's squeaking brakes brought the vehicle to a stop.

"Dr. Everly?" He leaned down, smiling into the window. He wore a brown Akubra hat, a light canvas jacket, and a shirt open at the collar. Something about him, the dark thin features, sent the briefest of warnings.

"Yes, but I can't chat now. Please, call my office and they will be most happy to . . ." The thin black pistol was centered between Brian's eyes.

"Do not move, Dr. Everly," the man's accented voice cooed. "Do not try to drive off. It will only get you killed."

Stunned, wordless, Brian was barely aware of the second man who walked up on the car's off side. It took all of his will to glance away from the gun when the door clicked open. A big man, also Arab-looking, had settled into the passenger seat to his left.

"You will follow my friend's instructions, Doctor, and you will not be hurt." The gunman smiled as he opened the rear door and slipped into the seat. "On the contrary, we want you to be very, very healthy."

1

The carpeted hallway was empty. Lymon Bridges double-checked to make sure as he stepped out of Sheela Marks' plush penthouse suite. He glanced up and down from long habit, checking for potential threats, and found none.

He turned, nodded to Dot McGuire—Sheela's publicist—and waited while she and Sheela stepped outside. Sheela Marks clutched her fake gold-plated plastic Oscar statue in her manicured hands. She was holding it upside down like a misshapen kitchen knife. Dot, in her midforties, walked behind in a tweed jacket and gray skirt.

Sheela was resplendent. Dot had dressed her in a sheer silvery sheath by Dolce and Gabbana that glistened with each step. It also accented the sensual curves of her hip and bust. She wore white michelle K stilettos that gave her another five inches—as if she needed them—and a white furry Dior boa wrapped around her shoulders. Her hair was immaculate, piled up on top with long reddish blond locks falling down her back. The entire image was to remind people of her best actress Oscar last month for *Blood Rage*.

A quick glance behind assured him that both Dot and Sheela were following as he led the way to the service elevator. Lymon liked the St. Regis. They were used to the needs of security and capable of lodging prominent people with their demanding requirements. Lymon lifted his left cuff, saying, "We're on the way to the elevator."

"Roger," Paul's voice assured in his earpiece. *"We're go. Limo's at the Door Three curb."*

Sheela asked Dot, "God, are we still on for that thing in Atlanta? I mean, we're two weeks into the promotion, the box office is down fifteen million from last week. What does the studio expect? That CNN can bring us back up? The buzz is on Tobey Maguire and his robot revenge flick now."

"Just do it," Dot chided. "You know the game. So does the studio, and so, too, does CNN. No sense in pissing them off with a no-show. Face time never hurts. Not for this box office, and not for the next. It's just one more day."

"And another hotel, and another airplane, and another room-service meal." Her beautiful face pained. "No, I'll be honest. Here's what I really hate: It's the same damn questions that I've been answering for the last three weeks." Her voice dropped to a journalist's slightly superior lilt. "'What's it like to work with Kevin Spacey?' 'Have you been seeing anyone since you broke up with de Giulio?' 'What is your next project?' 'What's *Jagged Cat* about?' 'Who stars?' Over and over and over again. Dot, can't we just send them the clips?"

Lymon's lips twitched at the note of frustration. Hey, it was the modern reality. Back in the good old days actors didn't have to globe-trot to build hype for a picture. Firms like his could consist of one to four guys and cover everything. Now people in his business had to be like a mini secret service, employing enough coverage to ensure a client's protection around the globe.

The elevator dinged, and Lymon positioned himself. As the doors opened, he blocked Sheela's body with his own until satisfied that the cage was empty. He held the door as they entered and placed himself to repulse anyone who might try to slip in at the last instant. Only then did he press the button for the first floor.

"Zemeckis is throwing a party Friday night," Sheela reminded. "It would be good exposure for us. Universal and DreamWorks are going to be there."

"Rex knows that." Dot frowned. "Look, we can do both. I'll talk to the producer at CNN, see if they can tape early. That means we fly in, shuttle to CNN Plaza, shoot the piece, and have you on the plane back to LA. Weather, CNN personnel, and the FAA permitting, you're at Zemeckis' by seven. Eight at the latest." She turned to Lymon. "Can you do that? Find us a jet back to LA on such short notice?"

"No problem," Lymon answered, mentally noting that he'd be on the phone to the Am-Ex Centurion travel service while Sheela was on camera.

The elevator slowed, settled, and stopped. Lymon was ready when the door opened and stepped out in a blocking stance. The hall was clear. He gave the briefest of nods and stepped in slightly behind Sheela's left shoulder as she started toward the door. The hallway wasn't long, no more than forty feet to the fire exit. He nodded at the security camera over the door. Hotel security had been notified of their route and supposedly were watching.

Past that last metal door, he had fifteen feet to the curb, and Paul would have the limo door unlocked for him to open.

"We're in the hallway," Lymon said into the sleeve mike.

"Roger," Paul returned. *"Sidewalk's clear. No visible threats."*

Routine.

The word had no more than formed in Lymon's head when a door opened to the right. A man stepped out.

Instinct led Lymon to take a half-step forward. In that brief moment he took the guy's measure: medium height, dark complexion, Middle Eastern or maybe Mexican, muscular and clean-shaven. The guy was dressed in the hotel's bell stand uniform. He was holding something in each hand that Lymon couldn't see. The man jerked a short but polite nod, the sort staff were supposed to give guests, and said, "Good day."

Lymon was stepping past him when their eyes met. It was something feral, excited—something that shouldn't have been in a hotel guy's eyes.

Lymon was moving to block him when the guy lunged at Sheela.

Lymon's arm caught the guy's chest, spinning him slightly off balance. He could feel the muscle, the athletic charge in the man's tensed body. One of the assailant's arms flashed up, the elbow catching Lymon on the cheek like a pile driver, batting him hard. The other shot out for Sheela.

It was the briefest glimpse: something glass or clear plastic, capped in blue with a needle tipping it. The attacker's arm had thrust out like a fencer's lancing the device at Sheela.

Lymon would remember the expression on her face, the look of shock in her eyes, as she stumbled backward, away from the assault.

Lymon caught his balance, planted a foot, and ducked under the outstretched arm. He jabbed with his own elbow, striking at the man's ribs. That quickly, the assailant twisted away and his other hand rose, a blocky black thing clutched there. He jabbed it at Lymon's side.

The jolt sent a spasm through Lymon's body; lightning flashed behind his eyes. Convulsing, he bucked backward into Sheela.

Dot was screaming at the top of her lungs. Lymon could hear Sheela's panicked gasp as she struggled under his weight.

The bellhop hesitated, a desperate expression on his face. Lymon caught his breath, willed his body to react, and bulled his way forward on rubbery muscles as Sheela pushed him from behind.

The bellhop dug at a pocket and pulled something—an aluminum can—free. Lymon saw the man's thumb as it popped a ring up. The guy dropped the can before turning to run.

Catch the son of a bitch! It took all of his self-control to hesitate. The gleaming aluminum canister was hissing as it rolled along the carpet. Dot was still screaming something unintelligible. Sheela looked like a spotlighted deer.

Lymon turned, bent, and drove his body into Sheela's, tumbling her backward and bowling Dot off her feet. The fake Oscar statue bounced across the carpet.

"Stay down!" he screamed as he threw himself on top of Sheela's squirming body. "Don't move!"

He stared into her terror-bright eyes, was aware of her open mouth, of her tongue so pink behind perfect white teeth.

Bang! Lightning strobed, blinding in intensity. Lymon's body jerked at the concussion, and something slapped painfully through his skull. He winced, cringed, and tried to press Sheela's body into his own. His ears hurt and rang—the way they did when someone shot a large-caliber handgun in a small room.

He could feel Sheela's body, looked into her famous blue

eyes, and watched her panic. Later, he would remember the pulse throbbing in her neck.

It seemed an eternity before he felt the hand on his shoulder, turned his head, and looked up. Paul was leaning down, his lips moving as if shouting, but only the horrible ringing filled Lymon's ears.

Dear God! What just happened here?

FBI HEADQUARTERS, PENNSYLVANIA AVENUE, WASHINGTON, DC

The clicking of the pen was slowly driving Special Agent Christal Anaya toward lethal violence. She was sitting next to Sid Harness—maybe her last friend in the world—and he kept clicking the damned ballpoint with his thumb. She was in enough trouble—her career balanced on the line. At best, she faced professional humiliation, at worst, outright dismissal. Nevertheless it took every fiber of being and will to keep from reaching out, twisting the pen out of Sid's hand, and driving it into his neck like a stiletto.

The conference room was on the seventh floor, mucky-muck territory where the suits lived. It had taken extraordinary measures to bring Christal here. Measures so extreme that she had drawn the personal attention of the assistant director himself. He sat at the far end of the polished mahogany table, armed with a yellow legal pad, a cup of coffee, and a stack of reports that outlined both the salient and sordid facts that had brought Christal to this room.

To the AD's right sat Special Agent in Charge Peter Wirthing, from the Washington Metro Field Office. To his right was Hank Abrams, agent in charge of the WMFO's RICO team, and the cause of Christal's current dilemma. Not once since she had taken a seat had the filthy *cabrón* even dared to look her in the eyes.

She was seeing an entirely different side of Hank Abrams now. How could a man who had been so on top of things, so in charge, have collapsed into this dripping *menudo*?

"Agent Anaya," Wirthing said, after meeting the AD's cool gray eyes. "We have reviewed every aspect of this current sit-

ation. Until the unfortunate incident in the surveillance van,
e couldn't have asked for more. Your work had been exemp-
ary. Everything was falling into place." He looked down at
e stack of glossy photos on the table in front of him. "After
aving received these, however, I'm afraid that we're going
have to drop our case against Gonzales."

Bill Smart, the federal prosecutor, who sat at the AD's
ft, nodded, looking down the table, past Sid and into
hristal's eyes. "The fact is, the case is blown. After Gonza-
s got his hands on those"—he indicated the photos—"we
aven't got a chance in hell of getting a conviction."

"In short," Wirthing said flatly, "everything we've worked
oward for a year and a half has just flown out the window."
is hard brown eyes met hers. "Bye-bye."

It was the way he said it. She swallowed hard, glancing at
ank. He just sat there, head down, eyes on his hands where
ey were clasped before him on the table. She could see
weat beading on his forehead. He looked like a man await-
ng the gallows. A penitent who had been condemned in
ite of his late-found piety and prayers.

She, however, refused to play that game. She kept her
ead up, glaring angrily. At least on the outside. Inside she
elt like someone had taken a weed eater to her guts. The
ck feeling, like she was going to throw up, just got worse.

"Agent Anaya, if you would excuse us for a moment?" the
ssistant director said. When she didn't move, he nodded ir-
tably toward the door.

Christal tensed, nodded, and said, "Yes. Of course." She
lanced miserably at Hank, but he just sat there, a whipped
uppy, staring at his sweaty hands.

Thankfully, her legs didn't betray her on that walk to the
oor. When she grasped the knob and opened it, she looked
ack. All eyes but Hank's were on her, seeing what? The
oman she was in the photos? Comparing them to her now?

Face rigid, she stepped out into the empty hallway,
rossed her arms, and rubbed her hands up and down the
leeves of her gray wool suit coat. Having nothing else to do,
he studied the faces on the portraits hanging from the walls.
ead white men. All of them. Smiling, gray-haired, looking

old and fat, like cats who had lived out of the can for so lon;
they had forgotten how to hunt.

How did it come to this? She tried to think past the gloor
and disbelief that clouded her mind. The last couple of day
had been one shock after another. It had all begun the firs
time she had seen the photos. *How did they do it? How di*
they get them?

The *why* wasn't an issue. With them, Enrique Gonzale
destroyed any chance the government had of prosecution
No grand jury on earth would indict. The slime was going t
walk. Because of her and Hank, and what they'd done in th
van that night. *Shit!*

She might have been standing there for an eternity—o
was it just seconds before Sid stepped out of the room an
walked over? He stopped beside her, staring at the same por
trait. He was antsy, rocking from his toes to his heels.

"So?" she asked softly.

He cleared his throat. "They think it would be best if yo
simply offered your resignation."

"And Hank?"

"He'll be taken care of."

"What?" she cried, whirling to stare. "Taken care of i
what way?"

Sid looked like he'd just eaten something covered wit
fuzzy gray mold. "Demotion. Transfer to North Dakota o
some such thing."

"Hey! He was *half* of it! That's his white butt sticking u
in those photos! What do they think? That I *raped* him
Huh? That I manipulated him?"

"Hey, Christal," Sid pleaded, "I know how it looks, bu
listen—"

"Listen, hell! These guys are setting themselves up fo
one hell of an EEO—"

"No!" Sid grabbed her hands, cupping them in his own a
he glared down into her hot eyes. "You don't want to pla
that card. Not even if it's only a threat."

"Why not? I get to resign? Hank gets a slap on the hand
Give me one fucking good reason why I don't file a sexua
discrimination suit against those bastards!"

"Because they'll hammer you! What's it been? Three years that you've been with the Bureau? You know how it works. This isn't some supervisor walking up and grabbing your ass! You and Hank literally screwed up an eighteen-month investigation. A major-league scumball is going to walk away from this without having to pay for what he did, or what he's going to keep right on doing. A lot of your fellow agents are going to be *really* pissed about that. Think about the kind of testimony Wirthing can compile. A lot of people are going to look at it as a way of getting back at you, Chris. Even . . . even old friends."

"You, Sid?"

He smiled sadly. "No. Not me. But I'll feel the heat."

She searched his eyes. "You really mean that, don't you?"

He shrugged. "You know, if I wasn't married . . ."

"It didn't stop Hank!"

"Yeah, yeah, well, you've always had really shitty taste in men."

She felt her soul slip down inside her. "They'd really do that? Go out of their way to destroy me?"

"Put yourself in their shoes. You know they would." Sid licked his lips. "And if you push it all the way to a hearing, you know those photos are going to be exhibit one. Center stage. I don't think you want that. Not if the press gets ahold of it." His eyes pleaded with her. "Take the easy way out. Fall on your sword. There's life after death."

"And if I fight for my life?"

"They'll see you in hell."

2

Paul wheeled the limo off the street into Sheela Marks'
drive, and hesitated as the security gates rolled open.
He waved up at the camera, aware that John was recording
their entrance.

"You know," Sheela called from the backseat, "I wonder
if it's worth it anymore."

"Pardon?" Lymon asked, turning in the passenger seat.

"All this." She waved at the gates as they drove through.
"The cameras, the gates and fences, the motion detectors.
God, I feel like I'm living in South Africa."

"It will all settle down into routine again," Lymon told
her. "You've just had a scare. Hell, I'm rattled too." Thank
God the ringing in his ears had finally gone away.

They passed the gardens and manicured lawn and pulled
up in the circular drive before the big house. Rex's Ferrari
and Dot's BMW were already parked off to the side. So was
Felix's Bentley. Apparently the life of a Hollywood lawyer
wasn't anything to sneeze at. Finally, Tony Zell's BMW Z8
was nosed in next to the rosebushes.

"Everyone's here," Sheela noted, voice a bit off. "Wring-
ing their hands over my health."

Lymon said nothing, but shared a glance with Paul when
he stopped the limo in front of the house's arching double
doors. The original owner had imported them from a
fourteenth-century Spanish cathedral. The wood was black
and cracked, hand-hewn out of sections of oak. The things
were so heavy they hung on special hinges, and the door
frame was a giant steel arch overlaid with stone.

Lymon got out and was reaching for the rear door when
Sheela opened it herself and stepped out. She wore one of

Marc Jacobs' white cotton blouses, beige Chloé trousers, and had a light cotton Bottega Veneta coat hung over her shoulders. As she stepped out she clasped a Fendi leather purse and gave Lymon a faint smile. A distance lay behind her eyes. "You ready for this?"

Lymon shrugged. "After you, ma'am."

He glanced back when the big limo purred to life. Paul waved, slipped the car into gear, and accelerated around the circle, headed for the garage out back.

Lymon followed her up the steps to the giant doors. As if on cue, the right-hand side swung open. Tomaso, head of the household staff, called, "Good to have you home, Ms. Marks."

"Thank you, Tomaso. Are they in the meeting room?"

"They are. Can I get you anything?" He tilted his head inquisitively.

"Sparkling water, thank you." She glanced back at Lymon. "Anything?"

"Coffee, if it wouldn't be too much trouble." It wouldn't, of course. It never was.

Lymon padded along behind Sheela on his cushioned shoes, feeling like a lion turned loose in the petting zoo. He barely glanced at the Southwestern artwork hanging on the white stucco walls, or the lacquered bronze sculptures resting in corners and in the hollow beneath the grand staircase. Underfoot, the marble tiles made a faint squishy sound under his rubber soles.

At the end of the hall Sheela made a left, leading him into the meeting room. Fifteen by thirty, the room was paneled in walnut with floor-to-ceiling bookshelves. A sixty-inch TV was built into one wall and attached to a satellite communications center for virtual conferences. A long and splendid maple table dominated the center, while leather-covered chairs with ample stuffing surrounded it. The small wet bar in one corner sported a rack of bottles, a tiny sink, and a built-in refrigerator. Gleaming chandeliers cast soft light on the hard people already seated at the table.

"What the hell happened back there?" Rex demanded before anyone else could speak. He fastened his bulldog eyes on Lymon. Rex Gerber had served as Sheela's manager for the last four years, riding her rising star like a Frontier Days cowboy in a Cheyenne bareback contest. At fifty-eight, he liked to think he was younger than his round belly, balding head, and fleshy nose indicated.

"We were ambushed in the hotel hallway." Lymon spoke professionally, refusing to go for the bait.

"What if he'd had a gun?" the lawyer, Felix Baylor, asked.

Lymon met the man's quick brown eyes. A sharp cookie and noted LA hotshot, Baylor had just turned forty-five. Along with his Bentley, he liked expensive trappings. The guy had a thing about being dressed to the nines; his shoes alone—custom-made Italian from a place on Rodeo Drive—would have paid a year's rent in west LA.

"Well, Felix, he could have killed Sheela, Dot, and me. Fortunately, you'll be happy to know that New York has even stricter gun laws than we do in California, so obviously he had to make do with a needle, a stun gun, and a flash-bang. Right?"

"Shit!" Tony Zell, Sheela's agent, muttered. His fingers were tapping a rhythm on a glass of iced scotch. Tony was blond, tall, blue-eyed, and fit. His thing was flash. He liked gold, be it chains, rings, or watches. When he wasn't doing power lunches, he liked to play tennis or golf. Rumor had it that some kid with dreams of being an actor detailed his Z8 once a day.

"Hey, the guy was in a hotel uniform," Dot shot back. She was sitting at the head of the table and had come dressed casually in a pink skirt, white blouse, and tennis shoes. "I was there. I looked the guy in the face and dismissed him. I still don't know how Lymon acted as fast as he did."

"Are you sure you're okay?" Rex turned to Sheela, rising from his chair.

"I'm fine. Lymon was on the guy," Sheela insisted as she and Lymon took seats.

"What about this needle?" Rex insisted. "Was he trying to inject you with something?"

"We don't know," Lymon said. "Nothing squirted out of it during the scuffle. I just got a glimpse, but it looked as if the plunger was down. I'd say it was empty."

"That's nuts!" Rex cried. "What was he after? Blood drive?"

"Have you given any thought to suing?" Felix asked as he squared his legal pad in front of him.

"Suing?" Lymon asked incredulously.

"It was a hotel uniform." Felix pulled a diamond-studded Montblanc from his pocket; thin white fingers caressed it like a tobaccoholic would a Cuban cigar. "They have responsibilities to their guests, and they obviously tripped all over themselves in Sheela's case. As a result of their negligence, Sheela Marks' life was placed in jeopardy."

"Bullshit!" Lymon shook his head. "So . . . you thinking about suing me, too?"

No humor lay behind Felix's eyes. "Lymon, we don't know what to think of your actions during the last forty-eight hours."

An old and familiar tightening began in Lymon's chest as his gaze burned into the lawyer's.

"Stop it!" Sheela slapped a hand on the table. "It wasn't Lymon's fault! Or the hotel's. We're not suing anybody."

Rex pushed a folded copy of the *Los Angeles Times* across the table. His thick thumb jabbed at a below-the-fold headline. The slug line read:

QUEEN OF SCREEN ASSAULTED:
SHEELA MARKS SHAKEN BUT UNHURT

A picture of her receiving her Oscar got as much space as the story. From what Lymon could glimpse, it was a rehashing of the police report.

"The hotel couldn't have prevented it," Lymon added softly. "This guy was a pro."

"Huh?" Rex and Felix muttered in unison. Tony had straightened, a quizzical look in his dreamy blue eyes.

"He was too good at his job." Lymon shoved the paper

back at Rex. "It wasn't any secret that Sheela was staying at the St. Regis. She had reporters up to the suite for three days before the assault. It didn't take a rocket scientist to figure out her departure time from the hotel. We'd advertised the fact she was doing the *Late Show*, and people know when it tapes. The studio sells tickets, right? Stars generally want to spend as little time as possible in the greenroom. So that gives the guy about a thirty-minute window to intercept Sheela. The hallway is the perfect choke point. I say the guy is a pro because he worked this out without me seeing him. His surveillance and planning were perfect."

"So he did his homework. That doesn't make him professional." Tony crossed his arms.

"The police never found a print. Everything was either wiped down, or smudged. The door he stepped out of was always locked, but when the guy went into that broom closet, he didn't jimmy the lock. He had a key. We watched on the security camera tapes later. He knew his target, knew what he wanted with her, and he damn near got it."

All eyes but Sheela's were on him.

"Why?" Felix asked, irritated.

"We don't know," Sheela said softly. "If he'd wanted to hurt me, he could have. And that grenade, dear God, you have no idea how terrifying that was. I couldn't hear, couldn't think, couldn't see. But for Lymon pushing me down, I hate to think what it would have been like."

Lymon spread his hands. "Paul heard the flash-bang go off at the same time the guy burst out the door. Our attacker ran all of twenty yards, dove into a cab, and was gone. Vanished."

Rex was still giving him the predatory eye. "Sheela is one of the hottest talents in film today, Lymon. She's worth thirty million a picture. Not to mention that she's a nice person. *Our* person. And you let someone get that close to her? What if that had been a real hand grenade?"

"We'd be dead," Lymon replied reasonably. "But he wasn't trying to kill her."

"But he *could* have!" Felix thundered. "For God's sake, man! That's why we pay you!"

"Enough!" Sheela cried, her blue eyes hardening. "I was *there*. I'm satisfied. I've been with Lymon ever since the event. He's done his job."

Rex, as always, was the first to back down. "Yeah, well, we're scared, that's all." He looked at the newspaper. "It could have been a lot worse than just a couple of canceled shows. And there's the upside. The phones have been ringing off the hooks. Everybody under the sun wants an interview. Larry King wants first crack at you. He said he'd bump whomever to get you."

"Screw him!" Dot cried. "Last time, he dumped Sheela for Julia Roberts. Paybacks are a bitch."

Felix continued to study Lymon. "You're sure the syringe was empty?"

Lymon shrugged. "I'm not sure of anything. I'm not even sure it was a syringe. It didn't look quite right. In the police report I told them it was 'syringelike.' When he jammed the stun gun into my ribs and I didn't go down, I think he got spooked. I had on enough layers that he didn't get a good connection on the electrodes. Sheela was behind me, supporting me so that I didn't fall. Then there was Dot—she was screaming her head off. I think the guy figured the attack was blown, so he dropped the flash-bang and ran."

"For God's sake, why?" Felix repeated the question that had been tormenting Lymon for two days.

"Who knows?" Dot looked from one to the next. "Maybe he's sitting in some bar at Lex and Twenty-fifth saying, 'Hey, wow! I just scared the shit out of Sheela Marks, man.'"

Felix cocked his head. "I don't get it."

"Neither do I," Lymon answered with a shrug. "It was just a glimpse, but like I say, the syringe looked empty."

"What does that mean?" Rex narrowed one eye into a threatening squint. "What good is an empty syringe?"

"I don't know." Lymon looked up as Tomaso stepped into the room bearing a tray. He placed a glass of sparkling water in front of Sheela and set a cup of coffee to Lymon's right. It was black, just the way he liked it.

"So, what do we do?" Tony leaned forward, a sharpening in his eyes. "*Jagged Cat* is in preproduction. Costuming wants Sheela in for fitting on Tuesday. Shooting starts on the first."

"So what?" Rex asked. "Sheela's there. What's the big deal? This is our turf." He glanced meaningfully at Lymon. "We can handle it, right?"

Lymon nodded.

Sheela had continued to stare absently at the table in front of her, the sparkling water fizzing by her hand. "It changes your life."

"What's that?" Felix asked.

"Knowing that someone can get that close to you."

"It won't happen again," Rex started, but Sheela raised a hand, cutting him off.

She looked at Lymon. "You've always told me that security wasn't a positive thing. That you could only lessen the odds."

Lymon nodded. "Just as with any system, there's always a way to beat it. Doing it, however, generally takes skill, money, power, luck, or some combination of them."

Sheela studied him thoughtfully. "Which of those do you think was responsible for what happened in New York?"

Lymon sipped his coffee, considering. "Luck is out. My guess is that we're looking at skill and money."

"Why?" Rex demanded.

"It was well planned, which means the guy wasn't counting on luck. The Bureau of Alcohol, Tobacco, Firearms and Explosives controls the sale of flash-bangs to military and police only. This guy had a CTS 7290. He didn't buy it on the corner of Twenty-second and Park Avenue. It took money to get that uniform. He didn't just lift it out of some guy's locker at the hotel. So, where'd he get it? Bribe someone in the laundry? Was it even real? Or did some tailor in Midtown make it based on photos of the real thing? Where did he get the key to the storeroom? The hotel ran inventory. None of their five keys for that room are unaccounted for. So, how did the guy know which key opened that door?"

"You're sure he didn't pick the lock?" Felix asked.

Lymon shook his head. "I watched him on the tape, Felix. You could see him reach down, insert it, and turn. It had to be a key. And the guy was cool. He didn't even look up at the camera. He knew he was being recorded, and not once did we get a full facial shot. During the attack his back is toward the camera. Afterward, he runs with his head down and tilted, sort of like a charging bull. Like I said: a pro."

"I don't like it," Rex added. "Thank God Sheela's safe."

"I want to know why," Sheela added, looking straight at Lymon. "Can you find out?"

Lymon carefully replaced his coffee cup. "Honestly, Sheela, I can try, but I can't promise anything."

"You have connections, don't you?"

"Yeah, sure. But those things cost—"

"I don't care." She used her screen presence, that commanding alto that had carried her to top billing on the marquis. *"Find out!"*

Sid Harness loosened his tie as he followed the hostess to a table in the back. He liked the Old Ebbitt Grill. The place had atmosphere. He glanced at the brown marble columns on the back bar with their golden chapiters. The stuffed African game heads glared down with fierce glass eyes. Dark wood trim accented the white panels, and the frosted glass dividers seemed to glow with an internal light. The effect was accented by real gas lamps that illuminated historical paintings of the Republic.

From old habit, he took inventory of the occupants: several prominent Washington reporters, one of the Congressmen from Ohio with several of his staff members, a basketball star with not one but two fawning blondes at his table. The usual eclectic Washington bunch.

The waitress led Sid to a booth on the back wall, a semi-private affair done in red leather with high seats. He slid onto the cushions across from Christal Anaya, took the menu, and smiled his thanks as the hostess retreated.

"Sorry I'm late."

Christal arched a thin eyebrow as she studied him from across the table. "If this had been anyplace but the Old Ebbitt Grill, I'd have left a long time ago."

"Development on a case," Sid muttered, and preempted the young man who came to ask if he'd like anything to drink. "A Foggy Bottom ale, please." Sid looked a question at Christal.

She placed a hand over the melted ice in her glass. "I've had enough for now."

After the young man left, Sid cocked his head, watching Christal watch him. God, she was striking. Her midnight black hair gleamed in the fancy gaslights, contrasting with the polished brass above the leather seats. She had a straight nose, sculpted cheeks, and perfect mouth, the sort that demanded a passionate kiss. Spirit lurked within her liquid dark eyes.

"If you're thinking of trying your luck"—her voice was husky with threat—"don't. I'm not big on men right now."

Sid shook his head, sighed, and leaned back, stretching out his arm. "No way, Chris."

The faintest trace of a smile ghosted around her full lips. "Then why would you bring me here?" She indicated the plush restaurant. "It's fancy and expensive, Sid. What's your game?" She narrowed an eye. "Your wife know you're here? With me?"

"Uh-huh."

"Really?" Christal leaned forward, dark locks spilling over her shoulders. "And just what does she know about me?"

"Everything."

A dark deviltry danced in her eyes. "Everything?"

"Yep. I told Claire I was going out to dinner with a beautiful femme fatale who'd been busted across the chops for something that might have been a simple mistake under other circumstances."

Christal leaned back then, suspicion in her eyes. "So, what's the gig?"

As the waiter stepped up, book in hand, Sid said, "I'd like the New York cut, medium well, baked potato, and Ranch dressing."

"The buffalo tenderloin special." Christal shot Sid a sly glance to see if he would recoil at the price. "Medium rare with garlic mashed and a Caesar salad with lots of anchovy."

The waiter stepped away, and she made a chastising gesture with one slim hand. "Normally, in a place like this, the woman is supposed to order first, you know?"

Sid yawned, scratched under his chin, and said, "Yeah. So, I'm a barbarian." He paused. "How you been?"

"Give me a break! How do you think I've been? I feel like hammered shit. When I finally get to sleep, I dream that last meeting in the director's office. I see that son of a bitch sitting there staring at his hands like he was a boy caught shoplifting." She shook her hair back. "I feel like I've been trashed, Sid. I feel like . . . Hell, I don't know what I feel like. Sick, I guess. Sick in the guts."

"Humiliated?"

"Humiliated." She rolled the drink glass with its ice back and forth. He watched her thin fingers, the bones so delicate under tanned skin. Her nails looked perfect. "I was headed for a really super career, you know."

At the tone in her voice, he added, "Yeah. Well, it doesn't seem like it, but the resignation was the right thing."

He figured she might have given a sewer rat that same loathing look. "Really?"

"Yeah, they'd have spitted you and roasted you alive. You might feel like shit this way, but you'd have felt like sour vomit the other."

"God, I'm glad you asked me to dinner! I feel so much better now."

"Good." He flipped a card out on the table. "I hear you're thinking about leaving DC. Going back west."

She picked up the card, glancing at it. "You can't be serious?"

"Yep."

"Cut the cowboy crap. Texans and Mexicans have a very long and not so nice history, remember?"

"You're from New Mexico."

"Yeah, well Texans and New Mexicans have a long-standing thing between them, too."

"I know. If God had meant for New Mexicans to ski, he would have given them money." Sid grinned. "I know all the old jokes." He paused, studying her. "About that card, I know the guy. He's always looking for good people. You're one of the best."

"Executive security?" she asked, slightly baffled. "Me? Like a bodyguard?"

Sid nodded.

"Forget it! The first time some skinny rich Anglo mouthed off, I'd bust the teeth out of his head."

"You'd probably be making twice what you are now."

"Was."

"Huh?"

"Twice what I *was* making."

"Oh, right." He proceeded cautiously. "So, what's your plan? Go back to Albuquerque to set up a legal practice? Christal Ayana, attorney at law? Maybe handle some divorces? Draw up estate plans?"

"Hey, I got the degree. A little study and I can re-up on the bar." Her lips twitched. "Even in New Mexico."

Sid grinned at her, reading her defensive smile. "I know. So, you graduated law school third in your class. And what? You slap an application on the FBI's desk first chance you get. You breeze through the qualification and zap, next thing, you're at Quantico; then you're graduated, and sworn in with rave reviews." He cocked his head. "You could have waltzed into a fancy law firm with a starting salary somewhere around a hundred grand. But you took the Bureau. Why?"

Christal studied the card between her fingers. "Do you know what's in all those law books that you see in a lawyer's office, Sid?"

"Cases, right?"

"Law," she answered. "Lawyers, at least good lawyers, spend most of their lives buried in those books. Applying their client's situations to those cases, working up alternatives based on legal decisions."

"Sure."

"I did the books all the way through law school." She glanced up. "And you know what?"

"What?"

For the first time, she actually smiled. "I *hated* it!" She laughed out loud. "Oh, I was good at it, because that's what I had to be. Hour after hour, I sat and read and memorized. I could quote so-and-so versus what's-his-name and The People versus Whozits. But to do it for the rest of my life?" She made a face.

"Do me a favor?" Sid asked.

The waiter appeared and set Christal's salad in front of her. "What?"

"Just call the guy. I think he could provide you with enough excitement to keep you from gagging."

As the waiter departed she poked at her Caesar with a fork, turning one of the brown anchovies over and over. "You're not trying to set me up or anything, are you?"

"Nope."

"Where do you know this guy from?"

"We were both Marine recon. Kosovo, Persian Gulf, Afghanistan. He went private while I stayed on the government's payroll. I think you'd like him. He's a no-bullshit kind of guy. Not only that, unlike some of the people in that room the other day, he works in the real world."

She was staring thoughtfully at the card, chewing. He could see her mind working. She asked, "Every job has its downside. What gives here?"

"Boredom. Fatigue." Sid shrugged. "Nothing you're not used to in the field. Hours of sitting on your butt, staying alert, followed by moments of frenetic action. Sometimes horrible hours, sometimes travel. Not that different than investigation, actually."

"He'll ask why I left the Bureau." He could see the air going out of her. "He'll want references, to speak to my supervisor."

Sid speared a bit of carrot. "Nope. He won't need to call anybody."

"What kind of guy is this? He'd just hire someone for a job like this without references?"

"Never."

"But you just said—"

"I've already called him about you. He knows the score,

Chris. Like I said, he's been in the real world. He could give
a good goddamn what the AD or SAC have to say. I vouched
for you."

Her eyes glistened, tears held back by force of will.
"Why, Sid?"

He gave her a crooked grin. "Because you're too good to
waste. Besides, who knows? Maybe someday you can save
my ass."

3

Reading traffic was an art. Lymon checked in both directions, made eye contact with the guy in the Chevy
truck, and eased the clutch out as he made a right onto
Wilshire Boulevard. Traffic was still light. The time 6:38 displayed on the fairing-mounted clock as Lymon tapped his
BMW into fourth.

The light changed to yellow and Lymon slowed, downshifting before putting his right foot down. The 1150 RT put-
tered happily, sending soft vibrations through the seat and
bodywork. A motorcycle could be a godsend when it came
to Los Angeles traffic. The Japanese crotch rockets might
have been faster, but the ass-in-the-air seating position was
excruciating. What was the point of looking racy if the position reminded you of a bug snuffling under a cow flop?

When the light turned, Lymon motored past familiar businesses and took a right for a half block to the alley. Turning
in, he passed the Dumpsters and waved at the two homeless
guys, Stewart and John, who lived under a blue polytarp behind the bakery. They weren't bad for homeless. They peed
and crapped in the storm drain, kept their lash-up neat, and
even did odd jobs for the street-front businesses.

Lymon idled into his small parking lot and killed the engine. Pulling off his gloves, he locked them in the tank-side
compartment, flipped out the sidestand, and locked the forks.

He pulled his helmet off as he climbed the steel steps to his second-floor offices. After unlocking the door he disarmed the security system and let himself into the back hallway.

He passed the small storeroom to his right, and then walked past the line of cubbyhole offices where his associates held court when they weren't on the job.

Lymon's empire consisted of twelve hundred square feet of the second floor. The rent wasn't bad, considering the location on Wilshire. He was minutes from Beverly Hills, Brentwood, and Pacific Palisades, where most of his clients lived. The second floor wasn't a deterrent to his business. He didn't need a high-traffic location, and most of his clients sent representatives if they came at all.

He stopped in the cubbyhole where the Capresso machine sat, pushed the button, and watched the lights glow to life. A faint wisp of steam rose from the grate on top. He retrieved his cup from his desk, filled it, and had just settled in to go through the mail in the in-box when a knock came at the back door.

He frowned at the clock—still ten to seven—and walked back. To his surprise, Mark Ensley stood on the narrow landing.

Lymon opened the thick security door. "You're about the last person I expected to find hanging out at my back door. Let me guess, you decided to give up on that two-by-twice outfit you run and come looking for a real job."

"Work for a chickenshit like you? Not a chance in hell. I'd rather hire on as watchman at a junkyard." Ensley stood five ten and appeared to be in his midthirties when in reality he was a fit and well-preserved forty-two. He wore an expensive silk sport jacket over a powder blue button-down shirt. Lymon supposed that the bundle in the right-hand coat pocket was the missing tie. Ensley jerked a nod as he stepped into the hallway. His dark eyes looked tired, and his hair was slightly mussed.

"That coffee I smell?" He had a smooth baritone.

"Yeah, and it looks like you need it." Lymon led the way. "Long night?"

"Yeah, weird." Ensley was rubbing the back of his neck. "I was headed home. Took a chance that you might be in early."

"Hey! Glad to be of service. Anything for the competition!" Lymon pulled a cup from the rack. "Strong?"

"Yeah. I need all the horsepower I can get."

While the machine ground, steamed, pressed, and dribbled, Lymon cataloged the stress reflected in Ensley's face. Handing him the cup, he led him to the conference room and snaked out a chair before dropping into it backward so he could rest his arms on the back.

The room was paneled in oak veneer with bulletin boards, chalkboards, a screen for PowerPoint and slide projections, as well as a foot locker full of toys. Actually they were props, used by Lymon's people for planning purposes. With the assortment of blocks, cardboard, and toy cars, they could create most any kind of scale model for route or location briefings.

Ensley flopped into one of the cushioned chairs and stared into his coffee. "What happened in New York? What's your side of the story?"

Lymon detailed it yet again.

When he had finished, Ensley looked up quizzically. "He tried to poke her with a needle? No shit? Like, to inject her with what? HIV? His sperm?"

Lymon shrugged. "You got me."

Ensley sipped at his coffee and raised an eyebrow. Lymon could see faint freckles on his skin. "Hey, that's good. If you keep losing clients, you can go head-to-head with Starbucks."

"I didn't lose my client," Lymon groused, irritated. "But the guy came awfully close." He met Ensley's eyes. "I can't swear to it—I just got the briefest glimpse—but it looked like the plunger was down on the syringe. Flipped out as it sounds, it was like he was going to try to suck something out her, not shoot it in. When he finally figured out that the attack was blown, he dropped a flash-bang and ran."

"Huh?" Ensley was skeptical.

"Standard CTS 7290. You might say he was fully committed to escape."

"Maybe it was drugs? Some wacko wanting to share his favorite high with his favorite actress?"

"Or maybe he wanted to inject her with something contagious, something only he had the antidote for? I don't know. Like I said, it looked to me like the plunger was down. Things were happening fast." Lymon settled his chin on his forearms. "So, what brings you to my door? Sure you're not looking for a job? I'll start you at five-fifty an hour taking out the trash."

Ensley grinned, but lost it too fast. "Julia had a break-in last night." Julia was Julia Roberts, Sheela's competition for highest-paid top-grossing female star and American icon. "Weird thing. Doesn't make any sense. It was a professional job."

"Julia Roberts has some of the best technology in the business. Sheela's thinking about upgrading to her system."

"Yeah, well, what if I told you some guy parachuted onto her roof last night? He left his chute dangling off the satellite dish just so we'd know for sure. He also left the pitonlike things he screwed into the roof under the tiles and the rope and harness he used to drop over the edge. He cut the screen out of an open third-floor window, and he was in."

"Where's Julia?"

"She had just left the house. She's got a six a.m. screen call and has to be out for costuming and makeup." Ensley turned the coffee cup in his hands. "The thing is, the guy must know this. You got me as to how. Maybe they were watching from the chopper. When her car pulled out of the drive, the guy dropped out the hatch."

"So what did he take?"

Ensley looked up. "That's the weird thing. He took her sheets. Right off the bed, still, like warm, you know? That, and the trash out of the bedroom wastebasket. What kind of guy steals dirty sheets and bedroom trash?"

"I'd start watching eBay. Maybe Julia's trash sells for a whole lot."

Ensley didn't look amused. "So, the guy bags up the sheets and trash, then climbs out the window. Up to now it's been a perfect job. Julia's people find out she's been hit because the helicopter comes in low, drops a line, and snags the guy off the roof. Woke up half the neighborhood."

Lymon rubbed his chin. "Like he didn't care if anyone found out that he'd been there?"

"Yeah. The police have already been in touch with the FAA. Did you know there were a hundred and thirty-seven helicopters flying in the LA Basin? Traffic control actually had the chopper on their screens for a while until they lost it against the San Gabriels." Ensley made a waving gesture. "Do you know how many private heliports there are up in those multimillion-dollar estates? He could have gone anywhere."

"I'd start checking with the rental companies. Not just everyone has a copter for hire. What about the house? The thief leave anything?"

Ensley sipped his coffee. "Police just finished going over Julia's room with a microscope. Nothing. *Nada.* Not a print, nor hair, nor bit of fabric. Nothing on the ropes, pitons, or parasail. It's all clean. You'd think it was the CIA or something."

"How's Julia?"

"I hear she's freaked. You got any idea how this is going to line out for her security guys?" He looked up, grinning weakly. "You may be up to your neck in job aps when she cans her protection."

"Once she settles down, she won't fire them, Mark. They couldn't have known some creep was going to parachute in, for God's sake." Lymon cocked his head. "It was too well planned. Not just some obsessive fan." He paused. "Shit."

"What?"

"I don't know. Just shit. Who'd want dirty sheets? I mean, why not take something really personal, like her Oscar, or jewelry, or a dress, or something?"

"I'm stumped, Lymon." He tossed off the last of his coffee. "I just needed to talk it over." He glanced at his watch. "For now, I'm headed home for a nap. Julia's got a meeting with her people at three this afternoon. This shit's gonna be all over the tube tonight, and I'd better be sharp enough to stick in the floor when it happens."

"Yeah." Lymon stood. "Listen, if there's anything we can do for you?"

Ensley grinned. "Nah. But if she cans her security team, I'll put in a good word for you. She's got to go somewhere."

The waiting was driving Christal mad. She had packed most of her small Alexandria apartment. The boxes sat in neat stacks in her living room. On the TV, the talking heads on Headline News were reviewing the sports world. For something to do, she'd taken up pacing both the length and breadth of her small apartment. She'd liked it here, had considered it home while she built a nest egg bank account in preparation for down payment on a real house one day.

Christal paused by the breakfast bar to stare at the phone. She tapped her fingernails on the countertop and sighed. Lifting the receiver, she punched the familiar numbers.

"Harness," the voice on the end said.

"Hey, Sid."

"Christal? What's up?"

"What are you doing?"

"Kidnapping. Young woman. Graduate student at Washington. Real hotshot. Hey, did you know there's a string of unsolved kidnappings going back five years?"

"No, Sid. I didn't know that." She glanced at the TV. "Most of the news is about Yoko Ono. Someone ripped off her penthouse. Took a lock of John Lennon's hair, can you imagine?"

"You haven't called Lymon yet."

"I've been packing."

"Where you going?"

"I don't know."

"Call Lymon. Me, I've got three more interviews to conduct. You wouldn't believe some of the things they can do with genetics these days." He chuckled. *"In theory, at least."*

"Sounds like fun." She hesitated. "Wish I was there." She meant it.

Sid heard the undertones. *"Call Lymon. I mean it. Meanwhile, I've got to figure out if my missing person is related to the sixteen priors."*

"Sixteen?" she asked, amazed. "God, why haven't we heard about this?"

"We're just putting it together. Call Lymon. I gotta go."

She heard the line go dead. Glancing at the television, she saw the camera was giving a shot of the street in front of Ono's ritzy building in New York.

Lymon really appreciated Sheela Marks' pool. It was huge—like everything else in the house—but when an A-list star like Sheela made twenty million a picture plus residuals, she could have a lot of perks.

The pool might have been a bit short of Olympic size, but the fitted-stone patio with its ivy-shaded trelliswork and overhanging live oak made for a cool and delightful sanctuary. A full-size Richard Greeves bronze of Sacagawea stood to the right, her face lifted to the sunlight. The few muted sounds of civilization—traffic and airplanes, mostly—that managed to seep past the high wall were drowned by the bubbling fountains that dominated the flower beds to either side.

Lymon stepped out of the double French doors after checking to make sure the wires to the security sensors were still attached and unfrayed. Old habits and all that.

Sheela sat in a lounge chair, a script in her hand. Lymon identified it by the brass brads in the three binding holes. She was in Balenciaga jeans and wearing a William B white cotton blouse unbuttoned over a turquoise tube top. Her red-blond hair had been done in a French braid. A glass of what looked like iced lemonade stood on the marble table beside her.

Lymon seated himself on the padded wrought-iron chair across from her and waited. Even after three years of association, she still affected him. Tall and long-legged, she carried herself with a sense of grace that no one would have associated with her obscure Canadian origins.

"Where do they get this shit?" she asked, smacking the pages she held. She looked up and fixed him with her irritated blue eyes.

"Got me. I don't write the things."

She shook her head and tossed the script onto the cement beside her. "I read it before it went into development. Good stuff, nice idea. Now, the execs have been having meetings, it's been through two rewrites by four people, and it's shit! I'm on page thirty, and I already know that by the third act my character is going to be raped by her father. So now I'm shooting him in the last scene? Duh!"

"Yeah, well, you shouldn't complain. I know for a fact that producers and studio execs don't get put in charge of really hot properties until their lobotomies have fully healed."

She grinned at that.

"What did you want to see me about?" Lymon rubbed his hands together. "Are my people on the ball?"

She lifted an eyebrow. "You come on your bike?"

Lymon nodded.

Sheela stood. "Come on." She led the way back into the house, calling to Tomaso as she passed, "Lymon and I are going out for a while. If Rex calls, he can get me on my cell."

"Yes, ma'am."

Lymon lifted a brow as they stopped by the front door. Sheela stepped into the coatroom and returned wearing a white leather jacket and carrying a pearlescent helmet.

"Sheela, just what the hell do you think you're doing?"

"We're going for a ride. You and me."

"Are you nuts?"

"Are you armed?" She pointed at his armpit, where he kept his HK .40 Compact in a Kramer undervest. "Of course you are. So, I'm well guarded and safe, right? Come on, Lymon. We need to talk, just you and me." She rolled her eyes to indicate the opulent surroundings. "Away from here." Her smile would have melted Kevlar. "And it's been years since I've been on a bike."

"What if something—"

"It's an *order,* Lymon. If I can't trust you, who the hell can I trust?"

"It's not a matter of trust. It's about variables that I can't control: drunk drivers, spilled oil on the road, an errant SUV with underinflated tires and a malfunctioning guidance system."

"Is that a harried housewife?"

"Generally."

"We're going."

With misgivings bubbling in his breast, he led the way out to the silver BMW. "In my professional opinion, I have to inform you that I think this is a bad idea. My job—"

"Is to keep your client happy," she shot back. "Aren't you the one who lives by the mantra 'The principal comes first'? Damn, I should have had Felix draw up a release, but that would have led to too many questions."

He stopped, taking his helmet off the handlebar. "We could have Paul bring the limo around. Anything you have—"

"Don't you get it?" Her eyes were pleading. "I'm tired of living in a can, Lymon. And you're the head canner!"

He helped her with her helmet, surprised that it was not only the right size, but DOT and Snell approved. "You've been planning this?"

"Ever since we got back from New York."

He straddled the bike, steadying it as she climbed on. "You've ridden before?"

"When I was a kid. Dad had a Harley and an old 250 Yamaha for farm work."

"Just do what I do. If we go down, hang on to me." He thumbed the starter, and the Beemer lit. Toeing it into gear, he let the clutch out and eased around the circle. At the gate, they waited while the heavy iron rolled back.

"I'll bet John's wondering who the second rider is."

She laughed. "Yeah, it's good for him."

"Where to?"

"Up to the Ventura, east to Glendale, and then take Highway Two over the Angeles Crest. After that, we'll make it up as we go."

She *had* planned it.

Lymon wound around, caught Beverly Glenn north to the Ventura Freeway, and matched speed with the traffic.

"Waahooo!" Sheela cried on the back as she raised her arms to the wind. "I am *free*!"

She's free, and I feel like I'm carrying a case of nitroglycerine in the tour pack! He didn't know how long it had been since he felt so nervous. Damn it! What if he dropped it with Sheela Marks on board? The woman sitting behind him was worth somewhere in the neighborhood of a billion dollars by the time you figured in future box office, residuals, and advertising revenue. The lawsuits would take years. This was lunacy!

"Doesn't this thing go any faster than fifty-five?" she called over his shoulder.

"I was just trying to calculate your net worth if I killed you."

"According to the latest figures Rex put together, about one point two billion. Now, take a deep breath, and let's move with the rest of the traffic."

He made a face, signaled, and felt the BMW surge as he accelerated into the fast lanes.

They made it to the twisty two-lane outside of La Canada Flintridge, and Lymon eased into the first of the corners.

"Doesn't this thing lean?" Sheela asked over his shoulder as she wrapped her arms around his waist. "You've got tread all the way up the sides of the tires. I saw it back at the house."

"Most strung-out actresses use pills," he muttered.

"What? Pills?"

"Yeah, you know, for committing suicide." With that, he figured himself for dead anyway, twisted the wick, and let the big twin do its thing.

4

How long had it been since she felt this relaxed? Sheela tilted her head back and looked up through the branches. It was a pine tree. Even she knew that much. The can of Dr. Pepper felt delightfully cool in her hands. A crystal creek was bubbling just to her left as she sat on a lichen-covered rock with her feet on a brown bed of needles.

"Perfect," she purred to herself. She could feel knots loosening in her muscles. For this one blissful moment, the world was fading, the pressure lessening.

She glanced at Lymon. He was standing to one side, looking antsy as he gazed back up the hill at the little gas station and store where they had pulled off the road. The sleek silver BMW was just visible at the edge of the parking lot.

"Relax, Lymon. Take yourself off the payroll for a minute."

He smiled at her, the action wary. "Can't, Sheela. It's just who I am. You've already talked me into a potential major-league fuckup."

She looked around at the trees and listened to the wind sighing in the branches. A loud car blasted past on the highway above them, exhaust howling. "So, how do you assess the risk here? High? We're on the edge of the forest. It's the wrong part of the country for *Deliverance,* and you don't look anything like Burt Reynolds."

"I guess I don't at that."

She studied him, trying to read his hard face. He had been a mystery since the first time she'd met him. Her previous security personnel had been pretty straightforward. They had cop personalities: That easy swagger, inside sense of kindred, and cynical approach to life she had known since her days as a teenager in Regina.

"You were a soldier," she remarked. "Special forces?"

"Recon. Same thing, but different." He looked at her. "Why are we doing this?"

She reached down for a pinecone and studied the brittle triangular petals. "I had to get away. I want to talk to you." That made him even more nervous.

She decided to let him off the hook. "Lymon, I want you to look into something for me."

He lifted a craggy eyebrow, waiting.

"This thing that happened in New York, it's been bothering me."

"Look, Sheela, we're instituting new procedures for the next time we're on the road."

She waved him down. "It's not that. I grew up in the real world. I know you can't stop everyone one hundred percent of the time. At least not and still let me do my job. I've got to go places, make appearances, and play the game."

"Okay, so?"

"So, I want you to figure out what this is all about."

He was frowning. "What have you heard?"

"Julia's bedsheets, John Lennon's hair, my attack, all high profile, all perfectly planned. Something you said at the meeting stuck with me: skill, power, money, and luck. Those were the things you said someone needed to beat a system. If we throw out luck, that leaves skill, power, and money."

"Uh-huh. So?"

"It doesn't make sense. Anyone with money and power who wanted to touch me, could. He could wrangle an invitation to a party, or put leverage on Tony or Rex. He could buy his way onto the set for *Jagged Cat,* or glad-hand his way into a fund-raiser or release party."

"I suppose."

"It wouldn't cost more than renting a helicopter, say, or figuring out how to break Yoko Ono's security system. I am assuming that those things can be had, but for a pretty hefty price."

He was watching her warily. "That's right."

"Lymon, part of my job is hype. I'm a product, marketed and sold. I know I have a certain charisma that translates on-screen. The rest of it is how I'm packaged. Hell, even a lot of the crap in the tabloids is manipulated by Dot and Rex."

"What are you trying to get at?"

"Marketing."

"I'm not sure I follow you."

"I'm not sure I follow me either. It's just a hunch." She tossed the pinecone to one side. "But it feels right."

He nodded, frowning. "Okay, so, marketing what? Weaknesses in security?"

"That's what I want you to find out." She stood, drinking down the last of her soda. "Now, while you think about it, let's go ride. I want to enjoy every second before they put me back in the can."

The air-conditioning was humming its familiar chant as Lymon sat at his desk. He kept running his day with Sheela over and over in his head when he was supposed to be concentrating on paperwork. Through the open door he could hear June Rosen, the secretary, talking on the phone out front. From her tone of voice—excruciatingly polite—he knew it wasn't good.

Neither was his current task. He hated accounting, and thanked God every day that June could do most of it. She wrote the checks for the electricity, water, rent, insurance, and the rest. She calculated the 941 payment, made sure that W-2s were up-to-date. She kept track of employee hours and tallied the expense report receipts, then calculated and sent the billing. The burden of double-checking schedules and making travel arrangements fell onto her shoulders, and like now, she answered the phone.

Lymon heard it click; then came the sound of June's pumps as she walked back and leaned in the door. She was a wholesome-looking thirty-two, two kids, single after a second divorce. Today she had her brown-blond hair up in something Lymon would have called a beehive. She wore a charcoal cotton pullover.

"That was *Daily Variety* again. They're still prying away

at the New York incident. They are wondering if it could be related to Julia's break-in."

Lymon tapped the expense reports with his pen. "Maybe Sandra Bullock and Nicole Kidman will get hit next? With Julia and Sheela, that's the big four."

He paused at that, remembering Sheela's insistence that it was all tied somehow to marketing.

"You okay?" June asked. "You've been preoccupied all day."

"Yeah, fine. Thanks." He smiled as she ducked back and clumped her way to the front desk.

Truth was, he'd been off his feed ever since that crazy ride with Sheela. After their soda stop, she'd insisted that they ride clear over to Santa Clarita before heading back. He had deposited her at her door a little before nine that night.

That look she had given him when she said "Thank you" had left him even more unsettled. Her eyes had been shining, intense—and they had looked straight into his soul.

Knock it off! She's business.

Security personnel didn't get involved with their principals. Not only was it morally irresponsible, it was downright dangerous. He was in enough trouble over the New York disaster.

His mind kept returning to that spirited ride. He'd been prudent, hadn't pushed the envelope, but once he'd relaxed, forgotten who was on the back, it had been fabulous.

The phone jangled at his elbow. He picked it up, hearing June: *"Sid Harness for you on line one."*

Lymon punched the button and said, "Sid? What's up?"

"Did Christal ever call you?"

"Nope."

"Oh, hell."

"Look, maybe she doesn't want the job."

"She's her own worst critic. Still blaming herself. I don't know, it's just that she's too good to lose. You know what I mean? She's young, and this is the first time she's really taken a hit. And it was a bad one. She's one of the best. Got a nose for what's really happening, you know? It's like she can sniff out motive. Hell, she was the one who broke the Gonzales case before it got FUBARed."

Lymon considered that. Motive? That was what was bothering him, Ensley, and Sheela. He tapped his pen on the reports. His people were trained to be guard dogs, not wolves.

"Lymon? You still there?"

"Sid? Maybe she's not right for executive protection. It's an art, a calling if you will, rather than a nine-to-five job. It takes a certain kind of personality. You know, someone who can whip a Lincoln through a J-turn one minute and walk the principal's dog the next. She's a street agent, right? Trained to stick her nose into trouble, not cover and evacuate a principal."

"She's got the brains for it, Lymon. Isn't that what you've always told me? That the job was really thinking out of the box? Planning? Advance study of a location or event?"

"Yeah, so? If she was that smart, how'd she get her tit in a wringer over this Gonzales thing?"

"What would have happened if someone had recorded your, um, indiscretion with that sultan's daughter?"

"I'd have been court-martialed then, and sitting in jail in Djibouti today." Lymon winced. "Hey, I was young. I've never fucked up since." An image of Sheela stared at him with cerulean eyes, and his heart skipped. Crap! He couldn't do it again. Wouldn't.

"Christal's young, too. Unlike you, she got busted. So tell me, you've been there. Second chances can make all the difference, can't they? Or have you stopped believing in learning from your mistakes?"

Sheela's words haunted him: *Lymon, I want you to figure out what this is all about.* He took a deep breath. "Sid, if I wanted her to do a little digging for me, maybe stuff that was OTR, off the record, could she do it?"

"In spades, buddy. I swear, she's as good as they come."

"What is she to you?"

There was a long pause. Finally, Sid said, *"Yeah, okay, maybe I'm a little bit in love with her. Just trust me on this, all right? When have I ever steered you wrong?"*

"Give me her number, Sid."

* * *

The tape made a ripping sound as Christal stripped it from the roll and sealed the last box. Using her teeth, she bit it off and patted it snug on the brown cardboard. Her apartment was cleaned, all trace of her gone but for the stack of brown boxes, each carefully labeled. The moving guys would be coming within the hour to load them into the van. Three days later they would unload them at her mother's house in Nambe, New Mexico. Whenever Christal was ready for them they'd be stacked in Mom's garage.

Her remaining personal possessions consisted of a pile of clothing to be hung in the back of her old battered '95 Nissan, her suitcase, two plants, and the radio that was playing on the breakfast bar.

She stood and tossed the roll of tape into her open suitcase. At the mention of Mel Gibson's name on the radio, she stopped short. She'd always liked his work.

"Sydney police remain baffled as they reconstruct the break-in at Sydney's prestigious Regent Hotel. Gibson certainly isn't in for a close shave in his next film, since it seems the erstwhile thieves only took the shaver head off of his electric razor."

Christal wrinkled her nose and tossed her thick black hair over her shoulder. She remembered the scuzzy stuff that an electric razor collected: bits of skin, chopped fragments of beard. Hell, if she was hitting Mel's place, she'd go for his checkbook, credit cards, and Swiss bank account—assuming he had one.

"Or, how about his agent's phone number while I'm at it, huh?"

She walked into the kitchen, opened the refrigerator door, and found a half-empty carton of orange juice. She set it on the counter before tossing opened jars of mustard, pickles, ketchup, and mayonnaise into the trash. When she lifted the lid on a plastic container in the far back, she found the green fuzzy remains of a month-old casserole. Good riddance. The nearly empty jar of Greek olives she kept, opening the lid and popping one into her mouth. She'd packed her glasses, so she tilted the orange juice carton back and chugged.

The phone rang. Wiping her mouth, she reached for the receiver. If it was the moving guys telling her they'd be late, she was going to raise hell.

"Hello?"

"Is this Christal Anaya?" The voice was male, competent sounding.

"Yeah. Who's this?"

"Sid Harness gave me your number. My name is Lymon Bridges, of Lymon Bridges Associates Personal Security, LLC. My business is—"

"Yeah, I know." She made a face. "Look, I don't know that I'd be any good at babysitting celebrities. You know, it's that bullshit factor."

To his credit, he laughed. *"Yeah, you get that on occasion, but not so much from the kind of people my agency works for. Most of them know the stakes."*

"Well, you see, Mr. Lymon—"

"Bridges. I'm Lymon Bridges."

"Mr. Bridges, the point I'd like to make is that I'm not in the market for a job right now."

"Previous offer? How much are they paying?"

She gave the phone a deadly smile, figuring, *What the hell?* "I don't think you could touch it."

"If you're as good as Sid says you are, and if everything works out, I'll start you at ten thousand a month plus expenses."

Christal stopped short. "What?"

"I think you heard—although the slip over my name doesn't lend credence to your investigative abilities."

"That was meant to irritate you."

"It worked." A pause. *"Are you as good as Sid says you are?"*

She shook her head, confused. "I don't know. Ten thousand a month? Just to keep some stuck-up spoiled movie star out of trouble? I don't have the ten-ton-gorilla physique. I'm five six and weigh one-fifteen."

"But you broke the Enrique Gonzales case open? Sid says you did that where the rest of the Bureau couldn't."

And blew it all! Aloud she asked, "Do you pay all of your bodyguards ten thousand?"

"No. Most of them are off-duty cops trying to make their bills. But you're not exactly going to be a part-time agent."

She felt her hackles rising. God, he hadn't seen the photos, had he? She tried to keep the rage out of her voice. "Just what did you have in mind?"

"Did you hear the news today? About Mel Gibson's razor?"

That left her off balance. "Yeah."

"There's an open E-ticket for you at Dulles. Delta counter. I'll have someone meet you at LAX soonest. Just give a call with your flight number and arrival time."

"Just like that? Fly to Los Angeles?"

"I have some people here I would like you to meet. There are things I want you to look into for us. If you are as good as Sid says, maybe you can do it. Then again, maybe you can't. Which is okay." A pause. *"Let me know which flight."*

Then the son of a bitch hung up.

Christal stared at the phone, listening to the dial tone. What the hell? Did he think she was just going to drop everything and fly to Los Angeles?

She cocked her head. Mel Gibson's razor? She could feel curiosity twirling around her spine like growing ivy.

"Bullshit! It's all bullshit."

June arched a critical eyebrow. "You didn't even give her our phone number."

Lymon leaned back in his chair and laced his fingers behind his head. "She's an investigator, isn't she? If she can't find our phone number, what the hell good is she?"

"She's not coming."

"She'll be walking off a jetway by noon tomorrow."

June shook her head. "Twenty bucks says no."

"You're on."

She gave him that suspicious look. "I don't get it. All you've got is Sid's word on this woman. She's just been canned at the FBI, so what makes you think she might be capable of doing this . . . whatever it is you're doing?"

Lymon shrugged. "One, I know Sid. He knows me, and he knows talent. I know what she did at the FBI, and Sid still vouches for her. That tells me that she might have fucked up, but it's not a genetic predisposition. Two, if she's not walking out of that jetway by noon tomorrow—or on the phone telling me she's delayed for a damn good reason—she's not the right person for the job. For twenty bucks it's cheap at twice the price."

"I don't want you around my boys," June told him as she started down the hall. "I'm trying to raise them to be decent and normal human beings."

"What? You think I'm like a lawyer or something?"

"More like a politician, actually."

"Hey! There's no reason to get ugly."

5

"In preparation for landing, please place your tray tables in their stowed position and return your seats to the upright position. All personal items must be stowed under the seat in front of you or in the overhead bins. At this time all personal electronic devices must be turned off. Thank you."

Christal found the button that made the footrest retract and brought her seat upright. She folded the table into the seat arm and turned off the reading light that hung by her ear. Once her laptop was zipped into its bag, she used her toe to shove it under the seat in front of her.

She glanced around, handing her used glass to the stewardess who walked past. If Lymon Bridges was trying to impress her, he was definitely on the right track. She'd almost gaped like the village idiot when the ticket agent told her that a first-class ticket was confirmed.

"Christal, what do you think about the Secret Service?" Sid had asked when she'd called him from Dulles. *"I mean the guys that oversee the president's safety. The real agents that do the actual work."*

When she'd given him an affirmative answer, he'd said, *"That's Lymon Bridges. That's the kind of work he does. He's one of the best, working for the best. I personally vouch for the guy. Trust me, if you don't think he's square, I'll buy your plane ticket back."*

She wondered if Sid knew he would have to shell out for first class.

Christal leaned her head back. Since seeing her belongings loaded into the van for New Mexico, her time had been spent on two subjects. First off, she caught herself wondering if this was such a good idea, and second, she had bought every news magazine in the WHSmith stand at Dulles to read up on celebrities. During the flight, she had used the first-class Internet access to do further research on her laptop.

The results had perplexed her. Mel Gibson's razor, John Lennon's lock of hair, Julia Roberts' sheets, Sheela Marks' odd assault—they all reeked of the bizarre. The thing that really aroused her curiosity as an FBI . . . okay, an ex-FBI agent, was that each of the crime scenes was clean. No clues had been left. Nothing. That, more than anything, made her whiskers quiver.

So, were they related? If so, how? What was the point? How much value did Julia Roberts' sheets have on the street? Christal made a face. She was definitely a Mel Gibson fan, but she wouldn't give a dented quarter for the chaff in his electric razor. Very well then, if you threw out cash, what was next?

It's some pervert with big bucks who's intent on sending them some kind of message. Then why didn't he call, write a letter, or e-mail? Pranksters liked to taunt in words as well as action.

A prank? Perhaps it was someone in the movie business?

Maybe some director or producer—one who had inadvertently misplaced his life somewhere along the way and had nothing better to do than think up weird nonsense like this?

She mulled the notion as the 767 banked on approach. Looking through the window she could see Los Angeles baking under the morning sun. Brown haze was packed up over San Bernardino and Riverside.

The sheer size of the sprawling megalopolis surprised her. She'd never seen it from the air before. The last time she had been in the city was as a little girl, when Mama had driven to Anaheim to see Aunt Maria. She remembered that trip as an eternity between potty breaks. She'd been hot, stuffed in the backseat with her unruly brothers. Aunt Maria had lived in a crowded apartment building. Christal and her brothers had been bored the entire time, fighting constantly and being yelled at. On top of it all, they hadn't gone to Disneyland.

She winced as the big jet touched down. A curious anticipation built as the plane taxied to its gate. She had that sense that her life was changing. Usually, when she felt this way, it was for a reason. She'd felt it the moment she submitted her application to law school, had felt it again when the FBI sent her a letter of acceptance, and felt it yet again the night she and Hank had made love in the surveillance van—though that had been one hell of a misinterpretation of presentiment.

As the bell rang and the seat belt sign went off, she stood, retrieved her laptop and carry-on from the bin, then filed out.

She didn't really expect anyone in the gate area, post-9/11 security being what it was, and LAX having been a constant target. To her surprise, she immediately saw the woman with the hand-lettered ANAYA sign.

She walked up, set her carry-on down, and extended her hand. "I'm Christal Anaya."

"June Rosen." Her smile had a wry quality, her handshake firm. "Welcome to LA. Do you have any other bags?"

"Just these. I travel light."

"This way then." She reached for the bag, but Christal snatched it up.

"I can carry it."

As they walked, she glanced sidelong at the woman. "I would have expected Mr. Bridges."

"Lymon, damn his hide, is in an advance meeting with Universal. They're ironing out the details for *Jagged Cat*."

"Excuse me? Why 'damn his hide,' and what's a jagged cat?"

June gave her a crooked grin. "Second question first. *Jagged Cat* is the client's new picture. They're in preproduction right now. That's costuming, building sets, and all the stuff that's got to be done before filming. The studios have pretty good security, but Lymon has to make sure that our people interface with theirs so that we can pick her up and drop her off, have the right passes, and so forth. We need to know the shooting schedule and where, if anywhere, we're going on location."

"Huh?"

"Are they shooting a scene in Portugal? If so, we have to be ready, advance the location, check the hotels, establish a relationship with local law enforcement, make reservations for our people, and book travel."

Christal thought about that. "Doesn't the studio do all that?"

"Sure, but what if Sheela wants to go sightseeing between scenes? Does she have transportation? Do we need local security? Special permits? Are there areas she shouldn't travel through? High-crime zones? What if she gets sick or is injured, maybe has an allergic reaction to something? That's our responsibility."

"I didn't know it was that complicated." She wondered who Sheila was.

"Sometimes more so."

"And the 'damn his hide'?"

"I bet the bastard twenty bucks you wouldn't show."

Christal smiled, deciding she liked June Rosen. "And what do you do for Lymon Bridges?"

"In official terms, I'm the secretary. In blunt actuality, I'm the business manager. I run the company." She shot Christal a communicative glance. "Fortunately for him, he's never asked me to sit on his lap, iron his shirts, or make coffee."

"How long have you been with the company?"

"Three years now."

"Is it a good springboard?"

June led her out through security. "Sure. But why would I go anywhere else? My boys are in good schools, and I get paid to work my ass off. Paid *well*."

Christal considered that as they passed the ticket counters and stepped out into the warm day. A black Lincoln sat at the curb, its four-ways flashing. June pressed a button on a key fob, and the lights flashed.

"You can just leave it in the Arrivals lane?"

"Special permit." June stepped to the trunk, opening it so Christal could place her bag inside.

Seating herself in the passenger seat, she looked around. Lincolns had never been her thing. She liked small, compact, and parkable. But then, she'd never had a special permit before.

June started the engine, fastened her seat belt, and waved at a cop who stopped oncoming vehicles to allow them into traffic.

"The special permit gets you into the concourses, too?"

"This is LAX. Lymon has done a lot of work fostering good relations with the TSA team here." She smiled and tapped her purse. "It helps that I'm a special deputy with LA County."

"Do I get a special permit?"

"You'll have to take that up with Lymon," June said cryptically. Then she turned her attention to driving as she accelerated northbound onto the San Diego Freeway. Christal noted that the woman held the wheel professionally and handled the big car with confident ease.

"First class, special permits, Lincolns—you people don't exactly keep a low profile, do you?"

"In this town, Ms. Anaya, image is marketing." She glanced at Christal. "How is your wardrobe?"

"I beg your pardon?"

"Depending on the nature of the principal's appearance, you will be required to dress in anything from professional to very formal. The problem with formal is to still look good but have freedom of movement in case things get, shall we say, athletic."

"I don't get it."

"Have you ever seen a Hollywood gala on TV?"

"Sure."

"Could you pick the bodyguards out of the crowd?"

"Well, yeah, sometimes. They're the big guys who look unhappy."

"How about the women?"

"I didn't know there were any."

June smiled dryly. "That's precisely what we're looking for."

"It's *not* going to happen!" Sheela's voice carried from the dressing room as Lymon walked onto the set where the wardrobe session was in progress. At first glance he saw Paul over in the corner under a stand of lights. The driver was sitting backward in a chair, a barely concealed grin struggling to creep past his iron control.

According to Lymon's watch, Sheela should be halfway through her fitting session. This was the first time the costume designers actually saw their creations on the stars.

Two assistants huddled to one side, slightly horrified expressions on their faces. Rex stood to the right, arms crossed over his belly and looking dour. Three different photographers were spotted here and there around the room with a plethora of cameras on tripods as well as hanging from straps on their necks.

The fitting room was studded with lights and reflectors focused on a raised dais. Mirrors were positioned so that the star could get a three-hundred-sixty-degree view of herself in costume. In the rear stood rack after rack of hanging dresses, blouses, suits, and jackets.

Lymon stopped short, seeing Sheela standing on the dais. Her face had that look of absolute disgust that he had grown passingly familiar with over the years. She was wearing a bright red sparkly gown with what he'd call "wings" sprouting off of each shoulder. It fit glove-tight at her slim waist, advertised her rounded breasts, and clung to her thighs.

"It's looov'ly," Fiona Borg cooed, a rapturous look on her wrinkled face. She had her gray hair tucked in a wretched hat—the sort of thing she would have paid a fortune to an obscure Italian designer for—and wore something that reminded Lymon of a silver sheet wrapped around her bony frame.

"I look like the princess in *Dune*!" Sheela countered. "The wings go . . . and the color can be anything but bright red."

"But vee 'ave already chosen. Bernard loooves it!"

Sheela whirled, her finger like a dagger. "Change it! I could give a shit what Bernard loves. This thing makes me look like the vampire whore in *Blood Guzzler*."

"But I—"

"Do I have to call Felix to read you the clause in the contract? The dress goes, or I do." She reached back and struggled for the clasps in the back.

"The dress is out, Fiona," Rex interjected with authority. "If Bernard's got questions, he can call."

"So, vhat?" Fiona asked, waving her thin arms. "Vee got vhat? Two veeks to shooting, huh? You vant me to conjure from t'in air?"

One of the assistants had sprung up to help Sheela with the clasps and zippers. Lymon could see Sheela's frustration in the tight movements of her arms as she wiggled out of the fabric. In a bra and panties, she stepped free, and then with a toe, kicked the gaudy creation off the stage. She noticed Lymon for the first time, smiled, and rolled her eyes in an indication of frustrated endurance.

For his part, he tried not to stare. Sure, he'd seen her body before, at fittings, when she was in the pool, and during photography. That was before that same body had been pressed so close to his on the bike. Before she'd given him that haunting look.

"We'll figure something out," Rex said, trying to placate Fiona. The woman had won two Oscars for costume design, which placed her in the sacred realm of the Hollywood gods.

"Ya, ya. You try dis, huh?" Fiona thrust a hand at the racks of clothing. "You t'ink dis is easy? Making de dress, makes de scene, ja?"

"We've got some problems with the screenplay as it is," Rex soothed. "Just find something Sheela likes. It's the wings, Fiona. She looks like an overbruised bat in them."

"And the color!" Sheela sang out.

"And the color," Rex agreed. "The set's basically painted what color? Blue or something?"

Sheela held up a hand. "I'll do red. Just not in that contraption." She glanced meaningfully at Lymon. "Give me five, people. I need to talk to Mr. Bridges for a moment. Business."

The assistants and Rex clustered around Fiona, all talking in serious voices as Sheela stepped off the dais, grabbed a white terry cloth robe, and wrapped it around herself before walking over to Lymon.

"I thought I'd give your eyeballs a break," she said with a smile. "I've never seen you look at me like that."

"Sorry," he muttered, hating himself for feeling slightly embarrassed. "Thought I'd let you know: We're square with the studio. Everything's set. Paul's your guard dog and gofer when you're on the lot. If you need anything special, just ask him. He calls the office, and we're on it. Like always, the more advance notice, the better off we are."

She nodded, looking back at the pile of red fabric with the two wings lying akimbo. "Can you imagine they wanted me to wear that? I'm supposed to shoot my father, for God's sake. Wearing that? What are they thinking of?"

"Tinkerbell goes vamp?" he wondered.

"Maybe." She turned back toward him. "And the other subject we discussed the other day?"

"June picked someone up at the airport. I'll be meeting with her as soon as everything is thumbs-up here."

"Who?"

"Someone an old friend turned me on to. Ex-FBI. Supposedly smart, talented, and motivated. I won't know until I actually talk to her."

"Her?" Sheela arched an eyebrow. "Isn't that a little unusual?"

"Maybe. Yeah." He shrugged, seeing the hesitant curiosity in her eyes.

"Bring her to the house. I want to meet her."

He frowned, meeting her probing blue eyes. "Yes, ma'am."

She narrowed an eye. "And stop the 'yes ma'am' stuff. It makes me nervous."

"Yes, ma'am."

She gave an exasperated sigh, pulling him farther off to the side. "Lymon, you're acting nervous. Was it the motorcycle ride?"

"Yes, ma'am."

"It's really irritating when you say that."

"Yes, ma'am."

Are you afraid that I might try to change our relationship?"

"Yes, ma'am."

"And you don't trust yourself to stay professional?"

"Ms. Marks, people in my profession—"

"Lymon, this isn't the time or place to have this discussion." She looked back to where Rex was still arguing with Fiona. "I've got to go." She reached for his left arm, turning his wrist so she could see the time. "Bring this person to the house. I should be there by three, which means I'll really be there by five."

"Yes, ma'am."

She gave him her million-dollar smile. "We'll talk about you and me some other time. It's not what you're afraid of."

Isn't it? The words echoed in his head as she turned and walked back to the knot around Fiona.

6

At precisely four that afternoon, Christal walked out of her unit. She appreciated the choice of a Marriott Residence Inn for her lodging. Not only did she have more room than in a hotel, but she had filled out the grocery list and looked forward to cooking her own breakfast. Having grown up in New Mexico, the average American breakfast of eggs, pig meat, potatoes, or cereal was just plain boring. She had grown up with *huevos rancheros,* blue corn cakes, salsa, and tortillas. Now that was breakfast.

She had dressed professionally in a gray knee-length skirt, white blouse, and matching gray cotton jacket. Dark nylons disappeared into polished black pumps. As she walked out to the parking lot, she realized she missed the familiar weight of the Sig Sauer in her now too-light purse.

The black Lincoln was waiting, engine running. She walked to the passenger door, opened it, and was surprised to find a sandy-haired man—moderately attractive in a rugged sort of way—sitting behind the steering wheel. He wore a light but well-tailored jacket and cotton slacks. She guessed his age at somewhere in his late thirties.

"Christal Anaya, I presume?" He reached out a firm hand. "I'm Lymon Bridges. Hop in."

She shook his hand, settling herself into the seat. He studied her for a moment through clear hazel eyes. "Have a nice flight?"

"Center seat," she told him. "I was stuck between a fat woman and her screaming child."

He grinned as he put the car into gear. "Do you always jack people around?"

"Depends."

"On what?" He waited for a gap in traffic before accelerating.

"On what I need to learn."

"So, what have you learned?"

"Your office manager is happy and loyal. That says a lot."

"I pay her to be nice to me. Some people will do anything for money."

"How much did you pay Sid?"

"If I could figure a way, I'd give him half of the federal budget." He seemed nonplussed as they stopped and started, inching along in the LA traffic. Heat mirages were dancing off the chrome and glass surrounding them.

She tried to see everything, watching the people on the sidewalks, reading the business signs. "How much did Sid tell you?"

"About you? Enough."

She started to push it, then hesitated. "Where are we off to now?"

"Meeting with the principal." He gave her that evaluative glance.

"Mel Gibson?"

"Nope. He's still in Australia pawing around among the didgeridoos looking for his lost razor." He took a right, following a winding road past sprawling white stucco houses. As they proceeded, the houses became more impressive.

"Where are we?"

"This"—Bridges gestured with the flat of his hand—"is Beverly Hills." He took a side road into a gated community. At the security booth, Bridges rolled down the window. The guard bent, got a good look, and nodded, saying, "Good day, Mr. Bridges."

Christal noted the cameras that watched them from both sides of the gate. Then she caught the guard staring into a computer monitor as he punched in numbers. "They record the plates?"

"They do," Lymon told her as the gate slipped silently open. "And the camera behind his window recorded my face. He typed in the license as we drove up; the computer flashed my image, Paul's, June's, and the rest of my team's."

"So much for big brother." She was watching the tall walls pass as the road wound around past additional gates that led to imposing houses among the trees. "Are these people paranoid, or what?"

Lymon chuckled humorlessly. "Let's just say that the life of a superstar comes with a pretty hefty price tag."

"It's like a prison in here."

"It is indeed. Palatial, but still a prison." He pressed a button on what looked like a garage door opener, and a gate opened on a recessed drive to their left. Lymon rolled his window down again, waving at the security camera as he passed.

Christal gaped as they drove down the tree-lined lane and

rounded the circle drive. Lymon stopped a short distance from a bright red Ferrari.

"Damn. Rex is here."

"Rex has a nice house." Christal stepped out, looking around at the manicured grounds. The huge three-story house was partially covered with ivy. She'd never been this close to a mansion before.

"Rex is Sheela's business manager."

"So, Sheila is the client?"

"Sheela Marks," he told her, watching her reaction.

"Sheela Marks? *The* Sheela Marks." Then she frowned. "Some guy with a needle and a stun gun attacked her in New York. Got through her security. *Your* security. Is that what this is all about?"

He smiled for the first time, as if she'd just passed some test. "Let's go in and see what you've got."

"Mr. Bridges' party is here." Tomaso's voice came through Sheela's intercom. *"I have placed them in the conference room."*

Sheela pressed the button. "Thank you, Tomaso. Please see to their needs."

"Yes, ma'am."

God, she was getting tired of "yes, ma'ams." She finished toweling off, closed the shower door behind her, and walked into her closet. She picked a leisure suit by Carolina Herrera consisting of white cotton trousers, an off-white blouse, and a matching short-cut jacket. As she dressed she wondered if Lymon would be imagining her half naked in the fitting room.

That look he had given her as she peeled out of that horrible red dress had burned right through her. Worse, she'd responded to it, surprised enough to grab the robe before walking over to speak with him.

"He's right," she muttered to herself. "It wouldn't work." Hell, Hollywood was filled with stories of celebs who married the common folk. It always came to grief.

I was common folk . . . once upon a time. That knowledge

had begun to haunt her. Not that anything would change. She was at the top. All it took was a glance across her opulent bedroom at the golden statue that stood on the marble table beside the bed. Not bad for a farm girl from Quill Lake, Saskatchewan. Who would have believed?

She finished buttoning the blouse, slipped her feet into comfortable sandals, and headed downstairs. Checking her watch, she had two hours before she had to dress for Bernard's party. It would take nearly an hour for Paul to drive her up to Bernard's place in Laurel Canyon. Take Rex? Or have him drive separately? If he went, they could discuss strategy and tactics on the way. But that meant waiting around to bring him back. Rex was a party animal who, despite his age, didn't pay attention to normal biorhythms.

She descended the stairs and walked to the conference room. Rex sat at his usual place at the table, a glass of scotch in his hand. Lymon, according to script, was drinking coffee. She studied the raven-haired beauty beside him as everyone stood upon her entry. Midtwenties, with dark eyes that could melt a man. A very attractive woman. She had dressed professionally and carried herself well, nothing frail about her. Definitely not fluff.

She glanced curiously at Lymon. God, bringing this Latina angel wasn't some sort of macho defense mechanism, was it?

"Sorry to be late. Fitting took a little longer than we expected." She gave Rex a smile. "But Fiona's mollified for the moment."

"I'd like you to meet Christal Anaya," Lymon said. "Christal, this is Sheela Marks."

"My pleasure," Christal said as she shook hands, the grip firm. Hard eyes met Sheela's. Good, she wasn't going to get the usual "I love your work" bullshit, or the fawning, tongue-tied admiration. But then, she wouldn't have made it this far past Lymon's penetrating radar if she wasn't professional.

"Let's get to it, shall we?" Rex said, taking his seat. "Lymon, what have you got?"

Lymon turned his attention to Christal. "A little over a week ago, Sheela was assaulted in a hallway at the St. Regis in New York. The assailant was almost able to stick some kind of needle into Sheela. He was also armed with a stun gun. When it became apparent that the attack was compromised, he dropped a flash-bang on the floor and ran. End of story. He left no clues."

Christal nodded, reaching into her purse to pull out a small notebook. "Did anyone at the hotel recognize the man?"

"No. He kept his face either averted from, or at an angle to, the security camera. A review of the previous two week's security tapes came up blank. If the place was scouted, he didn't do it in person."

"Did anyone try to do a computer enhancement on his face?"

Lymon shook his head. "It wasn't that high a priority. Sheela was unhurt. We were happy to be through with it. The police just considered it a typical prank against a celebrity. They dusted for prints, asked around the hotel, and did a preliminary investigation."

Christal jotted something in her notebook and looked up at Sheela. "You hadn't seen him anywhere before?"

"No. It was so quick. He had a dark face." She paused, frowning, wondering where the memory had come from. "He had excited eyes."

"Yeah," Lymon agreed. "Like he was victorious. Not obsessive eyes like so many fans have."

"Have you got a copy of the hotel's security tape?" Christal leaned back, frowning.

"We do. It's at the office. My people have been reviewing it, looking for ways to make sure it doesn't happen again."

"I'll want to see it." She twiddled the pen in her fingers. "I don't suppose we could get the police report. Not just on Ms. Marks, but on the other break-ins?"

"Uh, what are we leading towards here?" Rex asked uncomfortably.

Sheela placed her palms on the table. "I want to know what happened, Rex. Lymon and I are thinking of turning Ms. Anaya loose to see what she can dig up."

All eyes went to Rex when he said, "Don't you think that's going to be a distraction?"

"From what?" Sheela cried. "They've turned *Jagged Cat*

into crap with the rewrites. Personally, after reading the latest script, I think it ought to be called *Cat Litter*! That way we might get a jump on the reviews, don't you think? A distraction? The way it's written now, I could do it half stoned." She shook her head. "No, Rex, I *need* to know what happened in New York."

"It was some loony fan," Rex muttered.

"I don't think so," Christal said absently. She did with tone of voice what a shout couldn't. She fixed Rex's attention. "It's part of a pattern."

"What pattern?" Lymon asked.

Christal shrugged. "When I figure it out, I'll tell you."

"This is bullshit," Rex added, but he did it with less certainty.

"Humor me." Sheela used her hard look to put Rex in his place, then asked Anaya, "Tell me something about yourself."

Christal's dark eyes didn't waver. One thing about her: She didn't seem the insecure type. "There's not much to tell. I grew up in rural New Mexico, went from UNM to Princeton. After law school I placed an application with the FBI. I worked as a special agent handling drugs, racketeering, and money laundering."

"Why did you leave?"

Christal's eyes seemed to expand, but she didn't hesitate before saying, "I got entangled in an unfortunate relationship with a fellow agent. Bad judgment on my part."

"Bad judgment?" Rex asked as he shot an *I don't believe this* look at Lymon.

Anaya was bristling, her fists knotted, eyes slitted as she studied Rex as if he were some sort of insect. That, more than anything, tipped Sheela's balance. She turned on him. "As if *you* could talk, Rex." She grinned sardonically, avoiding a glance at Lymon. "As if *either* of us could!"

Lymon picked that moment to say, "I asked Christal to come out here for an interview because she has skills my people don't."

Sheela focused on the woman. "Can you do this? Figure it out on your own?"

Christal frowned down at her notepad. "Honestly, I don't

know. With the Bureau, I had certain resources, people with different expertise just a phone call away."

"People with the same skills are in the private sector," Lymon replied.

"But they're expensive—" Christal started, then glanced around at the opulent room as if she had just realized what she'd said.

Sheela appreciated her modesty. "Are we talking thousands, tens of thousands, hundreds of thousands, or millions?"

"Tens of thousands," Lymon stated. He glanced at Christal. "How long do you think it will take?"

She straightened. "Wait a minute, Mr. Bridges. I haven't said I'd do it yet."

"I haven't given you the job yet, either. I just asked how long it would take."

As Christal considered, she drew little circular doodles on her pad. "Do I get a date with Mel Gibson? Assuming I can find his razor?"

"Probably not," Rex muttered.

Lymon shook his head.

"I can guarantee coffee with Sheela Marks," Sheela said dryly. "I have an in with her business manager."

Christal raised her hands, looking uncomfortable for the first time. "Mr. Bridges, I can't give you a firm commitment on the time. If it's just a single event, a fan looking for a moment's fame, maybe a week. If it's what I think, part of a pattern, then who knows? A month? Maybe more. It would depend on the complexity of the case, the resources I have available. Sometimes, hell, it can boil down to dumb luck." She met Lymon's glance. "Sorry, that's the best I can do given the facts at hand."

Lymon nodded. "Thank you." He glanced at Sheela, then added, "Ms. Anaya, would you mind stepping out into the hall for a moment?"

Christal glanced back and forth, reading expressions; smiled professionally, and walked out, closing the door behind her.

Lymon frowned down at the table, his face a mask of indecision.

Rex blurted, "I think this is nuts!"

"You weren't there," Sheela said calmly. "You don't know what it felt like." She glanced at Lymon. "What do you think of her?"

He shrugged. "Right off the bat, I think she's smart, capable, and curious. She might be just what we're looking for."

"And this thing with the FBI?" Rex prodded. "What really happened, Lymon?"

"She was romantically involved with the AIC, uh, the agent in charge, during an active investigation. The bad guy found out and managed to get photos of them in a compromising situation. My source says that she fell on her sword to minimize the damage." Lymon smiled. "Sometimes people are just people, Rex."

Rex wasn't mollified. "Seriously, Lymon, wouldn't it be better if you just put her on a plane back to DC? We're blowing this thing out of proportion." He smiled. "Or, do you have *other* interests in the young lady? She's a nice piece."

Sheela saw Lymon's jaw harden, and quickly said, "My decision, gentlemen, is that we hire Ms. Anaya to look into the attack at the St. Regis." She tilted her head toward the door. "Lymon, would you ask her to step in, please?"

Sheela studied the woman as she returned. Anaya read the room's occupants, their expressions and body postures, with a single telling glance. She nodded at Sheela and took her seat, back straight, hands clasped, looking every inch a professional. Yes, she would do.

"Christal," Lymon began, "we would like to ask you to look into this, if you're willing."

"There are things I'll need," Christal replied with a cautious smile. "I assume that I'll have an expense account for travel?"

Sheela nodded. "See to Ms. Anaya's concerns, Lymon. I'll expect daily reports."

"Weekly," Christal said as she drew a line across her pad. "I don't want to have to stop everything I'm doing to run off and find a telephone." She looked up. "And another thing. I want you to understand there may not be anything to find. What happened to you in New York may be the work of a well-prepared fan. Maybe a maid was pulling a prank in Sydney. Julia Roberts' sheets might have been a practical joke." She paused, looking from person to person. "The final thing you must understand is that if there really is some kind of purpose and pattern to these events, I have to find evidence to discover the truth. In other words, some crimes, no matter how vigorously and professionally they are investigated, remain unsolved."

"So, we could be paying you for nothing?" Rex asked as he rattled the ice in his scotch.

Christal fixed him with a piercing intensity. "No, Mr. Gerber. You will be paying me for my dedication, ability, and expertise."

Sheela decided she liked Christal Anaya. It wasn't just anybody who could feed Rex his lunch like that.

"All right, people," Sheela said, getting to her feet. "I've got an hour to prepare for Bernard's party tonight. Rex, I'll see you there. Lymon, Ms. Anaya, thank you for coming. I'll be looking forward to your progress."

7

Bernard Antillio had attached himself to *Jagged Cat* when the studio first optioned the screenplay. He, along with Sheela, had been the leverage to green-light the picture. Bernard was considered a hot director. His last picture, *Three*, had been nominated for a Golden Globe, and swept away its competition at Cannes, Toronto, and Sundance.

The guy looked the part. He had shaggy black hair that he wore over his ears like a fuzzy helmet. He left his white oversized shirts unbuttoned at the top to display a thatch of black chest hair. A narrow face, darkly complected, was home to large brown eyes that projected a brooding intensity. A good distribution deal on *Three* had not only boosted Bernard to fame, but had paid for his new digs.

The house dominated a brush-covered lot atop the mountain on Miller Drive. The structure itself looked like haphazardly stacked triangles impossibly propped up with stainless steel columns that glittered in the lights. A wag had once said it looked like a pile of giant cement mousetraps that had been sprung and then filled in with glass.

From the highest of the pointed decks, one could see from La Cienega to the Valley. As Rex stood at the prow of one of the highest wedges—a combination of roof and deck—he nursed his scotch and stared out at the endless lights of the city spread so far below. They made an improbable seascape of twinkling yellow that illuminated the high clouds with a murky lemon glow.

His mind was knotted around Sheela's fixation on the New York attack. Now they had a what? A private investigator? And she would discover what? That a wacky fan had jumped at Sheela? Things like that happened. Adulation bred obsession. Stars like Sheela had to accept the lunatics, stalkers, and sycophants.

He chewed his lip, glanced back at the party visible through the windows, and listened to the music and chatter rising from the lower decks. A woman's high laughter carried over the babble of voices. They were mostly the movers and shakers from *Jagged Cat,* although the usual smattering of producers, execs, agents, stars, and wannabes had shown up. The place would have been packed but for a Russell Crowe gala in Bel Air.

Glancing down two levels, he could see Sheela in her pale blue dress. People crowded around her—supplicants in search of favor from the goddess of the moment. He wondered how she was bearing up under the demands. Adulation and parasitism had a great deal in common.

He turned his attention back to the view and recalled the afternoon. Rex couldn't help but grin at the memory of Christal Anaya's rich eyes. He would dream about her for a while. She had spunk—something he didn't see very much of these days.

Bernard came walking up, a drink in his right hand, his left arm draped suggestively over a young blond girl's shoulder. When Rex glanced at her, his first impression was of shining white teeth, vacuous beaming eyes, and tits that had absorbed too much Miracle-Gro.

"Hey, Rex," Bernard greeted, his smile that of a satisfied barracuda. "Good to see you. I hoped you'd come." He glanced over the railing at the people clustered around the bar on the lower deck. Down at ground level, a muscular young man dove cleanly into the pool. Knots and clusters of people could be seen chatting on the lower levels and through the tall windows. "Great party, huh?"

"Yeah, and if that kid working for the valet scratches my Ferrari, I'll have his liver flayed with a weed eater."

Bernard flashed his white teeth. "They've got insurance. I heard in advance that Felix was coming. Never piss off a lawyer who can afford a Bentley. Either he's very good, or he lucked into a tobacco settlement."

Rex nodded, smiling warily. "Yeah, I wanted Felix here." He pointed. Two levels down Felix was talking to Fillip Hart, the studio CFO. "As we speak, he's telling Fill that Sheela's on the way out."

"Out of what?" Bernard continued to grin, his teeth white against his dark narrow face. The blonde under his arm was beaming up at him, awe and anticipation in her wide blue eyes.

"You've read that latest crap they've written into the script?"

Bernard's eyes narrowed, and he took a slurp from his glass. The girl frowned, as if suddenly confused. Bernard chuckled, apparently unsure if he wanted to fire back at Rex or if it was a joke. "Valerie, let me introduce you to Rex Gerber. Rex, Valerie."

"Hi, ya," Rex granted, lifting his scotch glass in a mock salute.

"Rex is one of the last of the true Neanderthals."

Rex grinned. "So? Let me guess. You optioned the Scott Ferris story?" The grin died. "Don't fuck with the script, Bernard. You're not good at it."

"Fuck you, Rex! *Jagged Cat* needed more punch. That's what we added. In case you haven't been paying attention, box office is where it's at. The marketing research indicates—"

"Bernard." Rex lowered his voice. "I'll tell you just what

Felix is telling Fill. We're going back to the original screenplay, or Sheela's exercising her option to bug out."

"Rex, she signed the contract." It had finally soaked into Bernard's shaggy head that Rex was serious.

"She did, to do *Jagged Cat* the way it was way back when. Remember how it used to be a story instead of a blood fuck?"

"The public wants—"

"People want Sheela Marks doing what she does best. And it ain't being raped by her father before she chops him in two with a shotgun." He waved down Bernard's protest. "That's it. End. *Finis*." He smiled at the girl. "Nice to meet you." He left Bernard sputtering and cursing.

He walked through the rich aroma of pot where four people sat passing a joint in the shadow of a palmetto and stepped through the sliding doors into the house. He squinted in the lights just as Tony Zell caught his eye. Tony lifted a hand and excused himself from Jodie Foster's manager.

Either it was a trick of the lights, or Tony had put something in his blond hair to make it slightly iridescent. The gold chains around his tanned neck were visible inside a loose black silk shirt. Three gold rings adorned his right ear.

"Rex?" Tony greeted, taking his arm and pulling him off to the side. "Fill me in, buddy. I'm hearing stories."

"Yeah, it's true," Rex began. "Sheela's really cranked about it."

Tony made a pained face. "Why? I tell you, it's no big deal. So, it's a little publicity. It'll blow over. Not that it hurts, huh?"

"Bad publicity? I'd call it a bit more involved than that." Rex crossed his arms, looking into Tony's perplexed blue eyes. He waved away Aaron Purcell, who was walking up with a beaming smile on his thick lips. "Later, Aaron. Okay?"

"Yeah, see me." Aaron nodded happily at Tony and veered away.

"It's *not* a big thing!" Tony insisted. Then he asked, "Did Lymon put her up to this?"

Rex made a face. "What would Lymon care? And, yeah, it is a *big* thing. Sheela might be on top right now, but she's vulnerable. Women always are. She might survive one dunk-ing, but she's not a man. She can't take two."

"Why?" Tony looked worried as he fingered the gold ring on his left index finger. "Are there threats?"

"Nothing that Felix can't handle. Look, they don't want the publicity. If they don't handle this right now, it'll be in *Daily Variety*'s Monday edition. It'll be talked all over town that the screenplay's such a piece of shit that Sheela's walk-ing. That kind of negative . . . What?"

"What are we talking about?" Tony looked perplexed.

"*Jagged Cat*. What the hell did you think we were talking about?"

"Sheela's walking on *Jagged Cat*?"

"Haven't you been listening? I sent you a memo. Either they go back to the original story, or we're gone. Remember that clause that Felix put into the contract? We gave up two percent of box office for the right to ankle if anything pissed us off."

Tony nodded, thinking.

"What the hell were you talking about?"

"This thing at the St. Regis in New York." Tony shook his head. "I don't know why it weirded Sheela out so much. I mean, man, these things happen. She knows that."

"Yeah, well, Lymon found her a PI—a woman, no less. You'd think it was a movie. A real bitchin' number, too. Mexican, I'd guess. Like Jennifer Lopez, but more intense. Not J-Lo. Raquel, from the old days. Classic, with that fire in her eyes."

Tony's gaze had fixed on infinity. "She got a name?"

"Christal Anaya. Ex-FBI. Lymon gave me a thumbnail on her. She got caught fucking some of the Washington brass. They were going to kick her out, so she resigned rather than make a stink."

Tony gave him a careful scrutiny. "You think she can do anything?"

Rex shrugged. "Hell, how would I know? If you ask me, it's a waste of money. But, yeah, if there *is* anything there, I think she's a bloodhound. She'll sniff it out."

Tony had fixed his gaze on one of the bronze statues that stood in the corner of the room. It looked like green spaghetti that dripped water.

Rex rattled the ice in his glass. "Meanwhile, you might stop and have a nice chat with Fill. Just mention that we've still got a deal with him for two pictures. Ask him what he's got in mind for a replacement if Sheela legs on JC."

Tony nodded, and he fingered his gold chain. "Yeah, I'll do that." After a pause he glanced up. "FBI, huh? No shit?"

"Why are we here?" Christal asked as she looked around at the expensive furnishings in Morton's. The tablecloths, the centerpieces, the diners in fashionably tasteless dress left her uneasy. Something about the young beaming staff didn't seem right to her. They hustled about with an unaccustomed alacrity, smiling, seeming to be happier than circumstances warranted. And then she got it: They were too beautiful.

"I want you to get it out of your system." Lymon waved around. "Morton's is probably the most famous restaurant in Beverly Hills. So, here you are. This afternoon you sat across the table from Sheela Marks. Tonight you're where all of Hollywood's greats either eat or have eaten." He pointed to a booth in the back. "There's Governor Schwarzenegger with one of his managers. Evidently he's tired of the Capitol lunchroom up in Sacramento. That or he wanted to talk business with someone. As many movies are pitched, brainstormed, and green-lighted in places like this as in board rooms."

She chewed thoughtfully on her salad as she shot a furtive glimpse at Schwarzenegger. God, the guy was big! He looked older than he did in the movies. "Okay, so just what is it that I'm supposed to be learning here?"

"That once you get past all the hype, the money, and other bullshit, we're just dealing with a bunch of people. Stressed out, but still just people with all the baggage that entails. True, they're more egotistical and screwed up, but then they've got the means to support and reinforce their egotistical and screwed-upness."

"Sheela didn't seem screwed up."

"Nope. That's one of the reasons I like working for her. She still has horse sense."

"Horse sense?" Christal lifted a dark eyebrow. "Is that a bodyguard technical term?"

He stuck a fork tine into a tomato wedge. "Not yet . . . but it ought to be. I said horse sense because she comes from a Canadian farm where they raised horses—mares, more precisely—for urine. Some kind of estrogen source for menopausal women, or some such thing. And in the end result, you can't use the term common sense."

"Why not?"

He lifted the tomato, studying it. "Because sense is never common."

"No, I guess it isn't." The way he was looking at her made her nervous. "What is it, Lymon?"

"Did you have any training in witness protection, personal security, that kind of thing?"

"Some."

"Look, Christal, there are four main causes of danger in the personal protection business: Intentional injury, where someone comes gunning for your principal. Unintentional injury, where the attack is targeted on someone else and Sheela just happens to be in the wrong place at the wrong time; she's collateral damage, if you will. Third are silly accidents. Say she trips over a cable while receiving an award, or maybe just slips in the bathtub."

"And the fourth?" Christal asked as she finished her salad.

"The fourth is an invasion of the principal's privacy. Sheela is a very private woman that the whole world would like to keep under a fisheye lens." Lymon stabbed a chunk of romaine. "My job is to keep her safe from all four of the above-mentioned threats." He studied her as he chewed, swallowed, and said, "Do you understand that difference?"

"What difference?"

"The difference between keeping a person safe and being a cop."

"Well, yes, I think so."

"Cops make lousy bodyguards."

"Why?" She smiled up as one of the too-pretty young men took her salad plate.

"They see trouble coming, and have to stick their chins right into the middle of it. Where a cop is running in to collar the bad guy, a good personal security agent is already shagging his principal out the back door. I want you to learn these two words, Anaya: Cover and evacuate."

"Cover and evacuate," she answered. "I know that personal security is all defensive, but you hired me to dig up the reality behind these odd attacks, didn't you?"

"Yeah, but I want you to learn something about executive protection, too."

"Why?"

"Do you know how many women are in this business?"

"No."

"Damn few." He smiled. "You're going to need a job when this is all over. I want to see if you've got the right chops for a permanent position with LBA."

"I guess we'll see, won't we?" She paused. "So what got you from the Marines to the bodyguard business?"

He had a vacant look. "I'm not sure you'd understand."

"Try me."

She wondered what lay behind those crowbarlike eyes he turned on her. "All right. It was one of those things that happen to guys who do crazy shit. You start to balance on the edge of the abyss, taunting the dragons that lurk in the deep. A good friend told me I was either going to go over, or I had to get out."

"Go over how?"

"I'm an adrenaline junkie. Each mission is a high. You can be caught or killed any second. Your mind and body are so alert, so alive, it's an endorphin rush. After you are extracted, you decompress, but you no longer feel complete. Something's missing, and you can't wait for the next so you'll be whole again. You get desperate, waiting, hoping. The more dangerous the last mission was, the more you crave the next. It got so that every time I was out of the field I had to be training. If I was on enforced R and R I got crazy, started looking for trouble."

He tapped the side of his head. "I've got the kind of brain that gets addicted. It's a weird personality trait. Anything I do, I have to watch myself. I keep wanting more and more. A good friend figured it out before I did. So I had to quit before I got myself—and probably some other people—killed."

"I'd think working here would be just the opposite." She indicated the glitzy surroundings. "It's artificial. Fake. Arnold over there, he's not the real world. Reality is in Peoria, or Baltimore, or Denver, or somewhere."

"You're right. I'm here for balance," he replied. "But I don't expect you to understand. Like I said earlier, it's something inside my head."

The main course appeared, the impossibly pretty waiter placing her salmon on the table before stepping back for Lymon's lamb.

She picked up her fork. "You're sure it wasn't the glamorous lives of the stars? A chance to rub some of that glitter off onto your elbows?"

He chuckled before washing a cube of lamb down with red wine. "Maybe. Back in the beginning. That's another reason I like Sheela. She hasn't self-destructed yet."

"Yet?" She raised an eyebrow.

He watched her, those hard hazel eyes making her uncomfortable. As if he were seeing . . . what?

"There is an old saying." Lymon wiped his mouth on the cloth napkin. "Just before God decides to destroy you, he makes all of your wishes come true. Celebrity comes with a price, Christal. A terrible gut-wrenching cost to the body and the soul. Filmmaking is an alluring business filled with unpleasant people doing unpalatable things in an unattractive place."

"Uh, hey, boss, I don't want to rain on your parade, but that's a pretty fancy place Sheela lives in."

"Yeah. The walls are nice, but they're still walls." He picked at his lamb. "She wears a collar twenty-four/seven, and it's starting to chafe. She lives surrounded by twenty-four-hour security. We have restraining orders out on three different stalkers who have tried to get into her house. One, our good friend Krissy, was carrying a scalpel and a butcher shop bone saw last time she tried to get over the wall."

"For what purpose?"

"Krissy wouldn't say exactly—just that it had something to do with making sure Sheela understood how much Krissy loved her."

"God."

"Hey, nutty fans are the easy part. You only worry about them when you wake up at three in the morning and can't get back to sleep. The press, on the other hand, has her life under a microscope. Somehow paparazzi managed to get photos of her being intimate with each of her last two male friends. The average person in the streets takes their privacy for granted. Sheela's last romance began to flower at a private resort outside of Dallas. Someone managed to get a camera into her bedroom. The next day ... Are you all right?"

Christal forced herself to take a breath, aware that her facial muscles had tensed and her heart was pounding. "It's nothing. But, yeah, for the record let's say I *do* understand. What happened? The photos came with a note? Payment for nonpub?"

"Are you kidding? This was Sheela Marks and Ronaldo de Giulio, the Italian director. There they were, next day, splattered all over the tabloids. Front page. 'Sheela and Italian Flame Caught in Love Tryst!' It was a disaster."

Christal was scrambling to recover her thoughts. "So, someone got through your security?"

He shook his head. "She'd left in de Giulio's jet. His turf, not hers. But that doesn't mean that it wouldn't have wiggled past us. Maybe someone slipped the maintenance man a couple of C notes? Or the maid was offered a new car? Cameras these days are tiny. The digital revolution makes the invasion of privacy probable rather than merely possible."

"So, what happened with de Giulio and Sheela? They still together?"

Lymon shook his head. "Different shooting schedules. He was helming in Italy; she was in Manhattan doing *Rage*. And the press coverage was all over the two of them. Probing, prying. It was easier for both of them to let it pass than to deal with the pressure." A pause as he chewed. "People at the top have no private lives. The public eye is relentless in its scrutiny. Most of them work twenty hours a day, seven days a week. Do you really think Sheela wanted to go up to that party at Bernard's tonight?"

"She didn't? I thought all the stars did was run from one party to another." Christal speared a square of salmon.

"It's business," he answered. "Maintaining connections, being seen. It's who you know, how you look. Who you suck up to. In most professions they call it networking. She'll be there until after two tonight. Then she'll be on the lot tomorrow morning at six to continue with the wardrobe session. At noon she has to be at La Maison for lunch with Tony, Rex, and the studio bigwigs. At three, she'll be back on the lot going through makeup and cos-tuming for this afternoon's photo shoot for the marketing and publicity people. She'll probably be out by seven. We have her booked for a fund-raiser at the Beverly Hilton at eight. She'll make it home from that by one, if she's lucky. She's due at the lot again at five the next morning to pre-pare for a cast reading." He grimaced. "And it goes on, and on, and on. The worst is, she's always on stage, always having to perform for execs, producers, the press, photog-raphers, the public. Everyone but herself. Sometimes the only private moment she has to decompress is in the limo between events."

"Doesn't she get any time off?"

"Production starts next week. She'll have a trailer on the lot to catch catnaps in. It's noisy, small, and cramped. She won't rest until the picture's wrapped. She's a pro. She can't afford to do anything half-assed. Her performance in *Jagged Cat* has to be one hundred and ten percent. If not it could kill her. A male actor can screw up a picture without torpedoing his career. A woman can't. John Travolta still makes pic-tures. Kathleen Turner doesn't."

Christal gave him a skeptical look. "They pay her very

well for the stress. Didn't I hear that she's getting almost thirty million for *Jagged Cat*?"

"The IRS, Revenue Canada, and the state of California take about fifty percent right off the top," Lymon began, counting it off on his fingers. "Then her people get their cut of the gross. Tony gets ten percent. Rex gets fifteen. Felix picks up another ten percent. Dot gets somewhere around a hundred grand plus expenses. That's eighty-five percent of her gross income gone. Her accounting firm charged her two hundred and twenty thousand last year to keep it all straight. She pays somewhere in the neighborhood of three hundred and fifty thousand a year in salaries, workman's comp, FICA, and unemployment for the household staff, et cetera.

"Remember how she looked for the Oscars? By the time she shelled out for tanning, the makeup artist, manicure, facial, hair stylist, and her fashion stylist, she was into her checkbook for twenty-two grand. Just for that one night."

Christal gaped. "*Twenty-two thousand?* That's almost half of what I made for a whole year at the Bureau."

Lymon didn't blink. "Then she's got the physical trainers, voice and dialogue coaches. Then the caterers and research assistants all send in their invoices. Insurance runs another seventy-five thousand. She's got a whopping overhead for the maintenance of the house and grounds. She's in a time-share for the Gulfstream Three—that's five hundred fifty thousand a year." He cocked his head. "On top of that there's security, travel, and all the other nitpicky things. When you add it all up, the lady works for every red cent—and she can't quit."

Christal frowned. "Anyone can quit."

His smile was bitter. "She's in a race just to keep her place. If she took a couple of years off, Rex—who's one of the best, even if he is an asshole—would go elsewhere. She'd have to lay off half of her staff, and she couldn't keep the house and property up. She needs that jet. What if she can't make a last-minute meeting in New York? It could cost her the leading role in her next film." A pause. "Come on, Christal. You know how much pressure it puts on you when people are depending on you. Even if it's just the agents you work with in the field. You can't fuck up. You can't let them down. If it was easy to walk out, why did you take it so hard?"

She bristled. "What makes you think I did?"

His gaze was boring into hers. "We've known each other for almost eight hours now. Long enough for me to get a glimpse of the stuff you're made out of."

She smiled at that, leaning back, relaxing. "Okay, so I took it hard. What of it?"

"So, we're here. In Morton's." He waved around at the surroundings. "What I want you to take away is a feeling for the glamor and an understanding of the celebs in this business. They pay for success with little pieces of themselves. The film industry is a meat grinder. It demands more than most people can produce, body and soul. When they start to run out of gas, someone offers a pill, or a bottle, and they can keep the rpms up for a while longer, bear the pressure for another couple of months, or weeks, or days."

"And then?"

"Crash. Rehab if they're lucky. An ambulance and an obituary in the back of *Variety* if they're not." He smiled. "Most actors aren't stable to start with."

"Not like Marine recon guys, huh?" Christal asked.

He muttered, "Shit," not unkindly. "I just want you to see beneath Sheela's skin for a moment. Get an idea of the pressure. Under all the flashbulbs, fancy dresses, and long shiny cars, the world is feeding off of her blood and sucking at her soul. Then, just when it's really getting crazy, some guy tries to stick a needle into her in New York. Why?"

"Where do you want me to start?"

"That's your call. What do you think?"

"I'd like to talk to Ensley. And what about Gibson's security people? Can you arrange that?"

"I can."

She finished her salmon. "Let me follow my nose, Lymon."

"Just don't get it snapped off, Christal."

8

Christal's morning was spent in a flurry of paperwork, processing professional credentials—which June Rosen called "dog tags"—and "interfacing" with the local law enforcement. Application was made for a concealed carry firearms permit; she was fingerprinted and photographed for the background check. Then came the W-2s, introduction to expense forms, an American Express Business Platinum card, as well as a company Visa card.

"Have you got wheels?" June asked.

"Back in the lot at Dulles." She considered. "I'm headed back east soon anyway."

"Rent in the meantime."

So she had finally been dropped off at the Avis counter, where she picked up a shiny gold Chrysler Concorde. She had protested for a small, compact, easy-to-park model. Instead, June had coolly asked what she would do if she was driving in the rear blocking position and the limo had a flat. Did Christal want Sheela Marks transferring to the crowded backseat of a Neon?

Now, cut loose for the afternoon, Christal looked at her map and took a stab at honest-to-God LA traffic. While she ate a burger at Wendy's she pondered the question of where to get started. How did she find a man who may or may not be in New York? One who had jumped at Sheela Marks and run? Someone whom the NYPD couldn't even begin to place?

Christal sorted through the sheaf of paper June had provided. She stopped at a name, frowned, and punched the number into her cell phone.

"McGuire Publicity," a voice informed her.

"This is Christal Anaya for Dot."

"I'm sorry, Ms. McGuire is out of the office. Could I take a message?"

"Is she with Sheela?"

"I'm sorry, I can't say. I would be happy to—"

"I'm with Lymon Bridges Associates. I'm a special investigator working for Sheela Marks."

"One moment please."

The moment lasted nearly a minute.

"Ms. Anaya? This is Dot McGuire." Dot's voice sounded mechanical. *"How can I be of help?"*

"I'd like to ask you some questions, if you don't mind. It's about what happened in New York. Would you have any free time—"

"We're at the lot. Photo shoot. If you'd like, we could do it this afternoon."

Christal took down the directions, ended the conversation, and gobbled her burger. She thought DC traffic had inured her to anything. She was wrong. An hour later, she located the correct studio gate and pulled up at the security booth. The place looked like a maximum-security prison.

After flashing her new LBA ID and getting instructions from the guard, she placed a color-coded card on the dash and drove through a maze of buildings. Parking lot C-2 eluded her until she stopped a guy walking past with half of a gruesome-looking rubber corpse over his shoulder and asked for directions. After finding the parking lot, Christal got lost three times before she located door six in building C. Another security guard finally answered her buzz and led her through a maze of hallways into a small, brightly lit set. Hammers were banging somewhere in the background behind the moveable walls. The whine of power saws shearing wood made a muted cacophony.

Christal thanked the guy and stepped into the room. Sheela Marks stood beside a broken marble column. She was dressed in sleek black leather that emphasized the sexy curves of her body. Long unruly locks of gleaming penny-bright hair shone on her shoulders. She was glaring in a challenging but seductive way into a battery of tripod-mounted cameras that ran the gamut from thirty-five millimeter to large-format portrait jobs with accordion bellows. Three different photographers were snapping and squinting through the lenses. A knot of people stood to one side, some with clipboards, others with gadgets that looked like light meters. Calls of "Great!" "That's fine," "Looking good!" and "Fantastic!" were being called out against the construction noise.

"Makeup!" someone shouted. "She's starting to sweat."

Lymon's words from dinner at Morton's haunted her.

"Ms. Anaya?" A fortyish looking woman, professional in appearance, wearing beige cotton, appeared at her elbow. She studied Christal with harried brown eyes. "I'm Dot McGuire." After introductions, Dot gestured toward Sheela, saying, "What do you think?"

"It looks hot and boring," Christal replied. "Thank you for seeing me on such short notice."

Dot crossed her arms and shrugged. "At this stage of the game, I'm just here for moral support. My job gets hectic after the film is developed." She pointed to the knot of people with the clipboards. "For now, they're calling the shots, and we jump to the tune."

"What can you tell me about that day in New York?"

Dot sighed. "Hell, I don't know. What can I say? We got out of the elevator and started down the hall. Sheela and I were talking about Atlanta. She didn't want to do the spot on CNN."

"Why?"

"She was tired. We'd been on the road for three weeks."

"Promotion, right?"

"Right."

"Who sets that up?"

Dot gestured around. "The studio, mostly. It's written into the talent's contract. For *Blood Rage* Sheela had to do three weeks on the road concurrent with release. But there was an additional clause that if the pic garnered any awards—e.g., the Oscar—she'd do another three weeks during the re-release."

"So, anyone in the studio would have known Sheela's schedule?"

Dot gave her a weary blue-eyed look. "Hey, Christal, anyone on earth who knows the business could have gotten the schedule. Either through the studio, through the TV and radio stations, even through our Web site."

"You have a Web site?"

"Of course. Sheela Marks is big business. We average over two thousand hits a day. Our Web master updates it every two weeks. Where we're shooting, what we're shooting, personal interviews, critical reviews, DVD updates, where fans can find memorabilia, that sort of thing. Last December we even did a five-hour e-mail session where Sheela answered fans' questions."

"And her tour schedule was posted there?"

"Sure." Dot frowned. "Well, within reason. I mean we didn't post that we were staying at the St. Regis. Just that we'd be in New York and what events were scheduled."

Christal chewed her lip as she considered.

Someone called, "This one's a wrap!" Sheela stepped off the dais, and two assistants led her toward the rear of the set, where she disappeared between the panels.

"What are you thinking?" Dot had raised an eyebrow.

"If I called your office, like I did this morning, and said that I was with, oh, say a TV station, and I wanted to fax you some information, what would happen?"

"My assistant would give you the fax number where we were staying."

"The hotel fax?"

"Heavens no! Most hotels are good, and sometimes we even rely on them, but keep in mind, they're focused on running their hotel. Sometimes you don't get messages for several hours. The suites we rent are set up so that we can walk in, turn on the lights, and go to work. It isn't uncommon for us to have fax machines already waiting in the room."

Christal nodded. "In other words, it's not that hard to find out if Sheela's at a certain hotel. I mean, not if you know the ropes."

Dot's expression had tightened. "No, I suppose not."

"Can you go through your records, see if you received any direct communications to the hotel?"

"I can already tell you that we did. We were receiving

faxes the entire time we were there. I was on the room phone four hours a day when I wasn't on my cell. Publicists *live* on the phone."

"Talking to whom?"

"Everyone, dear. Confirming CNN for Atlanta, doing follow-up on interviews, ensuring that we were on the mailing list for recordings and photos, stroking the producers in hopes that they'd book us again in the future."

"Can you remember if anyone asked specifically where you were or what your schedule was?"

"Heavens, I couldn't tell you. Probably. No, surely. It wasn't a secret. Our job is to place Sheela's smiling face in front of as many people as we can. We had a ninety-three percent awareness before the release of *Blood Rage*."

Christal glanced at the man who stepped out from the panels. He looked so familiar. It took her a moment to place him. "My God, that's Manuel de Clerk!"

Dot gave her a wry look. "He's cast as the lead opposite Sheela in *Jagged Cat*."

Christal indicated the photographers as she tried to reset her switches to professionalism. "Why are they doing this? They haven't even shot the movie yet."

"Marketing." Dot indicated the cluster of people who helped de Clerk onto the little set. Amidst a babble of voices they were arranging him this way and that on the broken column. "Most of these stills go out to the marketing and sales people. They're preselling space in the film for advertising. Solicitations will be going to soft drink manufacturers, breweries, automakers, electronics companies, you name it. The highest bidder gets his products used as props on the set."

Christal rolled that around in her head for a moment. "So, let's say that You Betch'a Beverage outbids the competition to place their drink in Sheela Marks' hands. Could they get Sheela's itinerary?"

Dot lifted an eyebrow. "Darling, this is Hollywood. For a price, you can get anything. This whole town is for sale, and for the right price, all—and I do mean *all*—of the people in it can be had."

Christal nodded. "Well, since I can't have Mel Gibson, how much for Manuel de Clerk?"

Dot smiled. "As soon as they're finished over there, I'll be happy to take you over and introduce you." She gave Christal a calculating look. "You'd better decide now if you've got plans for later. With your looks and body, he's going to want to get up close and *very* personal."

"Just like that?"

Dot nodded soberly. "Just like that. This is Manny we're talking about." A measuring pause. "You interested?"

Christal swallowed hard. "Sorry, I'm working tonight." She stopped short, something clicking in her head. "This thing at the Hilton. A fund-raiser. Was that on the Web site, too?"

"Heavens, yes. We'll have a crowd of fans there. They get an 'I love Sheela' button for a donation. It's a benefit for multiple sclerosis. In fact, Sheela will be dropping a couple of bills into a young lady's collection can at the door, where the crowd can see her."

People retreated from de Clerk, and Christal watched the cameras clicking and whirring as her teenage heartthrob smiled into the lenses with a beguiling sexuality.

"Jack? How are we doing?" Lymon spoke into his sleeve mike as Tomaso opened Sheela Marks' massive front door.

"We're looking good, boss. Howard has given the fire doors a double check. Someone will be stationed on all the doors all the time. We've just finished a sweep with the hotel security. Nobody's hiding in the broom closets. We checked every nook and cranny. We didn't pry up the drain covers, but if they come up that way, we'll smell 'em first."

"Roger. I'm at Sheela's now. Paul has the car ready. I'll call as soon as we're on route."

"Roger."

Dot was trotting down the grand staircase, her purse bouncing, a leather briefcase hanging from her right hand.

"Hey, Lymon."

"Dot." He gestured up the stairs. "She ready?"

Dot gave him a look that said he ought to know better. "She slept through makeup. Try to keep her from flattening her hairdo when she nods off on the way, will you?"

Lymon nodded. "Any way we can slip out of this thing early tonight?"

Dot shrugged. "It's up to her."

"She's going to hurt herself," Lymon muttered.

Dot just watched him from the corner of her eye—a knowing stare. Then she added, "She said for you to go up when you arrived. Keep her safe tonight." Dot stepped past, bursting into her fast walk as she headed for the door.

"Yeah." Lymon tapped his palm on the handrail as he climbed the stairs. He walked down the long hallway with its intricate carpet and carved molding on the doors. The white walls were hung with Southwestern art. Paintings of pueblos, rainstorms over mesas, and dark-eyed Indians stared back at him. The subject didn't quite match the decor, but what the hell, it was Sheela's. It made her happy.

He stopped, knocked twice at the master suite, and heard "Come" from within.

The latch clicked under his hand, and he walked into a large airy parlor. Several chaise lounges, an easy chair, and a small wet bar stood across from a huge seventy-two-inch TV. Bookcases lined the walls, packed with volumes that he knew Sheela had never had time to crack.

The arched doors that led to the master bedroom were closed. To the right, he could see into the spacious dressing room. On one wall behind a raised barber's chair was a rack filled with cosmetics. Two big walk-in closets were open to reveal lines of dresses. Sheela was bent over the counter, examining her face up close in the mirror. She wore a Ralph Lauren "prairie" dress that George Blodwell had talked her into. White and lacy under a short-cut Spanish-style jacket, the ensemble looked absolutely stunning in contrast to the reddish copper of her hair.

"We're ready," Lymon called by way of greeting. His smile died when she turned to greet him. He could see the fatigue that even her expert beauticians couldn't hide.

"The studio gave in," she said wearily. "We've got the original screenplay back. Rex and Tony got them to fold." She gave him a hollow smile. "I can save this film, Lymon. I can make it work."

"I'm glad to hear that. You look like you're asleep on your feet." He asked, "Do you really have to do this?"

"My best friend from high school has MS. Yeah, I have to." She arched one of her famous eyebrows. "You really look concerned."

"It's mercenary. If you kill yourself, I've got to find another client."

"You lie well." She walked past him and into the parlor. "Tell me you rode here on your bike."

"Nope. Came in the Jaguar."

"Damn!" She turned after picking up her small beaded purse. "Wouldn't it be a rush, I mean riding up to the Hilton's front door on your BMW, dressed like this?" She struck a pose, her white dress swirling.

"The helmet would do abominable things to your hair."

"When I got into this, I should have cultivated a different image. Wild and unkempt. Why didn't I do diamonds and black leather, like Cher?"

"Doesn't suit you. How about ducking out early?" He offered her his arm as they headed toward the door. "I'll get you home for a little real shut-eye before tomorrow."

She stopped short, tightening her grip on him. "Lymon, God what I'd give for that. Can you do it?"

"Yeah. I promise."

"How?"

"What time do you want to leave?"

"Eleven?" She sounded so hopeful.

"I'll find you, slip up, and whisper something into your ear. You look suddenly excited, and we'll walk quietly but firmly for the door. At risk of getting your dress stained, we'll go out through the kitchen. Paul will have the limo at the employee entrance. By the time people notice, we'll be gone. Tomaso will take messages when your phone rings off the hook all night."

She searched his eyes, reading his soul. "Thank God. Do it, Lymon. Then I won't need these." She pressed two little white pills into his hand.

"Are those what I think they are?"

She shrugged. "I can't very well afford to fall asleep in my salad tonight, can I? People are paying three thousand a plate for the opportunity to eat in my presence."

Lymon tucked the pills into his pocket. "Where'd you get those?"

"A concerned and helpful friend. Does it matter?" Her lips tightened. "Come on, you know what goes down people's throats, up their noses, and into their veins at parties in this town."

"It's a one-way trip," he warned as he led her into the hall.

"I was told that those were all right. You should recognize them. Aren't they standard issue for the military?"

"Depends on the mission, but yeah. We call them 'Go' pills. Uncle Sugar thinks it's perfectly all right for a young soldier to screw with his metabolic rate when the alternative is seeing his dead body dragged naked through the streets by an angry crowd." He made a face. "Thing is, either way, the soldier is the one who ends up paying the price."

She gave him a curious glance as they started down the stairs. "Tell me, Lymon. Did you ever use any of those little pills?"

"Those and some other things you wouldn't want to know about."

"Did they work?"

Their eyes met as he said, "I'm alive today because of those little pills. They're one of the reasons I quit, Sheela. Yeah, you can stay awake. You can wring wonderful things out of your body when it's absolutely exhausted. What you've got to remember—the hitch, if you will—is that nothing comes for free. You're burning yourself, using your blood and meat and soul for fuel."

"So, what's the difference? I do that every day anyway. What's one way over the other? Maybe it's easier with pills."

Tomaso opened the door for them, bowing politely. "Good evening, ma'am."

"Thank you, Tomaso." Sheela gave him a smile.

On the steps Lymon added, "Easier? Is it? Don't you already have enough things feeding on you?"

He held the door for her, had started to close it when she beckoned him inside with her. "Go ahead, Paul," she called. "Lymon and I have some things to discuss."

As the car pulled away, she was frowning down at her gauzy white dress. "I want you to understand something. I've always had a strong will."

She waved him down when he started to speak. "Lymon, once, when I was fourteen, I got into trouble. Dad had an old Yamaha dirt bike he used to ride out to check the irrigation. It was missing one of the covers over the sprocket. I wasn't ever supposed to ride that motorcycle."

She leaned her head back, closing her eyes. "So, of course, once when Mom and Dad were gone to Regina for a horse auction, I got that damn bike started. The first thing I did was fall over. That chain pulled the inside of my leg right into that sprocket. It was a real mess—took a damn fortune in cosmetic surgery to fix it."

Her face had begun to relax as she looked back into the past. "I slapped a bandage on it—wrapped it in gauze we used for the horses' tails when we trailered them. God, I knew that Dad would be furious when he got home. I was scared silly about what he'd do and decided the only logical course of action was to run away from home until it healed."

She smiled. "Can you imagine that? You're not real smart at fourteen. Anyhow, I caught a ride to Saskatoon on a wheat truck. I was riding in the back. August, you know, eh? Hot. Sometime flies got under that bandage. It started stinking and itching. I was too scared to look."

He watched her throat work as she swallowed. "The police picked me up at a Tim Horton's two days later. When they took that bandage off, I threw up."

"Maggots?" he asked softly.

She gave a slight nod. "That experience freaked me out. To this day, I can't stand flies. It's made me very protective of my body." She hugged herself. "This is all that I have left. It's the only private me that I have to myself. The whole world has the outside. It's only the inside that is still all mine."

Her fatigued eyes opened, and she gave him a miserable stare. "So, no drugs unless I just can't help it. I'll try to keep me to myself no matter what the cost."

"Let me know if I can help."

She blinked, stretching and yawning. "You just did."

9

Christal parked the Chrysler in a lot off Peninsula four blocks from the Hilton. On the long walk she ruminated on the necessity of getting one of those parking permits from June when she finally got her car to California. Which gave her pause. Was her little squat Nissan still a prerequisite?

Don't ditch the past until you know you can pay for it.

Her mother's words echoed in her head as she remembered the time her father had traded in a perfectly good '79 Ford F-150 pickup for a shiny new '93 Chevy three-quarterton with all the stuff you could pack into a truck. Three weeks later his boss sacked him when he showed up for work drunk. When it was all said and done, the bank repossessed the shiny new Chevy, and Mom had to drive him around looking for another job. Six months later, she filed for divorce.

Christal frowned as she walked along the street, following in the wake of others trucking toward the Hilton. A breeze off the Pacific had sent the infamous brown cloud eastward over San Bernardino. The cool air was pleasing, not at all like the humid heat that mugged DC in the summer.

The palm trees, the brown-skinned people in low riders, the numbers of signs in Spanish reminded her of home. Truth was, LA was more like her kind of city. Sort of like Albuquerque on speed and steroids.

A crowd had already gathered at the drive into the Hilton.

She stopped by the sign pointing to registration and studied the people. She wasn't sure what she was looking for. The guys with the expensive-looking camera equipment had a veteran certainty about them. Something about their body language, the way they moved, reminded her of hunters. Paparazzi, she decided.

The fans she figured for the ones with the excitement in their eyes. Their cameras weren't Nikon F5s, but the cheaper and more portable point-and-shoot kind. Finally, she figured the tourists to be the ones carrying the disposable cardboard Kodak and Fuji boxes. The clothes seemed to bear this out.

Mingling with the crowd, Christal just walked and listened. A number of people were wearing I LOVE SHEELA pins. She caught bits of gossip, conversation about children, lots of discussion of movies and TV programs, some sports (particularly the Dodgers), a new restaurant on Wilshire, and bits and pieces of gossip about celebrity social life.

"I'm just so sad," one woman was saying to her friend as they gawked down the drive waiting for their glimpse of greatness. "De Giulio was just perfect for Sheela. God, what I'd give to have a guy like that crawl into my bed."

"He's too fast," her friend, a middle-aged woman in a pink stretch blouse, replied. "Trust me, you need a steady guy, not some slick who's gonna be sniffing out every muff in town."

Christal arched an eyebrow, remembering Lymon's description of Sheela's affair.

"Manuel de Clerk's really going to be here?" another young woman asked her friend. "I can't believe it!"

Didn't any of them have real lives? She thought back to the afternoon, to actually meeting de Clerk. Instead of giddy like her heart cried for, she had been professional, safe in her FBI mode.

That she had declined to give him her phone number when he asked brought home just how scarred the affair with Hank Abrams had left her. But it was more. That look in his eyes had sent a quiver down her spine. Damn it, he'd looked at her as if she was just another sure thing.

She walked on, hearing familiar names: Richard Dreyfuss, Jennifer Aniston, Michael Douglas, John Cusack, Mark Wahlberg, and Kate Hudson. At curbside, fit-looking men in suits stood at ease, eyes on the crowd. Obviously security.

A cheer went up.

Christal rose on tiptoes to see a long white limo round the corner. The crowd seemed to flow down the walk to the red velvet ropes. Christal stepped back, climbed onto a cement planter, and watched—not the occupant, Robin Williams, who stepped out to cheers—but the crowd.

The loners immediately caught her attention. Was it the fixed expression, the posture? She could almost sense their isolation as they stood packed shoulder to shoulder with other people. Her gift had been the ability to see scars on the psyche the way others saw them on the body.

Those are the ones to watch.

Then a moving head marked by a red cap caught her attention. Another cheer went up as another limo came gliding down the drive. Flashes popped, and voices called out in giddy excitement. "Shaquille O'Neal!"

Christal had no trouble seeing him tower over the crowd as he waved and called out, "Hey! Let's all give for MS!"

Another cheer went up.

The red cap was coursing through the press of bodies, an anomaly like a ripple crossing currents; it worked like an advertisement. And then, glancing across, she could see a second hat slipping through the crowd on the other side of the drive.

A single shriek set the stage as a black limo came ghosting down the drive.

"Sheela Marks!" a shrill voice called.

Christal balanced on precarious tiptoes, watching as the door opened and Lymon stepped out, his hard hazel eyes on the crowd. He glanced at the security, then reached inside to offer his hand to Sheela.

The popping strobes reminded Christal of full automatic muzzle flashes. Sheela smiled, waved, and threw a kiss to the ecstatic crowd. The roar drowned anything she said for the benefit of multiple sclerosis.

"You a Sheela Marks fan?" a voice asked.

Christal looked down, seeing one of the red hats. A young man, perhaps twenty, dark-haired, slightly bored looking, wore a white T-shirt stenciled with the words GENESIS ATHENA. A stack of fliers was in his hand, something photocopied on chartreuse paper.

"Yeah," she said. "Of course."

"Here." He handed her one of the papers before he turned away. She watched him walk from person to person, handing out the sheets.

She folded it between her fingers, looking back in time to see Sheela, in a lively white dress, step through the double doors, Lymon walking a step behind on the right.

By the time the last of the celebrities had arrived, teenagers were circulating through the crowds with ornately decorated coffee cans, soliciting donations.

Christal chipped in a five-dollar bill. Only then did she look down at the flashy green paper she held.

GENESIS ATHENA was prominently printed across the top.

"What would you give to share your life with the impossible?" she read. "GENESIS ATHENA makes dreams come true. You can bring her into your life."

Below the words was a picture of Sheela Marks. When she turned it over, the same words were written with a photo of Manuel de Clerk. A phone number and the Internet address www.genesisathena.com were printed at the bottom.

Lymon locked his BMW RT, undid the D rings on his helmet, and climbed the stairs to his office. The clock in the motorcycle's fairing had told him it was six-forty. He yawned, figuring that he could sneak home before noon and nap prior to meeting Paul at the studio. They needed to finalize arrangements for Sheela's trailer.

He slipped the key into the lock, stepped inside, and hung his helmet and leather jacket on the peg in the storeroom. Equipment was stacked on the shelves, and a big gun safe lurked in the rear. Walking down the hall, he was surprised to see a light on in his office. A greater surprise was finding

Christal seated at his desk. She was hunched over the computer monitor, her raven hair a jumbled mess falling over her shoulders. A half-empty cup of coffee rested to one side. Evidence she'd been there for a while. A yellow legal pad lay askew to her right as her fingers tapped keys.

"Make yourself at home."

She glanced over her shoulder; her large dark eyes might have looked right through him. "What is obsession worth?"

Lymon stepped in and walked over. "Whatever the market will bear." He flicked a finger back and forth. "You're in my chair, at my desk, using my computer."

Her gaze seemed to clear, and she looked up at him. "This is yours?"

"So, tell me, did you just make yourself at home in the SAC's office at the FBI? Or do things like your employer's privacy just not rate very highly on the Christal Anaya scale of propriety?"

An eyebrow arched, and he could see fatigue behind her shapely face. "Sorry, boss man. You should put a sign on the door. I didn't know this was yours. I needed a computer. June's looked daunting at the front desk. I know this model of Compaq."

"Dudette, you're getting a Dell." He waved his finger again. "Two questions. One, what the hell are you doing on my computer? Two, how long have you been here?"

She glanced at her watch. "Shit! Is that the time?"

He noted that half the yellow pad was folded under the backing. "Start at the beginning, Christal."

She pushed back in his chair, seemingly ignorant of her continued violation of his sovereign territory. A frown incised her forehead. "Have you ever looked at Sheela Marks' Web site?"

"Sure. Back when Dot first had it up and running. So what?"

"It's got a *lot* of information in it. Her whole career is there. It took me over an hour just to skim through it. Did you know that no less than fifteen different Web addresses are linked to her site?"

"You've lost me. Why is that important?"

"Because there is a whole Sheela Marks subculture on the Internet. I can take you to five different chat rooms dedicated to nothing but her. One of them, wow!"

"What does 'wow' mean?"

"The address is 'share-la-sheela.' It's sick." Christal studied him. "Did Sheela ever do porn films?"

"No."

"Then the nudes they run must be generated. You know, they put Sheela's face on a body that looks like hers ought to. For a price—sorry, boss, but I used the company Visa—you can have an image of yourself making whoopee with Sheela. All you have to do is copy a photo of yourself and they put it on the naked guy or gal doing the dirty with Sheela. You can download the whole thing, burn it onto a CD, and watch yourself porking away on your home big-screen TV."

Lymon felt a souring in his gut. "Can we find them?"

"Yeah, for a price." She was reading his expression. "But I can pretty much tell you right now that they're offshore."

"What else? Anything tied to the New York attack?"

She took a deep breath, stretching her arms in a way that an attractive young woman with a nice body in a tight black sweater shouldn't. "Mentions of it in the Web site, of course. Lots of chatter about it in the chat rooms." She made a face. "But nothing that pops out at me, you know? Most of it was 'Gee isn't it awful' mixed with 'What kind of nut would do that?' mixed with "If I got that close, I'd tell her how wonderful she is' kinds of things."

"This site with the naked Sheela—"

"And chat room to describe the experience."

"Right. Can we find that? Figure out who visits that site?"

Christal sipped at her coffee, grimaced, and said, "Cold. Damn. But that's a great coffee machine you've got." She put the cup down. "Let's put it like this: It's probably being run out of a little shop on a backstreet in Kuala Lumpur. You thinking about sending someone to break the guy's legs and politely request that he not do it again?"

"Something like that." It shouldn't be bothering him this much.

"If you found him, my bet is that the same program would crop up from somewhere else."

"We still find him."

"Want my advice?"

"Sure."

"I think the best way to handle this—God, an ex-agent, I don't believe I'm saying this!—is to put feelers out over at CIT, or up at San Jose. There's got to be someone who could write a virus, something that could be inserted into a man's photo."

He picked it up. "So when it was loaded, it would infect and destroy the program?"

She shrugged. "It would have to be handled with discretion."

He crossed his arms, liking Christal Anaya. "So, why would you suggest something like this?"

She tapped her notepad. "I like the lady. It pissed me off."

"You never answered the second of my questions. How long have you been here?"

She shrugged. "After the crowd began to fade at the Hilton I was intrigued. I needed a computer. Instead of going home I came here."

"You've been here all night," he noted. "Anything else that you need to report before I send you home?"

Her eyes had taken on that distant look again. "Nothing that's clear yet."

"When it comes into focus, tell me soonest. But for now, get the hell out of my chair."

She nodded, smiled at him as she collected her things, and stood. "See you, boss."

She was halfway out the door when she paused, reached into a pocket, and pulled out a bright green piece of paper. "Lymon? You ever heard of Genesis Athena?"

"Nope. Is it an escort service or a fitness spa?"

"It's neither. Sheela's site has a link, and there was a kid handing these out last night." She rattled the paper. "After I thought about it, I ran the kid down. He was hired through a temp agency. The temp agency gave him the flyers, paid him fifty bucks, and van-pooled the kids to the benefit."

Lymon looked at the wild green page. "So, what did you do?"

"Like I said, it's on Sheela's Web site. I used the hot key and took the link."

"What did you find?"

She gave him a perplexed look. "A questionnaire."

"Huh?"

"Yeah, you know, the sort that you get when you take a personality profile. It didn't make much sense, so I didn't stick around. I thought maybe you might know what it was."

"Ask Dot next time you see her. Meanwhile, get some sleep, huh?"

For long moments after she'd gone, he sat, staring absently at the computer. Then he thumbed through his Rolodex, punched a number into his phone, and waited. At the sleep-soggy voice on the end, he said, "I don't care what time it is. I need a name. Someone discreet who can write a killer computer virus."

Hank Abrams pulled into the drive of his Fairfax, Virginia, home and sighed. Marsha's red Honda Pilot SUV gleamed in its spot, looking freshly washed and waxed. On the other hand, he depended on the occasional rainstorm to keep his white '97 Buick clean. As to the car wash option, well, he'd had other priorities over the last couple of years.

He killed the ignition, listened to the engine diesel a couple of times, and sat for a moment, looking at the high-peaked roof of his gray-sided house. The freshly watered lawn sparkled in the hot afternoon sun. Marsha insisted on perfectly manicured grass. A timed sprinkler system and an expensive lawn service kept it looking immaculate.

Hank took a deep breath, feeling the heat begin to overtake the air-conditioning. What was it? Ninety-five out there? Not nearly as hot as it was going to be in the house when he told Marsha about his transfer and demotion. Pete

Wirthing had given him the news just after lunch. He'd lose a pay grade, and they were sending him to El Paso. West Texas.

Where the hell was El Paso? He'd had to look on a map. How could you get so far from anything and still be anywhere?

He opened the car door, grabbed up his briefcase, and stepped out into the sunshine. He could feel warm heat swirling around him. Clammy moisture stuck his shirt to his armpits. Was that the humidity or fear?

A month ago he'd been a hot new star in charge of his own investigation. Christal, with her uncanny ways, had broken Gonzales wide open. All the pieces of the puzzle had started to fall into place.

He hated the sinking sensation in his gut. Every nerve in his body had turned to rubber. God, how was he going to explain this to Marsha?

You don't mention Christal, you fool. No matter what.

He wet his lips. "Honey, I blew the investigation. It was my fault. I let a piece of information slide by." To his ear, it sounded good. Hell, she knew something was wrong. She'd asked him about it before bed last night.

He watched his black shoes rising and falling on the hot white cement and stepped up to the front door. On the second try he stabbed his key into the hole. The heavy door clicked and swung open. He slipped into the cool dimness of his house and closed the door behind him. It shut with a finality that sent a shiver through his guts.

"Marsha? I'm home."

Silence.

He found her in the dining room, sitting across the table where she could see him walk through the arched entry. Her back was straight, her black hair pulled back and clipped at the nape of her neck. She wore a sleeveless black pullover. A white pearl necklace that she'd bought in Paris duplicated the curve of the blouse top against her smooth chest. Her large brown eyes were smoldering, her mouth tight. He could see the muscles in her jaws, bunched and hard.

"Hank?" she asked in that silky voice of rage. "Good of you to come home again."

"Huh?" He glanced at the papers on the dark walnut table-top in front of her. His heart stopped, seemed to stutter, and began to pound against his chest wall. He could feel the blood draining from his face.

"Who is she?" Marsha asked in absolutely precise terms. He'd heard her use that tone when she deposed hostile witnesses. As an attorney she had few peers and was already well on the way to a partnership at her prestigious firm.

He felt his guts sliding down inside him, ready to drop right out the bottom but for the thin wall of his abdomen. With a shaking hand, he pulled out a chair and lowered himself into it before his legs gave out.

"How . . . ?" He swallowed hard, trying to keep his voice from quavering. "Where did you get those?"

"Manila envelope," she said softly, lifting it for him to see. "Taped to the door. My name is printed on the outside with black ink." A short silence. "You didn't answer my question. Who is she?"

"No one." At her look, he amended, "An agent. Someone under me."

"Yes." A twitch at the corner of her lips betrayed her iron control. "Very much under you, as the photos so clearly demonstrate. I'm glad to see that you are so on top of your duty."

"Marsha, don't. You have no idea how hard it's been."

"Apparently she knows how *hard* it's been, Hank." Marsha slapped the photos on the table. "So, come on, spill it. Got anything to say? Perhaps starting with the reason you decided to end our life together this way?"

He lowered his eyes and rubbed his sweaty hands together between his knees. "What do you want me to do?"

As the long silence passed, he stared miserably at his hands. They looked white and weak. He couldn't nerve himself to look her in the eyes. Wouldn't be able to stand what he'd see there.

Her voice was cool. "I've taken the liberty of making a

reservation for you at the Best Western. You know the one. Just before you get on the Belt Loop. I'll have your things packed by the end of the week. That allows you time to determine where to have them sent."

"El Paso," he muttered. "Send them to El Paso."

"Hank?"

"Yes."

"One last word of advice. Hire a *very* good lawyer."

10

Christal cranked an eye open, cursing the damn fool who wouldn't answer the knock at his door. The pounding came again, and she realized, to her chagrin, that it was her own door.

She flipped the covers off, fumbled for an extralong T-shirt, and pulled it over her shoulders. She pressed a hand against her full bladder, promising that it wouldn't be long.

She walked down the stairs in the half-light and squinted as she put her eye to the door peephole. She could see Lymon's face peering back, the nose distorted out of proportion by the small lens.

As he began another spate of knocking, she pulled the door open, squinting against the bright sunlight.

"Yeah?"

"Got a moment?" He stepped past her, a serious Dot McGuire walking behind. The woman's face was a study of upset and irritation.

"Do be my guest and come on in," she said to their backs, and took one last glance out at the day. From the angle of the sun, it had to be late afternoon. Closing the door, she walked over and cranked the curtains open. Lymon had walked straight into the kitchen, checked the coffee machine, and pushed the button.

"Good work, Christal," he called. "We thought we ought to have a meeting."

"It's . . ." She frowned at her wrist, realizing her watch was on the bedside table upstairs. "What time is it?"

"It's Hollywood, darling," Dot drawled as she pulled off her shoes and flopped into the easy chair. She tucked her nylon-clad legs under the knee-length skirt she was wearing.

"Can I get dressed?"

"Go for it. We're burning daylight," Lymon called from the kitchen.

Christal headed for the stairs. "Burning daylight? God, do people really say that?"

His shout interrupted her reverie. "Christal, dress formal. Black is preferred. Sequins acceptable. You're working tonight."

"Formal, right." She made her way back up the stairs, locked herself in the bathroom, and made peace with her bladder. By the time she had washed her face, found her best dress, and gotten most of herself together, she could smell coffee wafting up the stairs.

Lymon was perched on the sofa, a cup of steaming coffee on the low table in front of him. The television across the room was on CNN. Dot's eyes were fixed on it.

Christal poured a cup of coffee and strode in, seating herself at the end of the sofa, the cup cradled in her hand. "I take it this isn't a social call?"

Dot had raised a hand, then looked her way as a commercial aired. "Someone hit Sandra Bullock last night."

"Is she okay?" Christal asked. "Did they get the guy who assaulted her?"

"Not hit as in hit," Lymon explained. "Hit as in invaded her privacy and stole her toothbrush and hankies."

"Hankies? Toothbrush?" Christal realized she was still sleep-deprived.

"All that's left is Nicole Kidman," Dot said summarily. "The last of the big four."

"I'll right, I'll bite," Christal looked back and forth between them. "What's the big four?"

"The twenty-million club," Lymon supplied. "Only four actresses can demand over twenty million per film. Three of them: Julia Roberts, Sheela Marks, and Sandra Bullock have been . . . What? Attacked? Robbed? What do we call this, and why's it happening? Like Mel Gibson's razor. What's the point?"

"Tell me about the hankies." Christal leaned back, frowning.

"Sandy has a cold," Dot explained. "I talked to her publicity department. She was taking a long weekend at her house in Jackson Hole. Someone came in through the bathroom window in the middle of the night. Neutralized the security system and was actually in the room with her! Scared her to death. A voice called 'Good night' out of the darkness, and woke her up."

"Teton County sheriff's office was there within twenty minutes," Lymon added. "They found nothing."

"They won't," Christal answered, not quite realizing why she said it.

"Why?" Lymon leaned forward.

"Just a hunch," she muttered, covering.

"Like the computer stuff?" Dot asked. "Lymon called first thing this morning. My people have been all over that Web site. We had no idea it could take you so many places."

"Did you find the 'hump-a-Sheela' site?" She glanced cautiously at Lymon. God, the guy really had a case for his client. Was that good, given his position?

Lymon grinned unpleasantly. "It's being taken care of. It took a couple of phone calls, but by this evening we should be instituting countermeasures."

"I don't want to know about it," Dot said, sticking her fingers into her ears. But she went right on, saying, "We were shocked that someone could do that."

"If it was done once," Christal reminded, "it can pop up again at any time."

"I've got one of my staff detailed to spend a half day a week on the site, just following the traffic, you might say. Our Web master has been given the go-ahead to do a more thorough breakdown of who accesses the site, where they're from, and all the other statistics."

"How about the links?"

"Legit. As you know, most are studio links that take you to film information, and the others are charities." Dot clapped her hands.

"What's Genesis Athena?" Christal asked.

"We don't know." Dot frowned. "They actually paid us for the link, can you imagine? We get a thousand a month. I looked at their site. All I found was a questionnaire. I assume they're some sort of marketing research company."

"But you don't know?" Christal sipped her coffee.

"Well, for a thousand a month, they couldn't be too shady." Dot shrugged. "I checked. They're linked to other stars, too. We're not the only ones."

"Like who?"

"Manuel de Clerk, for one. Julia Roberts, Sandra Bullock, Mel Gibson, Denzel Washington, most of the A-list." Dot ignored the news as it came on again. A story about airport security.

"But nobody knows what Genesis Athena is?"

"It's a questionnaire," Dot repeated.

Lymon was watching Christal, a slight frown marring his forehead. "Is this another of your famous hunches?"

She tapped her coffee cup with a fingernail. "I'd just find out who was using my Web site, that's all."

"Right." Lymon nodded to Dot, as if to say, "Do it."

Dot missed it, musing, "Why would they take Sandy's toothbrush and used Kleenex tissues?"

"Always something personal. Like a *brujo* would take." Christal murmured to herself.

"A what? What's a brew-ho?" Lymon asked.

She smiled sheepishly. "It's superstition. *Un brujo* is a witch. Where I grew up, the older people still believed in witches. Hell, people even suspected my grandmother. Said she had powers. That she could see into men's souls."

"Right, like the Shadow? With the ability to cloud men's minds?" Dot asked, raising an eyebrow. "I remember the movie with Alec Baldwin."

Lymon's hazel eyes probed again.

"It's nothing." Christal tried to wave it off. "Have you had time to talk to—"

"No," Lymon interrupted. "I want to hear this. How did she see into souls?"

Christal winced. "Look, it's just old superstition, huh? Backcountry New Mexico is full of it. Grandma wasn't a witch anyway, she was a healer, a *curandera*."

Dot obviously wasn't buying any of it, but Lymon had leaned forward. "What about the personal items? You said what, that a witch would take things like that?"

Trapped, she admitted, "Well, yeah. If you're going to hurt someone, you need to possess a piece of them. A lock of hair, a fingernail clipping. Menstrual cloths were really big. So was a man's semen, assuming you could get it."

She stopped, feeling something nibbling at the edges of her consciousness.

"What?" Lymon asked.

Christal shook her head. "I don't know. It's as if something's just out there; something I can't quite grasp."

"About witches? You think Bullock, Gibson, and the rest were witched?"

"No." She tried to grasp the idea that lay just beyond her thoughts. "But that's on the right track. It's got something to do with possession."

"Bullshit!" Dot exploded. "You're not suggesting that we go to Madame Toulouse for a reading, are you?"

"God, no," Christal shot back. "I don't believe in that crap either. No, this is something that will make perfect sense when the right pieces fall into place."

Dot was building up to say something when Lymon waved her down. "Go with it, Christal. Hell, you've been here for twenty-four hours, and we've already got results."

"What?" Dot asked. "We'd have found that shit on the Web site eventually."

Lymon wondered, "But would we have dealt with it as effectively?"

"Hey!" Christal straightened. "You didn't take my advice, did you? I was dead tired. Not thinking."

Lymon gave her a soldier's grin. "Hey, Chris, this is the private sector. You're not a fed anymore. You get paid for results here. It would have been such a pain in the ass to travel all the way to Kuala Lumpur to bust the guy's legs and then have to speak politely to him. It would have hurt my facial muscles."

"Right. Glad to be of service, but the laws that control—"

"Come on, Christal." Lymon headed for the door. "We don't have time to chat. We're almost late as it is."

With fingertips, Hank Abrams drew designs in the moist surface of the glass. The bar's soft lighting cast amber tones through the bourbon. The tremble had left his hands. He still hated them.

Self-loathing was a terrible thing. He didn't understand it. Ever since Marsha had thrown him out of the house, he'd wanted to hurt himself. To take something jagged and sharp—a broken bottle, twisted rusty tin—and rake his arms and chest. He wanted to sting and bleed.

God, we're fucked-up creatures! He stared at his fingers as they traced figure eights on the sweating tumbler and tried to ignore the sounds of the bar. Patrons were talking in low tones, laughing. A table of men no more than two steps away were talking football. He fumed at the easy jocularity in their voices. They still had lives. Homes, wives, jobs to return to.

His eyes narrowed, remembering Christal. Her eyes were looking into his, smoky and challenging. He could remember the light in her ink-black hair, the set of her sharp cheeks. Narrow at the waist, she filled a pair of jeans perfectly. God, he'd wanted her from the moment he'd first seen her.

Enough to totally fuck up your life?

It shouldn't have happened that way. Hell, it had just been the two of them in the surveillance van. How had anyone been able to get pictures? Who would have known they'd fuck that night? It had been the first time—the only time. Nothing planned, really—it had just happened. As if the moon and stars had been in the right alignment.

In his misery he'd remained unaware of the man. Surprised, he looked up to see a thin dark-complected face, thick black eyebrows, a narrow nose, and terse mouth. The guy wore a fedora and a dark suit coat. His eyes looked like black marbles.

"Yeah?" Hank asked.

"May I sit?" The guy indicated the other chair.

"Uh, I'd appreciate it if you took one of those tables over there." He pointed across the bar. "Got someone coming, you know?"

The man's eyes never left Hank's as he pulled out a chair and sat. "You look like a man looking for a job."

On the verge of telling Fedora to fuck off, Hank hesitated. "And just what makes you think that?"

Fedora shrugged.

Hank flicked a finger to indicate the hat. "That's a little dated, isn't it? If you're trying to look like a 1930s gangster, you've got the part down pat. But for the twenty-first century it makes you look a little hokey."

"I am Salim, Mr. Abrams."

Hank's alarm bells began going off. He straightened. "Just how the hell would you know my name?"

"A mutual friend." Salim smiled. "For the moment his name need not concern us. Let us just say that he thinks you got a bum rap. He contacted me about your situation."

"And when I find out who, I'm going to bust his ass," Hank muttered darkly. "I *don't* need any son of a bitch fucking with my life just now. And I sure as hell don't need you and whatever your scheme is. I've got enough trouble."

Salim smiled. "I have no scheme, Mr. Abrams. I come to offer you a job." He touched the tips of his fingers together. "My sources tell me that you had Gonzales, but for an unfortunate circumstance. We were impressed by that."

Hank tightened his fingers around his glass. "You want to know something? Your loudmouthed friend in the Bureau is going to get his balls chopped off one of these days."

Salim shrugged. "Where are they going to transfer you to?"

"Why should I talk to you?" Even through the slight buzz, his cop's instincts were vibrating. "In fact, why shouldn't I just pick up the phone and call a couple of friends of mine? Here you are, whack, right out of the blue, knowing all about me, and no doubt about to pitch something that's too good to be true. Why do I smell shit?"

Salim smiled thinly. "This isn't a movie, Special Agent Abrams. I do not represent a drug cartel or money laundering ring looking to exploit a down-on-his-luck agent. Here's my card." He flipped out a business card. "Take some time. Do some research—through the Bureau, if you'd like."

Hank narrowed his eyes, feeling the tingle around his senses. Wishing now that the guy had shown up two drinks ago before the bourbon had slipped its muzzy fingers through his brain.

The card proclaimed VERELE SECURITY. It gave a New York City address and phone with an e-mail address.

"Security, huh?"

"We're licensed and registered. We specialize in executive protection." Salim gave him a faint smile. "We work for the good guys, too."

"So, why come to me?"

"Let me return to my question: Where are they transferring you to?"

"El Paso. You ever been to El Paso?"

Salim shook his head.

"Me neither. But, shit, I guess I'm going." He glanced up. "You know where I live?"

"I have your address. When I called there, Mrs. Abrams said she didn't know where you were, or care, for that matter."

"Right."

"Your personal relations do not concern me. I've been sent to see if you'd be interested in executive security. Finding people is never hard. Local police will generally work for us when they're off-duty. But finding *good* people is always a challenge. Depending on your capabilities, the wages can be quite good. And, well, how do I say this, the environment will be a great deal more salubrious than in El Paso."

Suspicion bubbled up in his blood. First the photos were taped to his door for Marsha to find. Now this guy shows up? It tasted like an ambush to him, but who was the leak in the Bureau?

"Before I go any further, I need to know who sent you to me."

Salim studied him for a moment with sharp brown eyes. "Fair enough. The assistant director. For reasons that I would hope you could understand, we would appreciate your discretion in this matter. Please don't charge into his office tomorrow morning demanding at the top of your lungs to know if he referred you to us."

Hank frowned. "The AD? The guy who just canned my ass?"

Salim sat back and removed his hat. "Agent Abrams, you have been around long enough to know that good people are often caught in situations that spiral out of control. The Gonzales case is one of those. As to how that camera got placed in the van, who knows? Gonzales didn't get to where he is by being an idiot. He knew you were closing in, and he fought back." He lifted a thoughtful eyebrow. "It's only a guess, Mr. Abrams, but I'd say that all things in perspective, professionally destroying you and Agent Anaya was his only way out. He wanted you beaten and broken . . . with your personal and professional lives destroyed."

Had Gonzales sent the photos to Marsha just like he'd sent them to Peter Wirthing? They'd been in a plain manila envelope, labeled in black ink. Both times. "I'll get the son of a bitch in the end."

Salim waited in respectful silence, then said, "Not from El Paso, you won't. And not through the Bureau. He's wise to you."

"Is that why you hunted me down? Because of Gonzales?"

"No. I'm here because you are a highly trained agent with skills that my company could use. As far as Mr. Gonzales is concerned, he's beaten you. You and he were playing a very high-stakes game. A smart man understands that. That he managed to exploit such a minor weakness is an example of not only his skill, but yours. You can let what happened crawl around under your skin until you end up broken, bitter, and ruined; or you can accept that at this time and place, Mr. Gonzales squeaked out the narrowest of victories. Your choice is to drown in self-pity or go on to bigger and better things."

"Which you are here to provide."

"Maybe. I haven't made up my mind yet. And the final decision will rest with my boss in New York. You're half drunk, surly, and depressed."

"What do you pay?"

"If you can convince us that you are worth it, we would start your salary at sixty thousand a year. Please remember the *if* in that sentence. You must prove your worth to us. If you've got chops, it would rise. Security supervisors in my company make between one hundred and one-fifty a year." He smiled. "That, of course, does not include any gratuities that our clients might feel obligated to bestow upon you for services rendered. Our clients include some of the richest men in the world. To some of them, a twenty-thousand-dollar tip is but a pittance."

"And all I have to do is sign on the bottom line?"

"It would depend on if you could satisfy my employer and me. Tell me, Agent Abrams, are you really any good, or are you a fuckup? Answer that question honestly. If you're the first, come look us up. If you're the latter, go to El Paso, bury yourself, and don't waste either our time or your superiors'." He stood, slipping his hat onto his head. "Good evening."

Hank Abrams watched him walk away, stunned and, truth be told, curious.

11

So, here I am, watchdog instead of wolf. The notion rolled around in Christal's head. Sid had been right. There was life after falling on the sword. If she'd gone to war with the Bureau, she'd have been up to her neck in lawyers, facing public instead of just professional humiliation, and making nowhere near three hundred dollars a day to stand around a

plush ballroom at the Regent Beverly Wilshire Hotel trying
to place names to faces she'd seen at the Cineplex down
from her Virginia apartment.

"It's simple," Lymon had explained to her. "All you have
to do is keep an eye on Sheela. Nothing intrusive, just be
close. Guests will be screened at the door, of course, and the
hotel has its house security on alert. We're just backup.
Howard and Jack worked a complete advance last night.
You'll be there with me, Salavatore, and Wu."

Salvatore fit the bill for the old adage of tall, dark, and
handsome; he had a strong jaw and fierce brown eyes. She
figured him for his midthirties, really fit, with a body-
builder's physique. If he hadn't been a football jock in college, she couldn't guess them. He worked part-time for
LBA. His day job, if you could call it that, was security for a
software company in Venice where he worked four ten-hour
shifts a week.

Wu was short for Yan Zan Wu, a barrel-chested Chinese
guy, late twenties, with a round and appropriately inscrutable face. He made her think of Odd Job in the Goldfin-
ger movie until she discovered he worked part-time for
LBA, too, while he finished his Ph.D. in physics at UCLA.

As she tagged along in Sheela's wake, she tried not to
look conspicuous and shot lethal glances in Lymon's direction. He was orbiting off Sheela's left, never more than five
quick paces away. She figured she could kill him later. Lymon hadn't thought to send her back upstairs for makeup
that afternoon. She'd donned her best dress, true, but now
she felt like a dolt being the only woman in the room except
for a bald female rock star, whose name she'd missed, without at least the benefit of blush.

In contrast, Sheela looked ravishing in a white Narciso
Rodriguez dress that complemented her red-blond hair. Her
face had been made up with Paula Dorf powder, iridescent
eyeliner, and apricot lip gloss.

"So, you're the fed?" A blond man interrupted her pique
as he stepped up to her side.

"Excuse me?" She took his measure: Blond, athletic, and
tanned, he looked really good. She liked the sparkle in his

blue eyes and the nonaggressive smile. Damn! The guy had enough gold hung around his neck to lure Coronado back from the grave.

"You don't look like a federal agent," he added, the smile displaying nice teeth.

"Do I know you?"

"Not yet. I'm Tony Zell." He offered his hand, adding, "Sheela's agent."

"Christal Anaya. Lymon Bridges Associates." She took a step to close the distance to Sheela. "I'm the FNG."

"FNG?" He looked confused.

"Fresh new girl," she punned, watching to see if he got it. He didn't, and she was unsure what to make of that.

"You're supposed to find out what happened to Sheela in New York."

"You don't sound enthusiastic about that."

He shrugged, waving at someone who called "Hiya Tony." "I don't know. I'm in the minority. It was probably just a fan getting his kicks. Bragging rights, you know."

"He hasn't been bragging yet," she said, walking slowly as Sheela moved. How did the woman do it? Sheela's smile never wavered, she seemed to know everyone, and a genuine excitement sparkled in her blue eyes. Every movement was poised, graceful, and sinuous.

"What? So, you've been to every bar in New York?"

She arched an eyebrow. "What makes you think New York?"

"Well, that's where it happened."

"Yeah, maybe."

"What do you mean, maybe? That's where Sheela got mugged, right?"

She shrugged. "Sheela's not the only celeb involved here."

He glanced around, adding, "Uh, it's not my place to judge, but what are you doing here?"

"Working," she added pleasantly as she led him another step, keeping her distance from Sheela's knot of people. "Lymon wants me to familiarize myself with this aspect of the business."

"You don't look anything like what a female FBI agent

should look like." He snagged two flutes of champagne from a passing tray, extending one in her direction.

"Sorry, I'm on duty. Apparently you didn't see *Miss Congeniality* or you'd know FBI agents can come in all sizes and shapes."

He laughed at that, still offering the champagne flute. "Here, at least hold it. You'll make me feel better."

She took it, looking past him, trying to concentrate on the people hovering around Sheela.

After sipping his drink, he asked, "Why do I get the feeling that you're only half here?"

"Because I'm on the job, Mr. Zell. Having you here, acting like we're having a discussion, removes attention from me. Therefore you're welcome to walk with me, assuming you don't get tired of talking to a wallflower."

"So, are you, like, always on the job?"

"They're paying me too much to waste precious time on myself."

"Hey, you've got to eat and sleep sometimes."

"Mr. Bridges doesn't seem to think so. He has developed this early habit of calling me at odd hours."

He seemed to digest that for a moment. "You ever think of films? Acting, I mean. You might try a screen test sometime."

That broke her concentration, and she stared flatly at him. "What? Are you kidding?"

He gave her an offhanded shrug. "I'm an agent. I'm always looking for new people. It's what I do. It wouldn't hurt to try. Talent comes from strange places. You're a beautiful woman. . . ." He made a face, as if searching for the right word. "Moxie. That's it. You've got moxie . . . a certain chutzpah that gives you presence."

She grinned crookedly before returning her attention to Sheela. "Are you hitting on me, Mr. Zell?"

"No." He backtracked too fast, adding to her amusement. "I'm serious about the screen test."

The auburn-haired woman caught Christal's attention. She couldn't have said why—just a quality in the woman's eyes, the way she moved. Call it predatory. Christal estimated her at five-foot-seven, tanned, with a classic Nordic face and burnished hair that streaked into sun-bleached yellow highlights. She wore a copper-colored form-fitting pantsuit that emphasized her muscular body. Skin-tight gloves covered her hands, and she held a flat purse the size of a hardback novel. More to the point, her serious gray eyes had fixed on Sheela with a feline intensity.

"Excuse me, Mr. Zell." She handed him back the untouched champagne.

He turned, following her gaze, and took a moment to study the woman. "Quite a number." He paused, and she could feel his gaze when it returned to her. "What is it about her that makes you nervous?"

"Just a hunch."

Christal stepped around a knot of tuxedo-dressed men and smiled when one asked, "Hey, Tony! Who's this?"

"Business associate," he answered smoothly. "I'll introduce you later."

The copper-headed woman had moved, calmly dismissing a young man who tried to talk to her. Bingo. She wasn't just socializing.

At that moment Sheela said something to the people surrounding her, gave them a gracious smile, and stepped away from her party. She clutched her handbag, walking purposely toward the women's restroom. Salvatore had picked her up, shadowing her right flank.

To Christal's surprise, Copperhead—as she'd tagged the woman—seemed to anticipate it and stepped into the ladies' room door a good ten seconds ahead of Sheela.

"Mr. Zell, it's been nice chatting with you."

"Hey"—he gestured with the untouched champagne—"I don't want to be a nuisance, but maybe dinner sometime? Nothing serious, just a chance—"

"Sure."

Salvatore had posted himself at one side to wait. He seemed completely at ease.

"Hole in your security, Lymon," she muttered as she skipped quickly to catch the door as it swung shut behind Sheela. Bright lights, mirrors, and red velvet-covered benches furnished the powder room. The three women who sat there seemed oblivious, patting and painting, applying lipstick amidst the usual facial gyrations as they gazed into the mirrors.

Copperhead was nowhere in sight. Sheela walked through the archway that separated the powder room from the toilets. Christal was two seconds behind her. Passing into the toilets, she found her quarry.

To her surprise, a short line waited: two women, Copperhead, then Sheela, and finally her. Bending at the waist, Christal assured herself that feet filled every stall.

"God," the first woman in line muttered. "This is taking forever."

"Nice reception, don't you think?" Copperhead turned to Sheela.

"Yes, it is."

"Sheela Marks, right?"

"Right. And you are?"

"Cindy Denton. I work with MCA, rights department." She hesitated. "I liked *Blood Rage*. Saw it last week."

Copperhead was giving Christal a thorough scrutiny. Christal didn't make eye contact, but fumbled with her purse for a distraction.

"Thanks, it was a fun film to make."

"Congratulations on the Oscar."

The toilet flushed, and a harried woman stepped out, pulling her skirt straight as she headed for the sinks.

"I wasn't expecting it," Sheela answered. "You always hope, but when it came, I just couldn't even think straight."

One by one, the line moved up. Copperhead stepped into the stall. Sheela glanced at Christal just as the woman in the adjoining stall flushed and stepped out. She was a mousy thing. Thin, dark-haired; the glance she gave Sheela was curious, evaluative.

Christal watched Sheela step in and close the door. She could hear fabric slough, a purse snapping, urine, then a flush. Another flush. Then another.

Finally, Sheela stepped out, pulled her dress straight, and shrugged as she walked past. Christal glanced into the stall. A tampon floated in reddened urine.

Copperhead stepped out unexpectedly, saying, "Excuse me. Please use that one." She pointed at the stall she'd just vacated as she pushed into Sheela's and flipped the door closed.

Christal stopped short. *What the hell?*

Sheela was at one of the sinks, bent to wash her hands as she checked herself in the mirror. The sounds from the stall made no sense whatsoever: the lid clunking as it was lifted . . . Then what? Christal couldn't place the noise as she pushed on the locked door. Was that plastic crackling and dripping water?

Moment's later, Copperhead opened the door, surprised when she found Christal still standing there. Their eyes locked, and Christal started forward, saying, "One moment, please."

Copperhead crouched, lowering her shoulder. She caught Christal off guard, driving her body back, off balance. Christal clawed for balance as Copperhead slammed her into the wall, then followed up with a hard blow to the solar plexus. Then another. And another.

Christal windmilled against the tiles as she tried to catch her balance. Her body jerked against the blows. She was gasping for breath, and then Copperhead was off, leaving at a run.

"Stop her!" Christal croaked, coughing as she pushed herself upright. Her guts were on fire. A glance showed her that the toilet bowl was white, the water clear.

Sheela and the other women had turned around to stare in disbelief as Copperhead ran past. The purse in the woman's hand was larger, and gripped as if it contained diamonds rather than a used tampon and urine.

Christal coughed again. Her lungs burned as she drew a breath and stumbled toward the door. She straight-armed a surprised woman who stepped into her way, pounded past the alarmed gazes of the women in the powder room, and smashed the door open. Salvatore was walking toward her, concern on his face.

"The woman!" Christal croaked, still out of breath. Then she saw her, that streaked-auburn head making straight through the crowd for the fire exit. "Stop her!"

Salavatore lifted his arm and spoke into the mike, a frown on his face. Christal forced herself forward, weaving through the surprised crowd. Across the packed room a fire door swung open. An alarm blared flatly.

Christal could hear Salvatore's feet thudding behind her as she dodged, weaved, and shoved people out of her way. The fire door clicked closed just as she bowled past the last of the gawking spectators and hammered her body against the crash bar. She might have hit a wall. Even the impact of Salvatore's thick body didn't budge it. For a long moment they hung there, thrusting, both of them, while the alarm blared its obnoxious wail.

Lieutenant Harris, of the Los Angeles Police Department, studied the rubber wedge inside the plastic Ziploc he held. It was a door stop, one of nearly thirty scattered around the hotel. They'd pried this one out of the fire door. "Who knows, maybe we'll get a print off it. Maybe it will even be from someone who doesn't work at the hotel."

"Don't get your hopes up." Christal had her butt propped on one of the wood-veneer tables as she looked around the small conference room. The walls were finished in beige and illuminated by overhead fluorescent panels. A podium stood in one corner; an easel with marketing diagrams had been left behind by some of the room's previous occupants. Outside, the press of media could be heard as two cops held them at bay in the hotel hallway.

Lymon stood with his arms crossed. The lieutenant and another detective sat at the table with the baggie. Sheela looked shocked and humiliated as she twisted her hands in her lap. The expensive Narciso Rodriguez dress seemed to shimmer in the light. Salvatore had a chastened look, as if he'd just come up impotent on his wedding night. For her part, Christal hugged her sore stomach and fumed.

"Why's that?" the lieutenant asked.

"It was too well planned. Right down to the fake legs in the stalls." Christal pointed her chin at the plastic trash bags full of shoe-covered mannequin legs. "Copperhead was wearing gloves. You're not going to lift anything from the women's room stalls or the fake legs, either."

"How can you be so sure?"

"Did you get anything at Julia Roberts'?" Lymon asked, picking up the threads. "How about at Bullock's in Wyoming? Ono's in New York?"

"You're saying this is related?" Harris looked from one to the other.

"Yeah." Christal took in the shocked expression on Sheela's face. She looked as if she'd just been raped. Maybe without the physical brutality, but the sense of psychological violation and humiliation reflected there made Christal's heart ache. "They didn't get their sample in New York. They had to come back."

"What? What sample?"

"Their piece of Sheela," Christal added.

Harris and Lymon both turned frowns toward Christal; the former asked, "What piece are we talking about?"

"A piece of her, a bit of Sheela."

"For what purpose?"

"We don't know," Lymon muttered.

A cop opened the door and leaned in accompanied by the sounds of melee in the hallway. "Lieutenant, there's no Cindy Denton at MCA. Not in the rights department, not anywhere."

"Thanks."

Christal could see a crush of reporters held back from the door behind the small knot of police personnel. They were calling questions as the cop pulled the door closed behind him.

Harris stared at the plastic trash bags on the floor. "Look, even if we figure this out, we're not going to be able to do much." He met their eyes sympathetically. "What's the crime? Theft of a tampon and urine?"

"Second-degree assault," Christal replied. "She hammered me three times after she shoved me against the wall."

He studied her thoughtfully. "We'll file it that way if

you're willing to press charges, but if it ever comes to court . . ."

"Yeah, yeah, I know. There's a hundred ways a good attorney could get an acquittal." She made a helpless gesture. "But what else have we got?"

For a moment, no one spoke.

Harris made a decision. "Ms. Anaya, we'll be sending a detective by tomorrow with a forensic artist and an old-fashioned mug book. It's obvious that the mousy woman and Copperhead, as you call her, were working together on this. If these things keep happening—"

"They will."

"—then at least we're doing something that might be proactive."

"How's the situation out there?" Sheela asked, looking sick to her stomach.

Lymon replied gently, "This has a bad smell, so the press has come in a swarm."

She closed her eyes, color draining from her cheeks. Christal stepped forward instinctively and reached out. At her touch, Sheela looked up and gave a brief shake of her head, raising an arm to stop her. "It's okay, Christal. I'm tougher than I look."

"Yeah," she answered. "I know."

Pain lay bright in her blue eyes. "If you hadn't been there, we'd never have known." A pause. "I wonder, would it have been better that way?"

The cell phone in Hank's pocket rang twice before he could stumble from the Marriott's bed to the chair where he'd flung his coat the night before. The hotel room had a brownish look in the dim light. Much nicer than the Best Western, and without any connection to Marsha. He glanced at the bedside clock: 8:23. Morning, he assumed, and wished he'd been easier on the bourbon last night.

"Yeah?"

"Abrams? That you?"

He recognized the voice. "Hey, Larry. What's happening in New York these days?"

"Just the usual. We've got half the Muslim population under surveillance. Kidnapping is up; drugs are down. I'm up to my ass in paperwork, and I've got a hot date with a grand jury on Friday. Which is why I'm in the office today. I got your voice mail."

"And?"

"Sure, we know about Verele Security. We work with them a lot. They're on the up-and-up. It's an international executive security firm. Big time. They specialize in high-profile personages. They had someone in our office last week. Some Saudi prince was in town for a bunch of medical procedures. Hush, hush, very sensitive. Maybe the guy had VD and didn't want the local mullahs back home to know. You get the picture?"

"Anything suspicious about them? You hear any rumors?"

"Nope. Why, you got something I should know for a heads-up?"

"Nah, it's just that, well, they've offered me a job. Sort of. If I pass the test."

"All I can tell you is that from our end, our dealings with them have been professional all the way. Especially with the ebbing and flowing of the terrorist threat. Like I say, they do a lot of Arab leaders, rich Asian businessmen, and that sort of thing. Mostly they try to keep their clients, and their clients' security, from rubbing with the public. Sometimes it's tied up with diplomatic stuff at the UN, and sometimes it's exiled leaders here for different reasons. If you got right down to it, I'm sure you'd find that some of their clientele are scum, but that just comes with the territory." A pause. *"You going to do this?"*

"I don't know. Larry, I'll level. I got my balls busted. Demotion and transfer to El Paso. Political, if you get my drift. The assistant director himself recommended Verele Security."

"Shit happens," Larry said neutrally. *"They've got an office in the city. Flatiron Building, I think."*

"Yeah." Hank looked down at his knees; his bare feet were kneading the carpet. "Listen, if they schedule an interview, how'd you like to do lunch? Or would you be seen in public with a pariah like me?"

"Call when you get here."

How many years had it been since Lymon had had butterflies like this in his stomach? Five at least since that last mission into Iran. It had been his final HELO—high-elevation, low-opening parachute drop—into a hostile environment. Naval intelligence needed positive identification of a chemical plant since the Iranians had built it in the middle of a residential area—and next door to an orphanage for good measure.

Lymon and his team had used a handheld laser targeting device to ensure that the navy jets hammered exactly the right building from exactly the right direction. They even had to dope the wind so that it carried the fumes away from the kids.

He felt the butterflies again as he walked down the hall, past the Southwestern art, and stopped at Sheela's door. He tapped lightly at the carved wood.

"Come," came the tired response.

Lymon opened the door, entered the parlor, and found Sheela curled on one of the chaise longues. Across from her, the giant TV displayed Russell Crowe in *Gladiator*. He was enthusiastically slicing, dicing, and lopping off limbs. Since the sound was off, it looked curiously surreal. Sheela, however, might have been oblivious as she stared vacantly into the corner. A half-empty cup of tea perched on a silver platter on the low table to her right.

"You asked for me?" He walked over and sat in the overstuffed couch across from her.

"Rex just left."

"I know. He sent me up."

"He thinks I should can you."

"If you would be more comfortable that way, I understand." She looked up with distaste. "Lymon, shut up!"

He lifted an eyebrow at the tone in her voice.

A faint smile appeared, then died at the corners of her mouth. "I need you too much right now."

"We haven't been doing such a hot job. First New York, then last night."

"That's not why I need you." A pause. "Well, yes, there's that too."

"Christal reamed me pretty good. She was wondering just why, exactly, I only had male security guys to keep track of a female principal." He paused. "She did a good job last night, didn't she?"

Sheela raised her eyes. "How's she feeling?"

"Sore. She showed me the bruises. Whatever Copperhead hit her with, I'm surprised she could go running in pursuit."

"Just a fist." Sheela shook her head. "I saw it. Saw her expression as that woman slugged her in the gut. It had to hurt. Is she still blaming herself?"

"Yeah. Like me, she seems to take these things personally."

Sheela seemed to fade. "You don't know what personal is. It's all over the papers."

"I know. Dot slammed an assortment of today's editions on the conference table. The slug lines were creative, to say the least."

Sheela's lips trembled. "Do you know how *creepy* it is? They maneuvered me right into that stall, lined it with plastic, and stole my . . . my . . ." Her eyes were imploring. "Who'd steal a woman's *tampon,* for God's sake? How sick can you get?"

"Well, do you want me to think about it for a while? I've got a wild and very creative imagination."

The attempt at humor succeeded in getting another quiver of her lips.

She took a deep breath, sighed, and slapped her hands onto her knees. "Hell, I should know better. It's just the price you pay in this business."

"It must feel like being raped."

She fixed him with a steady stare. "Believe me, it's very different." She saw through his stoic expression. "Why, Lymon, I've taken you by surprise! A woman who takes risks—like I always have—gets slapped down by life on occasion."

"On occasion?"

"The first time was in Saskatoon that time I ran away. One

night, under a bridge." She looked away, as if evaluating her past. "A great many things happened as a result of that forbidden motorcycle, didn't they?"

"I'm sorry. I'd change it for you if I could."

She waved it away. "I wouldn't let you. I wouldn't be who I am today, but for those events." She turned her eyes to his, watching for some sign. "Does it bother you? Knowing that I've been raped?"

He leaned forward, bracing his elbows on his knees. "Sure it does. You're important to me. I'd be a dirty liar if I said no and shrugged it off. But the past is the past. You are who you are, and that's who I've come to regard and respect."

"Regard and respect?" she asked dryly. "My, I couldn't have stated it any more sterilely with rubbing alcohol." She paused. "What would you say if I asked you to stay with me tonight?"

He could see the desperation in her eyes. "Sure. I'll set up camp out here. You've got a great library."

"What if I wanted you in there?" She indicated the closed double doors that led to her bedroom.

"I'd have to decline unless I could bring someone, maybe Christal, with me."

Her chuckle was humorless. "Ah, Lymon, always professional. It's okay. I won't ask you. Won't compromise your professional ethics."

"Look, Sheela, you're upset, off balance, and desperate to find some kind of stability. You don't want me. I'm not the man you think I am. Trust me on this, huh?"

She reached out for her tea. "Did you know there are people who make a hobby of memorizing the names of actors who have committed suicide and overdosed? Is that macabre, or what?"

"Why bring that up?"

"Because I finally understand way down in my bones why they do it. Not the counters, but the suicides." She sipped her tea, looking down into the brown liquid. "It caught me right out of left field, the biggest surprise of all."

"What's that?"

"I never anticipated the incredible loneliness that comes

with success. They're all standing in line, thousands of them, all wanting something from Sheela Marks. Since the Oscar, they've been hammering down Rex's door. It seems like the entire world wants me to give, but I, on the other hand, can't even share my only friend's company for a night."

"I'm not your only friend."

Amusement filled her. "Aren't you? Who else will give me a motorcycle ride? Do you have *any* idea how precious that day was to me? Damn, Lymon, for those few marvelous hours we were free, you and me. I was just a woman and you were just a man, and we were having fun."

"It was fun."

"When I'm harried, frustrated, scared, or angry, I take that memory out and play it from start to finish. From the moment you walked out by the pool, to the expression on your face when I came out with that helmet, to the gleam in your eyes when we stopped for soda." She paused. "The miracle is that there are people out there who can do that every day if they want."

"All right, some morning, when traffic's light, we'll sneak out and do it again."

"I want a life to go with my career, Lymon."

"Hey, that's pushing your luck."

"Yeah, well, instead of a life, I've got people humiliating me for all the world to see. Why would they take a tampon? It was soaked in urine. Hell, for that matter, how could they know I was having my period? Jeez, what are these people? Psychic freaks?"

"As far as I can tell, yeah. Look, we've got the whole team spread around the house. Paul is spelling John on the security cameras. The press is driving past in a constant caravan since the police have a patrol car parked out front to keep them moving. You're as secure as you can get short of pillboxes, sandbags, and a mine field."

"I'm feeling alone and violated, Lymon." She stared at him with weary eyes. "Cut me a deal. Just stay with me. You sit there. I'll sit here. We'll talk. About anything and everything. Watch movies all night . . . read books . . . hell, I don't care. Call for coffee every thirty minutes so that you know that the staff knows that you're being professional. Whatever you feel comfortable with." Her control began to collapse. *"I just need a friend. Is that too much to ask?"*

12

Christal blinked and glared at the computer screen. She was sitting on an uncomfortable chair at the kitchen table in her Residence Inn suite. After too many hours of bright Internet screens, a person started having visions. Her *curandera* grandmother would have approved. The effect was something akin to peyote but without the bitter taste and having to repeatedly throw up.

She yawned, shifting to get blood back into her butt. When she reached for her coffee cup, the last swallow was cold and bitter. Stains had dried around the rim, and rings marked the interior. How many hours had she been here, working so hard to find nothing?

The news stories abounded with accounts of the curious theft of Sheela's tampon. The press was titillated and the tabloids ecstatic. Public commentary was sporadic and, so far, found only in editorials. A lot of celebrity memorabilia was for sale on eBay and the other sites, but no one offered a used Sheela Marks' tampon.

Having exhausted everything else, she went back to Sheela's Web site and monitored the chat rooms. There, too, she found lots of conversations asking why their idol had been so publicly scorched. Christal monitored a couple of people who wished they could emulate the deed and wrote down their addresses.

In the end, she found herself back at the main menu, staring mindlessly at the screen. On impulse she linked to Genesis Athena and inspected their questionnaire. What was her name, her age, her sex? Was Sheela Marks her favorite actress? How many times a week did she watch Sheela Marks?

How many times a month? What was her salary? Her net financial worth? State her highest educational level. Had she ever written a fan letter? What were her views on adoption? On government regulation of biotech firms? Did she fear travel abroad? And so forth.

She was tired of questions—most notably of the question, "Why?"

Signing off, she stood and arched her back, trying to get the kinks out. The refrigerator hummed, and the TV in the living room flashed images from Headline News, the sound barely audible.

A vigorous knock came at her door.

"Lymon, if that's you, I'm going to kill you." She glanced at her watch. He might be paying her very well, but she'd been up all the previous night. That morning she'd done a turn with the LAPD forensic artist before returning to her apartment, where she'd spent five hours on the computer looking for clues. She had to sleep sometime.

At the peephole, she was surprised to see Rex Gerber standing with his hands in his expensive trouser pockets. Sunlight was shining on the scalp beneath his thinning black hair. His eyes were gleaming behind his fleshy nose. A tan jacket covered a light blue shirt.

"Good afternoon, Mr. Gerber," she said as she opened the door. "What's wrong?"

"Wrong? Nothing." He gave her a quizzical look as he stepped in. "You feeling okay?"

She nodded, leading him into the small living room. "Let me guess, my eyes look like Pennsylvania road maps, and I could bring groceries home in the bags under my eyes."

He looked around. "This is nice. I've never been in one before. Kitchen, couch, all the comforts of home."

"Have a seat. What can I do for you?"

Rex flopped back in the couch and bounced, evidently trying it out for comfort. Then he turned his attention to Christal. "I thought maybe we'd go out for a drink."

"Let me rain check. It's been too long since I caught a full eight hours. Lymon didn't let me off the night patrol until well after sunup. And then the day really started."

"So, what have you been doing?"

She indicated the computer at the kitchen table. "Research that had to be done immediately. The Web." She settled on the arm of the chair across from him. "If someone was making a point, something should have cropped up somewhere. Every search I've run has come up empty."

His fleshy face screwed up. "You're kidding? It's the talk of the town. My people have worn calluses on their ears answering the phones. Everyone wants to know what's going on."

"Oh, yeah, I found a lot of talk, Mr. Gerber. Lots of discussion of who, why, and what's next, but nothing from anybody who's saying, 'I got it! What am I bid?' "

He frowned. "I haven't mentioned this to Sheela, but the gals that did this might be really kinky, you know? Golden showers with Sheela's piss? And the tampon? What? Paint themselves? Flagellation? I don't wanna shock you, but sometimes people get really sick."

She clasped her hands together. "I suspect, Mr. Gerber, that I know more about deviant criminal behavior than you do. We have entire courses at the Bureau dedicated to it, but I don't think so. Not this time."

"Why not?"

"It's the second try at Sheela. The guy in New York didn't get the job done."

"Come on, that was clear across the country. He was a guy. This was two girls. You're saying there's three of them?"

"At least. Maybe more when you factor in the other celeb hits. All of them are taking something really personal. Sheets and toothbrushes, razor scuzz, and tampons are all pretty intimate. And with at least three people involved and striking from here to Australia, it's not just kinky sexual behavior."

"So what is it, Christal?"

"Mr. Gerber, I can't tell you yet. But it's going to be something really sensational."

"You know, I've been in this business for a long time. The lengths that some people will go to is astounding. There was a guy once who had himself shipped to one of my client's houses. Had himself nailed into a crate and delivered. Can you imagine? All that just so he could get inside the house.

Turns out the client was in England shooting a picture. The household staff got curious when the box started to smell like piss and shit, so they opened it. Good thing, too—the guy was half-dead from dehydration."

"Some people live for their obsessions, Mr. Gerber."

He gave her a penetrating look. "Can we get past this Mr. Gerber thing?"

Weary as she was, it took a moment to comprehend the interest in his brown eyes. *Crap. So that's why he's here.*

"Sure, Rex. Look, I'm sorry to be a spoilsport, but I've got to kick you out and get some shut-eye."

He hadn't moved, deporting himself as an alpha male, with his arm thrown back on the couch. "Yeah, Lymon's a slave driver."

"Scuttlebutt says you wanted Sheela to fire him."

He shrugged. "Someone got to my client. What can I say? I overreact sometimes. I know Lymon's the best, but I really care about Sheela. If it hadn't been for you, we'd have never known she'd even been tapped." He was giving her "the look" again.

"Come on," she told him as she stood. "Up and at 'em. I'll have that drink with you, but only after I figure this thing out."

He smiled, then eased onto his feet. "You know, I like you, Christal. You've got chops. I think you're going to go far in this business."

She smiled as she opened the door, a big hint that he was sharp enough to get. "I haven't proven myself yet."

"You have to me." He gave her a broad smile. "I'll be seeing you later."

"Good night, Rex."

"Yeah, you get some sleep, huh?"

She closed the door and slumped against it. Men. He had to have twenty-five years on her. He was older than her father would have been.

"Christ," she muttered as she locked the door.

* * *

Sid Harness searched the crowd as he cleared LAX security. A throng of people were waiting, some waving as they joined the effluvium of arriving passengers on their way to the baggage claim.

"Sid!" He heard Christal's voice at the same time he saw her wave. His bag in one hand, his coat over the other, he could only nod and smile as she worked through the press.

God, she looked good. He could see the fatigue around her eyes, but her posture was straight. Her hair was done up in an attractive style. Time had tricked his imagination; her perfect body was better than he remembered. She even looked a little tanned.

"Hey, Christal!" He gave her a partial hug, as much as his bag would allow. "So, how's LA?"

She laughed as she stepped in beside him. "I'm sick. In need of psychological counseling."

"Why's that?"

"Because I love it here. Oh, not the traffic and the crowds, but hey, that's a city anywhere, huh?"

"Yep." He glanced at her. "You're looking happy, Chris. I can't tell you how glad that makes me."

"Thanks to you. 'Fall on your sword,' you said. 'There's life after death.' So, yeah, I'm alive. But, by God, I'm going to get you for saddling me with that workaholic son of a bitch."

"That's my old buddy, Lymon, you're talking about."

She gave him a wry smile. "I gotta tell you, this private sector is a ball buster. Unlike the Bureau, when I mention overtime, Lymon just raises an eyebrow and asks, 'How much are we paying you?' "

Sid grinned, waving her off when she pointed questioningly at the baggage carousel. "I've got everything in the bag. Where are your wheels?"

"This way. I'm in short term. It's a bit of a walk. I couldn't get Lymon's Lincoln with the park-for-free-anywhere permit." She led the way out through the doors and across the pedestrian crossing. "How long are you in town?"

"Three days. I booked early so we could have some time.

First thing tomorrow I'm due in the LA Field Office. Unless something comes up, I'm out of here at oh-dark-thirty Wednesday morning."

"Where are you staying?"

"After tonight, I'm at the Hotel El-Cheapo just down the street from the FO. I've got the address here someplace. Lymon talked me into bunking with him tonight. Said he'd drop me off downtown *mañana*."

"You've known him a long time?"

"Yeah. *Semper fi.*" He smiled. "I owe the guy my life."

"What was he like back then? Intense?"

"That's a mild word for it." Sid glanced at her. "He had one speed: full throttle. And that last year he was headed straight for the proverbial brick wall." He paused. "So, tell me. What about it? Did I do right sending you here?"

She gave him that sloe-eyed glance that always teased his masculinity. "Yeah, Sid. I think. To tell you the truth, I've been running from the moment I got here." She paused. "As to Lymon, well, he's different. Right now he's got us all pushing. I'm supposed to be tracking down Sheela Marks' assailants, but I'm spending half my time at the principal's. She's a little freaked at having her personal waste lifted."

"I heard you took a couple of belts to the gut."

Her lip lifted, eyes hardening. "It won't happen again."

"I gotta know, what's Sheela Marks really like?"

"I like her." She glanced at Sid. "She's a lot like the roles she plays in her films. Tough and vulnerable. I'm worried about her."

"Why?"

"She's living in a pressure cooker. What happened on Friday doesn't help any. I think she'd like to take a week off to indulge in a nice emotional breakdown. Her manager won't schedule it for her."

"She's got a manager?"

"You bet. A real zirconium jewel. He wants to take me out for a drink and dinner. You know, get acquainted before he adds me to his list of conquests."

"Yeah?"

"He's in his fifties. And kind of an asshole. I've got better taste than that." She looked suddenly chastened. "Or, maybe come to think of it, I don't, huh?" After she took a breath, she asked, "So, speaking of assholes, how's Hank doing? Happy in his new assignment?"

"He's gone."

"What?"

"Resigned." Sid chuckled. "Would you believe it, he's working for an outfit called Verele Security out of New York. Who knows, you two might bump into each other on some movie set somewhere."

"That ought to be interesting. Do you think our clients will have the sense to get out of the way while I try to cut his balls off?"

"Marsha filed for divorce. Someone—probably Gonzales—sent her the photos. On top of that, Hank got dropped a pay grade and was being reassigned to El Paso."

"I like El Paso."

"Of course you'd like El Paso. You're from New Mexico. He's from Massachusetts."

"So, am I to assume he's coming here?"

"Nope. New York last I heard."

Sid did a double take when she stopped at a slick gold-painted Chrysler. "This is your ride?"

She was grinning. "It's just a rental. Job perk, you know?"

"I'm in the wrong business." He slid into the passenger seat, watching Christal out of the corner of his eye as she backed out, drove to the exit, and handed the ticket to the attendant. As they followed the signs to 405, he added, "I haven't seen you look this happy in a long time, Chris."

She ran fingers through her thick black hair. "I don't know why. Twenty-hour days can't be good for me." Then she flashed him a sexy grin and her eyes sparkled. "But, yeah, I'm having the time of my life. How about you?"

"Screwed," he muttered. "This abduction thing, if it is an abduction, is driving me nuts."

"So, tell me."

"What's to tell? I've got a graduate student, female, from over in Georgetown who just drops off the face of the earth.

One day she's there, about to defend her doctoral dissertation on manipulating phases of the cell cycle. What do I know about cell cycles? Hell, if a cell has a cycle, I assume it's a Suzuki, right?"

"What do you mean, 'dropped off the face of the earth'?"

"I mean, zero. *Nada.* She leaves her lab to go for a job interview with a biotech firm and never makes the appointment. She's gone. Keyser Soze gone."

"So why are you involved? It's a missing persons report; you don't have probable cause to make a kidnapping determination. Fifty-fifty says she got burned out and skipped, willing to give up the pressure-cooker bullshit of a Ph.D. program in return for sitting on a beach somewhere selling T-shirts."

"Yeah, maybe." He put his arm on the seat back. "Thing is, there's a pattern of this. Goes back five years. Over that time, no less than twenty-two hotshot young geneticists have vanished. Risen like smoke and drifted away. In each case there hasn't been a thing. Nothing. Not a body, not a ransom note. No sightings by acquaintances." He chewed at his lip. "Then, last Friday, just before you did the tango with that menstrual thief, a white male, Mike Harris, age twenty-four, leaves the UCLA genetics lab to take a whiz. What should have been a three-minute exercise has stretched into almost seventy-two hours now."

"Yeah, well a word of warning: You gotta watch out in these LA bathrooms."

He smiled. "Seriously, what do you think?"

"Seventy-two hours? That's a long time for a man to pee, and he's way too young for prostate problems."

13

The place was called Al's. Lymon had stumbled across it several years ago. The atmosphere was nice, with walls paneled in dark wood, and classical folk music played on the speakers. Not only that, Al had a deal with some Wyoming buffalo ranchers. He got a frozen package twice a week. Al's jalapeño-cheddar buffalo burgers were handmade, cooked to perfection, and melted in the mouth. He also made what he called "Sioux soup," which was buffalo meat, sunflower seeds, pumpkin seeds, squash, potatoes, blue corn flour, piñon nuts, and Anasazi beans. In addition to chili powder, he used fresh poblano peppers and cilantro. It could knock your socks off.

Lymon leaned back in the barrel-shaped chair and grinned at Sid as he finished his burger and washed it down with a glass of Anchor Porter. "Not bad, huh?"

"I could live like this." Sid made a face. "Those jalapeños, though, whew!"

"Homegrown." Lymon copped a glance at Christal. There were advantages to being raised New Mexican. You didn't break a sweat over something as innocuous as garden-raised peppers.

"So," Christal asked, "do the guys on the squad still hiss when they speak my name?"

Sid shrugged. "Yeah, some. Everybody's pissed because Gonzales got away." He paused. "The son of a bitch knows just how close we came to busting his ass. That's worth something."

Christal's eyes had clouded as she stared at her plate. She'd eaten a tender buffalo steak, medium rare. "If we can link him to the celebrity heists, we'll give you the goods on him."

"He's not into Michael Jordan's jockstrap, thank you." Sid wiped his lips with the napkin and sipped more beer. He glanced at Christal. "I don't know. You've got a nose for these things. What do you think? Trophies?"

Christal shook her head. "It's not right. Trophies suggest a victory. Taking something as a memento of a contest. If that's the case, what's the contest? Just breaking security? Why not take Roberts' Oscar, or Gibson's whole razor? Trophy taking by its very nature is the removal of something the target values. It indicates assertive-oriented behavior."

"So," Sid countered, "if it's not trophies, it's souvenirs."

Christal gave him a censorial glare. "You never were much for criminal psychology, Sid. Souvenirs are generally linked to reassurance-oriented behavior. The woman I dealt with in the ladies' john at the Wilshire didn't need much in the way of reassurance. Trust me on that. My abs are still tender to the touch."

"Really?" Sid asked with animation. "Can we feel?"

"I thought you had to be on a plane in three days."

"It won't take three days to feel your abs."

She gave him a look that would have warped titanium. "You'll be that long just getting out of intensive care."

"Meanwhile—getting back to the case—are we dealing with a symbolic action?" Lymon asked. "Taking someone's tampon has got to make some kind of point."

"Yeah?" Christal asked. "Symbolic of what? That Sheela Marks—along with most every other woman in the world—has a functioning reproductive tract?"

"At least you know she's not pregnant," Sid mused.

"We weren't worried about that," Lymon answered. "And if you assume these things are related, I don't think Mel Gibson was, either."

"If that's the case, there are way too many people for a sociopath to be involved." Sid fingered his beer glass.

"Unless it's a rich sociopath." Christal was staring into the distance. "Sid, I've just started to understand the things someone with money can do. If you pay enough, you can hire anyone to do anything. I mean, damn, how much does it take to get a camera into an FBI surveillance van? What's a tampon and some urine compared to that?"

Sid shook his head. "I don't know. Does stealing the kind of stuff we're talking about fit into any of the standard typologies?"

"It's definitely one hell of an invasion of privacy." Lymon pushed his empty bowl back and placed the spoon in it. With a finger he indicated to the waiter that the plates needed busing.

"Another round," Sid said as the man picked up the dishes.

Lymon noticed that Christal was on her second Sierra Nevada Pale Ale. "I'd started to come to the conclusion that she didn't drink. Sid, you're a good influence."

"Who? Chris? When she gets wound up, you need a funnel with a tube just to keep up with her."

"I don't do that anymore." Christal had lowered her eyes. Was that an embarrassed flush at her throat?

Sid shrugged. "No, I guess you don't."

"Want to fill me in?" Lymon asked gently.

"It was just a joke," Sid said bluffly. Hell, he didn't lie any better now than he did in the Corps.

Christal turned her dark eyes on his. "The last time I had too much I crawled into a surveillance van. Just me and my AIC."

"You don't have to do this," Sid said gently.

"Nope." Lymon sensed her discomfort.

Christal shrugged, fingering her beer. "It's all right. I made a mistake. Would I have made the mistake if I'd been stone-cold sober? I don't know. Maybe. Probably. I liked the guy."

"He was scuzz." Sid muttered, and gave Lymon a meaningful glance. "I don't get it. The guy's a dickhead, but women always fawn over him."

"It was his eyes," Christal told them. "The way he smiled. How he listened." She gave Sid a disapproving look. "It's a trick you might want to learn. When Hank is listening to a woman, he pays complete attention to her. He treats her like at that moment she is the single most important thing in his world."

"So? I listen to women."

"Yeah, Sid. With half an ear."

"But the guy was gutless!" Sid ended with a snort of derision as the waiter laid down another round.

Christal shrugged. "We didn't know that until the shit hit the fan. When it did, he took it like a whipped puppy."

Sid poured rich dark Anchor into his glass, studied the brown head, and said, "I think his time with Marsha was running out anyway. She was married to him. She knew what a loser he was. Flashy, with no guts. I'd bet he was whining when she threw him out."

"Whining is underrated," Lymon offered. "I whine a lot. It helps me get my way."

In the middle of a swallow, Sid laughed—and almost puked as he coughed and pawed for a napkin.

"You whine?" Christal asked. "When? Can I watch next time?"

"Sure. I think I have a whining session scheduled for next week. Check with June. She does the calendar."

Sid coughed again, belched, and placed a hand to his stomach. "Excuse me. Damn. You shouldn't do that, Lymon. Not when I'm vulnerable."

"You're always vulnerable. Speaking of which, when are you going to get off the government dole and come work with us real professionals?"

"If you're going to tempt a federal employee," Christal said, rising, "I'm off to the ladies' room."

"Keep an eye out for Copperhead," Lymon called.

Christal shot a look over her shoulder. "I hope she's there. She and I have this little thing that we need to settle."

They watched her walk to the hallway in the rear.

"Damn, that's a nice sight," Sid said with a sigh. "I really miss having her around. Not only is she just a good kid, but I used to spend half the day dreaming about that body."

Lymon chuckled. "You're married."

"So? I can still dream, can't I?" Sid refolded his napkin. "Okay, yeah, I guess I fell a little in love with Christal. Who wouldn't?"

"Hank?"

"Shit! But for him, she'd have had a dynamite career." Sid shook his head. "Weird thing. You and I both know it's not the first time a male and female agent made whoopee on surveillance; they just didn't do it when the target was Gonzales. We're still trying to figure out how the hell he got a camera into that van."

"Someone in the Bureau?"

"Probably." Sid looked up. "If Gonzales found out that Hank Abrams was in charge of the investigation, it wouldn't have taken him long to figure out just what kind of guy he was. Half the WMFO knew he was screwing around on Marsha." He made a face. "Fucking pretty boy."

"So why don't you ditch the bullshit? I could use a partner."

"Me? A partner?"

Lymon made a gesture of surrender. "Well, maybe. We'd have to see if June would hire you."

"That's the secretary?"

"Don't call her that to her face."

"Right." Sid paused, jerked his head toward the women's room. "So, how's she doing?"

"Good. You steered me right. If she likes the work, I'd like to keep her."

Sid seemed fascinated by a spot on the tablecloth when he said, "You thought about asking her out?"

Lymon gave him the evil eye when he finally looked up. "Is that why you sent her out here?"

"You seen a more beautiful woman recently?"

"I work for Sheela Marks." Lymon grinned at Sid's sudden discomfort and added, "I only owe you my life and my soul. Don't try to play matchmaker for me."

Christal returned a moment later and dropped into the chair with an easy grace. "So, did you guys get an angle on the celeb hits while I was gone, or did you spend the whole time talking about me?"

"Talked about you," Lymon said blandly. "You're a lot more interesting."

Sid had recovered completely, saying, "Well, if it's not profit motivated, it's payback, right?"

Lymon made a helpless gesture. "Sheela's never done a movie with any of those people."

"Any personal relationship with any of them?" Christal asked.

"Outside of bumping into each other at parties, no. Well, sure, there's the professional similarity, but that's about it. Are there mutual friends? You bet. It's the film business. Everybody knows everybody."

Sid leaned forward. "Maybe it's someone who got stepped on. An actor who lost a key role to Marks, or one of the others? Maybe it's something simple like they were repped by the same agency or something?"

Christal shrugged. "I can start checking on that." Her expression dropped. "One thing about the Bureau. You can always get people to do the scut work."

Sid cocked an eyebrow, lowering his voice. "So, Lymon. Assuming you find this guy, what are you going to do about him?"

Lymon tried to keep his voice calm when he said, "Paybacks are a bitch, aren't they?"

Christal was watching him, hearing more than he wanted to say. He tried to decipher the look she was giving him. Definitely evaluative.

"Be very, *very* careful, old friend." No levity could be heard in Sid's voice.

Sheela Marks' filmography consisted of no less than thirty-three titles, and it didn't take Christal long to figure out that this research, like so much that she had done as a federal agent, was tedious, long, and monotonous. Having the dates when the films were made was just the beginning. From there she went to *Daily Variety*, flipping through the editions looking for Sheela Marks' name. Then she painstakingly had to figure out who was in or out of the deals. After eight hours she had a list of several hundred names and that was just the actors. Including directors, she could add another fifty. Factor in another twenty-two when the producers were included.

She considered her list, tapped her pen, and glared at the stack of weeklies as she considered having to repeat the effort for each of the other names.

"Ma'am?" the librarian asked as she walked up to the carrel. "Are you about finished? We're closing in fifteen minutes."

"Yes. Thank you." Christal stood, feeling the ache in her back, and began collecting her things. "I'll see you in the morning."

Several names were rubbing against her thoughts as she stepped out into the tawny light of an LA sunset. One of them was Manuel de Clerk.

She pulled out her cell, dialed the office, and got the answering machine as it identified the company and stated the normal operating hours for Lymon Bridges Associates. June, it appeared, got to keep a normal human being's work hours. She called Lymon.

On the second ring he answered, *"Bridges."*

"Lymon? Anaya. I'm looking for Tony Zell's number."

"Agency or personal?"

"How do I get ahold of him tonight?"

"Got a pen?"

"Ten-four."

She scribbled the number he gave her on the corner of her legal pad where it stuck out of her purse. "Thanks, Lymon."

"Business or pleasure?"

"You're a funny man, boss. A stitch a minute. When would I have time for pleasure?"

"So what have you got?"

"Did you know that Sheela Marks got Manuel de Clerk bounced from *Blood Rage*? The guy was supposed to play the lead. Sheela insisted they find someone else."

"Yeah."

"She got him chopped out of a real juicy role."

"And you're thinking Manny's been holding a grudge?"

"I want to talk to the guy. I figure Tony can open the door for me. Does he represent de Clerk?"

"Nope. But he knows who does. Give Tony a call. Keep me informed."

"Right."

"Christal?"

"Yeah?"

"About de Clerk. Do me a favor. Be discreet, huh? Don't piss the guy off. It would really upset my digestion if his lawyer started baying outside of my bedroom window over some silly slander suit."

"Gotcha, boss."

She hit the *end* button and dialed Tony.

He answered on the third ring. Music was blaring in the background. *"This is Tony."*

"Mr. Zell? I don't know if you remember me. I'm Christal Anaya, working for—"

"*Cool! Christal! Hey, I've been thinking about you. You know, you promised me dinner, babe.*"

She made a face. Babe? "I was hoping you could direct me to Manuel de Clerk. I need to speak with him concerning the events at the Beverly Wilshire the other night. Nothing important, just some questions. Strictly business for LBA."

"*Yeah. Glad to help. It'll cost you, though.*"

"How's that?" she asked coolly.

He broke into hysterical laughter. "*Hey, Christal, you're too far out there! Chill out, babe. I don't need a bribe—at least not like that. Dinner. Tomorrow. Eight-thirty. You say yeah, I give you the number of Manny's digs and a phone call to let him know you're coming. Cool?*"

"Cool."

"*Fucking A! And don't forget, you already said yeah at the reception just before you hammered that bitch that tried to snag Sheela.*"

"I did?" Maybe he didn't remember who hammered whom?

"*Hey, I shoulda got it on tape, huh?*"

"I guess so."

"*Right! What's your number? Let me make a few calls. Maybe Manny can see you tonight. Just professional, huh? Don't make me jealous!*"

She lifted her lip, but said in a sweet voice, "I wouldn't think of it."

She hung up and waited. Within five minutes, her phone rang.

"*Hey ya, Christal? Tony here. I got it worked out.*"

"Okay. What, when, and where?"

"*His digs, babe. Nine o'clock tonight. Ring one long, two short and one long. The gate will open. He'll be at the big house.*"

"Thank you, Mr. Zell."

"*Hey, babe. It's Tony. No sweat. Dinner tomorrow, right?*"

14

Lymon's garage was a three-car affair. In one bay he kept a gray '92 Toyota Land Cruiser, in the next his personal car, a Jaguar S type, and finally his motorcycles. In the rear a pristine 1975 Moto Guzzi California Highway Patrol model rested on its center stand, the chrome fenders gleaming. His BMW stood closest to the door, the bodywork removed, the rocker boxes off to expose the oil-slicked valve assemblies. Finally a red-and-bronze 2003 Indian Chief Deluxe canted on its sidestand, the thick fenders waxed and shining. The leather saddle had a waxed look, and chromed diamonds glinted in the skirt. Two fringed leather saddlebags hung low at the rear.

A radio on a shelf in the back was set on KABC to make white noise as Lymon worked on the BMW. His red toolbox was open, several of the drawers at half-jut. He sat on an inverted bucket and used an Allen wrench to turn the BMW's crank to top dead center. Air sucked and puffed from the empty spark-plug holes as the valve springs compressed and then released. Lymon glanced in the inspection hole for the timing mark. As his fingers wiggled the rocker arms, he rolled the events of the last two weeks around inside his head. The thing that stuck with him was the look of terror in Sheela's eyes, the pulsing of the vein in her neck after the attack at the St. Regis. That was followed by her abject humiliation at the Wilshire. What in hell could he have done differently?

The soft whisper of an engine and the rasping of tires intruded. He looked up, seeing the long black nose of the limo rounding the curve of his drive and pulling to a stop.

He stood, grabbing a red rag and wiping his hands as he walked to the open door. Paul was giving him a worried look when he opened the driver's door and started around the front of the long vehicle.

"Paul? What the hell are you . . . ?" Lymon stopped short when the rear door opened and Sheela climbed out. She was carrying a canvas duffel bag with one hand, her purse hanging from her shoulder.

"He's doing what he's supposed to," she called, striding toward him. "Thank you, Paul. Please take the car home. Lymon can bring me when I'm finished."

"Hey," Lymon protested. "Sheela, are you nuts?"

She made a shooing gesture. "Bye, Paul. And thank you."

Paul looked back and forth, confused, and muttered, "Yes, ma'am" before walking back and slipping into the driver's seat. He put the long black car into reverse and backed slowly around the curve of the drive.

"This is my home," Lymon protested. "Sheela, what are you doing here?"

She was dressed in form-fitting jeans that hugged her round hips and long legs. Thick-soled black boots covered her feet. A gray long-sleeved blouse was tucked into her pants and did little to disguise her famous bustline. She had her red-gold hair in the French braid again. Wary blue eyes met his as she stepped past, frowning at the BMW with its sundry pieces scattered around the cement floor.

"What's wrong with your Beemer?"

"Nothing. It's just that you have to set the valve clearance every six thousand miles. While I was at it, I changed the oil. That's in that pan over there. I was just setting the intake side."

"So, it's not really broken."

"What are you doing here?"

She took a deep breath and turned. "I'm escaping, Lymon."

Her expression told him everything. The look she gave him melted his heart and overwhelmed his good sense. "Okay. So, you've escaped." He chuckled, wiping his hands. "Now what?"

She made a halfhearted gesture toward the disassembled RT. "Well, I was thinking of another soda up at that place on the other side of the Angeles Crest." She turned, frowning at the Indian. "What about that one?"

He glanced at the canvas war bag in her hand. "Let me guess, that's the helmet and leather jacket, right?"

She gave him a conspiratorial smile. "Could you do it for me, Lymon? Set me free again for a couple of hours?"

"It's not smart, you know."

She stepped closer to him, a desperate soul behind her searching blue eyes. "Hell, I know that. It's probably going to end in a wreck one way or another, Lymon, but God, if I don't do something I'm going to lose my mind."

"Yeah, well, when you get into trouble, it seems like there's always a motorcycle at the bottom of it." He indicated the sleek steel-blue Jaguar. "Sure you wouldn't rather save my heart a little wear and tear and take the Jag?"

She bent, unzipping the bag to pull out her helmet. "If I'm headed to hell, Lymon, I say go all the way."

"Can I at least finish the valves?"

His heart skipped at the joy reflected in her smile. "Sure. I can even help." She held up her long delicate fingers, manicured to perfection. "You'd be surprised. These have actually been oil stained. And I helped rebuild the injectors on a Massey Ferguson once."

"I'm all atwitter." Lymon smiled and returned to his bucket. God, this wasn't smart. But when he looked at Sheela, glowing with relief as she bent down to help him with the lock nuts and feeler gauges, he couldn't help himself.

Shit. I'm completely, totally, helplessly in love with her. "Just like every other red-blooded male in the world."

"What was that?" Sheela was sorting through the feeler gauges like dealing cards.

"Nothing that couldn't be cured by a bullet to the brain."

Christal wound her Chrysler through Brentwood's curving streets and slowed before a wooded lot. Behind a high wrought-iron fence, and through the trees, she could just glimpse an imposing Tudor-style house. She checked her watch: 8:32.

She pulled up at the curb and slipped the car into park. The last of sunset's glow was fading in the reddened west. Streetlights were flickering on. Rolling the driver's window down, she could hear insects and distant traffic on the evening air.

So, what was the right strategy? Drive up to the tall, spike-topped gate and ring the buzzer? Or wait until the designated time and act like a real professional?

She wasn't sure what the smart move was yet. This was different than working for the Bureau. Here, she had to operate with people's forbearance.

Her patience wore out at a quarter to nine when she turned the key, brought the Chrysler to life, and drove up to the gate. The metal box perched on a pole on the driver's side had a speaker, camera, and buzzer. She rolled her window down the rest of the way and reached out to ring long, short, short, long.

Like magic, the gate rolled back on its wheels, and Christal drove up the curving drive toward the imposing house. The tree-shrouded drive ended in a loop that surrounded flower gardens and a central cement fountain. Floodlights cast it all in a yellow sodium glow. A Porsche, a stretch Mercedes, and an Audi were parked at the side of the curve in front. The yards were manicured, and the dark grass looked recently mowed.

Christal grabbed her purse and notebook with its list of names and stepped out into the evening. The house lights blazed as she walked up the steps to the door. She was just about to stab the buzzer when a car door opened behind her. She turned, surprised to see a woman stepping out of the Audi's driver's door. She was small-framed, dark-haired, with a narrow face.

"Can I help you?" the woman asked, her voice thin. She was standing with her arms crossed tightly under her small breasts. She wore a white shirt and dark slacks. She might have weighed a full one hundred pounds, provided she'd had a big meal and had been hosed down.

Christal turned, stepping down the stone stairs. "Yes, I'm here for an appointment with Manuel de Clerk."

"He didn't have an appointment." The woman looked wary, suddenly nervous, tightening her crossed arms. She was squinting, and Christal realized the light was behind her.

"Excuse me, do you work for Mr. de Clerk?" Christal could feel her instincts begin to prickle. In that instant, she knew that face, had seen it when this same mousy-looking woman had stepped out of a toilet stall at the Wilshire but days past.

"Who are you?" Christal's tone sharpened. "Do you have any identification?"

The woman's eyes enlarged, and her thin mouth twisted into a faint smile. "I know you." Even as she was speaking she unfolded her arms and pointed a small silver revolver at Christal's midsection. "Just stand very still."

Christal experienced that electric lightness of the guts as she focused on the dark muzzle of the little snub-nosed revolver. Her skin crawled at the expectation of a bullet.

"Hey," she whispered, trying to get her breath. "Relax. I'm no threat."

"Who are you?" the mousy woman asked, her voice turning shrill.

"I'm Christal Anaya. I work for Sheela Marks." She swallowed hard. Shit, this little short-haired *vaina* wouldn't really shoot her, would she?

"What are you doing here?" Mouse's dark eyes were like stones in her pale face.

"I told you, I've got an appointment with Manuel de Clerk."

"Why?"

"Things for Sheela," she made up. "They're shooting *Jagged Cat*. Look, it's not worth me getting shot over. I'll leave." She took a step back, her arms half-raised.

"Stay where you are. You don't move." Mouse held eye contact as she leaned into the Audi, felt about with her other hand, and retrieved something off the dashboard. A little black box that looked like the remote for an automobile's door lock and security system. When Mouse thumbed the button, Christal heard nothing.

Christal made a gesture of surrender. "Look, this isn't my concern. If you're robbing the guy, I don't want any part of it."

Mouse smiled faintly. "Just stand still." She glanced past Christal toward the house, as if expecting someone. Who? Copperhead?

"So, what is it this time?" Christal asked. "I'd almost bet you're not getting a used tampon from Manny."

Mouse's expression reflected amusement, but she said nothing.

"Can I go?" Christal took another step back. "You've made your point."

"I said, don't move."

Christal nodded as she took another step back. Her brain was starting to work again, her training asserting itself. She was a good four steps from the front of her Chrysler. Two steps and a leap and she could be at the door. Did that give her time to pull it open and dive inside?

Was that even a smart option? The silver pistol looked like a .38, but it could just as easily be a .357. Maybe one of the compact Taurus or Smith and Wessons. They were building incredibly powerful pistols into small and lightweight packages. A .357 could make chowder out of auto glass.

Think! She studied the woman, seeing how the tendons stood out on Mouse's hand. She was gripping the pistol like she was squeezing a rubber ball. Christal could see it wiggling in the woman's overstressed grip.

So, what were the odds? Could the woman really shoot? Or was she the kind who had once emptied a box at the range?

God, what a thing to have to bet on!

Christal was running options through her head when she heard the door open behind her. She turned, seeing Copperhead as she came striding out of the house. The woman was tucking a blouse into the top of her skirt as her pumps tapped the stone steps. Her familiar purse hung from one shoulder.

"What's the. . . . ?" Her eyes fixed on Christal; a momentary puzzlement was replaced by a knowing smile.

"Ah? I know you. I think we're going to have a long chat, you and I."

Mouse had her gaze fixed on Copperhead. Christal bet the farm, spun on her heel, and ran. Feet pounding, arms pumping, she sprinted for the corner of the house, where shadows pooled under a weeping willow.

"Stop her!" Copperhead cried.

Christal couldn't separate the supersonic crack of a bullet from the report of the gun. She jinked right, took two steps, and jinked right again. She lost count of the cracking shots that split the air around her. Then she was in the shadows, darting from side to side. She pitched herself behind the bole of the tree, gasping for breath, heart hammering.

"What the hell are you doing!" Copperhead was screaming, her face contorted with rage.

"You said, 'Stop her!' " Mouse cried as she picked at the open cylinder of her gun.

"Damn! We don't need a murder! You *little fool!*"

"She's the same woman from the hotel! She followed us!"

"Come on!" Copperhead cried. "It's too late. The police will be here any second!" She was climbing into the driver's side.

"I think I hit her!" Mouse cried plaintively. "I've got to make sure!" She was slipping bullets into the cylinder, glancing back and forth from the gun to the shadows where Christal hunched behind the willow.

"I'm *leaving!*" Copperhead insisted as the Audi roared to life. "Get in, Gretchen! Or stay here."

Gretchen snapped the cylinder closed, made a face of indecision, and bolted, bracing herself on the moving Audi as she pelted around the rear and sprinted to pull the passenger door open and dive inside.

Christal sagged in the darkness, gasping for breath. Shit! She'd never been shot at before. Bureau training was one thing. It was another to actually have someone try and kill her!

Her hands trembled as she fumbled for her cell phone. The shakes were so bad it took all of her concentration just to punch 911.

"Emergency response, how can I help you?" a woman's metallic voice asked.

In the blur of an adrenaline high, Christal sputtered the address, noted that shots had been fired, that the subjects—two females wanted for questioning in regard to an incident at the Wilshire Hotel on Friday—were in a late-model Audi.

"Is anyone hurt?" the voice asked.

"My God, Manny!" Christal's legs had gone to rubber. She felt wobbly as she ran for the door. Copperhead had left it swinging wide.

"I'm in the foyer," Christal shouted into the phone. "I'm not touching anything." She raised her voice. "Hello? Is anyone here?"

A voice, faint, could be heard. "Hey! God! Help me!"

Christal ignored the questions the 911 operator was calling and took the carpeted steps two at a time to the top floor. She hurried down the long hall, past doorways that she assumed were bedrooms, to the final door.

"I'm coming!"

"She *cut* me!" the panicked voice cried. "God, cut me loose! *Help me!*"

Christal used her shoulder to push the last door open, taking a good look. She'd found a bedroom, all right. The room was bigger than the entire house she'd grown up in. Expensive white carpeting covered the floor. Most of the walls were mirrored, adding to the illusion of endless space. A huge walk-in closet opened off one side. The master bed was monstrous: a four-poster with a flat wooden canopy that looked like it was carved walnut. She could see the man, naked, spread-eagled. His head was up, the tendons straining in his gleaming neck, and he was staring at his crotch.

Christal's work at crime scenes caused her to pause, to notice the empty wine bottle on the nightstand, the glasses, one with wine still standing. On the vanity, a mirror was powdered with white and accented by a razor blade. A box of Trojans stood open beside it, with two torn wrappers on the floor beside the bed.

As Christal stepped closer, she could see that Manuel de Clerk was crying, his chest rising and falling with the sobs. Tears trickled down his sweat-slick cheeks. When he looked her way, it was with abject terror.

"She cut me!" he cried. "God, help me! Call an ambulance."

Christal stopped short. Each wrist and ankle had been tied off to one of the sturdy bedposts with a white nylon rope. His black pubic hair glistened, damp and matted. She winced at the dark red stain that had formed between the man's muscular thighs. As she watched, another drop of blood fell from the tip of de Clerk's limp penis.

15

When the light turned green, Lymon toed the shifter into first. The transmission made a metallic clunk, and the big Indian rumbled and shook as Lymon eased the clutch out and accelerated. He rolled the throttle, letting all sixteen hundred and thirty-eight ccs bellow. The Indian wasn't loud—Lymon hated loud pipes—but it had an authoritarian rumble that sent a tingle up his spine.

The lights on Santa Monica Boulevard seemed to pulse with brighter than usual color. Or was that just part of the high that came out of a nice night and being tuned to the bike and his passenger? He waved at people sitting in a sidewalk pizza place just because it was fun, and they were watching him ride past.

Sheela must have liked it, too; she tightened her hold on his waist. He fought the urge to reach down with his left hand and pat her leg where it rested against his hip.

"We should do this every night," Sheela called over his shoulder.

"You've got a schedule. Rex would go into apoplectic seizures. You're worth millions. You've got to take care of all your minions."

"I thought a minyan was ten Jews?"

"If you happen to be orthodox, it's ten *male* Jews. But that's spelled different."

"Details!" she cried.

"That's where the Devil is."

He enjoyed her crystal laughter, and found himself smiling. Using a handful of front brake, he hauled the Indian down for the next red, pulling in behind a Tahoe and leaving himself a bike length for escape as he watched a sedan slow behind him. Only when he was satisfied the car had stopped did he shift into neutral and let the big V twin drop into its *rumpity rumpity* idle.

Sheela reached up and wrapped her arms around his chest. He could feel her as she hugged him. "Thank you, Lymon. I really needed this."

"Hey, it's fun," he answered, trying to keep his voice light. "It's what I do for relaxation."

The light changed, and he accelerated with the traffic. The tranny shifted with a positive click. He was intimately aware of Sheela's body moving with his. They might have been matched, a curiously symbiotic twin sharing the night, the wind, and the sound. Part of it was the Indian's saddle. It forced the passenger to sit close. On the BMW she had been back, pretty much self-supported against the tour pack.

Damn his hide! His whole body seemed to be quivering, as if every nerve and muscle were aware of her. Even individual cells were howling out in primitive cognizance of the healthy female pressing against him.

Face it, it's more than just your hormones. His brain was piqued, too. Sure, she was beautiful, and probably laced with the kind of pheromones his receptors were perfectly geared for, but he liked her. Enjoyed her company. He always had, from the moment he had first taken an interview with her.

It won't work! he reminded himself sternly. She was a public lady, a superstar in a world where crossing the lines wasn't allowed. The few who had tried it had ended up as burned wreckage, picked over by the press and left to decompose.

"What?" she asked past the wind. "Did you say something?"

"Not out loud."

Her laughter was throaty. "Yeah, I can hear your thoughts, Lymon. Scary, huh?"

"Not as scary as the thoughts I was just thinking."

"About me?"

"You *can* read my mind."

He turned his head just far enough to give her a sidelong look. That's how the magazines should have photographed her, like that, with excitement and deviltry bubbling in her eyes, a natural blush on her perfect cheeks, and a delighted smile.

Dear God, I love you. The words came rolling out of his subconscious. Cowed, he returned his attention to the traffic.

If anything proved quantum uncertainty, Heisenberg, Schrödinger's cat, and chaos theory, it was LA drivers. Nothing could ever be predicted with any accuracy. Only the constantly wary survived. It was Darwin maxed to the tenth power. He had to concentrate on that. Whatever it took to keep his brain cells preoccupied with anything but the inevitability of biology.

"Now what are you thinking?"

"You can't tell?"

"Not at the moment."

"I'm knotting my brain with quantum physics."

"Why?"

"It's easier than Buddhism."

She seemed to consider that for a moment, then propped her chin on his shoulder and said, "I've been imagining left-handed tantra myself."

"What?"

"Ever read the *Kama Sutra*? Not the modern picture books, but the original?"

"We're not having this conversation."

To save himself he flipped on the turn signal, leaned into a right, and rolled the throttle, sure enough of the surface to scrape a floor board and the center stand.

Sheela tightened her grip and let out a shriek of delight. As they rolled down Coldwater, he heard his cell phone ring.

Pulling over, he toed the bike into neutral and slipped the phone out of his pocket. He asked, "Yeah?" as he killed the bike, trying to hear.

"Lymon?" Christal's voice was muffled by the foam of his helmet. *"There's trouble. It's Copperhead."*

"Where are you?"

"Manuel de Clerk's. The police are here."

"I know where he lives. I've got to make a drop-off, then I'll be right there."

"You might want to hurry."

He thumbed *end,* winced as a low rider rumbled past with loud exhaust and even louder bass speakers cracking the metallic blue paint off the car's body.

"You heard?" Lymon asked.

"Everybody in the western United States heard. I hate *Tejano* when it rattles my teeth. So, what's the drop-off?"

"You. Before I ride over to Manny's."

"I heard Christal say it was Copperhead."

"Yeah. So?"

"So, I'm going."

"Sheela, I don't need—"

"Punch the starter button there on the handlebar. That's the red one just up from your thumb. That's it."

The Indian chugged, popped, and rumbled to life.

"You work for me, Lymon," Sheela added curtly. "Your objections are duly noted for the record. Christal, however, also works for me."

"Oh, yeah? Who signs her checks?"

"You do, with my approval. I want to see what's happening. It's important to me." She tightened her hold as he found a hole in the traffic and unleashed the big engine's massive acceleration.

Sheela whooped in delight, tightening her arms around his chest. Then she propped her chin on his shoulder again, saying, "Here's the way it lines out. You're driving this thing, Lymon, so you could take me home. It's your motorcycle, so I couldn't do anything about it. Then, once you'd dropped me off, I'd just have to drive over to Manny's myself."

He gave her that half glance again, just to make sure she wasn't kidding. "You would, wouldn't you?"

"Just make it easier on both of us."

"You win," he relented, pulling into the left turn lane at Sunset.

As they waited at the light, she said in a soft voice, "Thank you, Lymon. You really are a sweetie, did you know?"

"Yeah. All sugar and honey, that's me." But his stomach was flipping like Mary Lou Retton on the uneven bars.

16

"God, it was weird!" Manuel de Clerk repeated in a half-panicked voice. He was sitting in one of the hulkingly plush leather chairs placed randomly in the great room downstairs. A white terry cloth bathrobe was wrapped around him and belted snugly at the waist. It covered his bandaged penis.

"Look, Mr. de Clerk," one of the cops was saying, "we don't know what we've got to go on. So, you've got a nick out of your dick? Big deal. Sometimes you play a little rough, shit happens, you know what I mean?"

Christal stood against the wall, arms crossed as she listened. The room contained a knot of officers, most killing time as they enjoyed a glance around Manny's opulently furnished house and considered the implications of the small wound to his most private. All but a few of them managed to keep from snickering out loud, but it was in each officer's eyes.

The cop shrugged. "You picked the lady up, you let her into your house. Maybe she snagged a tooth on your dick, huh? The thing we do have a problem with is the cocaine on your nightstand. Now, it's not much, be we can't just ignore that."

"My client doesn't have to address that at this time," Vincent Quill, Manny's lawyer, said from the side. He was a middle-aged man, balding. He wore a casual brown jacket and pressed cotton slacks. "He has already informed me that the woman brought the cocaine."

"The woman did?" The cop glanced at his companions, who shrugged.

"Hey, I told you." Manny dropped his head into his hands. "I just met her. She showed up at my table at lunch. Said her name was Lily Ann Gish. That she'd met me at a party at Bernard's. Didn't I remember her?"

"And you just invited her home?" the cop asked.

"Well, hey, she was . . ." He looked around, aware of the skepticism. "She was cool." It sounded really lame.

"So you let some woman you didn't know into your house. You let her tie you up for sex. Then you say she whipped out a little knife and cut off a piece of your dick. After that, she just got dressed and walked out?"

Manuel nodded sickly. "Yeah, that's it."

"End of story."

"End of story." He looked up. "But for the buzzer. The buzzer went off in her purse. She said, 'Sorry, Manny. Something's up. And it ain't you anymore.' And . . . she reached in her purse, pulled out that little knife, and . . ." He swallowed hard. "I thought she was going to castrate me! You wouldn't believe the look in her eyes."

"Triumphant?" Christal asked from the side.

"Yeah, God." Manny was running his hands through his sweaty black hair. "I asked her what she was doing. Shit, I was scared, you know? She just smiled, grabbed me, and sliced a piece off."

"Then what?" Christal asked. "Think about it. What did she do with the piece?"

The cops were giving her questioning looks. She raised a hand, stalling any outburst.

"Weird." Manny looked up, a slight frown on his handsome face. "She dropped it into one of the rubbers. She took both of the used rubbers, knotted them, you know? Like tying them off. And flipped them into her purse."

"She took the used rubbers?" the cop asked, glancing at the recorder.

"Yeah. I was screaming, telling her to let me loose. She just got dressed, never looked back, and walked away."

"Did you hear the gunshots?" Christal asked.

"*Bang. Bang. Bang.*" Manny nodded. "Yeah."

Christal took a deep breath. Copperhead took a piece of Manny—and two used condoms. Chock up another bizarre twist.

"Do you need me anymore?" Christal asked.

"We have your statement," the cop told her. "You'll have to fill out the paperwork if you still want to press charges against the woman."

"Yeah," Christal said woodenly. "The bitch was trying to kill me."

"Do you think you can prove that?" Manny's lawyer asked unexpectedly.

Christal stared at him. "Granted, I'm new here, and as people have been reminding me, LA isn't the East Coast. But doesn't the discharge of a weapon when it's pointed in the direction of a fleeing human being indicate intent to you?"

The lawyer watched her flatly as Christal walked out of the room, found the front door, and stepped out into the night. She took a deep breath of the cool air and realized that a small crowd had gathered in the drive. Most were police; others, she suspected, were Manuel de Clerk's staff: managers, publicists, and the rest of the cadre that A-list stars seemed to require. Three guys she immediately recognized as security were standing on the other side of the yellow tape, looking particularly sheepish.

At the corner of the house, two of the crime scene specialists were looking for bullet holes in the weeping willow's thick bole. Evidently Gretchen-Mouse hadn't dropped any of her spent brass.

"Christal!"

She raised her eyes, seeing Lymon and Sheela standing off to one side beside a big-fendered motorcycle. She pursed her lips and descended the steps before walking along the edge of the drive to the tape. She nodded at the cop there, ducked it, and walked over to where Lymon and Sheela waited.

"What the hell happened in there?" Lymon gestured at the house.

"How'd you get this far?"

Lymon grinned. "Connections with the department. That, and having an employee as a material witness helps."

Christal related the entire story, glancing curiously at Sheela when she got to the part about Copperhead. Sheela fixed on it like a terrier on a rat.

"Jesus," Lymon wondered. "She cut off Manny's dick and . . ."

"A small piece of foreskin actually," Christal corrected. "It bled like sixty, but the guy will hardly have a scar once it heals. The nutty thing is, she took two used condoms. What do you do with two used condoms? The sperm dies when the temperature drops."

"Souvenir?" Sheela asked, as if she didn't believe it.

"Witch," Christal blurted, hardly aware she'd spoken.

"Ah, here we go again." Lymon lifted an eyebrow. "We're back to broomsticks and black cats."

Christal flashed a self-conscious smile. "As in take a piece of your victim to focus the evil on his body or soul." She shook it off. "It's nothing. Tales of my childhood."

"Mouse shot at you?" Sheela stepped closer, worry on her face. "Are you sure you're all right?"

Christal shrugged. "Hey, it was the first time. Shots in anger, and all that. God, Lymon, if I'd had my pistol with me I might have brought this whole thing to a conclusion."

"Killing Mouse would have landed you in a pile of shit." Lymon pointed a hard finger at her. "Don't even *think* it!"

"I wouldn't have killed her. Not if I could help it. Hey, I maxed the qualification. They were talking about the FBI pistol team. Maybe even the national pistol championship at Camp Perry. If I could have anchored Mouse, taken out two of the Audi's tires, we'd have them."

"You'd have what? A gunfight over stolen rubbers and a tampon?" Lymon gestured with his hands. "Christal, this isn't the Bureau. We're *not* a law enforcement agency. Are you getting this wedged into your hard little head? We provide security . . . protection. Period! We don't take offensive actions. If you can't begin to think in terms of cover and evacuate instead of attack and subdue, you're going to have to look for another line of work."

Christal winced at the censure in his voice. "Yes, sir."

Sheela stepped close, taking her arm. "It's all right. You've done a super job so far, Christal."

"Have I?" she asked bitterly. "Doing what? Copperhead's still a jump ahead of us." She cocked her head, hearing the voices whispering from her subconscious.

"What?" Lymon read her sudden confusion.

"I don't believe in witchcraft, do I?"

"Why would you ask that?" Sheela was watching her, a faint frown on her smooth brow.

"I don't know. But something clicked somewhere. I'll let you know as soon as I figure out what it is." Yes, she could sense that she was on the verge of making the connection.

"Are you ready to head for the barn?" Lymon asked.

Christal gave him a deadpan glare. "Sorry, boss. I've got to make an appearance at the station to file a complaint. I have paperwork to do."

"Pressing charges?"

"I'm going to be running into them again." Christal raised her arms in surrender. "And you're right. I heard you. We're not the cops. But, Lymon, if something goes wrong, I want it on the record that, one, there was trouble, and two, they were the aggravating party."

"It was probably just coincidence that they were here." Sheela didn't sound sincere. "In the weeks ahead we'll all wonder what happened to them, what it was all about."

"No, I'll be seeing them again." Christal squinted into the darkness. She studied the bright lights at the end of the drive. The press was waiting like hungry lions. "Trust me. I can feel it."

The place was called Dusty Stewart's Santa Fe Grill. Christal had seen the sign as she drove down Sunset Boule-

vard and thought it was worth a try. Now she watched as the
waitress placed a heaping plate in front of her. She thanked
the woman and picked up her fork as she studied the steaming meal. The odor of corn tortillas and cumin had her sali-
vating as she reached for the side of diced jalapeño peppers.
She scooped them out over the enchiladas, creating a pattern
of green accents on the melted yellow cheddar and red
sauce.

The sounds of the restaurant covered Lymon's approach
as he walked up, pulled out a chair, and plopped himself
down beside her. He was wearing a brown blazer, sharply
creased cotton pants, and a professional button-down shirt
with a tan tie. His craggy face was creased with a smile, and
his sandy hair looked unkempt.

"Good evening," he greeted, rearranging his blue paper
napkin with its silverware. He glanced around at the piñatas,
guitars, and Mexican pottery that decorated the painted
stucco walls. Diluted strains of mariachi drifted down from
the speakers, competing with the clatter of plates and the
mumble of conversation.

"Hi, boss." Christal reached for the El Yucateco sauce in
the centerpiece.

"You get a good day's sleep?" He gave the waitress a
high sign. She was Hispanic, wearing a frilly white blouse,
low cut, and a black Mexican-style wraparound skirt.
"Smothered burrito," he told her, "and a Carta Blanca to
drink."

Christal told him, "Yeah, I slept like a rock. Even when
the yard crew was mowing the grass under my window. I finally woke up at five-thirty." She made a face. "I think I'm
turning into a bat."

"Glad to see you're breaking into the job. The schedule
can take over your entire life." He hesitated. "Did you get
my message?"

"That we're leaving for New York at midnight? That's for
real?"

"Yep."

"This is kind of last-minute, isn't it?"

He shrugged. "Get used to it. It's the way Hollywood

works. The bigwigs at the studio really want Sheela to attend a preem in New York. Her presence will bring certain benefits to the studio. Ergo, we leave at midnight."

"What's a preem?"

"A premiere showing of a new movie. It's a publicity thing where they bring in all the stars, the director, the producers, and lots of the film critics. The idea is to butter up the critics with hype, let them get chummy with the actors, and they'll write a good review of your movie."

"Right. Why am I going? I'm the new kid on the block."

"Because whatever it is that you're doing, you're kicking results out of the weeds. Maybe you'll see something in New York that we'd miss."

She poked her fork into her enchilada. "Excuse me, I'm starting my breakfast." She took a taste and nodded. "Not bad."

"Dusty Stewart's, huh? I've never been here before." He glanced around. "You can never tell about Mexican."

"Sure you can." Christal gestured with her fork. "Call ahead. If they have fresh jalapeños—like right off the bush—you're usually safe. If they say they have them in the cans, blow it off."

"That's the truth? Really?"

"Trust me. I'm one of the few New Mexicans who survived DC gustatorially unscathed."

He watched her just long enough to make her nervous. "Yes, boss? You want to ask me something?"

"You're from New Mexico."

"Right. I just said that. Born and bred. Who knows how many generations? I'm pure one hundred percent Southwestern mongrel: *Indio, Mexicano,* and Anglo all rolled into one."

He indicated her enchiladas. "Not everyone can eat that stuff with fresh peppers like that."

"Does this have a point?"

"Tell me more about your grandmother."

That stopped her short. "Why on earth would you ask about her?"

"You said she was a witch."

"Grandma was a *curandera,* a healer. Not a witch." She paused. "Well, ok . . . *maybe* not a witch. She was into the old folk remedies. You know, herbs for pains and aches. Taking sweat baths to purge evils from the blood. And, well, sometimes some things that were a little off the wall for the twentieth century, let alone the twenty-first."

"Such as?"

"She cured a guy of stomach cancer once." Christal balanced her fork in emphasis. "The doctors in Albuquerque told the guy that the cancer was too far gone. Told him to just go home and die. He didn't have anything left, so he came wandering up to Grandma's house one day. She lived in a little adobe off the road on the way up to Nambe. Had a garden, a ramada, the whole bit."

"And she cured him?" Lymon was looking skeptical.

Christal chewed, took a swig of her Coke, and shrugged. "The guy was a walking scarecrow—brown skin over bones. You kind of expected him to snap in two at a loud noise. But getting back to the story, Grandma did some things. I didn't understand the what or why of them. She walked around him, chanting in the old tongue, shaking a rattle and swatting him with a wand she'd made of sage, chamisa, and manzanita. She made him swallow some kind of concoction she'd brewed and sent him home."

"And that cured him?"

Christal shook her head. "No, she told him to eat rattlesnake."

"Rattlesnake?"

"Yep. And the guy did. He was all over that country looking for rattlesnakes. Offered five dollars apiece for them. I guess he ate rattlesnake fried, broiled and boiled, baked, fricasseed, smoked, steamed, microwaved, and every other way you could imagine."

Lymon made a face. "And *that* cured him?"

"He lived for more than five years after that. What the cancer failed to do, a Ford truck did. He was hit on his bicycle one Friday night by some kids who had been swigging their beer in quarts." She arched a challenging eyebrow. "The thing is, he'd gained weight, straightened out, and could ride all over the country on his bicycle. The physicians were mystified by his recovery. But for a pickup weaving out of its lane, who knows? He might still be pedaling around looking for rattlesnakes."

Lymon said nothing as his food arrived. He sipped his beer, then picked up his fork. "Did they do an autopsy?"

"What for? Cause of death was pretty straight forward. The guy had the letters *F-O-R-D* stamped into his chest."

Lymon gave her an amused look. "What about this witch stuff?"

"*Some* people called her a witch," Christal corrected. "It depended on if she liked you or not. Truth is, at times she scared the living bejesus out of me. The upper Rio Grande country is a funny part of the world, and Grandma was old school. I think she considered the 1846 American occupation of New Mexico as a passing inconvenience."

"So, why did you think of Copperhead as a witch last night?"

Christal scraped up a forkful of *refritos*. "I've been wondering that myself." She chewed for a while. "It's nothing I can say outright. I mean, these celeb hits, they're after a piece of the person. Does that mean I think that Copperhead and Mouse are locked away in some basement apartment, drawing pentagrams on the floor and repeating spells from *The Necronomicon*? No."

"So, what? What can a person do with Sheela's tampon?"

"Or a slip of de Clerk's foreskin?" She shrugged. "I don't know. They took Julia Roberts' sheets and garbage. Someone nabbed Sandra Bullock's dirty hankies; Mel Gibson lost the head of his razor. Those things are different than a small patch of foreskin."

"Are they?" Lymon hacked off a forkful of burrito.

"Bed linen isn't in the same league as part of a man's most precious."

"The press is all over this. The studio canceled shooting today." Lymon sipped his beer. "Manny is said to be a little distraught."

"If you think he's distraught now, you should have seen him staked out on that bed." She paused. "What are we missing here? They keep getting pieces of men. John Lennon's hair, Manny's foreskin, Mel Gibson's razor scuzz. With women, it's sheets, tissues, tampons, toothbrushes, hairbrushes, and fluids."

"It can't be to turn a buck. The bad guys walked right past a lot of stuff that would have fenced for a bundle."

"You know, Lymon, they're taking the kind of stuff that crime scene guys consider pure gold: DNA, HLA, hairs, blood type, fibers, lots of things."

"So, maybe it's DNA?"

"Sure, maybe. But that doesn't make sense."

"Why is that, Sherlock?"

"If it was DNA, why would they be involved in these high-profile assaults and burglaries? Do you know how easy it is to get someone's DNA? They could have done something as facile as grabbing Sheela's champagne flute at the Wilshire."

"Her champagne flute? How?"

"They could have isolated a couple of mesodermal cells from the lipstick smudge she left on the rim. Or, better, someone could have grabbed the paper towel she'd dried her hands on after she threw it in the trash. They didn't need to set up an elaborate hoax with fake legs and a plastic-lined toilet. In Julia Roberts' case, they didn't need to take the sheets. Cops pull DNA off of sticky-tape samples that pick up flakes of skin."

"But these aren't cops."

"No," Christal mused. "But if they *were* after DNA, they'd know how simple it is to get it."

"Okay, so DNA's out." He paused. "What would a witch want with any of this stuff?"

"You know how they give bloodhounds an article of clothing so they can track down the person? Evil magic works the same way. A witch needs to have something very personal and intimate to tie the curse to. Like an e-mail address to direct the evil to the right person."

"You know"—he gave her a level look—"I don't buy this witchcraft stuff."

"Neither do I. Despite my upbringing."

"Then, why are you looking so worried?"

"Because it's not what you or I believe that's at issue."

"Okay, I'll bite. Why?"

She gave him a grim smile. "Because all that matters is that someone *does* believe it. Figure out that core belief and this whole thing will make perfect sense."

He considered that. "Just like the stalkers. At least one in particular. I told you about her. She believes that Sheela is secretly in love with her."

"Krissy, right?"

"Right."

"Then you begin to understand."

"But that's a delusion. An obsession gone wrong. An example of the human brain making up rules when it operates dysfunctionally."

"And witchcraft isn't?"

"Hell, I don't know."

They ate in silence for a while. Finally, Lymon put his fork down. "Here's the thing. The guy in New York didn't look like a wacko."

"What did he look like?"

"Like a professional . . . doing a job."

"Yeah," she mumbled. "Just like Copperhead."

"So much for your theory."

Christal crunched a jalapeño between her teeth, savoring the burst of flavor. "Maybe not witchcraft, Lymon. But something similar, something parallel."

17

The water was colder than she had anticipated. A chill unlike anything she had ever experienced before ate through her, trying to numb her muscles. Above, the night sky seemed remote, cold as the water, and as heartless.

She swam on, glancing up on occasion to orient herself by

the bowl of the Big Dipper. Shivers were picking at the edges of her muscles. The midnight waters had an oily feel. From some vague corner of her mind, she was reminded that ocean swimmers greased their bodies.

Come on, Nancy. It can't be far. She'd seen the faint sparkles of lights just after dusk. She hadn't expected to see them from the water, not bobbing on the surface. Not until she got close.

Stroke after stroke, she forced herself forward. A leaden feeling had grown in her legs. Had it been so long since she'd been on the high school swim team?

It seemed a distant memory, as though from a dream life. She maintained the rhythm. Stroke and kick, stroke and kick. This race wasn't to the fast, but to the steady.

She had too much to live for. Not just herself, but the others. They all depended on her.

It would be so nice to stop, float, and rest for a bit.

Stroke and kick, stroke and kick.

She tried not to think of the black depths below. What did it matter? One hundred fathoms? Or fifty? All it would take in her condition was six feet.

Stroke and kick, stroke and kick.

She maintained her pace, doggedly panting as her muscles began to ache. A desperate fear had knotted in the back of her brain. What if she cramped?

Who would ever know?

No one. Only the black and lonely sea.

Stroke and kick. Stroke and kick.

Blessed God? Where are the lights? Please, just show me the lights!

Sheela glanced at Rex. He was in the window seat, his head lolled to the side, his mouth open. A faint snore was borne on each exhalation. The stubble on his dark cheeks marred the shiny texture of his skin. She could see where the oils in his hair and scalp had smudged the clear plastic of the window.

What was it about men that they were at their most

hideous when they were asleep in an airplane seat? Their breath seemed to taint the very air, thickening and fouling it with a faint odor.

She unbuckled her seat belt and stood, walking back in the hunched posture necessary to clear the Gulfstream III's low cabin. Dot was propped sideways in her seat, a pillow cushioning her hair. Her two makeup and wardrobe women were likewise slumped on their side of the aisle.

Sheela found Lymon and Christal sitting across the aisle from each other in the rear. Lymon had the reading lamp on and was scrutinizing papers. Christal was frowning down at her laptop as she periodically tapped the *scroll* key. The screen was glowing and the cables were plugged into the plane's Internet access. Sheela hunched down in the aisle between them. "What are you both doing awake?"

"Just double-checking the itinerary." Lymon tapped the papers on his lap. "We'll check into the St. Regis by nine—traffic and security willing. You can nap until three. Makeup and prep until five, when you've got a magazine interview. *Cosmo,* I think. At six-thirty Rex throws them out if they haven't left already. At seven, we leave for the premiere."

"I'm still a little hazy on this," Christal said. "We're flying to New York, checking into the hotel, watching a movie that Sheela didn't even star in, and flying back to LA the same night. Am I the only one who thinks that's a little nuts?"

"Fox is going to be there," Sheela said with a shrug. "I have to be there to smile and hug and schmooze. *Jagged Cat*'s producers want me sucking up to the Fox bigwigs. The company producing *Jagged Cat* still hasn't locked down the distribution rights. Universal and Paramount are dickering for them, and involving Fox adds heat to the deal."

"Don't they have people to do the selling?" Christal seemed confused. "You're an actress. You're supposed to be playing a character."

"Christal, you seriously don't think that they just pay me to act, do you?"

"Uh . . . yeah."

"Oh, you dear naïve girl." Sheela gave her a sympathetic smile. "This entire trip is targeted on three men who will be at the screening. They run Fox's film distribution. That means they put the movies into the theaters. My sole job is to smile and flirt, to snake my arm around their shoulders and bat my eyes suggestively. My people want pictures of me and the Fox management in *Variety, People,* and half the society pages in the country. By tomorrow morning rumors will be floated all over Hollywood that Fox is interested in distributing *Jagged Cat.*"

Christal pursed her lips, frowning. "Just how far will people go?"

Sheela caught the undercurrent. "Christal, these deals can be worth tens of millions of dollars, depending on the picture's success. It's just as ripe for abuse as any other deal when people stand to make or lose millions."

"I got it. Suddenly a midnight flight sounds perfectly reasonable." She paused, laughing. "Oh, hell!"

"What?" Lymon asked.

"I stood Tony Zell up. I promised him dinner tonight."

Lymon burst out laughing. "He'll be stewing! That's hilarious. Do you know when the last time was that a woman stood him up for dinner?"

"Nineteen ninety-six?" Sheela wondered. "Oh, Christal, what a blow to his overinflated ego. He's going to be drooling for you now."

"Lucky me."

"Make room." Sheela motioned Lymon over, aware of Christal's return to introspection. She was evaluating something, processing an idea based on something Sheela had said.

"What are you thinking?" Sheela asked.

"Brad Pitt was assaulted in New York tonight." Christal tapped her laptop suggestively. "He was getting into a cab with Angelina Jolie when some guy in the crowd outside a club on West Fifty-second shot him in the ass with some kind of dart gun. In the scuffle, someone else, a woman, yanked out a hank of Jolie's hair."

"That's a joke, right?"

Lymon, who had moved into the window seat, slowly shook his head. "No joke."

"Shit!" Sheela dropped into his vacated seat, feeling his body warmth. Reassured by it. "So, they grabbed the guy?"

Christal continued, "Witnesses said he looked Middle Eastern, dark complexion, medium build. When spectators tried to interfere, some kind of stun device was detonated. Probably just like the one that flattened you and Lymon at the St. Regis. In the confusion he got away. So did the woman who pulled Jolie's hair out."

"The dart is interesting, too," Lymon remarked. "Kind of like a harpoon, it apparently spools out, impales its victim, and is reeled back in."

"So, how's Brad?"

Christal was pensive. "They took him straight to the emergency ward. They're running tests now. Trying to see if anything was injected. They've got him on antibiotics and an HIV protocol, just in case."

"It's not an injection." Lymon gave Sheela a meaningful look. "It's another . . . what? Specimen retrieval? Just like snipping a bit of Manny's penis."

Christal added, "We can't be sure about what happened to Angelina Jolie. Was it an attack? Or just a scuffle? The details aren't clear."

Sheela leaned back, closing her eyes. "This doesn't make sense."

"Witchcraft," Lymon muttered as he stared down at his papers.

"Hey," Christal chided softly from her seat.

Sheela glanced back and forth between them. "That's the second time I've heard that brought up. You want to fill me in?"

Lymon rubbed his eyes, then looked at her. She liked the concern in his weary hazel gaze as he said, "How are you on soul possession? Targeted evil? Voodoo dolls and the like?"

"Not very. I don't believe in that sort of thing."

"Neither do we," Christal answered. "It's just something we're tossing around. It has to do with the personal nature of the things being taken." She made a helpless gesture. "It shows how baffled we are, Sheela. Surely you've heard the stories of witches collecting fingernail clippings, strands of hair, and navel lint. Taking some personal item to do sympathetic magic. It's the only comparison we can find. And it's silly."

"Is it?" Sheela felt a coldness in her breast. "Did Lymon tell you about my freaky fan? The one with the slice-and-dice course to unrequited love? She just knows that when I smile down from the screen, I'm talking straight to her."

"Must make you feel peculiar."

"Christal, until you've been there, I'm not sure I could ever make you understand. It curdles your soul. In a world full of six billion people, how many of them have wounded minds? How many were abused as children? How many brain damaged? How many have fried their synapses with drugs? How many have chemical imbalances? How many live for their fantasies, and how many would sell their souls to satisfy their delusions?"

"I've heard figures as high as one to two percent," Christal answered. "More, given the right circumstances."

Sheela barely nodded. "One of the most horrifying moments of my career was after I made my first film, *Joy's Girl*. My character was a young prostitute. I did a scene that was sexually explicit."

"I've seen it. That expression on your face is a heart-stopper. Was he really that attractive?"

"Hey, there were thirty people on set at the time. I hated the guy. The director knew it, so he told me to imagine that my favorite dessert was being dribbled on my face. That's where that look came from."

Christal laughed in delight. "Wow! It worked. The first time I saw that, I thought the screen was going to melt. Every man in the theater walked out weak-kneed."

Sheela shrugged. "I didn't understand the effect that scene would have. It was pieced together with bits from four days of brutal shooting. Do the shot, change the lighting, redo the shot, change the camera angle, redo the shot, change the color of the sheets, redo the shot. And on and on. You can only dream of chocolate soufflé for so long. After the first hour I felt as sexy as bread mold."

She glanced at Lymon, curious about how he was taking it. "It wasn't until the screening that I finally understood what a good film editor can do. I couldn't believe that was me up there on the screen. My manager at the time, Angel, leaned over and said, 'Well, kid, how about it? When this lays down in video, you're going to have a half million men playing it slow motion, over and over, while they slump on their couches and jack off.' "

"Yuck!" Christal gave her a disgusted look.

"Yeah. One of the perks of being a star, huh?" Sheela arched an eyebrow. "Sometimes, on really bad nights, I try to imagine that . . . all those men. I can picture them, illuminated in the television's glow, sweaty, hairy, their rumpled pants down around their knees, hands stroking up and down, and their wide eyes fixed obsessively on mine. How are they playing it in their minds? What are they doing to me? What would they give to turn that momentary fantasy into the real thing?"

Christal swallowed hard and looked away. "Jesus."

Sheela made a gesture of acceptance. "In that instant, they all want to possess me in one way or another. Maybe my soul, but always my body. So, guys, what's a little witchcraft compared with reality?"

Sid Harness strode down the hall, his coat flapping as he entered the New York City medical examiner's office. He was still blinking, wishing desperately for another cup of coffee, and decidedly sleep deprived. He'd had a whole blessed three hours of somnolence in his own bed, next to Claire's warm body, before the phone rang.

He'd left his wife sleeping, taken a quick shower, driven into the city, and parked his car in the long-term lot at Union Station. The morning train had taken him to New York's Penn Station. A cab had carried him to the ME's on the Lower East Side.

Now he hurried down the hall, found the right office,

and leaned in the already-open door. He tapped lightly, calling, "Hello? I'm Special Agent Sid Harness for Dr. Helen Lambout."

A middle-aged woman who sat at the desk looked up, peering over the tops of her glasses. Gray streaked her brown hair, and her face had a severe look. A green surgical smock covered a gray dress.

She smiled and nodded. "Yes. DC said someone was coming up. Come on in. Can I get you anything? Coffee?"

He grinned at that. "Yeah, I'm running on caffeine and nervous energy."

She studied him, apparently noting his swollen eyes and the lethargy that three hours of nodding to Amtrack's version of comfort had left imprinted in his face. "Come on. You'll want to see the lab results, too."

She led him back the way he'd come, down a flight of stairs, and along a hallway lined with examining rooms. They stopped in a small lunchroom with a table, chairs, a snack and pop machine, a microwave, and a stained coffeepot from which she withdrew a cup of something that looked like crankcase drippings.

Lifting the paper cup, she inspected it, peering down her nose through her glasses. "I don't know how fresh this is." She handed it to him with a shrug. "Creamer and sugar are there. While it's not necessary, any donation to the cause would be appreciated." She indicated a large coffee can marked DONATIONS with a slit in the plastic lid.

Sid fished out a dollar and slipped it through the slot. He sipped the coffee, struggled to keep his face straight, and went for creamer and sugar after all.

As he sipped cautiously he followed Dr. Lambout through double doors and into one of the forensic labs. He'd been in similar rooms before, but each time the surroundings sent a chill up his spine. The autopsy table with its lights, hoses, and drains always lurked like some ghost of the Inquisition. Light boards on the walls were for viewing X-rays. This room had a counter that sported a covered microscope, a small centrifuge, and glass-fronted cabinets full of test tubes, pipettes, beakers, boxes of rubber gloves, plastic specimen bags, and the other accouterments of necropsy. Even the air seemed chillier.

Helen Lambout led him to the counter, where a manila folder had the letters FBI marked prominently in black felt pen. She propped herself on one of the stools and flipped the cover open, asking, "Do you want to see the body, or are the photos sufficient?"

"The photos will do." He bent to peer at the glossy eight-by-tens. A naked woman lay on the table, eyes half-slitted in death. She looked incredibly pale, the whiteness a result of demise. Outside of being a floater, she appeared to be a typical Caucasoid woman of moderate build. He could see no immediate sign of trauma, no indication of any abnormality except that she was obviously dead. "Got a cause of death?"

"She drowned. Preliminary samples test positive for seawater. When we opened her up, we found no evidence of foul play. We're still looking for the more obscure pharmacology, but we came up negative on the usual: alcohol, marijuana, cocaine, heroin, and so forth. Internal organs look healthy."

"Stomach contents?" he asked.

"She had steak—beef, we think—at the last meal. Potato and broccoli were ingested about four hours before death. Again, the stomach contents tested negative for alcohol. Her lungs were fine, but deoxygenated from the salt water. We found no lesions on the skin, no evidence of injections or injuries. Vaginal swabs came back negative for semen or spermatozoa."

"Any scars?"

Lambout nodded. "A couple of faint scars around the hands." She flipped back to a diagram that reproduced them. "And one longitudinal scar on the right thigh."

"From the time she had her femur pinned after a car wreck when she was twelve," Sid finished. "Did the pins match?"

Lambout shuffled through the photos to a photocopy of an X-ray. "This is the shot we took. Attached to it with a paper clip is the fax her physician in California sent to us last night. That, along with the dental records, are pretty conclusive. We won't know on the DNA until next week at the earliest. Dermatoglyphics will be in sometime this afternoon."

"Where did you get a reference sample of her DNA?"

"She left a lot of it. All curated at the California lab." She tapped the folder with a narrow finger. "You want my opinion? I'm ninety-nine point nine percent positive that this is Nancy Hartlee's body."

Sid frowned as he flipped the pages back to show a photocopy of a nautical chart. "So, tell me, Doctor, where has Nancy Hartlee been for the last five years? And just why do you think her body was found floating ten miles out from the beach off Long Island?"

18

My God, have I ever been this tired? The question rolled around in Christal's head as Lymon walked back and opened the limo door for Sheela. The crowd exploded in applause and whistles as Sheela took Lymon's hand and stepped out into the New York night. Lymon wore a black tux, and Sheela was resplendent in a powder-blue Ungaro gown, her metallic red hair up, with ringlets falling about her pale shoulders.

Flashes of white lit the night, popping in the crowd like bottled lightning let loose. Christal could hear the frantic click of the shutters as she ducked out on Sheela's heels. Christal had outfitted herself in an off-the-rack black Ralph Lauren she'd found on sale during a last-minute panic trip to Bloomingdale's.

Reporters were calling out in a cacophony. "Sheela!" "Ms. Marks!" "Have they found your tampon?" "Sheela! Look this way!" "Sheela! How do you feel about the recent publicity?" "Sheela! Is it true that someone cut off Manuel de Clerk's penis?" "How do the recent assaults affect your shooting schedule?" "Sheela! Who are you seeing these days?"

"Remember." Lymon bent close, shouting into Christal's ear. "You have her left. Stay close behind her and keep your eyes open."

She did, forcing herself to concentrate, eyes on the crowd as she and Lymon followed a half pace behind Sheela. She wore an earpiece along with a throat mike at her collar. Somehow the fragile-looking velvet ropes held the mob at bay. Ahead of them, Sheela walked up the red carpet to the theater entrance. She was waving, nourishing the feeding horde with her famous smile.

"How does she do it?" Christal wondered as she squinted against the lights, searching for any sign of threat in the press of bodies behind the ropes. She kept the mantra in her head: Attacks always come from the third row back. It seemed like a sea of shining faces and glittering eyes. To her, they all looked like predators.

"Sheela's a pro," Lymon answered, his voice barely audible. How the hell had he heard her over the raucous babble?

Once they were checked through the theater's security, the lobby was crowded with black-tie-clad men in sharp tuxedos, women in exotic, expensive, and often revealing evening gowns, and liveried caterers passing through the throng like fish in seaweed with trays of champagne, caviar-heaped crackers, and other goodies. Every wall was covered with huge posters hawking *Night Stalker* and its stars.

Christal picked out faces: Gwyneth Paltrow, Jack Nicholson, Robert De Niro, and someone she thought might be Barbra Streisand beneath a garish hat. Halle Berry, clad in something that looked like cellophane, was surrounded by smiling men, some of whom pointed microphones toward her mouth.

The not-so-well-dressed carried pads of paper and tape recorders. Christal assumed these were the dreaded critics come to pass judgment on the final product. They seemed to move from star to star, talking, occasionally taking notes.

Then Christal fixed on the elegantly dressed men in the rear and off to the side. None of them looked distinctive, but each had a following. The moguls, perhaps?

"Sheela, *darling!*" an elderly woman in silver sequins cried; she flowed forward with an outstretched hand. "How perfectly *ghastly* that someone would do these things!" A throng rushed in on her wake, washing around Sheela.

Taking Lymon's cue, Christal followed him as he split off and walked toward the side of the room.

"From here on out," Lymon told her as they took a position under one of the huge posters that showed a hard-eyed Halle Berry staring down the sights of a huge silver semi-automatic pistol, "we just try to be unobtrusive."

Christal nodded, aware of the other wallflowers—mostly men, professionally dressed—who stood, watching alertly at the fringes. When their gazes crossed Lymon's, they would give a slight nod, then move on. Some spared Christal a great deal more than just a second glance. She could feel herself being sized up. The rest of the Brethren, she decided.

"How do you determine who's who?" she asked, indicating the people in the center of the room. Some were obvious sycophants; others seemed to be movers and shakers. Photographers slipped about like coyotes around a flock of sheep.

"Watch how much a person moves," Lymon answered. "The closer a person is to the top of the heap, the less he moves through the crowd. Those guys"—he pointed to a knot off to one side—"are the Fox bigwigs. They've got nothing to prove to anyone. They won't move until the curtain call. Watch Sheela. She'll drift her way over to them without seeming to. Power meeting power."

Christal studied Sheela, having seen her at the Wilshire reception but unaware of the social dynamics. A collection of people had gathered around her, laughing and smiling. Others worked their way through the press to take her hand, give her a slight hug, or that faint kiss of the cheeks. New Mexico–raised Christal still found that custom a little peculiar.

She was considering that when she saw the dark man; he didn't fit. Instead he stood to one side, his black eyes fixed, gleaming, and focused on Sheela Marks. He remained oblivious to everyone else in the room—even though Robert De Niro stood no more than two paces to his right. He was dressed immaculately in a black silk tuxedo that shimmered in the light like an insect's shell. She pegged him for a rich Arab by his facial features, complexion, and the regal way he held himself.

"Lymon?"

"Hmm?"

"Check out the guy. He's alone, standing five feet to Sheela's right. He's all by himself, detached, and if my instincts are right, he's not a movie type."

Lymon fixed on the man. "You're right. Not a movie type at all. I've never seen him before. He looks like oil money. A lot of rich oil Arabs invest in films. Hell, give me ten or twenty million worth of discretionary cash and I might, too." A pause. "He's sure holding a bead on Sheela, isn't he?"

"Trouble?"

Lymon gave a faint shake of the head, frowning as he watched the guy watching Sheela. "Probably not. At least, not that kind. You don't get in the door without an invitation." He paused. "Still, I don't like him, Christal. That expression on his face isn't right. Hell, he's not even blinking. Just keep an eye on him, okay? He can drool all he wants, just so he doesn't touch."

Christal's gaze kept going back to the hawkish Arab. In her grandmother's quaint vernacular, he made her whiskers vibrate. What was that look in his eyes? An almost obsessive gleam. She had seen men at livestock auctions stare at prize animals with that same careful appraisal.

"It's hardly a livestock auction," she muttered, forcing herself to turn her attention elsewhere.

"Pardon?" Lymon asked.

"Nothing."

"A livestock auction? Is that what I heard you say?"

"Yeah. Silly, huh?"

Sheela had managed to drift her cluster of admirers to within several feet of the Fox executives. Then, most artfully, she turned on her heel, seemed surprised, and rushed to greet the first of them. She kissed the man on the cheek, and over the babble of conversation, Christal heard ". . . So *glad* to see you!"

The photographers, like hunters from a blind, seemed to pop up from the very carpet, their cameras clicking. Sheela gave a little cry and skipped to her second target.

Christal gaped, even knowing it was an act. Sheela seemed to radiate joy at being in their presence.

"She's good, isn't she?" Lymon asked.

Sheela melted against another of the men, her posture a balance of restraint and provocation. Was that another of her arts? The ability to be both tasteful tease and provocative temptress in the same breath? Was that part of the A-list portfolio?

"So the trip's a success?" Christal asked.

"She'll work them all night." Was that weariness in Lymon's voice? "After the preem, Sheela will attend the Fox party. By the time she leaves, she'll have dates with each of those guys."

"No way!"

"Yeah, but none of them will happen. There are shooting schedules, conflicting business meetings, and last-minute cancellations, and what do you know? After a month has gone by, it's all forgotten but the goodwill."

Christal shot Lymon a sidelong look, aware of the hardness in his eyes and the muted tones of his voice. Puzzling at it, she was on the verge of revelation when her sixth sense made her glance back at the Arab. A second man had walked up to stand just out of sight behind the Arab's right elbow. Christal couldn't see his face, but he spoke in a confidential voice. The Arab leaned his head slightly to hear better, then nodded, a slight smile on his thin lips.

Christal craned her neck, trying to see the newcomer's face. Something about him haunted her: the way he moved, the set of his shoulders, and the gestures he made.

"Just a minute, Lymon." Christal moved out from the wall and angled behind the group that surrounded De Niro. The Arab and his shadow were moving now, heading toward the door. That walk! Damn it, yes. She *knew* him.

Christal hurried along the wall, paralleling the Arab's course, trying to thread her way through the packed bodies with as much decorum as she could.

The man was still on the Arab's off side. Christal had closed the distance, angling up on the right. She could smell the Arab: a perfumed scent, not unpleasant, but not attractive, either. He was tall, aloof, and walked with a liquid grace. A look of deep satisfaction, as if someone had just used oiled fingers to massage his soul, was betrayed by his lingering smile.

They were nearing the door, the Arab still blocking the view. "Excuse me," Christal called, stepping close.

The tall Arab turned rapturous black eyes on her, unfocused as if she had just interrupted a reverie.

"Oh, sorry," she said with a smile. "I thought you were Antonio Banderas." But her gaze went to the shorter man, who stepped past the Arab to see her. In that instant, their eyes locked and the world stopped.

Christal's heart skipped, then began to pound. He looked just as shocked as she did, those familiar eyes wide and disbelieving. An instant later a rush of loathing rose to replace the surprise in his face.

"Chris?" he stumbled. "What the hell . . . ?"

"Sorry, Hank," she managed through tight jaws. "Your friend here *isn't* the guy I'm looking for."

The Arab had turned confused eyes on Hank, then glanced back at Christal. He smiled then, saying in a whisper-accented voice, "She is a beautiful woman. Spirited. You know her?"

A feather of fear tickled her as a growing appreciation filled the Arab's eyes. He studied her face, bending slightly to stare at her breasts and the way her dress rode the curve of her waist and hips.

Shit! Mistake! Get the hell out of here! "Sorry to bother you, Hank. Have a nice night."

She spun on her heel and kept her back straight as she turned, walking back toward the side of the room. She could feel the Arab's hungry eyes; a creepy shiver crossed her skin, and a terrible sickness was spreading in her gut.

For some reason she couldn't comprehend, she joined the

periphery of De Niro's group. Maybe it was some primal urge—a search for safety in numbers. The muscles in her legs had gone rubbery. She clamped her jaw tight to keep it from trembling.

De Niro was saying, "What? Sure, I'm typecast. What do I care? If it's a good script . . ."

Taking a quick glance, she could see Hank Abrams talking rapidly, gesturing with his hands as he walked with the Arab out past the guards at the door. In that last instant, Hank shot a quick look over his shoulder, meeting Christal's gaze. A smothered rage burned there, seething and coiled.

"What's up?" Lymon seemed to appear like magic at her shoulder.

"I haven't got the foggiest idea." She glanced hesitantly at Lymon as she stepped away from De Niro's audience.

"You want to tell me who that guy is?"

"No." She could see the irritation growing behind Lymon's flinty expression. "But I guess I'm going to have to, huh?"

He paused. "I don't know. Why don't you tell me?"

"Yeah, later, all right? When I get my guts back."

She was saved when a voice called out, "Ladies and gentlemen, if you will take your seats, you are about to be part of filmmaking history! The premiere screening of *Night Stalker* is about to begin!"

A sporadic burst of applause and cheers was followed by people walking toward the doors on either side of the concession stand where harried caterers still poured champagne.

"What now?" Christal asked, taking a deep breath and centering her quavering soul.

"Now we wait." The question was hanging unanswered between them.

"We don't get to see the movie?"

"Sure, it's just that you've got to buy a ticket when it comes to a multiplex near you." He was watching her, the look evaluative. "Meanwhile, come on. I'll introduce you around. Like everything else, personal security is a small world."

Yeah, a world that has Hank Abrams squiring a mysterious Arab—one with a penchant for raping women with his eyes.

* * *

Ever since the Gonzales disaster, Hank Abrams had hated walking down halls to his supervisor's office, but here he was again, plodding down a much plusher hallway.

Verele Security's Manhattan headquarters dominated the entire twenty-second floor of the Flatiron Building where Broadway crossed Fifth Avenue. It was a successful company. The offices reflected that and were furnished with expensive decor, nice woodwork on the walls, thick carpeting, and occasional pieces of artwork that gave the place just the right cachet.

Once Hank Abrams had radiated in the attention of his superiors. Now their slightest notice of his existence sent the heebie-jeebies up his backbone. Dear God, why had Verele sent for him? He couldn't be sure, but he was afraid it was because of the very same woman who had ruined his career in the FBI.

A terrible ill feeling had settled on his stomach, heavy like a carry-out fast-food breakfast. The sensation in his too-tight nerves reminded him of the metallic sense of touching a nine-volt battery to his tongue.

He pushed open the frosted glass door to his boss's office and walked up to the glossy ebony desk where Trina, the secretary, held sway. She looked up, a knockout attractive black woman of thirty-five who had the most omniscient eyes of anyone—male or female—that Hank had ever known.

"Verele sent for me."

"Gotcha, Hank." She gave a smooth tilt of her head to indicate the door. "He's waiting for you."

"Thanks." Hank took a deep breath, squared his shoulders, and straightened his tie before he pushed the door open and walked into Verele's lair.

He had been here once before, when he was hired, but the place still set him back. The white carpeting had to be worth two hundred dollars a square yard. It was like walking on air. Whoever had designed the decor of black walnut, polished cherry, mirrors, and chrome had been a genius. It actually worked, each element complementing the other. Huge floor-to-ceiling windows gave a view up both Broadway and Fifth. Down below, traffic was flowing in slow starts and stops. The lower roofs of Midtown gave way to the upper Manhattan skyline in the hazy distance.

The big desk in the middle of the room was a composite of red cherrywood and chrome, its surface dominated by two computers, a modular communications system, and several telephones. An open laptop rested to one side. In a monstrous chair, upholstered with overstuffed soft maroon leather, sat a very small man.

Verele Yarrow was more than a midget and less than short. He stood four-foot-five-inches tall, his head oversized and nearly bald. Light blue eyes watched the world from a wide face, and the guy's nose was like a round ball. On this day he was dressed in a bluish silver silk suit.

When Hank had first met him, he'd almost made the mistake of judging Verele by his caricaturish looks. Then the man had spoken, and all doubt had vanished. His speech was precise, articulate, and his intellect cut like a hammer-forged Randall blade.

"Good day, Mr. Abrams," Verele began in his crisply formal way. "I thank you for your prompt arrival."

"Yes, sir." Hank felt the butterflies in his stomach.

"I would like to thank you for your excellent attention to the Sheik last night. You did very well in your first stint as a detail leader. The evaluation of your performance is excellent for your initial assignment in the hot seat. By the way, I think you've been informed that the Sheik will require your services again this evening."

A faint wave of relief washed through him. "Thank you, sir. Yes. My team picks him up at the Ritz-Carlton at six tonight. I understand that I'm to take him to one of the piers in Brooklyn."

"That is correct. As detail leader, you are to accompany him and his people. Take a small kit with you. Pack light. I'm not sure just how long this detail will take, but plan for several days at a minimum." The light blue eyes narrowed. "Whatever you see or hear is strictly confidential, do you understand?"

Hank swallowed hard. "Yes, sir." He winced. "Sir, I am an ex-FBI agent. I wouldn't want . . . I mean . . ."

"You will not be required to participate in anything illegal, Hank." Verele watched him intently. "Our mandate is the protection and safety of our clients. That is our only responsibility. Beyond that, we do not ask, we do not care. You should not be compromised in your service of the Sheik over the next couple of days." He paused, seeming to look right past Hank's defenses. "Do you have a problem when it comes to not asking and not caring?"

"No, sir."

"Good. Now, about last night. There was a woman?"

The relief was replaced with fear. "Yes, sir. I think I should explain, sir. She approached me. I did nothing to initiate contact."

"I'm sure that is the case. The Sheik reported that she actually approached him." A slight smile bent his broad lips. "Thought he was Antonio Banderas? The Sheik was flattered. He is also very interested in the woman."

"He is?" That caught Hank out of left field.

"You know her."

"Yes, sir." He swallowed hard. "She was at the Bureau when I was."

"We already know a little about her. Now we would like to know more. Tell me about her." The light blue eyes hardened like marbles. "*All* about her."

Hank winced. "Yes, sir." And the story began to pour out of him.

19

Christal and Lymon sat at their usual table in the back of Al's. She glanced sidelong at her boss. He was carefully scraping tamales from their corn husks, his fork peeling the steaming *masa* loose. She hovered over a medium-rare buffalo fillet with mashed sweet potatoes and wild rice. To drink she had selected a Sierra Nevada Pale Ale while Lymon nursed something called an Alaskan Smoked Porter. The color of it reminded her of the stuff mechanics drained out of engines.

They had only catnapped on the flight back from New York. She had been deposited at her room at just after one yesterday afternoon and would have slept clear through but for an annoying phone call from Tony last night at seven. She'd promised to call him back when her brain functioned again. Then, that morning, she had taken Lymon's call to have lunch at noon. By some not-so-subtle feminine instinct she knew exactly what he wanted to discuss.

"I think it was a combination of things," she said. "Hank was really on a roll. So was I. It was his first big investigation, and I was the spark plug that gave it combustion. I'd figured out the link that tied the entire Gonzales puzzle together." She glanced at Lymon. "We were both high on success, and it just kind of happened. Hank was handsome, smart, and full of confidence. Like I was telling Sid that night. Hank listened."

"And he was married."

"Yeah, I knew that." She lifted a weary eyebrow. "Lymon, sometimes that gets lost in the rush, you know? Especially on a long investigation. We were together day in and night out. I knew he wasn't . . . well, what I'd look for in a man. But he was there."

"You said he was a smart guy."

"Yeah. Really smart. I suspect he'd have eventually busted Gonzales without my input. He's got a good head for organization and detail. He's quick, methodical, and orderly. He ran a good operation. We didn't have many screwups in the field because Hank could keep all the balls in the air and know which one to toss up next."

"Was he the stick-to-it type?"

"More or less. Not really a bulldog, but I had him figured for promotion to special agent in charge within five years. Yeah, he was a real bright-burning candle, and when he looked at you right, those brown eyes would melt you."

"Is that what happened?"

Christal stared at the square of buffalo steak dangling on her fork. "We'd had a few drinks together just before we went on duty." A pause. "Well, maybe I had a few more than I should have. I don't normally do that, but we were flushed with success. That was Tuesday; by Friday, we were going to actually make the arrest. Hank had volunteered to change shifts with one of the other guys whose wife was having a baby. Hank asked if I wanted to take that shift with him. You know, just company. I said yeah."

She chewed thoughtfully as she replayed that night in her head. "We met at a place for a late dinner. It was just past ten. Maybe it was the hour. Maybe it was because I wasn't really going to be on duty—just standing in, you know? But I had a martini. I hate vodka. Then I had another. It was fun, Lymon. We were laughing—both of us on top of the world. It was a celebration."

She attacked the sweet potato. "When we relieved the guys in the van at midnight, we were still giddy. Nothing was happening. Gonzales' place was empty, the house completely dark. One of the guys we worked with had a bad back. He had one of those thin little blue foam pads rolled up on the floor." She sipped her soda. "It just happened. Him and me in the middle of the night. One minute we were sitting next to each other, watching the screens, and the next we were kissing; then we were on that blue mat."

She glanced at Lymon, seeing understanding in his eyes. "Would I have screwed him if I'd been stone-cold sober? Yeah, probably. I was attracted to the guy."

"Did anyone ever figure out how they compromised the van?"

"No. After the photos landed on the director's desk, they searched that van—and I mean thoroughly. They got squat. Whoever had put the camera in had taken it out again. From the resolution it was a very good camera." She avoided his eyes. "You can see everything. God, how humiliating."

"And then Hank shows up at the *Night Stalker* premiere in New York with an Arab who is fixed on Sheela like a Brittany spaniel on a pheasant." Lymon jabbed halfheartedly at his tamales. "If you'll remember, we were sitting right here when Sid said that Hank had taken a job with Verele Security."

"Escorting mucky-mucks."

"Yeah, mostly the hyperrich. There's specialization in this business. Multibillionaires have different concerns than actors do. Their biggest fear is either assassination or kidnapping. Sometimes it's corporate espionage. Their security is based on creating a safe buffer zone. Our job at LBA is tougher. We have to ensure personal privacy and bodily safety for very public people. In a lot of ways, their job is easier. They can build walls."

"He'd be good at that."

"Pardon me?"

"Hank Abrams. He'd be good at executive protection. Like I said, he's got a thing for the little stuff. In fact, he's a nut about details. He did things like plot the route we were going to take on an operation. He'd know the nearest hospital, have a list of alternatives, that sort of thing."

"Then he's a natural for executive protection. Good advancing is what it's all about. If you ever get jumped, have to use your cover-and-evacuate skills, it's already too late. You've screwed up."

"You can't always predict all the details."

"You can try." Lymon paused. "I did some checking. The Arab was Sheik Amud Abdulla. He's a Saudi national who lives in Qatar. He put twenty million into the production company that made *Night Stalker*. The funny thing is, he wasn't going to attend. Then, at the last minute, he flew in."

"And didn't stay for the movie."

"Maybe it's just me, but I thought he was just there to see Sheela."

"Almost like he walked in, got an eyeful, and walked out," she agreed. "I remember you saying he could drool, but not touch."

"You were the one who said it was like a livestock auction. What brought that on?"

"He was looking at her like she was a piece of meat." Christal shivered. "Lymon, I swear, he was looking right through my clothes when I stopped him at the door. He went from dreamy-eyed to rapacious. He was talking to Hank like I wasn't really there."

Lymon took a swig of his porter, pursed his lips, and frowned. "I'm going to mention it to Max. He's all wrapped up with the follow-through for the meetings he had on Wall Street. He used the trip for face time with the people who handle Sheela's investments. I think I ought to give him a heads-up."

"How come?"

"Just in case the good Sheik Abdulla wants to invest in one of Sheela's pictures."

Christal considered that. "You think ten or twenty million worth of investment would come with strings attached?"

He gave her a guarded look. "It's happened before. Funding for a fuck or two. It's all a weird game, mostly driven by power, by who can control whom. Think of the rush a certain type of man would get knowing that his money gave him control of Sheela Marks, even if just for a night or two. Is that Godlike, or what?"

"Why do people even get involved in this place?"

"Because balancing out the scum you will always find the ones who want to make movies: the artists and creators. They're the myth makers and storytellers—our tribal shamans. You know, the spiritual dreamers with the glow of universes in their eyes. They spin dreamlike fantasies to make people feel better about themselves. They give visions of hope to a society that is glutted with riches but suffering from a poverty of the soul."

He lifted a lip. "Then you have the parasites. The people in suits. They've figured out ways to make money off of and control the creators, dreamers, and doers. They're the brokers, lawyers, agents, accountants, and shady producers. In Hollywood, if someone has an MBA, count your fingers after you shake hands. Chances are, one of them will be missing."

She nodded. "I know the type. In my part of the world, they're called Anglo bankers. Somehow anyone who ever went to one for a loan ended up thrown off his land."

"Speaking of the sharks, how's Tony?"

"The guy's desperate, I guess. He left notes taped to my room door. I'm supposed to call him as soon as I get an off moment."

"Watch him."

She laughed at that. "Hey, he's not a Hank Abrams. Not even close. How on earth do I take someone who calls me 'babe' seriously?"

"He's one of the biggest agents in Hollywood." Lymon studied her thoughtfully. "With your looks, he's going to offer you a screen test. You know that, don't you?"

"He already has." She shrugged. "It's a ploy to get me into his bed. Maybe you'd better warn him that the last man I was involved with wasn't happy afterwards."

"Aren't you just a little curious?"

"About going to bed with Tony? Are you nuts?"

"No. About the screen test."

She smiled. "Maybe, Lymon, when this is all over. Sure. It would be fun. Just for kicks, you know? But I'm not fooling anyone. I'm not even close to Sheela Marks in caliber. Had I been in her place, those Fox executives would have seen right through me. They'd have laughed me out of the room, and I'd have blown the deal."

"False modesty doesn't become you." He smiled, changing the subject. "So, now we've added Pitt and Jolie to the list. Who's next?"

She considered that. "Something's been on my mind, Lymon. I keep coming back to Genesis Athena."

"I looked at their questionnaire. When I read the questions, they were just questions. Some of them, like the ones about the bathroom, seemed pretty silly."

"So, why does a company pay out as much as they do to support a Web site full of silly questions?"

"Got me. It's their money."

"I think," she said coolly, "that it's time to take the test, Lymon."

*　*　*

Sheela took a deep breath and held it as she stood on her cue under the burning set lights that illuminated the wrecked kitchen. All eyes fixed on Manuel de Clerk. The tension in the room was palpable, like a ticking bomb. Sheela tensed, pleading, *Come on, Manny, you can do it this time.*

For this scene she wore a short-cropped wig, and her face had been smudged by makeup. Her loose T-shirt was blood smeared and torn to give the slightest glimpse of her right breast. She was standing on a taped X in the ransacked kitchen. The table was turned over, flour had been thrown around, and silverware lay strewn across the countertop behind her. She gripped a rusty hunting knife as though ready to use it.

Across from her Manny de Clerk had stopped on his cue, made the half turn Bernard wanted, but the stern glare he was supposed to give the camera collapsed into a sad convulsion. A sob caught at the bottom of his throat, his mouth puckering.

"Cut!" Bernard called a moment before he let loose with a string of curses. Moans could be heard around the set. Then Bernard came storming out from behind the camera, a fist knotted and shaking as he stomped up to de Clerk, shouting, "God damn it! Get it together!"

"You don't understand!" Manny implored. "Dear God, I just see her. Smiling down at me. That knife in her hand!"

"Yeah, Sheela's got a knife. Remember the scene? She's supposed to chase your ass out of the kitchen with it!"

"No, I see that *woman*! She *cut* me!"

Bernard waved his arms. "That's fucking bullshit, Manny! I read the medical report! She nicked your dick! Ninety percent of the babies in this country get circumcised—and it's a hell of a lot more traumatic than what happened to you!"

"I'd say forty-five percent," Sheela offered flatly.

"Huh? What?" Bernard turned on her.

"More than half of those babies are girls, and a moderate percentage of boys aren't circumcised for various cultural reasons." Sheela tossed the knife up, catching it by the handle—a trick she'd learned in the filming of *Blood Rage*.

Manny continued to sob.

"What the hell do I have to do?" Bernard shook his head and lifted his hands imploringly to the lights that hung on the overhead scaffolding.

"Call it for today," Sheela said wearily. "Get the man some professional help while we shoot the scenes with me and Gene." She looked across to where de Clerk's double stood off camera. He nodded woodenly as Sheela continued, "Shoot the scenes with de Clerk later. Spot Manny in, and if worse comes to worst, fill it in with CG."

Bernard granted her a speculative look. "You think that would work?"

She lifted a challenging eyebrow. "I could oversee it, shepherd it through the process—but I'd want your cut of box office."

"What about costs? It'll be a fortune!"

"Bernard, if the rest of us hoof it, we can move ahead of schedule, right? Each day we save is a day's overhead you can move to FX."

De Clerk had wilted to the floor. Bernard's lip was quivering as he physically fought to keep from sneering. "Yeah, right." Turning, he called to his assistant, "Vern, call Manny's agent. Have him take care of this."

Sheela stuck the knife into the wooden countertop and pulled the close-cropped wig off. She tossed it to the costume assistant and pulled out the bobby pins before running her fingers through her hair. She shook it out as she walked off the set, passing the cameras.

Bernard followed behind, saying, "I just don't get it. What's with this guy?"

"He's a wimp," she told him, speaking so the grips and riggers couldn't hear. "I didn't want to do this picture with him, if you'll recall. And I can damn sure tell you I'd never have won that Oscar if he'd been in *Blood Rage* like they'd originally cast him."

"So, why'd you agree this time?" Bernard asked, a sour note in his voice.

"Because, you begged, Bernie. Remember?" She sounded jaded, and she knew it. At the stage door she paused. "Look, just change the schedule. We'll shoot all of my scenes and those with the rest of the cast. It'll be brutal, but it will get us ahead of schedule. And as for the stuff we've got to do on location, I'm serious: Use a stand-in and fix it in postproduction."

He hesitated, hanging in the doorway after she'd stepped out. "When it gets out, it could ruin his career."

"As if what he's doing in there isn't already accomplishing just that?" She met Bernard's worried eyes. "See you in the a.m."

She walked to her trailer and climbed the aluminum steps. When she entered, Lymon was kicked back on her couch, his legs up on the small coffee table as he flipped through *Daily Variety*. Glancing up, he read her expression and asked, "What's wrong?"

"Manny's a basket case. Bernard's panicking." She walked to the refrigerator and pulled out a beer, lifting it so he could see. "You want one?"

Lymon shook his head. "I'm working."

Sheela popped the top and walked over to settle on the couch beside him. She leaned her head back, took a deep breath, and sighed. "God, I'm tired. That's the bad news. The good news is that I used Manny's breakdown as a way of getting the schedule changed. If Bernard does it my way, I'm out of here in two weeks instead of a month."

"Have you ever heard of Sheik Amud Abdulla?"

She gave him a sidelong glance. "Should I have?"

"He was watching you at the *Night Stalker* preem. Christal picked up on it. If he gets in touch with you, let me know, all right?"

"Jealous?"

"Worried. The way he was watching you wasn't normal. I want you to keep your antenna up. Thing number two: Krissy sent an e-mail to your Web site. She wants you to know that she's having your baby."

Sheela couldn't help herself: She laughed, almost spilling her beer. "Well, at least that's an improvement. She's gone from sharp objects to pregnancy. Did she say just how she was having my child? Seems to me, last time I looked, the equipment was wrong—or am I missing something in the translation?"

Lymon pursed his lips. "Yeah, well if you were to ask me, I think your equipment looks pretty good—not that I'm an expert or anything."

"Oh, yeah? I've caught you studying my equipment a time or two in the past. As to being an expert, anyone who passes a high school biology class ought to have a pretty good idea of what goes where on a woman." She gave him a chiding look. "Or have you been holding out on me? At this late date are you trying to tell me that you only plug your current into male sockets?"

"I'm into the normal man-woman thing. Always have been. I was referring to your *private* equipment."

"God, I love it when you blush." She chugged more of her beer. "Lymon, when they finally put *Jagged Cat* in the can, why don't you and I go away somewhere and I'll let you run any kind of equipment checks you want."

She saw a stirring in the depths of his hazel eyes as he said, "Why on earth do you think you could stand me?"

"Because you're a man. A real one. I'm tired of all these artsy-fartsy, sensitive, soul-bleeding Hollywood types." She turned, pulling her knee up between her hands and looking him in the eyes. "Tell me, if some woman cut off a piece of your male part, would you break down and turn into a sniveling idiot?"

His grizzled smile sent a throb through her. "Lady, the woman ain't alive who could get that close to me with anything sharp. And if she did to me what she did to de Clerk, I'd be after her in a way she wouldn't want to consider in her baddest nightmares."

"You could hurt a woman?"

His expression had taken on a hard edge. "Oh, yeah." He paused and looked uncomfortably away. "You don't want to know."

"What if I do?"

He studied his hands for a moment, then picked at a fingernail. "You might not like me as much as you think you do."

"I'll take that chance."

"Forget it."

"Lymon, I'd like to know."

He gave her a long and intense look before he said, "A bunch of Al Qaeda got the bright idea that if they used women, they could get close to us. That we wouldn't suspect them. You know, given the Al Qaeda perspective on the sexes, and all. It worked, too. Three ladies in burkas. They walked right up the road, reached out from under their burkas, and tossed a bunch of grenades at us."

"And?"

His eyes were smoldering when he looked back at her. "Me and most of my guys walked away. They didn't. It's a simple equation."

"Does it bother you, this simple equation of yours?"

"Yes and no." When he saw she wasn't going to relent, he added, "Of course it bothers me. It bothers anyone normal when he has to kill people. I got out because I started to like it. As to those particular women, I waffle. Maybe they were innocent victims, told by men who had power over them to do this thing; and, having no other recourse, they did it. Or maybe they *wanted* to see us blown to bits. I don't know which is true. But in the final analysis they were trying to kill me and my people because we were Americans. In combat you do what you've got to do."

She decided to change the subject. "So, why does Krissy think she can have my baby?"

"I don't know. Krissy's nuts. Blow it off."

"Yeah, but if you'll recall, she's filthy rich as well as insane. That's a bad combination."

"Yeah, a bad combination, all right." He gave her that look that melted her insides. "Just like when security personnel mix with their clients."

20

GENESIS ATHENA. The words flashed on the screen. For background, a faint blue image of a robe-clad woman with a nice figure, a shield, and spear—Athena, perhaps?—could be seen superimposed on the forehead of a bearded man's face. Who? Zeus? What did that mean?

Christal sat in her kitchen, a half-empty cup of coffee to one side. She used her finger to move the cursor onto the words and watched as the arrow turned into a pointing finger. She tapped the pressure-sensitive mouse pad with her index finger and watched the letters dissolve to reveal the questionnaire.

Christal frowned, sipped her coffee, and read through the questions. They started innocuously enough. Name. Address. Sex. Occupation. Age. Level of education, and so forth.

On impulse, she pressed the *Print Screen* button and listened to her small printer whirring as it warmed up. Then, one by one, the pages slid out. She checked, just to see that it had indeed printed, and then returned to her screen.

"Do I want to do this?" She twitched her lips. "Sure, what have I got to lose?"

Under name, she typed in *Christal Anaya.*

At address, she gave her mother's post office box in Nambe. For occupation, she stated that she was self-employed. After all, what was the sense in being honest? This was just to see what happened, right?

Under marital status she typed *Single.*

Children? *None.*

Roommates? She hesitated, considering the wisdom of stating that she lived alone, and answered *Two.* Sex? popped up immediately afterward. She added *Female.*

In the yearly income column she arbitrarily typed in *$50,000.* Under assets, she listed that she owned her own home, valued at one hundred and fifty thousand. She said she was financing a Honda Accord. Further, she stated that she did not have outstanding loans, and owned no stocks, bonds, or investment real estate. Her sole form of income was from her employment.

Did she have a criminal record? *No.*

Had she been treated for mental disorders? *No.*

How often did she see a physician? *Once a year.*

What for? *Routine pelvic exam.*

She was asked to numerically rank her shopping venues. She listed going to the store as one, catalog as two, by telephone as three, and Internet as four.

How many credit cards did she have? *Two.*

Under hobbies, she facetiously typed *Stamp collecting, big game hunting, and reading romance novels.*

How many times a month, week, or day, did she leave her house? She said three times a day. Did she go alone? *Yes.*

How many times a week did she date? She grinned maliciously as she typed *Three.* Did she see one man, or several? She typed *Several* as she said, "I'm one hot chick."

The next question asked her to think carefully and answer honestly. How many people could she actually name that she would consider living with for a year in the same room? She thought for a while before typing *As of today, none.*

She was asked to imagine her bathroom. Rank the order in which the following were important to have. She chose: toilet-12, shower-11, sink-10, light-9, mirror-8, medicine cabinet-7, flooring-6, heater-5, tub-4, trash can-3, wall paper-2, window-1.

What on earth was that about? She sipped her coffee, perplexed at the nature of the question.

How often did she go to the movies? *Twice a month.*

Who were her two favorite stars? She chose *Sheela Marks* and *Manuel de Clerk.*

If she had to choose one movie on a given night, would she choose to see Sheela or de Clerk? Without hesitation she typed in Sheela's name.

How many times did she see Sheela on screen, VHS, TV,

or DVD in a given year, month, week, day? Christal opted for three times a year.

At that moment, a line of text appeared in bright blue, stating,

THANK YOU FOR YOUR COOPERATION IN TAKING THE
GENESIS ATHENA QUESTIONNAIRE. ALL INFORMATION
IS COMPLETELY CONFIDENTIAL AND USED FOR
GENESIS ATHENA'S ONGOING MARKET RESEARCH.
THANK YOU AGAIN FOR YOUR TIME.

Christal hit her *page up* button, but nothing happened. Then a small icon appeared at the lower left-hand corner—a box that said

EXIT NOW.

Christal clicked it, and the screen returned her to the Sheela Marks' Web site where she had originated. The little Genesis Athena patch key was now colorless. When Christal rolled the cursor down and tapped it, nothing happened.

"Now, that's weird," she muttered.

Leaning back she tossed off the last of her cold coffee and picked up the sheets she had copied with the *Print Screen* command. She started at the top, thinking about the answers she had given, and then stopped short.

"Wait a minute." Her frown deepened. "That's not the same question I was asked."

She stared, sure that she hadn't been asked how many close friends she had. Or to choose which of those friends she would tell an embarrassing secret.

She tapped the cursor again where it rested on the Genesis Athena patch. Still nothing.

"I don't get it. I *know* I didn't answer this question."

Scanning down the pages, she found others that she hadn't seen. If that was the case, if it wasn't just her faulty memory, what the hell did it mean?

* * *

Sid Harness took a sip from his cup and grimaced. He knew without asking that Sam Murphy had made the coffee. Murphy came from South Dakota. He had grown up on a cattle ranch on the fringe of the Black Hills. Supposedly cowboys made coffee that would "float a horseshoe." It was bullshit. People in the West made coffee like water. If a person wanted real coffee, he had to go to Seattle or the East Coast.

With his mind knotted around that, Sid walked to his small office and flipped on the lights. He was still burping Claire's breakfast of eggs and sausage. She liked the really spicy stuff.

Sid sat down at his desk and awakened his computer. His *In* basket had no more than five memos in it. A good day. But Pete Wirthing was out for the week, so the official BS had slowed to a trickle. Some papers sat in the rack on his fax, but he ignored them for the moment.

Pulling up his e-mail, Sid scanned through the communiqués from Los Angeles and Boston. Nothing had happened on the disappearance of the missing geneticists from either city.

He read through the official junk mail sent from the office of personnel, the Justice Department, as well as the Bureau per se, and ditched it.

Then a note with Christal's address popped up on the screen. Sid grinned and opened it. Christal, now there was a lady who knew how to make a breakfast.

Hi Sid:

I'm faxing a copy of a questionnaire that I pulled off of a Web page at genesisathena.com. When I filled out the questionnaire on screen the questions weren't the same. Could you do me a real big favor and send a copy down to the behavioral science guys at Quantico? Something about this isn't right. Which brings me to favor number two. Could you run Genesis Athena through ViCAP and NCIC when you get a spare mo-

ment? I'd be interested to know if it red-flags. I know
I'm out on a limb here, asking you this. Don't do any-
thing that could have you standing in for an investiga-
tion from the Office of Professional Responsibilities. If
you can't do this, just e-mail me back with a simple no.
I'll understand.

Forever the Best,
Christal

Genesis Athena? Sid stared at the name. He reached for
the pages in the metal carrier under the fax, discarded a couple of memos he had already read on-screen, and found the
pages referred to in Christal's e-mail.

He scanned the contents, then read the questions with a
greater interest. No, it wasn't quite right. He could see what
had tripped Christal's trigger. Something about the questions bothered him, too.

On impulse, he reached into a drawer, pulled out an envelope, and marked the delivery box NCAVC for National Center for the Analysis of Violent Crime—the old Behavioral
Science Unit at Quantico. What the hell. If anyone asked,
he'd just tell them he was following up on a hunch.

Then he ran the name "Genesis Athena" into the computers, feeling forever thankful that the Bureau had passed beyond the old Louis Freeh days when computers were
considered "optional equipment."

While the computer chewed on the name, he typed a response to Christal.

Dear Christal:
   Info sent. Computer working. No problem.
   You owe me dinner.

Best,
Sid

Genesis Athena? What the hell was that?

* * *

Hank Abrams kept a hand on the railing as he stood on the port side just behind the wheelhouse. That location kept him out of the wind and sea spray. The thirty-foot launch slowed on the swells as she approached the Coast Guard cutter. Hank had never been much for boats. He had managed the journey out past the twelve-mile limit and was now more than halfway back to shore. He hoped the Coast Guard wasn't going to take up too much time. His stomach was feeling just the least bit chancy with the rising and falling waves.

Sunset was burning a yellow halo across the New York skyline to the west. Several miles to the north, irregular white blocks of apartment buildings crowded the thin pale beach on the Long Island shore. The water here had a greenish brown tinge. Hank wondered how much of the color came from raw sewage.

As the launch pulled up abreast of the cutter, Hank studied the long gray boat with its distinctive red stripe. Uniformed crewmen were watching him through binoculars. The big fifty on the bow was shrouded in weather-protected tarping. Glancing behind, Hank could see Sheik Abdulla standing in his immaculate suit, his lawyer and two bodyguards to either side and behind him.

Don't ask, don't tell. But just what, he wondered, was he not supposed to tell? For two days he and the Sheik's personal bodyguards had been sequestered aboard the *ZoeGen* out beyond the twelve-mile limit. They had been given nicely furnished cabins on C Deck with access to the afterdeck. Food had been delivered to a nice dining room on D Deck. They had the use of a game room there with billiards, shuffleboard, and video games, as well as a small theater stocked with DVDs. Secure doors had restricted any access to the forward part of the ship. From their area, they couldn't even see anything forward. Hank had been told to stay aft, and he had obeyed orders, taking the time to lounge, read from the collection of paperback novels, and watch the television.

The Sheik had appeared as if by magic, told them to pack, and within a half hour they were headed back toward the wharf in Brooklyn.

At least until the Coast Guard had pulled alongside.

Should I be worried? About what? He shot a quick look at the slim launch. If it was drugs, they could be anywhere aboard, but no one seemed the slightest bit worried as the Guardsmen made the tricky crossing from the cutter. Hank watched them clamber up and over the railing.

Hank made his way to the midships, where the Guardsmen were asking for identification. They looked so young in their gray shirts and dark pants. The model 92 Berettas on their web belts, however, gave them an ominous presence.

"Your identification, sir?" a young man asked, watching him with serious brown eyes. The name WILLIAMSON was stenciled on the Guardsman's breast pocket.

Hank handed over his driver's license, realizing for the first time how professional politeness could effectively tell a person he wasn't jack shit.

"What is your citizenship, Mr. Abrams?" the young man asked, his brown eyes comparing the driver's license photo with Hank's face.

"American. I'm currently living in New York." Hank could see one of the other Guardsmen carefully checking the Sheik's passport and talking into the radio clipped to his shoulder.

"What is your business aboard this boat, sir?" came the crisp question.

"I work for Verele Security. Our offices are at 175 Fifth Avenue. The Sheik"—he pointed—"is a client. I was detailed to accompany him to the *ZoeGen*." He fished out one of his business cards.

"And your business aboard the *ZoeGen*?"

Hank spread his arms. "Honestly, Officer, I cannot tell you. I'm just the hired help. I didn't even see the Sheik until a couple of hours ago."

"I see." Williamson was tapping information into a hand-held computer unit. Then he glanced up and handed the driver's license back. "If you would step to the stern, sir, we will try not to detain you unreasonably."

Hank took his driver's license and walked back to where

the launch's captain and mate stood. Two of the young Coast Guardsmen were still working over the Sheik's documents.

Not only had post-9/11 security made everyone jumpy, it was even worse with a Saudi sheik piloting back and forth just offshore of New York City.

Hank watched as another crewman walked up and down the deck with a piece of electronic equipment—a sensor of some sort, no doubt sniffing for explosives, drugs, and who knew what other kinds of contraband.

"Does this happen a lot?" Hank asked the captain.

"Yeah. I told the Sheik to prepare. The way they watch the traffic anymore, I knew we'd get searched stem to stern. That ship out there"—he jerked his head—"it's just anchored off the limit. I've been ferrying people for the last week and a half. The Coast Guard's getting suspicious, but hey, we're clean and legal. What can they do?"

"Got me. I'm just protection." Hank paused. "You got any idea what happens on the *ZoeGen*?"

"You tell me. You were on that ship for two days."

"I played pool, learned snooker, watched a couple of movies, and farted around on the shuffleboard. Everything forward is off-limits. And I mean it's shut up tight."

"Then, pal, when it comes to that boat out there, you're way ahead of me."

For the next five minutes, the Coast Guard snooped around the launch. From where he stood, Hank could tell that Sheik Abdulla's lawyer was doing most of the talking.

In the end, the Coast Guard packed up and went back to their sleek gray cutter with its whirling radars and bristling antennae. As soon as they were aboard, the diesels thrummed and white billowed out from below the fantail as she veered off.

Hank caught a glimpse of the Sheik as he watched the cutter go. A clever smile lay on his lips, his dark eyes gleaming.

The rest of the short voyage passed without interest. When the launch finally pulled in at its slip Hank recognized Neal Gray waiting with his arms crossed. The man leaned against a large white box marked PERSONAL FLOTATION DEVICES. Hank wondered whatever had happened to "life preservers."

He liked Gray. Gray was the Sheik's man and gave orders to Hank's detail and squad leaders. He appeared to be in his early forties, a natty dresser, with blond hair that he kept neatly combed. In spite of his worried blue eyes, he seemed efficient, organized, and smart enough to let others do their jobs without trying to micromanage. A small black nylon satchel rested at Gray's feet.

Lines were cast, and the launch made fast. Able hands attached a walkway, and the Sheik followed Hank and his retinue off the launch.

That moment of awkwardness when he set foot on cement left Hank half-reeling after the pitching boat. Neal Gray straightened, picked up the satchel, and walked over, nodding to the Sheik as he stepped up to Hank's side.

"Any trouble?"

Hank shook his head. "It was more like vacation. The Coast Guard stopped us on the way back. No big deal."

"Good." Neal reached into the pocket of his snappy gray suit and produced an envelope. "Here you go. Instructions and a ticket. I've asked Verele if we could change your assignment, and he agreed. You're welcome to call him for verification if you'd like. Assuming you don't have any major objection, we'd like you to go home, catch a good night's sleep, and catch a plane to LA in the morning."

"What am I doing there? An advance for the Sheik?"

Gray's sober eyes took his measure. "Not an advance. Something quite different. You'll find instructions in the envelope. Actually, we need you to look someone up, make contact, and well, bring us a sample."

"A sample?"

"You'll see on the instructions." Gray smiled. "It's a little unusual, and please, we'll be happy to reward you for success." He smiled ironically and handed over the black nylon satchel. "Quite a handsome reward, if I do say so. Meanwhile, a credit card is enclosed along with a thousand dollars cash for tips and what have you."

"What kind of sample?"

Gray grinned. "Skin, actually, or a couple of strands of hair would do. Like I said, the instructions are inside. If you have any questions, call Salim. He's done this sort of thing for us before."

"That's it?"

"Pretty much. I'll debrief you when you get back."

"Who am I getting a sample of?"

"Your girlfriend." Neal's grin was suggestive. "She's tripped a couple of our switches and caught the Sheik's interest. We thought you were the guy to get a line on her."

"Huh? Why me? I mean, when we parted it wasn't exactly amicable."

"Yeah, well, I'm sure you'll think of something." In a mocking voice, he said, "Give my love to the stars."

With that Neal turned on his heel, walking to catch up with the Sheik's party.

Hank hefted the ballistic nylon bag. Maybe five pounds. Well, what the hell, the Sheik was the guy paying the bills.

Anaya! He couldn't wait to see her face.

21

Christal leaned forward after the plates were cleared and placed her elbows on the table. She gave Tony a clear-eyed appraisal as waiters bustled past their table and other diners bent to their conversations. The restaurant, called Madre's, belonged to Jennifer Lopez. Christal approved of that. She thought highly of any Latina, Chicana, or Hispanic, however defined, who made something of herself through hard work and brains. Never mind the mess with Ben Affleck.

Was Tony making some kind of politically correct statement in bringing her here? No matter. The food had been okay, and the atmosphere, if too frenetic, was still worth experiencing. If nothing else, she could tell her mother about it one day.

"So, Christal"—Tony leaned back—"you've made it. You're in LA. How does it feel to be part of the team?"

She studied him as she considered the question. He was wearing a blue Dewey and Durham blazer over a white silk shirt by Dior. The latter hung open down to the sternum. Probably to show off the golden necklace that covered his breastbone.

Tony's eyes betrayed a subtle excitement as he watched her. During the meal, he had gone to the restroom no less than three times for reasons she could only speculate on. Since he hadn't come back with white powder at the corners of his nostrils and his pupils seemed normal, she assumed it had been to double-check his appearance. That or his bladder was volumetrically challenged.

"Part of the team?"

"Sheela's team. You know, me, Rex, Dot, Lymon. All of us. I tell you, babe, we're—"

"Tony, how many times have I asked you not to call me 'babe'?"

"Yeah, well, like, it's a part of the language, you know? The way we talk out here. And it isn't just that you're a knockout. I mean, you can really sail out here, Christal."

"I get seasick."

"It's like . . . You . . . Huh? Seasick?"

"I was raised in New Mexico. The one time I rode a boat out on the ocean, I got sick. It wasn't pretty."

He looked confused. "What are we talking about?"

"You said I could really sail. I've seen those little sailboats down at the marinas. It looks bouncy."

"No way! You jacking me, Christal? I mean you could have it all. Do it right and you could take off like a rocket." He flashed her the kind of smile that made an orthodontist tingle with satisfaction. "You don't know it, but you've got a quality that I think would melt the lens. It's a no-bullshit presence. A sense of self. Strong, you know? Like a 'here I am' statement. Look at me. See me. Be me. Solid chutzpah, babe."

"Right. You think I could be a movie star?" She gave him a mocking look.

He leaned forward, challenge in his sparkling blue eyes. "You know, Christal, a lot of chicks would jump at a chance like this. You don't wanna stay in celebrity protection. I can see it in you. Not when you got a chance to reach out and pull in a chunk of the sky." He extended his arm, hand closing into a grasping fist. "Now, that's not to say it's gonna be easy. You get me? I mean, it isn't any trite figure of speech when I say it's a jungle out there."

"Let me guess, you're the great white hunter?" She arched an eyebrow. "If I just place myself in your hands, well, it might or might not work out, right?"

He gave her a grin. "I didn't do so bad with Sheela."

"Stow it, Tony. I'm not buying. If you're going to do the hard sell, try it with Patsy from Peoria. I've been around the block a time or two."

He cocked his head, the blue eyes narrowing. "You think this is all a gig to get into your pants?"

"Funny you should bring that up, but yeah, I do. And you know what? There's just room enough in my britches for me."

He threw his head back and laughed, genuinely amused. "You know, Christal, you're all right. Here you sit, in the presence of one of the most powerful men in Hollywood, and you're too cool!" He tapped long fingers on the table. "That wounds me. I'm one of the hottest agents in this biz, and you're blowing me off."

"Shit happens," she added sweetly.

"Okay, I'll bite. So why'd you say yes to dinner?"

"Because I promised, and I broke it. I keep my promises." She glanced around at the other patrons, mostly well dressed, manicured, and affluent. "Maybe that doesn't happen a lot in Hollywood, but I'm me. Call me a lamb among wolves."

His eyes had changed, cooling, calculating. For the first time she realized that he was indeed a man worth taking seriously. "Somehow, I don't think you're any innocent lamb, Christal."

"Hey. New Mexico kid in from the sticks, that kind of thing."

"I heard you were a lawyer."

"I've got a law degree, and once upon a time I passed the

New Mexico bar." She shrugged. "That's not really a lawyer."

"So, what, then?"

"I was looking for challenge."

"You're kidding! Leaving a law practice for the FBI? Let me get this straight. You thought working your way up in a law firm wasn't going to be a challenge?"

She ran her napkin through her fingers, folding it into pleats. "How do I say this so that you'll understand? I had something in my gut. No, maybe it was a chip on my shoulder. Do you know what lawyers, especially young ones like me, get stuck doing? It's a world of paper, of books and research. I was tired of offices and libraries. I wanted to get out in the world, find bad guys, and bust their balls."

He gave her an evaluative stare before saying, "What did he do to you?"

"Who?"

"The guy that set you off like this."

"It wasn't any one guy. Or girl, for that matter. The men in my life, going back to my father, have been good or bad, or a combination of each. I've dealt with my share of *cabrónes* as well as nice decent guys." She shook her head. "No, this was something different. Maybe wanderlust of the blood. I wanted to be able to look back and say, hey, I did that. Can you follow?"

"Yeah, I follow. You wanted high adventure."

"What about you? Did you wake up one morning and say 'I'm going to be a talent agent'?"

"Nah. I started as the receptionist." Tony made a disparaging gesture. "Day after day, I sat there, watching the people coming through the door, learning, you know? Producers would sit in the lobby, bitching or bragging, and I'd hear it." He smiled. "Hey, it was cool! I was working for peanuts. You know, just for the chance to be close to the action. At first it was for bragging rights. To tell the chicks that I knew what films Halle Berry was going to be starring in. Or that I'd heard Harold Becker tell Margaret Riley this dirty joke."

"You've made it a bit beyond the reception desk." She

could see the gleam in his eyes. Tony liked to talk about himself.

"That's the thing, babe. I started going in and telling the boss, 'Hey, this guy's hot for Drew Barrymore.' So I sort of worked my way into the system, and pretty soon I was being invited to lunches and parties. Just to circulate, listen, and report back to the boss. Then it was planning sessions. Say, maybe the Coens wanted one of our clients; how did we know when we'd reached a contract breaker?"

A soft smile rode his lips as he stared into the past. "Then, one day, I realized I was telling the old man more than he was telling me. It was epiphany, right? Wham! I'm actually *doing* this. Clients were feeling me out for what the boss was going to say. Did I think it was the right deal, the right role—I was dishing out the whole enchilada."

"So you were made a partner?"

Tony shook his head. "Nah, I laid my plans. Started dealing with the clients. When the leverage was right, I walked, and I took about half of them with me." He gave her a quizzical look. "Weird. You wouldn't believe how many stayed that I thought would come with me. But the ones who did were enough. I'd learned the ropes, you know. I knew which knot to pick at and how to retie it into a killer deal." He gave her an evil grin. "And, babe, I'm *good*!"

"Was Sheela with you from the beginning?"

"Nope. She was pissed at her agent at ICM. A little bird told me. Landing Sheela was like, the best, you know? Awesome. Tricky shit, but I was at the right place, at the right time, with the right deal. Cool."

His smile was infectious. Christal sat back, relaxing for the first time. "You want my opinion?"

"Sure."

"You're a rogue."

"Damn straight."

"But a charming one . . . once you stop dishing out that hotshot agent bullshit. Play that game with bimbos, Tony. Don't waste it on an intelligent woman."

One of his golden eyebrows rose. "So, wow! Does that

mean, like, I've still got a chance with the mysterious and enigmatic Christal?"

"Don't bet on it."

His grin was impish. "I'll take that as a challenge."

"Whatever. It's your funeral."

"Hey, babe, you're dealing with Tony Zell here. It's cool. I can bide my time, dazzle you with brilliance. Just wait, you'll see. I'm going to charm you like you've never been charmed before."

"Is that a fact?"

"Hey, I'm like one of those Indian fakirs with a flute. I'll get you out of your basket yet. I tell you, I can already imagine you swaying to the music."

"Uh-huh." She leaned forward, her hair spilling around her shoulders. "Just remember, Tony, I'm not one of your cobras."

"Yeah?"

"For sure. This time you've come face to face with a desert-tough New Mexican *culebra*."

"What's that?"

"More than you can handle."

He pushed back in the chair, laughing from deep in his belly. "You're a cool one, Christal. Really cool."

Lymon sat at his office desk going through the receipts. He had a cup of coffee within reach of his right hand. Behind him the computer screen glowed with his favorite screen saver, a series of motorcycles: some road racers, others touring bikes, an occasional flying motocross machine, and a trials rider balancing atop a huge boulder on a skinny Gas Gas. A Nanci Griffith CD was set just above the audible range to keep his emotions in check.

He needed Nanci Griffith's soothing voice. If he didn't do something to calm himself through the arduous process of dealing with the bits of paper, he'd go slightly berserk and break something.

Why did paperwork have to be such a miserable hassle?

He assumed it was because the people who wrote the tax laws, ran the IRS, and operated major accounting houses were both socially and sexually handicapped. Bug-eyed geeks with skinny arms and soft round bellies instead of real people.

He took a moment, imagining them: bald-headed, wearing white shirts with thin black ties and gray rumpled slacks. They were smooth-shaven and pale skinned. They carried shiny pens in their pockets. He could visualize their soft white fingers as they danced on the calculator keys and tape spooled out of the machines. Every now and then they would look across at each other and grin maliciously. It was because they knew that while they might be impotent wimps, they had the last laugh.

In the end all the tough guys like Lymon Bridges were doomed to spend endless and meaningless hours of their lives pushing paper, totaling columns, balancing books, and organizing receipts instead of enjoying their tough-stud, action-filled lives out in the sun.

"Maybe for fun I'll go beat up an accountant." Lymon savored the fantasy as he stapled a pile of New York receipts together for June's attention.

He leaned back, scowling at the different piles of paper on his desk. Someone had told him that the tax code was contained in bound books that stood eight feet high when stacked atop each other. If it demonstrated anything it was a measure of the success of the American economy. Nothing else would explain a GDP that could support so many nonproductive parasites feeding off the sweat of the productive few.

Voices carried down the hallway from June's desk, and he wondered who had come in.

He was halfway through Paul's expense report when the voices grew louder. Lymon lifted an eyebrow and waited.

He heard June's emphatic "No!" and pushed his chair back before getting to his feet. Stepping into the hallway he could see the man standing in front of June's desk. He was a handsome sort, midtwenties, maybe thirty, middle height, square shoulders, in a dark suit coat. The guy was dark-haired, shaven, but with that dark shadow to the cheeks that indicated a thick beard. He had a strong jaw, straight nose, and brown eyes that now locked with June's.

Lymon padded into June's office and asked, "Is there something here I should know about?"

June turned in her swivel chair, jerking a thumb over her shoulder. "This guy wants Christal's address."

Lymon raised his eyes. "Why?"

"Who're you?" The man had a competent way about him, as if he was used to authority.

"I'm Lymon Bridges. I run this place."

The man nodded, offering his hand. "Hank Abrams. I'm with Verele Security. Uh, I suppose you've heard of us?"

Hank Abrams? Lymon kept the surprise from his face. "Yeah, I've heard of Verele Security. They do good work. Are you here for personal or professional reasons?"

That took him back. Lymon could see him thinking through the possible answers.

"Professional," Abrams finally admitted.

"I see." Lymon smiled graciously. "If you will leave your phone number and address, I'll see that Christal gets them. After that, it's up to her if she decides to contact you."

Abrams gave him a hard evaluative look, then said, "I'd prefer to contact her on my own."

"I'm sure you would." Lymon kept his professional smile in place. "If I could offer some friendly advice, I'd say you might be better off to give her a little warning. Given your history, she might shoot first and wonder why you showed up after the fact."

Abrams gave him an icy smile as he put the pieces together. "I see. Thanks for the advice. That's real neighborly of you. Uh, you wouldn't have some ulterior motive yourself, would you?"

"Such as?" Lymon could feel June's curious gaze as she sat between them.

"Christal's an attractive lady."

"She's good at her job," Lymon countered.

"Are you trying to protect her?"

"She can protect herself."

"Then why won't you give me her address?"

"I already told you."

Abrams narrowed his eye, the smile never wavering. "What's wrong? Afraid I might just hire her away?"

"It's a free market."

"If you're worried, you're welcome to contact our New York office. My boss—"

"Verele doesn't concern me. You do. Just write your name, phone, and address there on the notepad. Christal will have it by tonight. My word on that. I'll tell her you're interested in hiring her. She can decide what she wants to do."

"That's it?"

"Sum and total."

Abrams glanced back and forth between Lymon and June, smiled in ill humor, and bent, jotting on the notepad at the corner of the desk.

As he finished and twisted his Montblanc to retract the ballpoint, Lymon asked, "Who was the Arab?"

Abrams started, and for that one instant Lymon could see him off balance. He recovered quickly, saying, "The Sheik is a client of ours."

Lymon replied, "And Sheela Marks is our client."

Abrams watched him for a moment, and then said, "From what I see in the news, you haven't been doing such a hot job protecting her recently." He flipped a mock salute. "Nice to have met you, Mr. Bridges." He turned on his heel, stepped to the door, opened it, and left. The sound of his feet on the steps grew fainter as he descended to the street level.

Lymon ground his teeth, glaring at the door, and stepped around to rip the paper from the pad. He glanced down, recognizing the address for the Hollywood Hilton.

"That was interesting," June told him evenly as she wheeled her chair around to face her desk again. "Would you mind telling me what just happened here? Turf fight? Or was that just two dominant males growling, bristling, and scratching the dirt?"

Lymon folded the paper. "It's deeper than that." He filled her in on the New York trip and then added, "Abrams and Christal were involved when they worked for the Bureau. It went bad enough to make Christal resign."

June studied him thoughtfully. "I see."

"Good. 'Cause I sure don't. What the hell was he doing here? And just why does he really want to see Christal?"

June shook her head. "I don't know, but if you think it has something to do with Sheela, maybe you'd better have a word or two with Christal, soonest."

22

Christal looked up from the stack of *Daily Variety* magazines she had been going through at her kitchen table. It was the sunlight off the Plexiglas windscreen on the silver BMW motorcycle that caught her attention. She watched through the window as Lymon parked the bike, leaned it onto the sidestand, and stepped off. He was unbuckling his helmet as he walked from the parking spot next to her Chrysler.

She met him at the door before he could knock and motioned him in, saying, "Not much new on this front. I've got some feelers out, but I'm drawing a bust looking for links between Sheela and the actors targeted by the celeb hits."

Then she got a good look at Lymon's face. "What's wrong?"

He tossed his helmet onto the couch and slipped out of his jacket. His eyes were smoky, as if something smoldered deep inside. He fished a folded piece of paper from his pocket and handed it to her before he turned and closed the door behind him.

Christal unfolded the paper, seeing the company logo at the top. She stopped at the familiar script. The note stated:

Christal: Contact me immediately. Most important! Hank.

A 212 area code telephone number—a cell, she assumed—and a Hollywood address followed.

She glanced up at Lymon. "Is this a joke?"

"I wish. He was in the office a couple of hours ago." Lymon watched her carefully. "Christal, I don't like it. Whatever is between the two of you isn't my business. But the fact that his client was so fixed on Sheela just might be. First we target the Sheik at the preem. Then your old boyfriend shows up as the Sheik is leaving. Then, bam! Abrams is walking in my door asking to see you. You tell me: Is this something I need to be concerned about?"

Christal took a deep breath, a cold feeling in her stomach. She perched her butt on the couch back. "Honestly, Lymon, I don't have the foggiest idea. It's nuts! Crazy! Too far out! What did he want? Did he say?"

"Only that it was professional. If it is, am I supposed to think it concerns Sheela? Is that the hidden agenda? Or is it just coincidence that he saw you in New York, got to thinking about his wife dumping him, and he talked Verele into trying to hire you so that you and he could get back together?"

Confusion came tumbling out of her brain, stopping any logical thought. "No way in hell!" she cried, crumpling the paper in her hand. "What? Does he think I'm a complete idiot, that I'd even want to be close to him?"

"I have no idea." Lymon cocked his head, apparently seeing through her struggle for control.

"I *don't* want to see him."

"It gets worse. I think he tried to follow me from the office."

Christal stopped short, staring. "Huh? Why would he do that?"

"To find you."

"That's even nuttier than . . ." She couldn't finish it, seeing the concern in Lymon's eyes. "Wait a minute. What makes you think he was trying to follow you?"

"A dark blue Ford Taurus followed me from the office parking lot." Lymon crossed his arms, pacing back and forth on the living room carpet. "It was parked back in the alley. I don't think he expected me to be on a bike. It must have been a shock when I threw a leg over the Beemer and motored off. This Ford pulled out after me. He did a good job, but his hand was tipped. There's no parking where the car had been sitting."

"Hey, Hank was trained by the Bureau. If he was following, it wouldn't have been a half-assed job."

"Yeah, trained to do a tail with a team, right? Lots of cars, passing, pulling off, keeping in touch by radio. That sort of thing. This time, he just had himself. It gets a little harder for one guy. Especially if he's having to make it up as he goes."

She glanced uncertainly at the window, half expecting to see a blue Ford pull into the space next to the BMW.

"Relax," Lymon told her. "Splitting lanes is legal in California. He's still back on Wilshire somewhere, sitting in traffic. I went around a couple of blocks and stopped to talk to the two homeless guys that live in the alley. Stewart and John. They described your Hank Abrams. He'd just pulled in and was waiting, figuring that you'd show up, I suppose. Or maybe that if you and I were involved—"

"What?"

Lymon chuckled. "That was one the things that crossed his mind when I wouldn't give him your address."

Christal shook her head, failing to see his humor in her current misery.

"Christal," Lymon added gently, "give him a call. See what he wants. If it involves that Sheik and Sheela, we need to know."

She nodded numbly. The thought came tumbling out of her stunned mind. "What if he offers me a job?"

"I'd ask for double the salary you're getting now. Any other fringe benefits are up to Hank and Verele."

"Thanks."

"No problem." He hesitated. "Listen, I hate to ask you to call this guy. Anything you need, we're here for you. Me, Paul, the rest of the guys. If it gets sticky, we'll take care of you. You know that, don't you?"

She nodded. "Yeah, I'll call him, Lymon. Just give me time to get myself together."

* * *

Hank Abrams had a sour feeling in his gut as he slowed, looked at his map, and frowned at the community gate that blocked his access to the street where Sheela Marks lived. Once again he cursed life without FBI credentials. That badge had opened a lot of doors. It would have passed him here, too, where he didn't think a Verele Security business card would. The guy at the guard shack would have asked where he was going and double-checked to see if Verele Security was making an advance at any of the houses up the road.

"Sheela Marks is our client," Bridges had told him. That meant that he might be able to pick up Christal when she went off shift at the principal's house.

He slowed as he considered the guard shack that stood in the middle of the road and noted the cameras that had been placed unobtrusively in the ornate shrubbery to either side.

Did he want a record of his presence here? It left him feeling awkward, somehow sordid. It wasn't as if what he was doing was illegal. The fact was, there were no laws against him completing his assignment.

Assault, the voice said in his head.

But it wasn't assault. Not in the classical sense. All he had to do was get close to Christal. He glanced at the small canvas kit bag on the seat behind him. He had checked out the special equipment it contained. The hand patch had been the most unusual; it stuck to the palm, and just by shaking hands, scrubbed off enough of the target's cells to be useful. The other stuff was no less esoteric, and each had its own particular uses.

Hell, if the instructions were correct, he didn't have to have physical contact with her, just find out where she lived. He'd committed the list of things he could take to memory: hairbrush, toothbrush, dirty clothes, used personal items, a sack full of her garbage, and so forth.

Theft, his legally trained mind countered.

Well, sure, by the strictest interpretation. But who would care? It wasn't like lifting a hairbrush was grand theft, for

God's sake. All he needed to do was get into her house, and from there, it was easy.

Breaking and entering.

Not if Christal invited him in, he countered. Hell, all he needed was her washcloth! If she didn't invite him in, the trash would do. But it wasn't as discreet; the samples could have come from anywhere with garbage. How would they know if a sample came from Christal, or a guest? But in a pinch it would do. He could wait until she took it out, and then he'd box it FedEx, check out of his hotel, and be on a plane that night.

He wheeled the Ford around and reluctantly drove away from the controlled access to Sheela Marks' community. As he passed the high-dollar houses he couldn't help but notice the tall walls that surrounded the large mansions. One by one he took the roads that surrounded the compound, figuring that the houses contained within sat on less than five acres. He could see the roofs through the gaps between the surrounding houses. Which one was Sheela Marks'?

The cell phone warbled in its melodious tone, and he pulled over to answer it.

"Hello?"

"Hank?" Christal's voice was controlled, toneless.

"Hey, Christal. It's good to hear you again."

"What do you want?" She sounded icy.

"Look, we need to talk. Something's come up."

"Yeah, I remember the last time you got it up. Somehow I ended up getting screwed twice."

He made a face. "Dear God, Christal. You have no idea how sorry I am. I never meant to hurt you. I never meant to hurt anyone."

"I know." She seemed to actually understand.

"If I could take my pound of flesh out of Gonzales, I would."

A pause. *"We just screwed up. That's all. He was ahead of us. I learned my lesson, Hank."*

"What lesson was that?"

"We weren't professional. That was the mistake I made that night. You can bet I'll never make it again."

He took a deep breath. "Yeah, that's two of us. That's why I need to see you." He paused. "Uh, Marsha has filed for a divorce."

"Make your offer." Her voice was emotionless.

He hesitated; obviously she wasn't into reconciliation. "What is Bridges paying you?"

"That's my business."

He winced. Then remembered Bridges' advice. "I think we can double it."

Her laughter caught him by surprise. Then she said, *"Hank, you couldn't afford me. Not that I'd work for you for any price."*

"You haven't heard my offer. Ten thousand a month." There. That ought to bring her around. At least get her to meet with him.

"You're not even close." More bitter laughter came rolling out of the earpiece. *"Have a nice life, Hank."*

"Wait! Christal, for God's sake, wait! Don't hang up!"

"You tracing this? Need to keep me on the line?"

"God, no! I swear." He shook his head, trying to figure out how it had gone so wrong. "Look, if you and Bridges are involved, that's fine. Here's the scoop: My boss is interested in seeing if you have what it takes to join our firm. That's all. No pressure, no strings. You can stay here in LA and handle our principals here."

"I'm with LBA now. I like working for Lymon. You know"— it sounded like a taunt— *"Sheela Marks is one of our clients."*

He frowned. "Would she be interested in changing security firms? Could you get me and my boss an interview?"

"Ah, so am I to believe that you want to use me to get close to Sheela? Is that it? You were always a deep player, Hank."

"Christal, just meet with me. I'll *buy* your time if I have to."

"What?"

"Pay you. Five thousand dollars. Just for the chance to . . ." He realized that he was listening to dead air.

With a pained look, he pressed the *end* button and stared thoughtfully through the Ford's windshield at the row of expensive houses.

"Yeah," he grumbled, "I'm a smart guy, I'll think of something." He threw the cell phone across the car, hardly aware that it shattered against the passenger window.

Sid leaned back in his office chair at the Washington Metro Field Office and stared at the bulletin board across from him. It showed a map of the world. Here and there, pins were stuck into it, marking where geneticists had disappeared over the last five years. Of all the cases he'd ever worked on, he'd never had one like this. It just seemed to lead nowhere. His counterparts contacted through Interpol had found the same thing, and they'd been working on some cases for five years.

He needed a break, anything to get his mind off the Gordian knot that his case had become. A picture caught his eye where it rested at the edge of his desk. Sid, Tim Paris—a fellow agent—and Christal Anaya stood behind a podium receiving a meritorious service award. He smiled, reached over, and lifted the phone. He glanced at his Rolodex and pressed in the numbers.

The distant ringing was followed by Christal's voice. *"Hello?"*

"Christal? It's Sid."

"What's up?"

"I'm bummed. One of our missing geneticists, Nancy Hartlee, was found floating off Long Island. I'm just hoping that Mike Harris, the guy from UCLA who had to take a pee, and Cindy Creedmore, my girl from George Washington U, aren't doing the same." He tried to cheer up. "But I've got news for you."

"What, Sid?"

"A couple of things. You asked me to get your car out of hock at Dulles. I got the keys you mailed me and had Andersen drop me off. I found the car, paid the chit, and drove it home. It's out beside my house. Claire isn't worried about it, and it's not hurting anything sitting there. No hurry. Pick it up whenever. Uh"—he glanced at the ticket on the corner of his desk—"you owe me fifty-four eighty-five."

"Thanks, Sid! You're a life saver. The check's in the mail as soon as I hang up."

"How's life in LA? Still sun, smog, and too much work?"

"We're leaving tomorrow for Toronto. Sheela's on location there. We're staying at the Toronto Westin Harbor Castle if you need us."

"Good. I like Toronto. Get to Tim Horton's for me, will you? Check out those chocolate donuts they make. And drink a bottle of Upper Canada Dark. You can only get it in Ontario. Along that line, I've got something for you."

"Is it fattening or alcoholic?"

"Neither. Genesis Athena. You wanted me to stick the name into my computer?"

"Yeah?"

"Biotech."

"What?"

"It's a biotech firm. The head offices are in Yemen, of all places. Not exactly what you'd call the steaming hub of biotechnological activity, but I guess they got a good deal on land or something. That, and looking at the prospectus, there's a lot of Arab ownership."

"So why would . . ." There was a pause. *"Arab, did you say?"*

"Have I developed a stutter, or is this just a bad connection?"

"Sid, can you fax me what you've got?"

"Yeah, Chris. Same fax number you told me before?"

"That's it."

"It's on the way."

"I owe you one."

"I can't wait to collect."

"Sid?"

"Yeah, Chris?"

"Has Hank been in touch?"

Sid frowned. "No. Should he have been?"

"He's here. Trying to find me. If he does call, you don't know anything. Nothing. Got that?"

"Uh, are you just being paranoid, or does this have a purpose?"

"We think he might have some interest in getting close to one of Lymon's principals. Nothing firm, mind you, and we doubt illegal, but, well, just keep it under your hat, all right?"

"Yeah, sure. Hey, you know I'd do anything for Lymon. As to Hank, well, when he calls, I haven't heard a thing since you left DC."

"You're a pal, Sid. I love you. Take care."

And then she was gone.

"You love me?" He smiled wistfully. "If I could only be so lucky."

23

The unions had driven a lot of filmmakers to Canada. Shooting costs were cheaper, the people more friendly, and, most ironic of all, the city lent itself to many different interpretations of the good old USA.

Sheela considered that irony as she sat in front of her penthouse window and looked out at the night. Her room was high in the Westin Harbor Castle. Three hundred feet below, she could see the marina hemmed by rocky jetties that enclosed a little harbor on the shores of Lake Ontario. Boats floated on black water illuminated by the city lights. She could see more dots of light out on Island Park where the last of the ferries had crossed.

To the west, just out of her view, red-and-white Air Canada planes periodically took off from a compact lake-side airport. They were small, mostly twin-engined or equipped with floats as they headed for the wild Canadian northland.

Looking out beyond Island Park and across the water, she could see several ships, their lights nothing more than yellow dots in the night. South and slightly west, across the international border, Buffalo, New York, radiated its light into the low clouds. South-southeast, she could see Rochester's telltale glow.

Toronto. *Home.* But was it? Yes, it was Canada, but it didn't feel like home. The red-and-white Canadian flags with her beloved maple leaf warmed her soul, as did the familiar sight of the big yellow Bay department store signs, the red Scotia Bank, and finding CBC on the television in the morning—although she had no idea who the hosts were these days.

The weight of the loonies and toonies in her hands weren't the same as dollars, and even though she had told the reporter from the *Globe and Mail* that it was good to be home, she now had to question the veracity of that.

Home had been Saskatchewan. Not Ontario. What was it about Canada that it seemed to be independent worlds separated by an even greater distance than she felt between Regina and LA? It was only after living in the States that she had come to see how fragmented the notion of unity really was in the Canadian psyche. Quebec, Ontario, and the western provinces might have been three different countries, with the maritime provinces as some peripheral satellites orbiting out there in the foggy east somewhere.

She turned at a slight knock. "Come in."

The door opened, and she could see the main room as Lymon entered with a six-pack of what looked like beer hanging from his hand. He was dressed neatly, wearing a blazer and tie, his legs in cotton trousers.

"I brought something."

"Beer?" she asked, squinting at the six-pack.

"Upper Canada Dark," he replied. "Something Christal said we had to try based upon an old friend's recommendation."

She gave him a look from under lowered brows. "I've got a screen call tomorrow at five a.m. Does that mean anything to you?"

He glanced around her room, took in the laid-back covers of the bed, smooth and folded as the turndown service had left them. Only a blind idiot could fail to notice that she was still fully dressed as she sat in her chair before the window.

In an inoffensive tone he said, "Apparently it means more to me than it does to you. If you had been sacked out according to plan, you wouldn't have heard that faintest of knocks."

"No, I suppose not." She pointed. "The opener is over there, assuming they're not twist offs."

He walked to the counter, pulled out two bottles, and levered the tops off, calling, "Glass?"

"No." She frowned as she took the bottle and studied it in the half-light. "You know, most Canadian beer is pretty weak. It's not like the microbrews you're used to."

"I'll take my chances." He lifted the long neck, sipped, and smiled.

Sheela lifted her bottle and washed some of the effervescent brew over her tongue. "That's really good."

Lymon stood silently, staring out at the dark lake below. "Quite a view."

"Your room doesn't have this?"

He shrugged. "I get the CN Tower, a glimpse of the white top of the ballpark, and a nice panorama of downtown." He turned. "How's the shooting going?"

"Funny you should ask." She used a toe to tap the script she'd dropped on the floor by the chair leg. "Without Manny, we've actually moved ahead of schedule. You tell me, Lymon, how does a prick like that get to be so important?"

"Women drool over him." He chuckled. "Christal said that even she had to do a double take when he walked out at the photo shoot."

"She's a pretty sharp cookie, isn't she?"

Lymon nodded. "I wish I could have hired her when I first started in this business."

"I haven't seen her for the last couple of days."

"Since we were shooting inside the Royal Ontario Museum security was tighter than on the street. I turned her loose to do her research."

"What's she found?"

"Why do you think a biotech firm would have a link to your Web site?"

Sheela closed her eyes as she leaned back in the padded

chair and sipped the mellow dark beer. "I have no idea, Ly-mon. The Web site is Dot's domain. What did she say?"

"She said that you don't look a gift horse in the mouth. Genesis Athena throws you pennies from heaven. Their check clears each month."

"Maybe I'll ask when I do *The Mike Bullard Show* tomor-row evening." She cracked an eye and glanced across at the clock next to her bed. "God, is that the time?"

"You have to be up in five hours." Lymon's voice was soft. "I was afraid that you weren't sleeping."

"Yes, Doctor. I'll just suck down my suds and collapse."

"I worry about you."

The way he said it warmed her heart. "I'll be fine, Ly-mon." She paused. "What's the word on your mysterious Arab?"

"Thankfully, there is nothing to report." He frowned. "Here's a curious twist. The day before we left, Christal's, uh, I guess you could call him 'ex,' showed up."

"The one from New York?"

"Yep. He wanted to see her something fierce. Offered her a job and, get this, even five grand just to meet with him."

Sheela opened her eyes and turned her head to stare. Ly-mon's craggy features were softly illuminated by the light fil-tering through the tall window. She could see the firm set of his lips, the way he rocked up on his toes. "That worries you?"

"He was with Sheik Abdulla in New York. Then he shows up trying to get a line on Christal. Why don't I like that scenario?"

"You think he'd try to use Christal to get to me?"

"Maybe. Not that it would do him much good. If he thinks that she'd tumble into his arms and help him do evil, he's a sadly mistaken young boy."

"Did you meet him?"

"He came to the office looking for her."

"What did you think?"

"Attractive, sharp, self-possessed, but not one hundred percent on his game. He tried to follow me to Christal's. Did a shabby job of it. Not what Christal's description would have led me to believe about his talents." He paused. "Curious, don't you think? First Christal goes into protection, and then he does? Is that just coincidence?"

"Maybe." She shrugged. "What else does an ex-FBI agent do? Private investigation? Police work? There aren't that many allied fields, are there?"

"No. I suppose not. I'm just concerned, is all. It's a pattern I can't explain. If I can't explain it, it makes me nervous. The more nervous I get, the more I want to explain things."

She placed the beer to one side and stood, walking on bare feet to stand behind him. Wrapping her arms around him, she placed her cheek on his shoulder. "It will be all right, Lymon. You will keep me safe. You always have."

"Ah, yes," he chided bitterly, "just like in that hallway in New York, and then, of course, there's my triumph in the ladies' room at the Beverly Wilshire."

"I wasn't hurt, was I?" she asked.

"You could have been."

She said nothing, tightening her hold, feeling the hard muscle lining his ribs and belly. For a long time, she stood like that, allowing his warmth to seep into her cool body.

Finally, she took a deep breath, let him go, and said, "I can sleep now, Lymon. Thank you."

He turned, brushed his lips across her hair, and walked silently to the door, where he let himself out into the main room.

The place was called Rotterdam, a microbrewery several blocks north of the Toronto Bluejays' ballpark. It didn't look like much from the outside; just a sign, the walls made of rough-sided ruddy brick. Inside, it was raucous, popular, and filled with the young and vigorous. Through gaps in the back wall Christal could see shiny stainless steel vats where various kinds of beer and ale were brewed. The white wood walls had been scarred by years of occupancy. Posters hung here and there on the walls, and a series of large blackboard menus listed various brews and foods, all chalked in with different-colored block letters.

A hockey game ensorcelled a clutch of husky young men at the far end of the main room. They wore numbered jerseys and were accompanied by two rather nubile young women wearing cutoff shorts and stretch shirts a size too small for the breasts they'd stuffed into them.

The wreckage of a fish-and-chips dinner basket was pushed off to Christal's left, and a half-full glass of the establishment's famed stout sat to her right. The bar napkin before her was stuck to the table, but still served to fulfill its God-given purpose as a notepad.

On the napkin top, she had printed GENESIS ATHENA. Then she had defined the terms. Genesis: to produce, to give birth to, to create. Athena: ancient Greek goddess of knowledge, first in war, symbol of the city of Athens, goddess of wisdom and knowledge, born fully formed from the forehead of Zeus.

She considered the relationship of the two words together. Athena, sprung full-blown from the forehead of Zeus; how had she been born?

"Use a fire ax?" she muttered, thinking about extracting Athena from Zeus' forehead bone. Did that mean heads had anything to do with the assaults? Mel Gibson's razor scuzz came from the head. But that flew in the face of Sheela's tampon and urine. Nor did it fit the harpoon shot at Brad Pitt's butt.

"A sample?" she asked under her breath. At that moment the room exploded with cries as someone scored a goal on the hockey game playing at the other end of the room.

What was it that Lymon had said about Hollywood celebrities? That they paid for their success with pieces of themselves? Pieces, like had been taken from Manny de Clerk's penis? She frowned, thinking of witches, and the desires that led them to possess.

Lymon's words returned to haunt her: *"Under all the flashbulbs, fancy dresses, and long shiny cars, the world is feeding off of her blood and sucking at her soul."*

Christal reached into her purse and pulled out the Genesis Athena flier that the kid had handed her at the benefit:

GENESIS ATHENA MAKES DREAMS COME TRUE.
YOU CAN BRING HER INTO YOUR LIFE.

Below was the image of Sheela Marks smiling out at the world.

"All right, I'll bite." Christal reached into her bag for her cell phone and dialed the 1-800 number on the flyer. She pressed *send* and waited through three rings before an automated voice said, *"Greetings! Welcome to Genesis Athena, the home of the stars! Please use the touch-tone pad on your telephone to enter the first name and then push the pound sign before entering the last name of the celebrity or star that you admire the most."*

Christal turned the phone so she could punch 7-4-3-3-5-2-#-6-2-7-5-7.

The automated voice said, *"According to your selection, you have chosen..."* Another voice supplied, *"Sheela Marks."*

Christal smiled. Then the first voice resumed, *"If this is correct, please press 1."*

Christal pushed the *1* on her keypad and heard the tone.

"For our free celebrity bio, press 1 now."

Christal repeated the operation.

"If you consider yourself to be Sheela's greatest fan, press 1 now."

Christal did.

"Sheela Marks has something special. When she smiles, the world is illuminated in light. If you dream of her night and day, press 1."

Christal made a face as she complied.

"We think you might have what it takes to join Sheela Marks' most exclusive circle of admirers. If you agree, press 1 now."

Christal pressed.

"Please enter your name and address starting with street, box, city, state, postal code, or zip now. Speak slowly and clearly for our voice recognition software."

Christal, caught off balance, sputtered, "Uh, I'm Lisa Bridges, 12256 Wilshire Boulevard, Suite Two, West Hollywood, California, 91210." She had only a moment to wonder if giving the LBA office address had been the right snap decision.

"Lisa Bridges, 12256 Wilshire Boulevard, Suite Two, West Hollywood, California, 91210." The voice repeated it perfectly. *"If this is correct, press 1 now."*

Christal punched the button.

"Enter your phone number now and press pound."

Christal entered her phone.

"Thank you for calling Genesis Athena and sharing your love of Sheela Marks. We will be mailing our Sheela Marks packet to you today. Please look for it in your box. If you do not receive it within the next week, please call this number again." A pause. *"We'll be sharing your dreams of Sheela."* Then a click indicated the end of the conversation.

The group at the far end whooped again as two hockey players slammed headlong into each other and tumbled onto the ice.

24

Sid Harness glanced at his watch. Twenty-eight minutes after noon. He still had two minutes before Lymon was supposed to call. Sid used the time to peel back the paper that wrapped his turkey-and-provolone sandwich. He was sitting at a white vinyl-clad table in a Subway off Thomas Circle. Looking out the window, he could just see the statue of the corroded general sitting on his dark bronze horse. Traffic wheeled around below the general's feet. He was scowling out, theoretically with the same grim determination that had held the line at Chickamauga, Franklin, and Nashville.

The lunch crowd clogged the small restaurant, and behind the glass counter, two dark-skinned people, perhaps Pakistani or Iranian, hustled back and forth, slapping meat, lettuce, peppers, cheeses, and tomatoes onto buns.

It was a good place. Loud, crowded, and hectic. If anyone overheard, they'd only get bits and pieces. Sid had wedged himself into a small corner table, his back to the room. He sipped at the Coke he'd bought and could barely hear the Commerce Department secretaries bitching about their boss at the crowded table behind him. The good-looking blonde kept banging his chair back with hers.

Sid's phone rang a half second after he'd taken his first bite. Swallowing, he washed it down with the Coke and opened his cell. "Harness."

"Sid? Lymon."

"I was just sitting here, thinking I ought to be billing you by the hour."

"Okay." Lymon paused. *"Is that legal?"*

"Hell no! But then, neither is what I'm doing for you. You'd think I was was working for LBA instead of you-know-who." He glanced around uneasily, satisfied that people were more interested in slamming lunch and getting back to the grind than eavesdropping on wayward FBI agents.

"Did you get what I need?"

"If I got your message correctly, you wanted to know where the toll-free number you gave me was physically located. Your tax dollars have allowed me to ascertain that that phone number is answered at 98376 Virginia Avenue in Broomfield, Colorado."

"Colorado?"

"That's what the divine oracle that lives inside the computer said. If you need to know more, you're going to have to cast tea leaves, or do a little old-fashioned detective-type footwork."

"Right. Thanks Sid. What about the Sheik?"

"He's a curious guy. Hails from warm, sunny, sandy Qatar. That's a small country about midway down the east side of the Persian Gulf."

"I know where Qatar is. We spent a weekend floating out in the harbor there, remember? R and R compliments of the good old USN."

"Yeah, I do seem to recall that, but then I have the keen

brain of a highly trained federal agent. You're just a marsh-mallow celebrity guard guy these days."

"Do you want to get to the point?"

"The Sheik's rich—owns a fleet of tankers and freighters that handle about ten percent of the shipping going in and out of the Persian Gulf. He also has major investments in real estate around the world. You might be interested to know that he's big in your business."

"Yeah, pictures, I know."

"He likes being seen with pretty women, especially movie stars and high-profile models. He likes to squire them around the world in his private 757." He lowered his voice. "Just between you and me, I heard that he does sensitive things for both the Bureau and the Company down at the big L."

The big L was Sid's personal slang for the Central Intelligence Agency in Langley.

"I see. Anything that you can tell me that might relate to my client?"

"No. He seems to be a legit Arab businessman who has decided that the future lies with the West rather than the dogmatic rag-heads who want to go back to the Middle Ages. No conspicuous ties to terrorism, Al Qaeda, bad guys in Iran, or anything that would blacklist him."

"How about biotech? Is he invested in that?"

"Odd that you should mention it. Yeah. He owns several companies that are into genetic engineering. They're agricultural. You know, drought-resistant corn and tomatoes, that sort of thing." Sid paused, wondering why it hadn't registered when he skimmed the memo he'd requested on Sheik Amud Abdulla. *Genetics?*

"Sid? Christal is here. She wants to know if you got any answer from the guys at Quantico about the questionnaire."

"Put her on."

He waited and heard Christal's voice. *"Hey, Sid. What's happening?"*

"My cold turkey sandwich is sitting undigested in front of me. It's a hot day in DC. My investigation is spinning its wheels in loose sand. I think Peter is going to make me shelve my kidnapped scientists if I don't have anything by the end of the week."

"Kidnapping cases don't suit you. What did the shrinks say?"

Sid pulled out his notepad and a pen. "Where can I fax the report to you?" She gave him a phone number, and he added, "You'll have to read the fine print, but head shrink Russ Tanner thought it was a test. You know, the sort psychologists give people to profile their personalities. He said that the changing questions were routine. If you answer something that gets a hit, the program changes to ask you more specific questions. Uh, say you've got a neurosis about being compulsively neat. It tailors itself to determine just how fucked up you really are."

"All this is in the report?"

"Yeah, I'll fax it to you as soon as I get back to the office. Do me a favor, huh? Deep-six the paperwork when you get it. I don't want anything coming back to haunt my sleep."

"For you, Sid, anything. Lymon and I will burn it in the trash can after we read it. Then we'll flush the ashes down the john."

He grinned as he took a bite of his sandwich. Through a mouthful he said, "You know, Chris, spy work really suits you."

The greenroom for *The Mike Bullard Show* at the studio in downtown Toronto was well stocked. Christal glanced past Lymon as Rob Sawyer, a Canadian science fiction author, opened the refrigerator and removed a can of pop. Sawyer was up next, having just won a Canadian literary award.

She reclined on a gray fabric-upholstered couch and glanced up at the television monitor as a round of applause broke out for Sheela. The television in the corner of the small room showed Sheela as she walked out on stage clad in a pastel blue Ungaro wraparound.

People in the greenroom went silent as Sheela walked up to Bullard and kissed him lightly on the cheek.

"That's my Sheela," Dot whispered. She sat in the chair opposite them, a sheaf of papers in her hands, reading glasses down on her nose as she watched Sheela take her seat and smile out at the live audience. The orchestra was playing the theme to *Blood Rage*. When the music died away, Bullard began teasing Sheela about her Oscar and why she had come to Toronto to shoot *Jagged Cat*.

Christal glanced at Lymon, seeing the longing in his expression as he watched Sheela on the monitor. "You okay?" she asked in a soft voice.

"Yeah," he muttered, tearing his attention from the screen. "It's been busy. What's Sid's fax look like?"

She tapped a roll of paper in her lap. "I failed the test, Lymon. That's why the Web site cut me off. It makes perfect sense."

"Explain. You were the one talking to Sid."

She glanced around the crowded room. Sheela had been the headline star. Everyone in the greenroom was fixed on the TV. "You've got to see the questionnaire for what it really is: some sort of a tool for evaluating the people taking it. Whatever Genesis Athena is looking for, I gave it the wrong information."

"Okay. Such as?"

"Well, for instance, I listed the wrong interests under hobbies. I think I said something flippant about stamp collecting and big game hunting. That's not what they were looking for."

"Right." Lymon frowned. "What do you think they're after?"

"I think they wanted obsession. That's why the bathroom questions were so important. I answered practically; their psychologists were looking for some different order in the importance of bathroom fixtures."

"Huh? You lost me." He crossed his arms.

"All right, let's say that someone compulsive filled out that questionnaire. After a toilet and sink, they might say a mirror was the next most important thing."

"Why?"

She was fishing, knowing that she was out of her league here. "Because an obsessive person might need to see themselves, to constantly be reassured that their hair is in place, that nothing is stuck in their teeth."

Lymon grinned. "Okay, so we should have had Tony take the test."

"Yeah, maybe." She frowned. "But my guess is that your old friend Krissy might have been a better choice."

Lymon started, his gaze prying at her. "Krissy's a nut. She's obsessed with . . ." He whistled softly. "Jesus, is that what you're getting at?"

"Look, it's just the way my mind works, okay? Grandma said I had the gift. It's the closest I can come to an explanation for a hunch like this."

"How often are your hunches proven right?"

She met his stare. "Often enough that I don't question them."

"So, you're thinking Genesis Athena is designed to recognize obsessive-compulsive disorders?"

She nodded. "I'm not sure why, Lymon. That part eludes me. I'm booked on a United flight to Denver in the morning. Maybe it will make sense when I find their offices. Broomfield? That's a curious place for their headquarters, but maybe by going there, I'll figure it out. If I find out it's a mental institution, some of the pieces will have fallen in place. If not, we'll see what comes in the mail when we get back to LA, but I'm betting that their Sheela packet will have something in it that will act as a lure for the lunatic fringe."

Lymon was staring off into the distance. "Did Krissy ever answer your e-mail asking about her having Sheela's baby?"

"No."

"We could have nailed her on that. Even sending an e-mail is in violation of her restraining order."

"Do you think Genesis Athena is run by one of Sheela's wacko fans?"

"After seeing the 'share-la-Sheela' site I guess I can believe anything. My inclination is that it's probably harmless." Worry lined his brow. "I'm more concerned about the Arab angle and what Abdulla wants. He's rich, powerful, and sniffing around Sheela. He's got my hackles up. He's a threat; I can just feel it."

"Yeah, me too." Christal rubbed her arms uncomfortably. "You weren't the one who got eye-raped right there in front of God and everyone."

Lymon nodded in concern. "On that line, maybe your buddy Hank is Abdulla's new bird dog. Sid said that the good Sheik likes pretty girls, right? If you'd taken that job you might be jetting around the world in posh luxury rather than sitting here waiting on the Mike and Sheela show."

The crowd burst out laughing as Sheela made a joke about the tampon theft. It seemed that the story still hadn't died.

"Get a life, boss. I'd rather be a maid at Motel Six in Albuquerque than spend a single second in that guy's presence. Grandma would have said he had *el mal ojo,* the evil eye. The man's bad news. End of story."

"Here, here."

Yes, evil, a voice whispered in Christal's head. *And he wants you!* A cold shiver ran through her. Out of nowhere, she asked, "Do you think he's behind the celeb hits?"

"What? Where did that come from?"

"I was just thinking how creepy Abdulla was, and it popped out."

Lymon glanced up as Mike Bullard and Sheela laughed together. They had moved on to telling some joke about ice fishing in Saskatchewan. Christal decided it was something peculiarly Canadian in humor.

Lymon said, "I could see some obsessed male Arab having an interest in a pretty woman's tampon. Kinky, but possible. As to Mel Gibson's razor scuzz and shooting a dart into Brad Pitt's butt? Well, there you've got me."

"You know," Christal mused, "Hank works for Abdulla. Maybe we should have met with him. We could have stripped him naked, hung him up by his thumbs, and squeezed him for information. I think he'd have spilled his guts with the right persuasion."

Lymon gave her a careful scrutiny. "Are you always this edgy?"

She fixed a plastic smile. "Only when I imagine the expression on Hank's face when I flick my Bic under his scrotum."

"You must really like the guy."

"I hate people who lead me astray. Mostly because they remind me how stupid I was. If I'm ever stupid, Lymon, don't remind me of it, okay?"

"Yeah. Images of butane lighters are filling my fertile imagination. I got the message." He lifted an eyebrow, hazel eyes attentive. "I've been meaning to ask: Do you think it's a coincidence that Hank goes into personal security just after you do?"

"I don't know," she answered honestly. "I had no contact with him after I left the Bureau. The only link between the two of us would have been Sid."

"And he wouldn't have said anything to Abrams." Lymon wiggled his shoulders as he scrunched lower into the seat. "The coincidence bothers me. I don't know, Christal; it's like we're dancing around the peripheries but not seeing what ties the whole puzzle together."

"If it's a puzzle," she countered. "I mean, you're just assuming that Genesis Athena, Sheik Abdulla, the celeb hits, and Hank are related."

He mulled it over. "All right, you're the one with the weird spooky gift and the brouhaha grandma. What's your take? Are they related, or not?"

"Related," she muttered, unhappy with herself for saying it. "For the life of me, I don't know why, but I think when it comes to me, it will all fit like a glove."

A wild burst of applause broke out as Sheela stood, waved to the crowd, and took Mike Bullard's hand.

"What about her?" Lymon's voice was barely a whisper. "Will she be safe, Christal?"

Christal paused, lowering her voice to match his. "You should marry her, Lymon."

"Sure," he breathed.

"Julia Roberts married Danny Moder, her cameraman. And Anne Heche married her cameraman, too. Sharon Stone married Phil Bronstein, a newspaper editor."

"Christal?"

"Huh?"

"Shut up." He rose too quickly to his feet, lifting his sleeve to say, "Paul, she's on the way. We'll meet you at the door within five."

In her earpiece, Christal heard, *"Roger, boss. Paparazzi are here in a drove. Tell Sheela to be on deck and ready for them."*

Christal rose, straightened her tweed skirt, and followed after Lymon. She would be slightly behind Sheela and to one side as they left the building. Dot had gathered her things and stepped into line as Lymon explained about the paparazzi.

Sheik Abdulla's face hung in the back of Christal's mind.

"¡El mal ojo!" her grandmother's voice spoke from beyond the grave. *"He is evil, child, and he wants you!"*

Hank Abrams sipped coffee from a disposable Tim Horton's cup and glanced around the spacious lobby of the Westin Harbor Castle. At this time of morning, the place was like a tomb. Only the desk clerk stood behind the polished counter. Passing the registration desk, he lifted one of the house phones from the receiver and punched *O*.

After three rings, a voice informed him, *"Hotel operator."*

"Yes, could you connect me with Christal Anaya's room, please?"

"One moment."

Hank pursed his lips and scowled uncertainly as he monitored the lobby. It had taken him two days to discover that Sheela Marks had packed up and flown to Toronto to film scenes on location. He'd scrambled to get here, then scrambled for another day and a half to find Christal's hotel.

Damn it, I'm headed for a fuckup again. He hated the feeling of inadequacy that had plagued him since the Gonzales fiasco. When he rubbed his cheeks he could feel stubble. Hell of a thing. He used to be perfectly groomed. The way he lived now, rustling from one motel to another, he barely had time to wash his clothes.

Now he had her located. All it would take was a touch, just a moment in her presence, and he could call it quits and return to New York. He ran the gimmick through his head: He'd say he was with building maintenance, eh? The phones had gone down—been hacked by pranksters, eh? Was she Melinda Arbuckle in room 4312? When she said no, he'd ask to which room he'd been connected.

The phone rang five times before the operator broke in to state, *"I'm sorry, sir. It appears that Ms. Anaya isn't in her room. Would you care to leave a message on her voice mail?"*

"No, thanks." He grimaced as he hung up the phone and glanced at his watch. It was a quarter to five. Where the hell was she? Christ, at this time of morning, the old Christal would have been lost in REM sleep.

He started to turn when the elevator dinged and Christal stepped out, a black nylon suitcase hanging from a strap at her shoulder. She was dressed in a professional pantsuit with a light gray cotton jacket.

Hank turned, facing the wall with the phone to his ear. From the corner of his eye, he watched as Christal crossed the lobby, her heels clicking on the polished floor. She stepped through the glass doors at the main entrance and out to the curb.

Hank hung up the phone and hurried after her, stopping just short of the door, where he could glance past the aluminum jam. The doorman had hailed a cab and was holding the door as Christal slipped into the backseat.

Hank waited until the cab began to roll before stepping out and running up to the doorman.

"Shit!" he cried in despair as he watched the cab take a right onto the street beyond. He turned to the surprised doorman. "Did Chris say where she was headed?" He reached into his pocket and pulled out a set of keys. "She left these, and she's going to be really upset when she realizes they're gone."

The doorman hesitated an instant, seeing the worry on Hank's face, then sputtered, "You'd better hurry, sir. She's on her way to the airport. I heard her say the international terminal."

"Great! Thanks!" Hank turned on his heel, sprinting for the line of cabs that waited in a line at the curve of the drive in.

Hell! If she was flying somewhere, he had to at least fig-

ure out where. If it was back to LA, well and good. He could
catch up with her there. If it was somewhere else, did he
dare let her out of his sight? What if he lost her again? Verele
would think he was a complete bumbling incompetent.

The cabdriver—a Sikh, given his turban—was half out of
his door when Hank yanked the passenger door open and
cried, "International terminal at the airport!"

He slammed the door and shook his head, wiping at the
coffee he'd spilled on his pants. The Tim Horton's cup was
half crushed in his hand.

25

Number 98376 Virginia Avenue was a white, prestressed
concrete building in a small industrial complex just off
128th Avenue on the far northern fringes of Denver, Colorado. The buildings were new, with long expanses of darkly
tinted glass. Thin strips of lawn were encompassed by white
cement walks that bordered the parking lot. The grass had
the manicured look of a professional lawn service, and several young trees were growing around a small pond with a
delightful little fountain.

Christal pulled into the lot and took one of the visitor's
spaces two down from the handicapped slot with its blue sign.

She put her Denver street map on the passenger seat and
checked herself in the mirror. The afternoon sun was already
starting to cook the inside of the car. Christal ran a brush
through her gleaming black hair, decided that nothing offensive was in her teeth, and closed her purse before stepping
out into the hot air.

God, have I really been up for twelve hours already? It
didn't seem right that she could feel used up, and it was just
after midday here. The flight in from Toronto had been tur-
bulent, just uncomfortable enough that the pilot had kept
people strapped in for most of it.

The DIA airport had been plugged with people. As she'd

waited in the bowels of the B concourse for one of the shuttles, someone had said that only two of the automated trains were running. The entire time, she'd felt as if eyes were locked on her. But when she had glanced around, it was only to see a sea of faces, all looking harried and irritated.

At least Avis had been up to their usual proficiency. Her car had been waiting after the shuttle bus dropped her at the right space. From there, the drive through Denver had been stop-and-go as the highway patrol cleaned up a wreck on I-76. The jam had given her time to really study her map. As a result she had driven straight to the address.

"All right, Genesis Athena, here I come." She walked up to the black glass door, gripped the aluminum handle, and pulled it open. Cool air washed over her as she stepped into a small lobby. Three chairs and a compact couch seemed to have surrounded and captured a small wooden table off to the right. In the corner a potted plant lived in tropical splendor under the fluorescent lights. To her left a stairway led up to the second floor, while a hallway was blocked off with a wooden double door.

Christal noticed a building directory on the wall beside the stairs and walked over. White plastic letters were inserted into a black background and denoted the occupants in different suites. Five businesses called the building home, but none of them was named Genesis Athena.

"The plot thickens," she whispered as she studied the choices. She immediately discarded the two engineering firms, decided that the fishing lure company was out, and hesitated as she studied the last two.

She discarded AlpenGlo Publishing and went with Cy-Bert as the most likely candidate. It was located in Suite 201. Christal climbed the textured cement stairs and passed through the fire door. Cy-Bert occupied the first suite of offices to the right. The door was wooden with a brass knob. A slit of window beside it gave her a view of a reception area and several doors leading into the rear.

Christal stepped in and walked to the desk, where a young woman in her early twenties looked up from a Kat Martin romance she was reading.

"Hello. Can I help you?" Excited blue eyes met Christal's.

"I hope so. I'm Christal Anaya," she replied as she laid a business card on the counter. "I'm with LBA. We're a security firm in Los Angeles. It is our understanding that Genesis Athena has a telephone number that is registered to this address."

The blue eyes grew serious, and the girl pursed thin pink lips. Christal could see the dusting of freckles on her nose. "Genesis Athena . . . let's see." She wheeled to one side and tapped at a computer console. After several seconds, she said, "Oh, yeah. Here it is." She turned the monitor so that Christal could see the name gleaming on the blue screen. The familiar phone number was listed, as well as an address.

Christal bent around so that she could read it. "Is that address right?"

"Uh, yeah," the young woman admitted. "Uh, I guess so. You'd have to talk to Bill and Simon. They run Cy-Bert. Uh, they're not here now. They're running a marathon in Boulder today."

"Do you mind if I write that down?" Christal was already jotting: Genesis Athena—643 Sa'Dah Street, Aden, Yemen.

"Uh, I guess."

Christal could feel a big chunk of the mystery slide into place. Yemen? That fit what Sid had told them. She asked, "So, how does a Yemeni company have a Colorado telephone address?"

"Oh"—the young woman waved it away—"we have over six hundred clients here, you know? It's like we do all the phones for them. You know, like if you want to have a number and give out information? We do all the ordering and things for telemarketing companies."

"Such as?"

"Well, like, you know, if you sell stuff, right? Like DVDs, or clothes, or stuff? You can call one of our numbers and our computers take your order. You know, they ask for, like, which product you saw in their catalog? Then you type in your account number, the item number, and your credit card number, and confirm your address, and the company warehouse sends you the thing you ordered."

"I see."

"Pretty cool, huh?"

"Do you have a number for Genesis Athena in Yemen?"

The ditzy blonde hesitated. "Wow. I don't know if I can give you that. It's like a company secret. Like, what if you're from another company that does the same thing that ours does?"

"I'm not. As the card says, LBA is a security firm. Our only interest is in keeping our clients safe. I swear, I'm not here to steal your clients. If you have any questions you can call our California office and get confirmation."

The blonde considered it for a moment. "Well, okay. You seem nice. It's like, we send the monthly bill out FedEx, and a check shows up the same way. I remember that now that I think about it. I have to sign for it."

"Do you do the setup here? You know, write the questions and add the voices?"

"We can." She glanced at the blue screen, her finger running down a line of numbers. "But not for Genesis Athena. They do all that in-house." She grinned. "But I got to be the voice for ColoHigh Fashions once."

"Wow!" Christal forced a smile. "So, I'm to understand that you're just a phone service? That's it?"

"Yeah, that's us. If, like, you guys at"—she squinted at the card—"at LBA need a system, we'd be, you know, really glad to be it. But you'll have to talk to Bill and Simon."

"When they get back from the marathon."

"Yeah, like, isn't that cool? You know? They're old—in their late thirties—and they can still run!"

"Yeah, cool."

Christal thanked the girl and turned. When she walked down the stairs, she shook her head. *Genesis Athena really is in Yemen, for God's sake?*

Yemen. Just catty-corner across the Arabian Peninsula from Qatar. Sheik Amud Abdulla called Qatar home. She was chewing on that thought as she climbed into her rental, closed the door, and started the engine to stimulate the air-conditioning.

She lifted her cell and punched in Lymon's number. He answered on the third ring.

"Bridges."

"Lymon? Anaya. Listen, I'm sitting in front of our address in Colorado. You're going to love it. The place is just a phone service. Genesis Athena isn't here."

"So, where are they?"

"You ready for this?"

"Shoot."

"Aden, as in Yemen. A country on the southwestern tip of the Arabian Peninsula. Sid was right; it wasn't a ruse." She related her visit to Cy-Bert and gave him the mailing address she'd taken from the computer.

A pause. *"Did you determine if our friend Abdulla has any connection?"*

"All they've got is a telephone contract with Genesis Athena. You should know, however, that if you ever need a phone service, the airhead at the desk will be happy to write LBA a contract. Lymon, my best guess is that this place is a cutout."

"So what do you think this means for us?"

"Well, for one thing, I think it's a cinch that whoever Genesis Athena is, they don't want to be easily found. And that, boss, really has my whiskers quivering, as Grandma used to say."

"I'll bring this up with Dot when I see her this afternoon."

"Right. Uh, what now? Do you want me back in Toronto, or to head for the barn?"

"Sheela's wrapping her shooting here tomorrow morning. It's up to you, Christal."

She was considering that when a dark blue Chevy Lumina pulled into the parking lot and rolled to a stop two spaces down from hers. The guy was jerking his door open as he killed the engine.

Christal blinked twice and gaped. "Lymon," she said in a sober voice, "Hank Abrams just drove in and jumped out of his car. He's headed right into the Cy-Bert building."

"What? Are you sure?"

She put her Buick into reverse and backed out, making sure she cleared the lot before she floored the accelerator.

"Christal?" Lymon was barking from halfway across the continent. *"Christal? Are you all right?"* For the moment she couldn't answer. Hank hadn't looked right. He'd been unshaven, his clothes rumpled and his hair mussed. That grainy expression reminded her of a man who wasn't sleeping well, someone haunted by depression and frustration.

"Christal? Are you there?"

"Lymon, I'm spooked," she added as she took a right onto 128th. "How the hell did he know I was going to be here?"

The lounge at the Hollywood Hilton had only a few patrons. Hank Abrams sat at a small table next to the far wall and hunched in the cloth-backed chair. He stared uneasily down at the glass of Glenfiddich, neat. Strains of sixties and seventies music drifted down from the speakers. Behind the bar, the bartender—dressed in a puffy white shirt and black slacks—was tapping keys on his computer register.

Staring into the amber fluid, Hank fought the desperate desire to upend his single malt and chug the contents. As of that moment, he could still expense the high-dollar scotch, but whether he'd be able to in a matter of minutes was anyone's guess.

God, what a relief it would be to down one after another and dull the growing ache in his soul. For those blissful hours, he could be smashed out of his head. The worry, the frustration, and disappointment would be gone.

Shit, six months ago, I was the fair-haired boy in the Bureau. Now it was all gone. He'd had a pretty wife, a nice house, a solid job. People had looked up to him as he rode the rocket to stardom.

How had he lost it all?

Christal! He closed his eyes, his hands grasping at the air, knotting until his forearms hurt.

Every failure, every fuckup, had Christal at the bottom of it. Jesus, what was she, the anti-Christ?

"Oh, yeah, like she was just here!" the cheery blonde had said. *"I mean, like, you should have seen her on the stairs, you know?"*

Hank rubbed his eyes. A sour churning in his stomach left him half-sick, a tickle of nausea at the bottom of this throat.

He looked up when he caught movement in his peripheral vision. Neal Gray, immaculate in a charcoal Brooks Brothers suit, white shirt, and matching tie, approached the table and pulled out the opposite chair.

"You look like hell," Neal told him as he took the drink list and scanned the offerings.

"I haven't gotten much sleep the last couple of days." The question had been burning inside him. "When I called you from Toronto and told you she was headed for Colorado, how the hell did you know she'd be going to that place?"

Neal looked up as the bartender approached and laid a napkin on the vinyl table. "Can you make a margarita? Nothing fancy, just on ice."

"Yeah, sure," the bartender replied, and turned back for the bar.

Neal leaned back, his fingers twisting the edge of the napkin into a spike. He gave Hank an appraising look as he coolly studied him. The man seemed to see right through the front, penetrating Hank's skin to read the growing desperation and fear. "Hank, your call from Toronto surprised us. How did you learn she was headed to Denver?"

"I managed to get close enough when she was checking in at the United counter. People don't look around when they're talking to the desk agents. It's as if they don't want to look suspicious or something. I overheard." He couldn't stand it any longer and blurted, "Look! I'm not a fuckup! I know it looks like I can't carry out a simple assignment, but the bitch won't even see me! Shit, I offered her five grand just to meet with me and she turned it down flat! And then, this Toronto thing, how was I supposed to know she'd be flying off with Sheela Marks? God, I swear, she's a fucking devil!"

"Hank"—Neal's voice was even—"take a break here. You're being too hard on yourself."

Hank gasped. It was too soon to believe he was off the hook. "I was ahead of her! Then, bang! I'm stuck in traffic behind a wreck on a Denver freeway. By the time I figure out just how to get to this place, she's already been there!"

Neal smiled. "Christal Anaya really gets to you, huh?"

Hank swallowed hard. "There are times, I swear, if I could reach out and wrap my hands around her throat . . ." He stared at the tendons standing out on the backs of his hands, his fingers tightening on the air above his scotch.

Neal leaned back. "It's okay. You did all right, Hank. Sure, we'd have liked to have had our sample by now, but warning us that she was headed to Colorado made up for that."

"It did?"

"She was already on one of our lists. She flagged one of our computer Web sites a couple of weeks ago. The lady is digging around at the edges of one of the Sheik's companies." Neal paused. "Tell me, do you think she's capable of industrial espionage?"

Hank leaned back, considering. "Christal? I don't know. I mean, she's not one to break the rules. She's kind of by-the-book, if you know what I mean."

Neal studied him. "You really thought I was coming to can you, didn't you?"

Hank swallowed hard. "Yeah."

Neal leaned forward. "What have you got left, Hank? Besides this job, I mean."

"Not much."

"Your mother's in a nursing home in upstate New York. Your support is the only thing between her and Medicare. Uh, just between the two of us, how do you think this thing with Marsha is going to work out? Will you get anything from the settlement?"

"Her firm's handling the divorce," Hank murmured. "She's offered a settlement if I don't fight it. Fifty grand, cut and dried, and I don't contest it."

"You going to take it?"

"Neal, if I fight it, she's going to clean me out. I'll be in hock to the lawyers alone for the next twenty years." Then, unable to help himself, he spilled the whole story about Gonzales, Christal, the night they'd screwed in the van.

After he'd run dry, Neal sat back, a pensive look on his face. "And they never figured out how Gonzales got a camera into the van?"

"No."

After a long silence, Neal's blue eyes narrowed. "Tell me something, Hank. How much of a stickler are you for the rule book?"

Hank straightened, a tickle of anxiety in his breast. "Where's this going?"

"Nowhere illegal, if that's what you're thinking." Neal grinned. "You might say that where we're going, there are no laws . . . but the pay is *real* good. I can assure you it's not drugs, or weapons, or any of the usual 'high risk' ventures. We do nothing that violates the law within the territorial borders of the United States." A pause. "How would you feel about making a hundred and twenty grand a year—not counting bonuses—as a starting salary?"

"Yeah?" He perked up. "What's the catch?"

"From our perspective, it might just be you." Neal smiled up at the bartender as the man placed the drink on the table. Neal handed him a credit card. "If you'd run a tab, I'd appreciate it."

"Yes, sir." The bartender retreated.

Neal sipped his drink and looked up. "Do you believe in quid pro quo? If I do something for you, you'll do something for me?"

"Like in the Mafia?"

Neal laughed. "We're trying to make up our minds if we want to invest in you for the long term. How would you feel if we looked into this Gonzales thing? Figured it out, if you will. Would that be worth anything to you?"

"Damn straight, it would."

Neal caught him off guard when he asked, "So, how does a top agent have such a hard time catching up to an unsuspecting woman? We thought you'd have obtained the sample within the first forty-eight hours."

Hank took a deep breath, feeling the ax hanging over his head. "I don't know. You'd think she was being protected by LBA rather than just working for them. Look, I can handle this. All I need is—"

"Christal Anaya has become a problem," Neal interrupted easily. "My people really need to talk to her. That's all. If you're with us, we'll let you in on the ground floor of something really big. It will mean leaving Verele . . . going to work for the Sheik."

Hank frowned, feeling the earth turning soft under his feet. "I don't understand. I'm just supposed to use one of your little gizmos to get a skin sample, right?"

"The plan has changed since then. It changed when Anaya walked into that telephone service in Colorado. There are bigger things afoot here. Things worth billions that I can't tell you about yet." Neal leaned forward, an earnest look on his face. "She's been jerking your chain, hasn't she? Come on, admit it: She's the reason you're in this mess."

He felt the resistance run out of him. "Yeah."

"My people need to talk to her, Hank. That's all. Just find her, help me and my crew get to her, and well, we'll talk about it later, all right?"

"You just want to talk?" Something had to be missing.

"Yep." Neal shrugged. "Hank, what the hell have you got left to lose?"

26

They occupied a spacious photographic studio in West Los Angeles. The photographers had just finished and were in the process of packing their film, dismantling their lights, and casing their cameras.

Christal watched as Sheela smiled and shook hands all the way around. The small group of Spanish businessmen, one by one, took their turns holding her hands and lavishing their thanks. Rex cleared his voice from the side—a signal for Dot, who smiled like a queen as she disengaged Sheela from her admirers and led her back toward the dressing room.

Rex stepped in smoothly, saying, "Gentlemen, that was fantastic! We have rarely had such a professional and flawless shooting session."

A babble of accented voices chimed in agreement. Christal smiled to herself. She'd listened to the three Spaniards as they had talked during the shoot. Their Castilian accent hadn't masked the sexual innuendo as they ogled Sheela during the photo session.

While the photographers continued to disassemble their equipment, a crew began collapsing the series of backdrops. The stage had alternately consisted of scenes from downtown Madrid, Toledo, Seville, and other Spanish cities. One in particular was of the Escorial illuminated by a wash of yellow light. Sheela had modeled various fashions before each, and the photographers had shot roll after roll of photos for the new catalog, billboards, and other media.

Electric fans on either side had created breezes to ruffle Sheela's hair and toss her coattails. That had been the last scene. Christal watched as the techs rolled the big backdrop into a long tube.

Rex caught Christal's eye and gave the slightest nod of his head before shooting a meaningful glance toward the dressing room.

Christal picked up her purse, walking wide around the tripods and stepping past the fan to take the narrow hallway to the rear. The dressing room was a haphazard affair: panels set up to screen Sheela from the main room.

Dot stood with her arms crossed, watching as Sheela slipped out of a long-knit MaxMara dress and handed it to a young woman who replaced it on a hanger and hung it on a wardrobe rack in the rear.

"How'd we do?" Sheela asked as she pulled on her slim denim Blujeanious pants and straightened.

Dot glanced back at Christal, nodded, then turned her attention to Sheela as she reached for a red-patterned top by

Guess. "Under all the hype, they're happy. Rex is going to stay behind and stroke their collective manhoods."

"Figuratively, I hope."

"Yeah, me, too," Dot said dryly.

"Whatever it takes." Sheela wearily pulled the top on and fluffed her red-blond hair over her shoulders. She glanced at Christal; with stunning quickness exhaustion had replaced the sparkle she'd shown during the session. "What do you think?"

"I don't see how you keep from falling over." Christal stopped short. "You about ready?"

"Get me home, James." Sheela stifled a yawn, grabbed up her Marc Jacobs purse, and pointed at the door. "Dot, I'll see you tomorrow at my trailer on the lot. You can brief me on my schedule then. I'm going home to fall into bed."

"See you then," Dot agreed.

Christal lifted her cuff mike and said, "Paul? We're on the way."

"Roger. Uh, Christal? There's a guy out here, looks like a lost electrician. He's across the alley . . . maybe ten yards away. He's got a toolbox and seems to be killing time. Just thought you should know."

"Right. I'll keep an eye out when we step out the back door." She gestured to Sheela. "We're ready."

Christal led the way down the narrow hallway to the sign that read EXIT. She pushed on the crash bar and stepped out. The alley was just off Santa Monica Boulevard, bounded by trash Dumpsters, bits of paper, and a couple of empty bottles. The alleged electrician stood across the alley and stared at her from across the hood of the polished limo. He had on a yellow hard hat; a leather tool belt filled with pliers, hammers, and such; and wore a gray sweatshirt and blue jeans over brown work boots.

"Come on, Sheela," Christal stepped over and opened the rear limo door.

"Ah, I love this job," Sheela was saying as she stepped outside. "The glamor of the alleys, hotel kitchens, back doors, and—"

The flash took Christal by complete surprise. She blinked,

wheeling to see the "electrician." His toolbox was open at his feet, and a large Nikon filled his hands. Instinctively Christal placed herself between Sheela and the paparazzo. The flash continued to pulse as the automatic camera captured Sheela's rapid duck into the limo.

"Hey!" Christal cried, her anger rising. "Just who the hell do you think you are?"

"It's a free country," the paparazzo called back, grinning from behind his lens. "God bless the First Amendment!"

"Maggot!" Christal slipped in behind Sheela and pulled the door shut as she clicked the locks down. "Shit!" She felt humiliated.

"Tricky," Paul called over his shoulder as he slipped the car into gear. "I've never seen that workman ruse before."

Sheela leaned back and closed her eyes. "It's all right. It was only one guy this time."

"God, they're like a bunch of mangy coyotes," Christal muttered as she studied Sheela with worried eyes. During the photo shoot Sheela had been electric. Then, in the dressing room, she had gone from glittering, smiling energy to sacked lint in an instant. Now she looked hollow and half-digested.

"You need some time off," Christal said softly. "It's none of my business, but given your schedule, I wouldn't have traded a day off for that photo session—no matter what it paid."

Sheela barely smiled, cracking one eye to study Christal. "So, you think I looked that bad?"

"No, you were stunning. I would have thought you lived for that moment alone. Now you're even more hammered than before."

"Christal, I had to do it. What, you don't think today was worth a million and a half? Not to mention they're boxing up everything I wore today and shipping it to the house. Freebies, you see. All the better if I happen to be wearing one of the pieces when the cameras go off."

Christal blinked. "You're kidding! A million and a whole fall wardrobe for six hours of photos?"

"That's right." Sheela closed her eyes.

"Man, am I in the wrong business. I guess a million five

makes up for all the hassle. On the way over here, I thought you were going to fall over from exhaustion. Then, all of a sudden, you were just burning at a hundred and ten watts."

"It's a trick. A thing you learn." Sheela shrugged it off. "As to the shoot, doing it is partly prestige. My face is going to be all over Spain. Gwyneth Paltrow, George Clooney, Sharon Stone—a lot of American actors have done the El Corte Inglés shoot. It's the most prestigious department store chain in charming España. Doing their shoot is one of those notches you cut into your pistol on the way up."

"But you just flew in with the morning doves." Christal glanced at her watch. "Uh, you didn't even get to go home before coming here."

Sheela gave her a wan smile. "What's the matter, Christal? Fame and fortune not all that you thought it would be?"

"It never is, is it?"

"No." She lowered her voice. "We had to schedule that shoot for this morning. I'm due on the set tomorrow at five. We only had today as a travel day. Bernard wants to finish up my scenes this week. It will put him four million and two weeks ahead on time and budget—and he's going to need every cent of that in postproduction to fix all the Manny scenes."

"That encounter with Copperhead really did him in, huh?"

"There wasn't that much there to start with." She seemed to be talking in her sleep. "He's a pretty face. No guts. They don't make many men with guts these days."

"Lymon included?" Christal ventured.

"Lymon is definitely *ex*cluded. He's the only man I—"

"Yeah, I know." Christal glanced out the tinted window as they turned onto Santa Monica Boulevard. Sunset was burning yellow through the smog and glistening off of the surrounding traffic. People were walking along the sidewalks, passing the businesses that alternately sold donuts, video disks, tattoos, lotions, cameras, and furniture from behind glass windows and beneath colorful signs. When she looked back, Sheela was watching her through heavy lids.

"You know?"

Christal nodded, feeling a pull on her long hair where the seat trapped it. "Is it really so impossible?"

Sheela closed her eyes again. "You remember that guy with the camera back there? *People* or *Us* or *National Enquirer* will hand him a couple of hundred for that roll." A pause. "Do you have any idea how much they'd pay for a shot of Lymon and me in an intimate situation?"

"A bundle, I suppose." She softly snapped her fingers to get Sheela to look at her before she made a slight nod toward Paul and lifted an inquiring eyebrow.

"He knows," Sheela answered softly. "But thank you for your discretion." She straightened, stretching her arms out in front of her. "Why am I telling you this? God I *am* tired. It's a warning of what I might blurt when I'm half-asleep."

"It's okay," Christal said. "Look, Sheela, if you ever need a confidante, I can keep my mouth shut."

Sheela cranked an eye half-open again. "You know . . . you could make a fortune with what you could learn. Any of the big rags would pay a bundle for an inside story on Sheela Marks."

Christal laughed out loud. "I could make a fortune smuggling coke in from Colombia, or doing hits for organized crime." She paused, giving Sheela a wry smile. "Sorry. Not a chance. Look, I'm a native New Mexican. We're genetically predisposed to both poverty and loyalty. I guess I'll just have to keep your secrets. Anything else would be a denial of my ethnic and cultural heritage."

Sheela smiled at that. "You're just all right, Christal Anaya. A good friend. I don't have many friends."

She paused. "If I'm going to be your friend, I've got to tell you, I think you're killing yourself with this schedule. You keep it up, and something's going to snap."

"I get a break as soon as we wrap *Jagged Cat*. If I get too woozy, there are always ways of keeping sharp."

"Chemicals?"

Sheela's eyes remained closed. "I hear censure in your voice."

"Yeah. How many stars OD or wind up so brain-fried on that stuff that they kill their careers?"

"Most," she whispered softly. "It's so easy. Just a little pill . . . and you're back. Sparkling like a Bulgari diamond and feeling as smooth as an Olay body rub. Suddenly, you're riding a jetting wave that carries you up and up, rising out of a dull grayness."

"And then it smacks you like a bug on a bumper unless you take another one."

"People just don't understand. I can't quit, can't call in sick. Too many people depend on me. Tomaso, Dot, Rex, Tony, Bernard, the studio." Her voice weakened. "I carry them all, Christal. Without me, they're nothing."

"You can't carry them all forever."

"I'm running out of me," Sheela murmured softly. "Running out . . . empty inside . . ."

"Hey, just get what sleep you can. I'll wake you when we're home."

Sheela said, "Thank you, Christal," before she nodded off.

Christal studied her face, wondering at the classic lines that had smiled down on millions from the screen. The woman made magic for the multitudes, was worshiped around the globe. So much so that a Spanish department store would chase her down and pay her a million and a half for wearing their clothes in front of a camera. All that, but Sheela couldn't be with the man she loved?

Is it worth it?

"You all right?" Lymon asked as Sheela wobbled on her feet. He caught her arm, steadying her.

She blinked and looked owlishly around the paved lot behind the studio. A row of trailers lurked along one of the high walls, each with a thick black electrical cable, water hose, and flexible sewer line running from beneath to fixtures in the pavement. The early-morning sky had an orange tone, deepened by pollution and the fires burning up in the Angeles forest. The weather guys said the wind would be changing sometime after noon to blow it all inland.

Sheela tightened her grip on Lymon and shook her head,

as if to rid herself of a bothersome insect. "Just tired, Lymon. Look, get me to my trailer. That's all. I've got time to
sleep while the grips and set designers do their thing."

He tightened his hold on her arm as he walked her toward
her trailer. His BMW was perched on its center stand just
under the trailer's awning. "You worry me."

She gave the motorcycle a hollow-eyed stare. "That was
one of the most memorable days of my life, Lymon. No matter what, never forget that."

"It was just a ride, Sheela."

"Yes . . . pure paradise."

As they walked by the silver machine, the trailer door
opened and Rex leaned out. "Good! Back before I'd thought
you'd be."

"What are you doing here?" Sheela's voice reflected
weary acceptance.

"Tomaso wouldn't let me see you last night," Rex muttered. "You're going to have to do something with that guy,
Sheela." He jammed a thumb into his chest. "I'm *not* the
hired help. I'm your manager, not some pastry chef he
can . . . Hey, you okay?"

"Tired," she said, leaning harder against Lymon. "I just
need a nap."

"Too many twenty-hour days," Lymon added, knowing it
wasn't his turf, but unable to keep his trap shut.

Rex cued on the protective tone in Lymon's voice, his
eyes sharpening as he noticed the way Sheela had clamped
onto Lymon's arm. "Yeah, well, I've got business. Tony's
had two offers. One from Jerry Bruckheimer, another from
Donald Petrie. They're both casting for projects that you attached yourself to. Preproduction starts for both within the
week. We've got decisions to make."

Lymon almost lifted Sheela up the steps and walked her
back to the small bedroom, elbowing Rex to the side in the
process.

"Sheela? You hear me?"

"Later," Lymon said gently, but shooting Rex a look that
would have chilled milk.

"God, give me a break, Rex," Sheela added. "I almost didn't get through that last scene. Bernard's pushing like a maniac. I owe him in return for scrapping that bullshit he'd written into the script."

Rex made a sweeping gesture to include the two brad-clipped scripts and a clutter of paper that he'd placed on the table in the small booth. "Yeah, well what about—"

"Later!" Lymon snapped, and maneuvered Sheela into the small bedroom.

She smiled up at him. "Thanks, Lymon. Wake me a half hour before my call, all right? Hot coffee? And maybe time to run through my lines before I have to walk over for makeup?"

"Yeah, you've got it." He smiled at her, running his thumb over her eyebrow. "For now, you sleep."

"You'll be here?" Her fatigued eyes pleaded with his.

"I'll be here. And the coffee will be ready. Strong and black."

"See you soon," she murmured, and turned before flopping on the bed. He wasn't sure, but he thought she was already asleep as he pulled her pumps off of her feet.

He closed the door, passed the mirror-lined dressing room, and found Rex in the small kitchen. The manager was seated half out of the booth, his tie loose over a powder-pink shirt, his suit coat hanging open. Rex was watching him as if seeing him for the first time.

"Cut her some slack, Rex. She's walking wounded."

Rex's eyes had turned a cold blue; the set of worry and distaste lay on his lips. "Lymon, what the *hell* are you doing here?"

"Doing?"

Rex waved a hand at the bedroom. "You acting as her assistant now, as well as her bodyguard? Maybe thinking a little Whitney Houston and Costner gig is going to fall into your lap?"

Lymon managed a narrow smile as he bent, opened the fridge, and pulled out a can of the nasty light beer that Sheela kept there. He popped the top, took a swig, and made a face. He tapped the can with a finger. "You know, if it wasn't for marketing, they'd never sell this swill."

"Is that a fact?" Rex was looking even more hostile.

"Yeah, but you hire a firecracker ad agency, pay some big-name football players enough, write a cute script for them, and you can even convince all those hardworking blue-collar stiffs that watered-down pilsner tastes good."

Rex might have been looking at a bug. "So, just what are you trying to sell me?"

"Nothing, Rex. Not a single thing."

"Right. What is this shit you're pulling with Sheela?" His expression hardened. "You're the hired help, Lymon. The muscle. Period. You getting me?"

"You're not telling me anything I don't already know." Lymon took another swig of the beer and sat down across the table from Rex, meeting his eyes across the scripts and paperwork.

Rex broke contact first, leaning back and slapping his hands on his legs. "I don't want her hurt."

"Then give her a break," Lymon indicated the paper cluttering the table surface. "Come on, tell me the truth: Can't that wait until next week? The lady is killing herself. She wasn't kidding. She was like shredded paper in that last scene. She could barely manage her lines. She was on the verge of collapse. Bernard didn't notice. He thought she was spot-on—given that she was supposed to be whacked-out after running from the police for days—but everyone else in the room was holding their breath with their fingers crossed."

"Wait just a fucking minute! Who appointed you as her keeper?" He blinked, as if struck by something. "God, you're not in love with her, are you?"

"Fuck you, Rex."

"You poor deluded idiot! You listen to me, and you listen well. If you're in over your head, it's time for LBA to move on, and I'll find someone else to see to Sheela's security."

Lymon felt himself starting to bristle. "I don't work for you, Rex."

"Oh, yes you do, buddy. I'm the guy who brought you in, remember? It's my signature on your check. I run Sheela's affairs."

Lymon rolled the fragile aluminum can between his fingers. "Okay, go ahead and fire me." He glanced back at the closed bedroom door. "But do it after she finishes shooting, will you? Like, maybe after the cast party? The studio has rented Dan Tana's for all of Friday."

"Then, you're history, pal."

Lymon arched an eyebrow. "We'll cross that bridge when we get there. But, I don't think so. You're forgetting, you may sign my checks, but the lady back there brings in the bucks. In the end, we both work for her."

Rex smiled thinly. "You don't want to push this, Bridges. When it comes right down to where the shit hits road, she'll back me. She *needs* me a hell of a lot more than she needs you. She might be the talent, but I'm the brains behind her business empire."

"What? Make her choose? Me or you? Bullshit! I stopped playing that game in the fifth grade. She needs both of us. Just as we are, not fighting over her like twelve-year-olds." He leaned forward, pointing a finger. "So, here it is. You do what you do, and I'll do what I do, and we'll both do what's best for the lady, all right?"

Rex watched him in distasteful silence for a moment, then said, "Yeah, right." He used his left hand to scoop up the stack of papers, pointedly leaving the screenplays behind. "When you think it's all right, could I make an appointment with Sheela to go over her investment portfolio? And maybe you could schedule those two scripts into her free time? Bruckheimer and Petrie really need an answer . . . if you think you could get around to it."

Lymon shook his head. "You're being an asshole, Rex."

"And you're not?" He stopped at the trailer door. "Who's the asshole here? Me? You're the one who thinks you can romance Sheela. Let me remind you of something. If you remember Houston and Costner in *The Bodyguard*, you'll recall that it didn't end well for either of them."

27

Hank was walking down yet another hallway to another meeting. This time it was a hallway at the Hilton, but the eerie feeling of trouble had started chewing on his gut. He stopped at the door and knocked softly as he glanced up and down. A maid stepped out to the cart he had passed and gave him but a cursory notice as she lifted a stack of towels.

Hank hesitated for an instant when the door opened. Instead of Neal Gray, a striking woman stepped back, saying, "Come in."

Hank walked past her, fully aware of her fascinating gray eyes and hair like freshly spun copper. She had pulled it back into a French braid that hung partway down her back. She wore an elastic tank top that flattered her breasts and tight brown cotton slacks were molded to her legs in a way that left little to the imagination. Expensive sandals hugged her feet.

The lady-killer smile he gave her was instinctual. She smiled back, eyes measuring, but interested. Ah, she was one of those—one of those few women who were completely satisfied with themselves. She knew just who and what she was, and God help the man who tried to play silly games with her. She'd shut him down like a Disney ride in the rain.

"Hank Abrams," he said as she closed the door behind him.

"April Hayes," she returned. Her accent was cultured, educated, perhaps with a hint of Midwestern twang, but he couldn't be sure.

He entered the room to find the couch occupied by a short-statured dark-haired woman with an intense face. She wore a white blouse and gray jeans. Her shoes were loafers. "Gretchen Smith," the shorter woman told him as she stood to shake his hand. Her dark brown eyes were probing, antagonistic. He pegged her as just the opposite—a woman who had never found herself. The intense expression was meant as cover for a deep-seated insecurity.

"My pleasure." He looked around, trying to keep from glancing at April again. "Is Neal here?"

"In a moment," April told him easily as she walked to the small bar. "Drink?"

"Scotch, if you've got it."

"We do." She shot him a knowing smile that sent a tingle along his backbone. "Single malt, neat, with a water back, right?"

"Right," he agreed, playing along with the game. He tried to ignore the head-to-toe scrutiny Gretchen was giving him. "How long have you been with Verele Security?"

Gretchen's face went sour. April's smile remained warm and welcoming as she said, "We're not. We work for Genesis Athena." She poured from a bottle of Glenlivet. "I was in law enforcement. LAPD." She handed him the scotch, their fingers touching for the briefest of instants. It felt like electricity.

He saw her pupils react. Interesting. For a moment their eyes held. "So, you didn't like LAPD?"

Her smile teased. "I was on the fast track to detective. A chance meeting with the Sheik changed my direction, my paycheck, and the amount of bullshit in my life."

"Cool!" Gretchen quipped as she seated herself at the couch again. "It's life-story time."

Hank turned, a pleasant smile on his face as he took in the woman. "And you? Been with the Sheik for long?"

Gretchen frowned as she looked up at him, trying, no doubt, to figure what he was angling for. "Three years. Genesis Athena hired me because of my brain." She said it as if that was her only asset.

At that moment the door to the rear opened, and Neal Gray stepped out. Hank caught a glimpse of an ornate bedroom, the sheets rumpled and askew. So, did that mean that Neal and April were an item?

"Hey, Hank," Neal greeted. He was wearing a white shirt, narrow gray tie, and wool slacks. His taffy-blond hair was mussed uncharacteristically as if he hadn't run a comb through it that morning. "Did you meet everyone?"

"I did." Hank sipped his scotch. "I've got to confess, I thought it was you and me."

"This is the LA team." Neal was grinning, a secret in his eyes. "They handle some of our special operations. Counterparts to Salim and his group back East. April and Gretchen have collected some of our most promising specimens."

"Specimens?" Hank asked.

"Like you were doing out here. At the time it seemed like you were a more logical choice to go after Anaya."

"You might say we're proactive," Gretchen declared. "Do you have a problem with that?"

"Uh, no." Hank tried to keep his face neutral. God, what was she? The Wicked Witch of the West's evil doppleganger?

"Our mutual problem," Neal said as he took a seat, "in this instance is Christal Anaya." He glanced at Hank. "She was a pretty good investigator, wasn't she?"

Hank took a chair across from the coffee table, choosing the spot so that he would be in April's immediate line of sight. He smiled, affecting a knowing attitude. "Christal Anaya is one of the best field agents I've ever worked with. She has an uncanny ability to fill in missing data. It's . . . I don't know, almost like magic. The first time you hear her begin to fit things together, you'd swear she was nuts, but as the data begin to come in, you discover she's been right all along."

"Intuitive?" Neal asked.

"Spooky intuitive," Hank agreed. Then he smiled, using the boyish one that women found so attractive. "You know, her grandmother was a witch."

"What?" Gretchen asked in a grating voice. "That's absurd."

Hank glanced first at Neal, then at April. The woman was watching him with level gray eyes, her fine face betraying nothing. He shrugged. "Say what you will, but there are times when you work around Christal that you can't help but wonder. She does have an ability that almost goes beyond science when it comes to solving cases."

"So," Neal mused, "if she's digging at our corporate secrets, do you think it's a good bet that she'll figure them out?"

Hank shifted, affecting complete assurance. "If Christal were sniffing around doors that I wanted kept closed, yeah, I'd be worried."

April shot a communicative glance at Neal and arched her eyebrow as if to say, "I told you so."

Neal, for his part, frowned and laced his fingers together. "Maybe it's lucky for us that Hank's here."

"I just hope I can help."

"Do we know where she is?" Gretchen asked pointedly. "I'm tired of putting up with the bitch."

"I'm on it," Hank added. "It's just a matter of—"

"We've got her," Neal replied softly. "She's staying at a Marriott Residence Inn near here. Word is that she's checking out next week. My sources say that she's probably going to be looking for an apartment on her off time."

Hank started, jerking up straight. "How the hell do you know that? I've been chasing my ass off trying to get a line on her."

Neal's smile was the Cheshire cat kind. "It's all right, Hank. We've got our sources. When you tailed Anaya to Colorado, you brought the seriousness of the situation to our attention."

"Thanks for telling me," he said dryly.

"I just tapped my source this morning," Neal added. "It's not one I use except in extreme circumstances."

"Maybe you should read your memos," Gretchen muttered. "We've bumped into Anaya twice now. It was all in the reports."

"But nothing that would have indicated a direct threat to Genesis Athena," April amended, obviously to Gretchen's displeasure. "Our contacts with her have been in what we assumed to be the parameters of her job with LBA."

"What about de Clerk's?" Gretchen shot back. "Why the hell was she there? Huh? His security was supposed to be off that night."

"It was," April snapped. "I think he made a date with her and forgot."

Hank watched the interplay with interest, but Neal stopped it when he raised his hands. "Forget it, ladies. I've checked. It's a matter of the right hand not knowing what the left was doing. So, forget it. Let's move on to Friday night."

Gretchen leaned down and picked up a cardboard folder. This she opened, taking a diagram out and spreading it on the table. It looked like a floor plan to Hank. He could see a unit, parking lot, stairs, windows, and doors marked. A big green mass was labeled TREE.

"This is Anaya's room at the Residence Inn," Gretchen began. "It's a piece of cake. We can leave the vehicle in the lot here." She pointed to the parking lot. "I've already called the manager. Two of the units on either side of Anaya's will be empty on Friday night. I took the liberty of renting them. The third room in the building"—she indicated the room diagonally—"is already rented, so we'll have to keep the noise down."

Gretchen seemed to be enjoying this.

She continued, "We can enter at any time. The lock takes a standard magnetic card. The tree beside the walk will provide us with some cover from the main office. Even if we're seen, no one is going to pay much attention."

Hank leaned forward. "Let me get this straight. We're going to break into Christal's room?"

Neal looked up. "Do you have a problem with that?"

Hank pursed his lips, aware that April was watching him with hawklike intensity. Did he dare let her think he was bothered by a little thing like breaking and entering? Besides, it was a hotel! And better yet, it was his chance to show Christal that she shouldn't be prying away at one of their clients!

He smiled as he imagined Christal's face when he stepped out into the room. "I think it would be wise to do this when she's gone. If you walk up and ring the bell, Christal's not going to let you in."

Neal's expression was neutral. "According to my source, Sheela Marks and her cast are going to be at Dan Tana's for most of the evening. Anaya shouldn't be off shift until sometime in the very early morning, but we should be ready early—just in case."

"Good." Hank leaned forward, looking at the diagram. "Then I suggest that we have coffee ready when she walks in the door. Not only that, but we need someone outside, to follow her up the stairs in case something tips her off and she bolts." He pointed. "This unit next to hers shares the same stairway, right?"

"Yes," Gretchen told him distrustfully.

"Good. And we've rented it?"

"Yes."

"Then when Christal opens her door, it wouldn't be out of line for someone to step out right across from her as a blocker in the event she runs."

"I like that," April said as she leaned forward. "Good call, Hank."

Gretchen looked even more sour.

"That's it, then," Neal said, and glanced up at Hank. "Anything else about Anaya that I should know?"

Hank shrugged. "She's going to be really pissed about this. You'd better not count on her just taking a warning and backing off. She's not that kind of agent."

Neal's lips puckered, and he nodded. "I'll keep that in mind. Any other questions? No? Then I'll see you at eight tomorrow. We'll do a drive-by and check in to our next-door rental as soon as we know Anaya's gone. See you then."

They all stood, Hank feeling good about himself. He was headed to the door, his mind knotted on Christal and how she was going to take a rebuke from strangers.

"Abrams?" April asked, matching his step. "You got time for a drink?"

Something about her appealed to him. Maybe it was the danger that lurked in the corners of her dry smile. Or perhaps she was just a damn good-looking woman, and she was coming on to him. Or was it the hint of challenge that lay so deep in her smoldering gray eyes?

"Sure. They make a mean margarita here. Or, if you prefer, we could go somewhere else."

"I know someplace private."

Hank bowed. "It'll be my pleasure."

As they walked out into the hall, she gave her head a slight tilt. It reminded him of Lauren Bacall. "You never know," she said, "we might both enjoy it."

* * *

A weary Sheela rubbed the back of her neck as she walked from the studio to her trailer. The lot was hot, baking under the sun. She had heard that a peculiar high-pressure system had built over the Mojave, that it was kicking the scorching desert air back over LA.

The weather guy didn't know what high pressure was.

A headache ground away at the back of her brain, and her eyes burned, perhaps from the smog, or perhaps from the fatigue that lay so heavily in her bones, blood, muscle, and soul.

She had finished her last scene, God willing, if some editor didn't find a flaw that would cause Bernard to recall her.

But that would be sometime in the amorphous future. On beyond zebra, in another lifetime that started after she woke up from a zombie's somnolence that would start after the festivities on Friday.

The cast party was a thespian's tradition that reached back into the dim and distant past. A celebration of the hard work, the good times and bad, that had occasioned a group of strangers to become a short-term family.

I'm done! She smiled wearily and looked down at her purse. The amphetamines lay unused, but for a couple of tablets. She was still in control. Her body might have felt like scorched toast, but her self-discipline had held.

The pills in her purse mocked her. She could feel them, whispering, calling, chiding her. Relief lay just a swallow away. She'd be fresh again, ready to take on the world instead of being this brain-dead hulk of ambulatory tissue.

Sleep is almost yours.

She waved as she passed a flock of extras dressed as Civil War Confederates and rounded the corner that led to her lot trailer. The awning cast a solitary square of shade over the lawn chairs and small table. The muted puttering of the air conditioners rose from the long line of trailers.

Sheela plodded up to the steps and opened her door—then

sighed wearily as she stepped inside and waved halfheartedly at Rex, who sat at the table in the small booth.

"We're finished," she told him. "I wrapped my last scene. Bernard's doing some short intercuts with the extras, and then he'll get what he can out of Manny, but that's not my problem anymore." She grinned. "So, it's Thursday afternoon, and I'm headed home to fall face-first into bed."

Rex smiled. "Glad to hear that. You and I have some things to talk about."

"Not now, Rex. I can't think . . . let alone pay attention."

He tapped the two screenplays on the table. "Did you get a chance to go through either of these?"

"Get real!"

"We need an answer. Tony thinks you ought to bail on the Petrie property and go with Bruckheimer. I tend to agree. The role suits you better."

"I want some time off," she said as she slumped into the booth across from him. "Rex, I'm roadkill. It took everything I had to get through *Jagged Cat*. I can't keep up with this schedule."

He tilted his head. "I thought I got you something for that."

She reached into her purse and pulled out the little pill bottle. "I took three. I don't like them."

His flat stare bored into her. "Sheela, do you know what it means to be on the A-list?" He tapped the screenplays again. "I've talked to the producers. You've got your choice. Twenty million up front, or fifteen percent of the box office. Your decision."

"Rex, I . . . ." She shook her head. "They start preproduction next week, right?"

"Bruckheimer wants you on Thursday for a preliminary meeting. Petrie has his scheduled for Friday."

She closed her eyes, whispering, "I just can't do it."

She could feel his eyes, hard, unbending. "Sheela," he said softly, "I've gotta know which one."

"Neither," she told him as she nerved herself to look him in the eye. "Tell Jerry if he'll wait for a month, I'll do it."

"What?" Rex snapped. "You want me to tell Bruckheimer

to put a two-hundred-million-dollar project on hold while you take a nap?"

"You heard me!" The shrill note in her voice surprised her. She hesitated, rubbing her masklike face. Her skin felt wooden from the caking of makeup. "God, I'm sorry, Rex. I don't mean to be a shrew."

He smiled, half-forgiving. "It's okay, Sheela. Yeah, get some rest. I'll drop by tomorrow and we'll make a final decision. About nine, then?"

She gave him an empty look. "Why are you pushing this?"

He stood, collecting his papers. "Because you're hot. Come on. You're in your thirties now. This is Hollywood, babe. Get it? You've got ten years. That's it. When you hit forty, you're history. By the time you turn forty-one, they're gonna need an archaeologist to dig you up."

She blinked, feeling the twinge of fear.

"Hey," Rex relented as he snapped his briefcase closed on the papers. "It's okay. We just gotta make hay while the cutting's good." He pointed to the pill bottle. "They're there if you need them." A smile. "You can rest next decade, right?"

"Yeah, right." Shit, the way she felt now, she wasn't going to wake up until she was forty-three.

"Sheela," Rex cooed in a gentler voice, "it's not just you that we're talking about. Crying 'Me! Me! Me!' won't cut it."

She could feel the sense of guilt come toppling down, like stones on a swimming woman.

Rex got halfway to the door and stopped, his briefcase under his arm. He turned, a pensive look on his face. "Tell me, this 'time off' thing . . . Did Lymon suggest it?"

She shrugged. "He's worried about me."

A flicker crossed his eyes. "Yeah, I'm sure he is."

Then Rex was gone.

Sheela rolled the bottle of pills between her fingers. If she only took one, she could finish the scripts this afternoon. She fought for a deep breath, feeling sick. Pieces of her were shrinking.

Going away.

Getting ever smaller.

Everyone depends on me. The whole fucking world.

28

Friday afternoon had started hot under a searing sun. Christal pulled her Chrysler into the circle drive and tried to park as inconspicuously as possible. She glanced at her watch, seeing that it was five till one. The vegetation cast cool pools of shade that barely masked the heat rolling down from the San Gabriels.

Christal took a moment to check herself in the mirror. Good, nothing in her teeth, and she looked presentable. Not bad for as rapidly as she'd gotten ready for this assignment.

"Christal?" Lymon had asked, curiosity in his voice. *"I just got a call from Sheela. She wondered if I could send you over at one this afternoon. Said there were some things she wanted to discuss with you."*

When she'd prodded, Lymon had given no more details, but had sounded puzzled himself.

"Christal?" he had finished. *"Be quick, huh? She's got a heavy schedule tonight. Try not to take too much of her time. Let her get all the rest she can."*

So, here she had come, shuffling through the half-coagulated LA traffic to Sheela's opulent mansion. She had checked in with neighborhood security and then buzzed in at Sheela's gate.

Crystal emerged from her Chrysler and walked up to the huge wooden doors. She hadn't even rung when Tomaso opened the right-hand portal and welcomed her.

"This way, Ms. Anaya," Tomaso said, leading Christal not to the meeting room that she was familiar with but up the stairs. She lagged, trying to see the artwork. The familiar colors of the Southwest were warm and reassuring. A single glowing Reid Christie painting showed sunlight glowing off of bison backs. In another, by Santiago Pérez, a colorful New Mexican rider dashed his horse below a saint-filled sky.

"I didn't know Sheela had such an interest in this kind of art," she offered as Tomaso led her past the closed doors to the end of the hallway.

"Yes, she tries to go to Santa Fe at least once a year." Tomaso smiled, lifted a hand, and knocked before opening the door and announcing, "Ms. Anaya to see you, ma'am."

"Thank you, Tomaso," Sheela called as Christal stepped into the . . . what? Ante-bedroom? Christal stared at the huge TV, the books and videos. Looking straight back through the opened doors she could see Sheela's huge bedroom; to the right she had a glimpse of the well-equipped dressing room.

"Christal!" Sheela rose from a chaise and crossed the floor to take her hands. "Thank you for coming."

Christal started to smile, and hesitated, fixing on the puffiness in Sheela's red-rimmed eyes. "Hey, you all right?"

"Tired as hell," Sheela muttered. "Can I get you something? A drink? Have you eaten?"

"Yeah, I fixed a bite at my place. The Residence Inn is neat that way. Each of the suites has a kitchen. They're little apartments, actually."

Sheela motioned to the chair across from hers and resettled herself. "Did you see the news this morning? About what happened in Paris?"

Christal leaned forward in the overstuffed chair. "You mean about Princess Diana? Yeah."

During the night, someone had broken into the forensic lab that curated specimens taken from the body of Diana, the princess of Wales, during the investigations after her fatal car crash in 1997. The Sûreté was investigating, and was particularly curious as to how a French radio station had been tipped off within hours of the break-in. News clips had shown outrage throughout England as the story broke. The Spencer family had already voiced their dismay. No statement had been forthcoming from the royal family on the matter.

"What do you think?" Sheela asked softly.

"I don't know yet." Christal made a gesture. "Maybe it's

related, maybe not. She wasn't Hollywood. Not a film star like you and the others."

Sheela nodded. "I want to know what you've found out about the celeb hits. Everything. Lymon has been giving me reports, but I want it from the horse's mouth."

Christal leaned back and started at the beginning, relating everything that she knew, then added, "I think it's all coming together. And I don't like where it's going."

"How's that?"

"I think Sheik Abdulla, Genesis Athena, and the bizarre thefts are part of the same thing." She winced slightly. "It's as if I can feel it all moving in unison. Kind of like something breathing just out of sight. You can't help but know it's a monster of some kind. You see, the thing is, Lymon's right. There are too many coincidences. Why Hank? Why did Sheik Abdulla cancel everything at the last minute to fly to New York just to see you? Why is Genesis Athena in Yemen, while he has his offices in Qatar? You, Julia Roberts, Sandra Bullock, Brad Pitt, Mel Gibson, Manny de Clerk—all the big stars. All high profile. It's like a fan wish list from *Us* or *People* magazines."

"So, you think the Sheik is . . . what? Gaining leverage for pictures by stealing my tampon? Or just angling for magazine ink?"

"No." Christal clarified, "but I think he's figuring to make a great deal of money somehow. That, and it's an ego thing. Something to do with control and power."

"Ah, we're back to witches again?"

Christal cocked an eyebrow and nodded. "Yes . . . no. I've got a gut feeling that it's similar to what my ancestors fretted about, but with a very different twenty-first-century twist. Power and greed—just like in ancient Southwestern witchcraft—lie at the bottom of this. It's about feeding a craving hunger, and the hunger is called desire."

"It frightens me that I've been in this business long enough to think you're right." She rubbed her face, a dull pain behind her eyes.

"You look terrible. You taking uppers?" Christal asked,

and immediately regretted it. Damn it, her mouth had been getting her in trouble all of her life.

"Some," Sheela admitted, pointing to the scripts on the floor at her feet. "Rex is after me to make a decision. Hell, I can't even remember what I read." She picked up a pill bottle from the table, rolling it between her fingertips. The little pills inside rattled like Death's whisper. "If he wasn't pushing so damned hard I . . . God, there's just not enough of me to go around." Her eyes sharpened. "It goes against my principles—taking these things."

Christal studied her, seeing the fragility in her eyes, in the set of her shoulders. The woman was ready to fall into a thousand pieces. What the hell was the matter with these people? "I may be out of place asking, but why are you doing this? I mean, treating yourself this way?"

"People depend on me." She said it with all the sorrow of the saints. Then she asked, "What do you think about honor, Christal?"

"That's not a question I get asked every day."

"I guess today is your day."

Christal straightened, rubbing her hands together. "Very well, I think honor is the root of integrity. It comes with certain core principles that govern every waking moment of our lives. I'm a Catholic at heart—from the old church, the one that says you're going to have to pay for every sin you commit."

"Do you have principles, Christal?"

She smiled wryly. "Unfortunately. They keep getting in my way. The last time I violated them, I got slapped down pretty hard. I'm working overtime to keep from paying for any more mistakes."

Sheela nodded, then asked another curious question. "Do you depend on me?"

"God, no! What kind of silly question is that? I have a great deal of respect for you. In fact, I wonder how in hell you can keep it together with all this shit coming down. Depend? No. Sorry. I have my own life, thank you."

Sheela stared into the distance, and Christal saw the brittleness, the cracks that were running through her psyche.

This was a glimpse of what Sheela Marks would look like when she was old and worn through by life.

Christal asked, "Doesn't Rex see what's happening to you? Doesn't anyone care if they push you into the abyss?"

A chilling smile lay on Sheela's lips. "I'm property. A trademark. Like Rex says, I may only have ten years left."

"You'll be charred carrion if you don't do something for yourself."

"I can't let everyone down. I did that once. Never again."

The resignation in her voice set Christal off. She leapt to her feet. "Maybe I ought to go down, lift Rex up by his tie, and have a little talk with him. Shit, he's treating you like you're his own private little hunting dog! So what if runs you to death, he's Rex fucking Gerber, he can always get another dog, huh?"

Sheela laughed out loud, the sound of insanity barely hidden in the peals. And then, to Christal's amazement, Sheela's swollen eyes began to leak tears.

"Hey, it's okay." Christal knelt in front of her and took her hands. Mother trucker, what did she do now? Sheela's tears left her oddly uncomfortable, embarrassed. She'd never been a good one for hand patting and consolation. "Sheela?"

The woman sniffed, pulled her hands away, and wiped at the tears. Christal watched as Sheela Marks pulled herself together with Herculean effort.

Sheela took a deep breath, then whispered, "Sorry. I don't know where that came from."

"It's okay."

Sheela shook her head. "Isn't it funny? Surrounded by all these people, and I have to call you to fall apart in front of." A grin. "I could have a therapist, like all the rest. You can't throw an apple core into the bushes here without hitting one." A pause. "Somehow that just doesn't suit my practical Saskatchewan upbringing."

"My New Mexican one either."

"Well, thanks for listening." A pause. "Would you do something for me, Christal? Something personal?"

"It would depend. Don't forget that I come from a law enforcement background."

Sheela looked up, desperation in her eyes. "I need to get away for a couple of days. I need to go someplace where no one can find me. I just need time to myself. Can you help me with that?"

"Sure. I mean, maybe. I'd have to know where you were going. My first concern would be for your safety."

"I'll be very safe. I'll have protection close at hand."

"I'd have to tell Lymon."

"Yes, but only him."

"Okay, so, just where is this safe place?"

She sounded like a little girl when she asked, "Could I come and stay with you for a couple of days?"

"*What?* Why me?"

Sheela took a deep breath. "Because, Christal, I just want to be a real person for a while. They're slowly draining me away. If I don't get out, find something to grab ahold of, I'm going to lose myself."

Christal shook her head as if to throw the idea off. "You want to come stay with me . . . in a hotel?"

Sheela nodded, her eyes down. "What if I told you that there was no one else I could depend on?"

"What about Lymon?"

"I'm asking this as one woman to another. I *need* to get away for a couple of days. Away from Rex, away from Tony, someplace where I can just sleep, watch TV, read a book, and be anybody but Sheela Marks." She looked up, eyes glittering with desperation.

"Yeah, I'm in. Let's do it," Christal declared hotly. "And if Rex or Tony show up blustering, I'll eighty-six their asses right out of the place."

Sheela seemed to melt in relief. "Thank you. You don't know what this means to me."

Christal nodded, feeling the pieces of something falling into place deep in her mind. "One condition."

"What's that?"

Christal pointed. "You toss those pills into that toilet back there—and my place is yours."

Sheela stood, walked back to the dressing room toilet, and upended the bottle. Pills cascaded into the bowl before she ceremonially pressed the lever to flush them. When she reentered she looked more alive, a faint sparkle in her eyes. Artfully, she tossed the empty plastic bottle to Christal. "It's a deal."

Christal frowned. "Just one little problem: How are we going to do this? Sneaking you out of here is going to be like breaking you out of the federal pen."

Sheela hesitated before she said, "I've got a plan."

29

"Boss, we've got a problem," Christal announced as she burst into Lymon's LBA office and closed the door meaningfully behind her.

He had been at wit's end, double-checking the figures his accountant had forwarded. The federal government wanted a bigger chunk than he had expected for the quarterly taxes. Bigger to the tune of fifteen thousand dollars. He'd been wondering how he was going to broach the question of a bigger bill to Rex.

Thus it was that the last thing he needed was Anaya stomping in with "a problem." He gave her what he hoped was an appropriate glare of reprimand as he tapped the fingers of one hand on the adding machine and shuffled the piles of paper stacked here and there with the other.

"Have you ever considered knocking politely and asking permission before barging in like one of Hannibal's elephants?"

Anaya didn't register it as she plopped herself into the chair next to his desk. "It's about Sheela." She looked around. "Is this place safe? Can we talk?"

"Yeah, provided your vocal cords work, which they seem to. You mind telling me what's so important that you can interrupt my private self-flagellation at the IRS's behest?"

"Sheela's on the verge of a breakdown." She raised a hand. "Hear me out, huh? You remember when she asked me over this afternoon? The woman's at wit's end. She needed someone to talk to. I was it."

"Why you?" He sat back, slightly irritated.

"Because I'm . . . I'm safe. A neutral party, if you will. She doesn't have to worry about offending me, about biasing a preconception. I'm peripheral enough that if it doesn't work, if I betray her confidence, the blow won't kill her soul. You get it, boss? I'm an expendable nobody."

"Rex has been at her again?"

"Yeah, he's pushing really hard over some movie deal that Sheela has to make her mind up about yesterday."

"That son of a bitch."

"We're on the same wavelength there, boss. No doubt about it."

Lymon closed his eyes and sighed before reaching for the phone. "Thanks, I'll deal with it."

"No." Christal surprised him by placing her hand on his atop the phone. "It's taken care of."

"Would you mind explaining that?" Damn it, not only was Sheela his client, but *he* was in charge of LBA, not some two-week-old employee.

"Here's the deal, Sheela's going to spend the weekend at my place."

"What?"

"Yeah, that's the problem." Christal raised her hands. "Don't get on your high horse. I'm here to find a solution that's going to keep Sheela safe and still give her the privacy she needs right now." Her dark gaze bored into his. "Lymon, you weren't there. You didn't see the expression on her face. One wrong knock and she's going to shatter. Just the same as if you dropped a Swarovski crystal onto a slab of cement."

"I wish you'd talked to me before—"

"Rex has her on uppers," Christal continued. "He's trying to squeeze everything he can out of her."

Lymon ground his teeth.

"So, we have to make this happen. Sheela's got a plan. I want to put a couple of wrinkles into it."

Lymon gave her a dead stare. "Christal, this isn't just an

exercise; you're playing with dynamite. This is a very important woman's life you're talking about."

"I know," she answered honestly. "She's everyone's golden goose, but they're so busy gnawing on her drumsticks that she's going to be bones on the plate before anyone notices. So, boss, this weekend she's coming to my place to just be a regular person."

Lymon leaned back in his chair. "I don't know whether to strangle you, or give you a raise."

Christal rose, bracing her hands on his desk as if she were about to leap over it. "Answer me something, boss. You care for the lady, don't you?"

"Look, Christal, this is the real world, not some movie, or novel, or something. I have professional responsibilities."

"What about your responsibilities as a man?"

Lymon stared at her, fighting the desire to stand up and bust her across the mouth. "You're treading on dangerous ground here."

"Yep."

He had butterflies in his stomach as he said, "All right, smart-ass, what have you got in mind?"

For the *Jagged Cat* party, Bernard had rented Dan Tana's, a small two-room Italian steak house in the nine thousand block of Santa Monica Boulevard. The Friday night gathering was intimate, the cast's chance to share the final familial bonds they had forged during the short but intense shooting schedule.

Red-and-white checked tablecloths, red leather booths, and hanging Chianti bottles decorated the rooms. Celebrity artwork, movie posters, and photos hung on the crimson walls. The fare was New York steak marinated in a special Italian tomato sauce; rolls, many of which were used as projectiles; and all the wine the cast could drink.

Sheela had hooted and clapped as Bernard conducted the impromptu awards ceremony. For her gag gift, she had received a bent carving knife to commemorate the scene where she chased her father around the kitchen. Then she had turned to the familiar faces, told them what a pleasure it had been to work with them, and blown them all kisses before retaking her seat and listening appreciatively to the others as they took the floor and received their gag gifts.

Manny de Clerk sat in a booth in the back, surrounded by his agent and manager, a somber look on his face. He had just smiled and waved when Bernard gave him a framed photo.

Poor Manny. Sheela had covered her sympathy with a smile. When the real world had broken through his fake self-image, he had cratered. *What about yourself?* she asked. *If someone penetrated the walls you've built, could you do any better?*

She swallowed hard and rolled the cloth napkin between her fingers. Her heart was beating, anticipation sending tingles through her muscles. God, she felt like she was a girl again, stealing her father's motorcycle.

That's silly! You're a grown woman. Yeah, one who was sneaking away for a weekend of sin. Or so she hoped.

She glanced across the room to the door, knowing that she was coming up on time to leave. She could still back out, call Christal and tell her that she'd changed her mind.

"Anyone else got anything to say?" Bernard demanded. "No? Then I guess that does it for me. Again, thank you all. You're the best, most professional cast I've ever had the pleasure of working with. God bless you all."

They all applauded, whistled, and stomped.

"If anyone's interested," Bernard answered, "I'll be serving drinks up at my place. You're all welcome."

More whistles and cheers.

As they stood, Sheela made the rounds, kissing cheeks, hugging, making the pleasant chatter expected of her. She reached into her purse, thumbing the button on her cell. Plugging her other ear with a finger, she said, "Paul? I'm ready."

"I'll be there soonest," he said. *"The door security will call for you when the limo is out front."*

Sheela mingled in the knot at the door, smiling, feeling alive for the first time since she and Lymon had gone tootling around on the Indian. Sapping fatigue lay there, deep in her brain and body, but the adrenaline rush held it at bay.

What's happened to you? she wondered. *When did your courage dissolve into water?*

Thank God for Christal. *"You can depend on me."* The woman's words repeated as if engraved on Sheela's soul.

What was Lymon's reaction going to be? He'd be pissed at first. She smiled at that, both pleased and irritated that he was ever the professional. Just once, couldn't he let himself see beyond his duty? Dimming the noise and bodies around her, she imagined the two of them, alone, intimate, just holding each other.

"Manuel de Clerk?" the door security called.

Manny's agent acted like a battering ram, opening the way to the door. Sheela could see flashes as the paparazzi captured Manny, one hand raised, fleeing down the cordoned rope lines to the open door of his limo.

Shit, they were like locusts. She frowned, looking down at her black leather pants and tall black boots. Would they guess? No. It was too far-out.

"Sheela Marks!" came the call.

She excused herself, smiling, as she stepped to the door—and out into the strobes and clatter of the cameras. Two of the security guys made sure that no one crossed the velvet ropes leading to curbside.

"Sheela!" "Ms. Marks!" "Look this way!" "Sheela, over here!" She smiled, waving, trying to oblige them all, knowing full well that the wrong expression was captured forever.

The limo door was open, and she slipped inside with one last wave. The door shut, and she held her posture as Paul pulled away from the curb. Only then did she collapse.

"Thank you, Paul," she called.

"No trouble, ma'am." He kept his head forward. "The bag is on the floor as you requested."

She experienced a flood of relief. She was only moments from freedom.

* * *

Marc Delangelo slipped from the crowd blocking the sidewalk in front of Dan Tana's. He raised his hand, waving; a bright red Porsche Boxster, the top down, swerved toward him.

He vaulted into the seat, pointing. "There, that limo. That's her."

Jennifer, his girlfriend, glanced at him in the illumination cast by Santa Monica Boulevard. "You're sure it's her?"

"Yeah." He grinned. "She's up to something. I've watched her a lot of times. She doesn't dress like this unless something's up. I mean, leather pants? That's not her style. And that denim long-sleeved shirt? This is Sheela Marks, not Gwyneth Paltrow."

"So?"

"So," Marc replied, "if we keep them in sight, I think we're going to catch America's sweetheart doing something really cool. And, like, that's a couple of months' rent if I can get it on film."

She glanced at the infrared camera that he pulled from a bag. "You'd better. I'm still pissed at what you paid for that thing."

"Hey, babe, it's the coming thing!" He gestured ahead. "You just stay a couple of lengths back from that limo."

Genesis Athena. Christal rolled the name around in her head as she pushed the plastic grocery cart. According to her watch it was just after ten, and the store was almost empty. A few other patrons cruised up and down the brightly lit aisles of the Albertson's. They were casually dressed, no doubt picking up the last few things before the weekend. That, or like Christal, they worked unusual hours.

She glanced at her watch, figuring that Sheela would duck out of the *Jagged Cat* party as early as she could. She had promised to be at Christal's by eleven. The woman who had pleaded so passionately with such a look of desperation in her eyes wouldn't be partying on until all hours of the night.

Christal had checked to be sure that Sheela made her party at Dan Tana's, then had taken her Concorde to do some last-minute shopping. It had occurred to her in a stupendous flash that she was about to have a most auspicious houseguest—and her refrigerator was stocked with what she considered the barest necessities of survival: refried beans, tomatillos, cheese, poblano and jalapeño peppers, corn tortillas, eggs, and burger. Whatever Sheela liked, Christal could just about be assured that the famous actress' spice cabinet didn't just consist of cayenne pepper, cumin, cilantro, and garlic like Christal's did.

Genesis Athena. The thought intruded, as if trying to lever itself into her mind. An image flashed: that bit of Manny de Clerk's foreskin. Christal was trying to force it away and concentrate on Canadian-friendly recipes when her eyes fell on the sausages in the meat cooler. Reddish and mottled—like a bloody tampon. Where in the hell had *that* come from?

She could hear her grandmother's voice, whispering encouragement from just beyond her perception.

"What is it, Grandmother? What are you trying to tell me?"

Christal stopped short, a coldness washing through her as her brain made the curious connection. Foreskin? The mottling on a tampon? *Tissue!*

Menstrual blood contained bits of tissue from the sloughing uterine lining. And what was razor scuzz but bits of skin and beard hair? *Tissue!*

Sandra Bullock's hankies and toothbrush? They'd be loaded with cells. Some from the nose, others the delicate cheek cells inside the mouth. Just like Julia Roberts' sheets—full of skin cells and hair scuffed off by friction as she slept.

They'd taken a more direct and blunt approach with Pitt and Jolie. They'd chopped a piece out of Brad's butt, and pulled Angelina's hair out by the roots—and collected their tissue samples!

She could sense the answer, just beyond her grasp, like the

perfumed hint of flowers born on a summer night's breeze. She thought of Sheik Amud Abdulla. What did a man who was obsessed with control and power do with bits and pieces of other people's bodies? Power was the key, wasn't it?

What does a witch do with the pieces he collects?

"He uses them to gain more power and control," she mused aloud as she passed the processed meats and picked a small frozen turkey out of the freezer. She'd bet that Sheela hadn't had a stuffed turkey dinner any time recently.

What kind of power would a man like Abdulla seek?

"Wealth," she answered. "But how does he get more wealth from pieces of other people's bodies? How does he sell that to others? And better yet, what kind of control does he achieve?"

And therein lay the rub.

Nevertheless, Christal smiled as she walked the aisles. She had it! She could feel the rightness of it. Abdulla accrued the wealth and control, and Genesis Athena was the vehicle through which he did it.

But how? Why did the questionnaire screen out people like Christal? Who was it meant to pass? And why?

When she picked that final lock, the whole thing would fall into place. She tossed a small sack of pine nuts into the basket for stuffing, then added black rye bread. She'd make Sheela a stuffed turkey like she'd never had before.

It wasn't ransom. None of the celebrities would pay to get their bits of tissue back. Nor had any demands been made. So, what did Abdulla get? What was the prize contained within those often-microscopic bits of flesh?

DNA.

But they'd thought of DNA. Considered it, and abandoned it. Abdulla could have obtained his samples at minimal risk. With ludicrous ease, actually. Evidence recovery teams recovered DNA every day from crime scenes all across the country. People left DNA everywhere they went. Instead of swiping Sheela's tampon in that ridiculously involved sham in the ladies' room, Copperhead could have waited, and simply stolen Sheela's champagne flute when she set it down. A moderately competent technician could have recovered more than enough cells from the smear on the glass to develop a complete DNA profile.

"So, why grandstand?" Christal mused. What could be gained by taking such terrible risks? The smallest of mistakes could have landed Copperhead and Mouse in the can. Then the whole thing would have been compromised.

"Or would it?" She frowned as she rolled her cart to the checkout and began placing items on the conveyor for the checker. It wasn't like the police could have held either Copperhead or Mouse for more than a night until they made bail for trespass. They could have claimed it was a prank gone wrong, apologized, paid the fines and restitution, and walked.

Christal swiped her credit card and wheeled her load of plastic sacks out into the warm night. The sky was glowing a yellowish brown. The Los Angeles Basin, it seemed, never experienced true darkness. *And I am just starting to see the light!*

Christal slipped behind the wheel, a giddy thrill running through her. It was all coming clear. Sheik Abdulla was a witch, all right. Just a different kind of witch than the ones she had grown up hearing about. He, too, wanted souls to control. It was only the way of it that eluded her.

She turned on the map light and pulled the small blue notebook from her purse. Steadying it on the steering wheel, she began jotting down the basics. God, it was all coming together. And in a moment of epiphany, she had it!

Why hadn't anyone expected this? It was the logical next step given the leaps and bounds in which genetics and biotech had been evolving.

She scanned the notes, thinking back to the expression on Sheela's face that night they'd stolen her tampon. At the end of her list, she printed one last haunting question before jamming her notebook partially into her purse.

"I'm going to get you," she promised as she slipped the big Chrysler into drive and headed for her apartment. "By the time Sheela leaves on Sunday, Mr. Sheik, I'm going to have you by the *cojones.*"

30

L
ymon caught up with Sheela's limo as it turned onto
Coldwater Canyon. He pulled up beside the driver's
window and gave Paul a thumbs-up. Against the reflection of
the lights on the car's glass, he could barely make out Paul's
nod and grin.

Glancing behind, Lymon couldn't see anything out of the
ordinary in the traffic. Switching lanes, he maneuvered to
the car's right side and stayed even with Paul as they slowed
for a red light. He rolled to a stop across from the right rear
passenger door and looked over expectantly. Even before the
stretched Cadillac came to a complete stop, Sheela opened
the door, stepped out, helmet on her head, and slammed the
door shut behind her. In a flash, she was on behind Lymon,
her arms tight about his middle.

"Let's go!" she cried, glee filling her voice.

When the light turned, Lymon waved at Paul and rolled
the throttle, letting the big Indian bellow as he pulled away.
He signaled, pulled into the right lane, and turned off on a
side road. "Want to go straight to Christal's, or ride for a
while?"

She was laughing, the little-girl sound of it filling his soul
with joy.

"God, Lymon! I'm really doing this! I feel free! Free,
free, free!" She whooped, raising her arms to the night and
jiggling the bike.

"Hey! Let's not wreck us in the process, all right?"

"God, no! This is too good to be true!" She snugged her
arms around him and squeezed the breath out of him. "I
want to ride for a while. But we do have to go by Christal's
first. I told her I'd be there at around eleven. She'll worry if
we don't check in."

"Right." Lymon flicked the turn signal and bent them into
a turn, heading around the block and back toward Christal's.

"Hey," Sheela said as she leaned her chin on his shoulder.

"Hey," he answered gently.

"It was really good to see you pull up alongside, Lymon. When Christal told me to stow my helmet and leathers in the limo, I was just hoping against hope."

He sighed. "Yeah, well, I'm an accomplice now. Rex will skin me alive if ever figures this out."

"Rex can go screw himself," Sheela muttered. "I don't know, Lymon, should I fire him?"

"He's the best in the business."

"At what price?" she wondered. "When I talked to him this afternoon, he hinted that I might want to think about changing security firms. He said you stiffed him for another ten thousand in your bill."

"Yeah, and I'll bet he didn't tell you I ate five thousand of the twenty the IRS hit me for. I divided it with you since part of the fault was Rex's for prepaying me last month. He didn't think of what that would make the quarterly earnings look like. If I'm down at the end of this quarter, you'll get the benefit then, too."

"Do we have to talk business?"

"No." He signaled for a left and slowed to wait out traffic at the entrance to Christal's Residence Inn. At the first break in the oncoming cars, he slipped the clutch and pulled into the lot, aware of a Porsche hot on his heels. He noticed that the sleek car pulled into the registration space and a young man leapt out, watching the Indian as Lymon rounded the end of the speed bump and idled toward Christal's.

People noticed the Indian. It was unique, with the styled fenders and the huge engine. People didn't walk up to it thinking it was just another Harley.

He started to pull into the space before Christal's, then noticed the van, its side door open. A knot of people were hurrying down the walk, a limp-looking body propped in their midst.

"What the hell?"

"It looks like someone had one too many to drink," Sheela said as Lymon slowed and put a foot down.

The bike dropped into its loping idle, shaking beneath

him as he watched. They were loading the person into the door. Lymon saw a swaying of hair. Something about the woman's slim form . . .

"Hey!" He let the clutch out, rolling forward. "What the hell's going on here?"

A man turned, tall, blond-headed. He looked handsome in the glow of the sodium lights. "Nothing that's your business. My wife just drank a little too much, that's all."

Lymon eased to a stop several feet from the van, craning his head to see inside. He could feel Sheela tense behind him. "Christal?" he called.

His only warning was a blur as the man leaped, caught him on the shoulder with both hands, and tumbled Lymon, Sheela, and the Indian onto the pavement.

Lymon's body slammed hard, his helmet cracking loudly against the asphalt. He got his hand under him, pushing up, only to feel the weight of the Indian trapping his calf and foot.

"Son of a bitch!" He heard an engine roar, looked up past the bike, and saw the van careen back, lurch to a stop, and then squeal the tires as it rocketed ahead, hammered the speed bump, and screeched into the night.

"Sheela? Are you all right?"

"Fine." She was wiggling behind him. "Shit! What happened?"

He flopped like a trapped fish, got a hand up to press the chicken switch on the handlebar, and heard the big twin chug to a stop. "Someone just took Christal." He threw himself desperately against the weight of the big motorcycle. "I don't fucking believe it!"

"Hang on," Sheela muttered. "I've about got my foot loose."

Lymon turned his head at the sound of footsteps. He could see the young man running across from the registration building. He held a big blocky camera before him, stopping to shoot a couple of quick pictures before saying, "Hey, shit! Sheela Marks! What a hit!" Then he lifted the camera to shoot another couple of frames.

* * *

Friday night in the summer was always a busy time at the police station in Beverly Hills. This one was no exception. Lymon barely managed to keep a shackled drunk from puking on Sheela as they made their way down the hallway.

The interview room they had been taken to was off a hallway, soundproofed, and apparently wired for sound. The room, painted off-white, wasn't more than ten by eight with the proverbial one-way mirror framed into one wall. A thick and heavy metal table dominated the center; each leg had been bolted securely to the cement floor. The cubicle felt decidedly cramped with six people in it.

"I don't get it," Lymon growled as he shifted from foot to foot. To Sheela he looked like a caged lion. Something in the set of his face, in the rage behind his eyes, both fascinated and repelled her. Her own adrenaline was still rushing through her veins like a tonic.

Two uniformed cops sat on the other side of the battered gunmetal gray table and stared uneasily at Sheela where she leaned against the far wall. In reply, she stared back.

The paparazzo, a freelance photographer named Marc Delangelo, glowed; while his girlfriend, Jennifer Schmidt, looked sheepish as they sat in two of the plastic chairs.

"I got it all." Marc was beaming. "I mean, I ran half a roll of those people carrying that woman to the van."

"It's dark," Hurley, one of the cops, protested.

"It's an IR camera, man," Marc cried as he tapped a finger on the heavy camera resting on the table. "I don't need flash, get it? I can shoot in any light."

The second cop—Randisi, according to his tag—said, "Look, you've got no proof that this Christal Anaya was abducted. These might have been friends of hers who were taking care of her."

"She was new to town," Lymon replied. "She didn't have friends here."

"Yes, she did," Sheela interjected. "She had me!" A fire

was burning within her. "And she had you, Lymon. Then there's that FBI agent."

"Sid Harness. But he's in Washington."

"FBI?" Randisi asked.

"A mutual friend." Lymon was grinding his teeth.

Sheela pushed off the wall and stepped over. "Look, Officer, maybe she wasn't abducted. We'll have a better idea when we process Mr. Delangelo's film."

"Hey, it's *my* film! My personal property. Protected under the First Amendment."

"It may be evidence," Hurley corrected.

Sheela felt her blood begin to boil as she turned on the photographer. "What's it worth to you? Huh? I'll give you fifty thousand right now. Sight unseen. Hell, you might have left the lens cap on. Forgot to put film in the camera. Who knows?"

Delangelo swallowed hard. "Seventy-five thousand."

"Bullshit!" Lymon exploded, wheeling around.

The look in his face sent a cold shiver down Sheela's spine. She raised a hand, blocking him. "Easy, Lymon. Take a breath."

He did, keeping the maniacal rage from boiling over. She looked past him at the two cops. She could read their expressions: wary, as if sensing the stakes and unsure who to finger for the coming explosion.

"Gentlemen," Sheela said professionally, "I would appreciate it if your crime scene people could go over Ms. Anaya's apartment. I realize that you might have budget concerns, but if you will call your chief, I believe I can find some sort of reasonable compensation for the department."

The two cops glanced at each other, and Randisi made a slight tilt of the head. Hurley stood, nodded, and let himself out into the hall.

Lymon was thinking now; she could see it. He said, "You've got a file on Christal. She pressed charges a couple of weeks ago during the Manuel de Clerk thing. She identified the same woman at de Clerk's who took Ms. Marks' tampon at the Regent Beverly Wilshire. If I were you, I think I'd start there."

Randisi watched them through half-lidded eyes, his fingers tapping on the statements they had just signed.

"Hey, I'm outta here," Delangelo muttered, "Come on, Jennifer."

"You'll leave when I tell you to," Sheela barked, using her stage voice. "I'm not done with you."

"Bullshit!" Delangelo cried. "I'm sitting on the biggest shot of my life here."

Sheela walked up to stare into his eyes. "What if I told you there was more here than the simple abduction of a security agent? What if I told you that you're sitting on the biggest story of the decade?"

"Are you shitting me?"

"Oh, it's not Nine/eleven, or Afghanistan, or Iraq, but it's some-thing that could make your career. If you're interested, you'll play ball. If not, I'll write you a check for seventy-five thousand for that camera right now."

He hesitated, frowned, and she read him like a comic book. He didn't even have complicated illustrations.

"This is bullshit."

"No bullshit," Sheela replied. "You in or out?"

Delangelo glanced at Jennifer, who was shaking her head no. He licked his lips, the frown line deepening in his forehead. "Seventy-five thou? No shit?"

"Done." Sheela stuck out her hand. "Rex will have a check for you in the morning. Security will let you through." She reached for the camera.

"Hey." Randisi gestured at the camera. "That's not leaving this room until I say it is."

Sheela tossed him the heavy camera. "How long will it take your people to develop infrared film?"

He caught it by instinct and grunted as the weight rocked him back in his chair. "We can have it in a couple of hours if it's a rush."

"It's a rush," Lymon said, leaning over the table to stare into Randisi's eyes.

* * *

Hank stared down at Christal's bound body and wondered how it had all gone so wrong. The van slowly worked its way through the desultory late-night traffic. He rode in the back, seated on one of the benches while April held his hand. Her fingers were drawing designs on his palm. Something about her excited him in a way that no other woman ever had. She was mixture of dare, challenge, and sensuality. Hell, she was Sharon Stone in *Basic Instinct*. Hank had never understood that character until he looked into April's saucy gaze and saw her soul sway with his.

He needed only to close his eyes and his dick began to tingle. Images of their afternoon lovemaking replayed in his head. He could see her golden body, so perfect, rising and falling sinuously as she held his wrists down. When she'd come, her breasts had tightened, straining at the air. In that instant his body had exploded with a pulsing orgasm that left him bucking under her weight with every nerve on fire.

So, does it matter? We've got Christal. She'll talk. That's all we want. Just a little talk.

He turned to smile at April, his guilt assuaged, and then he looked down at Christal, remembering another night, another van. That time, he'd lain atop her. He remembered moaning when he came. Remembered her tightening around him to make it better. How were they supposed to know they were being recorded? That a few days later, surrounded by his colleagues, he would watch his bare buttocks rising and falling in a black-and-white nightmare. The camera angle had recorded Christal's face when she finally came, had caught her open mouth, her eyes closed in delight and her throat working as pleasure pulsed through her.

As he stared down in the dimly lit van, her slack expression reminded him of that night.

We just want to talk. He swallowed. *Yeah, sure.*

Shit, what had he done? He glanced at April, words of

protest rising, only to be blunted and fall away in confusion as she leaned over to kiss him on the lips.

The plan had worked like proverbial clockwork at the Residence Inn. He had watched Christal climb the steps a little before eleven that night. Three plastic bags of groceries hung from her hands. Slipping them onto her left arm, she had fished her key out of her purse, slid it into the lock, and walked into her apartment.

Hank had stepped out the door of the opposing unit and had been right behind her, his presence as a blocker unnecessary. Christal had flipped on the lights and walked into her room. It was only when she turned to close the door that he had seen the surprise in her eyes.

"Hank?"

"We've got to talk," he told her, stepping in and shutting the door behind him. He watched the sudden anger in her face and raised his hands, distracting her as Neal walked up from behind on crepe-soled shoes.

"We've got nothing to talk about." Christal's hands knotted on her grocery bags. Some thought flashed in her eyes, an understanding that something was dreadfully wrong. She started to turn when Neal reached out and pulled her back. As she started to scream, he had neatly inserted a syringe into her neck and depressed the plunger.

"What is that stuff?" Hank asked, worried for the first time.

"Just a little oil for the system." Neal back-heeled Christal to the couch, keeping one hand pressed over her mouth as she bucked in his strong arms. The grocery bags tumbled to the floor. The turkey made a hollow thump. Cans and bottles rolled across the white vinyl. Her purse bounced off the corner of the couch and spilled open.

April and Gretchen stepped out into the main room, each smiling down at Christal. "Got you at last, bitch," Gretchen snarled. She drew back a foot for a kick.

April stopped her, saying, "Not now." She glanced at Hank, praise in her gray eyes. "Nice work, Hank. She never suspected a thing. You're good."

He glowed at the compliment. "Glad to be of service."

Christal's struggles had gone weak, rage draining from her dark eyes to be replaced by a dreamy look. Neal took his hand from her mouth and looked down at the blood welling on his palm. "She bit me."

"Hope you've had your shots," April chided.

Hank stared. Christal's face had gone slack, blood on her lips. "Must have hurt like hell."

"Not the worst I've ever gotten." Neal walked over to the sink, found the paper towels, and began dabbing at his hand.

April leaned down, staring into Christal's eyes. "We're from Genesis Athena."

Hank saw the change in Christal's face.

"Ah, you know," April said in a friendly voice. "That's why you went to Colorado, isn't it?"

Christal blinked and frowned, as if having trouble following the conversation.

"Do you know what Genesis Athena is?"

"Yes," Christal murmured. "You're . . . witches. . . ."

April laughed at that. "Do you know what we're doing?"

Christal blinked hard, made a face, and said, "You're stealing souls."

April patted her kindly on the shoulder. "Oh, we're stealing more than that." Then she straightened. "All right, let's get her to the van."

"The van?" Hank asked, surprised. "You said you wanted to talk to her."

April walked up to him, her slender fingers arranging his collar. "We do, but not here. We need someplace a little more private."

"Jesus, do you know what you're playing with? One wrong move and you're involved in felony abduction!"

She turned, asking, "Christal, if we give you some answers, will you come with us?"

Christal blinked, seemed to be struggling with the question, and slowly nodded.

April's eyes illuminated as she turned back to Hank. "There, see? You can't abduct a willing participant. It's that easy."

And it had been, right up to the moment the lone motorcycle had pulled up. He'd looked, half expecting the silver bullet-looking thing that Bridges rode, but had seen instead some sort of sleek cruiser with two riders. Hank had never been big on motorcycles, and this one had picked a lousy time to rumble up.

"Do you think the guy on the bike is going to be trouble?" Hank asked as he glanced back over his shoulder at the traffic.

"Nah," Neal called from the front seat. "It'll be days before anyone comes looking for Anaya. It's not like the guy got a good look at me. For the moment he thinks he pissed some guy off by sticking his nose where it didn't belong."

"You know," Hank reminded, "I made my living in the Bureau interviewing people like the guy on that bike. Between him and the woman, they could put together a pretty good picture of what happened."

"Hank," April whispered, "trust us. We're good at this. If a problem crops up, we'll solve it. We're not doing anything illegal."

He started to say something, aware of the weight of Christal's body at his feet, but April had reached over, her hand slipping along his thigh to send tingles through his penis. "For later." Her whisper deepened. "Trust me, you'll never regret it."

Hank closed his eyes and nodded, trying to keep from moaning as her fingers found him through the soft fabric of his pants. In that state, he wasn't looking out the window as they drove into the private airport.

31

In his dreams, Sid was sledding across sparkling blue Bahamian water. He rode some sort of engine-powered surfboard. Dreams were magical that way. His super surfboard didn't even need a surf. It just jetted across the crystal waves, a foamy wake washing behind. He kept looking over to the white beach backed by lush green trees. A woman stood there, her gaze fastened on him. She was a beauty with long black hair, sparkling obsidian eyes—her perfectly tanned body covered only by a skimpy yellow bikini. Sid grinned, and waved, angling the surfboard toward her, knowing that paradise lay there, just across that short stretch of water. As he neared, she reached up, slipping the straps of her bikini from her brown shoulders and—

The phone rang loudly. The dream shredded and left Sid clawing for the nightstand. He jerked around in his bed. Bits of beach, sun, water, and girl drained away as he fumbled for the receiver and rasped, "Yeah?"

"Sid? It's Lymon."

"Fuck! It's . . . uh, five in the morning!" He got one eye half focused on the digital alarm clock beside the bed.

"It's about Christal. . . . She's been kidnapped."

"What?" Sid sat up, aware of Claire groaning as she rearranged her pillow and curled away from him. "Who'd kidnap Christal?"

"There was a paparazzo there. He got pictures. A whole roll of them. It's a bunch of people loading Christal into a van. She looks drugged, drunk, or otherwise not herself. Oh, and Sid?"

Sid ran a hand over his face. "Yeah?" His mind was staggering, trying to comprehend through the cobwebs of sleep. He kept stumbling over how nonsensical it sounded.

"One of the guys manhandling her into the van is Hank Abrams."

Lymon rode his big Indian into the circular drive fronting Sheela's house and pulled to a stop behind Tony's Z8 BMW. Rex's red Ferrari squatted like a menacing wedge at the edge of the steps.

"Well," Lymon quipped as he kicked the sidestand out and turned off the ignition, "the Bobbsey Twins are here."

"Right! Just what I need after the last twenty hours." Sheela straightened a leg and stepped off before she began fiddling with the D rings on her helmet. "Maybe they're busy at the pool and we can sneak in without them knowing. We'll tiptoe up to my room and crash."

"After what we've been through, do you think you could sleep?"

"Sleep? In the classical sense? No. But I'm going to fall face-first onto the floor if I don't lie down." She lifted her helmet off and shook her head to free her braid. Her face looked lined and gray, making her appear ten years older than she was. "God, I'm worried sick, and I don't think I've ever felt his exhausted and wrung out."

At that moment, Rex Gerber opened the front door.

"Trick or treat," Lymon said softly as he stepped off the bike and undid his own helmet. He could feel the heat in Rex's gaze as he followed Sheela up the steps. Something in the man's look reminded him of the time he'd got an under-aged date back to her father's house two hours after midnight. On irate impulse, Lymon said, "Hi, Dad," as he passed Rex.

"Yuck it up, asshole," Rex muttered. Then he turned to Sheela, who stepped into the coatroom and hung up her helmet and leather jacket. "Sheela, can I have a word with you."

It surprised Lymon when she whirled, a finger spearing toward Rex's face. "I'm not up for your bullshit right now, Rex. Someone kidnapped Christal last night."

Rex backed away from the finger, frowned, and then blinked. "What?"

"You heard me. Lymon and I saw it." She reached back and began pulling her hair out of the French braid. "We've got pictures."

"Kidnapped?" Rex repeated.

"Someone got into her apartment last night and carried her away. We've spent the whole night alternately talking to the police and the FBI. Like I said, we've got it on film. And Rex, you're going to love this. The woman that Christal calls Copperhead, the one that sliced a chunk out of Manny's dick and copped my tampon? She's there. So is the mousy one, the one Christal said was called Gretchen. The paparazzo that snapped the pictures was using a really good infrared film."

"You're not kidding?"

"Sorry, Rex." Lymon set his helmet on the foyer's marble table. "It's as real as it gets."

Rex seemed to mull over the words, then nodded to himself. "Well, I'm sorry to hear that. I liked her. Lymon, I hope you get her back."

"That's it?" Lymon asked, propping his hands on his hips.

"Well, she's your employee. I don't see where this should involve Sheela."

"But it does," Sheela shot back. "I hired her. I made that decision that day in the meeting room. We sent her after the people who tried to mug me in the hotel in New York. Then she stumbled over them at the Wilshire, and again at Manny's. Now, it appears, she made them a little too nervous. She's in this mess because of me!"

Rex put out placating hands. "Yes, yes, all right. We'll put the best people we can on it. But Sheela, let's talk to Dot first, see what kind of spin we can put on this. There ought to be a way to make a win-win situation out of it."

Sheela blinked, wavered on her feet, and would have flown at Rex but for Lymon's restraining hand. He calmed her, saying, "Easy, Sheela."

Rex backpedaled, smiling. "Hey, I'm sorry. I didn't know it was so rough. All night with the police? The FBI? Damn, Sheela, I wish you would have called. I could have come down, lent my weight to—"

"Shut up, Rex. I'm tired. It's been a long two weeks, okay? When a guy named Delangelo shows up please have a check for seventy-five thousand for him. I bought his camera."

"Seventy-five thousand? *For a camera?*"

She waved him off, starting for the stairs, only to have Tony walk out of the main room, a script in his hand.

"Hey, cool! Sheela, babe, we gotta talk! I've been on the phone with Jerry. He *really* wants to spot you for *Giant*. You read the script, right? I mean, it cooks! I think you ought to jump on this, babe. It's got your fingerprints all over it."

"Tony," she muttered, "fuck off." She started up the stairs, then hesitated, looked back, and said, "Lymon? You coming?"

"Right behind you," he added, shooting Rex a neutral glance.

"What the hell's that all about?" Tony asked.

"Someone put the bag on Christal last night," Rex said. He sounded confused.

"Huh? What do you mean put the bag on?"

"As in kidnapped. You got that? Someone abducted Christal."

"No way!" Then a short pause, and Tony said, "Abducted? Seriously? Weird shit, man."

Lymon shook his head, following on Sheela's heels. At the top of the stairs, he glanced back. Tony had a deeply pensive expression, his brow furrowed as if processing unsettling information. The look in Rex's eyes barely veiled the anger and frustration seething within him.

Anger? Sure. Lymon seemed to have the inside track. But where had the frustration come from?

When he closed the bedroom door behind him, he stopped short, suddenly terribly unsure of himself. Where the hell was this leading? Sheela seemed completely oblivious to the way this was going to look to the folks downstairs as she called, "Lock the door."

Lymon found the latch and watched her as she collapsed onto the chaise and bent to pull her heavy boots off. After the last one thumped onto the floor, she stared at him, face haggard, eyes listless, her hands hanging limply from her knees. "I'm worn through, Lymon. I have nothing left. If I have to deal with one more crisis, no matter how small, I'm going to break down and bawl like a baby."

He walked over and offered his hand. "Come on, let's get you to bed."

Instead she lifted one leg suggestively. "These leather pants are a bitch. Pull."

He did, helping her to slide them off. Then she stood and began unbuttoning her blouse as she walked toward the rear. "Come on, Lymon. It's not the way I always dreamed of leading you to my bedroom. It was always supposed to be a romantic seduction with expensive cognac, candlelight, and soft music."

He followed her into her refuge, staring around at the beautiful furnishings. The room was soft, white, and large. Against one wall a fluffy canopy bed sported huge frilly pillows. The dressers held knickknacks and photos of her family and old friends. The only other star to be seen was Morgan Freeman. When Sheela saw him looking at it, she added, "He saved my life once. Talked me through a bad situation."

Sheela dropped her shirt on the floor and walked over to the bed. Her nimble fingers unplugged the cord from the back of the phone. She tossed one of the big pillows to the side and threw back the covers. Unabashed, she undid her bra and let it slip away before pulling an oversized T-shirt from a top drawer. She glanced at him as she pulled it on. "Are you as tired as I am?"

He shrugged. "I couldn't sleep. I'm too worried."

She crawled under the covers, patting the bed. "Come lie here beside me. Clothes on or off, I don't care. I just need you close, Lymon. I have to know you're here."

"Sheela, if I crawl in there . . ."

"It'll be like necrophilia," she replied, closing her eyes. "I won't feel a thing. I'll be asleep before you can pry my legs apart."

He frowned, kicked off his boots, and slid under the covers, feeling awkward in his clothes. It seemed sacrilege to be wearing street clothes while encased in her spotless white linens—but a whole lot safer than the alternative. A curious giddy feeling tightened at the base of his throat. The sheets were smooth, scented, and his hard body sank in the bedding.

She made a purring sound. "Promise me you'll stay close?"

"I promise."

She snuggled against him, her hand slipping across his chest. He was remembering her body as she changed into her sleep shirt. She'd looked like a goddess. But an image of Christal wedged into his weary brain. Here he was, safe and comfortable beside the woman he loved. And Christal? Where was she? Scared? Frightened? To torment him, his imagination pictured her bound, gagged, as one man after another crawled on top of her naked body.

"She's my friend, Lymon," Sheela whispered, as if she shared his thoughts. "She never asked anything of me. She didn't want anything from me. Just you, and her, in the whole world."

"We'll find her," he said softly. "She's one of my people. I don't leave my people behind."

"Just hold me." Sheela pressed her body against him.

"I might embarrass myself," he said, kissing the side of her head.

"Lymon, I'm so tired, I'll never remember, but it's nice to know." A pause, then a sleep-softened, "I love you."

"I love you, too."

She was asleep that quickly.

Lymon lay there, painfully aroused, his heart thudding against his ribs. The woman he loved more than life lay beside him, her body heat stirring a sexual desire like he had never felt before. And that added guilt to his whirling thoughts. How could he feel like that while Christal was undergoing . . . what?

He blinked up at the ceiling, forcing himself to imagine Christal's face, wondering where she was.

Be safe, Christal. He swallowed hard. What would it be like if she wasn't? What if they found her body in a ditch somewhere out beyond San Bernardino? No one should die like that. Alone, frightened, degraded, and abandoned.

Sheela's breath purled on his cheek.

The shit's in the fire now.

32

In for a penny, in for a pound, Hank Abrams thought. Where had that saying come from? How many years had passed since anything worthwhile sold for a penny a pound? He looked down from the Gulfstream II's window. The Rocky Mountains were glowing in the morning light.

April slipped into the seat beside him. She flipped her

burnished red hair over her shoulder and gave him that challenging smile that made his blood race. "Neal and Gretchen are asleep in the front seats. Anaya's going to be out for at least another couple of hours." She pulled her muscular leg up, propping it on the seat back in front of her. "So, how's it feel to be in the six-figure salary bracket?"

He shot a look past her to where Christal lay propped uncomfortably across the aisle, her mouth hanging open. Drool had dried on her shirt. Her arms were bound to her body with silver duct tape. Her eyes, half-open and slightly dried, reminded him of a dead woman's, the stare empty.

"That's what she's worth? A hundred grand?"

April seemed to find that amusing. "Probably a lot more. The Sheik found her enchanting. He's got a thing for women. He's fascinated by blondes and redheads, but—I think it's something cultural—he just craters for a brunette."

"Wait a minute. You mean we stole Christal for . . . what? A harem?"

April twirled a long lock of hair, a knowing amusement in her eyes. "I like you, Hank. You really have a sense of indignation. A harem? No. At least, I doubt it. Maybe, if Anaya's into it, she might make a play for him. The Sheik's a little different. He's a watcher."

Hank swallowed hard. "You guys are white slavers? Is that it?"

She turned, leaning so her face was close to his. Her steely gray eyes were alive with excitement. "No. We're not going to hurt Anaya. We just need to find out what she knows. That's all. If she's not a threat, we'll take a sample, reimburse her for her time, fear, and inconvenience, and let her be on her way." She ran a finger along his temple. "God, what do you think we are?"

"I don't know. You tell me." He took her hand in his, pulling it down and folding it in his so she wouldn't remind him of his sexuality—or hers. "I think it's time you tell me just what Genesis Athena is all about."

April nodded. "That's how we drum up business. It's the hook that brings in the clients."

"Clients?"

April freed her hand and settled back in her seat. "What you became part of last night is one of the world's newest and potentially most profitable businesses. I told you, we don't do anything illegal."

"Just kidnapping and transportation across state lines. That's major jail time that we're into right now."

April shrugged. "Not if she's released with compensation. Like I say, the Sheik's interested in her."

"Yeah, so what? He watches her? Then gives her a couple of bucks and lets her go?" He snapped his fingers. "Just like that, Christal Anaya forgets she was lifted from her apartment and hauled across the country against her will?"

"Probably so." April watched him speculatively. "You see, we don't want her body. We just want her DNA."

"Excuse me?" Then it hit him. "That's what the little devices you gave me were for?"

"Uh-huh, and had she not tapped our phone service in Colorado, we'd have taken our sample, added her to our catalog, and she'd never have been the wiser."

"So, what do you do with the DNA? Patent her genetics?"

"Sometimes, yes, depending on different genes people have."

"I thought that was the province of biotech labs. That drug companies and things were filing those kinds of patents."

April leaned back and took a deep breath. Hank couldn't help but watch her breasts swell the fabric on her thin silk shirt. "You're thinking about US patents. Hank, there's a whole world out there. Genesis Athena is an international company. We have labs in the Persian Gulf, in Africa, Europe, and Australia. We even have a ship, a large—"

"*ZoeGen*," he whispered.

"That's right. You've been aboard. With the Sheik, right?"

"Uh-huh."

"So," she asked, "now that you're getting the idea, are you in, or out?"

"Why me?"

"You're Bureau trained. You did a good job with Anaya. We watched you. That was smart action on your part when she dropped everything and went to Toronto. Even smarter when you followed her to Colorado. Sometimes in multinational companies like ours, simple things are forgotten. We didn't think of putting a warning system in place in Colorado. Now, we're notified immediately if anyone walks in the door and starts asking questions about Genesis Athena. Finally, you were right about the planning at Anaya's. You handled her perfectly. She never knew what hit her. In short, if you decide to throw in with us, we think you'll be a formidable asset."

"And how does Verele fit in?"

"He's legit. His company provides security when we have people in New York. That's all. He doesn't ask questions; we don't speak out of turn."

Hank felt a fluttering in his gut. "So, what happens if I say yes?"

Her nose wrinkled with her smile. "I've been looking for a partner. Gretchen's good, but, you know, she's got issues. I like you, Hank. I think you've got potential. I mean, you were great in the sack. It's been a long time since I've made love with a man who wasn't intimidated by me."

"Besides great sex, what's it pay?"

"We receive fifty thousand a job plus royalties."

"Royalties?"

"Two percent of what the company makes per specimen. For Julia Roberts alone, Gretchen and I stand to make a couple million."

"What do you mean, Julia Roberts?"

"Remember when her sheets and trash were stolen? That was us. I did the parasail jump from the helicopter. We got plenty of good solid Roberts DNA out of her sheets and the tissues she used to wipe her makeup off."

"Jesus Christ!"

"We'd love to do him, too. Imagine what he'd be worth! The problem is finding a sample. And you've got to prove who he is. You know, people won't fork out that kind of money unless they know they're getting the real thing."

"Wow."

"The clincher is there's no law against taking another person's DNA for profit."

"Yeah, but there's a whole slew of laws against cloning. Not just in the US, but around the world."

"Not in Yemen," she reminded, "and certainly not on the high seas. That's what I meant when I said that we're not breaking any laws, strictly speaking." She jerked her head toward Christal. "And we'll make sure that she doesn't bear a grudge by the time we're through. Trust me on that."

Hank glanced unsurely at Christal. "And if I say no?"

"We ask you to sign a nondisclosure agreement, pay you a hundred grand for your silence, time, and consideration, and hope you'll think it over and change your mind. I'll be sure to give you a number where you can reach us."

He chewed his lip for a moment, aware of the challenge in her eyes. "So, how's Gretchen going to take you finding a new partner?"

April leaned close and kissed him. "She'll get over it."

"Uh-huh."

She traced her tongue around his ear. "When we get to the *ZoeGen* I've got a private cabin and a couple of weeks of vacation. It'll be like being on our very own cruise ship."

"I hate waiting that long."

She rose up in the seat, glancing forward. "You ever had sex at forty thousand feet?"

"Nope. The Bureau made us fly economy class. It's tough when you're folded into a center seat next to a little old lady."

She reached over and unbuckled his seat belt, pulling him after her. "Come on. There's a fold-down bed back here. We'll have to be quiet, but they'll be out for hours."

"Are you crazy?" he asked, glancing back at where Neal and Gretchen's heads were lolled two rows away.

"It's the only way to be." She led him back to the rear and folded down the little couch across from the tiny galley. Before he could protest again, she had his belt unbuckled, his pants unsnapped, and his fly down.

April wrapped her long fingers around his stiffening penis. Her eyes were agleam, and her lips had parted in anticipation. His hands—of their own volition—began fumbling at the snap on her jeans, then shoved them down over her round hips. His heart hammered in his chest, breath hot and racing in his lungs. She clamped her mouth on his, her tongue flicking and teasing. He bit off a moan as her grip tightened painfully on his erection.

God, he had never known a woman like her.

Then they were on the cushions.

He was staring into her eyes, saw her pupils expand, dark and eternal, as his throbbing penis slid into her silky sheath. She shuddered, her muscular body arching as she tightened her vaginal muscles.

"Join us, Hank," she whispered.

"Yes. *God, yes!*" He gasped.

Lymon checked his watch. The digital numbers 2:16 flashed at him. He turned his head to see Sheela, curled on her side. Her red hair spooled over her pillow in a soft wave. She was sleeping hard enough that she didn't move as he slowly lowered his feet to the floor, picked up his shoes, and padded out to the anteroom. He closed the doors behind him before using the toilet in the dressing room.

He stepped into the hallway, glancing down toward the stairs, and saw no one. On silent feet he passed the paintings and sculptures and eased down the curving stairs.

"Lymon?" Rex's sharp voice barked as he walked over to the little marble-topped table and reached for his helmet.

"Yeah, Rex?" Lymon turned. Rex stood by the doorway that led through the parlor and out to the pool.

"You and I had better talk." Rex made a jerking movement with his head. "Not here. Outside. Just the two of us."

Lymon bit off a rueful smile, nodded, and followed Rex out to the poolside. There, Sheela's manager had set up camp. Melting ice cubes floated in a half-empty glass of scotch. Two scripts were piled atop each other, and file folders held copies of stapled contracts. Rex dropped onto one of the white lounge chairs. He waved to the chair across from him.

"She's still asleep?" Rex asked gruffly.

"Yeah. And, please, leave her alone. She needs the rest."

Rex's hard stare bored into his. "What are you doing, Lymon?"

"Taking care of my client."

"Really? Sneaking around so you can slip your dick into your client? Is that how you take care of her, Lymon?"

Lymon leaned forward, anger welling. "Rex, I'm going to tell you this once. I don't have sex with my clients. I never have, and I never will."

"Yeah, right." He threw a gesture toward the house. "What the hell just happened up there? You read Grimm's fairy tales to each other, made tea, and—"

"Do you have trouble with the English language, Rex? I told you, I do not have sex with my clients. Period."

Rex just stared at him like he was some kind of bug. "You're fucking fired. Get lost. I don't want you here anymore."

"That's not your decision."

"Lymon, I've told you before, you don't want to cross me. You don't want to put Sheela in the position of choosing between you and me. You'll lose, pal."

"Don't be an asshole, Rex." Lymon sat back in the chair. "I'm not playing this game. For the moment, I've got a bigger problem. One of my people was taken last night. Christal may not be anyone important to you, but she is to me. Now, if you're finished swinging your dick, I'm going to check on what they've found out about Christal, and what I can do."

Rex's flat stare didn't waver. "Stop the bullshit, Lymon. Oh, yeah, you're concerned, all right. Have any trouble getting it up while you were worrying about Christal? Or did that just make it all the more exciting?"

"You're a real shithead, Rex." Lymon pointed a hard finger. "And since you can't seem to understand that I could have just caught forty winks up there, here's how it lays out. If I ever . . ." He shook his head. "Forget it. It's none of your business." He got to his feet. "I've got things to do."

"Lymon!" Rex called from behind him. "Lymon! Don't you walk out on me!"

Lymon shut the door behind him, nodding to Tomaso, who was coming toward him, another scotch on a tray. He said, "Sheela wants to rest. If Rex demands to see her, tell him to go to hell. You got that?"

Tomaso, generally so very in charge of himself, started. "Sir?"

Lymon gave him a pat on the shoulder. "Just do it, all right? If you don't, he's going to kill her."

Tomaso's dark eyes held his for a moment, and he finally nodded. "Yes, sir."

"Good." Lymon made his way through the house, out past the foyer table, where he collected his helmet, and into the yard. Afternoon light cast a yellow glow through the trees as he pulled his cell phone from his pocket, turned it on, and punched the number for the West LA station handling Christal's case.

Come on, Christal, let them tell me you've been found safe and are at the station giving a statement.

But she wasn't. The police had nothing to report.

33

Sid was starting to think he'd been taken for a ride. The cabdriver he'd hired at LAX didn't speak English. Sid didn't speak Spanish. He hadn't remembered that it took so long to get from the airport to Wilshire Boulevard. But then, he'd been riding with Christal last time, sharing conversation, laughing, enjoying the odd moments of just looking at her and thinking how pretty she was.

This time he was in the back of the cab, his suitcase propped under one arm, while traffic moved, stopped, and moved again. The slightly pungent tang that periodically rose up from the floorboards suggested that the greasy-looking stain between his shoes must have had its origins inside a human digestive tract. When he rolled the window down, all he could smell was traffic. And the Mexican cab-driver called back that he was doing something to the *frio,* whatever that was.

Sid tried to think about other things.

So, it was with relief that the cab finally took a left onto Wilshire, proceeded another three blocks, and pulled up at the curb beside a fire hydrant.

"Estas aquí," the driver told him. *"¿Es el número, no?"* He pointed at the address on a jewelry shop window.

"Yeah, we ought to be three doors down." He hoped he was right. Lymon had taken him in the back way. The obnoxious odor rising from the floor made his decision for him. He forked out the thirty-five bucks, opened the back door, and hung his travel bag over his shoulder. As the cab pulled away, he took stock of the sidewalk, then started down the block. Not every business had a number over the door, but Sid had the general idea.

LYMON BRIDGES ASSOCIATES was printed in block letters on a sign screwed into a brick wall. Sid sighed with relief, opened the aluminum-clad glass door, and thumped his way up the wooden steps. At the top he opened a security door and stepped into Lymon's office. He could smell coffee, the odor of wood and dust, and the slight mustiness of carpeting.

June's fortress of a desk stood empty, its surface cluttered with a computer screen and keyboard, a blotter, a stand of pens and pencils, telephone, and all the other impedimenta of a good cleric.

Soft voices were coming from the rear. Sid dropped his bag on the leather-upholstered couch beside the door and walked past June's desk.

He found Lymon's office occupied. Lymon himself sat behind the desk. June was half-perched on one corner, staring down at the computer monitor. Another guy, a darkly complected, fit-looking young man, lounged in Lymon's office chair. They all looked worried as they glanced up.

"Sid?" Lymon cried in surprise, rising to his feet.

"What's the matter with you? Don't you check your machine?" Sid asked. "I called just before my flight left DC."

He got a good look at Lymon's face, seeing the stress. "What's the news?"

"Nothing," Lymon answered, then gestured around. "I think you know everyone here but Salvatore."

"Sid Harness," he said, taking the man's hand and feeling the bundled strength implied by the grip.

"My pleasure. I've heard a lot about you."

Sid jabbed a thumb in Lymon's direction. "He lies."

Salvatore grinned. "Then so does Christal. She told the same stories."

"What are you doing here?" Lymon asked, coming around the desk. "How did you get here?" He looked puzzled. "Why?"

Sid shrugged. "It's Saturday. I've got a slew of annual leave coming. I thought you might need a little help on this end. Having a tame FBI guy in the closet can be helpful." He scuffed his toe for effect. "And on top of all that, Christal's my friend."

A knowing smile molded Lymon's lips. "Yeah, I thought so. You eaten?"

"Not on airplanes these days. I grabbed a donut at the Winchell's down the block from my house. That was a little before seven this morning."

Lymon turned to June. "Call Al's. Have him make up a to-go order of burgers." He looked at Salvatore.

"I'm on it, boss." The muscular man rose to his feet, nodded to Sid, and stepped out.

June picked Lymon's phone off the cradle and tapped numbers by memory.

"What happened?" Sid asked as June spoke carefully into the phone.

"Here're the photos. Take a look for yourself." Lymon led him to a work table in the office's back corner.

As Lymon narrated the events, Sid fingered the photos. Each had that slightly off color of an infrared shot. The image quality was remarkably good. The guy taking the photos had started with a party walking down the sidewalk. Sid could see a figure being carried. From the postures, Christal was completely limp. Alive, or dead? He couldn't tell.

The series of photos led to an open van door, then pulled back, showing a motorcycle pulling up.

"You and Ms. Marks?" Sid asked.

Lymon nodded. "Sheela was going to spend the weekend with Christal."

"Huh?"

"It's complicated."

Sid read the look in Lymon's eyes, let it go, and flipped through the rest of the photos. The most telling was of a tall man shoving Lymon and Sheela over, while in the background, a familiar face was caught full-on. Hank Abrams had been in the process of dragging Christal's limp body into the van, but had looked up in time to see the man push Lymon's bike over. Hank's expression reflected worry and distress.

"What do you think?"

Sid thumbed through the rest as the van motored off. "Is that a license number?"

"Yeah, a Ryder rental. The local FBI is working on it."

Sid tapped the stack of photos against his palm. "How'd you get all this?"

Lymon chuckled, tension in his voice. "Sheela did it. She managed to enlist the service of the paparazzo who shot this. Look, it was just fortuitous. The guy caught on that Sheela was doing something, tailed us, and took these photos."

"What?"

Lymon's shadowed eyes held no humor. "It's how people live out here, Sid. Sheela wanted time to relax. She talked Christal into letting her spend the weekend in her hotel room. We just happened to ride in at the right moment to see it all happening."

"You're sure it's Christal these guys were after? Maybe they got wind of it, thought they were getting Sheela?"

Lymon bent and picked up a gaudy green flyer. Sid took it and unfolded the paper. The big letters jumped out at him. "Genesis Athena." Looking up, he asked, "You think that's what this is all about?"

Lymon crossed his arms, glanced at June, and shrugged. "It's the best we've got."

"Why?"

"Answer that, my friend, and we'll know what Christal was on the verge of discovering."

"What about Hank?" Sid asked.

"I called his boss this morning. Verele says he knows nothing about any kidnapping. According to him, Hank is no longer in his employ. He says he took a position with a client."

"Sheik Amud Abdulla?" Sid said, remembering. "You believe that?"

"Look, I know Verele. Verele Security isn't into breaking the law. My take is that Genesis Athena offered Abrams a better deal. I think the good Sheik just lifted Christal. Did she tell you about the first time he saw her?"

"About that night in New York? A little. I did some research for her."

"We know." He tapped a file folder that lay closed on the desk. "Genesis Athena. What is it, Sid? What's the Sheik doing? Why'd he grab Christal? What did she discover that scared them so?"

Sid could feel June's probing gaze as she studied him. He shrugged, glancing at the woman. Lymon had a thing about surrounding himself with attractive women. "You got me, cowboy. I just ran some stuff through the computer." He heard the rear door open and close down the hall. Salvatore had been really fast. "She faxed me some papers, a questionnaire. I had the psych guys down at Quantico look at it. They thought it was a test of some sort. A sort of psychological evaluation."

"To evaluate what?" a fine contralto asked from behind him.

Sid wheeled, and stared into the most bewitching blue eyes he'd ever seen. They pinned him like a study moth, and it took his floundering mind a moment to realize that he knew that perfect face. Had seen it staring down at him with rapt wonder from the screen.

"Jesus Christ," he mumbled.

"Not even close." The goddess was offering her hand. "I'm Sheela Marks. And you are?"

"Sid Harness," Lymon called from behind when Sid's words failed him. "He's a very dear and very old friend."

Sid swallowed hard, managed to shake Sheela Marks' hand, and watched as Lymon pushed past, a frown on his face.

"What's happened?" Sheela asked.

"What are you doing here?" He looked past her to the tall handsome man who waited in the hallway. "Hello, Paul."

"Mr. Bridges," the man replied respectfully.

And then Sheela Marks put her hands on Lymon's shoulders, looking into his eyes. "Lymon, I have to know what's happened. Have the police called? The FBI? They won't talk to me, but I know that you have connections."

"Nothing, Sheela. Not a word. No one has called here or even to her mother in New Mexico, for that matter." He seemed to harden. "She might have just dropped off the face of the earth."

Sid could feel the electricity flowing between them, could read the body language. For a long moment they looked into each other's eyes, and then Sheela Marks said, "I have to find her, Lymon. No matter what it takes."

Gray dreams began to shred, giving way to a terrible sweetly metallic taste that clung to Christal's dry tongue. She shifted, vaguely aware that her body had the gritty feel of numbed cotton. A faint ache lurked behind her eyes. For the moment, it was fine to lie in the safe grayness, hanging halfway between wakefulness and the fragments of fleeing dreams. Some voice deep within urged her to surrender to the dream again. Fall back into the mist of unconsciousness. It would be so much easier that way.

Easier? Than what? A slippery premonition goaded her to blink. A white haze glared when she flicked her gritty eyelids. The fluffy muzziness in her brain refused to give way to thought.

She pulled her hand up, hearing it rasp across linen. Rubbing her eyes, she blinked again. Shit, was she hungover?

Her tongue moved dryly, and swallowing was almost impossible. The first saliva tasted foul—really foul.

She made a face.

Pushing with rubbery muscles, Christal sat up, aware that she wore only panties and a brassiere. Her glazed vision had trouble coming into focus, so she massaged her rheumy eyes with her palms until she could make out the small white room. Her new cosmos consisted of a solid metal door, a table with a plastic drinking glass and water pitcher, a round window, and her bunk. A smaller wooden door led where? To a closet?

"What the . . . ?" She struggled with her brain. Thought seemed to be such a flexible problem. *Where the hell am I?*

She pinched the bridge of her nose, trying to pin her mind in place. Home was the Residence Inn in west LA. She had been doing what? Getting ready for Sheela to come and stay the weekend with her.

She had been where? Headed home after doing some last-minute shopping. She could remember walking the supermarket aisles, selecting things to cook, things she thought Sheela might like to try.

Then, a faint memory stirred. First it was the emotional recollection of fear, and then the hazy images of Hank Abrams, his hands up, a pleading expression on his face as he glanced at something behind her shoulder. A hand had clapped over her mouth, dragging her back. The sting in her neck . . .

"God, where am I?" She swung her feet over the edge of the bunk and stared down. Her shoes were resting side by side on the gray-carpeted floor. Her clothes were neatly folded on a small nightstand at the head of the bed.

She swayed as she stood, bracing one hand against the cold wall, and felt unforgiving steel beneath. A hard rap with her knuckles confirmed the fact. Her slim brown fingers contrasted against the white paint.

Steadying herself, she turned to the round window and stared out in disbelief. The sun was either rising or setting, capping the waves with yellow, hollow troughs dark and rippling as the muscular swells rose and fell.

Shit! She was in the middle of the Pacific! On what? A ship? She pressed her nose to the glass, bending her face this way and that as she tried to see to either side. Endless water rolled off to the golden horizon.

She made a face as she poked and prodded her stomach and abdomen. Why the hell were her insides so tender? Taking inventory, she could see a bruise on the back of her hand. From what? An IV? Her arms and shoulders were sore. What the hell had they done? Dragged her like a corpse?

The effort of pulling on her pants almost tumbled her face-first onto the floor. Finding the sleeves in her blue blouse almost defeated her. Her coordination wasn't what it should be. She took a deep breath, stretching, feeling the dull ache in her muscles. Then she grabbed the handle on the metal door and twisted. Locked.

She glanced around, cocking her head. What the hell had Hank done to her? She tried the smaller door, opening it to find a compact toilet and sink.

She turned back and hammered on the big steel door with the flat of her hand, yelling, "Hey! Open this up!" The heavy portal seemed to suck up the worst of her violence.

She stopped, listening, as panic rose in her breast. She could only hear a faint humming, the noise that of distant engines.

"Hank! You asshole!" She hauled off and kicked the door, feeling a spear of pain in her foot.

How long did she stand there? Her room had grown dark. So the sun had been setting? Then she'd lost an entire day? Or had it been more? A terrible fear, like nothing she had ever known, slipped needles along her spine.

She had noticed the switch on the wall, pressed it, and was relieved when the recessed safety light in the ceiling came on. She tried the pitcher. It contained water. Gratefully she drank, aware of her dehydration. Then, opening the toilet door, she stepped in and relieved herself. Urinating proved uncomfortable enough that she checked for blood, and was relieved to find none. The bathroom wasn't much bigger than a phone booth. Outside of the sink a toilet paper dispenser was the only furnishing.

She stood, pulled up her pants, tried the sink, and was rewarded with hot and cold water.

"So, I won't die of thirst," she muttered before walking back to stare out the porthole at the darkness. She turned off the light to see better. Out there, on the ocean, she could see no lights, nothing but an endless darkness.

Swallowing hard, she whispered, "Dear God, I'm scared."

34

Given his name, Sean O'Grady should have had red hair, freckles, and mischievous green eyes. Instead the Bahamian native looked anything but Irish, with his smooth black skin, angular jaw, bony face, and African features. He had agreed to meet with Lymon and Sheela through Sid's intercession. The "tame FBI guy" was already proving his worth.

O'Grady and Harness sat across the booth from Lymon and Sheela. O'Grady had picked a Studio City Burger King for the meeting. The wreckage of the agent's dinner consisted of a Double Whopper wrapper, empty box of fries, and a soft drink cup, half-full, on the plastic tray.

Sid sipped at a cup of coffee and kept a notebook in his hand. Lymon and Sheela shared an order of fries, having eaten earlier. Sheela had dressed in stealth mode, wearing a loose Lakers T-shirt, faded jeans, sunglasses, and a scarf over her head. She looked more like a housewife than an internationally known film star.

"We got this," O'Grady said, reaching into the pocket of his coat to pull out a little blue spiral-bound notebook. "Recognize it?"

"Yeah . . . well, maybe," Lymon granted. "Christal used one that looked something like that."

O'Grady passed it across. "Flip through to the last page."

Lymon thumbed through the pages, seeing Anaya's neat script. He noted that true to her Bureau training, each notation recorded the place and time of her writings. The last page—dated as 22:15 hours on the date of her abduction—consisted of a series of quickly jotted notes under the heading "Genesis Athena."

He read: Genesis Athena. Athena sprang full-blown
            from the head of Zeus. Sheik didn't pick
            that from random. DNA is the key. He's the
            twenty-first-century version of the
            traditional Southwestern witch. But he is
            stealing more than just a person's soul—he
            wants it all. DNA from the rich and
            famous? What the old-time witches would
            have given for this technology!
            ?: If DNA is so easy to get, why make such
            a production of stealing it?
            ?: How much would an obsessed fan pay for
            a celebrity baby?
            ?: How do I break this to Sheela?

Lymon frowned, glanced at Sheela, and tried to decipher her pensive expression.

"That mean anything to you?" O'Grady asked. Sid had stood, stepping around the table to peer over Lymon's shoulder.

Under his breath, Lymon whispered, "Son of a bitch."

"What?" Sid asked, bending closer to stare at the page on the notebook.

"Where'd you find this?" Lymon tapped the notebook as he looked up.

"The floor. When the ERT went through Anaya's room at Residence Inn, it was under the couch along with a tube of lipstick. The only prints we've lifted off it are Anaya's. We went through her place from top to bottom. In the process we got a blood sample on a paper towel, a couple of smudged prints, several hairs, and some evidence from the registration desk that we're running down. Rubber from the scratch they laid in the parking lot matches the compound in the rental van's tires." He smiled. "Someone hosed the inside of that van down with bleach and a high-pressure system before they returned it. The credit card it was rented under led us to a PO box in Long Beach. Somebody named Lily Ann Gish had rented it."

"Lillian Gish," Sheela said softly.

"You know her?" Sid asked, slipping back into the booth beside O'Grady.

Sheela gave him a faint smile. "It's an alias. They're playing with us. Lillian Gish was one of Hollywood's first superstar actresses back in the black-and-white silent film days."

"Same name Copperhead gave Manny, wasn't it?" Lymon asked, trying to remember everything Christal had told him. He glanced at O'Grady. "You might check the police report. See if that matches."

O'Grady nodded, writing in his notebook. "That business in the notebook press any of your buttons? About the DNA, I mean?"

Sheela took a deep breath. "I can tell you how much an obsessed fan would pay for a celebrity baby."

"How much?" Sid asked.

"As much as they could leverage," she answered flatly. "People would mortgage their houses, sell their cars, take out all the loans they could." She turned her sunglasses on Sid. "Some would sell their souls, not to mention their bodies, and the very blood in their veins."

Sid frowned. "And the business about DNA?"

"Christal thinks the celeb hits were about stealing DNA," Lymon supplied. "But if you'll recall, we've had that conversation . . . and discarded it."

"Stealing . . . DNA?" Sid asked absently, his face tightening in that old expression Lymon knew so well. Damn it, he was onto something.

"The problem is," Lymon continued, "like Christal says in her notes, why go to the trouble and risks? You can steal someone's DNA without sticking your neck out. You want Sheela's DNA? Swipe the napkin off her table at Morton's when she's done with lunch."

"Do you think that's really it?" Sheela asked softly, her head lowered.

Lymon glanced around the table and shrugged. "Hell, I don't know."

"It's wild, but possible," Sid muttered, reading Sheela's deflated posture. "You'd be surprised what people can do with DNA these days."

"Like what?" O'Grady asked.

Sid made an open gesture with his hands. "I've been working a series of kidnappings. Geneticists. In the process I've had to learn something about the science. Some of the things they can do? You wouldn't believe it. Remember Dolly, the sheep? That was just the tip of the iceberg."

Sid had their attention, so he leaned back, one arm on the seat back. "Look, you've heard the bits and pieces on the news, right? Ted Williams being frozen? Those extinct marsupial wolves in Australia? The frozen mammoth in Japan? The news is always telling us about something. Remember the calf they cloned from a piece of steak? The jellyfish genes in the monkey?"

"Man, those are just animals!" O'Grady muttered derisively.

Sid gave him a flat look. "You think there's a difference between cloning a sheep and a human?"

"Well, it ain't the same thing! I mean, man, people are a whole lot more complicated than any sheep!"

Sid slowly shook his head. "That's your emotional reaction, Sean, not reality."

"Well, bro, you fill me in, then." O'Grady had set his bulldog chin.

"When you're dealing with DNA, a sheep is every bit as complicated as a human being. Sometimes, even more so. One of the guys we've been looking for cloned extinct marsupials in Australia. Used DNA extracted from museum specimens. Now, that, let me tell you, was complicated shit compared to taking a sample from living tissue, isolating the DNA, and inserting it into another woman's egg."

Sheela seemed to be wilting as Sid talked. Lymon placed a hand on her shoulder. "What is it?"

In a small voice, Sheela said, "It's all starting to make sense, Lymon. All of it. Christal just handed it to us."

"How's that?" O'Grady asked. "You know why she was abducted?"

Sheela barely nodded as she stared down at her lap, head bowed as if in prayer. "Marketing."

"Huh?" Sid asked. "How does stealing Christal equate with marketing? Marketing what? Felonious behavior?"

Sheela took a deep breath, lifting her head and removing her dark glasses. She looked from one to another, the deadness in her eyes affecting Lymon as no words could. "DNA is easy to obtain—I understand that. But if someone like Krissy wanted a Sheela Marks baby, how do you prove you can actually provide it?"

Lymon felt a cold wash of understanding. "Oh, my God!"

"That's right," Sheela said woodenly. "You've got to be able to *prove* the DNA comes from the person you say it does. The customer has to know beyond a doubt that you've got the real thing; that he's not being bilked."

"I'm dense," O'Grady growled. "What the hell are we talking about?"

"The reason for the celebrity hits." Lymon swallowed hard. "It's advertising. Don't you get it? If you're going to offer your client a chance to have a baby with Mel Gibson's DNA, you have to prove it's the right stuff. I mean, you can't show someone a pile of DNA and say, 'That's it. Meet Mel Gibson's DNA.'"

"Son of a bitch," Sid whispered, a half-vacant expression on his face as his mind worked it over. He sat back, stiff-armed, unblinking.

"The questionnaire," Lymon added, another piece falling into place. "Christal wondered what they were screening for."

"Excuse me?" O'Grady asked as he scribbled furiously in his notebook. "What questionnaire?"

"It's the Genesis Athena web site," Sid filled in. "I sent a copy to Tanner down at Quantico. We're going to want to access that site and have Tanner play with it for a while."

O'Grady chewed at his lip, his dark face furrowed. "You're telling me that someone is stealing DNA from movie stars, and . . . what? Selling it to whom? People to have babies with? Now, I don't know that much, but doesn't having a baby mean you've got to have a sperm and an egg?" He gestured with one hand. "It's not like a piece of skin or a hair follicle can get a woman pregnant. You read?"

Sid worked his jaw back and forth. "That was then, Sean. You ought to see the things they can do now."

"But, sure, that sheep Dolly and all. But it takes a laboratory, right?"

"Yeah," Sid agreed. "These cutting-edge labs can mix and match, do just about anything with DNA. It's like ordering a car made to custom specs. You can choose everything."

"So," O'Grady asked, "where's the laboratory?"

Sheela whispered, "Find Krissy, and you'll know."

"Who?" Sid asked.

"The lunatic who's having my baby," Sheela said softly.

But, beneath it, Lymon could hear the cracked-glass tone in her voice.

Christal was contemplating her growling stomach when a low knock brought her bolt upright and out of bed. She was on her feet, prepared for anything when the door—or was it a hatch?—opened and swung back.

A young man stood just beyond the threshold. The first thing she noticed was his inquisitive brown eyes. They seemed to sparkle with anticipation. She figured him for his midthirties, with sandy blond hair, a strong-jawed face, and a tentative smile. Two muscular men in coveralls stood behind him, darkly visaged, with close-cropped hair. Arabs? They had a menacing air about them. Security, perhaps?

"Ms. Anaya?" the brown-eyed man's voice was laced with a seasoning of Scottish. He wore a white-knit sweater and brown cotton pants.

"Who wants to know?" She propped her hands on her hips, knees flexed, ready to flee or fight.

"Dr. Gregor McEwan, at your service." His smile deepened. "Hungry, perhaps?"

"Why would I be hungry?"

"It's been two days since ye've eaten. Come, then. Let's take you off to the cafeteria."

She glanced over his shoulder, and he read her concern as she eyed the guards. "Oh, don't be worrying about them, now. They're more for my protection than yours."

"Really?"

"What if it turns out that ye're not friendly? Ex-FBI? Against a marshmallow like me? You could probably pull my arms out of their sockets and twist off my head." He waved her out. "Come. Let's eat. Surely you can't plan your escape on an empty stomach." His smile mocked her, an unsettling arrogance in his sparkling eyes.

Christal considered her options. Her belly wasn't going to fill itself based on the dreams she'd been having of steak, enchiladas, and cheeseburgers. Nor would she gain any understanding of her situation by staring at the walls of her prison. "Sure."

When she stepped out into a white corridor the air seemed fresher. The steel walls were lined with piping, thick wire, and welded braces, all covered with a heavy coat of paint.

"This way, then." McEwan started off, motioning her to walk at his side. The corridor was just wide enough for the two of them.

"So, where am I?"

"Aboard ship. Her name's the *ZoeGen*."

"And just where are we, exactly?"

"I can't say . . . exactly. Navigation's not my thing. Somewhere in the middle of the Atlantic. Well, maybe a couple of hundred miles off the Maine coast, actually."

She gave him a skeptical look. "How long was I unconscious?"

"Aboot twenty-four hours. Maybe a tad longer."

"Why did you kidnap me?"

He gave her a sheepish sidelong look. "I'm afraid some of our people panicked."

"Panicked? That's an understatement. Do you know what you just unleashed? People are going to miss me. That means federal as well as local police involvement. Hank and his little band of friends are going to be at the center of a hurricane." They stepped through a bulkhead and took a right into a wider companionway. She glanced over her shoulder, aware of the lurking presence of the guards. They watched her with flat brown eyes, faces expressionless.

"Nothing we can't make amends for," he said hopefully. "I really do apologize. We'll see what happens, and it's currently under discussion, but I'm sure we can reach some agreement that will be mutually acceptable."

Was he a lunatic? Or just plain nuts? "Gregor, you can't kidnap a person, drug her, transport her across state lines— hell, out of the country—and not expect a whole ration of shit to fall on you!"

"Oh, I don't know. They took me in the beginning. Bagged me right in front o' me own house. It was only after I understood the potentials and the money to be made that I took over running the program for the Sheik. And a good choice it was. I'm now in charge of research and laboratory operations."

"Wait. You mean you changed sides—in spite of what they did to you?"

"Ach, what? Hold a little kidnap against them when I could be in charge of the most advanced genetics laboratory in the world? What others do in theory, we do in practice! Lass, I don't even have to write a grant proposal here."

He chuckled at that and pushed open a large double door. Inside Christal found a rather mundane-looking cafeteria— perhaps thirty by forty—packed with tables, plastic chairs, and a food line of steam tables staffed by four women, also Arab, if she was any judge of such things. She counted fifteen people, still more Arabs given their looks and the sibilant tongue they spoke, who sat at the tables, eating. They were dressed in lab wear: green smocks, pants, and the women all had loose headwear that could be draped over the face. Females, she noted, sat strictly to themselves at a back table, and cast curious glances her way.

"Help yourself," he instructed as he led her to the line, picked a tray out of a rack, and added silverware, napkin, and a plate from their various stacks and holders.

She was famished, no doubt of it. No doubt, too, that she needed to keep her strength up. The fare was mostly European in nature: roast beef, lamb, potatoes, gravy, steamed cabbage, bread, and cheese—but couscous, hummus, falafel, and other dishes smacked of different appetites by the other diners. She opted for Coke, while he took juice from the machine at the end of the line.

She followed Gregor to a chair, settling herself across from him. The table was a Formica-topped ubiquitous model that might have been found in any institutional lunchroom in the world. Neither of the guards had taken a tray. Instead they discreetly seated themselves far enough away for privacy, close enough to be there in case Christal lunged for McEwan's throat. Her days with LBA had heightened her sense of awareness about these things.

"Who are the Arabs?" She inclined her head toward the others and attacked her plate.

"Geneticists. Lab techs. They're the muscle and bone of Genesis Athena." That flare of arrogance betrayed itself again. "Most of them, I trained. So they're the best in the business."

As she wolfed her food, she asked, "I don't get it. Why steal celebrity DNA?"

McEwan studied her thoughtfully as he neatly cut roast beef into cubes, skewered them with his fork, and chewed. "We want to be the first."

"To steal DNA?"

"Not to steal it, to *patent* it, Ms. Anaya."

"You can't *patent* someone's DNA! It's, well, it's *personal*!"

He laughed at that, genuinely delighted. "Do you know that no law, in any country, protects a person's exclusive right to their own DNA? Not even in your dearly provincial USA."

"Bullshit!"

"Oddly, bullshit is protected. You can't walk off with a wheelbarrow of manure from someone's bull paddock. That's theft. But once your DNA is out of your body, it belongs to anyone who can lay hold of it." He spread his fingers wide. "Poof! Gone. It's no longer yours."

"I don't believe that."

"Well, I can't affect your beliefs, lass, but when you do go home again, you may be well advised to check the statutes. See if you find DNA listed anywhere in the definitions of personal property. Meantime, however, let's just say I'm right, hmm? There is a huge precedent in law as well as in practice."

"What? I can tell you that as a graduate of—"

"How often have you had a blood test? Oh, say for cholesterol? Perhaps for a blood chemistry board? You know, to measure lipids, bilirubin, hematocrit, things like that."

"A few, why?"

"What happened to the extra blood?"

"What do you mean?"

"I mean they may have needed a tenth of a milliliter— that's less than a drop, eh? But they took a syringe full. That's an extra three or four whole milliliters of blood. What did they do with it?"

"Threw it out?"

"Hardly! They sold it! Some they distilled for plasma, some for insulin, some for albumin—lots of things. Right! So let's take the insulin, for example. Your body produced it, eh? It was part of you. Does anyone think once it's drawn that it still belongs to you?"

She could only stare at him in disbelief. "DNA is different. I mean, as I understand it, I'm still using my DNA. Cells are synthesizing proteins, dividing, things like that."

"And all that insulin and plasma? You weren't using that as well?"

She stared.

He chuckled as he spooned up mashed potatoes. "Sorry, lass. No one cares. Laboratories all over the world are taking DNA samples from patients. And, sure as to be, the very second they're coded, they're put up for patent. Some come from folk with resistance to diseases, others from people with a tolerance for certain environments, some even from athletes who show certain kinds of muscle tissue. It's a mad scramble, lass, to see who can get what first. A gold rush like in the wild West. Companies are falling all over themselves staking claims. And, just like those long-ago miners, no one knows which genes are going to be the mother lode!"

She stared at him, food half-chewed in her mouth. Finally she swallowed and managed to say, "It's illegal to . . ." *What? Patent another person's DNA?*

McGregor stabbed another square of meat. "No, lass. Most governments around the world have only passed laws banning *cloning*. You know, the artificial *reproduction* of another human being. They've said nothing aboot the DNA. In fact, by taking the stance that you c'not reproduce yer own DNA, they have told you ipso facto that the state has more right to regulate your DNA than you do."

"I don't follow."

"Indeed?" He took a drink of juice from his tumbler. "Think of it this way: You're of the opinion that yer DNA belongs to you and you alone. What's a clone? A copy of yourself. It's your own DNA that you're copying. Not mine, not the president's, but yours. Now, if that was really the case, could the government regulate it?"

"But that's not the same!"

"Isn't it? Fact is, you have the right to believe in whatever God you want, read whatever book you want, join any political party—but not to control yer own DNA. If you want privacy, stick to your beliefs, but don't look to your body, lass." The twinkle was back in his eye.

"But laws against cloning—"

"Are laws that regulate your use of your own personal DNA. In your opinion, you think you should have the say over yer own DNA. I understand that. Most people—bless their simple souls—think they do. What they don't understand is that through fear that someone might clone himself, they've given that control over to the government, business, and, most onerous of all, *investors*."

"How did that happen?"

"Sheer unadulterated fear, lass. That, and the social conservatives, of course. God bless the Christian religious right, wherever they live. They've given Genesis Athena a monopoly."

Christal's mind stumbled over the implications.

"You see," McEwan continued, "all these technologies, going way back . . ." He gestured with his knife. "Take insulin, again. No one objected to processing insulin from human blood that was going to be thrown away anyhow. Doing so was in the best interest of society. Insulin used to be a touchy thing. You couldn't mix sheep with human with artificial and not have a reaction. The sources had to be pure. Millions of diabetics benefited, and still do. It was the precedent, you see. DNA just got folded into the same blanket, if you get my drift."

She glared at him. "So why kidnap me? Why did you have to break the law if this whole operation is legal?"

He chuckled. "Aye, the grandstanding. Why, advertising, of course. We've got the product. Oh, to be sure, we'll be sending little apologies, and even checks in the mail as things begin to fall into place. Admitting to our stunts, as it were, and offering reparation. Legal division's already been hard at work over that."

"Legal division? You've lost me again."

McEwan waved his greasy knife. "It's all going to come out in the next year or so. The clients can't be expected to keep their silence. What's the point of having a little Julia Roberts running around the kitchen if you can't brag aboot her t'yer friends, eh? When it does break, it's going to be one of the biggest stories since Bin Laden. Thing is, we don't want to look like simple criminals, so we'll make restitution to the aggrieved parties." His expression sobered. "It's just the right thing to do. Image, and all that."

"Wait a minute. You stole all these people's DNA, you're going to patent it, and then send them some sort of pittance to make it right?"

"Aye."

"Why not just stick a check in the mail now? It's cheaper if they don't have time to think about how they've been gypped." she said sarcastically.

"Because the less they know now, the easier it will be to get our samples. After the story breaks, things might get a wee bit trickier. People will be more careful—not that it will do them much good, mind you. The common folk in the streets have no idea how much DNA they leave around in restaurants, hotels, their clothes, cars, even when they lick an envelope."

Christal shook her head. "I'm still not understanding how this works. You take the DNA, patent it, and then what?"

"Sell it, of course."

"To whom?"

"Anyone who will pay for it."

"Give me an example."

McEwan leaned back, pushing his empty plate away. "Well, take Princess Diana of Wales. Our marketing research determined her to be one of the most beloved women of all time. Getting the sample was the riskiest operation we ever undertook. I'm sure you heard of it."

She jerked a quick nod. "The lab in Paris where her forensic samples were curated."

"We had a huge list of applicants just waiting for us to succeed. We've done brilliantly. The first embryos have been implanted in the clients. We've already got a list of close to two hundred candidates for implantation. We've banked over a million and a half in deposits alone."

"Embryos?" Christal asked, her fork halfway to her mouth. "Damn it, it just sank in. You meant it when you said 'little Julia Roberts' earlier."

"Aye," McEwan said, reading her confusion. "You see, Ms. Anaya, we're not just selling the DNA in a bottle or anything like that. When we sell it, it's alive and ready to be implanted into the host mother."

35

Hank tried to put the last forty-eight hours into perspective. Genesis Athena, he'd discovered, was nothing if not organized. He'd been surprised to find his luggage unloaded from the cargo hold of the aircraft that had carried them to Teterboro, New Jersey. April assured him his room charge at the Hilton had been taken care of. A physician had met their flight, checked on Christal's condition, inserted an IV drip, and given her another sedative. The helicopter flight to the marina at Eastham, on Cape Cod, had been both quick and efficient. He and Neal had carried Christal's somnolent body aboard a sleek cigarette boat; and an hour later, they had watched her lifted aboard the *ZoeGen* by capable crewmen. Hank had scrambled onto the lowered ladder and up into a hatch that opened in the cruise ship's side.

April had led him to her cabin, a snug room with wooden paneling, a plush bed, and most of the amenities. Sex had led to sleep that had led to more sex, and so forth.

Now, showered, shaved, and rested as he hadn't been in months, Hank found himself sitting across from April in her cabin, eating breakfast from a room service cart a steward had brought. Pale midday light glowed through the single porthole.

"Happy?" April asked as she lifted a forkful of scrambled eggs from her plate and balanced them. Her robe hung open far enough that he could see the soft curve of her breast.

Hank finished chewing his bacon, washed it down with a shot of black coffee, and wiped his lips. "I think I've fallen through the looking glass." He chuckled, opening his arms wide to take in the surroundings. He wore a white terry cloth robe belted at the waist.

April scraped up the last of her eggs, used her napkin, and asked, "Want to see the rest of the ship?"

He gave her a thoughtful look. "Beyond the infamous bulkhead?"

Her sober eyes took his measure. "First, I have to know. Are you in? All the way?"

He chewed his lip, gave a curt nod, and stood. "Yeah, I'm in."

"Why?" she demanded. "What would convince you to do this? You used to be a federal agent. Sometimes, working for Genesis Athena, you'll have to skirt the law. Why would you sell your soul? For a payback?"

"Nah, I'm smarter than that." He gestured around at the

plush quarters. "I like the way you do business. Charter air-craft, your own ship, and capable personnel? I could be an asset to you. And I'm assuming you weren't blowing smoke about the salary."

"No smoke."

"Things went so fast the other night. Until now I never understood that you can just get swept away. I mean, we kidnapped Christal. It's a felony, April. Whatever it was that we did, we can't go back. Can't rethink it and change it."

"You feeling trapped?" she asked as she stood and slipped her robe off.

He stopped short, watching her perfect body. A dancer had a body like that, toned and agile. She stepped to her dresser, pulled the top drawer open, and fished out a bra and panties. He watched one long tanned leg after the other slide through the openings.

She glanced at him as she snapped her bra and slipped her arms through the straps. The question hung between them. Trapped? Hell, how did he answer that?

"Sure. But I was part of the entrapment. I knew what I was doing, setting Christal up. When we packed her out of that place, I had a momentary hesitation. I was doing everything I'd ever been trained to prevent; but you know, I haven't lost any sleep over it."

She laughed as she pulled gray cotton slacks on. "I keep telling you, we're not doing anything illegal. People may disagree with our methods, but there are no laws—"

"Kidnapping—"

"Shit!" she snapped. "Cut it out, Hank. Remember? I asked her. She said she'd go if we answered her questions. You heard her."

"She was drugged! A good DA would—"

April walked up to him, slipped her hands inside his robe, and pressed her palms against his chest. They were cool on his warm skin. "We'll make it right with her. She won't press charges when we're through. We've paid her back in a way she'll never forget. Genesis Athena has the resources to fix almost anything. We're here for the long term—with a prod-

THE ATHENA FACTOR 321

uct no one else is going to be able to provide." A smile curled her lips. "Trust me."

He hesitated, staring into those marvelous eyes. Then he nodded. What the hell. "Yeah, like I said, I'm in." He gave her a sly grin. "And I could get real used to the lifestyle."

"Come on," she added impishly. "Get dressed. Let me show you why you've made the best decision of your life. You're in on the ground floor of the biggest industry of the twenty-first century."

Moments later they rolled the cart with their demolished breakfast out into the narrow companionway for the staff to pick up, and April led him through one of the hatches and into a major corridor.

"As you've no doubt guessed, *ZoeGen* is an old cruise ship. Greek, originally, and perfect for our needs. She provides us with accommodations for fifteen hundred clients at a time. Currently we have over three hundred staff and crew on board. They berth in the lower decks. We do everything from genetic scans, genetic engineering, gene replacement and therapy, molecular engineering, all the way to providing complete reproductive services for any client, male or female."

"What do you mean, male? How does a man reproduce himself?"

"Our geneticists retrieve one of his germ cells from the testes before it divides into sperm. They remove the nucleus and insert it into a host woman's denucleated egg. Once it's implanted in her womb, she carries the fetus to term, delivers it, and after we're sure the child is healthy, it's given to the father."

"You have women who will do this?"

"For a price, Hank. It's a big world out there, and you'd be surprised what an incentive a couple thousand US can be in a place like Bangkok. None of this comes cheaply, but what some people will pay for an exact genetic copy of themselves would amaze you. It's the ultimate narcissism on a mobile platform we can take anywhere in the world."

"As long as you stay in international waters."

"That's right. That's our ace in the hole." She had pulled

her reddish hair into a ponytail that bobbed as she nodded. "We have a full legal team, but sometimes even they can't keep up with the laws in individual countries. The high seas are open territory for Genesis Athena."

She stopped at a hatch, pressed a series of numbers into a keypad, and opened the sealed door.

Hank stepped through into what had once been an open two-story room, perhaps fifty feet across and sixty long. The balcony where he stood was now glassed, providing a view of the floor a story below.

"This used to be the ballroom," April said, taking a position on the railing before the glass. "You're looking down onto one of the G Deck labs."

Hank could see white-clad people seated at counters around what was clearly a laboratory. Racks of test tubes, beakers, tubing, and trays were everywhere. He could identify the microscopes, of course, but the rest of the equipment baffled him. "The last time I took science was in college. I was in the criminal justice program, not biology. What is all this stuff?"

April shrugged. "I haven't the slightest idea. What you're seeing is where the real heart of Genesis Athena lies. Those people down there are the brains that make it all possible."

"Okay, enough of the melodrama. What am I seeing?"

She gave him a sidelong glance as she said, "You would call it cloning, Hank. Pure and simple. The world market for molecular biology, gene therapy, infertility, and genetic engineering is huge. Billions huge, and I'm talking dollars, euros, pounds, what have you."

"So, what was Christal doing that hacked you off?"

"She was nosing her way onto my particular turf."

"And that is?"

"Obtaining DNA."

Hank frowned. "Whose DNA?"

"My biggest single acquisition was Elvis Presley."

"Get off it! The guy's dead."

Her laughter sounded musical. "His body, yes. We used a truck-mounted drill to bore a hole through his tomb. Center-punched his casket and inserted a probe into the corpse. By employing the correct procedures, our techs can recover intact nuclear DNA despite the mortuary preservative."

"How come I didn't hear about it? Drilling a hole in Presley's grave, I mean."

"Because Graceland covered it up. They didn't want the publicity. Put yourself in their place. Would you want the whole world to know that someone had violated your security, drilled a hole in your hero, and walked off with a piece of him? It might tarnish the myth, or worse, encourage someone else to try."

"You drilled a hole . . ." He shook his head, baffled.

April stared down pensively. "Since then we've changed our methodology. Now we don't leave any doubt about the validity of our samples. As to Elvis, it's okay. You remember that eBay auction of Elvis' hair a couple of years back? We've got rock-solid provenance, and can cross-compare the DNA from that to our Graceland sample. We've got a waiting list of clients scheduled for implantation for the foreseeable future."

"For tubes of dead Elvis DNA?" He was looking out at the laboratory, thinking of how much money people spent for things like Elvis' guitar.

"Tubes of . . . Hardly! You still don't get it, do you?"

"Get what?"

She teased him with her eyes. "Do you remember the line in the movie *Men in Black*? The one where they're driving on the roof of the tunnel?"

"Yeah, Tommy Lee Jones says that Elvis isn't dead, he's just gone home."

April gave him a bewitching smile. "Our first Elvis clone was born last week. The host mother is a rich widow from Indianapolis. So you see, the movie was right. He went home—but now he's back."

"This is a joke, right?"

"Do you remember the Tasmanian wolves a few years back? One of our people pioneered that process. DNA is only a molecule, a code. It doesn't die along with the body. If it's preserved, the code can be reactivated."

He stared, openmouthed.

April's eyes seemed to enlarge as she shook her head. "Now, Hank, are you beginning to understand the power behind Genesis Athena and why people will pay millions for DNA that we control the patents to?"

After a night of unrelenting nightmares, Sheela sat on her poolside recliner. In the cool protection of the shade, she watched turquoise water lap at the white cement walls. "The cement pond," the Beverly Hillbillies had called it. How appropriate for a Saskatchewan girl's final retreat. The only standing water she had known for her first fourteen years had been the clear water in the dugouts where the horses and cattle drank.

How did I get here? Looking back through the kaleidoscope of her tumultuous life, she might have been carried off by a tornado. Batted this way and that by the winds of opportunity, fortune, and plain dumb luck, she had come out on top.

How much of myself did I sell on the way? She pursed her lips, shifting her gaze to the fountain in the flower bed, where water bubbled and danced in a delighted spray beneath the Sacagawea statue.

Not as much as most do, she decided. Truly talented people always wrestled with the green-eyed demon of insecurity. She too was constantly plagued as the beast hung its scaled head over her shoulder to whisper that she wasn't any good anymore, that she could never conjure an Oscar-worthy character like Cassie Evens in *Blood Rage* again. That *Jagged Cat* was going to be released to howls of derision. It would land at the box office stillborn, the dissection of its carcass celebrated by the wags in *Time, Newsweek, Daily Variety,* and *The Hollywood Reporter.*

"Washed up!" the headlines would decry.

How did I let Christal down? She rubbed her right thumb across the smooth back of her left hand, feeling the skin, bone, and tendons slipping beneath. *If I had taken the meeting Rex wanted me to, would it have been different?*

Had it been the gods staring down from their aeries on high? Had they seen her desperation to change her life? To save herself? Her belief in the capriciousness of fate was tragically Greek in nature. For any good thing, some terrible price ultimately had to be paid.

"Sheela?" Felix's soft voice interrupted.

She glanced over her shoulder as he came walking out in an expensive silk suit that rippled like a rainbow trapped inside gray. "Hello, Felix. Come, sit."

She watched his lean body as he bent, fingered the fabric-upholstered pad to ensure that no lotions, oils, or other liquids could soil his suit, and seated himself.

An image of her father flashed in the back of her mind: He was bent behind a cow in the squeeze chute; his arms buried up to his elbows in her rear; blood, amniotic fluid, urine, and manure dripping down his brown-duck Carhartts. She could see the expression on his face as he struggled to turn a breeched calf to free a stuck leg.

The image came from light-years beyond Felix Baylor and his immaculately tailored three-thousand-dollar suits.

What kind of men have we bred in this business? Aloud, she asked, "What have you found out?"

Felix straightened his white cuffs where they protruded from his suit coat. "Genesis Athena is quite an organization." His brown eyes were thoughtful. "You asked me to contact them, see what kind of information they had on Sheela Marks. Well, it appears to be substantial. They forwarded a fairly complete biography of you and your achievements. The document we received would have done Dot proud."

"Flattering or derogatory?"

"Most flattering." His expression left little doubt about that. "Sheela, you asked me to contact them in behalf of the name Jennifer Weaver. May I ask why?"

"A hunch, Felix." She gave him a weary appraisal, then asked, "Who are you?"

"What?"

"I asked who you are, Felix. Really, deep down inside your bones and soul, who are you?"

"I . . ." He shrugged, perplexed. "I'm an attorney. Your attorney. Um, the father of three. Some of my cases—"

"Yes, yes, but do you *know* yourself? If I stripped all that away, dropped you on a desert island like Tom Hanks in *Castaway,* would you know yourself? Would you still have that kernel of 'self' on the inside to cling to? Or are you a paste-up of your various images? A collection of events and actions stuck together with no discernible order to become this rendition of Felix Baylor?"

"What the hell are you talking about?"

She studied his wary expression, reading complete bafflement in his brown eyes. "I'm talking about *being,* Felix. Not just, What am I? Or, What do I do? But what I *am* inside, at the heart, the soul, in the marrow of the bones."

He blinked, expression thinning. "Oh, I get it. You're doing some sort of preparation for a role. Rex wanted me to talk to you about—"

"Fuck him. Fuck you, too." She closed her eyes, rubbing them. "Felix, I'll tell you this once. I'm tired. Exhausted. I've done three films a year for the last ten years. Through all of that, I've clung to something, deep down inside. It was a piece of me." She tapped her breastbone. "Way down in here. Deep. Do you understand?"

He just listened with no change of expression.

"A couple of days ago, I asked Christal Anaya if she, too, depended on me. And do you know what?" She didn't wait for his blank look. "She honestly told me no. Finally, one person had the balls to tell me no. But more than that, that same woman told me that if I wanted, I could depend on her. And she really meant it. Now, isn't that a switch?"

"But she's the one who's missing."

"No shit!" Sheela narrowed her eyes. "I'm at a real rocky place in my life right now. I checked the accounts. You and your firm have made a little more than three and a half million off me and my production companies. That doesn't count the additional work that my reputation has brought your firm."

"But that—"

"I'm *not* complaining. You earned every cent of it that you didn't get by padding the billing." She gave him a wry smile. "And you'll be paid for your time now."

"And that is to do what? This Jennifer Weaver thing?"

Sheela nodded. "Pay attention. Here is what you need to know: Jennifer Weaver is thirty-four, single. With the sale of her deceased father's cattle ranch, she has a portfolio worth a little more than ten million. She lives in LA and has been fascinated with Sheela Marks for the last ten years. She has seen all of my movies at least ten times. She attends every venue she can, hoping to get a glimpse of me. She wants to know if Genesis Athena can get her close to Sheela Marks."

Felix looked confused again. "But, I don't get it."

"That's your assignment. Make it happen, Felix. I don't care what you have to do. Build an identity for Jennifer Weaver. Driver's license, passport, address, billing history, whatever it takes. You can make it happen."

"What's the point?" He spread his arms. "Genesis Athena is a big company; we've checked their stats. Financially, they're huge, but they're not players. If someone wanted to get close—"

"They're players, Felix." She narrowed her eyes, using all of her skill to hide her fragile and wounded soul. "They've stolen part of me. Part of that core knowledge of who and what I am. They've stolen part of my essence, my being, if you will."

"Sheela, this sounds nuts! Maybe you should talk this over with a friend of mine. She's a psychologist. A real one from Stanford. Not one of these astro-babble psychotherapists, but the genuine—"

"You are not to discuss this with anyone. Period. Every shred of attorney-client privilege is now in effect. If you so much as breathe a word, even to Rex, I'll have your balls."

He made a pained expression. "So what am I going to do?"

"You're going to make it so that I can find them. Genesis Athena is doing something with DNA. *My* DNA. Genetics, cloning, whatever. You're going to set it up so that Jennifer Weaver can buy whatever kind of piece of Sheela Marks that they're selling."

She watched him finally glom onto the realization that whatever happened, legal action was looming at the end of it.

He said, "Let's say they take the Jennifer Weaver bait."

"Then you set up an appointment for Ms. Weaver."

"Sheela, you're one of the most recognizable—"

"I'm also an actress. Just in case you've forgotten. And, in spite of what some of the critics say, a damn brilliant one! I'm going after them. Then, when I find out everything, you can have them." She gave him a predatory smile. "If they're as well fixed as your research indicates, you could clean up a tidy bundle—and add to your reputation by making some interesting new law, too."

"It could be dangerous."

"The key to this game is deception. And no matter what your objections, or the counseling you're going to feel obliged to give regarding my safety and ethics, and all the other bullshit, I'm doing this."

"Sheela—"

"Dammit! Don't you understand?" She felt a tear in her soul. "If I don't, *I'm going to lose what little is left of me!*"

36

The knock was louder this time, more demanding. Christal sat up on her bunk and called, "Come on in! It's only locked from the inside."

She wasn't terribly surprised when the portal swung open and Hank Abrams stepped in. He was dressed in a dark blue blazer, light blue button-down shirt, Dockers, and white running shoes. His hair looked slightly mussed, as if he'd been standing out in the sea wind. A faint flush lingered on his cheeks, and his eyes gleamed as he studied her.

"Hey, Christal. How's it going?"

She balled her fists, gauging the distance, wondering if she could stand, swing her leg back, and land a kick in his crotch hard enough to blast his testicles up past his ears.

He read her expression, and stepped back with enough haste that she decided her opportunity had vanished.

"Look," he said softly, hands out, "I'm sorry. You had some people worried."

"Yeah, well, perhaps you've forgotten the things you used to know in your old job, Hank. Like the statutes on abduction . . . legal curiosities like the Mann Act, reckless endangerment, breaking and entering, assault, and a whole list of fractured or broken legal codes I'm only beginning to get hints of."

"I told them that they'd be wasting their time."

"Who's wasting their time?" She narrowed an eye. "Copperhead?"

"Who?"

"The redheaded bitch that accompanied you to my apartment."

"Ah, April."

"She your latest, Hank? Wow! After Marsha, you've fallen to new lows."

A faint quiver of his lips betrayed him. "I wouldn't bring up the women I've fucked. You might be surprised at who we'd discover was right up front in that list."

Christal let it go, watching him, struggling to see inside his skin. "I don't get it. Did I really read you that wrong? This whole time were you really just a shit? Or did you cover it so well that no one guessed? I mean, damn, it's not just that you fooled me, but the whole Bureau: Wirthing, Harness, even the folks in the academy who are trained to spot bad apples."

"You know, I was just as dedicated as anyone else." His eyes hardened. "And I was doing a damn fine job until I ran into you. You fucking wrecked my life, Anaya. I tell you, it was God damn biblical! You're the damned anti-Christ. One minute I was on top of the world. Then you fucked me blind that night in the van. When I could finally see again, I'd lost everything. My wife, my career, my self-esteem. Everything." He made an explosive gesture with his hand. "Slam-bam! Gone."

"Gee, Hank, I'm going all weepy for you. I remember that

night in the van really well, but my hearing must have been bad, 'cause I don't remember you crying 'no' over and over as you ran your hands up under my bra, or when you un-snapped my pants. I don't remember you battling mightily against my wiles as you slipped your erection inside me. And, come to think of it, you didn't pull out again until long after you came. Even then you lay there until I reminded you we didn't want to make a mess on Ben's pad. As I recall, we spent another two hours talking about how good it had been. Re-member that? You were half of the postcoital conversation—you, with that idiotic happy expression on your face."

"You bitch!"

She waved it away. "Forget it. Gonzales won. You landed on your feet, flush in your new career as a big-league felon. You know, I'm going to have the time of my life when I fi-nally bring you down."

He crossed his arms. "Christal, they don't want a fight with you. They want to come to some sort of settlement."

"What? Bribe me? It was a bad choice, sending you down here to negotiate."

He sighed in mock despair. "You know that we're in the middle of the fucking ocean, don't you? You've got a lot of time to think about it. I'm going to say this one more time: No one wants any trouble."

"They got it the first time your sweet April slugged me in the gut. They got more of it when mousy Gretchen shot at me. And, on top of that, I'm not inclined to forget that some bastard stuck a needle into my neck and carted me off to . . . where the hell are we? The Atlantic?"

"They just want a little more time, that's all. They'll pay you for the insult done to you, for your inconvenience, and, it seems, for the privilege of patenting your DNA."

"You don't get it, do you?"

"Get what?" He spread his arms. "Christal, Genesis Athena is the coming thing! I've seen their lab. Jesus! It's amazing some of the things they can do."

"Yeah, cloning the dead? Your pal the Sheik just back-handed Dr. Frankenstein right across the chops. Talk about one-upmanship."

"Christal, it's not just that." He was grinning at her now in the old way that used to excite her. This time it only incited fury. "The technology is the thing. It's about who actually has the right to control DNA. Genesis—"

"Bullshit! It's about money! The right to control DNA? They stole Sheela's. Snatched it right off her tampon! They're involved in theft! Grand larceny. You're a bunch of fucking witches!"

"Huh?"

"Soul stealers. Predators of the body and heart. Raising the dead for unsavory purposes, just like in the old stories. You're purveyors of the ancient evil. Grandmother's old-time Pueblo witches, but you're wearing modern clothes, doing it with twenty-first-century technology."

"Oh, shit! Here we go again. Not good old Grandma and her quaint Mexican ways! I heard enough of that crap to last me a lifetime."

"But this is different," Christal continued stubbornly. "It used to be superstition, metaphysical tales told to raise the hackles on dark winter nights. No, you're right uptown now. Santa Monica Boulevard, doing it for real." She narrowed her eyes. "Why, Hank? Why are you on the other side now?"

He stared at her floor for a moment, shrugged, and said, "Because, as you no doubt recall, I've got nothing else. Not only that, but as I came to find out so recently, it's inevitable. The Raelians and Clonaid, with their little publicity stunt, were just the harbingers of things to come. Genesis Athena—or some other company like it—is the coming thing. Big, funded, multinational, they'll be to molecular genetics what Microsoft is to computers."

"You really believe that?"

"The technology is here. It will be used. You can't stop it. So just accept it."

"What? Without even thinking about what it means to people?" She tried to see past his calm. "Something else is driving you, Hank. What? Pissed because you got your hand slapped? Is that it? You got caught with your pecker dripping, and now you'll pay back the whole world?"

"Fuck you!"

She paused. "That's right, isn't it? In your whole life, you've never been knocked down before. Never took a fall. You were a golden-haired boy who never had to learn what it was to lose, to fail and have to live with it."

"God! You, of all people, have a hell of a lot of nerve to analyze *my* life. Why don't you go straight to fucking hell?"

"Or is it just the money? Huh? You sold out for bucks? Is that it? Money over legalities?"

"We're not breaking any laws. Look, we're in international waters. You're riding in a legally registered vessel flying the Yemeni flag. Genesis Athena has a second lab—bigger and better—in Yemen, where this is all legal. They have corporate offices in Doha, Qatar, where there are also no laws against it."

"Seems to me I recall Genesis Athena operating on American soil, where we've got laws. As a federal agent, you damn well know it."

He chuckled. "Look, there's no winning an argument with you. As to the ethics, I don't know. If someone wants to buy one of Sandra Bullock's clones, why should I care? What's DNA anyway? It's a molecule. Like water, or benzene, or a polymer. You blast thousands of DNA molecules out every time you sneeze. That night in the van I filled you full of eight million little copies of my DNA. But for a matter of timing—and your IUD—your DNA and mine might have wrapped around each other and made someone new. It's what life's all about, right?"

"Go to hell, Hank."

"I already did. And it was you who took me there. Believe me, I've paid through the nose for it." He slapped the wall absently, looking around her small cabin. "Think about what it would take to settle with Genesis Athena. They want to make things right. Find an amicable solution. They'll be reasonable if you will." He turned to the door. "The one thing you've got plenty of right now is time."

And with that he was gone.

In anger, she threw her pillow, watching it bounce harmlessly off the cold steel.

* * *

Rex sat at the Formosa bar, elbows propped, his butt on a red leather stool. Across from him, he caught his partial reflection through the bottles shelved in front of the back bar mirror. His broken reflection displayed a man with a sour disposition. A glass of Macallan, neat, and a water back stood before him. He toyed with the scotch glass, rocking the amber fluid back and forth.

For this meeting Rex had chosen a dark blue Armani sport coat over a light blue pinstriped shirt. Gray flannel slacks were snugged with an ostrich-hide belt.

He was making faces into the partially obscured mirror, trying to understand what had jerked the rug out from under him, when Tony Zell came striding through the door, slowed to look around, and met Rex's eye.

Zell's golden jewelry caught the light, shining from his neck, wrists, and watch. White leather loafers contrasted with the wood as he walked across the parquet floor. A white sport coat over a blousy black shirt accented his faded jeans.

"What's up, Rex? Sorry I'm late. Had a thing with a client, you know?" He smiled, white teeth flashing in his perfectly tanned face.

Tony slid onto the barstool to Rex's left. "Got your message. Bruckheimer's bummed. He's going with Catherine Zeta-Jones. Can you imagine? It's like, wham! Out of the blue, Sheela just craters. It's not like her." He turned, waving to the bartender. "Hey! Got a Remy XO?"

"Yes, sir," the man called, turning to reach for a high bottle.

Rex spread his fingers wide, seeing the contrast between his skin and the bar wood. "She's falling apart. It's a lot of things, I guess. A big one in particular."

"Anything I can do?" Tony was watching him, wide-eyed, as if expecting some truth to come tumbling out like wisdom from the Buddha.

"Can you walk up behind Lymon fucking Bridges, slit his throat, and dump his guts on the ground in a pile?"

"Lymon, huh? What's he got your rice steamed over?"

"I think he's porking Sheela on the side."

"No shit?" He paused, thinking about it. "So? Why should we care who greases Sheela's snatch?"

"He's playing out of bounds. He's the hired help, for God's sake!"

"Uh-huh," Tony agreed solicitously as the bartender placed a brandy snifter on a napkin before him.

"My tab," Rex told the man, who nodded and walked back to the end of the bar. "Hell, it's more than that. It's bad enough that he's screwing her. Worse, he's trying to wrap his damned wings around her. I'm starting to feel like I need Lymon's permission if I want to see my client."

"That's what went sour on the Bruckheimer deal?"

"Yeah. Part of it, at least. I know for a fact he was telling her not to do it." Rex balled a fist. "We just watched the bodyguard tell Sheela to kiss off a twenty-million-dollar deal."

Tony frowned down at his drink, picked up the snifter, and scented the aroma before he took a swallow. "You're sure about this? About Lymon, I mean? You're sure it's not just the publicity? The thing with her tampon and all the shit that came down after that?"

"Stuff like that happens in this business. The nuts are everywhere. Sheela's been through shit like this before. Maybe not so personal, but, you know, times she and her lovers were splashed on the front pages. She never folded then."

"What's the deal about Christal's disappearance?"

"Sheela's taking it pretty hard. Did you know that Lymon and Sheela saw it happen? They were out flitting around on Lymon's bike. What's he doing running her around town in the middle of the night? And on a motorcycle, for God's sake? His job is to protect her, not get her killed."

Tony straightened. "They *saw* Christal's abduction?"

"Yeah, and that's another thing: What were they doing there? Huh? I mean, what's Lymon doing taking her to one of his employee's hotel rooms?"

"You're sure they saw it?" Tony was watching him with a sudden curiosity.

"Yeah. In fact, they got an ID on one of the muggers. Get

a load of this: It was such a fuckup on Lymon's part that a paparazzo followed him and Sheela on their little ride. The guy had an IR camera . . . got photos. They got a facial shot of an ex-FBI guy. One of Christal's old boyfriends, or some such thing."

Tony pursed his lips, eyes unfocused. "No shit?"

"No shit. Look, I wanted to get together and let you know the score. I'm at the end of my rope. Bridges is butting into Sheela's business. We just lost a major film."

"They looking for this guy? The FBI guy?"

"I assume. Tony, are you listening? We've got trouble brewing here. Sheela's at the top of her trajectory. She can't take time off—if she does, she loses leverage. Leverage means money in our pockets, mine and yours. You getting this? So, what does she have on tap? How many options with how many producers?"

Tony frowned, lifted his cognac, and sipped. "For the time being, she can pretty much write her own ticket."

"For how long?"

Tony considered. "To keep her current contract, she's got a couple of months before her value starts to slip. That's depending on what happens with the release of *Jagged Cat*. If they market it right, position it right in the schedule, if they can cover for Manny's breakdown, if the postproduction and editing work . . ." He shrugged. "You know the variables. A film's a crapshoot, Rex. With lots of different people throwing dice. If any one of them makes a bad cast, they can scuttle it."

"So, you're telling me that Sheela's career rests on this picture's box office?"

"That's the film biz." Tony sniffed, rubbed his nose, and gave Rex a serious look. "I saw some of the dailies. Sheela was brilliant. My impression is that Bernard's got chops as director. Now it's up to the editors, but my gut tells me that Sheela's performance is going to keep the thing afloat."

"But your gut could be wrong."

After a long and pensive silence, Tony asked, "You thinking about bailing, Rex?"

He lifted his scotch, tossing back a full swallow. The amber god warmed his throat with its sweet burn. "If I told Sheela she had to pick between me and Lymon, what would she do?"

"Hell, I don't know." A pause. "Is the guy really that big a problem?"

"Yeah."

"You sure this is all professional?" Tony lifted an eyebrow. "Like . . . maybe there's some jealousy here? You know, the old bull is walking stiff legged because a younger bull is mounting the lead cow?"

"Fuck you."

"Okay, so now that we've got that figured out, what do you want me to do?"

"Put pressure on Sheela. Let her know that she's flushing her career. I want her back on track, Tony. She's got another ten years, fifteen at the most, before she's a has-been."

Tony smiled, amused. "Yeah, I get it. Not only is she getting fucked under your nose, but your own mortality is chewing at the edges of your well-being. Greed, jealousy, and desperation. You're a sad case, Rex." He paused. "So, what's my incentive to convince her to ditch Lymon?"

"About ten million if we can keep her working for another ten years." As Rex stared into his scotch he could feel Tony's probing eyes, and asked, "What?"

"Last time I saw Sheela, she looked pretty ragged. I've seen 'em crash before, Rex. They go down in flames and explode when they hit the ground. You can squeeze only so much out of a person. Some take it better than others. As to Sheela, you sure this is the time to press?"

"At twenty million a picture, you tell me."

"What if she has a breakdown? What if she snaps? You know, you can kill a goose by forcing it to lay too many golden eggs."

"There are ways to handle stress."

Tony chuckled. "Yeah, pills, drugs, booze. It's the old Hollywood dance. Wring 'em dry before they burn out." He slapped the bar. "Damn, Rex, you're the only man in this town who's shittier than I am."

"You going to tell her?"

Tony lifted his snifter, clinking the rim on Rex's scotch glass. "To partners."

37

Christal made a fierce face and ignored her burning muscles as she finished her last reps. She pulled her knees up, gasping after her seventy-five sit-ups.

Falling back, she pulled strands of sweaty hair to one side, rolled over, and began her battery of push-ups. Outside of staring at the whitewashed steel walls, there wasn't much else to do, so she had determined to shape up. And, who knew, it might be her ticket off this ship of fools.

All she needed was an opportunity.

Her shoulders bunched as she pushed herself up, lowered, pushed herself up, and stopped as a hesitant rapping sounded on her door.

She jumped to her feet, clawed her long black hair back out of the way, and said, "Yeah? What's up?"

The lock clicked, and a fit-looking young man glanced uncertainly around before stepping into her cabin. "You alone?" he asked quickly in a voice literally dripping with Australian.

"Nobody here but us mice. Who are you?"

"Brian Everly." He closed the door behind him, leaving it ajar. He stopped short, staring at her as if he'd never seen a sweaty, panting, and disheveled human female before.

She used the moment to take his measure. Tall, square-shouldered, he had longish sandy blond hair, weathered skin that betrayed faded freckles, and the most fascinating pale blue eyes. A sheepish smile teased the lips of a decidedly masculine mouth. His red-checked flannel shirt couldn't hide the deep chest that tapered to a thin waist where it was tucked into faded Levis. Buff leather shoes with crepe souls shod his feet.

"God," he whispered. "You're . . ."

"Yes?" She wiped at the perspiration that trickled down the fine hairs at her temple.

He seemed to catch himself on the verge of doing something foolish; and was that a hint of embarrassment that
crossed his pale eyes? "Sorry, but you look a little, well,
flushed."

"You caught me exercising." She arched a brow. "Uh, you
got a reason for barging in? Or were you just in the neighborhood checking out the latest kidnap victims?"

He smiled, shifting from foot to foot as if nervous. "Oh,
yes, sorry for that." He seemed genuinely contrite. "I'm
one of the fellow inmates here, actually." He glanced back
at the door. "I'm not supposed to be here. Talking to you, I
mean."

"Really?" She crossed her arms, feeling the heat from her
exertion through her damp clothing. Having nothing but the
tiny sink to wash it in, she was suddenly aware of a warm
odor rising from the fabric.

"Yes, you see, I've been working on your DNA. That's
how I found out you were aboard. Um, your name is
Christal, right?"

"Yeah. Christal Anaya."

"Beautiful name." He seemed to mean it.

"Thank you," she said dryly, tilting her head in a questioning manner.

He took a step forward, hands spread in supplication.
"Look, I just need information. You came from the United
States, right?"

"Uh-huh."

"Did you hear anything about a woman, Nancy Hartlee?
She would have swum ashore off New York about a week
and a half ago."

Christal stared at him. The name rang a bell, but where
had she . . . Sid. On the phone. "Nancy Hartlee? A young
woman? Geneticist?"

He nodded, hope in his eyes.

"She drowned."

She watched the hope in his eyes crumble to despair. He
looked away, shoulders dropping. "Damn."

"She was a friend of yours?"

He nodded faintly. "What . . . what did you hear?"

"A friend of mine, an FBI agent, went to New York. He's working on missing geneticists. She was on his list. When the medical examiner's office in New York alerted the Bureau as to a possible ID, he went up to verify it."

Grief had mixed with hope when Brian looked up. "You're part of the investigation? Is that why you're here? They're looking for the *ZoeGen*?"

"Not that I know of. If they are, my source didn't mention it to me."

His intent stare left her uneasy. "You're in a great deal of danger."

She kept trying to see past his concern. Real? Or faked? "Why should you care? For that matter, who are you? What are you doing here? Why shouldn't I throw you out of here like I should have done with Hank?"

He gave her a fond look. "Good point. I'm a geneticist. Like Nancy was . . . and the others of us here. Like you, I can't leave. They need my skills, at least for the time being. You, on the other hand, are entirely dispensable. We've got our sample."

"Then, why am I here?"

"They're waiting for the Sheik. As I understand it, he wants to see you."

She felt a cold flush down deep in her guts. "Does he?" She hesitated, seeing the worry in his eyes. "You can tell me, Brian. I gave up on fairy tales a long time ago. What's the rest? I'm supposed to take my place in his seraglio? Is that it? A little rape before they throw me to the sharks like your friend Nancy?"

"Oh, no. Not like that. First off, Nancy dove overboard on her own. She was a brilliant swimmer, right? In high school. She thought she might make it to shore, tell the authorities what was going on out here. Perhaps save us all."

"And the Sheik?"

Brian averted his eyes. "You're not a virgin, are you?"

"What?" Christal glared. "What kind of question is that?"

"If you're not a virgin, he's not interested."

She just stared at him, hands clenched at her sides. Fear pumped adrenal unease through every vein.

Brian added, "It's something to do with his cultural upbringing, I believe. He won't take anything but a virgin to his bed. Before he'll have intercourse, she must be pure. His alone." He made a dismissive gesture. "The stories are that he can't stand the idea of lying where another man has already lain."

If anything her fear worsened. "Then, what on earth does he want with me? I haven't been a virgin since I was sixteen."

"He wants to see exactly what you look like. I mean, how you will look when you finally go to his bed."

"Whoa!" She raised her hands. "You lost me there."

Brian wearily rubbed the back of his neck. "Look, Christal, you're going to be hearing a lot of shocking things, but the fact is, the Sheik isn't interested in you, but in how your duplicate will be when she comes to his bed in another fifteen years or so."

Confused and wordless, she could only stare. He managed to look everywhere in the small cabin except into her eyes.

Her voice cracked as she asked, "You seem like a decent guy. How can you be part of this?"

He swallowed hard, turned away, and stepped to the porthole, where he looked out at the rolling ocean. "In the beginning, we were just afraid. We looked at our work as a way to buy time, to wait for an opportunity to escape. At first we didn't understand the amount of influence that Genesis Athena could wield. We always believed that the world would catch on. That the Royal Marines would land on the deck, and we'd be turned loose to expose this whole asinine mess. Time passes; things change."

"Your friend McEwan doesn't seem to share your sentiments."

In his profile she could see disgust. "Yes, well, Gregor would have been a shit no matter where he worked, or who he worked for. Most of us, the Westerners, have been replaced over the years with the Sheik's people. They came, studied the procedures, and have taken over the lab." A grim smile played. "Smart lad, Gregor. He's cut his security risk down to just me."

"Smart? He seems to be one of them."

"He is. He went right over to them when we figured out the potentials."

"Why?"

"For a share of the profits, of course. Do you realize the potential this industry has? Genesis Athena controls the modern science of genetics. We can reproduce any organism that has ever lived if the DNA's intact; cure most of the genetic diseases. Technology developed here has been licensed to labs around the world. We're talking in terms of billions of dollars from that alone. Not to mention people who have lost children and want them back, or those who have lost a spouse. People will pay incredible sums for a second chance. They'll pawn their souls to cure a dying loved one."

"And the celebrity DNA? Gregor mentioned Princess Diana."

"That's what we call the luxury market. People like our dear Sheik. By the time he's done, his collection of the world's most beautiful women will be unmatched."

"But they have to grow up first, right?"

Brian shrugged. "The Sheik is a very rich and powerful man who also happens to be young. He's smarter than so many of his peers in the Arab world. Most Arab leaders want to make life the way it was in the tenth century—reestablish the caliphate—and they're doomed to failure. With fuel cell technology, petroleum will eventually fade. The Gulf States that have lived off oil profits will have nothing to offer. The Sheik, however, wants to create the future. He expects to be one of the most powerful men in the world. If you ask me, it's as if he's challenging the Prophet himself."

"These are *human beings* we're talking about! Not just cattle!"

"Is there any greater power, Christal, than the ability to control people? We're talking the ability to create, modify, utilize, and dispose of them. To own them, body and soul. That is the ultimate power, matched with unlimited money. The Sheik holds the future of humanity in his hands."

Christal sank onto her bunk, trying to comprehend the immensity of Genesis Athena. Finally she asked, "How do they keep you? I mean, can't you jump overboard when the ship docks?"

"Docks where?" he asked. "*ZoeGen* puts in at select ports: Aden, Doha, Karachi, Bandar-e-Abbas, Tripoli. These places raise any flags? You'd be surprised how tight security can be."

"Doesn't anything ever break? Don't they need parts? Something?"

"The machine shop is downstairs and aft. Out of bounds for us. Just like the Royal Australian Navy, we're supplied at sea by a tender. Food, water, fuel—it's all piped aboard, right?" He gestured around. "You have no idea what a perfect prison a ship can make. You're currently in the old crew section. It's completely sealed from the rest of the ship. There's one access in and out, and it's locked and guarded twenty-four hours a day. The other hatches are welded. The ventilation system is barred with titanium grating, but you'll trigger the pressure sensors under the ductwork before you get that far."

"What about the cafeteria staff? How do they get in and out?"

He crossed his arms as he turned her way. "They're implanted with small subcutaneous chips. They don't make it past the controlled entry unless they provide a fingerprint, retinal scan, and the chip reads correctly." The corners of his lips curled. "We thought about taking a sample and cloning one to get the fingerprint and retina, but the chip would still elude us."

"I'm surprised you're not all nuts."

"Oh, they take pretty good care of us. We get the latest movies, supervised access to the Internet, time off to read or study. The latter is encouraged, by the way. And we teach."

"Teach?"

"Members of the Sheik's extended family, mostly. Them, and some other young people from around the Persian Gulf who are likely prospects."

"What do you mean, likely prospects?"

"As I said, the Sheik knows that petroleum is only a temporary means of wealth. The world will find alternative sources of energy. When it does, the elite families in the Gulf will collapse like a house of cards. The Sheik's family and friends will be right there when it happens, but instead of oil, their monopoly will be molecular biology. If you want a cure for cancer, you'll be coming to the Sheik."

"This is a nightmare."

"Wasn't there a song? 'Welcome to my Nightmare'?"

At the sound of his doorbell, Lymon padded down the hallway, crossed his living room, and looked through the small window in his front door. Movement had already activated his porch light; he could see Sheela standing there, expression pinched, her hair shining like flame in the light.

"Sheela?" Lymon asked as he opened the door. "What's wrong? What are you doing here?"

She stepped in, glanced around, and walked into his arms after he closed the door. "I needed to see you."

He stood, holding her close, feeling her cool body against his. "You could have called. I would have—"

"No. I wanted out, Lymon. The dreams . . . God, nightmares, I mean." She shook her head where it was buried against his shoulder.

He had just tightened his grip when Sid stepped around the corner, caught a glimpse, and spun on his heel to beat a quick retreat.

Lymon called, "It's all right, Sid. You don't have to go."

When Sheela glanced up, startled, he could see that an unwanted third person was the last thing she'd counted on.

Sid hesitated, and Sheela turned, waving, "Go away, Sid. Lymon is attempting to protect himself."

"Huh?" Sid was poised on one foot.

"From me," Sheela added, stepping away, her voice dropping. "He's doing his damnedest to maintain his professional distance . . . and it's driving me berserk!"

Sid was canny enough that he promptly fled back down the hallway for the guest bedroom. Sheela met Lymon's eyes, a glittering desperation there. "We've got to talk."

"What happened?"

She took another step and turned. "Remember *Joy's Girl*? I was told after I played Jennifer Weaver that men would be masturbating to that scene. Did I ever tell you about that? About the image of them that plays over and over in my mind? About how creepy it is?"

He sighed, nodded, and walked over, placing an arm over her shoulder. "Yeah, I know. Can I get you a drink? Scotch? Orange juice? Coffee?"

She shook her head. "No, thanks. I was trying to sleep. But the images, Lymon. You wouldn't believe what my mind can create when it's half turned off, free to conjure."

He glanced across at the clock. "It's three in the morning. That's when the world looks the bleakest."

She placed her hands on his chest as she looked into his eyes. "I could live with the knowledge that men watched that film and masturbated. I mean, I know enough about biology to understand about males being visually stimulated. I'm an attractive woman. I sell my sexual image for a lot of money. I play sexual roles. It's part of the bargain, part of what I'm paid for."

"So what did your imagination come up with that was different this time?"

She searched his face, as if willing him to understand. "Genesis Athena. They took my DNA to make little clones of me. I was thinking about why, Lymon. I was conjuring all of the ramifications. Why would someone want a little copy of me? Or of Nicole Kidman, or Sandra Bullock? What would they *do* with them?"

"Sheela—"

She took an agonized breath. "They're breeding copies of *me*, Lymon. Selling them to people like Krissy. She said she was going to have my baby, right? How could she not have known about Genesis Athena? It was right there, tied to my Web site."

"We'll deal with it, I promise."

Sheela made an anxious step, her fingers locked in her hair. "I keep imagining what Krissy will do to that little girl. It's like Pandora's box when you start to think about it. People who want my clone . . . God, that's a terrible word! This is a child! This is me! My hand, my body, my brain and heart." She placed a hand to her breast. "A breathing, feeling being. A being who's what? Going to be made into a little sexual experiment? Is Krissy going to cut that little baby into pieces to show her how much she loves her?"

"Sheela, you don't know—"

"*Bullshit!* Think about it, Lymon. Do normal people go out to buy a Sheela Marks clone? No, they want their *own* babies. They want a product of their DNA and their spouse's. A child conceived in love, as part of a relationship!"

"Sheela, settle down." He disentangled her hand from her hair, and held it. "We'll deal with it."

"Will we?" she asked in a small voice. "How, Lymon? We don't even know where they are. What if we can't stop it? What if I have to live the rest of my life knowing that because of what I did on-screen, some pervert is tormenting an innocent little girl? Can you imagine?"

"Yeah, I know what happens to pretty little girls when psychosexually ill people get ahold of them."

"They won't understand that I am a product of my own history. They won't understand all the things that made me who I am. The mess I got into in Saskatoon. Finding my father's body . . ." Tears began to trickle down her perfect face. "What's a clone, Lymon? Is it like an identical twin, just one that's delayed for a while? Or is it different? Does the soul make an imprint on a person's DNA? Some essence that's passed down?"

"I don't know."

"Neither do I, and it's driving me insane."

38

An unfamiliar pillow pressed against her cheek as Sheela blinked awake in confusion. Horrifying images spun away as the last of her irrational dreams faded into shreds. In that last instant, she had seen her father as she had that last day—seen him hanging in midair, as if frozen in an aerial dance. His head cocked at an unnatural angle, his tongue protruding as if to blow a raspberry at the entire world, his eyes, bugged out but the pupils gray. He hung there, a broken puppet tied to the barn beam with a red length of plastic baling twine.

I let you down, Daddy. I'm so sorry.

She turned, pulling her legs up into her belly, and looked around in relief. Lymon's bedroom was Spartan, male, and neat. She could see his clothes in the open closet, and turning her head, could draw in his rich scent from the bedding.

She blinked hard, struggling to shove the memory of that long-ago day in the barn back into the recesses of her mind.

Lymon. Concentrate on Lymon.

He had led her here, holding her in a spooned position as she cried. Now, in the morning light, she lay like a gutted fish, limp, with nothing left inside the arched cathedral of her ribs.

Did she have any tears left? Or had she cried enough for all of them? How many? One? Ten? A hundred? Or would there eventually be thousands of little Sheelas being implanted in strange women?

Are they mirrors?

Would they see reflections of her life? Would they know that terrible day when she had walked into the barn to find her father's body?

How much of me is really in my genes?

She had no idea. For the first time, she wasn't even sure

what it was to be alive. The notion of personhood had been irrevocably changed, mutated, and taken into another dimension.

She pushed the sheet back and looked down at her body. She was wearing the blouse she'd donned in such a rush last night, and the white cotton pants she'd bought at Jones New York. She stood, walked to the full-length mirror on the closet door, and inspected herself.

"What do they see?" She traced her fingers up her thighs, around the curve of her hips. She followed the narrowing of her waist and raised her hands to support her breasts. Her nipples raised the thin fabric of her shirt.

Why is a body like this worth anything? She tried to comprehend the notion that people would pay to reproduce this flesh—her flesh. They would sacrifice so much to grow it inside their own bodies. Releasing her breasts, she ran her slim fingers along her face, following the indentation of her cheeks, along the bony sides of her eyes, and pulled back her thick mass of red-blond hair. She leaned close, trying to see into the depths of her blue eyes, to scry what really lurked there in the blackness of the pupils, and found nothing. Only the familiarity she'd seen in mirrors ever since she could remember.

What do I do next? Where do I go from here?

In defeat, she turned, staring at Lymon's bed, remembering his body against hers. That was twice now that she'd had him in a bed. The first time, she'd been too ridden with fatigue. This time, it had been the horror of her nightmare that had come between them.

"What's it going to take, Lymon?" She walked into his adjoining bathroom and pulled down her pants. She squatted and relieved herself in his toilet. At the sink, she washed her face, dried on his towel, and used his comb to make order of her ratty hair.

She did a final check in the mirror, wished for a toothbrush, but declined the use of his. Some things just remained inviolately personal.

Her shoes waited at the side of his bed where she'd left them. Steeling herself, she walked out into the hallway. Male voices could be heard from the kitchen

As she approached the arch that separated kitchen from dining room, she hesitated. Yes, that was Rex's faulty alto. He was saying, ". . . I don't care. It's got to stop."

Sheela stepped through the arch and asked, "What does, Rex?" Both men looked up: Rex with distaste, Lymon with worry. Sid was apparently—and probably most wisely—elsewhere.

She passed the stove and counters to where Lymon and Rex sat across from each other at a small table, two cups of coffee between them. Lymon's was half-empty, Rex's still full.

"You and Lymon." Rex gestured with his hands. "I know it's your life, Sheela, but it's going to get out."

"What is?" She crossed her arms, leaning back against the counter.

"I repeat: You and Lymon."

"What about us."

"Do I have to spell it out? You're an adult, sure. You ought to be able to have sex with anyone you want."

The explosion came from deep in her wounded soul. In a leap she was on him, bending over him, finger jabbing at his face. "We're not having sex, Rex! I wish to God we were, *but we're not!* You got that?"

Rex swallowed hard, trying to back away. "Then, what are you doing here?"

From the corner of her eye she caught the amused expression poorly hidden on Lymon's face, but centered her hot gaze on Rex's half-panicked visage. "I'm here because I needed to talk to someone I could trust." She could see the incomprehension in his eyes, and that, more than anything, defused her. "You just don't get it, do you?"

"Get what?" he almost squeaked.

She took a deep breath and backed away, met Lymon's neutral eyes, and shook her head. Turning, she walked to the cabinets and started rummaging from door to door.

"What are you looking for?" Lymon asked.

"Coffee cups."

"Third from the left."

She found a cup, walked over to Lymon's Capresso machine, and pushed the green button until all the lights were flashing. As the machine ground, hissed, and filled her cup, she let herself fume.

When she turned back, Rex had a slightly chastened look on his face. Sheela stalked across, pulled out a third chair, and seated herself. She gave Rex a frosty glance. "What if Lymon and I decide to take our relationship to the next level?"

Rex looked uneasily back and forth. "Sheela, I don't want to—"

"Just answer the question. What? You'd quit? Out of what? Jealousy? Is that what we're talking about here? Or would it be insecurity?" She slapped the table. "Damn! Don't tell me you're in love with me! Is that it? You couldn't stand to think of Lymon and me together?"

Rex made a wounded face. "No."

"Then, what?"

He sighed, lifted his coffee, and sipped. Buying time, no doubt. "Look, you do whatever you want with whomever you want, all right. I'll keep my nose out of it."

"Then what's your problem?"

"Are you going back to work?" Rex said it so hopefully.

Sheela chuckled dryly. "Oh, God, is that it? You're seeing your cash cow stumble?"

"Look, we've had this conversation."

"I'll call Felix. Have him nullify our contract. You're free, Rex. No penalties. I won't make a fuss."

Rex stopped short, sputtered, and seemed to have suddenly discovered an upset in his stomach.

"Wait a minute, Sheela, I'm not saying I want out."

"Then why are you here, and why are we having this conversation?"

Rex closed his eyes, reopened them to glance uneasily at Lymon, and asked, "Do we have to talk about this now?"

Sheela smacked her lips and said, "Yep."

Lymon was halfway to his feet. "I could—"

She reached out, grasping him by the wrist. "You're staying."

Lymon looked slightly uncomfortable as he reseated himself. She decided that she liked that. "You are the two most

important men in my life right now. Here's the word: I'm not
doing another movie for a while. I need some time for myself. I have things I need to see to. You are either with me, or
against me. Lymon, I already know is with me. Where are
you, Rex?"

She knew the look she was giving him; she'd used it with
great effect on-screen. Apparently it worked just as well in
person. Rex began to squirm.

"With you."

"Good. You're sure?"

"Yes."

"Because, Rex, if you're not, I can still make that call to
Felix."

He nodded, unhappy, but apparently on board. "I know.
It's not necessary."

She released Lymon's arm and took a sip of coffee.
"Good. I want you to call Dot and make sure that my schedule is cleared for the next month."

"Cleared for . . ." Rex began hotly, then caught himself.
"Okay, Sheela. What about after that?"

She smiled wearily. "Then I'll do whatever picture you
and Tony can come up with." That, or, who knew, she might
be anything. Even dead.

Christal shoveled food into her mouth as she studied Gregor
McEwan. Since taking up her regimen of strenuous exercising, her appetite had grown accordingly. With the revela-
tions given her by Brian Everly, her interest in McEwan had
blossomed.

He had brought her to the cafeteria, apparently during the
dinner hour because most of the other tables were filled
with casually garbed technicians. A group of neatly
groomed young men talked and laughed in the back as they
bent over one of those little games played with black and
white marbles.

"I'm not sure that holding you is such a good idea," McEwan noted, a thoughtful expression on his angular face. "The cost in food alone is exorbitant."

"So, let me go," she countered as she raised a spoonful of bangers and mash.

He lifted an eyebrow. "Not until we can come to some sort of agreement."

"You know Hank?"

"Who?"

"Hank Abrams. The guy who caught me, along with April and Gretchen."

He grunted, nodding. "They're a different part of the team. They work for Neal Gray. He's in charge of obtaining the samples. Why?"

"Hank said they wanted to make a deal with me. Up to now, no one has given me an incentive. And, Greg, I've—"

"Gregor, please. Greg makes my teeth hurt."

"Gotcha. No dentist on board, huh?" Christal chewed and balanced her spoon. "As I was saying, Gregor, locking me up in that little room where I can only stare at the walls and a round hole of ocean isn't buttering me up. It's pissing me off even more than I was pissed off to start with."

"Christal, I'm sorry, but you're considered a security risk. Put yourself in our position; would you just let someone with your capabilities wander around loose? To get into what kind of mischief?"

She wiped her mouth with her napkin and attacked the slice of apple pie. A gleam of interest lay behind his eyes. She knew that look, had seen it in men's eyes since she'd turned twelve.

All right, she'd use any vulnerability she could. She smiled. "Gregor, the point I'm trying to make is that you're a piss-poor salesman. Sending Hank down to try and bargain didn't start you off on your best foot. Get my drift?"

He warmed to her smile. "Then, I'm to understand that you'd be reasonable?"

"Sure." Her fork clattered on the empty plate. The two bodyguards were watching from their seats down the table. "Look, I'm as reasonable as the next person. But let's lay out the way it is, all right?"

"I'm listening."

"You guys steal my client's DNA. April socks me in the gut. Then Gretchen whizzes a slug past my head. Hank and April drug and kidnap me and carry me off to the *ZoeGen*, where you lock me into a tiny cubicle—enforced solitary confinement, right?"

He gave a slight wince.

Christal pointed a finger at him. "Now I've got a shitload to explain to my boss. The LA police, the FBI, my family—everybody's alerted to my abduction. I can tell you my mother is absolutely frantic by now. In short, this Neal Gray fellow just made a major fuckup."

"I see your point."

"Do you?" Christal leaned back. "Gregor, let's say I want to play ball. Like I said, I'm reasonable. Not only that, I'm ex-FBI. I know the system. I know how deep you guys are in now. As I see it, you've got two choices."

He leaned forward, elbows on the table. "And they are?"

"One, you keep me bottled up in my little room until the Sheik comes to check out his latest prize; then you wrap chain around my neck and throw me overboard to go sight-see on the *Titanic*. The problem with that is that Christal Anaya has vanished forever, and unlike your missing geneticists, I've got powerful friends with money who probably aren't going to let loose of this thing."

"And the second option?"

"We come to an agreement." She shrugged. "It'll cost you, but I can go back, assure everyone that I had to make a split-second business decision. That I'm sorry for upsetting people, but Genesis Athena made me an offer I couldn't refuse. I can turn the official wrath so that Lymon Bridges, my previous employer, takes most of the heat. I make amends with my family, buy mom a new car, and apologize for worrying her."

He narrowed his eyes. "Why would you do this?"

She chuckled, gesturing around. "For the same reason you did. Come on, tell me, Gregor, you were abducted in the beginning, weren't you?"

He sighed, giving in. "Aye. They came out of the mist one morning when I was dying of a hangover. I was terrified, hauled off at gunpoint, and drugged. Much as you were. It wasn't until I began to see what they were doing, realized the possibilities . . ." His eyes had taken on a glow. "Christal, there's a bloody fortune to be made here! What the twentieth century was to technology, the twenty-first will be for biotech. Imagine being in on the ground floor of a company like General Electric or Microsoft. That's what Genesis Athena will be. But more, because today we're talking global, not just national."

"Okay, but I'm still a little hazy on how this all works."

He grinned arrogantly. "All right, think of it like this: We have nearly six billion people in the world, but they're still people. They have the same old human desires for health, family, and security. People will *pay* to obtain those things."

"And Genesis Athena can guarantee security?"

"Maybe not complete security, but security from illness, from birth defects, augmented immune systems, resistance to certain diseases"—he grinned—"the return of a dead loved one."

She frowned at that.

"Oh, come on, Christal! Think about it. The greatest single tragedy in human history is that of the lost child—the young adult taken before their time. Society as a whole can bemoan the notion of cloning a dead infant. It's a different story when it's *your* infant, whom you loved and cherished, whom you would give your very life, your soul, to bring back."

"Maybe for some."

"Maybe for all, once the notion gets around." Gregor waved it away. "Part of the resistance to the idea of creating life out of someone's cellular DNA is that it's still too new, reeking of the impossible. Of black magic, if you will."

"And it's not?"

"Heavens, no!" Gregor leaned forward again. "We're not

talking wacko Raelians here. It's the future, Christal. It's adaptive. Look ahead into the next hundred years. As the population continues to grow, life will become ever more competitive. We're nearing a cap on our global resources. Maximizing productivity, knowledge, and redistribution of resources is the key to long-term survival. I'm not just talking at the individual level, but at the corporate, governmental, national, and international levels. It's a matter of positioning, of pooling talent and employing it."

"To do what?"

"Let's say a country pours fifteen percent of its GDP into health in the prevention of contagious diseases, for degenerative and metabolic disorders, treatment of alcoholism and genetic disorders, not to mention care for the aged and infirm. For the sake of argument, we'll give our government an annual budget of one hundred billion. That being the case, fifteen billion is going to health care."

"Uh-huh. So what can Genesis Athena do?"

"What if we could approach that government with a genetic screening program that would save them ten billion a year?"

Christal blinked. "You're joking!"

"No joke. Oh, granted, we can't do anything about traumatic injury. People will continue to fall off buildings, crash their cars, get in fights, and burn themselves. No, what we *can* eliminate are the contagious, metabolic, and degenerative diseases. How? By simple gene therapies, by rapid genotypic scanning of fetal tissue from amniotic fluid. What would the government of South Africa pay to stop HIV cold? We can do that for them."

"No way!"

"Way," Gregor said flatly. "And here it is: We've isolated the gene sequence on the ape chromosome that makes chimpanzees resistant to HIV. For roughly two billion we can build the labs, equip them, and guarantee that no child born with that additional complex of ape genes will be HIV positive in South Africa again."

She stared at him. "You're serious."

"Very much so. And that's just the tip of the iceberg. You ever been to South Africa? Roughly a third of the population is HIV positive. Johannesburg will change your comprehension. On one side of the street, I've seen a thirty-story glass-and-steel skyscraper. It might have been transplanted from downtown London, Frankfurt, or Hong Kong. The parking lot is filled with Mercedes, BMWs, and shiny Lexus autos. Across the street—I kid you not—is a refugee camp filled with a thousand people living in cardboard, tin, and plastic tarp shanties. They bathe and drink in the same ditch they defecate in."

"Why?" Christal shook her head. "Why do they do it?"

"Because Africa is teetering on the verge of catastrophe. In the old days, the ANC was granted asylum by other countries. Now, they refuse to deny any refugee a similar chance at the future. Their borders are open to persecuted people fleeing the tyranny of demented egomaniacal leaders in Zambia, Zimbabwe, and Angola. So today in South Africa the First World exists in a patchwork crazy quilt with the Third, often only separated by a single boulevard. It has to be seen to be believed."

"And Genesis Athena can fix that?"

"We can help." Gregor tilted his head, inquisitive eyes on Christal's. "Let's go back to our hypothetical model. What could they do with another ten billion a year? Build infrastructure? Educate their people? Develop industries and train new workers? Perhaps put it into agricultural production to feed their people?"

"Let me get this straight. You're telling me that Genesis Athena is out to save the world? That all this"—she waved around at the ship—"is part of a mission for mankind?"

Gregor stared thoughtfully at the table in front of him. "The brutal truth is that we're a business. No better and no worse than any other. We intend to make a profit. We're no different than a hospital, and in a sense, we offer the same services. Health in return for payment for services rendered."

"And the cloning?" Did she dare mention the things Brian had told her? No. Not until she understood the dynamics.

"That's what we call vanity, or luxury services." He searched her eyes intently. "Like I said, it's a business. We're in a race to patent as many genotypes as we can. The same with the genes themselves, like the chimpanzee immune sequence I mentioned earlier. Meanwhile, we have people paying small fortunes to have us re-create a dead child. Our Elvis clones sell for one hundred thousand dollars apiece. We've cashed checks for over ten million on Elvis alone."

Christal gaped. "Ten *million*? Just for Elvis? It's hard to comprehend."

"Imagine trying to explain automobiles and airplanes to someone in Victorian England in the 1890s. People would have thought you daft. In fact, they'd have looked much the way you do right now, Christal Anaya. They'd have had that same skeptical look in their eyes."

"Do you really think you can do this?"

"Aye." He smiled fondly. "That's why I went with Genesis Athena. In another fifty years my name will be spoken alongside Bill Gates, Thomas Edison, and Henry Ford. My processes will have banished HIV, multiple sclerosis, Huntington's chorea, cystic fibrosis, and even susceptibility to such common diseases as tuberculosis, rubella, influenza, and rhinoviruses. My replicative procedures will be the standard for millions who wish to duplicate themselves. Lass, it's going to revolutionize everything."

Christal sensed his vulnerability. "I want to see this."

He glanced up. "I beg your pardon?"

She waved around at the cafeteria. "I'm in a secure part of the ship, right?"

"To put it mildly, I think you'd be harder pressed to get into the White House than out of here."

"Then let me see. Let me meet people." She glared when he started to object, stating, "Gregor, *I mean it.* What if you're not just blowing smoke? What if it's really true and you can do all these things?"

"It is."

"Then why can't I make my own decision if I want in or not?"

39

Sheela sat across from Felix Baylor in her first-floor meeting room. The polished wooden table was already littered with papers from Felix's open leather briefcase.

"Jesus," Sheela whispered as she scanned one of the stapled sheets Felix had given her.

"That's just the tip of the iceberg." Felix's voice pinched. "As near as my people can determine, Genesis Athena has somewhere in the neighborhood of forty million in assets in their publicly held corporation. My guess is that many of the entities who are major shareholders have even deeper pockets."

"And this Sheik Amud Abdulla?"

"He's the public figure. There are others, Sheela, people back in the shadows. I can't even begin to guess at this point." He hesitated. "And I'm not sure I want to."

She looked up. "Excuse me?"

Felix fitted the tips of his fingers together. "You asked me to set up a hypothetical inquiry from Jennifer Weaver. I did that. There was no risk involved for either you or me. I don't want to dig any deeper, Sheela. If I do, flags are going to go up."

"Meaning what?"

He shrugged, creasing his sleek silk suit. "I'm not sure myself. I can tell you, however, that after years in this business, I can sense trouble when I'm sniffing at its door. If I send my people to ferret out the big guns behind Genesis Athena, I don't think we're going to like the results."

Sheela sat back in her chair. "I've never seen you scared before."

Felix took a deep breath. "I've never tripped over anything like this before. A great deal of wealth from Saudi Arabia, Kuwait, Qatar, Iran, Italy, the US, Argentina, Peru, and Great Britain is involved here. Even one Texas billionaire with a really unsavory reputation when it comes to outside interference in his affairs is seriously involved."

Sheela laid the sheet in front of her. "Thank you, Felix. I won't ask you to do more for the time being."

He gave her a sidelong glance. "It doesn't mean that we can't sue, Sheela. Given what I've discovered"—he gestured at the papers before her—"we can still file. These people invaded your privacy, stole your DNA for profit. What they're doing is morally, ethically, and legally reprehensible."

"You just told me you wouldn't want to tangle with these people."

"That's in a different realm." Felix smiled warily. "If we file suit, it will be a matter of record in a court of law. That's according to the rules, if you will. Then, during discovery, we can drag out the other names. That, too, will be according to the rules. They won't mess with the judicial system because of the unwanted attention it will bring them."

"Such subtle nuances."

"That's law. But if we go that route you had better be prepared to settle out of court with a literal mountain of nondisclosure forms. They're going to want to bind that settlement up in iron chains."

She picked up the report again, reading through the several pages. "So, this is really it?"

"That's it."

"Christal hit it on the head, didn't she?" Sheela tapped her fingers on the paper. "Jesus, Felix, they're selling my DNA." She glanced up. "Can they really do that? Technically, I mean. Implant little copies of me into some other woman's womb?"

"Apparently. Yeah, I guess. They've done it with sheep, cattle, cats, monkeys, and apes. The popular story is that there are too many variables for reliable cloning of a human being. You remember the Clonaid thing with the Raelians? After that people said it was too dangerous, that too many unknowns made it unreliable."

"Unless Genesis Athena knows something the rest of the world doesn't."

His expression was serious. "Given the amount of money they seem to have poured into this, they could be light-years beyond the current state of knowledge in university labs."

"Thank you, Felix." She indicated the report. "If you could set this up so easily, anyone else could, too. I need to think for a while. I'll be in touch."

Felix nodded, stood, and began replacing papers into his briefcase. "Sheela, I think it would be a good idea to let Rex know what we've discovered."

She stared at the neat paragraphs on the report, her heart like lead in her chest. "I'll tell him when I think the time is right."

"All right, but I want you to know that in my professional—"

"Yes, yes, I know." She waved him away. "But I'll keep my own counsel on this. Thank you again, Felix."

She watched him snap his briefcase closed, nod, and walk to the door. Only after it had clicked shut did she reach for her telephone. "Keep the faith, Christal, wherever you are. You're going to be part of the settlement."

She dialed a 1-800 number and picked up one of the bound reports Felix had left behind. When the voice on the other end said, *"Genesis Athena. Melinda speaking. How may I help you?"* Sheela answered, "My name is Jennifer Weaver. My case number is 94-4443."

"One moment please." A pause. *"I see that you're interested in a procedure for a Sheela Marks baby."*

"Yes. I'd like to book a procedure, please." She made a face. "I'm afraid time is something of a problem. Could we do this soon?"

From the *ZoeGen*'s high railing Hank watched the white launch approach the ship. The small launch bobbed on the North Atlantic's deep blue swells. It seemed like an eternity since he, himself, had been one of the baffled visitors. From his vantage point on the rail, Hank watched the people clamber down the ladder to the craft. One was a petite blond woman wearing a white windbreaker and slim jeans. She looked slightly unnerved as she leaped into the rising and falling boat. One by one he watched, counting no less than thirty-one passengers. Assuming fifty thousand a day as an average, that was a 1.6 million-dollar boatload down there. And the launches arrived three times a day for delivery and pickup.

He raised his eyes, looking out to the west. The cool breeze was blowing into his face, carrying with it the smells of salt, sea, and far-off land. He squinted past the razor-sharp horizon. There, somewhere just beyond the curve of the Atlantic, lay Halifax, Nova Scotia.

April appeared, a white sweater masking the thrust of her breasts but accenting her square shoulders. The wind whipped her copper-colored hair back. She looked over the railing, catching sight of the blonde, and remarked, "*Cha-ching!* There's another big chunk of change into the till. I just hope she was one of mine."

"One of yours?"

"The embryo she was implanted with. If it was one of my recoveries—say, Julia Roberts or Sheela Marks—I'm a couple of thousand dollars richer."

"That's your royalty, right?"

"Right." April leaned her head back, breathing deeply through her nose. "Rumor is that we've got another three big-dollar clients down in the lab. All Canadians. One of them for a child replication. The other two are enhancement jobs for rich kids."

"An enhancement?"

"Something about changing one of the base pairs to modify a sugar molecule on the brain cells." April made a face. "I'm way out of my area of expertise, but I think it's supposed to make the brain grow larger. Our people are into things like that. Simple little changes that give cells a slightly higher performance."

"What if it backfires? I'm just starting to understand the risks involved in fooling with people's genetics."

"There's risk in everything, Hank. You didn't go into the FBI without accepting a little risk."

"No, I guess I didn't." He smiled at that. "Funny, isn't it? The last place I'd have thought I was going to end up was on a ship in the Atlantic, preparing to steal other people's DNA."

"You'll retire rich."

"If we don't get busted first."

"We have insurance in the form of a crack legal team. Sometime it'll happen. As inevitable as rain. Cost of doing business and all. When it does, keep your mouth shut, call our attorneys, and let them settle. We've got some of the biggest guns in the business."

"Assuming we can come to terms with Christal. Kidnapping isn't just trespass."

Neal's voice came from behind. "We're working on her. The head of our genetics department has been talking to her. He seems to think she's coming around." Neal stepped up and looked down just as the launch cast off. White foam boiled under the stern as the launch bucked into the waves and headed for the invisible western shore.

"What's the plan?" April asked. "Vacation's fine, but I'm not adding to my investment by sitting out here, pleasant though it might be."

Neal leaned forward, staring down at the swells that rose and lapped so far below. "There's a complication."

"Why don't I like the way you said that?" Hank asked, turning, crossing his arms.

"You remember that motorcycle when we grabbed Anaya?"

"Yeah. The one you knocked over. I think I told you at the time it was a dumb thing to do."

Neal turned, his blond hair flipping in the wind. A coldness lay behind his blue eyes. "Want to take a guess as to who was on that bike?"

"Ronald Reagan. But since he had Alzheimer's he couldn't remember a thing."

"Try Sheela Marks. The driver was her bodyguard. I think you made his acquaintance."

Hank made a face. "Neal, I want you to know right off: The guy's trouble. He's not just some rent-a-cop. Neither is he the usual stupid no-neck muscle guy recruited from a gym. He's the real thing. Don't underestimate him."

Neal pursed his lips. April was watching him, a cool appraisal in her eyes.

"It gets worse," Neal added. "It seems there was a paparazzo with a camera. The guy got photos."

"Shit." Hank turned, slapped his palm on the rail, and glared out at the endless expanse of water. The sun was riding high, well into its summer path. A group of gulls wheeled and ducked, checking them out before following the deck aft.

"What does that mean?" April asked.

"It means that Neal fucked up," Hank muttered.

"Hey! Don't start pointing the finger at me!" Neal barked. "You were the one who coordinated that whole operation, remember?"

Hank raised a hand. "Stop it! We're in the shit, Neal. You're the one who walked over and knocked the bike over. Prior to that, everything was explainable. But I'm not going to get into a pissing contest." He turned, glaring alternately at Neal and April. "I've been down this road before, so believe me, let's admit that we had a screwup, deal with it as a team, and go about fixing the problem instead of cutting each other's throats."

Neal was still hot, his face red and angry. "Right, smart guy. You got any ideas?"

Hank bit his lip, avoided Neal's eyes, and gave April a slight wink. She seemed to be hanging all her hopes on that. After a moment, he said, "The key to this is Anaya."

"Yeah," Neal said roughly. "I say we go down, walk her up here, and let her see if she can swim home."

"An injection would be quicker," April added. "We could dissect her in one of the labs and drop the pieces overboard. If you'll recall, they found Nancy Hartlee and identified her."

"Whoa, Nelly!" Hank raised his hands. "Jesus! It's a miracle you've made it this far. You're about to compound one crime with another? You guys aren't any smarter than the damn hick criminals I've spent half my life slapping cuffs on!"

He had their attention now; even Neal was calming down. Hank smiled. "Look, the thing is, you can't let it escalate. You start to panic, and intelligence goes out the door so fast it sucks logic and sense right out behind it. No, what we have to do is handle Anaya. Buy her off, convert her, brainwash her, I don't care; but the fact is that you've got to get her back to Los Angeles with a story that the cops can believe."

Neal looked unconvinced. "A bullet to the brain—"

"Don't even think it!" Hank growled. "From here on out, put that thought out of your mind. Banish it! Be smarter. That's the tough thing."

"Smart how?" April asked. The chill had sharpened her complexion.

"A thousand ways," Hank answered. "She came here doped to the gills; she could leave the same way." He snapped his fingers as he looked around the ship. "All right, just for example, what would happen if our Christal was found two weeks from now passed out on a street in Kingston, Jamaica? Let's say she was injected with cocaine and ecstasy and with a blood alcohol content of two-point-two, so that when the cops dropped her at the hospital, her toxicology read like a junkie's dream recipe. Meanwhile, someone calls her mom in New Mexico asking if Christal's there. When mom says no, our caller says, 'Well, she ripped off two hundred bucks from me in Key West, and I ain't gonna forget it!' When mom asks who this is, our caller says, 'Hey, I just party with the lady in LA, you know?' And we hang up."

Neal had begun to smile. April had lowered her chin, complicated thoughts shuttling back and forth behind her gray eyes. She asked, "Do you think that would work?"

"With a little embellishing, yeah. I mean, we'll have to fine-tune it, but it's got all the right ingredients. If she wants to babble about a ship, the feds will think it was a regular cruise ship. They've got an excuse to think she wasn't kidnapped. Instead, she was doing drugs, went AWOL with partying friends, and came to in Jamaica, or wherever the hell

we leave her. End of story, and we all go back to work."
Hank lifted an eyebrow. "We've got the resources, right?"

"Uh-huh," Neal agreed. "Sure, we can do it. But what
about Anaya? She was after Genesis Athena in the beginning. She's going to know when she sobers up and flushes
out that she was set up."

"Let her." Hank shrugged. "Look, the lady's got a bad
rep with the Bureau. They'll be glad to wash their hands of
her. As to her boss, he's an arrogant prick. If it looks like
he's going to be tarred by her actions I think he'll fire her
butt and make sure she stays a thousand miles from Sheela
Marks. The LAPD is going to read the FBI report and figure that Anaya just wasted a pile of their precious time.
Without resources, Christal can say anything she wants.
Who's going to believe her? Her credibility, along with a
buck fifty, will get her a cup of coffee at Denny's, and
that's that."

April looked at Neal. "When can we do this?"

Neal shrugged. "That depends on whether the Sheik
wants to make a special trip out to see her. For the present,
as soon as we finish with the last Canadian, we're heading
south again. Reservations has another sixty clients coming
out of New York for procedures. Depending on what the
Sheik wants to do, I'd say that we wait for another week,
set up the arrangements, and initiate the plan. It will take a
while to score the drugs, review the plan, and figure out
how to move Anaya from here to there. I'll want to talk to
McEwan, make sure that what we sedate her with won't
leave a fingerprint." He glanced at Hank. "Is this time-
critical?"

Hank shrugged. "I can't say. Probably not. The longer
they look until they find her, the more pissed at her they're
going to be."

April laughed suddenly, causing Hank to ask, "What?"

"You're going to enjoy this, aren't you?"

"Hey," he told her, "paybacks are a bitch."

*   *   *

That night, Mozart's Symphony no. 40 was playing on the sound system in Felix Baylor's oak-paneled home office at his 4.5 million-dollar mansion perched high on the flank of the Santa Monica Mountains just off Canyon Drive. He sat behind his huge teak desk, a snifter of Camus Borderies XO to his right. He had his laptop open, a copy of a contract glowing on the screen. If he looked to his left he could see through the large picture window and down the brush-choked slope to the city. The lights twinkled and shimmered. He could see the Beverly Hilton glowing near where Whittier merged with Wilshire. Across the room—flanked by floor-to-ceiling bookcases—a large red cordovan couch with carved armrests dominated the wall.

Returning his attention to the contract, he frowned as he studied one of the clauses covering residuals and bent to the keyboard, overstriking a series of Xs over the offending part. What the hell did the studio take him for? A brainless idiot? Leaving that wording would have let them weasel their way into several million in DVD sales.

He reached for the cognac, lifted the crystal bulb, and sipped. The door clicked, and he looked up, irritated. "Becky, I've told you . . ."

Lymon Bridges came striding into the room followed by a burly man in his midthirties, black-haired, in a casual coat and tie. The stranger closed the door behind him, flipping the lock home as Lymon crossed the floor.

"What the hell?" Felix stood, glaring. "Get the *hell* out of my house! Damn you, Lymon, you don't just show up here without some sort of appointment! I don't give a foggy damn what you told Becky—"

Bridges stepped around the desk, caught Felix's arm, and twisted. Felix screamed as a spear of pain lanced through his shoulder. He bent, following Lymon's lead as the man bulled him across the room and stuffed him face-forward into the plush red leather Spanish couch.

Stunned, half-panicked, Felix heard the second man say, "So this is how the other half live? Nice office. From the thickness of the walls, I'd say pretty much soundproof, too. No one'll hear the screams."

"Where is she?" Lymon demanded, bending down to growl into Felix's ear. He added torsion to the strained arm, and Felix screamed into the leather.

"I want to know it all, Felix. Every last bit of it. *Where is she?*"

"What are you . . ." His whimper was stifled as Lymon jammed a hard hand behind his neck and pressed his head deeper into the suffocating leather. Felix flopped, trying to kick out with his legs, feeling his shoes slip across the waxed maple floor.

"Uh, boss, you might let him catch a breath," the accomplice said mildly. "If you suffocate him, it'll take hours to rummage through all of his papers to find the right notes."

"Right, Sid." Lymon let up, allowing Felix to turn his head far enough to gasp a quick breath.

Sid—looking big in the corner of Felix's vision—bent down to stare. The look of disdain in those hard brown eyes sent a shiver through the lawyer's soul. He might have been an insect—one with interesting wings, but an insect nevertheless.

"Where is she?" Lymon repeated, a bit more leniently this time. "Where did she go?"

"I can't tell you. Lawyer-client priv—" He ended in a scream as Lymon twisted him into the leather again.

"That doesn't help," Sid chastised from the side. "You don't want to piss Lymon off. I've seen him rip a guy's arm clean out of the socket when he gets really pissed. We had an Al Qaeda rag-head one time that cried for a day and half before Lymon finally lost his temper and broke his neck." A pause. "You know, the CO was so torqued off we had to walk patrol for two weeks in the hills after that." His voice dropped. "Are you feeling careless yet, Lymon?"

"I just might be."

Sid added, "Mr. Baylor, maybe you'd better just tell him. That way you avoid all the pain, the surgery, the pills, the time in physical therapy."

"Where is she?" Lymon hissed into Felix's ear.

"Lymon, you're making a terrible mistake," Felix managed to mutter against the leather. "I'll have you up on charges for—" Lymon pushed his face into the cushions and wrenched the arm. Leather stifled the scream.

"Felix," Lymon said softly, "I'll tell you this once. Whatever she's gotten herself into, she's not up to it. So, you're going to tell me what she's doing . . . where she's gone. I don't give a rat's ass about privilege, because if anything's happened to her, I'm going to break your silly little neck."

"I'd listen to him, boss," Sid added solicitously. "Lymon's the kind of guy who'll twist your head off, shit down your neck, then screw your head on backwards just out of sheer cussedness."

"How'd you get in here?" Felix's stumbling mind tried to latch onto something, anything, to give him a lever on the way to recovery.

"Locks were a hobby of mine in the military," Sid answered. "Yours weren't very challenging."

"Felix? You going to tell?" Lymon added.

The last of Felix's resolve drained away. He went limp, tears of frustration beaded at the edge of his vision. "Genesis Athena. She's after them."

Lymon released his hold, grabbing Felix's collar and turning him so that he sat facing forward on the couch. Looking up into those eyes gave Felix's stomach a cramp. "She asked me to set up an account under the name Jennifer Weaver."

"After the character she played in *Joy's Girl*?"

"Yes." Felix closed his eyes, looking down at his rumpled shirt. The fine silk suit coat still looked pristine.

"Where did she go?"

Felix shook his head. "I don't know. Honest, Lymon. She didn't tell me. She had me set up an account, obtain an ID, credit cards . . . Hell, I built an entire identity for her. Driver's license, everything."

Lymon drove a fist into a hard palm. It sounded like an oak beam snapping. Felix flinched. "She's going to have your ass, Lymon. Just like I'm going to."

"I want the file. You've got a copy."

"At the office."

"Then we're going to the office."

Felix swallowed hard, his mouth dry. A terrible violence

lay behind Lymon's eyes, a look he'd never seen there before. "Why are you *doing* this?"

"Because she's in way over her head." The faintest thaw hovered around Lymon's lips. "Bless her heart, she thinks she can do something about it, maybe figure a way to get Christal back, but she's walking into a snake's den."

"She didn't want you to know," Felix added. "Not you, not Rex, not Tony, nobody."

"Yeah," Lymon muttered. "I figured that out. But for the fact that Tomaso loves the lady almost as much as I do, she might even have gotten away with it. She scared the shit out of him when she made him drive her to the airport in his little Toyota."

Felix raised a hand in defeat. "Let me up, Lymon. Don't hurt me again. It's in my computer. I'll print you a copy of everything I've got."

Lymon reached down, pulled him to his feet, holding him close so that he could stare into Felix's eyes. It sent a deeper chill down Felix's spine. "One last thing, Felix. What happened here tonight, it's between you and me. Alone. Do you understand?"

Felix nodded, averted his eyes, and almost stumbled as he walked toward his desk to retrieve the files.

40

Lymon led the way up the back steps to his second-floor office. Sid's heavy feet thudded on the metal behind him. As Lymon fished for his key, he asked, "Are you sure you want to be part of this?"

Sid stopped on the next stair down, his round face illuminated by the yellow security light. The night was alive with the sound of traffic, distant sirens, and the hum of the building fans. In the parking lot below, Lymon's Jaguar gleamed in the light.

"Yeah. I helped get Christal into this mess."

Lymon turned, slid his key into the lock, and opened the door. He took a right, flipping on the light as he walked through the storeroom to the safe in the back corner. He heard Sid lock the outside door before following him.

The dial turned as Lymon input the combination. "You're a government employee, Sid. A federal agent. If this gets sticky, you don't have the approval of your supervisor. They could get real nasty with you." He looked back as he turned the handle to undog the latches.

Sid had a pensive look on his face. "Sometimes, Lymon, things just get out of hand. It's the LA Field Office's case, but this Genesis Athena thing, it's related to my stuff. I can feel it in my gut."

"You know what they do to agents who go out on a limb?"

"They whack it off just to see how far they fall." Sid rolled his lips over his teeth. "I don't have time to fill out the 302s and jump through the hoops. If this works out, I'll get a reprimand, but I'll still break the case." He grinned sheepishly. "Uh, if you'll recall, we've had reprimands before."

"The problem is, we've got to be right. You understand that, don't you? You break the rules and fuck up at the same time, they hammer your ass."

"If it gets that bad, I hear that there's some guy in California wants to offer me a job."

"If you really fuck up big league, they throw you in jail."

"Let's try not to fuck up that much, okay?"

Lymon turned his attention to the safe. A rack of six HK Compact .40-caliber pistols rested on the padded top shelf. Boxes of CorBon .40 S&W cartridges were stacked next to a collection of high-capacity magazines. The lower shelves were filled with files of confidential correspondence, several sacks of bundled bills, agreements, and official LBA documents. In the bottom rested a black plastic case secured with a combination lock. This, Lymon bent and retrieved.

Sid frowned. "Is that what I think it is?"

"Yep." Lymon turned, plucking two of the magazines from the shelf and dropping them into his pocket. He then added a box of .40-caliber ammunition and finally slipped one of the HK pistols into his coat pocket. Locking the safe door, he lifted the lid on a storage box by his feet and retrieved a shoulder holster before leading the way to the hall and on to his office.

Sid was eyeing the heavy black plastic case that hung from Lymon's right hand. "I'm not going to ask if you've got a Class Three license for that thing."

"I do. All nice and legal." Lymon walked into his office, flopped the heavy black case on the desk, and unloaded his pockets of pistol, mags, and ammo before sloughing his coat off. He slipped his arms through the holster straps, opened the box of ammunition, and began thumbing cartridges into a magazine.

"So," Sid asked, "what's the plan? You know, since Nine/-eleven, you're not walking onto any airplane with a holster rig and magazines, no matter what you're licensed for."

Lymon glanced up as he slipped a magazine into the HK, worked the slide, and dropped the mag to top it off. "She's traveling under the name Jennifer Weaver. We've got her account number at Genesis Athena. When I pushed the redial on her phone, I got Delta Airlines reservations. They confirmed she boarded the five p.m. flight for New York. Work it out."

"We're going to New York?" Sid made a face as he studied the black case. "You're outfitting for an operation into the Biqa' Valley, not the Big Apple. I don't want to be the one to rain on your parade, but you don't have any legal leg to stand on if they catch you there with a pistol and an MP5." He pointed to the black case. "Assuming, that is, that you can even get past airport security with that stuff."

Lymon's grizzled brows lifted. "Oh, ye of little faith." He slipped the loaded pistol into the holster riding under his left arm, flipped through his Rolodex, and began punching numbers on the desk phone. He smiled at Sid as he raised the receiver to his ear.

It rang three times before a familiar voice answered, *"Hi. Vol Aviation. Bernie here."*

"Bernie? It's Lymon Bridges," Lymon began. "We've got an emergency. How soon can we be in the air for New York?"

"An hour and a half," Bernie answered after a slight hesitation. *"Uh, where did you say we were going again?"*

"New Jersey, actually. Teterboro."

"Right. I'll get the flight plan filed . . . fuel the jet. How many people?"

"Two."

"Right. Any special considerations?"

"Nope."

"I'll be ready."

"See you then." Lymon hung up the phone, grinning at Sid. "Charter, my friend. It's expensive as all hell, no security hassles, and I can guarantee you, the food's better."

Sid cracked a smile for the first time. "I could get to like this. Assuming, that is, that we don't get our tits into one hell of a ringer."

"You've read the files." Lymon finished loading his second magazine and dropped it into the holster's magazine pouch. "We've got to get to that marina in Brooklyn. We'll find her there."

"You'd better hope."

"Yeah, well, if not—if they pick her up first—Verele's going to have a very bad day until he spills his guts about Genesis Athena."

Sheela sat in seat 4A and stared vacantly out the plastic window. She had seen the Mississippi pass below before the overcast closed in over Illinois. Now as she looked down, it was to watch a blanket of fluffy moonlit clouds roll slowly under her high-flying 767. The paperback novel she held remained unread. She'd picked it up at the newsstand—something about archaeology and Southwestern witchcraft. The subject had made her think of Christal, but try as she might, she couldn't keep her attention on the story.

To her consternation, the in-flight movie was *Blood Rage*. She did everything she could to avoid seeing her image on the small screens at each of the other seats. Would anyone glance up from their little glowing screens, notice her, and begin pointing?

She reached up, absently fingering the brown wig she

wore. It was a quality job, as good as money could buy—
and God alone knew she'd had enough experience with the
finest makeup artists in the world to know how to make a
wig look real.

She fought the urge to get up and walk to the lavatory.
She'd already been there twice to see that her brown contacts hadn't slipped, to check her makeup and ensure that
she hadn't smudged the olive complexion she'd so labori-
ously applied.

She was Jennifer Weaver now, a desperate and lonely
woman traveling cross-country to fulfill a fantasy.

Bullshit! With each passing minute she was growing ever
more frightened, wondering what passing insanity had
driven her to attempt this foolishness.

I won't let you down, Christal. The image of her father's
bloated face floated in the back of her mind. It left a tight-
ness around her heart.

She ran her fingers along the edges of the paperback
novel, looking at the stylized image of Kokopelli embossed
on the foiled cover. *Where are you, Christal? What are you
doing?*

She closed her eyes, thinking back to Christal's self-
assured smile that day. God, she'd seemed invincible. But
twenty-four hours later she'd been spirited away to where?
The nightmare fantasies kept spinning in Sheela's mind.
They were filled with brutality and rape. In each, Christal
suffered in filthy and degrading conditions.

"I'll make them give you back," she whispered under her
breath.

A sudden image of Lymon levered its way into her wheeling thoughts. She could see his disapproving expression,
trace the lines of worry that would be forming there in the
next day or so when he finally discovered that she'd disappeared. He'd be frantic. They all would. But she could count
on Felix to keep a lid on it. He'd make sure they didn't do
anything silly, like report her as a missing person.

Not telling Lymon hurt the worst. But she'd make it up to
him. In the end, they'd have their day. She'd go, find out
about Genesis Athena, decline their service at the last mo-

ment, and pay them enough to make it all right. Then she'd have the inside story. From there, Felix and his minions could apply the screws and break the whole damn thing wide open.

She closed her eyes. For the first time in years, she was doing something. Not for others, but for herself. For Christal, who'd offered her friendship without strings. For the little babies who would be born of this malicious procedure. Yes, it was worth being frightened,

By God, a person's DNA should be sacrosanct, private and personal! It was hers, as it was Julia's, and Sandra's, and Mel's, and Brad's, and all the others. Intimately part of their lives and bodies and souls. Why had no one seen this coming? Why had Congress, in all of its hearings, with all of its expert testimony, not preempted this? Where the hell had the Solons been when the news percolated with stories of genetics?

If only she weren't so scared. If the fear would just loosen from around her guts. Damn it, this wasn't a movie. This was for real, with people who'd dared to kidnap someone as tough as Christal Anaya from right under their noses.

Genesis Athena had no idea that Jennifer Weaver was anything but what she seemed. It would be the role of a lifetime—only no one would ever know.

No one but me—and after all, who the hell else is there in the end?

One by one she thumbed the pages of the novel, the words unseen on the pages as her jet whisked ever eastward.

Christal reveled in her newfound freedom. Earlier that morning McEwan had shown her the length and breadth of her current universe. After seeing the security arrangements, she wondered why the hell they'd bothered to lock her into her cubicle in the first place.

Her world now consisted of a small segment of H Deck on the ship's port side. A series of cabins were inhabited by various staff, most of whom Gregor had introduced her to.

Each had been pleasant, professional, and reserved. English was obviously their second language, and from their reaction to her, Christal could tell that outside of the same coloration and complexion, they were from different worlds.

She had played dumb when Gregor introduced her to Brian Everly. It was apparent from Brian's expression that he'd rather engage in an intimate relationship with cholera than be in the same room with the Scottish geneticist. Two points for Brian.

There was one way in, and one way out, and it passed through a monitored "go, no-go" steel hatch. The thing had been modified like the common jail access where only one door could be opened at a time, and then only when a security officer pressed the right button. The hallways were studded with video cameras. She could now walk to the cafeteria, to a small home theater with a DVD collection of the latest movies, to a common lounge with its TV, comfortable chairs, pool table, and games. A compact but complete gym and the attached women's locker room with its attendant showers was also available for her use.

The security camera in the women's shower had caused her some concern. She had to assume that it worked and that some man was watching. Modesty won out. She glowered up at the camera, then down at the stained pits on her blue blouse. It wasn't like they'd brought a wardrobe for her. She had what she'd been wearing the night they'd kidnapped her.

After McEwan had left, she'd availed herself of the gym, pounding out her aggression on the weight machines and treadmill. Flushed and dehydrated, she walked out into the hallway. With the towel hung over her shoulders, she dabbed at the perspiration beading on her face and throat. Her muscles had a deliciously loose and warm feel, and she absently studied the hoses, cables, and pipes that ran along the companionway ceiling. Was there some way she could exploit them? How?

"Christal?" a familiar voice called. She turned to see Brian Everly stepping out of a cabin.

"Brian." She let her towel hang and held her hands up.

"Look! I'm free! Ready to fly away just as soon as I can cut a hole through the hull."

"What have you been doing?"

"Exercising. I'm hot, sweaty, and smelly, but I refuse to use the women's shower with that damned TV camera staring down."

He glanced around. "They know you're out?"

"Gregor unlocked my door." She stepped in beside him. "He thinks he's got a chance to convert me to the side of money, greed, and corruption. That or throw me over the side to the sharks." She motioned around. "Besides, I've been up and down the halls. I'm not seeing anything I can fashion into a clever tool to make an escape."

He chuckled. "Good on you. But believe me we've been at it for five years. If there were a way, we'd have found it. I'm off for the cafeteria. You up for a bite?"

"Sure. Uh, provided you can either sit upwind or don't mind the smell."

Something in his smile sent a tickle through her. "Oh, I think I can endure. You have a nice scent."

"Liar." She walked at his side, glancing at him. "So, for five years no one has broken out of here?"

"Nancy Hartlee. And look where that got her."

"What about McEwan?"

"What about him? He's one of *them*. He can come and go as he pleases."

"How does he motivate you? I mean, you and the rest, you could just sit down and say 'Up yours' and refuse to lift a finger. Go on strike, if you will."

He gave her a sympathetic glance. "Have you ever heard the name Albert Speer?"

"Who?"

"Nazi general. He was the genius who kept Hitler's war machine running through the last years of the war. A brilliant man, actually. While the Allies bombed German industry into rubble, he decentralized it, moved it underground, and kept a couple of million slave laborers producing munitions and aircraft." He smiled sadly. "McEwan is that sort. Bloody fucking brilliant."

"You could sabotage things."

He gave her a thoughtful look. "What if you were given a choice? That you could work and produce, or be the subject of ebola research?"

"No shit?"

"Speer had bad guys in uniforms walking up and down the factory floors. If his workers failed to meet their quota, they were shot in the head. On the *ZoeGen* there are other means, just as persuasive, at McEwan's disposal." Brian smiled sourly. "Nowadays there are few of us left. The recently nabbed people, like Mike Harris and the rest, are at the facility in Yemen. If we don't take the buyout, who knows what will happen to us. There are two schools of thought on the matter. One is that after they pay us a bloody small fortune and we sign their nondisclosure agreement, they really will let us go. The second is that it will be cheaper to simply give us a sedative and sink our weighted bodies into the Rockall Trough."

"The where?"

"A really deep hole in the middle of the Atlantic."

"Oh."

He held the door to the cafeteria for her. "But, moving on to more delightful conversation, tell me about yourself. How on earth did you get here?"

Christal nodded at some of the now-familiar Arab technicians who sat at the end of one of the tables, drinking coffee. "I was researching Genesis Athena for my employer. Apparently I got too close. That and I caught the Sheik's eye at a New York film premiere. But we've talked about that already. I'd rather hear about what you're doing." She walked over and took a tray and silverware. As they went through the line, selecting items, she said, "I mean, I've come to understand the why of it. Billions of dollars can be made. Where there's money, there's a way. But, like, why kidnap you people? Why not just hire you?"

He piled mashed potatoes on his plate. "Because of the legalities. Oh, I don't just mean the work itself, but, well, take Nancy's nanoscalpel. The University of California at Davis had filed on the patent. By stealing Nancy, Genesis Athena got all the information on how to build one of their own.

They now hold the patent on a machine far in advance of the UC Davis device. Nancy's technology, coupled with Gregor's work on maintaining cytoplasm integrity in the oocyte, gave them the technique. I had a patent pending on my procedure for introducing nuclear DNA from dead cells into living ones. Mitch Harvey had isolated and perfected the procedure for isolating and introducing spermatozoic phospholipase C into—"

"Huh?" She gave him an askance look as they carried their trays to a table. "Talk English, all right?"

He grinned as he sat. "It's been years since I've had to describe things to the uninitiated, so stop me if I get too technical."

"Count on it."

He made a sphere with his hands. "Think of a cell as a complex functioning organism, which, in a sense, it is. It has a skin that surrounds it and the equivalency of organs—called organelles—functioning inside it. At the heart is the nucleus—the center, where the DNA is. That's like the central computer. The cell itself is filled with cytoplasm, the nutrient-rich fluid in which the organelles float . . . No, that's a bad analogy. Let's say it's a gel in which the organelles are both suspended and interconnected—a chemical mix that has a great deal to do with the health and well-being of the cell itself."

"Right, I remember most of this from my biology class. But why was floating such a bad analogy?"

"Because in the beginning we didn't have any idea how important or intricate the cytoplasmic structure was when we were sucking nuclear DNA out of one cell and squirting it into another. It would be like sucking your heart out with a giant vacuum cleaner and blowing it into another person's chest. Think you'd survive the surgery?"

"God, no!"

"Right. You want to know why it took thousands of attempts to create Dolly way back in the nineties? It's because we didn't understand that we had to *carefully* extract the DNA without altering the delicate balance between the cytoplasm and organelles."

"You know, for years I've been losing sleep over that very question," she told him dryly.

He managed a grin. "It turns out that a cell is a lot like a factory. Raw materials go in; finished products and wastes come out. When we were sucking the nucleus out with a micropipette, it was like tearing the head office out with bulldozers. We were ruining the assembly lines, spilling product and goods here and there, pushing the machinery this way and that, and tearing great gaping holes in the factory wall. McEwan—bushranger that he is—was the first to figure out how critical the systemic organization and structure of the cytoplasm and organelles was. Nancy Hartlee, way across the world in California, devised her nanoscalpel, which allowed us to make an incision in the plasma membrane, the vitelline space, and the zona pellucida."

At her look of incomprehension, he added, "Those are the structures that make up the cellular wall of an oocyte—a human egg cell. Prior to that, we were literally crashing our way through, damaging the cell in the process."

"Okay, I get the picture. By cutting you kept the shock to the egg cell down, right?"

"Right. Go back to the vacuum-cleaner heart surgery we talked about. You want to traumatize the patient as little as possible. Cells, like animals, are tough and resistant, but they can only deal with so much trauma."

"You've covered McEwan and Hartlee. What was your contribution?" She thought his accent was musical and exotic.

He cut a piece of steak, saying, "I was the team leader on the first successful re-creation of an extinct species. You remember the Tasmanian wolves?"

"Yes! And the research leader disappeared. That was you?"

He made a mock bow. "At your service. Granted, we were still using the old shotgun approach, but we'd discovered that light and temperature affected cellular reproduction."

"Huh?"

He studied her over a forked broccoli. "Where does conception take place?"

"Well, as I understand it, in the fallopian tubes between the ovaries and uterus."

"Right, and tell me, Christal Anaya, how many fluorescent lights do you have in your fallopian tubes?"

"None of your business."

"Do you keep them at room temperature, or do you set your reproductive thermostat to body normal?"

"That depends on the man I'm with. For some, I keep it ice cold."

"And the others?"

"That's on a need-to-know basis, and as of now, you don't need to know." To change the subject, she said, "Okay, I get it. It's warm and dark inside."

"Brilliant! You've just hit on my part of the miracle. You see, cells are alive. They react to stimuli. My team proved that exposure to light changed a cell's function. Caused it to react differently."

He took a moment to eat his broccoli. Oddly disturbed by the recent sexual banter, Christal studied him. Despite his current circumstance, some internal spirit buoyed him. He looked fit, and she couldn't help but notice the kindness behind his pale blue eyes.

"The thing you must understand," he began, "is that cells have complicated metabolisms. Just like the organs in your body, each organelle in a cell serves a particular function. The DNA is something like the brain and blueprint. It carries the instructions for operation. Surrounding it is the endoplasmic reticulum—the factory floor, if you will—where the cell builds proteins and synthesizes lipids, uh, the fats. The plasma membrane is the skin. Structures called mitochondria produce the energy, while the ribosomes manufacture various proteins the cell is tasked to make. Golgi bodies process and sort lipids as well as synthesize polysaccharides—a sort of structural sugar molecule."

"I didn't realize it was that complicated."

"Believe me, we're just scratching the surface of the structural components. We haven't even started with the intricate and delicate system of intracellular chemistry. It was there that my team made their contribution in the cloning of the Tasmanian wolves."

"I should have known."

"Don't be an irritant, Christal. It ill behooves a woman of your beauty and grace."

She was trying to decide how to respond when he continued with, "Light, you see, is energy. Plants, after all, live off it. While animal cells don't have chloroplasts—the organelles that handle photosynthesis in plant cells—why should we have been surprised that bright laboratory light, especially fluorescent light that pulses, affected discrete functions in the organelles?"

"So, you did it in the dark?"

"Right." He shrugged. "Couple that with McEwan's work, Nancy's nanoscalpel, and Harvey's PLCs—"

"Whoa! PLCs?"

"Phospholipase C. The small-case 's' stands for spermatozoa. If you'll recall, the last time I mentioned that, I got a similar perplexed look from you. You should look that way more often. It gives you a vulnerable quality that balances the normal man-killer fire in your eyes."

She started at the tone; that light jest masked deeper things. She remembered the look in his eyes that day when he'd first walked into her cabin: awe mixed with appreciation. So, what did she think about that? "Why don't you get back to this prophylactic CS."

"Phospholipase, not prophylactic. Though in a sense you might say they are related. The latter can be obtained in a little packet from a men's room wall dispenser while—all things coming to their natural conclusion—the former eventually ends up inside that selfsame latex."

He was playing with her, a twinkle in his eyes. Her confusion over the subject and her reaction to him just egged him on. To cover her fluster, she used a professional voice to ask, "Are you trying to make a point?"

"About PLCs? Yes. It's an enzyme, Christal. Mike Harris discovered that a very specific form of PLC is found only in spermatozoa."

"And why is that important?"

"Because it liberates calcium in the egg cell."

"I knew that. Imagine eggs without calcium: the shells

would be rubbery, and you couldn't crack them on a frying pan."

He ignored her. "In the simplest terms, PLCs tells the oocyte that it has been fertilized. It's a catalyst, a biological switch, one that releases a rush of calcium, which in turn tells a zygote—a fertilized egg—that it can start turning itself into an embryo."

He sipped at his coffee. "In the old days, we used electricity, and guess what? We didn't always get the result we wanted. Cells didn't like the electrical charge any more than you like putting your finger in a light socket. Harris' PLCs provided us with nature's much kinder and gentler key to boot the system."

"So, what you've been telling me is that you've managed to fix most of the problems that caused clones to fail?"

"Welcome to Genesis Athena."

"Put this into perspective. Where are you compared to other labs?"

"Christal, we're light-years ahead. I've only given you a thumbnail sketch. Some of the applications are so technical you'd be lost by the descriptions of the chemistry alone. And then there's another whole universe in epigenetics."

"Epigenetics?"

"The nonprotein coding in DNA. We used to call it 'junk' DNA. Wait, let's go back. DNA codes for the production of different proteins, right?"

"Right."

"But if all the genes in your body worked twenty-four/seven making all the proteins coded for in your DNA, there wouldn't be a difference between your liver and your big toe, would there?"

"I guess not."

"Each cell in your body carries your entire genetic code, be it an epithelial cheek cell, or a liver cell. So, what tells those cells how to be different? What to make? How much to make? And when to stop making it?"

"You wouldn't have brought up junk DNA unless it was there."

"Right. All those bits of old viral DNA, fossil genes, and apparent coding nonsense interact with signals from the cytoplasm to amplify or mute individual gene expression. This is done by something called methylation, literally tagging sections of DNA with methyl molecules that act as on-off switches. When something tampers with methylation in the noncoding DNA, the system goes haywire. It's the root of most cancers and all developmental and metabolic problems. We had to map and control the epigenetics before we could produce reliable clones."

"How does making a clone flip the wrong switches?"

"Individual cells react to trauma just like organisms do. In the early days when we removed or inserted nuclear DNA, the cell's cytoplasm and organelles were traumatized. They sent enzyme signals to the nucleus that popped methyl off entire gene sequences as the cell sought to repair itself. Think of thousands of switches being thrown randomly, lights going on and off, systems powering up and shutting down. We had to catalog the methyl tags before we could understand what we were doing to the oocyte."

"How many of these methyl tags have you found?"

"Over ten million. And with them, we are closing in on the cure for most cancers. That alone will make the Sheik the richest man on earth."

"So, what's your success rate with clones?"

"Close to one hundred percent."

"Come on, conception doesn't even come close to that when it's left to nature."

All traces of humor left his face when he told her, "Nature is random, full of error and chance. With our control of epigenetics we are slowly and surely removing those variables from the system."

"You're telling me that you can control the human genome?"

"Genesis Athena is about control, Christal. And don't you ever forget it."

41

The woman had called from the Hilton lobby. She would be knocking on the hotel room door within minutes.

Sheela took a deep breath, nerving herself, falling into her character. She was Jennifer Weaver, thirty-two, daughter of a domineering but mostly absent and very dead father and an overindulgent mother who had overdosed herself with sleeping pills when Jennifer was twelve. She knew this role, had played it so well years before that it had catapulted her into fame and fortune.

She had chosen a suite at the New York Hilton for her visit. The room had a view of the facing buildings on Fifty-fourth Street, and by craning her neck she could just see traffic clogging Avenue of the Americas. She would have preferred the Plaza, or the Four Seasons, but even disguised, she feared that someone would recognize her. No, better to play it safe here, where she'd never stayed before.

The rapping at the door was professionally brief. Sheela stepped across, opened the door, and looked uncertainly at the woman who stood there. She wore a neat gray wool suit with a midlength skirt, white conservative blouse, and coat tailored to her full figure. She might have been forty, with a round face and brown hair tastefully curled. Black pumps shod her feet, and a large leather case hung from her left hand.

"Jennifer?" the woman asked hopefully.

"Yes?" Sheela smiled uneasily, barely meeting the woman's eyes.

"Hello, I'm Mary Abernathy with Genesis Athena. May I come in?" Her smile was warm and reassuring, perfectly matching the friendliness in her eyes. She stepped forward, offering her hand.

Sheela gave it a limp shake before retreating to the small couch. Abernathy took the chair that made up one corner of the triangle created by the TV, chair, and couch. "Let me begin by telling you a little about myself. I'm a registered nurse working with Genesis Athena. I'm here to do a preinterview to get an idea about your general health, take a few samples for tests, and determine what we need to do to make you happy. I'm also here to answer any questions that you have; so please, don't hesitate, no matter how personal. Everything that happens here today is completely and totally confidential."

Jennifer Weaver nodded, smiled shyly, and fidgeted with her hands. "Okay."

"All right, first, let's get some baseline information." Nurse Abernathy reached into her leather case and withdrew a clipboard. "Most of the information has already been provided by your law firm. You're thirty-two, single, and living alone in Los Angeles, correct?"

"Uh-huh."

"Are you taking any drugs? Anything? From aspirin to LSD—we have to know."

"No. I've got aspirin and antihistamines in my purse. But I'm not on any prescription."

"No marijuana, cocaine, ecstasy, anything like that?"

"No." She shrugged. "Not recently. I mean in the last year or so. I'm clean. You'd find it in the blood test if I lied."

"Have you ever been pregnant before?"

Jennifer Weaver hesitated.

"It's all right," Abernathy confided, leaning forward over her clipboard, knowing eyes on Jennifer's. "By the time I was your age, I'd had a 'situation' myself."

"Yeah," Jennifer admitted, eyes downcast. "Once when I was fifteen, and again when I was nineteen."

"Did you abort or carry to term?"

"Abortion."

"At a regular clinic?"

"Yes. I had help. Daddy never knew." She sniffed angrily. "As if he'd given a damn."

Abernathy smiled sympathetically as she jotted something on her form. "What do fathers know, huh?" She looked up. "Tell me about your periods. Bad cramps?"

"No, well, sometimes."

"How would you describe your flow? Heavy, medium, light?"

She shrugged. "Uh, medium, I guess."

"Any tenderness associated with either menses or ovulation?"

"A little, maybe. I don't know. I mean, I never take pills, or anything."

"Ever had STDs?"

"Yeah."

"When?"

"When I was younger. You know. I was a kid then. I didn't give a damn."

"What kind?"

"I had the clap when I was sixteen. Then a doctor told me I'd had chlamydia. He put me on pills for a couple of weeks."

"Did you take them all, or save some for later?"

"I took them all." She shook her head. "I didn't want the disease, you know? It's like being a whore or something when you've got disease."

"Well, before we do the procedure we'll double-check and make sure everything's okay. Jennifer, have you had a pelvic exam recently?"

"Last November. Everything came back normal."

"Those times you were pregnant, how long did you wait before the abortion?"

She made a wincing face. "Four months with the first one. I was like really young, you know? I didn't know what to do. I was scared. The second time, I knew—I mean, I'd been through it before, so I only had that one for a little over a month. You know, just long enough that I knew I'd skipped. Then I got the test."

"No problems or complications?"

"No." She shrugged. "I didn't even bleed much afterwards. I thought, you know, that I'd be laid up for days or something."

Abernathy smiled. "You look like a very fit young woman. How long since your last period? Can you give me a date?"

"Almost two weeks." She bit back any reaction as she thought of her stolen tampon.

Mary made the notation on her form. "So you're almost ready to ovulate. Have you noticed any indication that you're close? Tenderness in the ovaries, vaginal discharge?"

"Not yet." She appeared to think. "But it should be soon."

"We might want to hurry you forward." Mary Abernathy looked up. "Outside of pregnancy, have you ever skipped periods?"

"Yeah, back when . . ." She looked away. "It was before Dad died. Before the trust was set up. He wanted to have me locked away. Sent off. Anywhere but where he was. You know. It wasn't a happy time in my life."

"So it was stress related you think?"

"Yes."

Abernathy didn't look up as she made notes on her form. "But nothing since?"

"No."

"I'm going to read off a list of diseases and health conditions. I need to know if you or anyone in your family has ever had any of these."

Through the long list that followed, Jennifer Weaver answered no to some, and yes to others, building the profile of her rich but unhappy life. Mary Abernathy dutifully noted each on her form.

Finally she looked up. "Okay, Jennifer, that's it for the paperwork. Next I need to do a quick physical. It's nothing to worry about." A smile. "I'll warm the stethoscope. The worst part is taking a routine blood sample for the lab. That will provide us with a baseline blood chemistry board, ensure that you're not having some problem, and confirm that your baby's immune system will be compatible with yours."

Jennifer swallowed. "Okay." She tried to look listless as Mary took her blood pressure, listened to her heart and lungs, but flinched when the blood sample was taken.

As Abernathy finished sealing and labeling her samples she looked up. "Now, that wasn't so bad, was it?"

"No." Jennifer actually managed a weak smile.

"One last thing to do." Mary removed a plastic cup from her case, along with a plastic bag. Jennifer could see a Q-Tip inside. "I need you to walk back to the bathroom and give me a urine sample. Seal the cup when you're done. Finally, I want you to put your foot up on the toilet, just like inserting a tampon, and very carefully insert the Q-Tip and swab the inside of your vagina."

"Huh?" the request caught Sheela by surprise. She blinked the confusion away, pulled Jennifer's character back into place, and nodded reluctantly.

Mary Abernathy's expression turned serious. "If you'd like, I could help you."

"No." Jennifer stood, reaching for the cup and baggie. "That's all right. I think I've got the idea."

"Just be very careful not to contaminate either of them, okay? Don't lay the Q-Tip on the sink or toilet. Just drop it straight into the baggie when you're done and seal it."

As she went through the process, Sheela had to wonder. Urine samples, well, sure. But the other? She made a face as she swabbed herself then dropped the Q-Tip into the baggie and sealed it.

Stepping out, she gave the samples to Abernathy and watched the woman write on them before she placed them in her case.

"Any questions?" Abernathy asked.

"Will it hurt?"

"The procedure? No." The nurse smiled. "You won't even know it happened."

"When will we do it?"

Abernathy shuffled through her papers. "If you're as close to ovulation as we think—and we'll know from hormone levels in the blood and urine samples—the sooner the better. Our lab ship, the *ZoeGen,* has just arrived off Long Island. I'm going to recommend that you leave as soon as possible. Can you do that? Go at a moment's notice?"

Jennifer nodded. "I'll be right here. Waiting, you know? I don't have any friends in New York."

At her expression, the nurse's professional demeanor

seemed to crack the slightest bit, only to be replaced by the personable smile. "We'll be in touch, then."

"And the billing?" Jennifer asked. "That will all be handled through my attorney?"

"That's what I was told. Your deposit has been received, and your credit is approved. Provided that the tests don't indicate any problem, you'll be home in a week and pregnant with your new baby."

"It's that easy?"

The woman nodded. "It's that easy. We guarantee that your baby will be free of any genetic defects. But you are going to be warned so many times, you'll have it memorized, so I'll start now: Jennifer, you must understand. We can't be responsible for what you do to yourself and your baby once you leave our facilities. Alcohol, tobacco, drugs, stimulants, certain foods, chemicals, poisons, and things like mercury that you introduce into your system can cause irreparable harm and are beyond our control."

"I know."

"Good. Be sure that you do," Mary Abernathy told her firmly. "Jennifer, I'll be honest. We guarantee our work and the health of the fetus. We know our business well enough that we'll know if you cheat, understand? Our doctors will be giving you periodic checkups throughout your pregnancy. We are going to monitor both you and the baby very carefully. If you work with us and follow the rules, everything will end in a perfect delivery and a remarkable child."

"Will you be there?" Jennifer glanced away. "At the procedure, I mean?"

She nodded. "If you'd like. We're here for you, Jennifer. You're paying for the finest care and service on earth."

Jennifer looked uncertainly at Mary. "If . . . I mean . . ."

"Yes?"

In a small voice, she asked, "What if . . . if at the last minute, I change my mind?"

"It will be all right," Abernathy replied gently. "We'll deal with it when the time comes. This is a big decision. If you decide, for whatever reason, that you're uncomfortable, we'll call it off. No one will say anything. It's happened before. We want you happy so that when the time is right, you'll come back to us."

Sheela clenched her fist. "They said it would be a Sheela Marks baby. That's what they promised. That's who my little girl will be, right?"

"Oh, yes," Nurse Abernathy answered. "We took her DNA right off of her tampon. Remember when that happened?"

"How could I forget?" she said too coldly.

Rex sat fuming in Tony's plush reception area. ZTA, Zell Talent Agency, had its offices on the eighth and ninth floor of a high-rise off Melrose. A polished white marble floor gleamed under the lights, and the furniture was designer stuff Tony had picked up in London. A balcony hung over the waiting room where Rex fidgeted on one of the couches. Access to the sacred upper spaces where Tony hovered like God was gained by way of a sculpted staircase behind the reception desk.

Across from him a woman in her forties, dressed in a brown Gucci concoction, held a huge brown leather purse in her lap while she consoled a pouting teenage boy dressed in baggy gray canvas. The kid had chunks of metal sticking out of his lips, nose, cheeks, and brows, as well as spiky black hair that stood out in all directions.

Rex shot a hard look at the receptionist, whose radar immediately picked up on it. She smiled, saying, "It will be just a moment longer, Mr. Gerber. Are you sure you wouldn't like anything? Coffee perhaps? Sparkling water?"

"I want Tony," he growled.

"Yo!" Tony called from above, his white leather shoes appearing on the steps as he descended and bent to peer down at Rex. "You've got him. Come on up, Rex."

"Hey!" the bratty teenager bitched. "I's here first, man."

Rex shot him the same sort of look he would have given an unwashed beggar pushing a grocery cart down Santa Monica Boulevard. The older woman was trying to hush the kid, hissing something about success and paying dues.

Rex flashed an empty smile at the receptionist as he hurried to the stairs and took them two at a time to Tony's upper level.

"I thought 'Yo' was out of style these days."

Tony grinned. "You never know. I might bring it back. So, Rex, what's up, babe? You look like, you know, bad shit's happening? I had to cut short a—"

"Can it," Rex muttered, leading the way down the hallway, past the assistants who watched from lowered eyes, past Tony's personal secretary, and into his large corner office. Rex made the 'close it' gesture with his finger, and Tony shut the door behind them.

"Sheela's missing." Rex stopped short, whirling, hands braced on his hips.

Tony stood with one hand on the doorknob, a confused look on his sleek tanned face. Two thick gold chains could be seen behind the open throat of his shirt. "Missing?"

"Yeah, as in I can't find her." Rex jabbed a finger at Tony. "Tell me you've heard something. That she's called, left an e-mail, messengered you, sent flowers, anything."

"Hey, man, the lady's been on my radar, but not since we had that meeting, you know? What's Lymon say?"

"The prick's gone, too. No one home. When I collared Tomaso—that Cuban dickhead that works for her—he just shrugged and said 'Sheela left for a vacation.' End of story."

"A vacation?" Tony asked, amazed.

"Bullshit! It's all bullshit."

"What's Dot—"

"Nothing. She's still pissed about clearing Sheela's schedule. I called you about that, right?"

"Yeah, I got your message. I called Sheela's, but it was late. No answer." Tony looked up. "You're sure Dot doesn't know where she is?"

"Nope." Rex pursed his lips. "But I think Felix does."

Tony rubbed his face with a tanned hand as he walked over to the window that looked out toward the Hollywood Hills. "Give it a break, Rex. I think the lady pushed herself too hard."

"Excuse me?"

"She was burning out. Thing is, she was smart enough to see it coming. If you ask me, she's gone somewhere to lie on a beach without a phone, drink some good booze, and chill. You know what I mean?"

"If you'd let me finish, Felix knows something. I could hear it in his voice. When I asked about Lymon, he almost burst a vein. 'That son of a bitch! What did he tell you?' That's what Felix said, and he said it in a voice like I'd never heard him use before."

"I've heard you use that tone of voice before when Lymon's concerned."

"Genesis Athena," Rex stated bluntly.

"What?"

"The thing Christal Anaya was working on."

Tony smiled. "Yeah, Christal. They got any leads on her yet?"

"Nope." Rex paused. "What's that look for?"

"I'll never get to see if she was as good as she looked." Tony seemed to return to the conversation. "What about Genesis Athena?"

"I just came from Lymon's office. I said I needed to get in and find a file. That hyena woman that works for him was breathing over my shoulder the entire time to make sure that I didn't get into anything I shouldn't. When she started to get suspicious I said that Lymon must have the file and I'd get it from him."

"So where did Genesis Athena come from?"

"It was written on a notepad by Lymon's computer in big block letters, you know, like he was scratching it right through the paper. You know, the way people do when they're mad."

Tony frowned. "Wait a minute. You think that Sheela and Lymon are doing what? Chasing down Genesis Athena?"

Rex chewed his lip as he thought. "I don't know. But like I said, Felix does. When I mentioned Genesis Athena, he told me to go fuck myself."

"Felix said that?" Tony looked ever more thoughtful.

"Yeah. Not quite his style, huh?"

Tony reached out a hand and placed it on Rex's shoulder. "Hey, you've been working too damn hard. Fuck it. If Sheela and Lymon are out having a little tryst, more power to them, huh? You said that she practically admitted they were lovers that day at Lymon's. You're overreacting. Sheela wanted her calendar cleared so she and Lymon could disappear someplace where they could get it on in private. After what happened with de Giulio, I don't blame her."

Rex chewed harder on the inside of his lip, then shook his head. "I don't buy it. Sheela was pretty broken up about Anaya's kidnapping. She had that look. You know, the one that said she wasn't going to let it go."

"Fine, go wear yourself out, Rex." He walked to his desk, dropping into the easy chair. "Look, if the lady calls, I'll tell her you're worried. I promise, as soon as she hangs up, I'll use my caller ID to get the number, ring you, and you can get back to her. It's your funeral."

"Just hope it isn't hers, Tony."

He had already shrugged it off. "Only if the media gets hold of it. They'll have color photos of her and Lymon in flagrante around the world within hours."

"So, you're going to do nothing?"

"Call me when you've really got something to worry about, Rex."

42

The chatter of a helicopter beat its way through the *Zoe-Gen*'s maze of decks and companionways. Christal blinked her eyes open, yawned, and stretched. She sat up on her hard bunk. Pale morning light was streaming in through the porthole. She threw off her blanket, stumbled over, and squinted out at the day. She could see the chopper, one of the fancy Sea Kings; it dropped out of the morning sky, slowing. She lost it as it drifted out of her limited line of sight to settle on a helipad somewhere above. The chopper's chatter and whine died away to be replaced by the now-familiar ship's hum.

Christal rubbed her eyes and walked into her small bathroom. She used the toilet and splashed water in her face. She was feeling her damp shirt and pants—washed in her little sink the night before—when a knock came at her door.

"Just a minute!" she called, grabbing down her damp things. She whirled in anger when her door swung open. "Hey! I said *just a minute*!"

To her surprise, Copperhead—dressed in a flattering pantsuit—stepped in and closed the cabin door behind her. She gave Christal a curious appraisal, noting the crumpled clothing Christal now held in a futile attempt at modesty.

"You look like a drowned rat," Copperhead stated frankly.

"Get the hell out of here!"

The woman smiled, her hands loosely at her side, her weight perched on the balls of her feet. She wrinkled her nose. "Is that you, or is there something wrong with the plumbing?"

Christal's fingers cramped where they bunched her clothing. She considered flinging the whole mass at the woman as a distraction before she beat her to death.

"Go on," Copperhead said easily. "Get dressed. I'll meet you outside."

"Why?"

"You're wanted." With that, Copperhead laughed softly to herself, opened the door, and stepped out into the companionway.

Christal took a deep breath, shook her head, and began dressing. When she stepped out into the companionway, Copperhead was leaned against the far wall, her arms crossed. She pushed off, looking Christal up and down. "Come on. This way." She started down the hallway. "We didn't think to bring you anything else to wear."

"Inconsiderate of you, don't you think, April?"

"If we ever do it again, we'll know."

"What? Kidnapping's not a normal activity?"

"Actually, you were the first. Change that. Let's say you were the first fully developed adult that we ever snatched.

Some cells here and there don't count, right?" She gave her a wry smile. "Look, I'm sorry. Anaya, I don't have anything against you. Fact is, if you weren't good, we'd have never crossed swords in the first place."

"One of these days, I'm going to pay you back for those punches you gave me that day in the women's room. And I'm going to bust your dear little mousy Gretchen, too. I've never been shot at before—let alone with intent."

April took the turn that led to the only way out. "All I can tell you is that she won't be a problem in the future. She's been transferred."

"Transferred where? Gestapo charm school?"

"Tokyo. Among her several outstanding talents, she speaks both Japanese and Chinese. We project our Asian market to explode as Genesis Athena's capabilities become known. That's especially true of China and India, where population control implies limits on fecundity. The point is, if you can only have one child, why not have exactly what you want? And, I'm sure you know they're generating a great deal of wealth in the Orient these days. Within twenty years we expect it to be our largest market."

"Where are we going?" Christal asked as they approached the security door.

April entered a quick sequence on the keypad, leaned to look into a retinal scanner, then waved her wrist over it. She pressed her finger to the pad and waved at the camera, calling out, "It's the woman I told you about, Hans. Please pass us."

The door clicked, and Christal followed April into the small box. One wall was made up of thick glass, behind which sat a muscular blond man. Christal could see monitors off to either side displaying familiar images of the corridors, cafeteria, a laboratory, and the security door they'd just passed. He tapped instructions into a large control panel.

The outer door clicked, and April led the way into another of the companionways.

"Was that the women's shower room I saw in one of his monitors?" Christal asked.

April nodded, indicating that Christal should precede her.

"I hadn't thought of that. I suppose the others are so used to it they never give it a second thought anymore." She smiled ironically. "Hans, and Max, who works the night shift, could care less. They're lovers when they can manage to find the time."

Christal filed that away as she walked perhaps fifty yards and was directed to her right. "Take that first lift, if you will. Press the button for the B Deck."

When the doors opened, Christal stepped inside. Another of the ubiquitous security cameras glared down with a bulbous glass lens. She gestured toward it. "Doesn't that bother you? Being in the fisheye all the time?"

"We take security very seriously," April said as she stepped in across from Christal. "And if you're thinking of jumping me and making a break for it, we're about thirty miles offshore. If you're lucky the water temperature is fifty degrees Fahrenheit. Instead of trying something that will end up making you look ridiculous, why don't you just cooperate for a while longer, and let the lawyers make their pitch."

Christal pressed the B button. "What's the pitch?"

"The cost of your current inconvenience and future silence."

"What if you can't afford it?"

The look April gave Christal was anything but reassuring. "Ms. Anaya, you're thirty miles out into the Atlantic. No one back on the mainland has the faintest idea of where you are. Hank says that you're a very bright woman, and my experience up to this point bears that out. We will be reasonable if you will. It's a simple equation."

The door slid open. Christal sighed as she stepped out into a lavishly appointed corridor. The walls looked like they were done in hand-waxed teak. Golden sconces lit the rich carpeting and arched ceiling. The doors off to either side were wooden with gold handles. "Pretty chic," Christal muttered. "Is this part of the deal?"

"That's up to you. Just because circumstances put us on opposite sides doesn't mean it has to stay that way." April followed just behind her left shoulder. "Next door to the right."

Christal grabbed a slim handle, turned it, and stepped into what might have passed for a small lobby at a top-end hotel. Marble columns supported a sculptured ceiling. Gold filigree was everywhere. The floor was a combination of marble and sections of thick Persian rug. The furniture was immaculate, worth a fortune, and looked immanently comfortable.

"To your right. That door in the corner," April told her.

As Christal crossed the room, she looked out the tall windows that lined the far wall. She could see silver-blue ocean gleaming in the summer sunlight. Nothing marred the water's surface. Not a ship, not even a bit of flotsam.

The doorway led her into, of all things, a small locker room with a tiled floor. On one wall a redwood bench was backed by a full-length mirror. Floor-to-ceiling stainless steel lockers covered the other. Vanities filled the spaces to either side of the doors on either end of the room. They were accompanied by mirrors, hair dryers, and small sinks, all looking fully equipped.

April closed the door behind them. "If you'll remove your clothes and open that locker on the right, you'll see that we've taken the liberty of supplying you with a wardrobe. I think the size is right." She cocked her head. "Would you like to take a shower? One without a camera?"

Christal had taken up a position across from her. "What's up? Why are you doing this?"

"Some of our people would like to talk to you. We thought you might like to clean up and dress appropriately. You've got about an hour until they're scheduled to see you. If you want to go looking like you've just come off a two-week camping trip in the Guatemalan high country, who am I to complain? If not, there are clothes here and a shower room just beyond that door. You're welcome to clean up, wash, dry, and fix your hair. Whatever."

"And you?"

April pressed a key on the pad near the door they'd entered through. A solid-sounding click could be heard.

"I'm going for a swim." April bent her leg, slipped a shoe off, and began undressing. She looked at Christal with amusement as she peeled out of her pantsuit. "Like I said, we've got an hour. Use it anyway you'd like. Me, I'm taking it in the pool." She inclined her head toward the door at Christal's right.

Christal frowned, then opened it to see the sort of shower a Roman emperor might have designed. The place was tiled in white marble with three sets of matching sculpted golden showerheads. When she looked back, April was naked, hanging her clothing in one of the lockers. The woman padded past on bare feet, walked calmly into the shower room, and turned on the water at one of the showers.

So what are you going to do now? Christal looked warily around the locker room, searching the corners for small cameras, microphones, or anything that might be suspicious. Back through the doorway, Christal could see April soaping her hair. If she was going to take her, now would be the time. Talk about vulnerability. Copperhead would never see her coming.

Her people want to talk to me? She reached up to finger her stringy black hair. It felt tacky from the film left by the hand soap she used when she washed in her tiny cubicle sink. Then she glanced around at the opulent surroundings. Was this really legit?

What the hell. Christal flipped out of her pumps and opened the locker April had indicated. Two white blouses, a gray wool skirt and jacket, and a neatly pressed pair of matching designer slacks hung there.

Maybe it wasn't the right decision, but she peeled out of her still-damp shirt and pants, laid them neatly on the red-wood bench, undid her bra, and dropped her panties.

Vulnerable. Right. That's just how she felt as she walked through the door to the shower room. Damn! Talk about sybaritic! She hadn't seen that one full wall was mirrored. She took the faucet farthest from April, cranked the handles, and fiddled with the water until the temperature was right. The soap, shampoo, and conditioner were contained in a gold-plated European-style dispenser with push buttons.

God; it felt heavenly. From under the spray she watched April's reflection in the mirror as the muscular woman turned off the water, shook out her hair, and stepped to a far

door. When April walked through, Christal could see the
smooth turquoise surface of a pool under a glass-paned ceiling beyond.

Leaving the water running, Christal immediately slipped
back into the locker room and tried the far door. Yep, locked
all right. She returned to the shower room and turned off the
water. Dripping her way to the pool room door, she opened it
just a crack to peek out. April was churning her way through
the water, stroking powerfully.

Christal glanced this way and that, seeing round life preservers here and there along the walls. Lounge chairs, small
tables and benches, and several closed cabinets stood on the
poolside patio. A diving board jutted out over the deep end
closest to her.

"It's okay," April called where she trod water in the center
of the pool. "We're not going to be disturbed. At least, not by
anybody who will live through it if they do."

"Uh, I don't know."

"Suit yourself." April flipped over, diving like a dolphin,
her feet rising from the water as she slid down to kick otter-
like across the pool floor.

Christal could hear the voices, whispering, warning, as
she glanced around, searching again for any sign of cameras, of observation.

Oh, do it! she chided herself. After all, April was buck-
assed naked, and as she had pointed out, she wasn't the kind
to take an infringement without serious consequences.

Christal stepped through the door, running to make a
clean dive. As she speared into the water, a voice asked, *But
what do you really know about her? This is Copperhead!
Maybe she was a lap dancer at a strip club before she became a felon?*

Too late now. She was in the water. Her head broke the
surface, and she flipped her wet hair aside.

April stroked past, floating on her back. "Feels good,
doesn't it?"

"Whose place is this?" Christal found footing and braced
herself, water modestly up to her neck.

"We have a lot of rich clients." April pulled her feet under her and stood in the chest-deep water. "That's why I brought you here. I thought you could use a break and some softening up before the lawyers get to you."

"Is that what this is, softening up?"

"Well, it's not a full-body massage, but it helps." April slicked the water from her face and pulled her wet hair back. She could have passed for Ursula Andress in *Doctor No*. "You want the truth?"

"Sure. Not that I'm betting I'll get it."

"Genesis Athena is a huge, bulky, and often unwieldy corporation. Sometimes management makes decisions that people in the field don't approve of. In your case, my bosses panicked. Hank didn't help matters any. He gave them a full report on you. Gretchen made a mess of the Manny de Clerk collection—and right after that you walked into the answering service in Colorado. God knows how you put that together, but it blew everyone's minds. They had convinced themselves that you were going to be motoring up to the *ZoeGen* in a Zodiac boat and doing some sort of GI Jane commando raid by the next morning."

"Good idea. Anything explosive around here?"

"Just reality, Anaya. And sometimes that's more volatile than any chemical. Management didn't think that the public at large was ready for our reality to become common knowledge, and you might be the one to spill it. We want to introduce Genesis Athena in warm drips and drops, not scald the world with the whole giant corporate pot. We'll let people get used to the idea, and then reveal a little more of our capability. By the time ten years have passed, people will be as comfortable with our abilities as they are with space flight."

Christal pushed off, sidestroking. April matched her pace. The woman seemed half porpoise. Where Christal had grown up, the deepest water was the chocolate-colored stuff that ran during the summer in the waist-deep acequia.

"What about the guys McEwan has locked up downstairs? They part of the business plan?"

"They'll be compensated."

"Uh-huh, how? Just like Nancy Hartlee?"

April pulled up, treading water in the deep end. "How did you hear about her?"

"Read the paper. The *New York Times* placed her story just under the fold. You know, wondering how she'd gotten from California five years ago to a watery grave off Long Island."

April jackknifed and dove; Christal splashed as she paddled around and started back for the shallow end.

April rose like Aphrodite in her path and sleeked her water-dark hair back with slim shining hands. "You check the followup?"

"What do you mean?"

"About her family? The insurance?"

"Never heard of it."

"No, probably not. It didn't make the news that Nancy Hartlee had an unknown insurance policy. Assuming you decide to take our settlement, check it out when you get back." April pointed a hard finger, looking as dangerous as she ever had. "I know what you're thinking. No! We didn't drown her, throw her overboard, or anything else. It was her decision to go over the side. She was the one who tried to swim ashore. The miracle is that she made it as far as she did."

Christal stood, water coursing down her sides. "So what? I'm supposed to think Genesis Athena is run by a bunch of angels? Bullshit!"

"Angels? Not on your life, Anaya." April cocked her head, water running down her tanned skin and dripping from her breasts. "We're a business. An international corporation worth billions that's struggling to be worth trillions. It's about global power and competition to be the world's foremost in biotech."

"And that justifies kidnapping? Stealing people's lives the way you stole Nancy Hartlee, Brian Everly, and the others? That gives you the right to humiliate Sheela Marks and terrify Manny de Clerk?"

"Look, I don't agree with everything they're doing. Just like I'm sure you didn't agree with everything the Bureau has done, is doing, or will do in the future. You've been around the block, Anaya. You're not some simple Pollyanna hick from New Mexico." She chuckled then, as if laughing at herself. "Look, we're a lot alike, you and me."

"Don't count on it."

"Oh yeah? You were with the Bureau, one of their young hotshots. I was with LAPD. You got bounced by bad luck, coupled with a bit of bad timing."

"You seem to know a lot about me. Hank tell you all that?"

"My case is somewhat similar. I didn't get caught with my pants down. Instead it turned out that my superiors were more interested in my body than my brains. With Genesis Athena I can get as far as my wits and looks can take me." Challenge filled her eyes. "What about you, Christal?"

"What about me?"

"Genesis Athena could make you a very rich woman."

"As long as I didn't mind overlooking some things like kidnapping, extortion, theft, conspiracy, and a few niggling little ethical concerns?"

A faint smile graced April's perfect lips. "Nothing in life comes without compromise. But don't make that decision now. Take your time, hear what our people have to say. Then you need to think seriously about it."

"What, being bought off or dropped overboard?"

"We're not going to kill you." April leaned forward, stroking in a circle as Christal leaned back to float. "But you'd better know, if you force us into it, we'll ruin you to protect ourselves. Paying you for your silence is the second option; but the first, the one we'd prefer, is that you consider a change in employment."

"Go to work for you? After what I've seen."

"Yeah. That's just what I'm saying. You're talented. You wouldn't have to do anything you didn't want to. Stealing DNA just happens to appeal to me personally, but we've got to provide security for clients, do research, lots of things that would suit your skills. I'm not trying to whitewash some of the things Genesis Athena does, but on the other hand, you could retire in twenty years with stock options and a couple of million in the bank."

"Just as long as I don't mind bending a few principles along the way."

April twisted sensuously in the water. "You'll bend them no matter what you choose concerning us. Life does that to people—forces them to compromise between utopia and reality. I'm willing to bet your tax dollars go to fund programs and policies that you find ethically reprehensible, but I don't see you leaving the United States."

Christal slipped sideways in the water. "There's nothing I can do about what the government does with my tax dollars."

"Bullshit. You've just made that particular deal with the Devil, Christal. You're comfortable with it. You get to live in familiar surroundings with certain services and protections, knowing at the same time that your government is buying off reptilian dictators, propping up sadistic governments, and hiding international murderers because they back us in the war on terrorism or turn over drug rivals or sell us cheap oil. Every day we make international criminals into millionaires and give them credibility—people that we'd arrest, convict, and lethally inject if they were on our streets. Or didn't you discover that during your days at the Bureau?"

"You're telling me it's the same thing with Genesis Athena?"

"Right down to the charity gene treatments we do for poor kids." April turned onto her back, spreading her arms, floating with her face and breasts out of the water. "Genesis Athena is like your beloved American government—down to the last moral compromise. We do some bad things, some neutral deeds, and a lot of good stuff as well."

"Right."

"By the end of the next decade no person on earth will have to be born with a genetic disease. That's twenty million lives lived without mongolism, trisomy G, Huntington's, cystic fibrosis, Tay-Sachs, PKU, sickle cell, or thalassemia. No more ALS or muscular dystrophy."

"For a price."

"You ever been to the emergency room? There's always a price."

"I still don't think you're angels."

April kicked and regained her feet. "We're not." She waded close, where she could look into Christal's eyes. "But keep something in mind while you think about it. You're right. The cheapest thing would be for us to tie a chunk of metal around your ankle and drop you overboard, but you know what? We're not going to do that. We're offering to make amends, settle for the inconvenience."

"Why?"

"Because you've still got a surprise or two coming. Time's about up. You've got a meeting." April climbed out of the pool, striding for the shower room.

Christal flipped back her wet hair as she waded for the steps. She wiped water from her olive skin and stared thoughtfully at the wet footprints she followed.

A business. Did she believe that? That Genesis Athena was just a huge amoral Goliath crashing its way through people's lives?

April was already under the shower, rinsing the chlorine away. She turned her back to the spray as Christal walked in.

"Here's the deal, Anaya. Somewhere down the line Genesis Athena and its personnel will be held responsible for their actions. Time and money, along with charitable actions, can lessen the blow, dull the sharp tongue of censure, but we'll still have to face the music."

"Damn right." Crystal twisted the knobs and rinsed under the warm water. She felt truly clean for the first time in days.

April shut off her faucet, water trickling down her tanned skin. The beads of it glistened in the bright overhead lights. She stood defiantly, head back, breasts high, her firm thighs slightly apart. "We're not fools. Everything that we're doing now will eventually come out. At least, that's how we have to plan for the future. Knowing that, it will serve us in the long run to make amends for our mistakes now."

Christal turned off the water and walked over to face her. "Is that what you told Nancy Hartlee? What about the other slaves you've got locked up down below?"

April stepped over and pressed a tile beside the mirrored wall.

Christal jumped as warm dry air began blowing out of

slim vents artfully fitted between the sections of mirror. She braced herself, squinting into the warm rush. In awe she watched her mirrored reflection. Her skin was moving as if under an invisible caress. As the jets changed, her breasts slowly lifted and rolled. The pressure sharpened her cheekbones, outlined her abs, and lifted her black hair. As it dried, it began to flow out behind her in a raven wave. She had never seen herself like this: a Native goddess, firm and slim, brown and muscular.

"Quite the thing, isn't it?" April asked beside her. "Lean into it. Shake your hair out. If you turn, it will slick the water away."

Eyes slitted against the wind, Christal studied the woman as she posed before the mirrors, her actions slow, graceful, almost like tai chi. Copperhead laughed aloud as the waves of air rolled over her body.

Christal tried to match her movements, turning slowly, trying to balance gracefully against the pushing air. It felt great. No wonder the rich lived like they did.

April touched the tile again; the warm air vanished as if but a memory. She was looking Christal up and down as if she were a prize racehorse rather than a security risk. A faint smile curled the woman's lips. "Bottom line: It's business. We'd prefer to fix the problem now rather than take the loss in the long run."

Christal walked into the locker room, gaze fixing dismally on her grungy clothes where they lay on the redwood bench.

"Put on the new ones." April might have been reading her mind. "Leave those. I'll have them laundered and delivered to you later."

As Christal inspected the locker's contents, she found a new brassiere and panties, still in packaging. When she dressed in one of the new white blouses, she wasn't surprised to discover it was her size exactly. *Fix the problem? Take the loss in the long run? Just what, exactly, was Copperhead after?*

"What would it take?" April asked as she hooked her bra clips. "Our terms, once you boil down all the bullshit lawyer talk, are that you drop any and all charges, that you sign a nondisclosure agreement, and that you never reveal any of the things you have learned here or elsewhere about Genesis Athena."

Christal considered for a moment and said, "Five million."

April laughed. "Not a chance."

"So, what's your counteroffer?"

"Two hundred thousand."

"What makes you think I wouldn't take it and spill my guts later anyway?"

April's gray gaze cut like diamond. "Because we're a business, Anaya. You have a basic understanding of our capabilities, resources, and resolve. I think you know that we'll use them if we have to. We'll keep our end of the bargain only as long as you keep yours."

"I'll think about it." Christal pulled the classy gray skirt up and zipped it. "Let's go have this meeting."

April worked her arms into her pantsuit and stopped long enough to pull a brush from one of the vanity drawers to brush her shoulder-length hair.

"You ready?"

"Yes."

April reached over and pressed the keypad on the door lock plate. She opened it and led the way out into the marble-columned lobby. Christal barely cleared the door before she came up short.

Sheik Amud Abdulla—backed by two sturdy-looking men—stood waiting for them. He was dressed in a sleek black silk suit and was smiling, a gleam in his dark brown eyes. He nodded to April as though in satisfied approbation.

Christal's guts squirmed when the man turned his raptorial attention to her. He started with her feet, gaze slowly rising, savoring, as he took in her legs, the fitted skirt, white blouse, and tailored suit coat. Christal swallowed hard when he fixed on her face, a dreamy smile on his lips.

"Your meeting is canceled," the Sheik said in perfect English. "Miss Hayes, please take Miss Anaya back to her quarters. We wouldn't want to cause her fatigue in her current condition."

43

June Rosen answered on the first ring: *"Lymon Bridges Associates. How may I help you?"*

Lymon leaned back behind the steering wheel in his rental car. He and Sid had picked a small commercial lot across the street from the Brooklyn charter boat service, paid the shop owner to let them sit, and set up camp. "It's Lymon. I was just checking in. Anything happening I should know about?"

"The police called. They've still got nothing on Christal's disappearance. On the same subject, her mother called twice yesterday asking if there was news. Agent Harness' wife called—"

"Yeah, Sid checked in with Claire a little while ago." Lymon glanced across the seat and out the passenger window at the taunting gates of the charter service. "He's got his home fires covered, but his squad supervisor in Washington is starting to chafe at his continued use of personal time."

"And last, but definitely not least, Rex was here yesterday. He insisted that you had a file of his on your desk. I took him back and watched him like a hawk to make sure he didn't get into anything."

"Was he a good boy?"

"For the most part. He seemed to fix on your notepad, and frowned. You'd scribbled 'Genesis Athena' there."

Lymon considered that. "I think it's all right."

"Where are you?"

"Waiting in a parking lot across from the charter service in Brooklyn. We've seen people going in and out all morning, but none of them was Sheela. It's been long enough we're wondering if we made the right move."

"If you need moral support, call. In the meantime, I've got two new clients. I'm sending Salvatore as detail leader to cover one and Wu for the other."

"Good work, June. Do what you have to."

"You, too."

Lymon canceled the call just as Sid came walking up with a box of donuts and two cups of coffee in a carrier. He opened the passenger door and slipped into the seat. "Sorry, boss, but the only chocolate donuts had those little sprinkles on them, so that's what you got. But me, I got my crème-filled."

"Got the receipt?" Lymon asked as he took coffee and a donut.

Sid handed it over, and Lymon carefully noted the expense, folded it double, and placed it in his pocket. "Did you know that IRS stands for Invasive Rectal Service?"

Sid gave him a sidelong glance. "Huh?"

"You know, that feeling you get every April fifteenth when you bend over and spread."

"Do I detect a note of latent hostility?"

"You don't have to deal with the paperwork. Yet."

Sid sipped his coffee. "There you go again, trying to woo me away from serving my country with—Whoa! Cab pulling up."

"Yeah, I got it." Lymon reached for the binoculars and watched as a brown-haired woman in the backseat leaned to the little drawer and paid the driver. The trunk sprang open. Next the cabbie got out and walked around to remove a familiar suitcase. The woman had stepped out from behind the cab.

"It's her!" Lymon snapped the binoculars down and shoved them into his pocket. "Brown wig and darker complexion, but I'd know that walk anywhere."

"Let's roll," Sid said as he popped the door open.

Lymon was already out, striding purposefully across the street. He could hear Sid's steps ringing on the pavement behind him.

A middle-aged woman they had watched arrive earlier stepped out of the covered walkway smiling. Lymon was close enough to hear her say, "Jennifer! I'm so glad you made it! Any trouble?"

Jennifer? Was she still pretending to be Jennifer Weaver? Using the account Felix had told them about?

"No trouble," Sheela's voice answered as she faced the woman. But not Sheela's voice. She sounded somehow small, insecure.

"Excuse me!" Lymon called, quickening his step. He saw Sheela turn—recognized her face despite the brown hair, but the brown eyes would have fooled him. *Play along, Lymon, until you know what's coming down.*

Sheela gasped with recognition as Lymon said, "Jennifer? Can we have a word?"

The middle-aged woman stepped forward, a frown on her face. "Who are you?"

"Jennifer's security firm, ma'am." Lymon pointed to Sid. "This is Agent Harness, and I'm Detail Leader Bridges. Jennifer is our principal."

The woman was watching him with a hawklike intensity, trying to gauge his veracity. Sheela, on the other hand, looked like a spotlighted deer: anger, confusion, and disbelief all boiling under her pinched expression.

"Lymon," she finally hissed, "what *are* you doing here?"

He gave her a bluff smile. "Look, Jennifer, when you hired us, you hired the best. We're just doing what we're paid to do."

"Lymon!" she cried, trying to find the words. He could see incipient panic on her face. Every instinct in his body and soul was to grab her, cover, and run.

"Jennifer, it's all right." He held his hands up. "You didn't hire us to make moral or ethical judgments on your life. We're not priests, we're protection. Period." He glanced at the middle-aged woman. "She's not doing anything illegal, is she?"

"What? No!" the woman cried. "Ms. Weaver is here on personal business."

"Then there's no call for alarm." Lymon shrugged. He recalled the character, saw the vampish insecurity she was projecting straight from her stellar on-screen performance in *Joy's Girl.*

"Lymon," Sheela growled, "I don't have time for this now! I have a boat to catch."

Lymon glanced at the other woman. She had her arms

crossed, clearly on the verge of calling for help. "How long are you going to be gone for?"

By now, Sheela was recovering. He'd seen that steely glint before, knew that hardening of the mouth. She was getting pissed. No way he'd be able to talk her out of this. Instead, he nodded at Sid. "Go get our bags."

"What?" Sheela cried.

"Ma'am, my job is your personal safety. If you have a problem with that, you can fire me right now. Right here." He hoped his eyes communicated his desperation as his stare bored into her brown contacts. "I don't know what you're into, but as your security, I advise against it."

She seemed to waver, on the verge of actually telling him to go to hell. "All right, Lymon. Come on." She turned. "There's lodging for them?"

The hard woman was watching him through eyes that would have burned holes in cement. "There will be an additional charge, Ms. Weaver, but yes."

"It's all right. I can pay." Arrogance was in Sheela's voice as she waved it off as a minor annoyance. She seemed to be firmly back in character.

Sid was already waddling back across the street, various bags under both arms as he dodged a garbage truck that came barreling down the street.

Lymon gave a professional nod, wondering what the hell Sheela was doing. He was unable to read the emotion behind her dark brown contacts. From the set of her mouth, however, he figured he was in for a real tongue-lashing when they finally had some privacy.

Did she reach up, grab him by the throat, and choke the living daylights out of him, or did she throw her arms around him and kiss him full on the lips?

Sheela considered both options as she sat on the cushions inside the covered cabin on the forty-foot launch. She was one of sixteen passengers aboard. Lymon and Sid Harness leaned against the rail at the stern, no more than ten feet behind her. They might have been passengers on a pleasure cruise for all the concern they showed. Their luggage was piled next to hers on the deck.

On the right, across the murky water, the lower Manhattan skyline passed, and Long Island's blocky buildings crowded the shoreline to the left.

Among the other passengers were two very pregnant young women on the opposite bench. They acted as if they knew each other, but Sheela couldn't hear their conversation over the roar of the twin engines. In the front, a sickly looking man who might have been in his midtwenties was traveling with a woman who seemed to be his nurse. A young couple sat immediately across from her—a man and his wife—both in their midtwenties. They had been introduced as Bill and Wyla Smith.

When Sheela had asked whose baby they were going to have, Wyla had replied, "Why, our own, of course. My father died of Huntington's, and I'm going to have it as well."

"How do you know?"

"Genetic screening. I have three too many trinucleotides on my fourth chromosome. Through Genesis Athena, Bill and I can make sure that our baby won't face my fate and my father's."

They went on, explaining about something called CAG nucleotide repeats that were completely beyond Sheela's comprehension. To cut the lecture short, she asked Wyla, "But you've already got it? Can't they do something about it? Cure it?"

Bill smiled at his wife and tightened his hold on her hand. "We've been talking to the people at Genesis Athena. They say they can cure it through a gene therapy they're working on. It's still experimental. For the time being, we can afford to have the baby fixed. We'll go back and treat Wyla when we can pay for the rest of the procedure." A pause. "And you, Ms. Weaver?"

She gave them an uncomfortable smile. "I'm having a Sheela Marks baby."

They gave her a blank look, as if they didn't understand.

Sheela avoided their eyes, looking at the stern. Lymon and Sid were talking to each other. What was Sid Harness, the FBI agent, doing here? Was the Bureau involved now? A thousand questions were boiling inside her.

She caught the furtive glances they shot her way, and literally itched to stomp back there and demand to know how they had found her, what they were doing in New York, and more to the point, why the hell they hadn't blown her cover.

"Jennifer?" Mary Abernathy asked, coming to sit on the bench next to her. "Are you all right?" She glanced back at the men, irritation in her eyes.

"Furious. Confused," Sheela admitted, falling back into her role. "They treat me like a baby."

"I've called ahead to make quarters available for them the way you requested." She paused. "We've put them in a suite next door to yours, but it's a waste of money. I promise you, you won't need your security. You'll be under the literal nose of our excellent protective services. You are more than welcome to order your people to return to shore. You'll have plenty of time to have them meet you at the dock when you return."

Sheela made a face, as if mulling it over. "No, it's all right. They're just doing what I pay them for. It's just that sometimes . . ." She glanced up, eyes hollow and vulnerable. "You know, being rich isn't all that most people think. For me, it's like living in a cage! I can't just be normal! Everyone wants something from me."

After a pause, Mary asked, "I do have to know one thing: Are they discreet?"

Sheela answered with blunt honesty. "Believe me, there are times when I wish Lymon wasn't such a perfect damned professional."

"Well, don't worry about them." Mary watched the bridge pass overhead. "We have relations with a lot of clients who have privacy concerns. Many of them come with security details a great deal bigger and more cumbersome than yours, believe me."

"Thanks." She lowered her head, looking meek. "I'd better go back and make peace. I acted like a real shit. It was a diversion that allowed me to slip away."

"Then," Mary Abernathy mused, "how did they find you?"

"Something incredible, no doubt. Lymon's a magician. He probably pulled a white rabbit out of his hat and it ratted me out."

She got to her feet and took a moment to adjust to the pitch and roll of the launch as it rose and fell on the swells. The breeze was cool off the water, wind tugging at her brown wig. Seagulls hovered off the lee, watching to see if the incomprehensible humans had food.

To steady herself, Sheela kept one hand on the gunwale as she made her way astern. Sid cued Lymon, who turned, nodding, his face inscrutable.

"Lymon," she said wearily, "how the hell did you find me?"

He glanced toward where Mary Abernathy watched before returning his stare to the billowing white wake behind them. "Could you turn your back to those people while you're talking to me?"

"What?" She placed her hands on the fantail, complying. "Why?"

"Hell, Sheela, I don't know. Just a hunch. Who is that woman, the one with the beady little Attila eyes?"

"Mary Abernathy. She's a nurse. She came and checked me out, set up the appointment."

He shot her a worried look. "Just what the hell do you think you're doing?"

"First you tell me how you found me."

"You scared the shit out of Tomaso when you made him drive you to the airport. I think it was the disguise that weirded him out. He called and said you were up to something dangerous, that Felix was involved."

"Felix?" She lifted a hand to her throat.

"Yeah. By the way, despite his tough-guy image, it turns out that he's a real wimp when it comes to pain. And last, but not least, you should clear the redial on your phone."

She considered what he'd said—not just the words, but the tone in his voice. She hated the flat control, as if he were keeping a careful rein. When she looked hard into his eyes, she could see it brewing there: fear mixing with growing desperation.

Her chest tightened when he said, "Now it's my turn. What are you doing here? Why are you playing Jennifer Weaver games with Genesis Athena? What if they see through your brown hair and eyes? Why are you taking silly chances and putting yourself at risk?"

"I'm going right to their heart." She swallowed hard. "And when I get there, I'm going to tear it out."

"Holy shit," Sid whispered from Lymon's other side.

"Can you get out of it?" Lymon asked tersely. "Stop this nonsense before you get hurt?"

"Of course. I'm going to back out at the last minute. I'm going to say I just can't do it. That I'm not ready. I'll apologize in a most pathetic manner and maybe cry a little. I'll offer them a big enough settlement to make it all right, and then when I get back to LA Felix is going to file suit. We're going to blow this thing wide open. And Christal's going to be part of the settlement."

"Assuming they don't find out about it," Sid muttered. "If Nancy Hartlee is any indication, these guys play for keeps."

Lymon shot his friend a nervous glance. "Yeah, I think you're right."

"What are you two talking about?" Sheela demanded, more threads of fear winding through her. "Damn it, Sid, are you here investigating for the FBI?"

"Well . . . yes and no." He made a wry face. "Actually, more no than yes. I'm just as far out on the wobbly limb as you are, Ms. Marks."

"Where the hell are we going?" Lymon asked. "Where's this boat taking us?"

"To a ship," she told them, gesturing forward. "Somewhere out there in the ocean."

"And what happens once we get there?"

"Jennifer Weaver will supposedly have Genesis Athena impregnate her with a Sheela Marks baby. I mean, I'm obviously not going through with the procedure, but don't you see? It's the proof we need to sue the shit out of these bastards. And that's where they do it. Out at sea on a ship."

"Damn it, Sheela! What if they figure out who you are? I know Felix did the background work and set this up, but so many things could go wrong! We're talking about real bad shit here."

"They'll never know, Lymon." She gave him a nervous smile, trying to mask the fact that she was more scared than she had ever been. "I know this role. I can do it in my sleep. I mean, who's to tell them? You and Sid surely won't say anything. Just play the part. Be yourselves. Big, tough, security guys."

"You're sure they'll let you walk out?" Sid asked skeptically. He looked like a man with a bad feeling stuck sideways in his gut.

"Why wouldn't they?" Sheela shrugged. "To them I'm a psychologically disturbed rich girl living on a bloated trust fund. At the last minute, I break down, change my mind, and say I won't do it. Trust me, it's in Jennifer's character. As long as they get paid, why would they care?"

"If they don't, if it goes bad," Lymon warned softly, "you be sure we're close. You understand?"

Sheela nodded, the thudding of fear beating at the base of her throat. That look of desperation in his eyes kept eroding more and more of her courage. "It'll be fine, Lymon. Trust me."

"A ship," Sid muttered. "An oceangoing laboratory where they do genetic procedures." He paused suddenly, stiffening. "You know, Nancy Hartlee was found floating right out here, somewhere."

"You mentioned her before. Who's Nancy Hartlee?" Sheela asked, a hollow feeling in her gut.

"One of Sid's missing geneticists." Lymon's worried eyes sent a tremor through her. "No one could figure out how she'd drowned so far offshore."

"It's all starting to make sense." Sid balled a fist, back hunched as if the muscles were taut. "Fuck!"

"Double fuck," Sheela said glumly.

"Yeah," Lymon agreed. "Times three."

44

Hank had just finished a workout on the weight machine in the E Deck fitness center. He stepped out of the locker room showers, reaching for one of the towels that rested on the rack. He buried his face in the soft terry and rubbed it dry. It was when he started on his head that he realized he wasn't alone. April stood brazenly, arms crossed, head cocked, right in the middle of the men's locker room.

"Uh, you supposed to be here?"

She laughed, reading his sudden discomfort. "Why, I'm surprised at you." She stepped forward, using her fingertip to wipe up a droplet of water from his left nipple. He followed it as she raised it to her mouth and touched it to the tip of her tongue.

"Hey, sweetheart, it's not me. What if some other guy was in here? You might make him blush."

When her eyes met his it was with a feral curiosity. "And you don't blush?"

He pulled her to him, heedless of her expensive pantsuit, and kissed her hard. He could feel the strength in her body as she stiffened and arched against him. In the end he let her push back. She gave him that fiery look, and his soul began to swell. Damn, she was saucy when she was mad.

She broke away and stepped back, looking down. Her natty pantsuit was dampened over the breasts, belly, and thighs. "You bastard!"

Hank chuckled and continued toweling himself off. He made sure she was watching as he spread his thighs and rolled the towel around his heat-distended genitals. "Hey, April, you come walking into the men's locker room, you take dangerous chances. Shit happens. Especially when male hormones have been loosened up in the gym."

She flipped her metal-red hair back and studied him through narrowed eyes. "So, you had a good workout?"

He tossed the towel into the hamper and walked to where his clothes were laid out across a bench. "I worry myself."

"No wonder." She was staring down at the wet spots. "Keep pulling shit like this . . . I'll kill you."

"April, I haven't felt this good in years." He turned to look at her as he stepped into his briefs and let the elastic snap around his waist. "I feel alive in a way that I never have. I'm doing something for the first time in my life."

"And what is that?" She reached for another of the towels, patting it on her breasts and belly to dry the stain.

"I'm working for me." He ran his arms into his shirt. "Better, I'm working for a team I can believe in. I mean, this isn't the Bureau. This is real. Results count, not political bullshit. I'm rested, I haven't spent the night worrying about a house payment, or what I'd done to piss fucking Marsha off, or whether I was in or out at the office."

April balled her towel and flung it at the hamper. "Pull your pants on. I want you to see something."

He zipped his jeans and tugged on his running shoes. When he stood, she was giving him that probing look. What was this shit? Was she about to pass judgment on him again? Part of his euphoria evaporated.

"I hate it when you start staring at me like that."

"I want your opinion on something."

"Why do I get the feeling I'm being set up?"

She grinned at him, stepping close and lancing a long fingernail under his chin; a predatory curiosity lay behind the expanded pupils in her gray eyes. "I can't say for certain, but my guess is that you'll like it."

He trapped her finger, pulled it up to his lips, and kissed the tip as he traded gaze for gaze. "Lead forth."

He followed as she led the way to the door and pushed it open. She took his arm, pulling it around her shoulder. "I've booked the movie room for us. First off, there's something I want you to see. Second, it'll give my clothes time to dry out, and third, it will give me time to decide if I still want to slap the shit out of you."

He grinned where she couldn't see it.

"Sexy movie? You know, males are visually stimulated."

In a dry voice she said, "No shit? Bam! Revelation! After all these years I finally understand why men go completely brainless when they see my tits. Until now I thought it was just some bizarre form of innate stupidity."

She stopped at the movie room door and let him push it open. Hank stepped inside, surprised to find Neal Gray in one of the seats.

Neal looked up, nodding. "Hey, Hank."

"What's up, Neal?"

"More of the same. We're still trying to gauge damage control on the Anaya thing." He glanced at April, eyes fixing on her damp breasts. "What happened to you?"

"Don't ask."

"It would never cross my mind." He waved at the screen. "We'll fast-forward through the meaningless parts. Have a seat, guys."

Hank settled himself into one of the comfortable chairs. April couldn't be too pissed at him, because she slid in beside him. The lights dimmed, and the big screen that filled one wall illuminated as cameras followed April and a woman that Hank immediately recognized as Christal into what appeared to be a small but elegant locker room.

"This was taken this morning," Neal said. "It's part of a film the marketing team will be using for our 'Zea' series."

"Huh?" Hank asked, watching as April's screen voice said, *"If you'll remove your clothes and open that locker on the right, you'll see that we've taken the liberty of supplying you with a wardrobe. I think the size is right."*

Neal replied, "Zea is a series of females we'll be producing from Anaya's DNA. Now, obviously, we're not going to call them the 'Christal' series. If she chooses to settle, we'd rather not have her coming back asking for royalty in the future."

Hank watched the on-screen April say, *"I'm going for a swim."* Christal watched skeptically as April slipped off her shoes and began undressing. *"Like I said, we've got an hour. Use it anyway you'd like. Me, I'm taking it in the pool."*

Hank glanced at April. "You told her no cameras."

"She'll never know. The Sheik arrived this morning. He wanted a chance to look over his investment. What you can't see is that the shower room has a one-way mirrored wall through which this was filmed. The same with the pool. Underwater cameras are hidden behind the lights. It's quite a sophisticated system. Top-of-the-line technology."

They watched Christal stare suspiciously around the room, sometimes peering straight into the camera. She checked the locker, hesitated, then reluctantly undressed. Hank swallowed hard, watching her as she padded to the door to stare longingly at the shower where April washed.

"We kept her in pretty Spartan quarters," April said. "She was ready for the opportunity."

The view changed as Christal stepped into the shower room, glancing in surprise at the camera. "She's just discovered the mirrored wall," April added with amusement. "Marketing is going to love that expression of wonder and awe. It gives her a sense of excitement, don't you think?"

Hank shifted as the camera closed on Christal's body. He might have screwed her, but he'd never seen her naked before. It was like Christmas—April and Christal, side by side for comparison: April, a little more full-breasted, pale with a dancer's supple body, beside long-limbed Christal, darker, brown, muscular, and lithe.

April and Neal laughed when April stepped out and Christal immediately scurried out to try the locker room door. "Now," Neal added, "tell me that wasn't expected?"

When Christal finally took the plunge, the camera angles changed again, following her as she crossed the poolside at a run and dove. Immediately, the underwater lenses picked her up, her perfect body lancing into the frame in a rush of white bubbles.

Hank fought the urge to shift again as the camera zoomed in on Christal's body, then backed away as April slipped past with eel-like grace. He could feel April's curious glance, and tried to keep his expression nonchalant.

"This is what we want your opinion on," Neal said.

The cameras changed, focusing on Christal's face as April discussed the relative merits of Genesis Athena.

"Watch her," April added. "Study her closely, and tell me what you think."

Christal listened to April's comparison between the US government and Genesis Athena.

April leaned to ask, "What do you think? Is she buying it?"

"It's irritating her. You can see it in her mouth."

"Watch this," April indicated the screen as Christal declared: *"There's nothing I can do about what the government does with my tax dollars."*

"Bullshit." April shot back *"You've just made that particular deal with the Devil, Christal. You're comfortable with it."*

Hank leaned forward, watching Christal's familiar expression. The clarity of the picture was awesome. He could see her pupils, the faintest of tension at the corners of her mouth. He saw the reaction. "There! You got to her when you brought up the government funding of bad guys." A moment later, he saw her expression turn thoughtful again, when April told her that it would be cheaper to deep-six her, but that they wouldn't. "She's chewing on that."

He watched as Christal, oblivious now, climbed up out of the pool. Her face was pensive as she walked along the poolside to the showers. Damn, she was one fine-looking woman.

"Marketing is going to like this part," Neal added. "You can see her natural grace, here. She's vulnerable, but looking intelligent."

The scene shifted to the shower room. Hank watched as the women showered, the discussion continuing.

He started when April reached over on-screen and touched the wall. "What the . . . ?"

Beside him, she laughed in amusement. "It's a big blow dryer. I'll take you sometime. You wouldn't believe how stimulating it is."

I believe! He couldn't help gaping like an idiot as Christal's skin moved as if massaged. It did the most marvelous things with her breasts and belly. The air pressure gave her face an exotic look, sharpening her cheeks, black hair rippling out in a wave. Her narrowed eyes added to the effect, like something from an animator's pen. When it stopped, he was rigid in his seat, hands clasped on the armrests.

"This is the important part," Neal said. Was that a tremor in his voice? Damn, the man would have to be made of wood not to have been affected.

Hank managed to breathe again as he watched Christal and April dressing.

"Here!" Neal called as April asked what it would take.

Christal took a moment to consider. *"Five million."*

April's laugh was mocking. *"Not a chance."*

With an evaluative stare, Christal asked, *"So, what's your counteroffer?"*

"Two hundred thousand."

The camera was centered on Christal's expression when she said, *"What makes you think I wouldn't take it and spill my guts later anyway?"*

On-screen, April told her, *"Because we're a business, Anaya. You have a basic understanding of our capabilities, resources, and resolve. I think you know that we'll use them if we have to. We'll keep our end of the bargain only as long as you keep yours."*

After a thoughtful hesitation, Christal said, *"I'll think about it."*

The screen went blank and the lights came up. Neal turned in his chair. "You know her, Hank. What do you think? Will she buy it, or do we go with the Jamaica option?"

Images of Christal's body undulating in the wind stream dominated his thoughts. *Shit!* "I don't know."

"Want to see it again?" April asked slyly, her gaze half-lidded and knowing.

See it again? Hell, he'd be dreaming that vision for the rest of his life! Hank shook his head, answering, "Actually, yeah. She'll go for it if it's handled right." Knowing full well she wouldn't. He frowned. What in hell had prompted him to say that?

"Paybacks are a bitch," Neal quipped. "And Gregor has made sure she'll never forget."

"Come on," April said, standing and reaching down to pull him to his feet. "I need to go to my cabin. Some hairy ape spoiled my outfit."

He stood, hoping his knees weren't wobbly. April's lips

curled, reading his weakness. The excitement in her hooded gray eyes added to the stirring in his loins. It was shaping up to be an exciting afternoon.

The *ZoeGen* looked huge as the launch motored into the ship's lee and the engines reversed. The only thing on the empty ocean, it might have been its own continent. Lymon glanced up, watching a platform and ladder lower from a hatch that opened in the great ship's side.

Dear God, I hope this was a good idea. Setting foot aboard that ship went against every instinct. He reached down for the handles on his locked plastic case.

Sheela looked pale despite her makeup and brown wig. She gave him an uncertain smile, as if the reality of what she had plunged them into was dropping home like an anvil.

"This is going to be interesting," Sid muttered. He'd been on the verge of seasickness for most of the trip.

The launch rose and fell, rubbing on fenders as it came to rest beside the lowered landing. While the huge bulk of the ship blocked the prevailing wind and the swells, it still appeared dubious to Sid.

"If you'll each just wait until the surfaces match," one of the deckhands said, "we'll have you step right across."

Lymon met Sheela's wide-eyed stare with an encouraging smile. "Want to go back now?"

She shook her head too fast. "See it through."

"It's your call."

They watched as one by one the other passengers climbed up, held the handrails, and easily stepped across. After the two pregnant women, Sheela took her turn, stepping across as the launch rose. One of the *ZoeGen*'s crew women steadied her hand, then gestured her up the short set of steps to the hatch.

Lymon tightened his grip on the black plastic case, climbed up, and smoothly stepped across, declining the young woman's hand. He turned back, calling, "It's easy."

"What if I miss?" Sid replied.

"The water's only a thousand feet deep here. You'll have lots of time to think about it on the way to the bottom. And once you're there, it'll be so dark you won't be able to see just how bad your situation really is."

"Asshole!"

Lymon climbed the steps, his case in hand, and glanced back just in time to see Sid scurry from the launch's deck to the platform.

The corridor that Lymon entered might have been a hallway at the Four Seasons. Sheela was waiting beside a uniformed crewman—a smiling young man this time. He wore a neat blue jacket with brass buttons, white pressed pants, and held his hands clasped before him. His name tag read PETER.

The young man was saying, "Everything is ready, Ms. Weaver. As soon as you wish, we can proceed to your quarters and get you settled in."

"The luggage?" Lymon asked.

"That will be delivered by our staff. Would you like me to take that case for you, sir?"

"Thanks, but this is my responsibility." He gave Peter a *You know how it is* smile.

"Thank God! This thing doesn't move." Sid came barging in, muttering under his breath and looking green. Lymon noticed that perspiration was beading on his forehead.

"He's the last of our party," Sheela said in her irritated Jennifer tone. "We can go now."

Lymon took up station behind and to Sheela's right. Sid, not knowing the drill—or too close to puking—just followed along behind. Lymon could hear him sucking great gulps of air. Sometimes even that helped.

Despite the opulent nature of the corridor they followed, Lymon noted that small security cameras had been tastefully incorporated into the decor. Which got him to thinking: What if they had to get out of here in a hurry? A knot was pulling tight in his gut.

"You going to be any good if we land in the shit?" Lymon muttered over his shoulder.

"Point me in the right direction," Sid mumbled, "and I'll throw up all over them."

They entered a wood-paneled lift trimmed in polished brass. Sheela was fidgeting around in her purse, muttering, "My compact. God, I didn't forget my compact!"

"We have a well-stocked commissary," the steward told her. "And the launch makes several round trips each day. Feel free to contact me if you need anything at all." He gave them a professional smile. "Some of our clients have been known to charter a helicopter just to go to dinner ashore."

Lymon kept his face straight as Sheela stopped her rooting and glanced up. "What? You don't have food?" she asked.

"Oh, we have a gourmet chef and a full kitchen. Your people even approved a menu for your stay. Once you're settled, we can go over it. If there are any changes you would like to make, we'll be happy to accommodate them."

The lift opened and Lymon stepped out, checking the corridor. He made way for Sheela, glaring at Sid, who was still sentient enough to realize Lymon was trying to tell him something. With a hand signal Lymon put him into position as they started down an even fancier hallway, the wood here looking like teak. The polish was so deep he could see his reflection.

"This will be your quarters for the next week," the steward said as he stopped before a door on the left and opened it. Lymon followed Sheela inside and promptly stepped around her, surveying the room. This was the only advance he was going to get.

The place was large, airy, perhaps twenty by thirty feet with a ten-foot ceiling paneled in skylights framed by thick black timbers. The furniture looked Victorian, with polished wood and expensive fabric. Concessions to the twenty-first century included a big-screen home theater unit as sophisticated as Sheela's own dominating one wall. A computer desk stood in one corner with a monitor, keyboard, and fax/printer looking like they'd just been lifted out of a corporate office. A cordless phone sat in its cradle. Where the floor was exposed beyond the thick red carpet, it was waxed wood. Two large picture windows filled the opposite wall, and a weather door let out onto a spacious balcony. Lymon checked the door, leaving it for later. He walked across the suite, noting the ornate wet bar in the corner, and opened the corner door that accessed the bedroom. Behind him the steward began explaining the bar's capabilities and demonstrating the refrigerator and microwave to Sheela.

Lymon found a king-sized bed atop a boxed frame. Another phone rested on the nightstand along with a TV remote for the plasma screen on the far wall. An alcove to the right was fitted out with a settee that allowed its occupant to stare out over the ocean through a huge glass window. In the bedroom, Lymon quickly went through the built-in dresser drawers, checked the nightstands, and stepped into the spacious bathroom. He found white marble tiling and counters, golden faucets, a whirlpool tub, and a glassed-in shower. A gleaming toilet stood next to the bidet. The towels were clean and perfectly folded, and the toilet paper was full in the gold-plated holder.

A quick look over the place showed nothing amiss. But, as Anaya would have said, his whiskers were vibrating. It looked like any of the luxury suites Sheela had occupied around the world. Why then, did he have this uneasy feeling of hidden threat?

He walked back through to the main room and found the steward involved in teaching Sheela the intricacies of the TV remote control.

Sid was out on the balcony. Lymon stepped out, looking around. "Feeling better?"

"Yeah." Sid had leaned on the rounded steel of the railing. "Funny, looking at the ocean doesn't bother me from up here."

"Glad you're recovering. You're not acting up to snuff for the security business." He looked around, taking in the deck chairs and tables. Looking over the side, he found a straight drop down to the ocean, what, eighty feet below? Leaning out, he could see that another balcony was below, while a deck railing appeared to be just above.

"Nice digs." Sid stuffed his hands in his pockets and looked around.

"Come on. You're going to learn the security business."

Lymon led the way back in and managed to catch the steward's attention. "Excuse me, Peter, could we have a quick word with you?"

"Sure." The steward stepped over while Sheela was stabbing at the remote. Headline News was playing.

Lymon gave the man his best smile. "Could you contact your head of security and set up an appointment as soon as possible? We'd also like a map of the ship, something detailing the various decks and corridors, with escape routes, directions to the dining room, and other venues highlighted. We need to know the location of the closest lifeboats, personal flotation devices, medical facilities, fire extinguishers, and first aid kits. I'd also like a list of shipboard contacts for emergencies, phone numbers for medical personnel, security, your equivalent of a concierge, and room service. We would like a schedule of Ms. Weaver's planned activities and a schematic of where they are to take place. If you could provide us with a list of other guests aboard, and their security personnel, I would be happy to meet—"

"Whoa!" The steward threw his hands up. "I'll have Neal Gray, our head of security, contact you as soon as he can."

"Thanks." Lymon backed off, slipping the steward a fifty-dollar bill.

Sid had taken that in, wide-eyed. He followed Lymon over to the wet bar in the corner. As Lymon began sorting through the stock of drinks, snacks, and accessories, Sid whispered, "A fifty? Are you nuts?"

Lymon gave him a subtle grin as he continued his inspection, making sure the packaging hadn't been tampered with and that the bottles still had their factory seals. "It's cheap at twice the price. If I have to ask this guy for a box of Cracker Jack, he's going to move mountains to find it for me."

"He'd have probably done it for ten."

"Maybe." Lymon shrugged. "If we were lodging on D Deck downstairs. But up here on B Deck we might just end up needing more than Cracker Jack before we're out of here. You get my drift?"

"Uh, maybe."

"What if She . . . Ms. Weaver decides at three in the

morning that she wants to blow this berg? How much cooperation am I going to get from Pete?"

"Right. You get what you pay for. I'm starting to catch on.
So, what's next?"

"I want you to go over this room carefully. See what's
here. Memorize this suite and then we'll take a walk and
learn our way around. You need to be familiar enough with
the ship that you can find your way around in an emergency
without floundering."

Pete had taken Sheela on a tour of the bedroom.

"Our job," Lymon continued, "is to be ready for any con-
tingency. Normally we figure this out in advance, meeting
the people, touring the facilities, and learning the picky little
details. The rule here is that we hurry a little harder since
we're behind." He dropped his voice. "And you defer to any
of *Ms. Weaver's* demands."

"Right," Sid said, catching on. He still didn't look fit, but
at least his mind was working again. "What's your initial
take, boss?"

"Look around. Something's not right about this place."

"Yeah, I'm starting to think that, too."

"Good. Think of it as a crime scene, Sid. Look this place
over with the same care you would use at the scene of a
triple homicide."

"Got it. I just hope you're not being prophetic."

45

Using Nancy Hartlee's nanotechnology always delighted
Gregor McEwan. He'd tried to score with the lady in
the first couple of months after she'd been brought to
Yemen. Back in those days, before the *ZoeGen*, they'd been
a small, tightly bound nucleus of brainpower stuck on the
edge of the Arabian desert. A camaraderie had built among
them, and despite the reality of their incarceration, it had

been a period of incredible cross-fertilization of ideas, theories, and conceptual applications.

He and Nancy had hit it off, at least until she began to grasp just how brilliant he really was. Perhaps if she'd stuck with him instead of walking out, she'd be sharing in the glory. Instead, Nancy Hartlee was dead and buried, while no less than fifteen of her little clones were spread here and there around the world. Several had been placed in scientific-oriented families to see if her doppelgangers developed the same keen brain. That was one of the fascinating things: seeing how the duplicates developed. Talk about a laboratory for behavioral genetics!

Gregor concentrated on the image projected on the screen. His fingers turned the knobs that manipulated the nanoscalpel, the cellular dam, and pipette. In the pale green image, the cell appeared something like a translucent jellyfish. The oocyte's organelles were defined by diffracted infrared light to minimize cellular photosensitivity. The photons in turn were intensified and converted into the screen image.

The nanoscalpel methodically slit the structures of the cellular wall, and Gregor turned the knob that directed the nanodam into place. Another of Nancy's inventions, it kept the cytoplasm from sagging and losing its integrity. To date, he was the only person who insisted on calling it a speculum. Well, it was an egg, wasn't it?

Using the nanodam he eased the cytoplasm aside and made another incision through the layers of the endoplasmic reticulum. In many ways, this was the trickiest part. The ER, as they called it, had the same qualities as corrugated paper, and was just about as delicate. If too much pressure was applied, it could fold up on itself, destroying its integrity and damaging the cell's ability to function. The ER had to be eased open to expose the nuclear membrane before inserting the nanodam. Doing so was more of an art than a science, and over the years, Gregor had developed a feel for the equipment that remained unmatched, although Ibrahim was getting close.

Finally, he had the nucleus exposed. On the screen, he used a grease pencil to mark location of the nucleolus in relation to the centrioles, the poles to which the chromosomes attached for meiotic division. Only then did he insert the micropipette to the nuclear wall. Applying light suction, he turned the nucleus, watching it move in relation to the centrioles. Reaching out on the control board, Gregor changed the image perspective to the rear. With a dial he inserted a nanopipette to the backside of the nuclear membrane. Then, as he began retraction of the nucleus through the incision, he slowly pumped purified, anaerobic, neutral pH water into the space created by the retreating nucleus.

Having successfully extracted the nucleus, he retracted it and spun the controls that brought the replacement into position. This he eased forward into the incision and, encountering the water-filled nuclear cavity, reversed suction, allowing vacuum to pull the new nucleus into the cavity. All that remained was to spin the nucleus so that its orientation with the centrioles was as close to the original's as the new nuclear morphology would allow.

Gregor smiled with a delighted sense of satisfaction when he withdrew the pipettes and nanodam. Changing the angle on the screen, he compared the images. The organelles near the incision had a three percent variation from their original location.

Gregor rolled his chair back from the control panel and jotted his observations and procedures into the master notebook. Under the bottom, he wrote the word SUCCESSFUL! and underlined it twice. All the oocyte needed now was a dash of PLCs and a nutrient-rich uterine wall to stick to.

"Sir?" Ibrahim said, leaning into the room. "Something has come up that we think you should see."

"Indeed?"

"Yes, sir." Ibrahim was in his late twenties, darker than the rest of the Sheik's kin, with a profound brain. He was the most adept of the trainees, and Gregor's personal favorite. "It is either a most remarkable coincidence, or someone has done something very wrong."

* * *

BBC World News was playing on the lounge television. Christal sat on one of the couches, her right leg pulled up, a magazine in her hands. Had she been asked, she couldn't have said what had been on the news, nor could she have even named the magazine in her slim brown fingers. Instead, she stared absently across the empty room, running the events of the morning through her mind.

Movement at the corner of her eye caused her to stir. Brian Everly had leaned his head in. "There you are! Missed you in the cafeteria. Hungry?"

She smiled, and felt it slip away. "No. But I probably ought to eat."

He had stepped into the room. "What? New clothes? Don't tell me you made a trip to the QVC in Sydney for a little shopping while I wasn't looking?"

She closed the magazine and tossed it onto the coffee table in front of her. "No. I had a little adventure this morning. Copperhead came to take me upstairs—allegedly for a meeting, but I'm not so sure anymore."

"Copperhead?"

"April Hayes."

"Ah?" He stepped around the coffee table and seated himself at the far end of the couch. "How much did they offer, and for what?"

"Two hundred thousand to drop any charges and keep my mouth shut."

He wove his fingers together. "You going to take it?"

"How the hell do I know?" The worry that had been churning in her gut rose to the surface. "What are my options, Brian? If I say no, do you think they're going to let me spend the rest of my life down here eating their food, taking up space, and being a security risk?"

"Then take it and be glad." He stared down at his hands. "But if you do, Christal, don't ever ever say a word. Not to anyone. Not ever."

She gave him a sidelong glance. "You think they'd really do it? Pay me and let me go?"

He gave her a weary smile. "For whatever reason, they'd rather have you outside and mum, rather than dead."

"Copperhead said that they'd rather pay now than later. I can understand that. People will begin asking questions when I don't reappear. I left them some information, you see. And I'd had run-ins with Copperhead that involved the police. That's a lot of loose ends."

"Take it, Christal."

She turned suspicious eyes on him. "Why, Brian? You part of this?"

The weary smile deepened. "I'd expect smarter questions from a woman as bright as you, Christal Anaya, but no, not in the way you think."

"How, then?" Why hadn't she noticed what a handsome man he was? She liked the gentle concern in his odd pale eyes, the easy way that he sat. Something about him made her feel comfortable when she was in his presence.

"Because I'd rather have you safe."

It was the tone in his voice, the way he managed to shyly avoid her eyes.

"Gallantry?"

The faintest of shrugs lifted his shoulders. Then he laughed at himself and sat forward to rub his hands together. They were muscular hands, eminently male, veined, with strong tendons.

"I might even go with you."

"What?" She tried to see past the careful expression on his face.

"I've never had a reason to join them."

"What are you talking about?"

"I've been here for five years." He turned sad eyes on her. "They took me out of my car and stole me away from my life. They locked me up here and put me to work, making sure I knew that I either produced, or they would destroy me. I watched colleagues wither and die in this place. Here, and at the lab in Yemen, we rewrote the rules. We changed the bloody world as it hasn't been changed since the first atomic bomb detonated in your New Mexico."

He gestured toward the BBC anchorwoman who talked so thoughtfully into the camera. "They don't understand. Nothing's the same. Within thirty years, people will be ordering their children like they do motor cars."

"Come on."

Ironic humor tugged at his lips. "Color is one of the easier options: white, brown, or black? We also mix and match for any shade in-between. We have a special on eyes this month. Personally, I like yours. Oh, right! Then we have strength. Do you want fast or slow muscle?"

"Huh?"

"By programming for a preponderance of slow myosin—that's one of the contractive muscle proteins—we can make your child a world-class weightlifter. If you want a sprinter, we can change the DNA to produce fast Two-a and Two-x myosins. You, incidentally, have a preponderance of slow myosin. You're better at endurance over the long run. I'd like the chance to test that out one of these days."

"That's a joke, right? About the muscles, I mean."

"Sorry. Fact is, it's one of the simple qualities we can tailor into your child. Other things, like resistance to a communicable disease, get a bit more dicey. Something that people don't understand is that in nature, everything becomes a trade-off. If we tinker with the immunogenetics to build a resistance to certain gram-negative streptococcal bacteria on one hand, we increase susceptibility to infectious bacilli on the other. What is taken in one place, must be given back somewhere else."

"Good God, you're not joking."

"You, my dear Christal, have a susceptibility to multiple sclerosis. I'm not saying that you're going to get it—odds are that you won't—but with the right preconditions, the proper viral vector, and a stressed immune system, you could. It's because of a protein inconsistency in the myelin sheath in your nerves. It's easily fixable so that your descendants won't have it."

She shifted, tensing. "You found that in that sample of mine you've been working on?"

He glanced away again. "We fixed your disposition to osteoarthritis, too. It was a simple base-pair substitution that will add elasticity to the hyaline cartilage. On the other hand, I did nothing to change your sebaceous and maxillary glands."

"Huh?"

"I like the way you smell, Anaya."

"*¡Madre de Dios!*"

"Sorry, I guess I shouldn't have said that."

She reached out, laying a slim hand on his arm. "I'm a little stunned is all. Talk about Alice through the looking glass! One minute I'm running an investigation in LA and the next I'm talking to the Cheshire cat." She shook her head. "I don't understand. These things you're doing? Stealing DNA, changing it? Curing diseases and selling babies? My God, how come no one is screaming their head off? Where's the Church? What's the Pope say? Where's the righteous indignation of the president, the senators, and Congress? *Why doesn't anybody care?*"

"Easy, Anaya." He reached out and caught the balled fist she was clenching.

She stared angrily into his eyes. "Well?"

He gave a paternal smile that soothed some of the ruffle in her feathers. "You know Senator Baber? The one on the Senate ethics committee?"

"Tennessee, right?"

"I think so. He was here last year."

"Huh?"

"We cloned a new prostate for him. His old one was enlarged and precancerous. The story I heard was that he'd rather have a new one than lose his sexual potency."

"Cloned a new prostate? Wait a minute! Nobody transplants prostates!"

"At Genesis Athena we do. He had to fly to Yemen for the procedure."

"Sexual potency? He's sixty!"

"The young lady accompanying him—I think he called her a 'staffer'—wasn't nearly that old." His smile widened. "If you'll recall, Baber's wife died of amyotrophic lateral sclerosis. You would know that better as Lou Gehrig's disease. It's not a pretty way to go, and it tore Baber apart. So, at the same time we implanted his new prostate, we did a simple gene scan on his daughter, Marissa. On her twenty-first chromosome we found a missense mutation at the q22.1 location—a SOD1 condition for the autosomal dominant trait."

"That's not English," Christal objected.

"Oh, yes, right. Sorry. It means she got the ALS gene from her mother and it would override its allele. That's the functioning gene from her father's chromosome. In short, she was perhaps five years from the onset of the disease, so we ran a gene therapy, using a tailored viral vector to replace the malfunctioning gene. As time passes, the inserted gene will produce enough enzymes to break down the toxins that cause ALS. Baber won't have to watch his daughter die in agony the way his wife did."

"So, what are you saying?"

"I'm saying that just like my example with bacterial resistance earlier demonstrated, what you lose on one hand, is taken on the other. In short, do you expect world leaders to decry Genesis Athena in public while in private we're restoring the gift of life to them and their loved ones?"

Christal sat back. "But these other things!"

"What?" Brian lifted his hand as a supplicant. "You're drooling mad that they're going to sell your DNA? That people like me have been held against our wills? Do you think that Senator Baber is going to call out the dogs? Genesis Athena gave him back his sex and his daughter. Where do you think he's going to come down?"

"There are other leaders."

"Ah? The director of your FBI had a procedure done at Bethesda Naval Hospital last year, remember?"

"Yes. Something about deterioration of the optic nerve. After a couple of months he was back to twenty-twenty vision."

"Want to take a stab at who licensed that procedure? That was actually our beloved Gregor's brainchild. He was the one who thought to utilize that particular protein matrix for delivery to the degenerating cells. The point being that if push came to shove, would your FBI director have his heart and balls behind an investigation of Genesis Athena?" He paused. "Gregor even hinted that your director may have been responsible for your friend Hank's recruitment. Well, for the initial phone call at least."

At her stunned look, he added, "It's more than just the *ZoeGen*, Christal. It's hospitals, pharmaceuticals, gene therapies, and a thousand patents in molecular biology. Their tentacles extend throughout the medical field. They offer life and hope where there hasn't been before."

"So what do we do?"

He stared down at his hands again. "I've spent five years fighting them, and what's it got me? My friends are gone, my life has been stolen, and my universe is this little patch of deck in the guts of the *ZoeGen*." He reached out, tentatively touching her hair. "For the first time, I've found something that I want. A reason to finally say all right, take their bloody settlement, and go someplace to try to rebuild my life."

She didn't understand at first. The sadness mixed with hope deep in his eyes sent a flutter through her. "God, Brian, you hardly know me!"

"Right. And I'm not trying to be a boor. A woman like you has guys hitting on her all the time. It's not like that. From the moment I first saw you, all hot and sweaty, I was stopped short in my tracks." He withdrew his hand. "But, no matter what, take their offer, Christal. For me. Get the hell out of here, bite your bloody tongue, and be glad of having your life back."

"What about you?"

He looked away. "Assuming they actually believe me, I'd like to look you up out there. On the outside. When there's just the two of us. You know, maybe do dinner and the movies. Just to see if I find you so wondrously attractive as I do in this bloody hole." A shrug. "I want a chance to be normal with you, that's all."

"You don't think they'll let you go?"

"I fought them a long time, Christal. McEwan once told me he'd see me rot in hell before I'd breathe unfiltered air."

She bit her lip, frowning as she considered. "No matter what, Brian, I'm not leaving here without you."

"Now that," McEwan's familiar voice interrupted, "might be quite a feat."

They turned to see McEwan leaning in the door. He stepped in, one eyebrow raised. "Thinking about leaving? Really?"

Brian sighed wearily. "Oddly, I've been trying to talk Ms. Anaya into accepting the offer she's been made." His voice dropped. "I've been thinking of accepting, too."

"You, Brian?" McEwan's voice mocked. "After all your years of protestation and principle?"

Brian's soft chuckle was heavy with resignation. "What am I going to do? Sit here in the bowels of this ship for the rest of my life? You've won, McEwan. You and Genesis Athena." He paused as McEwan studied his expression. "I'm tired."

"Yes," McEwan agreed. "I suppose you are. But why should we believe that you'll play by our rules?"

"Maybe because I've never had a reason before."

McEwan turned his attention to Christal, as if seeing her anew. She tensed under his probing eyes. He said, "Ibrahim and I were just running a few tests on a blood and tissue sample taken from a client. You know, to test for compatibility? We've just made a fascinating discovery. Too bad you weren't there, Brian."

"Oh?"

McEwan's eyes hadn't left Christal's face. "The client is already aboard. A Ms. Jennifer Weaver here for an implantation. That name mean anything to you?"

Christal caught herself, struggling to keep her face straight. *Jennifer Weaver?*

"No." Brian answered absently, "Should it?"

"Maybe not now, but she's going to make history soon. She's here for a Sheela Marks copy."

Christal imagined Sheela's face staring down from the screen. *For a Sheela Marks implant?* Sheela hadn't come here, had she? Dear God, was she aboard the *ZoeGen*?

"Oh, it's a little coincidental, that's all." McEwan's eyes never wavered. "We've just never seen a perfect match between a client and a donor before. It was one hundred percent the same. Right down to point mutations."

"What?" Brian sounded perplexed. "That's impossible!"

"Yes. Quite."

Christal's heart began to hammer. She had no idea what McEwan was reading from her expression. Jennifer Weaver? God, it had to be! Was Lymon with her? Had they tracked her down? If so, then it was only a matter of time until the cavalry appeared.

"There's got to be a mistake," Brian said irritably. "Someone mixed the samples. It's a joke."

"Oh, it's not a joke." McEwan smiled at Christal with a subtle satisfaction. "As Ms. Anaya will be able to tell you soon enough, I have a very sophisticated sense of humor. One with a wee bit o' time delay."

Brian was frowning as McEwan turned on his heel and strode from the room.

"What was that all about?" Christal tried to control her racing pulse.

"The bit about time delay? I have no idea, but there's only one way a donor and client can have a perfect match."

She placed a hand on his arm, chafing under the scrutiny of the security cameras. Would they be watching her? Recording her reaction? "Explain."

"Prior to beginning the process of implanting an embryo into a host mother, we do a series of simple tests to determine compatibility. The first thing we look at is blood type, since blood is the interface between mother's uterus and the fetal placenta. We want to know if Rh is a factor, as well as any of a number of other genetic predispositions. If we find no conflicts, our physicians will give the woman a complete physical, and inject her to stimulate ovulation and the release of multiple oocytes, egg cells from the ovaries. After we collect the eggs, we'll evaluate them for morphology and resources, choose the best, and replace the nuclear DNA with the donor's."

"Yes, I know all that. What did McEwan mean they matched?"

"Christal, the only way they can match one hundred percent is if they come from the same person."

She felt the blood draining from her face. "Brian, we've got to talk." She glanced meaningfully up at the camera. "There's got to be a place."

46

When Peter finished with Sheela, he looked at Lymon and Sid, asking, "Would you gentlemen like to see your room?"

Lymon, Sid in tow, followed Peter down the B Deck hall to the next suite. This proved to be a duplicate of Sheela's, right down to the stock of fine liquors in the bar.

"Is this right?" Lymon asked. "Generally quarters for security are somewhat, well, less expensive."

Pete clasped his hands, his perfect professional smile unblemished. "This was done at Ms. Weaver's request, sir. If you would like other quarters, we would be more than happy to comply, but as I'm sure you can understand, it will have to come through her."

"I'm sure this will be fine, Peter." He slipped another fifty from his money clip and handed it over. "Thank you very much for your courtesy to Ms. Weaver."

"Thank you, sir. Is there anything else?"

"No, that will be all."

Sid, in the meantime, had taken to wandering around the room, looking carefully at the walls and ornamentation. "Quite the digs. I could get used to this business." A hesitation. "Uh, that is if you think I work out, sir."

At the old familiar tone in his voice, Lymon turned wary. "It's not always like this."

"I would hope not," Sid added cryptically as he turned away from one of the wall sconces. "Uh, you said something about checking out the corridors? Getting the lay of the land? Maybe we'd better be doing that."

"I did." Lymon bent, laying his plastic case on the table. As he began undoing the combination lock, Sid leaned close to whisper, "If there's anything there you don't want seen, you'd better not open it."

Lymon froze, reading Sid's eyes. "Right." Instead, he strode over to the phone and lifted the receiver.

"Operator. How may I help you?"

"Ms. Weaver's suite, please."

On the second ring, Sheela answered, *"Hello?"*

"Ms. Weaver, it's Lymon. We'll be advancing the hallways. If you need anything, please ring my pager."

"Thank you, Lymon. Sometime soon I must talk to you. We have some things to clear up."

"Yes, ma'am." He tried to sound contrite and hung up. Looking at Sid, he said, "Let's go."

He was turning when a knock sounded. Lymon met Sid's curious gaze and shrugged. Opening the door, he admitted an attractive man in a gray suit, white shirt, and tie. The blond hair had been combed back to reveal a high forehead. He had a professional smile under his wary blue eyes.

"Hello. I'm Neal Gray, head of *ZoeGen* security."

Lymon hesitated for the slightest instant, and recovered immediately as he recognized the guy. He'd last seen him in the parking lot outside Christal's Marriott. Lymon forced his most bluff smile, extending his hand. "Lymon Bridges, and my partner, Sid Harness. We work for June Rosen's security firm. Glad to meet you."

The man's shake was firm as Lymon searched his eyes for any hint of recognition. Would he know him? Lymon had been wearing a three-quarter helmet that night, with a full-face visor. While Gray's face had been clearly visible in the sodium lights, how much of his own could have been seen?

"What can we do for you, Mr. Bridges? I came just as soon as I could after receiving Peter's call. I trust everything's been satisfactory so far."

"It has. You have excellent staff." Lymon thrust his hands into his pockets. "We just wanted to introduce ourselves, let you know who we were. Familiarize ourselves with your system, and see if there was anything we could do to make your job easier."

"We appreciate that. Peter should have shown you your

rooms. If you have a minute, why don't we take a tour of the ship? Your advance, if you will."

"We'd like that." Lymon kept his smile in place. "After you."

They followed Gray out into the hallway as the man said, "In all honesty, I don't think you guys are going to have much to do. Believe me, we've got all the bases covered. Look at this assignment as having your own semiprivate cruise ship. And since your principal was gracious enough to provide a suite, I think you're going to enjoy your stay."

"Are we expected to share the king bed?" Sid asked dourly, eyes hooded.

"Peter didn't tell you? The love seat across from the TV folds out. Or we could have a second bed brought up."

"The foldout will be fine." Sid grinned humorlessly. "Boss, I'd actually prefer the foldout."

"That's it, suck up," Lymon chided, trying to stay in character.

Gray pointed at the hallway. "I'm sure you've already noticed that we have security cameras up and down the hallways. As a result we can control movement and access through any part of the visitors' portion of the ship. B Deck is yours to roam, gentlemen. Please feel free to use any of the facilities. We have a weight and exercise room." He pointed to a door marked with a golden barbell. "The nearest fire extinguishers are at either end of the hallway."

"What about first aid?" Lymon asked.

"You didn't bring a kit?" Gray asked innocently.

"In my suitcase," Lymon replied dryly.

"As I thought." Gray clasped his hands together. "Dial zero on any phone. The operator is on duty twenty-four/seven. Simply state the nature of the medical emergency and your location. Two trained EMTs will be on-site within minutes if not seconds. Because of the nature of our work, we have a small hospital on board. We can handle anything from heart attacks to hangnails."

"Quite an operation."

"You'd be surprised." The man's voice was filled with irony. Did he mean medically, or the ship? Gray pointed at another of the wooden doors. The shape of a pool table had been engraved on the gold plate. "This is the game room. Pool, snooker, card tables, the latest video games, that sort of thing."

As they proceeded down the hallway, they were shown the dining room, library, business center, and small lounge with a dark bar in the rear.

"Should I call ahead?" Lymon asked as he eyed the empty room.

"If you'd like. We can have her favorite beverage waiting, assuming the medical people clear it." Gray pointed to one of the cameras. "Otherwise feel free to just drop in and we'll know immediately and have someone coming on the run."

"I'll bet you don't get much business from the ACLU," Sid observed matter-of-factly.

Gray laughed. "Mr. Harness, we're not a public institution. This is a private and very professional clinic. While we treat people's privacy with the utmost care, believe me, we take our responsibilities for their safety most seriously. Your principal is spending a small fortune to come here for a procedure. We will make sure that she is satisfied."

"Yeah, right," Lymon said woodenly.

At Gray's curious look, he added, "Mr. Gray, don't misunderstand. The lady's my principal, and I'm a professional. But then, so are you, so let me give you a heads-up. A courtesy, if you will, from one pro to another. Let's just say that Ms. Weaver is a little, um, flighty. She's not one to stick things out, if you know what I mean." He glanced at Sid. "What do you think? Fifty-fifty?"

Sid shrugged. "Maybe."

"Meaning?" Gray asked.

"Meaning that we might get a call from Ms. Weaver at midnight tonight asking—no *demanding*—that we get her out of here." Lymon shrugged. "It's our job. What we're paid for. If she decides she doesn't want to go through with this procedure of hers, what's the drill?"

Gray frowned, lips pursed. "If she doesn't, it will complicate things. A lot of people have gone to a lot of trouble to set this up."

Lymon glanced away, lowering his voice. "The people who run her trust are used to, shall we say, 'situations.' My job is to see that we accede to her demands. If we need a helicopter, can we get one?"

"It'll be expensive."

Lymon laughed. "She can afford it. And it's always in the middle of the night."

"If we can't use the helicopter that's currently aboard, I'll be able to summon one from the mainland. It might take as much as a couple of hours, or she could go by means of one of the ship's launches, if necessary."

"Thanks. That's good to know."

"What's down there?" Sid asked as they passed a stairway leading down. A substantial steel grating barred passage. It reminded Lymon of one of the scarier scenes in the movie *Titanic.*

"That leads to the lower decks." Gray turned, a fist in his palm. "Gentlemen, your access is restricted to B Deck. If you wish to visit other areas of the ship, please don't hesitate to call my office and a guide will be assigned. We are happy to accommodate visits to places like the engine room, the bridge, and galley. Because of the sensitive and *private* nature of our work, some portions of the ship are off-limits to unauthorized personnel." He gave a forced smile. "We have had people in the past who, for reasons of their own, tried to break our security. It is our standing rule that anyone who does so will be confined, and removed from this vessel at first opportunity. Am I understood?"

"Fair enough," Lymon replied easily.

At the end of the corridor Gray opened the large double doors and led them out onto an open deck surrounded by white steel railings. A large pool dominated the center, surrounded by lounge chairs and tables. Another bar was covered by the overhang to the right of the doors. A healthy-looking man and an attractive brunette woman were lounging in a small whirlpool to one side. They looked up, smiled, and waved.

"More clients?"

"Yes. Leaving tomorrow, actually. Traveled down from Canada with us." Gray pointed overhead. "Up the steps you will find the tennis courts." He indicated the davits that could just be seen beyond the railing. "Lifeboats are just there on either side of the ship. Peter would have already shown you where flotation devices are located in your room closets. These large cabinets to either side contain others in case we have to evacuate when you're away from the room."

"What about the other guests?" Sid asked.

"We'd like a list if we could," Lymon added. "It would give us an opportunity to interface with their security, let them know who we are and vice versa."

"As of this moment, you are the only party aboard with security." Gray gave him a sharp look. "As I said, we take our clients' security very seriously. There are currently no persons aboard who could be considered threats to your principal. Given our monitoring, we will be on top of it in an instant if there is."

"Sounds good." Lymon looked around, seeing nothing but empty ocean beyond. It wasn't a new vista. He and Sid had spent weeks looking out at water from ships in the Persian Gulf. The afternoon sky had taken on a brassy look.

"Is this your first time on a ship?" Gray asked, reading his expression.

"Not hardly."

Gray's beeper went off, and he lifted a small radio from his belt, flipping it open. "Yes?"

"Sir, when you can, we need you in the barn. There's a situation you should be aware of."

"On my way." Gray reholstered his radio. "Gentlemen, if you need anything, dial the operator. I, or one of my staff, will be back to you immediately." He gave a brief nod. "And thanks for the heads-up on your principal. I'll make sure the proper people are notified in case she changes her mind." He looked back and forth between them. "Anything else?"

"Not at the moment."

"Then, if you will excuse me, I'll get back to the grind."

Gray shook hands again and disappeared through the double doors into the hallway.

"What do you make of that?" Sid asked.

"Top of the line, right down to the helicopter. You think he recognized me?"

"Who?" Then Sid made a chopping gesture, warning in his dark eyes. "Hold that thought and follow me."

Sid led the way to the railing farthest from the bathing couple. As they faced out at the ocean, where swells were shining in the late-afternoon sun, Sid said between gritted teeth, "The room's bugged. We're under a fucking microscope."

"You sure?" Lymon asked as he looked down at the water rippling along the steel hull so far below.

"Yeah, I found what I think is a Super Vanguard Sciax system in both Jennifer's room and ours. The thing uses top-of-the-line fiberoptics, microlensing, and computer-enhanced resolution, as well as superb directional audio capability. You can hear someone digesting a pizza from across the room. We considered it for surveillance, but it got axed in the budget. Absolutely incredible what it will do. Hell, for all I know, they've got a long-range microphone on us now. Be careful, Lymon. Tell Jennifer to be careful."

"Right."

Sid shook his head. "You and your crime scene. Shit. You can't pass a fart in this place without someone knowing." A pause. "What were you going to say back there?"

"You recognize Gray?"

"Should I?"

"You've seen his picture. LA, at Christal's apartment the night she got grabbed."

Sid's face hardened. "He didn't place you?"

"Not that I could see. If he did, he was better at hiding it than I would have been."

"Think Christal's here?"

"Got me." Lymon frowned down at the shifting waters. "But with this kind of security, I don't think they're going to let us go poking around looking for her."

"Shit! We gotta get the hell out of here."

444 W. MICHAEL GEAR

"Yeah, let's just hope that helicopter is ready when Jennifer throws her fit."

"Amen." Sid looked at him. "Lymon, if your friend Gray wanted to keep us here, what could we do about it?"

"Got me. Whatever it is that we'd have do, it wouldn't be pretty."

"Whu-up!" Sid answered in military slang.

47

At the knock on the door, Sheela was surprised to find Mary Abernathy standing there. Something seemed to have changed. The woman studied Sheela with a strange new intensity, as if seeing her for the first time. "May I come in?"

Sheela wore her shy Jennifer smile and nodded, stepping back.

Abernathy entered with the self-assurance of an M1 battle tank. In a clipped voice she said, "Our Mr. Gray is providing orientation for your security. I thought we should have a little chat."

As Abernathy took a seat, Sheela settled herself on the overstuffed chair just opposite her. "Okay."

"How are your quarters here?" Where did the hostile tone in her voice come from?

"Just fine. I was expecting, oh, I don't know. Like hammocks and little round portholes. Not like a real hotel."

"Had anything to eat?"

"No. And I'm starved."

Abernathy leaned forward, her smile oddly forced. "Outside of starvation, how are you feeling?"

Sheela took a moment to fidget, then let her glance slide sideways. "I'm fine."

"You're sure?"

Sheela managed a trite Jennifer nod. "Who were the pregnant women? You know, this morning on the launch. . . . There were two pregnant women."

Abernathy hesitated. "Not all of our clients are young and healthy like you are. And some, believe it or not, are actually male. For a fee Genesis Athena will próvide a surrogate mother. It's expensive, but for many people it's the only option."

"I see." She made it plain that she didn't.

"All right." Abernathy pressed her hands together. "What if you're a single father and your son dies suddenly? What if you want another child? What if that bereaved man feels like you do, Jennifer? What if he wants a *specific* child? Should we deny him when we can help you?"

"Well, I, uh . . ."

"No!" Abernathy waved it away as if it were an irritation. "And it's not just men. We know of women, who for reasons of age, or biology, cannot have children. Maybe they've had cancer or had a hysterectomy. Perhaps they're female corporate executives who can't take time out for a pregnancy. Do we deny them but only help people like the Smith couple you met this morning?"

"Well, I don't know."

Abernathy leaned back, one eyebrow lifted. "Jennifer, do you believe in equality?"

"Sure."

"Then why is it, when it comes to reproductive biology, only some people are allowed to reproduce, and others aren't?"

Sheela frowned, actually disturbed by the way Mary Abernathy had phrased the question. "It's not a matter of being allowed, is it?"

"Can a man have a child without a female partner?"

"No."

"Is it right?"

"Well . . . it's how God made us."

"Ah! Of course. God. But, Jennifer, we've been interfering with the way God made us for centuries now. In most cases a baby born prematurely will die without medical intervention. With modern technology we can save it and it will grow up to have a normal and happy life. Or would you let it die?"

"Of course I'd save it."

"What if it has a perforated septum in its heart? What's your choice? Do you operate to save it, or let it die?"

"Operate."

"But that's interfering with the way God made that baby."

"But reproducing is different, isn't it? I mean, men were born men."

"Why should a man not be allowed the same rights a woman has? In the past, our hypothetical baby would have died because we couldn't do anything to save it. We didn't have the technology. Until now, a man couldn't reproduce himself. Genesis Athena makes that possible. If we can provide our service to you, why can't we provide the same service for a man? The end result is the same: You, or he, will have a healthy baby to raise, to be your child. You have a right to a family, Jennifer. Why doesn't a man?"

She put a hand to her mouth. "I guess . . ."

"Yes, I think you understand. It's a matter of essential equality. At Genesis Athena, we're leveling the playing field for the first time in human history."

Sheela sat back. "So, it's all just a matter of technology? Of tools and science? You're saying that because we can, we should?"

Abernathy smiled kindly. "What you're asking is, Where do you draw the line? No, that's not the real issue, is it? The question is, Why should you draw a line at all?"

Sheela frowned. "I guess, since I'm here, I'm not the one to ask that."

"Good." Mary stood. "Are you settled?"

Sheela nodded, looking around. "I'm unpacked. And, well, I don't know. All of a sudden, I've kind of . . ."

"A little scared?" Abernathy asked as if she knew full well what Jennifer was going to answer.

"I guess."

"Come on. Let's go for a short walk. I want to show you

something, and introduce you to some people you'll be working with."

Sheela hesitated. On the one hand, she wanted Lymon close by. On the other, if, as she suspected, they were going to do the usual doctor-patient chat where everything was explained in detail, it would give her the excuse she needed to back out.

"Will it take long?"

"Barring complications, half an hour, if that. We'll treat you to a marvelous dinner when we're finished."

Sheela seemed to mull it over. "Sure. Let me contact Lymon so he doesn't tear the ship apart looking for me."

"Use the phone." Abernathy pointed. "He'll find the voice message when he and Mr. Gray return from their tour."

She gave the woman her insecure Jennifer smile and reached for the phone. After leaving a message for Lymon, she followed Abernathy out into the corridor and to the right, where one of the elevators waited, doors open.

Sheela stepped inside. She watched Abernathy press the button for H Deck. "You're going to like the people who will be working with you. We've found that if instead of waiting out the first night alone, you socialize with the staff, you'll feel better about the procedure."

"I see."

Abernathy studied her thoughtfully as the lift slowed, dinged, and the door opened. "We've also determined from the blood sample I took in New York that our window is very narrow."

Sheela followed her out into a white corridor. "What window is that?"

"A most curious biological one. This way."

Two men in white uniforms, both darkly complected, stepped out, nodding at Mary Abernathy. They dropped in behind Sheela as Mary started off down the hall.

Sheela glanced nervously at the men following behind, wondering if Jennifer should say anything, or just take this in stride.

Abernathy seemed brusque, oddly tense. Or was it just

that things had happened so fast? She hadn't had time to just sit and think, to put the plan in order.

Abernathy stopped before a door marked EXAMINATION and opened it. "If you'd step inside, Jennifer."

Sheela entered to find a wood-veneer paneled waiting room with comfortable couches, a coffee table, and magazines. Soft music drifted down from the speakers. It could have been lifted from any doctor's office in the country.

Abernathy gave a signal to the two men, who remained outside, and closed the door. "The nice thing"—Abernathy gestured Sheela to follow her—"is that we don't have to wait. Come on. We're all set."

"For what?" Sheela asked as she stepped into a hallway and was led down to a small room. Here, what looked like a dentist's chair dominated a small examining room. The noxious odors of medical chemicals stung her nose.

"Take a seat," Abernathy told her. "It's the most comfortable one in the house." She made a face. "Oh, don't worry. We just need to take a blood sample. Simple really. It has to be done while you've got an empty stomach. As soon as we do the vampire thing, we'll be off for dinner with our specialists so that you have a chance to relax."

As Sheela uncertainly settled into the seat, an attractive young woman of either Middle Eastern or Indian descent entered. She was perhaps thirty, with high cheeks and sleek black hair pulled back and clipped. Her white uniform was slightly baggy, somewhat Oriental in style. "Hello, Ms. Weaver. I'm Asza. This will only take a moment." She walked up and smiled down at Sheela in a reassuring manner. "You'll barely feel a thing."

Sheela glanced down at the syringe in the woman's hand. "Uh, I don't know if I want to—"

"Shhh!" Abernathy put a playful finger to her lips. "It's just a hormone to prepare your system. Trust me, it won't hurt a bit. It won't affect you at all. Well, sometimes women have minor hot flashes the next day, but that's about it."

"Wait!" Sheela said as Asza leaned down and swabbed her arm with alcohol. "I'm not ready for this!"

"The empty stomach," Abernathy said, leaning down and

insisting. "It's very important. And then, in a shake, we're off to dinner. I think you'll enjoy it. We've got a baked halibut that's marinated in . . ."

Sheela missed the rest as she looked down. Asza had slipped the sharp needle into Sheela's arm. She watched in horror as the plunger injected a clear fluid into her vein.

Hank and April bent over the small table studying their latest assignment: obtaining a sample from George Clooney. The actor was currently shooting a film in New York. Hank and April had been perusing the street maps, comparing them with the locations the production company had filed with the New York film commission, and trying to decipher the security at the New York Four Seasons Hotel.

"There are a million ways to do this. It's DNA, for God's sake!"

"It has to be high-profile," April insisted. "People have to *know* that we've got the real thing."

The room phone rang. April lifted the receiver, listened, and said, "We've got to go. Security center. Now."

"What's up?"

"Security alert. Something big's coming down."

Next thing they were in the hall, Hank following on her heels. He liked hurrying along behind April. The view from the rear was delightful.

Their route took them up two decks and down a long central corridor. A large metal hatch was marked SECURITY CENTER. April ran her fingers over a numerical keypad, then spun the wheel.

"We've got a problem," Neal told them as they entered. He stood in front of a bank of glowing monitors in the security center. Each screen showed different parts of the ship. The feed from each camera was monitored by the central computer. As long as no movement was detected, the computer ignored that image. It was a neat system, smart, and helped avoid errors that came from boredom on the operator's part.

For the moment, the single large screen in the center of

the complex displayed an attractive woman reclining in a chair as white-dressed nurses scurried about her, hooking up monitors, IVs, and other assorted medical apparatus.

Hank and April slid in behind the two work tables with five of the other security guys.

"I wanted you two since you've both had experience with Sheela Marks." Neal was looking back and forth between April and Hank.

"What?" April asked, straightening in her chair. "That was weeks ago."

"Who is that, April?" Neal pointed to where one of the nurses peeled a brunette wig from a tightly coiffed red-blond head. Hank could see another of the nurses teasing brown contacts from a glassy blue eye.

"Shit!" April spat. "How'd she get here?"

"She slipped right past us." Neal crossed his arms. "She's registered as Jennifer Weaver, come to have a procedure. I just got a call from my source in California with a heads-up that she might be headed our way."

"What would she want with us?" April asked, a frown deepening between her delicate brows.

"Better yet," Neal asked, "what are we going to do with her?"

For a moment the room was silent, expressions grim. Hank could understand the dilemma. This wasn't a blip on the radar. Not a Crystal Anaya who could disappear if necessary. If they deep-sixed Sheela Marks, someone *would* come looking.

"Jennifer Weaver." Neal glanced up from a sheaf of notes he'd picked up. "Apparently one of her screen characters."

Hank remembered: the saucy if insecure vixen from *Joy's Girl*.

"Her attorney—Felix Baylor, a big gun in the LA legal world—set up an account for her alias and paid down a pretty big deposit." Neal glanced from one to the other. "A lot of firepower could be leveled at us if this isn't handled just right."

"How did you finger her?" Hank asked.

"We might even have missed her with the tip, but apparently the woman knows more about acting than she does about genetics. She asked for implantation of one of her own clones."

April burst out laughing.

"What's the joke?" Hank asked from the side of his mouth.

"They'd chart identically in the lab. Like a crook submitting his own fingerprint when he volunteered to help solve his own crime."

"Right." Hank frowned.

"So, people, what do we do?" Neal gestured at the screen. "She doesn't know we're onto her. She's under sedation and out of trouble while we figure out how to handle this thing."

"I say she has an accident," one of the shipboard guys said. "Maybe the launch has a little bad luck? An explosion just before she and her party docks at the pier in Brooklyn?"

"No way," Hank countered. "The launch is already under Coast Guard scrutiny. Right now they know that something's going on under their nose. The first time I was here, I was stopped by them. Believe me, they know that high-profile people are traveling out here, and maybe even have a hint at what we're doing. But until they get a flag, they're not going to show up to do a 'safety inspection' and search of the ship."

Neal nodded. "For the time being, they know we carry enough senators, judges, and congressmen out here to cut us a little slack. Hank's right. Let's not make more trouble for ourselves that way."

"What about the Anaya option?" Hank asked.

All eyes turned his way.

Hank spread his hands. "We were going to drop Anaya in Kingston, Jamaica, stoned on good dope, and let her wake up in the local pokey. The cover was that she ditched her friends back in California for a drug binge. It gave us deniability when she tried to finger us for jacking her."

April gave him a thoughtful look. "You mean just substitute Sheela Marks? What about the law firm, this Felix character? He'd know."

"What would he know?" Hank shot back. "With the right

spin, we could say that Marks did this sort of thing on occasion, always with a well-rehearsed alibi for being where she was not. She might have scheduled an elective 'medical' procedure with Genesis Athena, but at the last minute, booked a flight from New York to Kingston as Jennifer Weaver to let her hair down out of the spotlight."

Neal had listened with pursed lips. "You think you could put that together and make it stick?"

"Yeah." Hank leaned back. "Sure. It would take a little setup, but it could be done." He glanced at April. "You've got a little darker hair, gray instead of blue eyes, but with the right makeup, you could pass for her. We could fly down on the first available flight, score some drugs, throw some wild parties, and book it all to Weaver's credit card. We sneak Marks in, tailor a drug cocktail, and call the hospital to report an OD on our way out of town."

April was nodding, putting it together in her mind. He could see the quickening of anticipation in her eyes. "Damn, I'll miss getting a piece of George Clooney. He's supposed to have such a way with women."

"One hitch," Neal replied. "What about Marks' security?"

"Piece of cake," April said. "We got by those guys twice. Once in New York, once in LA, so we can do it again."

"And almost got nicked," Neal added. "Both times."

Hank tensed, remembering the hard-eyed look Lymon Bridges had given him in the LBA offices that day.

"That second time was Anaya," April replied. "And if you'll recall, she's belowdecks."

"Who's with Marks?" Hank asked. "Show me."

Neal turned to the young bearded man sitting at the monitor control panel. "Vince? Could you give me a visual of the Weaver security detail?"

Within seconds the monitor changed, Sheela Marks vanishing to be replaced by a shot of Lymon Bridges prowling down the B Deck corridor. He walked in easy strides, like a muscular predator. Behind him, a thickset man followed a half step behind, arms swinging slowly. Hank stood, rounding the table to stare. "I don't fucking believe it!"

"What?" April and Neal asked in unison.

"People, take a close look. That's Special Agent Sid Harness of the Washington Metro Field Office. FBI."

"You're sure?" Neal asked, coming to stand beside him.

"Yeah. Real sure." Hank took a deep breath. "Game time, folks. The feds are here. Things just got a whole lot trickier."

"So, what do we do?" Neal asked.

Hank chewed on his lip as he thought. "Let me make some calls. I might have an idea."

48

The cramped bathroom was in quarters belonging to a female nurse named Asza, whereabouts currently unknown. Christal stepped in to straddle the toilet as Brian closed the door behind them. A white technician's uniform hung from a hook in the door. It looked clean, crisp, and freshly pressed.

Brian gave her a grin, that sexy twinkle in his eyes. His Australian accent seemed to have thickened in the close quarters. "You see, the thing is, Asza is one of the Sheik's nieces. He wouldn't dare allow a camera to monitor her during her private moments. And, fortunately for us, she never locks her quarters."

"Brian? How did Nancy Hartlee get out of here?"

The twinkle died. "She was involved with one of the guards at the controlled entry. She worked on it for a long time. You know, just going for casual conversations. After a couple of months, he started sneaking in, spending the nights in her quarters. No one gave it much thought. Just two people having an affair."

"So what happened?"

"One night she came to me. Brought me here." Pain reflected in Brian's eyes. "She said she was going up top, that she'd talked the guy into letting her see the stars. He took her out. Got her past the security somehow. It was like camel crap hitting the road the next morning when Nancy didn't show up for work. The guards were replaced by Max and Hans—the two gay guys—and we didn't hear another word about Nancy until you confirmed her body was identified."

Christal felt her guts drop. "Damn, I thought maybe it was through some vent or something."

"Sorry." He seemed to be musing. "You know, over the years, almost everything's been tried at least once. That's why most of the staff's been replaced with trained members of the Sheik's family."

"Security-friendly."

"What's this thing with Jennifer Weaver?"

She took his hand, reassured just to touch him. "I work for her. Or, I should say my company does. Jennifer Weaver is Sheela Marks. Weaver was her breakout role. She must have gotten her hands on the information I've compiled about Genesis Athena. At least, that's my guess. Just shooting from the hip, I'd say she set up an appointment for one of your cloning procedures, figuring she'd come right to the source and find out what it was all about. She's probably got my boss and some of his people following in tow." She gave him a wicked grin. "Brian, if there was ever a time to get the hell out of Dodge, this is it."

"Where's Dodge?"

"It's a bit north of Alice Springs."

"Christal, I don't wish rain on your parade here, but how are you planning to get past the controlled entrance? You saw that, right? How it works? And then there are the security cameras in the hallways. It's a bleeding fortress, and you're smack in the center of it!"

"Uh, you don't have a couple of Arnold Schwarzenegger clones hanging around, do you? Maybe with a couple of M79 grenade launchers?"

"Sorry. We don't do Terminators here."

"How about Linda Hamilton?"

"I'm afraid not. At least we haven't seen her sample come through yet."

"She did pretty well with just a paper clip."

"I don't follow."

"Wait a minute." She tilted her head, weaving her fingers into his. "McEwan can come and go as he wants, right?"

"Forget it, he's *not* going to sign you a pass. He's the biggest prick on the boat. No way he'll take a fall—and you can't bribe him."

"Who's his superior?"

"No one. He reports straight to the Sheik. He's the head of the biological section."

"So he can do anything he wants, anytime?"

"Pretty much. Like I say, he's thick with them."

"You know him, Brian. If it came down to him or Genesis Athena, what would he do?"

"He'd save his neck."

She was thinking hard on that, aware suddenly that he was staring at her mouth. "What?"

"Do you know that you stick your tongue out of the corner of your mouth when you're concentrating?"

"I've heard that before."

He reached out, running his other hand down her sleek hair. "I'd love to tell you that McEwan had a weakness other than his vanity. Dickless shit, he already acts like he sits immediately to the right of God's throne. To hear him tell it, he *is* Genesis Athena, and the world has yet to understand how great he is."

It began to click in Christal's mind. "Brian? How desperate are you?"

"Desperate enough to take their buyout. Desperate enough to take a chance on you."

"You mean that?" And oddly, his answer was important to her.

"God help me, I don't think I could stay here now. I'd give the world for a chance to get to know you."

"I don't need the world, Brian." She reached up and took his other hand in hers. "Just a little help from you, and a little bit of courage."

"What? About taking their buyout?"

She shook her head. "McEwan knows that Sheela's aboard. Copperhead—your April Hayes—knows that I work for her. They're putting the pieces together as we speak, so we've got to move fast."

"It's going to be dangerous, isn't it?"

Christal nodded.

He smiled shyly at her. "Whatever it takes, I'm here for you."

She reached her arms around his neck, pulling him to her. His lips met hers gently, and she turned into his kiss. Her heart began to beat, and her breasts felt sensitive as they brushed his chest. She let her memory linger on the dashing light that sometimes filled his eyes, and how those lips on hers bent into that devilish smile.

Finally she leaned back, sighing. "I could get to like that."

"Me, too," he whispered. "Now, just what do you have in mind?"

"Hand me that uniform hanging on the door. If I'm not mistaken, Asza is about my size."

"This is bullshit," Lymon growled as he knocked on Sheela's suite door. "She wouldn't have charged off and left a trite little phone message on the machine." He rattled the handle, finding it locked.

"It sounded like a prissy little girl," Sid reminded him as he watched up and down the corridor. "Lymon, what do you really know about her?"

"Enough." He shot a hard glare at Sid.

"Yeah, so?"

"So"—he lowered his voice—"someone was there, with her, when she left that message."

In an equally rough whisper, Sid replied, "She might have been playing to the audience: you. Come on, Lymon. She ditched you in LA so she could come here. Maybe she's doing just what she wants to."

Lymon glared, voice hoarse. "You mean that? Or are you playing to the audience, too?" He jerked his head toward the closest security camera.

Sid shrugged. "You tell me."

"I *know* the lady."

"You're in love with her. That's different."

"Shut up, Sid." Lymon turned on his heel, striding down to their door; a building panic was fueled by anger in his gut. They hadn't even had a chance to get their stories straight, and poof! She was gone. Vanished into the bowels of the *ZoeGen*.

"If they figure this out," Sid muttered as he leaned close, "she'd make one hell of a hostage."

"I said, shut up." Lymon crossed his suite in long steps and picked up the phone, dialing zero. At the voice, he said, "This Lymon Bridges, Ms. Weaver's security. Give me Neal Gray, please."

"One moment."

The moment lasted three long minutes, during which Lymon's desperation quotient got jacked up another couple of notches.

A voice said, *"This is Vince Harmon. I'm sorry, Mr. Gray isn't available. May I be of assistance?"*

"I need to know the location of Ms. Weaver."

"One moment." A slight pause. *"She's currently in conference with our counselors."*

"Can you put me through? I need to speak with her."

"I'm sorry, sir. She can't be interrupted. I'll contact our floor security and make sure that she is notified of your call as soon as she's out of her session."

"No, Vince. You'll put me through right now." He tried to keep his voice flat and emotionless. From Sid's expression, it didn't work.

"I'm sorry, sir. The counseling conference cannot be interrupted. I will have her call you the moment she's finished. That's the best I can do."

"Hey, pal! It's not good enough!"

Sid was shaking his head in warning.

"Make sure she calls!" Lymon bellowed before he hung up. "What?"

"What are you going to do? Charge forth, beating down doors until you find her? You know the score here. You're a smart guy, Lymon. Do you really think you can get off this deck without Gray's goons mobbing you and bundling your butt back here? You're not thinking." A pause. "It's not like you."

"No, I suppose not." Someone had once told him that human beings were just oversophisticated chimpanzees. He considered that as he stepped away from the phone instead of ripping it out of the wall and throwing it. "What's the look for?"

Sid's face had softened. "I hope that she's worth it. That's all."

"Worth what?"

"All the love you have for her."

"Yeah, well, sometimes, Sid, it ain't all it's cracked up to be." Lymon started for the door. "I can't just sit here like a bug in a jar. I need to figure out how to get into my tactical case; then we're going out."

"We going to get into trouble?"

"What do you think?"

At his chair in the security center, Vince Harmon watched Lymon Bridges as he walked into the bedroom, threw his black plastic case on the bed, and then pulled the cover over himself. The other guy, the one he'd been told was FBI, yawned and stretched.

Vince changed the camera angle, switching from one fiber-optic lens to the next. No matter how good the system, he couldn't see through the bedspread.

Report it?

Even as he considered, Bridges threw the spread back, made a negative gesture to Harness, and stalked out of the room, his suit coat neat and a determined look on his face.

Vince played with his controls, flashing back to the bed. The case sat half-exposed, still locked.

"Come on," Vince whispered. "Give it a try. You can't beat our system, asshole."

* * *

Gregor stepped out of the Sheik's opulent suite on A Deck and closed the door behind him. He nodded to the two security guards who stood outside; sinister black machine guns hung from straps at their shoulders. The guns came as a surprise. That was a new twist, but then, this was a curious new development: the first infiltration by an outsider that they were aware of.

Gregor straightened his smock and walked to the lift that would take him from the Sheik's palatial quarters down into the bowels of the ship. He pressed the button and waited until the doors slipped open.

Inside the lift, he thumbed the button and watched the lights flicker until the lift stopped on H Deck. Stepping out, he padded down the illuminated white hall past doorways; passing staff nodded politely, often giving him faint smiles.

He shouldn't be bursting with this sort of excitement, but he felt absolutely exhilarated. They had known that someday they would be faced with this situation. Gregor was actually amazed that it had taken this long before someone finally wised up.

"Everything in its time," the Sheik had said calmly, his dark eyes glowing. "This, my dear Gregor, is our time."

"What are we going to do?" he had asked.

The Sheik had steepled his long brown fingers, smiled, and replied, "Let it play out as it is meant to, Doctor."

Gregor smacked a fist into his palm as he found the right door, flashed his implanted wrist over the lock plate, and entered. He walked up to a glass partition and was raising his hand to the intercom when his PDA buzzed in his pocket.

Pulling it out, he flipped it open and accessed his personal channel. Brian Everly was staring out at him with worried eyes. "Gregor? Do you have a minute? Something's come up."

"Such as?"

"An irregularity."

"Brian, I'm right in the middle of something."

Everly gave him that old familiar "You're an idiot" look that had grated on Gregor's nerves from the moment they'd met.

"What is it?"

"Something that you apparently missed on the Sheela Marks' chromosome six. But, what the hell, what are a couple of spare nucleotides? It's probably nothing, right, mate?"

"Where are you?"

"Lab six."

"Be right there." Brian flipped his PDA closed, gave one last look through the window, and headed for the door.

"Asshole Aussie! Who does he think he is? Crocodile Dundee?"

Past the tennis courts on B Deck, Lymon led them to a blank wall. The steel here had been painted white, but he could see where all the windows but one had been welded over with steel plate. An armed guard stood before the only door, a serious-looking hatch with a sophisticated lock plate and numerical pad. The guard was a big guy, and he held an MP5 sub gun in both hands. His smoky dark brown eyes seemed to say "Try me" as he watched Lymon and Sid approach. He spoke softly into a collar mike, the sibilant Arabic barely audible.

"What now, boss?" Sid asked, eyeing the guy.

"We smile . . . and try something else." Lymon did just that, trying to act nonchalant as he stared around, noting the cameras and the two stairways that led to the roof. Both were closed off with the metal-grated doors. Above, just visible over the lip of the roof, was the unmistakable protrusion of a helicopter blade.

"Looks to me like that's our ride out of here." Lymon gave the slightest nod, but Sid had already picked it up. "Yeah, assuming we can get someone to fly the thing."

"You still tuned up from our stint in the Marines?" Lymon turned, leading the way back past the tennis courts.

"Hey," Sid answered. "That was for five minutes, with a real pilot in the other seat. We don't even know what kind of machine that is up there. I'd kill us faster in that helicopter than that goon back there would with that sub gun."

"Just a thought." Lymon led the way down the stairs to the B Deck. This time it was empty, the bathing couple having gone in. The dining room had been occupied as they went out. Supper time. Lymon's belly kept reminding him.

"How's your ability with locks?"

"Damn good, as you well know."

"That was a handy little skill you picked up. Saved our asses a couple of times, if you'll recall. Not to mention the advantages it gave us in getting into the AAFES warehouse at Camp Bondsteel."

"We damn near got hung over that, too."

"Yeah, but we didn't." Lymon stopped by the pool, picking up one of the sections of aluminum rod from the cleaning accessories. "Let's see how far we get."

"We're gonna regret this."

"There's only one camera that points at the grating leading down to C Deck." Lymon ran the pole back and forth in his hands. "The lock looked like a simple one. If I jar that camera just a bit out of alignment . . ."

"I hope Claire's satisfied with my life insurance and pension."

"I guess she'll have to be, huh?"

49

On two different occasions in the post-9/11 world, Christal had run headlong into racial discrimination. The first time was in December of 2001 when she was asked to deplane from a commuter plane taking her from DIA in Denver to Albuquerque. The pilot, a guy with a Massachusetts accent, had said he was uncomfortable with her aboard. Only her FBI credentials and the assent of the other passengers, most of them locals who knew what Hispanics looked like, had allowed her to continue the flight.

The second time had been in Charlotte, North Carolina, a couple of months later, when she was singled out and taken into a back room, where a female security officer had had her undress while her luggage was dismantled piece by piece because she looked "suspicious." That time they had tried to take her FBI shield and folder to see if it had been "reproduced."

A call to the Charlotte Field Office—where she'd been visiting—finally got her off the hook to fly, fuming, back to DC. Now, for the first time, she could actually use her dark complexion to her advantage. If all those screeners could be wrong, so, too, might the *ZoeGen* security guy, Hans.

Assuming this doesn't just get me killed. But then, if she was going to get the hell out of there, risks had to be taken. God knew, Sheela was taking one hell of a chance just setting foot on the *ZoeGen*.

The white uniform fit a little tighter than Christal would have liked. It hugged her hips and breasts a little too snugly for comfort. Nevertheless, she stood slightly behind Brian Everly where he sat peering into a microscope, and tried to look like she was jotting notes in a folder he had given her.

Surreptitiously, she glanced from the corner of her eye, seeing the camera that clung to the corner of the ceiling like a malevolent gremlin. The bulge in her skirt pocket was unsettling, as much for what it was as for what it represented.

Am I going to be able to do this? God, it was one thing to think about it, to rehearse it in the mind's eye, but quite another to carry it out.

She took a deep breath, trying to still the pounding of her heart. In the polished surface of a stainless steel autoclave she checked her reflection: white uniform, her dark hair secured modestly behind her neck, and a pinned white technician's hat. A facial mask hung at half-staff, Brian having informed her that it was part of the uniform, as were the latex gloves protruding from her left pocket.

"Where the hell is he?" Brian muttered under his breath.

"It hasn't been but a couple of minutes since you called."
She glanced at the clock on the far wall. "Less than two,
actually."

He looked up at her, eyes pleading. "Are you sure you
want to do this? Wouldn't it be better if it were me?"

"Have you ever had to kill someone, Brian?"

"No." He cocked his head. "Have you?"

She gave a slight shake of the head, keeping her voice
low. "But at least I was trained to. And I made the decision
long ago that if I ever had to, I would."

"Pray it doesn't come to that, right?"

She screwed her lips up, twisting the pronunciation to
something similar to the Australian "Right, mate!"

A second later, the lab door whipped open and Gregor
came striding in. In the quick glance Christal managed before
she averted her face, he looked irritated. She concentrated on
jotting nonsense in her folder as he crossed the room.

"Very well, Brian. This had better be good. Just what the
hell is so damn important. Don't tell me it's some silly point
mutation in an alu or something."

"Take a look," Brian said, tension dripping from his
voice.

Later, Christal was sure it was nerves, rather than acting,
that had made it sound so ominous, but Gregor slipped into
the chair as Brian made way. Gregor's fingers went to the
microscope focus as he rested his forehead against the
viewer.

Brian gave Christal a pleading look as she reached into
her pocket and removed the syringe. In answer she shot him
a reassuring smile and stepped beside Gregor McEwan
where he peered into the hooded microscope. "I don't see a
bloody damned—"

Christal leaned down and jabbed the needle into his side
just above the hip bone, saying, "Stand up, Gregor, and
don't make a fucking move, or I'll squirt this shit right inside you."

He froze, face still pressed against the viewer. "What the
hell?"

"I said, stand up, and do it slowly. We wrapped elastic

around the plunger. That means if you twist away, the plunger drops. You get it?"

Gregor carefully pulled his head back, raising his eyes to meet Christal's. "Whatever you think you're doing, it's not going to work."

"It's worked before," Brian said too quickly. "It's your invention, after all. I filled the syringe with five ccs of your CAT delivery system. The one you developed for the psychologists."

Gregor had stiffened. "*Five* ccs! You idiot, that would kill me!"

"Yes, quite," Brian continued. "And in a most unpleasant way."

"What's it do?" Christal asked. "You didn't have time to fill me in on all the details."

"A small virus delivers a ribosomal RNA strand that inhibits the production of acetylcholine in the nerve cells. Without ACh, as it's called, the nerves cease to function. Gregor's dosage was infinitesimal, measured in microliters. It was just enough to put the brakes on choline acetyltransferase, or CAT, in people with overactive production."

"Right." Christal nodded. "Whatever you said."

"What do you want?" Gregor asked, smart enough to get with the program.

Christal leaned close, whispering, "I want you to stand up. As you do, you're going to put your arm around my waist. You know, just like I was your girlfriend. Get the picture? Then you and I are going to walk out of here, smiling and laughing like the old friends we are. After we're past the security door, you're going to take us to Sheela Marks' quarters. When we get there, we'll give you further instructions."

Gregor closed his eyes, body stiff. She could almost hear his brain running through alternate endings to his current dilemma.

"Come on, Gregor," she told him gently. "We're standing up now. If you don't come when I lift you, this plunger might drop a little, you know, from the awkward position and all."

He came, rising slowly, gently, letting Christal wind her arm around his side. Brian, perspiration beading on his pale skin, took a moment to place a small towel over the offending needle so that it appeared to be draped over Christal's arm.

"You know, just a few microliters will cause me serious physiological damage, Brian."

"Oh, yes. I'm quite aware." Brian rubbed his hands together nervously. "I'm sure you're worried about seepage from the large-gauge needle, but we took the precaution of placing a small wax plug in the channel. Not much—just enough to ensure that if you cooperate, you'll be able to enjoy a long and prosperous future."

Gregor took a deep breath. Christal could feel the fear radiating out of him. She could almost smell it, sour and acidic. When he looked down he could see the elastic-wrapped syringe protruding from just above his hip.

"Put your arm around me," she insisted. "Do it slowly, gently." She gave him a smile. "You were interested in me once, Gregor. I saw it in your eyes. What happened? Did I lose my charm?"

"You *can't* get off the ship! Neither can Marks and her people! This *isn't* going to work!"

"You'd better help us figure out a way to make it work, then," Brian said, gesturing toward the door. "After you. Oh, and when we get to the box, you just tell Max to let us past, and that I'm wanted upstairs, you got that?"

"And if you don't"—Christal placed her lips next to his ear—"the plunger goes down. After that, you're dead, and we make up whatever story we want to."

Gregor stared down at the hidden syringe. "Aye, I get the picture. Let's go. The sooner this is over, the sooner I get that damn thing oot o' my side."

Gregor tried to swallow but couldn't. His mouth had gone dry, and his tongue stuck. With each step, he could feel the sting as the needle shifted in his flesh. Dear God, what if they hadn't really plugged it? Would he begin to malfunction? Would his brain and muscles turn sluggish and then simply shut off?

He shot a glance at Brian. The man looked on the verge of doing something rash. The bunching of his jaw muscles, the fevered quickness of eye—it all bespoke a terrible desperation.

When he got a good look at Anaya's face, he could see a simple clear determination in the flesh of her dark brown eyes. Why the hell had he ever let her have the run of the deck down here? Of all the stupid mistakes! He almost tripped as panic built inside him.

"Easy," Christal said smoothly, tightening her arm around his waist. "Don't miss a step. If you fall, this could all go very wrong."

"You have no idea." Sweat was beading on his face and trickling down from his armpits. What a horrible way to die. Having the nerves just shut off. His brain, his marvelous brain, would go inert, just become a gray-white blob of protein and fat from which no more dreams would be spun. All of it, everything he hadn't written down, would simply cease, locked forever between mute nerves that slowly suffocated in the lonely darkness of isolation.

"Last chance for a check," Brian said as they rounded the corner to the security entrance. "You're sweating, Gregor."

"I'm not the only one."

"Take the towel. Wipe him off." Christal indicated the cloth draped over the syringe.

Brian did, his pale blue eyes reflecting how close he was to panic. His movements were too quick, blocky. "Frightened, Brian?"

"You bet I am. If this goes wrong, we're all fucked, mate."

"You always were a spineless shit," Gregor answered as Brian replaced the towel.

"Yes," Brian admitted, straightening. "I suppose so. But what the hell have I got to lose? You've seen to that, Gregor, so I suppose that you and I have finally come to the end of our little Greek tragedy. So, let's go play it out, shall we?"

"Move it," Anaya said grimly, and her arm propelled Gregor forward. "It's up to you, Greg. The next five minutes are going to determine how you live out your future. Your decision, buddy. Long and happy, or really short and miserable."

He stopped before the lock plate, reaching out with a trembling arm. "I choose long and happy." He pressed the button and leaned awkwardly, carefully, forward for the retinal scan. "Max? It's Gregor, open up."

The door clicked, and Gregor summoned all of his courage to step into the box. He found a grin from somewhere, tightening his hold on Anaya's waist, and looked through the glass. Max was scrutinizing Brian, who looked terribly uncomfortable as he followed them in. He flinched as if at a gunshot when the heavy door clicked shut behind him.

"It's all right, Max," Gregor called. "Brian's wanted upstairs. The Sheik wants to have a little discussion with him."

"Sir?" Max asked, hesitating.

"I authorize it, all right? Don't take all fucking night!" Gregor roared, losing his patience. "I've got things to do!" He indicated Christal, who had her head half averted, as if embarrassed by his attentions.

The door clicked, and Gregor muttered under his breath as they stepped out into the hallway. His legs turned suddenly rubbery. Christal's supporting arm tightened reflexively.

"Good work," Christal told him. "You even convinced me."

"Fuck! Right. Thanks for nothing, you mean."

"That's my Gregor," Brian added from behind. "Pissy as an ant, even when he's getting a bleeding compliment. Which way?"

"Down the hall and to the right," Christal said. "There shouldn't be any trouble going the way I went last time, right, Gregor?"

"Right. Whatever."

"Yeah," Christal agreed. "I'd hate like hell to step off the lift into a mass of gun-toting security guys. It might make me let loose of this plunger."

"I just want this thing out of my side!" Gregor heard the whimper in his voice.

To his relief, the lift was waiting. They walked inside, Christal giving him a curious look. "B Deck?"

"Oddly enough, you're correct."

"The suite with the swimming pool?"

"No. Across the hall."

"Too bad," she answered wryly as Brian pressed the button. "I could get used to that."

To his complete surprise, Gregor had to fight back a smile as the image of Anaya's naked body formed in his mind. She still had no idea of what he'd done to her. Of his little joke. And that knowledge, insignificant as it might seem on the surface, gave him the first tiny ray of hope. He glanced up at the camera in the corner; the glassy round eye was staring down at him with a benevolence he could feel. Was Vince watching him, even now? He stared up at the lens, his mouth moving slowly to form the word "Help!"

It was at that moment that Christal Anaya kissed him full on the lips.

50

Lymon lifted the aluminum pole and jabbed at the camera. With satisfaction he saw that he'd jimmied it off to one side. He nodded to Sid, who bent over the lock, his picks sliding into the slot. Lymon took a deep breath. God, his hands were sweaty, and his nerves were tingling.

What the hell has happened to you? In the old days, he'd been wound tight but fearless during a mission. He'd lived for that adrenaline high that came with the closing presence of danger. Now his overstretched nerves left him feeling sick and spineless.

To make matters worse, his imagination was playing with him, spinning out images of Sheela. None of them were happy. What were they doing to her? He remembered the Sheik's fixation that night in New York, that gleam of anticipation in his eyes. He could see Sheela—his Sheela—forced to accede to any perversion. And how would she react?

Would her soul retreat, flee back to a shadowed bridge abutment somewhere in Saskatoon?

"Come on, Sid." He couldn't keep the fear out of his voice.

"Just a second. There's only one more tumbler."

That's when it fell apart. Three of them, wearing suits and sunglasses, came in through the double doors. Two more rounded the far corner of the B Deck hallway, striding purposefully forward.

"We're fucked!" Lymon hissed as Sid straightened, palming his lockpicks.

The three Arabs stood shoulder to shoulder; each held an HK MP5, the SD model with a built-in sound suppressor, in the ready position. They stopped no more than five feet away, the first—in accented English—ordered, "Put your hands up, please."

"Hey, wait a minute!" Lymon protested. "We're here with Jennifer Weaver. She's a client. You guys back off, and we'll have Neal Gray straighten this out."

"Sorry, he's busy right now," Hank Abrams said as he strode through the doors behind the three guards.

Lymon shot a glance over his shoulder to see the two blockers firmly in position, weapons at half-mast. Shit!

Abrams walked up behind the suited Arabs, saying, "If you would simply walk down the corridor, gentlemen, we won't have to cause any disturbance. Our other guests are at supper, and it would really piss me off if we upset them."

"Hey, Hank, what's up?" Sid asked.

"Hello, Sid. I'm afraid you're up, kind of like a sore thumb." He gestured. "Let's move, people. And quietly. If you make a scene, I promise I'll pay you back for it big time. Be good, guys, and maybe we can come to some sort of peaceful resolution, huh?"

"Yeah." Sid turned, hands up, and Lymon followed.

The blockers had moved up to their suite door; one of them opened it and stepped inside. The other took a half-step back, his weapon at the ready.

"Nice work. Who trained these guys?" Sid asked.

"Neal did," Abrams said from the rear. "He doesn't like fuckups. Something you might want to seriously contemplate. Step into your room, please, gentlemen, and do it in a way that won't cause my guy in there to cut you in half with a burst."

"Right," Lymon agreed. He had that cold sweaty feeling of impending disaster. What the hell were they going to do now? He took a moment to study the guards: Each was alert, his thumb resting on the fire selectors. Now wasn't the time to try anything stupid. Lymon walked to the middle of the room, Sid coming to stand beside him.

Hank entered last. He gave them a knowing smile and shook his head sadly. "I knew it. The second I recognized you, Sid, I just knew you were going to push it." He shifted his attention to Lymon. "And you, Mr. God-almighty Bridges—I feel like I owe you one."

"How's that?"

"For jacking me around in your office that day. You didn't have to do that, you know. You could have just given me Christal's address, and maybe we could have avoided a whole pile of shit."

Sid interjected sourly, "Yeah, a kidnapping with witnesses just isn't the same as a good clean snatch, huh? Forget it, Hank. It's out of control. They got photos of you and Neal that night. Why do you think we're here?"

"Maybe you were in the market for a pleasure cruise?" Hank gestured to one of his guards. "Pat them down from top to bottom. Turn their pockets inside out, and take their belts. Now, Sid, Bridges, if you make this difficult we can search you just as easily if you're unconscious and bleeding from the scalp."

"You'll fuck up the carpet," Lymon noted as he tapped the thick Persian with his foot.

"Housecleaning has a big steam cleaner." Hank nodded to his goons. "Go."

"You know how the Bureau hates to have one of its own go bad." Sid made a *tsk*ing sound with his tongue as thorough hands relieved him of the HK Compact and spare magazine. Then his lockpicks, belt, and pockets were "liberated." Sid continued, "We're after you, buddy. If we'd known you were aboard, the Coast Guard would be swarming this tub from top to bottom trying to sniff you out."

Hank crossed his arms. "So, what are you suggesting? That I just stick my arms out, let you slap the cuffs on, and go willingly?"

The guards followed suit with Lymon, taking his HK, the flash-bang he'd tucked into an inside pocket, and the portable satellite phone he'd clipped to the back of his belt. Their accumulated possessions were piled onto a towel.

"Take that up to the security center," Hank ordered one of the men. "And don't forget the case on the bed in the back."

Lymon watched the towel neatly tied into a bundle before it and his black tactical case vanished through the door.

"We could work something out." Sid cocked his head, indicating the gun-toting guards. "You don't need them. Why don't we just mosey over to the bar, crack a couple of those fancy bottles, and figure out what it would take to bring this to a satisfactory conclusion?"

"Why would I do that?" Hank walked a slow circle of the room, glancing at the ornate fixtures with mild interest. "Seems to me I've got you. Better, I've got every other card in your deck, including Bridges, Marks, and Anaya. I've even got an unseen hole card, Sid. I happen to know that nobody back at the barn knows where you are, or better yet, what you're working on."

Sid made a buzzer noise with his tongue, adding, "Wrong! No points for Hank this round. Sean O'Grady at the LAFO knows. It's all over the country. One lead after another piped from field office to field office."

"Nice bluff." Hank smiled. "We've had feelers out. No one's certain yet that we really kidnapped Christal. They'd just like to talk to us. We've been considering damage-control options. What if it turns out that sweet Christal went willingly?"

"Yeah, right," Lymon interjected. "You should have seen O'Grady's face when we told him you'd offered five grand just to see her."

"What makes you think she didn't take it?" Hank's mocking tone antagonized Lymon's sense of impotent rage.

Sid propped his hands on his hips. "I know Chris. Whatever you've done with her, she's not going to play ball."

Lymon saw the faintest hesitation in the guy's eyes. Yeah, he knew that, didn't he?

Hank turned, walking to stare out at the ocean through the large windows. "You people being here makes it a little more difficult. That's all. Not only that, Sid, you're on your own. Nobody in the Bureau is talking about Sheela Marks as bait—and you know they would. It's an agency—as hungry for juicy gossip as any other bunch of half-frustrated people." He laughed. "Hell, Marks' own business manager doesn't know what's coming off, or why!"

"And that's another screwup," Sid continued. "This is *Sheela Marks* we're talking about. Not just some grunt off the street. She's wise to you, and you can bet that people are going to be listening to her when she gets off this floating den of perversion."

Hank frowned. "You make a very good point. We're going to have to give that some thought. If we let you all go, can we count on you to take it to the press? Do that and by the end of the week every person in the civilized world is going to know our name. When the swarms of reporters come clambering aboard, we can demonstrate our gene therapies, our enhancements, and successes in IVF. We couldn't *pay* for that kind of publicity."

"You'll be shut down within days. Your vessel confiscated, and each of you slapped with charges like you've never even imagined," Lymon added.

Hank whirled, a gleam in his eyes. "Oh, really? I don't think so."

"Why's that?" Sid asked.

"This is a Yemeni-flagged vessel in international waters. We are operating in compliance with Yemeni law. Yemen, if you'll recall, is an ally in the war against terrorism. They're strategically located, providing us with bases of operation into the Red Sea, the Persian Gulf, and the Horn of Africa. Their government hands over suspected Islamic fundamentalists with terrorist ties. With all that at stake, do you really think Washington is going to compromise that relationship over a few strands of celebrity DNA?"

"You might be surprised," Sid said dryly.

"So might you." Hank cocked his head. "One of the things you're unaware of is how many Washington bigwigs the Sheik has treated aboard the *ZoeGen* or at the facility in Yemen. I was actually stunned when I read the list."

Lymon had been watching him, reading his body language. Damn it, either the guy was one hell of a poker player, or he really believed he held all the cards. He wasn't just bullshitting; he was bragging. And that, more than anything else, sent a shiver along Lymon's spine.

"Sheela Marks has a pretty loud voice herself," Lymon said. "And so, too, do Julia Roberts, Mel Gibson, Brad Pitt, and the rest of the people whose DNA you've stolen. I think they can make it pretty hot for you."

Hank shrugged. "The average American thinks they're spoiled, rich, shallow, and for the most part, as moral as dock rats. You ever read the bios? Who's going to garner more sympathy? Ben Affleck, or a twelve-year-old little girl whose life Genesis Athena just saved through one of our miracle therapies?"

"The key is still Christal," Sid said doggedly. "That's kidnapping, and we'll get you for that."

Hank chuckled. "What makes you so sure about Christal? How do you know we haven't made her an offer she can't refuse? If we could pay five grand just to talk to her, what would we be willing to offer in return for her cooperation?" He stepped close, looking into Sid's eyes. "And we don't need Christal, Sid. What about you? For a million in cold hard cash, would you be willing to sign a statement that Christal told you she was here of her own free will?"

"Fuck you." Sid crossed his arms.

"Please, old friend, hands where we can see them. That's it." Hank leaned close. "Two million?"

Sid hesitated, the first uncertainty reflected in his expression. "You're shitting!"

"First thing every morning after a spicy meal," Hank

replied. "But I'm not kidding about our ability to reward the people who work for us. Only one thing, Sid—you're going to have to prove you're worth it."

The door opened, and an attractive woman stuck her head in. She looked Lymon and Sid over with curious gray eyes, her long red hair falling around her shoulders. "Hank? We're set. The passengers are all in the dining room. The hallway is cleared."

"Thanks April." Hank gestured at Lymon and Sid. "All right, you two, while you think over our offer, let's go."

"Where?" Sid asked, propping his feet as if to root himself in the rich carpet.

"Someplace safe," Hank answered. "Where you won't be upsetting our other passengers."

The Arab guards lifted their heavy black weapons. Lymon had seen that look before; it didn't bode well for him. Reluctantly, he waved Sid forward and started for the door.

51

Visions spun and rolled behind Sheela's eyes. Her dreams seemed chaotic—pastiches of scenes acted, roles played, and people she'd known. She saw her father's face, smiling, worried . . . dead. Rex, beaming as he took her hand for the first time and said, "Sheela Marks, I think I can be of great service to you." Bernard, arms waving as he cried, "My God! That's masterful! Cut! Cut!" The weight of the Oscar—so cold and heavy in her hand—as thunderous ovation rolled up from the Kodak Theatre floor.

It all gave way to an image of Lymon: tall, muscular, his craggy face lit by a smile. He was reaching for her, his hand outstretched as he straddled his silver BMW. All she needed was to take his hand, step up on the passenger peg, and he'd wheel her away to forever: just the two of them and the magical motorcycle that sped her toward Nirvana.

Awareness came from her physical body. Her attempt to

swallow ended in disaster. Her tongue caught on the back of her mouth, almost choking her. She started, coughed, and blinked her dry eyes open.

The light was bleary, white, and streaked. She tried to swallow again and failed.

"Easy," a gentle female voice told her. "Let me help you."

A hand slipped behind her head, easing her forward. "Here's water. Just take a sip."

Sheela felt a glass touch her lips, and cool liquid washed around her tongue. When she swallowed, the water rolled through her chest and stomach like a wave.

Blinking again, the room slowly came into focus. And what a room! Marble columns, gold filigree in polished dark wood, thick Persian carpets, and what looked like a diamond-encrusted chandelier overhead. She lay on a velvet-upholstered chaise longue, the woodwork polished and engraved. Bright white light came from large windows behind her.

She tried to place the white-clad nurse. "You are . . . ?" her voice cracked.

"Asza. You're aboard the *ZoeGen,* Ms. Marks."

Sheela groaned as she forced herself to sit up, arms bracing her on the cushions. She was half reclined on a couch of some sort. "Why am I here?"

A sibilant voice came from behind her left shoulder. "Because you paid us to impregnate you with a Sheela Marks embryo."

The nurse stepped back and Sheela turned, seeing a dark and handsome man in an expensive silk suit. He had neatly combed black hair that gleamed in the chandelier's light while half silhouetted by sunlight shining through the windows. He looked Arab from his complexion, with a fine-boned face, intelligent eyes, and a smile that flashed perfect white teeth. A golden espresso machine sat atop an intricately carved wooden stand.

He spoke softly, barely audible over the hiss of the machine. "Imagine our surprise when we discovered that Jennifer Weaver's and Sheela Marks' DNA matched exactly. Only one of O. J. Simpson's jurors would have believed that we were dealing with two different people. Fortunately, we discovered the situation before serious consequences could occur. So, no harm has been done."

Sheela reached up, rubbing her face. Her skin had the feel of dry latex.

He stepped forward, reaching out a hand. "I am Sheik Amud Abdulla, founder and president of Genesis Athena. Welcome aboard the *ZoeGen*, Ms. Marks. If I had known you were coming, I would have made a special effort to have greeted you as you came aboard. I have admired your work for years."

"Thank you." It was coming back, now. The *ZoeGen* . . . Genesis Athena . . . a party of people bearing Christal away in the dead of night. "Why are you doing this?"

"I am building this century's quintessential service and health industry. Science has always laid the foundations for every great empire. You need only think of Alexander's iron swords, or Roman architecture and engineering, the English colonial factory system, or the modern American military industrial complex. Personally, I would have preferred to develop the space industry. It would have been a much more natural extrapolation from my family's expertise in shipping across oceans to the transportation of goods across the solar system. Marshaling the capital, however, was not only prohibitive, but others are so far ahead of us."

"Let me get this straight, you steal DNA because you can't go to space?"

"Each is part of mankind's future," the Sheik told her amiably as he worked the levers on the coffee machine and steam hissed. "Our world is becoming increasingly competitive. In the past humans have focused on making ever more intricate, improved, and sophisticated tools. I offer the next step: that of producing ever better humans to use them."

"And for that you needed *my* DNA?"

"To be sure, Ms. Marks. You are a most beautiful and intelligent woman. The same traits which make you so attractive, add value to your DNA." As the machine sputtered he raised a slim index finger to his chin, as though in deep thought. "What is celebrity?"

"It's a pain in the ass."

He might not have heard her snide remark. "It is envy; and what people envy, they wish to emulate. Through you, they live vicariously, be it by means of your screen presence, or—with the help of Genesis Athena—your very genes."

"That's sick."

"I make no judgments. I simply provide a product in return for a fee. Our latest survey indicates that three percent of the American people will pay to have a baby based on their favorite celebrity's DNA. Three percent! And that is without advertising, without incentives of any sort. Most, alas, are from lower-income, lower-educational demographics, but taken in total they represent a substantial market. And that is just America. China, India, Indonesia, and Thailand, where cloning isn't viewed with as much suspicion, are worth billions more to us in the long run."

"Then why start with Americans?"

"In the modern world, Ms. Marks, marketing is everything, as you and your publicist well know."

"And the Web site? The questionnaire?"

"It allows us to rank-order potential clients. We can immediately discard the frivolous and closed-minded while concentrating on persons with both the predisposition and ability to afford our services."

"The way you talk of cloning it's another form of slavery."

He paced to one of the windows and stared out. "We are helping people to have children . . . nothing more, nothing less. The only difference between natural reproduction and our IVF service is the genotype of the child. It is still a life, Ms. Marks. As prized—or despised—by its parents as any other."

"That's the entire point!"

He turned, silhouetted by the glow. "Is there a difference between a life based on your DNA versus a child conceived of any other two people's? Six *billion* human beings exist on this planet; until recently, each of them was created by the chance mixture of parental DNA. You were created that way. Are you going to try and tell me that DNA that was good enough for you isn't good enough for someone else?"

"It's *my* DNA!"

"You had no part in its design, composition, or character. You received it from your biological parents, who in return, received theirs from their parents, and so on. If DNA is anyone's, it is God's."

"I don't see it the way you do."

"Ah, you would have me believe that your soul acted to choose your DNA? Perhaps pointed in the darkness of your mother's womb, saying, 'There! I want that sperm, and only that sperm, with those discrete genes to fertilize this egg, and this egg alone!' "

"Don't be preposterous."

"Who," he asked mildly, "is being preposterous? You developed from a random association of deoxyribonucleic acids that programmed the synthesis of proteins into a specific pattern of organic compounds. You are the building, not the blueprint. And since you, yourself, didn't draw the blueprint, what do you care if we initiate the construction of additional buildings?"

"I'm going to tear you apart over this."

He chuckled, stepping back to watch as Sheela swung her feet unsteadily to the floor. Asza glanced at the Sheik, who made a small gesture with his fingers. The nurse bowed, walking on noiseless white shoes to let herself out through an ornate door. Sheela caught a glimpse of a suited guard outside. An automatic weapon hung ominously from a strap over his shoulder.

An armed guard? What was he afraid of? *Lymon!*

"Ms. Marks," the Sheik said as he filled a small cup with steaming coffee, "I am not an unreasonable man. I understand and feel for your confusion. As we speak, the world is unprepared for the reality of Genesis Athena."

"Got that right." She placed a hand to her stomach. That empty nauseous feeling had to be hunger. How long had it been since she'd eaten? She considered trying to stand and gave it up, her head still woozy.

"Eventually, perhaps, there will be some consensus in international law about the disposition of an individual's DNA. Most governments, however, have been reluctant to venture into such murky and obscure waters."

"Why?"

He turned back to the machine, supple fingers plying the levers. "Politicians, for the most part, are not particularly bright or creative people. By nature they are deal makers, looking for the lowest common denominator which will maintain social stability. They do not take kindly to tackling intellectual challenges which will redefine the human condition. Thinking, especially about philosophical matters, causes them a great deal of distress. For the moment they believe it is easier—and benefits society—to allow anyone who wishes to patent any sequences of DNA they happen discover. Think of it as the carrot offered to biotech firms for their investment in recording the human genome and discovering a host of other medical applications."

"There's still time to change it." She smiled grimly. "Who knows, I might just be the woman to push it through."

He shook his head as he filled a second cup of coffee. "I think not, Ms. Marks. The cat is out of the sack, and it would be way too much trouble to chase it down again." He looked up. "Cream or sugar?"

She felt a subtle vibration, and barely sensed movement. The Sheik, too, seemed to hesitate, a faint frown marring his forehead. Then he dismissed it, and lifted an eyebrow. "This is my own special blend, Ms. Marks. You must be famished by now."

"Black, please." Sheela gave in. The smell of the coffee might have been the most wonderful thing she'd ever experienced. Her stomach growled.

As he handed her one of the delicate blue and white cups, he added, "I am also a realist. I understand that the value placed on your DNA is the result of your hard work, risk, and perseverance. In essence, but for your energy and talent, it would only be so many nucleic acids strung between pentase sugars. A mere one of six billion, if you will."

"What a delightful way to think of it."

"But valid, nonetheless."

"And?"

"And I am willing to offer you a royalty on all revenues we make off your genotype. If you involve yourself in the sales and marketing, we would be happy to offer you a higher percentage, one negotiated on your participation. But for now, if we assume all obligation for marketing and publicity, we will send you a statement biannually for three percent of our net."

Shit! He was serious. *He wanted her to help sell her clones!*

"I'm sorry it can't be more, but one never knows. You might take some action which damages the value before we recoup our investment in you."

"Such as?"

His shoulder lifted slightly. "We know the genetic and degenerative diseases you are predisposed to and can compensate for them, but what if you ruin our investment through a willful act?"

"How could I do that?" She tried to keep the anticipation out of her voice.

"Suicide."

An image of her father's face flashed in her mind as she said flatly, "Not a chance."

"Questionable religious or political associations could damage your value." His lips quirked. "Say, a newfound affiliation with the Raelians."

"Raelians? I think that's a bit unlikely. As to the politics, I'll keep that in mind next time ambitious Democrats swing through town on a fund-raiser."

"You might become involved in criminal activity such as drug dealing, involvement in homicide, or sexual aberrations with children or livestock."

Livestock?

She shook her head and made a face. "Maybe you've guessed, but I didn't come here looking for money."

"Indeed?" He gave her a grim smile. "Then what?" Before she could answer, he said, "Ah, but of course, justice! The great grail to which we all aspire in the end." His thin lips curled. "And just how, Ms. Marks, did you intend on obtaining your justice? Perhaps through a legal suit, since your attorney was the only party privy to your arrival?"

"How did you know that?"

He shrugged off her question. "We operate in international waters. You would have to file suit against us in a Yemeni court. I am a personal friend and supporter of President Salih. Our law is Islamic. I don't think you would appreciate or approve of the final judgment."

"Your people stole my DNA in the United States."

"For which I deeply apologize, and offer a financial restitution." He shrugged. "What is your embarrassment worth, Ms. Marks? Perhaps I could make a fifty percent investment in your next film?"

"Look, I want my stolen DNA destroyed. I want your guarantee that you won't use it to make little Sheela babies. You do that, and I'll collect my people—including Christal Anaya—and be out of here on the next boat. After that, you and I will have no further association. Deal?"

He studied her through half-lidded eyes. "Ms. Marks, you are a formidable woman, but you are not in any position to be making demands. Genesis Athena has fulfilled its obligations to you. I have given you my offer. I think it is a very generous one." His smile sharpened. "Do you wish to accept?"

"No, actually, I think we'll do this the hard way. In the courts." She tried to stand, swayed, and sat down again, clutching at her empty coffee cup.

"You will need time to recover from the anesthetic, Ms. Marks," the Sheik observed dryly. "Perhaps we will talk again when you're feeling a little better." He raised his voice, calling, *"Achmed!"*

The door opened to reveal the armed guard. A quick mix of Arabic passed between them, and Asza appeared with a wheelchair. She smiled as she locked the wheels in front of Sheela, asking, "Are you ready, Ms. Marks?"

"For what?"

"I'm here to take you back to your quarters. You'll feel a great deal better after you've eaten and slept."

She helped Sheela move into the wheelchair. "Thanks for the coffee," Sheela called over her shoulder. "But we're not through yet."

His waspish smile mocked her. "No. But we will be . . . and very soon, Ms. Marks."

The door cut off any reply.

52

By placing heel to toe, Lymon could make eight steps in one direction and five in the other. The cramped steel cubicle had been painted in thick layers of white, and a single recessed bulb glowed from behind a wire mesh screwed to the ceiling. The heavy waterproof hatch that opened to the corridor had been firmly dogged. Whoever the thoughtful party had been who had remodeled it, he'd forgotten to leave a handle on the inside.

The room was naked of fixtures or furniture. Sid squatted in one corner, a tired look on his face. His hands were limply propped on his knees, wrists protruding from his rumpled suit coat. Standing above him, Lymon could see Sid's scalp beginning to gleam through sparse dark hair on the top of his head. God, Sid was too fucking young to be going bald.

"Sorry I got you into this," Lymon told him hollowly.

"Wasn't your fault, boss. I sent Christal to you, if you'll recall." He smiled sheepishly. "Funny thing about Christal. Shit just happens around her. But for her, we'd have never found the lynchpin that tied my geneticists to your tampon theft. It's like—hell, I don't know—she's some sort of lightning magnet, you know?"

"Believe me, I've been figuring that out." Lymon paced anxiously back to the door, shoving on it with all his might. That did him about as much good as dining on dinosaurs.

Lymon felt a faint vibration through the hull and a subtle shift in his balance. They were moving. Headed where? Farther out to sea where the bodies wouldn't be washing into the shipping lanes like Nancy Hartlee's?

Sid said, "You know, I believe that story about her grandma being a witch. It has to be some deep-seated occult thing. Nobody else could draw this much shit down." He frowned. "Assuming Christal's here."

"She's here. Her kidnappers are here, which means they probably brought her here." Lymon smacked the thick hatch with the meaty bottom of his fist. "No, actually, I hope she's someplace else. This is starting to look a little grim. You felt this thing start to move?"

"Yep. And I don't think they're headed in to the navy pier in Manhattan, either." A pause. "How do you think they got onto us so fast? Neal Gray?"

"Maybe. Hell, it could have been Hank. He might have seen us come aboard." Lymon shook his head. "They were ahead of us from step one. As soon as they had us separated, they took Sheela. Then, when they had the other clients safely out of the way, they swept us up like bugs on a waxed hardwood floor."

Sid smacked his lips, the frown deepening on his forehead. Finally he asked, "So, what do you think they're going to do with us?"

"What can they do to us? Charge us with bringing guns aboard?" Lymon slapped his arms to his side, lying: "Nah, my guess is that they're putting pressure on Sheela, and when it's all finished and she agrees to whatever they want, we'll be bundled aboard that launch and sent back to shore."

Sid gave him a flat look.

"What else can they do?" Lymon cried, trying to believe it himself. "You're an FBI agent. People are going to be missing you. There's a kidnapping involved. *Sheela* is here. They've got to cut some kind of deal with her. Whatever it is, we'll be part of it."

"Uh-huh." Sid stared at his hands, expression tight. "You know, I never did right by Claire."

"What the hell brought that in out of the blue?"

"I should have treated her better." He looked away. "She always hated DC."

"So, when you get out of here, move someplace else."

"I will." But he said it flatly, then looked up. "Lymon, let's be honest, shall we? We know an awful lot about them. Who their people are, what they're doing."

"You're a federal agent. They won't mess with you."

"Joe Hanson, one of the guys at the WMFO, was taken out when I first got assigned there. Held hostage for a couple of days; the bad guys liquored him up and drove him off a cliff. Being an agent isn't always sacrosanct."

"Sheela will work it out." Lymon rubbed the back of his neck. "It's going to mean a chunk out of her hide, one way or another, but she'll do it."

"And then?"

"You and I will spend the rest of our lives worshiping at her feet. I don't know what they'll ask of her, but you can bet it won't be easy."

Sid was watching him. "She'd do that? Sell her soul to save us?"

Lymon sighed, nodded reluctantly, and sank down on the cold steel floor beside Sid. "You don't know her like I do. It's the price she's always had to pay to do what had to be done. She gives up little pieces of her soul for other people all the time. Most of them, like Rex, are sophisticated cannibals who devour her bit by tiny bit. It's a wonder she's not a hollow shell these days."

"Yeah, well, I hope for both our sakes that you're right."

For long moments Lymon fixed his gaze on the endless white of their tiny cell. "It's all backwards. I'm supposed to be saving her. It's my job."

Silence.

Sid softly asked, "You think Christal's all right?"

"Yeah." But he didn't mean it. "How'd Hank Abrams end up being such a shit?"

"Bad genes."

They stared at each other for a moment.

"The guy's always been an asshole!" Sid exclaimed. "You

just cut an asshole a little more slack if he happens to be on your team."

"What turned him to the Dark side?"

"Money, ambition, the chance to screw Christal . . ." Sid went white. "Shit, you don't think . . ."

Lymon pursed his lips. "Maybe. It's a crummy world. Assuming we're all dropped someplace with our hearts still beating and allowed to go home, we're going to have to treat those ladies with a great deal of compassion and care."

"You think that's the price of our freedom?"

Lymon studied the calluses on his hands. "If that's what it takes to buy our freedom, Sheela will go through with it. But what about later? What do you say when you're looking her in the eyes? 'Thank you' sounds a little trite. Where do you find the words to tell them the things in your soul?"

"Beats me."

They stared at the walls in silence then, waiting, for . . . what?

"Think they'll ever feed us?"

"Hank didn't strike me as a compassionate, caring kind of guy."

Lymon took a deep breath and closed his eyes. He just sat, one finger on the pulse in his wrist. He was fully aware of each beat of his heart. How much longer was he going to be able to enjoy that sensation?

Truth was, Sid had a high probability of being right. It would be just as easy to march them to the railing in the middle of the night, pop a cap into each of their skulls, and let them drop over the side. As to Sheela, she could disappear into some mansion in the Yemeni back country, and no one would be the wiser. Christal? For all he knew, she'd already fallen prey to something terrible.

He was so lost in his thoughts he didn't hear the greased dogs on the hatch slide back. It was Sid's elbow that brought him to his feet. He started and gaped.

Christal stood in the open hatch, a heavy bag hanging from one hand. She was decked out in a too-tight white nurse's uniform. Grinning, she said, "Hi, boss. Hi, Sid. So, tell me, did I miss much?"

As Christal swung the heavy bag across the room to Lymon, she said, "I found that on a table in the security center. All those guns and a flash-bang! I'd never have guessed they were yours except for the billfolds, and I'd know Sid's lock-picks anywhere."

"How the hell did you find us?" Sid cried, stepping forward to throw his arms around her.

"I was having the most fascinating talk with a guy named Vince up in the security center. Did you know that they've got the most incredible system of cameras and microphones on this boat? You can hear a mouse fart three decks away."

She watched Lymon work the slide to check the round in the chamber, and then shove the HK into its underarm holster.

Sid—grinning from ear to ear—let her loose, asking, "Are you all right?" as he took his turn at the bag. He grinned as he stuffed his precious lockpicks and his billfold into pockets. Last came a set of keys, a small Maglite, and a Spyderco folder.

"Fine, but we'd better be rolling. We're two decks down from the security center. It's not far, but it's still dicey. I could have left you here, safe, but I took a chance on springing you when I did. It's a gamble either way."

"Where's the other gun?" Sid asked as he shoved his billfold into his back pocket.

"I've got it. Let's beat feet." She turned, starting down the corridor and pulling the HK Compact from her right hip pocket. "This isn't a sure thing by any means. A whole lot of shit could still come down."

"Where are Hank and his goons?" Lymon asked from behind her.

"Right now they're in a strategy session with the Sheik. Sheela was up in his stateroom, or whatever the hell you call it. It's like a castle atop the A Deck behind the stack. Pretty ritzy place, I'd guess. It's also the only place on this hulk that isn't wired."

"You saw Sheela?"

"Yeah." Christal shot a hard look over her shoulder. "She looks a little wobbly. Just a guess, mind you, but I think they're keeping her disoriented, maybe as a means of softening her up, or maybe it's just for security reasons."

"How long have you been here?" Sid asked.

"Seems like forever. I don't know. Last thing I remember was going home with groceries in LA, seeing Hank behind me on the steps, and *bam!* waking up here."

"They just let you wander around?" Lymon asked as he stuffed things from the bag into his pockets.

She gave him the look she reserved for idiots, and added, "Boss, if they catch any of us, they'll shoot first and ask questions later."

Lymon was eyeing the cameras they hurried past.

"It's all right," Christal told him. "As long as our luck holds, no one's at the monitors. But we sure as hell don't want to loaf."

"What about your friend, Vince?" Lymon shot a fast glance back the way they'd come. "I've had conversations with him before. He didn't seem like the fun and forgiving kind."

"He's having a very close-up and personal encounter with a roll of duct tape." She led them up a stairway. "Boss, there's one thing you need to know."

"Lay it on me."

"No matter what happens, no matter to whom it happens, we've got to keep them distracted for another hour and fifteen minutes. Do you understand?"

"What happens in an hour and fifteen minutes?" Sid asked.

"If we last that long, life is going to get really interesting for Genesis Athena."

Christal trotted up a second stairway, took a hard right, and stopped at a thick steel door marked SECURITY. "Pray for a miracle," she muttered, raising the pistol with one hand

W. MICHAEL GEAR

and pushing with the other. A thick fold of paper fell away as the door swung inward.

"Whew!" she exhaled as she stepped through, covering the room with the powerful HK pistol. "Nobody here but us mice. Get the door, Sid. Make sure it's closed." She stepped over to where she could see Vince behind one table. He still looked like a silver pupa. Behind the other, Gregor McEwan stared up from the duct tape like a bug-eyed worm.

"What's this?" Lymon had the fold of paper in his hand.

"To keep the door from locking behind me."

Sid and Lymon were staring, wide-eyed, at the entire wall covered with monitors showing various views of the corridors, decks, and hatches. Here and there, images flipped from one scene to another as someone walked into the camera's eye.

"Sid," she called, "keep an eye on the monitors. The security hatch is the one in the upper left. Holler if anyone tries to get in. Vince wouldn't tell me whether anybody can open the door. It's got a lock plate on the outside, and who knows how many people have the code."

"Neal Gray for sure," Lymon said, striding up to look down at the bound and gagged men. "Friends of yours?"

"That's Vince," she said, pointing. "He's the one who looks like a silver mummy. Sort of handsome, actually, but you can only see his eyes. He's got a short beard, but I'm betted three-to-one odds that most of it goes when someone finally pulls the tape off."

Vince's eyes rolled in an unsettled manner, and he made mumbling sounds through the little hole where his nostrils weren't covered.

"And this is?" Lymon indicated the second man.

"Meet Dr. Gregor McEwan. Late head of the Genesis Athena genetics program."

"McEwan?" Sid asked, looking up from the huge bank of monitors. "Scottish? Midthirties, light brown hair, brown eyes, kind of a round face?"

"That's him."

"Yahoo! He's one of my kidnap victims!"

"Not anymore. He changed sides." Christal tapped her pistol meaningfully as Gregor watched.

Lymon studied the security system, looking from the monitors down to the knobs. "Where's Sheela?"

"One of the nurses was wheeling her down to her room last I saw." Christal glanced up. "Time was short. You were closer and didn't have an armed guard following behind you."

Lymon tapped something into the computer and muttered, "Whoops" when the screens went dark. He hit *Esc* and they came on again.

"Don't fart around, boss," Sid growled at him.

Lymon turned to Christal. "How'd you get here?"

She sighed, fingering the polymer grip of the HK pistol. "A friend of mine gave me an idea. I was down in the high-security area when I asked him if they'd cloned any Terminators, you know, from the movie? He said no, but I remembered Linda Hamilton sticking a needle full of drain cleaner into a bad guy's neck. So the next time Gregor came in, we stuck a needle into his side, and he walked us out. I was playing his girlfriend in the elevator when I saw him staring hopefully at the security camera."

"So you came here first?" Lymon asked.

"We couldn't do anything until we controlled the security center. Gregor very persuasively talked Vince into opening the door." She gestured at the monitors. "This is the high ground, boss."

"You said you had a partner?" Sid asked.

"Yeah, Brian Everly, he's—"

"The Australian geneticist?" Sid asked, turning. "The guy who disappeared from Australia?"

"Yeah, that's him." She lifted an eyebrow. "Nice guy, too. For the time being, he's cooling his heels and staying out of trouble in—"

"Whoa!" Lymon interrupted, pointing. "Bad guy alert! We've got movement! That's Neal Gray, and there's our friend Hank Abrams stepping into the elevator along with the redhead."

Christal followed his finger to a monitor displaying a group of people as the elevator doors slid shut. "The woman is April Hayes. She's my Copperhead from LA. They're kind of the Genesis Athena brain trust for covert operations."

They watched the monitor as the cage descended. Christal felt her gut tightening as she studied the faces. At that moment, a white dot appeared at the corner of the screen, and Sid cried, "Got it!" He was fiddling with a mouse on a pad beside the control board.

A half second later, the image shifted to the big central screen and the audio kicked on.

Neal Gray was saying, "... *Depends on Marks. In the meantime, April, I want you to run down to H Deck and find out where McEwan is. It's not like that asshole to miss a meeting.*"

"*On my way,*" April said as the elevator door slid open. Text at the bottom of the screen told them the cage was on C Deck.

Abrams and Gray stepped out, and Christal saw them emerge onto one of the smaller monitors.

"Which one do we follow?" Sid asked.

"Go for Hank and Neal," Lymon replied.

"I'll keep an eye on Copperhead." Christal watched as the monitors shifted. Hayes rode the lift down to H Deck and stepped out. The image on the monitor constantly shifted, as one by one, the complicated computer program sorted from camera to camera as it followed her the short distance, and around the corner. Christal watched Copperhead approach the security entrance and ring her way through.

Hayes stopped short in the box, staring through the glass at Max. Her mouth worked, and Max spoke in reply, hunching his shoulders as if in confusion.

Hayes frowned, asking something further.

Max bent down, fingers running over the control board as he watched the various monitors to either side. After a moment, he shook his head.

Christal could almost read Copperhead's lips as she said, "Then where is he?"

"Trouble, people." Christal straightened as Max lifted a phone to his ear and punched a number. The phone by Lymon's left hand bleated.

"That's Max," Christal said. "He's calling, trying to find out where Gregor is."

"So?"

"So, answer it! Pretend you're Vince and say that Gregor went to his quarters to boff his sweetie."

"What makes you think I can sound like Vince?" But Lymon was already lifting the receiver, saying in a bored voice, "Security center, what do you need, Max?"

Lymon listened as Christal watched the face on the monitor. Max looked slightly puzzled, but was talking.

"He's in his quarters doing his girl." Lymon spoke with a slight wryness to his voice. After a pause, he said, "Got me." And hung up.

Max was staring thoughtfully at the phone; then he looked straight into the monitor, as if trying to see behind the camera. Christal would have given anything to hear what he said to Copperhead, who in turn stared up at the camera with thoughtful eyes.

"Can we switch this?" Christal asked.

"Wait." Sid was watching Abrams and Gray as they entered what appeared to be a lounge. A big conference table was surrounded by chairs. Several men, Arab from their looks, sat drinking sodas, smoking cigarettes, and talking. They looked up when Hank and Neal entered.

"*Heads up,*" Neal said as he stopped at the table. "*We've got a situation developing.*"

"There's got to be a way to listen to both monitors at once!" Christal growled as she stared impotently at the keyboard controls. Glancing up, she watched as Copperhead stepped out of the controlled entrance and fiddled with a lock plate. Before the camera went dead, Christal got a glimpse into the control room where Max was sitting. The screen obligingly switched to an Arab woman scrubbing a section of I Deck.

"Damn!" Christal knotted a fist, glaring at the monitor.

"We don't know yet what our options are going to be. Marks may or may not cooperate. If she doesn't, the police are going to find her drugged to incoherence in her hotel room in Jamaica. We'll leave enough cocaine scattered around to keep her and her lawyers entertained for a decade."

"What about her security?" one of the Arab guys asked.

"We haven't decided that yet. If they can't be bought off cheaply, it may be more economical for the LAPD to find a stash of drugs in Bridges' house. They'll tie it to Marks' Jamaican binge. We can accomplish that for as little as ten thousand paid to the right people."

"Sons of bitches!" Sid bellowed.

"I need to get Copperhead back," Christal said, frantically reaching down to tap the *Backspace* button on the control keyboard. Nothing happened. She could hear Vince snickering against the tape from behind the table. For an instant she considered walking back and booting him real hard in the ribs, but gave it up as the sound of a pager came through the speakers. On-screen Neal Gray reached for his small belt radio.

Copperhead's voice barked from one of the control room speakers, saying, *"Neal? Cracked Castle. Go now."*

They watched Neal switch channels on his belt radio before lifting it to his ear. After saying, *"Yeah," "Uh-huh,"* and *"Keep me informed,"* Gray turned, saying to Abrams, *"April and Max can't find Anaya. They think she's out with Everly and McEwan. She and Max are reviewing the tapes right now."*

Hank frowned, lifting his own belt radio and pressing a button. Hank's voice asked, "Vince?" from the speaker.

Lymon gave Sid a knowing glance and picked up the microphone, saying, "Security, Vince."

Christal heard Hank ask, *"Do you have the location of . . ."* Hank frowned on-screen, glancing up as if to stare at them through the monitor. *"Who is this?"*

"Vince," Lymon said in a bored voice. "Just like every day at this time. What do you need, Hank?"

Christal was staring into Hank's eyes as his frown deepened and he lowered the phone. She could see his mind racing, trying to put the pieces together. "He's not buying it."

"Oh, shit," Lymon muttered as he set the mike back on the desk. Abrams had leaned close to Gray's ear, whispering. Then they both turned to stare up at the camera.

53

Lymon glanced around the security center as Abrams and Gray continued their whispered conversation on the main monitor, then started around the room, whispering into the ears of each of the other security personnel. As they did, one by one, black pairs of eyes turned toward the camera. The expressions were anything but friendly.

Lymon stepped to the cabinets at the back of the room, finding electrical equipment, assorted cables, and conduit in one, life jackets in another, tools and what looked like spare parts in a third, paper supplies in a fourth. Another held gas masks and protective gear. A fire extinguisher hung on a bracket beside the hatch. "Christal, when you arrived here, our guns and stuff were on one of the tables, right?"

"Affirmative. That one there." She pointed.

"But was there a big black plastic case?"

"Sorry, boss, it's already up on the bridge."

"Damn!" He slammed the last locker and glanced down at the duct-tape-swathed men. Vince had wiggled slightly to one side. From the amount of tape wrapped around him, he wasn't getting free anytime soon. McEwan just stared with a glum resignation in his worried brown eyes. Most likely considering what the Sheik was going to do to him for letting Christal out.

"If we're going to do something, we'd better be on it fast," Christal called. "Copperhead is on the move, and she's talking into her radio. It's not coming through here. Cracked Castle must be their code to change band lengths." She studied the complicated control board. "If we only knew how to use this."

"Evidently she's in contact with Gray," Sid replied, "because he's whispering into his as well."

"We're moving," Lymon decided. "We've got seconds to wreck this place and go."

"Negative," Christal said, jabbing her thumb over her shoulder. "We've got McEwan. He's a major player. Worth a bundle to us as a hostage."

"And they'll have Sheela if we don't get to her ASAP," Lymon shot back sharply.

"You go," Christal told him, reading his sudden desperation. She reached into one of the lockers he'd opened and lifted a pair of the belt radios. Pressing the button, she said, "Testing." One of the room speakers crackled and repeated it. She tossed him the belt radio. "I'll hold the fort here and try to break their communications frequency."

Sid stood, taking the other radio. "I'm with Lymon."

"No!" Lymon shot him a knowing smile. "Get the hell off this thing. Someone's got to get the facts to the authorities."

"Hurry!" Christal cried, watching the monitors. "They're headed this way. You've only got seconds."

Sid stepped to the hatch, undogged it, and leaped out into the hallway. Lymon was hot on his heels. When the heavy hatch swung shut, the lock clicked with finality. Christal watched as the security system followed their flight.

They were in the middle of C Deck. Sheela was aft on B Deck, past the security hatches. Here and there in the cameras, men were emerging from cabins and hurrying along the corridors. For the moment, Lymon and Sid seemed to have a straight shot aft, through the security hatch, and up the stairs.

So, what needed to be done? Christal studied the big hatch, her point of vulnerability. Shore it up? A thick wad of electrical cable had spilled out of one of the lockers Lymon had pulled open. This she dragged to the hatch, along with several lengths of metal conduit. She pulled out a drawer on one side and wedged the conduit behind the fire extinguisher bracket on the wall on the other. Then she used the electrical cable to lash the conduit across the hatch wheel so that it couldn't be turned from the outside. Finally she took one of the chairs, cramming it under the wheel for additional bracing.

Only then did she slip into the command chair and stare up at the monitors. Lymon and Sid were running full bore down a corridor listed as C Left on the screen.

In the screen above them two guys in suits—security from the lounge—were running the opposite way in B Left.

"I get it," Christal whispered as she studied the screens. Each level of screens matched the different decks. She was watching figures on the left side, no doubt for the port side of the ship.

She lifted the large microphone that rested to the side, and keyed it. Anyone with a radio would overhear her. "Lymon? You there?"

She watched him lift his radio. *"Here!"*

"Bogies at twelve o'clock. B Deck."

He seemed to get it. *"Roger."*

In the right-hand monitor that covered C Deck, she could see Copperhead stepping out of the elevator before hurrying down the hallway and taking a right. Christal watched the woman come to a stop right outside the security center hatch.

"Knock, knock," Christal said softly as she picked up the HK Compact, rocked the slide back to visually check the chamber, and let it slip back over the reassuring gleam of brass.

April Hayes punched a short sequence into the lock plate, saw it gleam green, and tried to turn the wheel that would open the hatch.

Christal watched the wheel move a couple of degrees before it bound tight on the electrical cable. In the monitor, April was straining against it, face in a grimace. Then she stepped back to raise her belt radio.

"Oh, my," Christal said sympathetically. "We just don't look happy today, do we?"

She glanced at the clock. They had forty minutes left. Time enough for everything to go terribly wrong.

Sheela ate like she'd been away from food for days. The nurse, Asza, fiddled with the room service cart that had been delivered to the suite. Just inside the door, Achmed stood at ease, his ominous black HK submachine gun hanging from its sling. His face remained expressionless, eyes flat.

As if I were some sort of threat! Sheela shook the thought off and continued cutting sections of steak into cubes before wolfing them. She had no idea what the future was going to bring, but the opportunity to eat couldn't be turned down. Supper consisted of creamed corn, beef steak, mashed potatoes, and lobster tail.

As she ate, she could feel herself coming alert again as her blood sugars began to rise. The last of the lethargy created by the anesthetic was wearing off. Still, she had a feeling of fatigue, as if the stress were nibbling at her bones. An unfamiliar tenderness lay deep within her belly. Aftereffects of the hormone shot?

"Why are you involved in this?" she asked Asza.

"I serve my family," the woman told her evenly. "It is a great opportunity for me. Here I am valued, well paid, and I get to see so much of the world."

"Stealing other people's souls is valued work?"

Asza looked back quizzically. "I do not steal anyone's soul." She tapped her breast. "The soul is in here."

"What of the babies you plant in other women?"

"Allah will give them each a soul of their own." Asza lifted a spoon from one of the dishes on the cart. "Would you like some more corn?"

"I want the hell out of here." She indicated the guard. "What's his purpose? To shoot me if I try to leave?"

"He is here for your protection."

"Right."

She was considering testing the limits of her protection when her door opened and two men burst into the room. Sheela froze, her fork halfway to her mouth.

"Get her up, and get her out of here!" the first, a tall blond man in an immaculate suit, ordered.

"Just who do you think you are?" Sheela demanded as the second man—younger, brunette, with a handsome face—rounded the table, waved Asza aside, and grasped Sheela's elbow.

"Ms. Marks," he said, "I'm afraid we're going to have to cut supper short."

"But I—" She was jerked to her feet, almost fell as her chair toppled backward, and was shoved forward, reeling to catch her balance.

"Get her out of here, Hank!" the gray-clad man told the younger. "To the Sheik's. Fast!"

"On the way," Hank agreed. "Asza, keep an eye out behind us. Good luck, Neal."

Asza followed behind as the young man hurried Sheela toward the door.

"You," Neal told the guard, who was looking uncertainly back and forth. "Give me a hand."

The last thing Sheela saw as she was dragged through the door was Neal and her guard upending the dinner table, spilling plates and food all over the floor. As she stumbled down the hallway, a door opened, and Wyla Smith gaped, her mouth round with surprise.

"Call nine one one," Sheela called, only to have Hank twist her arm until she screamed. Whatever was happening, it wasn't going to be good.

"Lymon! You've got goons coming your way from both directions!" Christal's voice came over the radio. *"Find a hole, if you can."*

"Roger." He glanced at Sid as they hurried down a Spartan hallway marred by sturdy-looking wooden doors. He gestured. "Try your side." And started rattling knobs on the left.

Sid grabbed knob after knob as they ran. "Here!" He found an open one on the left, leaping inside as Lymon, catching sight of the hatch opening ahead of them, pivoted on a foot and threw himself in behind Sid.

Sid clicked the door shut and leaned against it. They were both panting for breath as Lymon turned to survey their retreat. The first thing he noticed was that it looked like a small living room—the sort one might find in a mobile home. A TV in one corner was playing a daytime soap. On opposite ends of an overstuffed couch sat two women, staring wide-eyed and clearly startled by Lymon's sudden appearance. Each suckled an infant on an exposed breast.

Even as he gaped, both women pawed frantically to cover themselves, disrupting the babies, who bawled out in frustration.

"Sorry!" Lymon said, raising his hands—only to be brutally aware of the radio in one, and pistol in the other. "Security, ma'am," he made up, trying to grin sheepishly.

"Who are you?" the first young woman, a twenty-something brunette, managed. Her eyes were fixed on Lymon's pistol, as if she were staring at her own impending execution. She had the squalling baby tucked tightly against her stomach, where it kicked and punched from around the protection of her arms.

"I'm Rick, and he's Louie," Lymon lied between panted breaths. "Please, relax. This is just a training exercise."

"Where's the bogie?" Sid asked into his radio, eyes on the door.

"Still in the hall," Christal's voice returned. *"They're proceeding slowly, carefully. They've just spotted the second party and are moving toward them."*

"What model is that?" Lymon asked, indicating the brunette's infant.

She shot a quick glance at the blonde across from her, then said uneasily, "Elvis. They both are. We just delivered last week." She frowned. "You're sure you're security?"

"Yeah, Neal's got us on an exercise. Training, you know. Tactical evasion." He grinned, having almost caught his breath. "Hey, look, we apologize for just bursting in on you like this, but it's one of those 'make it up as you go along' things."

Sid was staring incredulously at the two women and there babies. "Elvis? As in Presley?"

Both women nodded, wariness barely abated.

"Yours?" Lymon asked, as if just making conversation. "I mean you both delivered in the normal way?"

Both women nodded in unison.

"Why Elvis?" Sid asked.

"He's the king," the brunette said as if that explained everything. "Look, don't you guys ever knock?" She was starting to recover. "I mean, damn! Dr. Morris said we'd have our privacy until we finished our postnatal physicals."

"Look, sorry." Lymon gave Sid a meaningful glance as he raised his phone to ask, "Central, sit-rep, please."

"Bogie is at end of corridor. One moment. You're clear for the moment. Be aware of moving patrols."

"Roger." Lymon indicated the door. "Let's go, Louie."

Sid waved toward the women. "Good luck. Hope he can sing when he grows up."

Lymon cracked the door and glanced out to find the hallway empty. Sid closed the door behind them on the way out, then asked, "Rick and Louie?"

"Didn't you ever watch *Casablanca*?"

"I prefer car chases and explosions." Then, as they ran, "You believe that crap, that those kids were Elvis knockoffs?"

"The really scary thing is, yeah, I believe it." Lymon trotted for the hatch, and grabbed the wheel, turned it. This was the moment of truth. They knew it was locked from the other direction. The dogs slid, and he stepped through, seeing an intersection of corridors along with a stairway leading up to B Deck. Evidently access wasn't restricted as you went aft. He glanced at the lock pad as the hatch clicked behind them. Going back wasn't going to be so easy.

"If our guesses are correct, we're right below—"

The radio crackled. *"Lymon! Bad news. They've got Sheela. She's one deck up. Better hurry."*

Lymon charged across the hallway, hammering his way up the staircase. He rounded the landing, heading up the last flight, and ran smack into one of the steel gratings. He could hear the ding as the elevator door clicked shut.

"Shit!" He gestured at the lock. "Get on it, Sid. Faster this time."

Sid fumbled out his lockpicks and bent to the task.

Lymon lifted the radio. "Where are they taking her? Can you tell?"

"Hang on, boss. I got troubles of my own."

* * *

Christal watched four muscular men join up with Copperhead in the corridor outside the security center. As the latter glared up at the camera, one of the men punched in the security code; then all four massed their weight against the wheel.

With a sense of desperation, Christal took a deep breath and leveled her pistol on the hatch. "No matter what," she promised, "you're not coming through."

The wheel turned, straining the cable tighter around the conduit. She could see the wheel shivering as the cable stretched, resisted, and held. The hatch remained inviolate until the men finally released it and shook their heads.

Christal sighed with relief, letting the adrenaline seep out of her muscles.

April raised her radio, changed channels, and said through the speakers, *"I assume that is you in there, Ms. Anaya."*

Christal lifted the radio. "Two things, April: One, I'll shoot the first bastard to walk through that door—assuming, that is, that you can force it. Two, before you take me out, I'll put a bullet in Gregor McEwan's head."

Copperhead's stalwart gaze seemed to burn right through the lens. *"Let me talk to Gregor."*

"I think not. Bad form and all. You might have some other silly code like 'Cracked Castle.' "

"Then how do I know you've got him?"

"Sometimes you just have to take things on faith." She smiled ironically. "Or the fact that you can't find him anywhere else in the ship."

"You know you can't win. Not in the end. Eventually you're going to run out of water, food, perhaps even oxygen."

"We'll deal with that when we get there."

She glanced at the line of monitors, watching as Lymon and Sid slid a steel grating aside to pile out onto the B Deck. Lymon turned, headed toward Sheela's quarters. Christal keyed her mike. "Lymon! Don't do it! She's not there."

Lymon slid to a halt, pausing uncertainly as he raised his radio. *"Where'd they take her?"*

"Deck A. The Sheik's."

In the hatch monitor, Copperhead was talking into her radio.

Christal felt the tension rising. "Lymon, April heard that. Beat feet, boss. Get the hell out of Dodge. Be aware that all communications are monitored from here on out."

"Ten-four." She watched as Lymon and Sid talked, then split, each running a different way down the corridor.

"So"—Copperhead's voice came through the system— *"Bridges and Harness are loose? My, but you are a pain in the ass, Anaya."* April held the radio at an angle beside her jaw, a wry look on her face. *"Are you sure you wouldn't like to go to work for us? Anyone as talented and adventurous as you would make an incredible asset to the organization."*

Christal glanced up at the clock. Shit, the second hand seemed to crawl across the face. "How much?"

"Five hundred thousand a year, plus bonuses and royalties."

"Last I heard, it was two hundred grand."

"I think we misjudged your initial worth."

"Yeah, keep right on misjudging." She watched as Lymon slid to a halt and pressed the button beside the elevator. Two men were approaching the B Deck security hatch from the forward corridor. Christal cued her mike. "Run Lymon. No time."

He turned, beating down the hallway, feet flying. It was at that moment that Neal Gray and a second man stepped out of Sheela's door. The agent who followed dropped into position, the black sub gun centering on Lymon's chest.

"No!" Christal cried, starting out of the chair.

At precisely that moment the second team rounded the corner and charged into the corridor behind him. The shooter hesitated, afraid his burst would hit his companions.

"Give up, Lymon!" Christal said woodenly into her mike. "They've got you boxed, and you were just a couple of ounces away from being hamburger."

She could see the defeat reflected on his face as he let the pistol drop and raised his hands. Gray and the others closed on him. In a knot, they hustled him along to the elevator, waited for the door, and then Christal watched Lymon being lifted to the A Deck. The last she saw, he disappeared into the Sheik's quarters.

"Well, Anaya"—Copperhead's voice came smoothly through the system—*"your assets are being whittled away. Do you still want to do this the hard way?"*

Christal glanced up at the clock. "You bet, bitch."

Sid was hurrying down C Deck, testing doors as he went. But in the monitors, Christal could see ever-increasing numbers of security personnel trotting down the corridors.

It was just a matter of time.

54

It could have been déjà vu. Once they had hustled her up to the Sheik's opulent quarters, Hank Abrams indicated that Sheela take a seat on the ornate chaise longue. The Sheik stood at his coffee machine—while light from the large windows gleamed off of his immaculate black silk suit. This time she could see his diamond cuff links as he worked the levers of the espresso machine.

"Black again, Ms. Marks?" he asked in his clipped English.

"Sure," she said warily, wishing her heart wasn't hammering against her ribs. "What's the matter? You missed my company?"

"A bit of a problem, actually," he answered. "Your people are causing a measure of distress." He glanced at her, his flat black eyes unforgiving as stone. "It will be good for us in the long run, I think. Security has become a little lax over the last couple of years. Isolation creates the illusion of invulnerability. Your arrival, auspicious as it is, is indicative that those days are now passed. Where you now intrude, so too will a curious media, authors, private investigators, and a host of others, not to mention several of our business rivals anxious to scoop one of our patents."

"I'm thrilled to be of service."

The coffee machine hissed as he filled a cup, placed it on a delicate saucer. Hank carried it across the thick carpet to her. The Sheik gave her the same smile the fat woman gave the turkey on the day before Thanksgiving. "Please, enjoy. You may not have much time."

Hank Abrams had stepped over by the door where Achmed stood at his post. Abrams had a radio to the side of his head, an intent expression on his face as he listened, and then talked. He turned. "We've got Bridges, sir. Where would you like him?"

Sheela's heart leaped. It took all of her concentration to keep her expression under control. Lymon's wry smile and sparkling eyes teased from her memory. She was going to hate to hear his muttered, "I told you so"s.

The Sheik narrowed an eye, glanced at her, and then said, "Bring him here. I want them all together in one place. I take it there has been no progress at the SC?"

Abrams might have been a battlefield lieutenant given his rod-stiff posture. "No, sir. Ms. Hayes is working on it. Apparently Anaya has the hatch secured some way."

Sheela straightened. *Christal!* So, she'd been here all along! The SC? What could that be? Sheela took a deep breath, pursing her lips as she took inventory of the ornate room. There had to be something here that she could use when the time came.

"The SC was designed to be secure against unauthorized entry," the Sheik said in a voice all the more ominous for its curious gentility. "How did she get past the hatch? Where did the error occur?"

"I don't know, sir. When this situation is under control, we'll make a very detailed analysis: how it developed—and how to ensure it doesn't happen again."

The Sheik's smile carried a predatory confidence. "I'm sure you will, Mr. Abrams. You seem quite adept at solving *past* problems."

Abrams' expression turned grim. "Yes, sir." He turned away, the radio to his ear. "Agent Hayes is currently bargaining with Anaya, sir. Do you have any specific instructions for her?"

The Sheik stepped over to stare down into Sheela's face. Marshaling all of her will, she lifted her eyebrow into an inquisitive arch.

"It's a fascinating strategic and tactical problem," Abdulla told her. "Your Ms. Anaya has some of my people, and I have some of hers. Don't you wish this was one of your movies? We would know how it ended, hmm?"

The door opened—breaking the war of wills—and blond-haired Neal led the party as Lymon was marched into the room. The grim expression on his face was one she'd never seen before: stressed, and clearly worried. Another of the security men, a flat-faced guy with a thick black beard, held an HK machine gun tight against Lymon's back. Sheela stood, her cup of coffee in hand. Thank God he looked all right. When their eyes met, she couldn't help drawing a breath. A glittering desperation lay behind his eyes.

It was unlike him. What did he know that she didn't?

With a stiff hand Neal shoved Lymon backward into one of the overstuffed chairs that lined the paneled wall. "If he so much as gets out of that chair, Aziz, you shoot him, understand?"

Aziz jerked a quick nod and grinned as he hovered over Lymon's left shoulder, the HK's suppressor inches from Lymon's head.

Sheela knew that weapon, had handled it on the set of *Moon of Falling Leaves* several years before. Not exactly a box office flop, but not one of her stellar roles either, the picture had been about a housewife accidentally caught up in the drug trade. Yes, she knew the MP5. While prepping for the role, the weapons expert had given her a rundown on why it was the world's most successful submachine gun.

"Lymon?" she asked in a carefully modulated voice. "Are you all right?"

"Fine, Ms. Weaver."

"Cut the crap, asshole!" Neal Gray told him. "We know who she is, who you are, and who Sid Harness is, too."

"How about the White Rabbit?" Lymon asked. "You got him pegged, too?"

At a gesture from Neal, the guard pulled the heavy automatic weapon back and drove it hard, muzzle first, into the side of Lymon's head. Sheela heard the impact, saw Lymon's head snap sideways, and started forward.

"Stop that! Right now!" she commanded, her finger stabbing out like a knife.

The guard pulled the gun back, turning it so its black muzzle pointed at her. She felt her belly go hollow and crawly as the gaping bore centered on it.

"Enough!" the Sheik ordered as both Abrams and Gray stepped between Sheela and Lymon. Behind them she could see Lymon making a face, one eye squinting under the pain as his torn temple darkened with blood.

"You asshole!" She glared across Abrams' shoulder at Aziz, who stared emotionlessly in return.

Before anyone could react, Sheela lifted her little cup of coffee and dashed it over Gray's shoulder so that the hot liquid spattered on the guard's face.

Gray and Abrams rushed her, bearing her back to the fainting couch. After they'd flung her into the cushions, she got a glimpse of Lymon halfway to his feet, frozen as the gun-wielding Aziz glared at him over the sights. She could read rage in the Arab's bulging jaw as hot coffee dripped down his face and into his beard.

"I said, *enough!*" the Sheik barked. In a milder voice, he said, "You do like to take chances, Ms. Marks."

"You and your people," she told him as she gathered herself into a sitting posture, "are just digging yourselves in deeper."

The Sheik glanced at Lymon and snapped his fingers. "Attend to him. I don't want him bleeding all over the furniture."

Sheela could see the first stream of red leaking down from Lymon's temple and along the line of his jaw. He gave her the faintest shake of the head, as if warning her against any further foolishness.

She ground her teeth and turned her attention to the Sheik. "What do you want from me?"

He took the empty cup and saucer from her hands and walked back to the big table in the middle of the room. "For the moment, I would like you to coax Ms. Anaya out of my security center." He shot her a long, evaluative look. "Would you do that?"

She stood again and crossed her arms defiantly. "Why the hell should I?"

"Let us say that by doing so, you will be fostering trust, yes?" He cocked his head, a spider's smile on his lips. "And, you must admit that just as I and my people are, as you say, 'digging ourselves in deeper,' so are you and yours."

"What's the trade?" she asked, narrowing her eyes as Abrams stepped out of the bathroom with a damp washcloth in his hand and started dabbing at Lymon's head.

The Sheik stared thoughtfully at her. "Your lives, Ms. Marks. The chance for you to go on and make movies. Even for Mr. Bridges to continue to work in your employ. You might actually have the opportunity to enjoy this relationship you have just begun. I hear it's been platonic until now."

How could he know that? She stiffened, a flicker of anger glowing against the cold fear inside her. "My personal life is none of your business."

His fingers rolled her empty coffee cup back and forth on its saucer. "Your actions directly affect the value of your genotype. For instance, if you take up prostitution on Santa Monica Boulevard, you will destroy the market for your embryos."

"Then maybe you had just better let us go while I can still maintain my value."

The smile died on his lips. "That is indeed one option. But, by doing so, I must have assurances that you and your people would not dedicate yourselves to impeding Genesis Athena. Can you promise that? Hmm?"

He read her defiant expression and laughed. "Ah, yes, that's what I thought. So, you see, when it comes to perceived value, other strategies might prove to be more effective. Perhaps if your bodies were found in a small rental yacht adrift off the Florida Keys? Shall we say, asphyxiated by an unfortunate leak from the exhaust system?"

Sheela searched his hard black eyes. He meant it! She hurried to say, "No more movies, that way. No future for your investment."

"That is correct; we would just have to make do with the Sheela Marks legend, and hope, as with Marilyn Monroe, that a death cult of fascination developed." He gave a faint shrug. "Genesis Athena's marketing abilities are substantial, and in many ways, virtually untapped. Handled correctly, given just the right spin in the media, you might just be worth a great deal more to us dead than alive."

Sheela felt a cold rush travel down her spine. "You'd never get away with it."

"No?" He chuckled softly as he worked the levers on his coffee machine and filled yet another of the cups. "I suppose I wouldn't have much chance of obtaining Sandra Bullock's DNA from her bedside either. And I'd never manage something as impossible as obtaining your menstrual tissue from the ladies' room at a crowded Hollywood gala."

"Let's cut the bullshit, shall we?" Lymon was pressing the blood-soaked washcloth to his temple, keeping pressure on the wound. "Let's look at this as a business proposition, okay? Killing us involves a lot of risk and expense. Any way you cut it, it's complicated. Kill us now, and you have to move the bodies to the scene. If you decide to kill us there, you've got to transport us alive, and hope nothing goes wrong. As the complexity rises, so does the probability for a fuckup. Stupid small things can go wrong. Stuff you can't plan for. Some pump jockey might recognize one of your people when he's fueling the yacht, or you might have a flat tire at an inopportune time while transporting the bodies. Maybe the Coast Guard picks that moment to do a safety inspection. In the real world, shit happens. Why take the chance?"

"Yes, and?"

"You want our silence and cooperation," Lymon said with a slight shrug. Water from the washrag was mixing with his blood, sending pink ribbons down his neck. "We want to go back and take up our lives where we left off."

"How do I know you will do that?"

Lymon's smile was bitter. "Because you've won. We all know that."

"Lymon!" Sheela cried. "What's the matter with you?"

He said in an offhanded manner, "Sheela, what's the point? The Sheik's outfit is big, well funded, and superbly organized. You can't stop it, so you might as well make the best of it. Trust me on this."

Confused, she tried to understand. Was this really her Lymon? Or had that blow to the head taken something out of him? Rattled his brain? Perhaps given him a concussion or something?

"What do you have in mind?" Neal Gray asked.

Lymon broke eye contact with Sheela, giving a nonchalant shrug. "Say you ship Sheela, Sid, and Anaya back to the mainland, and keep me for insurance. In the meantime, I'll get on the phone to Rex Gerber, Sheela's business agent, and tell him we're buying into Genesis Athena. Say he sends you a check for maybe . . . two million? We put that in an escrow account under both of our names."

Sheela stared, openmouthed, then cried, "What the *hell* are you doing, Lymon?"

"It's business," he told her bluntly, then directed his remarks to Gray. "Sheela and the rest go back to living their lives. Sid writes up a negative 302—that's the FBI's brand of favorite paperwork—and everything's back to normal."

"Lymon, I *won't* have anything to do with this!" Sheela told him sharply.

"Sure you will," he answered, as if willing her to obey, "because I'll stay here. If you guys break your agreement, the Sheik can do whatever he wants to with me, and can withdraw the two million to boot."

"No!" Sheela brazenly walked over to look down at him. She ignored the guard's angry stare. Beads of coffee still gleamed in the guy's beard. "I see what you're doing. No, Lymon. You're not buying my life with yours. We'll do this together, whatever it is."

"Touching," Hank Abrams said, his radio still to his ear.

"But it appears that our people have cornered Sid Harness. He was in one of the crèches. They're bringing him up now."

Sheela could see Lymon's expression tightening.

"Ah," the Sheik said amiably, "it appears that the only problem remaining is Anaya. Let's solve that, shall we?"

"How, sir?" Gray asked. "She's barricaded in."

"It seems that we have all of her people. Perhaps it is time to use them."

"Mffffutt!" Vince called.

Christal rolled her chair back, turning to see him as he struggled against the tape. No way he was getting free. She shifted in her chair and returned her attention to the wall of monitors. In the big central screen, April waited calmly in the hallway, her radio to her ear. The four goons were standing around and giving the world brooding looks that promised violence and mayhem. It had been long and fretful minutes since she'd seen Sid Harness bundled into the Sheik's quarters.

Vince made a muffled sound again. Since nothing was happening outside, Christal stepped over, bent down, and ripped the tape from his mouth. He screamed at the mustache hairs that went with it.

"You got a problem?" she asked.

"God, that hurt!"

"Besides that?"

"I gotta go to the bathroom."

"Right." She slapped the tape back across his mouth. "Go ahead. I won't watch."

Before returning to her seat, she checked Gregor's tape and made sure he wasn't working anything loose. He stared up at her with pleading eyes.

"You okay?"

"Mffft!" The tape worked under his nose.

"You know, you and Vince have the same accent."

She slipped into her chair just as Lymon's face formed on

one of the monitors. *"Christal? You there?"* His voice came over the speaker as he spoke into one of the radios.

"Here, boss. What's the situation?"

"We're putting the final touches on a deal."

"Let me guess. The Sheik and all his companions in sin deliver themselves to us in cuffs with signed confessions, right?"

"This isn't the time for your questionable humor." Lymon's eyes narrowed. *"I want you to get ready to leave the security center. You will proceed under guard to one of the hatches, where you and Sid and Sheela will be taken by boat back to the mainland. After that, you will take a charter flight back to LA."*

"And what happens to you?"

"I'm staying here for the time being."

"Hostage, eh?"

"Volunteer," he corrected.

She glanced up at the clock. "Sorry, sir. I can't do that."

"It's an order, Christal."

"Yes, sir. But, as of this moment, consider me to be fired. Or I resign. Whatever."

"Christal, I'm dead serious. I want you out of that control room."

She stared at his face, reading his desperation. The hair on one side of his head was mussed and damp. The flesh looked swollen, and if she wasn't mistaken, weren't those blood-stains on his collar?

She keyed the mike. "Lymon, you're speaking under duress. Since I'm no longer in your employ, I've got to make my own calls. I think you understand the stakes here."

"Christal, you've got to trust me. It's over. We've all come to an agreement. Everyone's happy with it, so I want you to leave the control center now." A pause. *"Christal? Christal? Can you hear me?"*

Hank Abrams stepped into view, moving Lymon to one side and taking the radio. *"Hey, Christal, what's happening?"*

She keyed the mike. "Not a hell of a lot—which is how I like it. I was just sitting here watching Copperhead on one of the monitors. She and her goons are looking a little upset.

You might want to come up and offer some comfort and consolation."

His eyebrows twitched in the familiar way they always did when she annoyed him. *"The time for banter is up. You know, we could get nasty about this, but Christal, you don't want to pay the price if we do."*

"Why's that?" She glanced up at the clock.

"Because it's real hard to live out the rest of your life remembering the look on Mr. Bridges' face when I put a bullet in his brain. That's going to weigh on you, Christal. It's going to fill your nightmares until the day you finally die." He smiled into the camera. *"Take a moment. Think about how it will be. For the rest of your life you'll see it as I raise a gun to his head. That interminable instant will pass, and—bang! You'll replay that in your dreams, in all your waking moments. It will be your own private hell, Christal."*

"Go fuck yourself, Hank."

"You sure you want to play the hard-on when people's lives are at stake?"

She nodded, then glanced up at the clock. Something was wrong. It should have happened by now.

"Christal? You just going to let him die?"

She caught the faint whiff of something sweetly metallic and clamped a hand to her nose. Turning, she could see Vince's head lolled to the side, his eyes half-closed, chest rising and falling.

She leaped from the chair, lungs starting to burn, and found the open locker. Bending, she pulled out one of the gas masks, fumbled at the straps, and found the filter cartridges in separate containers in a box. Her heart was pounding, lungs sucking at the base of her throat as she ripped one of the cardboard boxes open and unscrewed the filter canister.

She got the round canister inserted, its neoprene seal tight, and screwed the canister closed.

God, help me! She fought the urge to take a deep breath, to expel the sour air in her lungs as she fumbled the thing over her head and tried to adjust the straps.

In desperation, she clasped the mask to her head and gasped, stumbling to her chair and flopping down. The mask had a rubbery smell. She blinked her eyes and tried to determine if her senses were impaired.

Yes, sleepy—she could feel it—and stood, walking slowly to and fro, slapping her arms to her sides, willing herself to stay alert.

In the monitors, Hank was talking, his expression filled with that earnestness she'd once associated with optimism. She shook her head, feeling the tendrils of lethargy at the edge of her mind.

Picking up the mike, she said, "Can you hear me?"

"Sure, Christal. You're muffled but audible," Hank replied. *"Now, did I make my point?"*

"Sorry, Hank." She smiled wryly behind the mask. "I was a little busy." She could see April and her goons stepping back as a small acetylene welder was rolled into position by the door. "Hank? You'd better tell your sweetie, Copperhead, that I'll shoot Vince the second they put that torch against the hinges."

"What are you talking about?" Hank's face had turned serious again.

"I'm talking about shooting one of my hostages. You torch my door, I'll shoot Vince. You shoot Lymon, I'll shoot McEwan. *Qué lástima.*"

He seemed to be thinking; then, with a smile, he lifted the radio. *"You and I just got crossways, Christal. It doesn't have to stay that way, you know. We used to be friends. I genuinely liked you. What's changed?"*

"Remember when they sacrificed my ass over the Gonzales case? Did I hear you say a word in that hearing? Huh? Anything to indicate that you were just as culpable as I was?"

"Yeah, I know." He glanced up, concentrating on the monitor. *"It was Marsha."*

"Give me a break! You weren't a human being because of Marsha?" She could feel her thoughts starting to clear. Maybe she hadn't gotten nearly the dose that had laid Vince and Gregor out on the floor.

"Neal made some phone calls. Did you know that Marsha's firm represented several of Gonzales' accounts?"

She stopped short, frowning behind the mask. "No. I didn't. Why didn't you? She was your wife."

"She never told me her business."

"So how'd she get the camera into the van?"

"Turns out she dropped by just before we went on shift. Said she was looking for me. Tom Paris let her in. When she left, she said not to say anything, that she'd be back later and wanted to surprise me. My guess is that Tom didn't think anything about it. Then, when the shit started to come down, he kept his mouth shut. Or she found a way to help him keep his mouth shut."

"Son of a bitch!"

"Yeah." She could hear the question in his voice. *"Good old Marsha. Fucked us all. You, me, even the Bureau. Hey, you know, when this is all over, we could go pay her a visit, just you and me."* A pause. *"You ever think of that?"*

"Your playmate, April, might disapprove." Christal looked at the monitor where the hall gang—as she'd come to call them—waited with their cutting torch.

Christal watched as April lifted her radio and said, *"It's not working, Hank. It's been more than enough time. That change in her voice, it wasn't the gas."*

"Bingo! Five points to Copperhead." Christal glanced up at the clock, shaking her head. What the hell had gone wrong? "Whatever kind of shit you're pumping in here, you'd better hope it doesn't kill Gregor and Vince. I didn't put a mask on either of them."

She could see the irritation in Hank's eyes. *"Then I guess we're back to shooting Lymon; and after that, Sid's next."*

"You're not thinking, Hank. You shoot Lymon, I shoot Vince. You shoot Sid, I shoot Gregor. Then what? You going to shoot Sheela? Are you sure you want to run the stakes up that high?"

He stepped back, dragging Lymon into the picture. He lifted a stainless HK 40 that she recognized as Lymon's and placed it against Bridges' temple. His thumb flicked the control lever to the fire position. *"What's it going to be, Christal?"*

She pressed the key on the mike, saying, "Go fuck yourself, Hank." Then she closed her eyes, a miserable sense of failure and premonition crashing down on her soul. It was past time. They'd failed. The witches were going to win.

55

Sheela stared in disbelief as Hank Abrams raised his gun to Lymon's battered head. Hank's expression was pinched, hollow-eyed, as if he himself couldn't believe what he was about to do.

Achmed held the camera as if it were a grail, his hands cupped about it to make sure it took in the whole image. He'd laid his MP5 on the table, ready to reach.

"It will be a shame to ruin that piece of carpet," the Sheik said from the side. "And please, back him up against the wall. That caliber bullet will probably blow the back of his skull out, and it will be easier to clean up if the wall stops most of it."

"No!" Sheela cried, starting forward. Aziz cut her off, his eyes promising something nasty. She could see blisters on his face where the coffee had scalded.

"For God's sake!" Sid said where they'd placed him in the corner. "Let me talk to Christal! I can reason with her."

Lymon suddenly smiled as he stared into the camera and shouted, "Go for it, Christal! God bless you!"

"Inshallah!" the Sheik muttered. "Just *shoot* him! We'll clean up later."

Sheela bent down and sank her teeth into the hand that clasped her shoulder. As the guard howled and flung her aside, she barely noticed Neal Gray, a look of amazement on his face as he stared out through one of the large windows.

"What the hell?" Gray said, taking another step toward the glass.

Sheela scuttled back and fell, hearing Aziz roar as he grabbed for her.

"Kill him!" The Sheik took another step toward Hank Abrams and raised his fist. "Do it! Or do I have to do it for you?"

From the floor, Sheela reached out, crying, "No! Lymon! No!"

Sweat had started to bead on Abrams' face, and he slowly shook his head. His hand wavered, and he lowered the pistol. "No," he said. "Not me."

Sheik Abdulla uttered some terrible curse in Arabic and wrenched the pistol out of Hank's hand before thrusting him backward, out of the way.

He turned to the camera, eyes fierce and hot. *"You will get out of my control room, you bitch!"* He jammed the pistol against Lymon's swollen head.

"I'll do anything!" Sheela shouted, leaping to her feet. "Whatever it takes to—"

"Fuck!" Gray shouted. *"I don't fucking believe this!"*

In the brief instant before the room lurched sideways, Sheela would have sworn she heard a crumpling sound, felt a shiver. A low rumble could be heard. Then, as if scattered by the fist of God, people were reeling, things were falling, and shouts broke out.

Amidst the clatter and crash of falling dishes, crystal, and breaking glass, Sheela scrambled for balance. Loud snaps, like breaking wood, split the air. The great table slid, folding up thick Persian carpet like crinoline. Huge and heavy, it came within inches of crushing her against the trembling wall. She would remember the crazy sight of Achmed hitting the wall headfirst to slump in the wreckage. The Sheik and Lymon staggered, slammed into the wood-paneled wall, and the pistol blasted thunder into the rumbling chaos.

Earthquake! The first thought caught in Sheela's recoiling mind. She struggled against the folds of carpet that had rolled around her. The table tilted sideways, and something heavy hammered her in the middle of the back.

She reached around, feeling cold steel.

* * *

When the world canted and heaved, Lymon grabbed Sheik Abdulla, feet milling against the vibrating floor. Together they crashed into the wall, Lymon managing to raise an arm as they tottered. The pistol went off as he shoved the Sheik's gun hand up; then they fell, each twisting and struggling to find footing in the wadded carpet.

The pistol! Get the damned pistol! Lymon drove his elbow into the Sheik's side, then again, and again, as the man howled. What the fuck had happened? One minute, he'd been staring right into Death's face, eternally proud of Christal's defiance, and the next they were rolling around on the floor while a deafening rumble filled the air and the floor bucked up and down like a Humvee on a mountain two-track.

Abdulla's head rose inches from Lymon's as he tried to turn the pistol. Lymon pulled back, and jerked forward, butting his forehead into Abdulla's face. He felt and heard the bones breaking in the man's nose.

"Asshole! I'm gonna kill you!" he howled as he got one hand around Abdulla's throat. His other hand clamped on the flailing wrist below the gun hand.

The Sheik was muttering something in Arabic when Lymon's iron grip choked it off.

"What the fuck!" Hank Abrams was shouting as he picked himself up off the floor. "What the fuck happened here?"

"We're grounded!" Neal Gray screamed. "We're grounded off some damn beach!"

The Sheik hammered a knee into Lymon's crotch. He gasped, writhed, and felt Abdulla twist free long enough to gasp, "Help me!"

Lymon roared in rage, flopping his body onto the Sheik's. Another shot rang out as the man's hand reflexively pulled the trigger.

A harsh order sounded, and Lymon looked up to see the bearded Aziz, somehow on his feet in the wadded carpet, staring down over the sights of an HK MP5.

Lymon swallowed hard and nodded, letting the Sheik go.

The man flailed away from Lymon's grip and scuttled over Achmed's slumped body. In the process, he stuck his hand in the hot water seeping from the spilled espresso machine and shrieked.

Lymon rolled onto his side. The room was in shambles: shaken, not stirred. One of the marble columns was splintered, the ceiling hanging, and several of the smaller tables lay on their sides. Two of the large windows had shattered.

"Kill him!" Abdulla hissed, trying to hold the pistol and cradle his burned hand at the same time.

Lymon's nerves went cold as the guard smiled through his black beard—and flipped the safety off. A gleam filled the man's black eyes as the sound-suppressed muzzle rose above Lymon.

The staccato burst was too loud. It almost broke his eardrums, and couldn't have come from the suppressed MP5. It took a moment for his brain to catch up with the vision, but the guard's sides were jumping frantically, his eyes impossibly wide, and bits of red were making haze in the air.

Aziz seemed to weave in the sudden silence; and the heavy HK rolled out of his grasp as if in slow motion. Then his knees went. He collapsed straight down, then slipped sideways into his own gore.

In the voice that had stopped countless cinematic bad guys, Sheela Marks ordered, *"Don't even think it!"*

Lymon lifted his head to see Sheela wading out of the accordioned carpet. She held an MP5 in the finest SWAT team entry form. Her face was a mask of determination as she centered the sights on the Sheik.

"Please relieve Abdulla of that pistol." Without breaking her gaze, she asked, "Lymon? Are you all right?"

Getting to his feet, he gave her a panic-induced grin. "Yeah." And reached out to snag the pistol from Abdulla's hand. "Nice gun work. Where'd you learn that?"

"Weapons expert on the set of *Moon of Falling Leaves*. But this one shoots real bullets."

"Hey!" Sid roared as Neal Gray scrambled for the door. "One move and I take you apart myself."

Lymon tossed his pistol to Sid. "Keep an eye on him." To

the stunned Sheik, he said, "Sorry, pal, but the party's over."
He bent to slip the remaining MP5's sling from the dead
Aziz's shoulder.

Then—adrenaline pumping with the postcombat jitters—
he walked to Sheela, bent to kiss her lips, and said, "God, I
love you."

She spared him a quick smile. "I love you, too." A slight
frown. "But what the hell just happened here?"

Together, they made their way to the shattered windows.
Through the spears of hanging glass he could see a long
gleaming stretch of beach. Behind the littoral, an irregular
line of trees was cloaked in green through which the afternoon sun shone. People were already appearing on the
shore, looking small as they pointed. And yes, wasn't that a
park ranger's four-wheel-drive truck flying down the sand,
light bar winking?

"What the hell happened?" Sheela asked, her MP5 still
covering the Sheik.

"I think we just landed in New Jersey," he told her in an
awed voice.

"I've never liked Jersey," Sid muttered as he stood up
from checking the dead guard's body. "God, is my boss
gonna give me shit over this."

56

Christal sat quietly in the darkness and dangled the
weight of the gas mask from one hand. She replayed
that last instant over and over. Seeing the monitors going
black, feeling the shudder and then the jolt. Her chair had
thrown her against the control board, and the room had gone
black in an instant.

Oddly, the last monitor to go had been the one that
showed Copperhead and her four goons tumbling down the
corridor floor like broken dolls. It was even better than giv-

ing the bitch three good solid belts to the stomach! Paybacks were hell.

Then a silent and eternal night had fallen.

The worst part had been the waiting. Was Lymon alive? Had the Sheik killed him?

She smiled grimly in the darkness, and said, "Hank, you always were a wuss." She'd seen it in his eyes as he held the gun to Lymon's head. So, he'd done the right thing, but had it been for the right reasons?

A groan came softly out of the darkness. "Shit!"

"Good morning, Gregor." She wondered it if was morning. Her universe might have been stopped in time, frozen like existence at the edge of a black hole.

"What the hell? Where am I?"

"Security center."

"Turn the fucking lights on. I can't see a thing."

"Power's cut." She made a mocking face in the darkness.

"God, they've gone to that extreme? How long have I been out?"

"I haven't the faintest idea. Hours."

He shuffled in the darkness. "How on earth could I have gone to sleep?"

"Gas. Anesthetic, I think. They pumped it into the ventilation. I barely got to the gas masks in time." She smiled wryly. "Be glad they didn't use anything lethal. You'd be dead, bucko."

"You won't win, you know. They'll starve you out in the end."

"Sorry, Greg—"

"Gregor," he insisted.

"—but you've already lost."

"What?"

"You slept through being slid across the floor." She leaned back in the darkness. "I don't know how the hell they're going to get this thing off the beach."

"What are you talking about? Beach?"

"Yeah, Brian and I decided on Sandy Hook."

"What? Where's that?"

"New Jersey. It sticks up like a thumb on the south side of New York Harbor. It's a national recreation area. We thought it was perfect."

"Oh, come now! Stop the bluff."

She chuckled at the sincerity in his voice. "Greg, you've got no idea. You're through, buddy. Coast Guard is probably swarming around like fleas out there even as we speak."

"Right, lass, and if that were indeed the case"—he let his brogue deepen—"ye'd not be sitting in here on yer hands in the dark."

"Got that right. Problem is, the hatch is jammed. I tried it. You can turn the wheel, but I think the dogs are bent."

"No way!"

"Way." She took a deep breath. "Air's gone stale too. Ventilation's gone. I hear bangs and creaks every so often, but not much else. This hole's pretty soundproof. I think it was an eternity ago I heard a clang on the door. God knows what that meant."

"Assuming you're not lying through yer teeth, you think they've forgotten us?"

"That's a possibility. They might have their hands full. It was quite a jolt when we beached. Brian would have had them throttle up just before we ran aground."

"And why would the captain have done that?"

"You remember that black case that sat on the table when you first got us in here?"

"Aye."

"Turns out it belonged to Lymon. It had a Heckler and Koch subgun and some other equipment in it. Enough that the bridge crew didn't hesitate when Brian ordered them to set a new course." She paused. "I hope he didn't have to kill any of them."

"Ach, are you trying to tell me that Brian fucking Everly had the guts to commandeer the bridge? And that nobody noticed?"

"Who'd know anything was amiss?" She resettled herself in the darkness. "Look: Neal Gray, Hank, and April were intensely occupied trying to run Lymon and Sid down at the same time they were trying to pry me out of here. My only concern was the Sheik. He was the guy who had the windows, who might have been able to see what was happening and react in time to stop it." She smiled in the dark. "But God bless Sheela, she played the role of a lifetime. Kept him occupied and didn't even know it."

"So, yer telling me that we're beached in New Jersey, that you and Brian did this all on yer own?"

"*Claro que sí.* That's the way it is."

"Bullshit!"

A slight moan came from behind Vince's tape. Christal wondered if he'd ever managed to relieve the pressure in his bladder. She sniffed, but wasn't sure she'd recognize the odor of urine in the stuffy air. She might have already grown used to it.

"Why don't you pull this tape off me, and we'll both try to open the damn hatch?"

"Just lie there in the darkness and shut up."

"Go ahead. Be smug. In the end I've had the best of you, Anaya. How will you choose, you sanctimonious bitch? Will you give it life or—"

The clang was so loud she jumped. "Shit!"

"Aye. Someone knows we're here."

A slight glow turned from dark to cherry, to light red, then faded.

"What's that?" Gregor asked.

"I think they're cutting the hinges, Greg."

A lower glow could barely be made out, and then it, too, faded. Metal on metal rang out; then a grinding sound came through the steel. A high-pitched whine ended with a drill poking through and being withdrawn.

Christal grinned when a thin voice thick with Australian accent called, "Anybody alive in there?"

"Nobody but us mice," she shouted back at the hole.

"Be clear of the hatch. It's going to fall inward when we pry it."

Christal stumbled across the dark floor, feeling for Gregor's and Vince's bodies. Then she shouted, "Clear!"

The grinding sounded, and a thin line of light widened as the heavy hatch leaned, then crashed inward.

Christal blinked in the white light as Brian's tall shape stepped in, followed by two gray-clad Guardsmen.

Christal grinned as she stepped into Brian's arms. "Hey, it's good to see you."

"Good to see you, too. You all right?"

"Couldn't be better." She turned to the Guardsmen, pointing. "Those two need to be cuffed and confined ASAP. The charges are conspiracy to commit kidnapping, attempted murder, breaking and entering, tax evasion, and any kind of violation of maritime law you want to throw at them."

Then she reached up and kissed Brian Everly firmly on the lips.

57

TWO DAYS LATER

Sheela padded across the carpet in her corner suite at the Plaza. Through the windows, she could see the street below: Manhattan traffic starting and stopping, joggers making dots of color as they trotted along the winding paths visible through the trees in the park.

On the television, CNN continued to document the evacuation of the *ZoeGen* as, by groups of ten, the frightened passengers were removed, loaded into vans, and hauled off to the INS detention center for processing.

The press was in the midst of an incredible feeding frenzy. Each story that emerged fed an ever-greater appetite.

"*Information on Sheik Amud Abdulla continues to trickle in,*" the commentator said. "*Apparently, he has been a strong supporter of US policies in the Gulf, playing a hand in the pacification and rebuilding of Iraq. He has been instrumental in helping to stabilize the Gulf during building tensions with Iran. Senior White House officials are hinting that the Sheik, despite the grounding of his ship, has been cooperative and forthcoming during this investigation.*"

Dot, looking harried, walked into the room. "God, you wouldn't believe it! How do they figure these things out?"

"What now?"

"Somehow, angels alone know how, Letterman's producer has figured out that you were aboard the *ZoeGen*." Dot cocked her head. "Do you want to do the interview?"

"Tell him yes, but later. After things have settled down." She waved at the TV. "Dot, anything I say is just going to complicate matters."

Dot gave her a thoughtful look. "You understand, don't you? You couldn't *buy* better publicity."

"Good, because right now, that's the *last* thing I'd spend money on."

The frown deepened on Dot's forehead. "Tony called. I know you said you didn't want to talk to anyone, but he's on pins and needles to speak with you. I have him and Letterman holding."

Sheela made a face. "Right. Tell Letterman that the next interview I do will be his, and I'll take Tony's call here."

She walked over, settled herself in a settee beside a half-drunk cup of tea, and lifted the receiver. "Hello, Tony."

"Hey, babe! Wow! Is this some story or what, huh? Listen. I've got Soderbergh on the other line. We've been talking. You know, throwing some pitches around. He's hot to do your story. You know, the whole thing! Like from the tampon incident to you traveling incognito to snoop out Genesis Athena. It's like, name your price, babe! You can produce, whatever. Just give the word!"

"I need to think about it, Tony."

"Hey, babe! It's okay. Still too close, huh? Take a day or two to let it sit and digest. This stuff just keeps growing like mold in the refrigerator. I been talking to Benny. He thinks we can cast Patricia Velasquez to play Christal, and maybe even Tom Hanks as Lymon. Wouldn't that be a rip?"

"Tony, take a break."

"It's cool, babe. We're already working on the script. You

know, just things I know. We'll have a treatment ready by the time you land in LA."

She hung up, rubbing her eyes and trying to shake off the sense of premonition. "This is going to be a nightmare."

Dot was watching with neutral eyes. "You were the one who wanted to take a month off."

"Why the hell doesn't Lymon call?"

Dot smiled. "Listen, you're just lucky that Sid Harness managed to get you extricated from that mess. Lymon and Christal are going to have their hands full for days. They're giving statements, talking to lawyers, filling in details. Thank God you were smart enough to fly Felix out to look after them. And what about this dead guy?" Dot's face tightened. "Did you really shoot him?"

Sheela glanced up, her face like a mask. "Dot, I think you have things to do. And while you're about them, make sure that we have a plane ready the moment the government cuts our people loose."

"Yes, ma'am."

After Dot left, Sheela looked down, barely bending her right index finger. In her mind, she could feel the gun vibrating in her hands.

"A short burst," she whispered, remembering the weapons training she'd received in preparation for *Moon of the Falling Leaves*. "So short. But now, everything's eternally different."

On the TV, photos of Elvis Presley and Princess Diana were being overlaid atop the beaming faces of two little babies.

"Are these cloned children really created from Elvis Presley and Princess Diana of Wales? As of this report, we have no reaction from either the Spencer family or the Presley estate."

Sheela gasped, staring in disbelieving horror at the young woman's face on TV. Krissy was smiling into the camera, that crazy gleam in her eyes. *"Oh, yes,"* she was saying. *"I went to Genesis Athena months ago."* The camera pulled back to show Krissy pressing her hands to a swelling abdomen. *"Mine's a Sheela Marks baby! And I want everyone to know that I'm going to love her . . . the same way I love Sheela Marks!"*

For a moment time seemed to stop. Sheela pressed a hand to her mouth, stifling a scream. Then, in horror, she bolted from the room, Krissy's madly gleeful expression burned into her brain.

58

BEVERLY HILLS — TWO MONTHS LATER

"*In the end I've had the best of you, Anaya.*" Gregor's words echoed hollowly.

The cold rage had continued to grow. Christal considered that as she put the Concorde in park and killed the ignition. "*Don't go there.*" Brian's words hung in her ears.

"Got to," she muttered, aware of the coiled rage that was growing like a cancer inside her.

"*How will you choose, you sanctimonious bitch?*"

She had been raised Catholic. In the old church where the *santos* stared down from the walls. Down deep in her bones she believed in heaven and hell, in the consignment to flames of woe. The decision she now faced tore her soul in two. But the choice couldn't be made—not yet; not until she had placed her foot atop the serpent's head and heard him squeal.

"*Will you give it life or . . .*" Death? Christal finally understood the choice Gregor had left her to make.

She stepped out of her car and walked down between the manicured hedges. Her heavy hiking boots looked peculiar against the brushed cement of the walk. The place was a sprawling angular mansion of white cement, soaring windows, and great views of the surrounding mountains that gave way to the city. In the hazy distance, through the smog, the brassy gleam of the Pacific under afternoon sun could be seen.

What was the moral choice? She hated herself for having to make a decision that her upbringing, even her legal education, left her so ill prepared for. One way she was a murderer in the eyes of her church, the other, an accomplice in the propagation of sin. Or, if she went through with it, wouldn't it be a form of suicide?

It is me . . . and it is not. But, who are you, Christal Anaya? What are you?

The anger, the injustice of it, deepened as Christal stepped up to the great black door sunk in the white stucco wall. With a slim brown finger she rang the buzzer at the call box, then leaned down, announcing, "It's Christal."

"Cool, babe. Be there in a sec," Tony's voice answered.

She hung over the abyss, lost and alone, facing eternal damnation. How did one atone? She could hear Grandmother's distant voice hissing at her from somewhere beyond the grave.

Within moments Tony opened the door and stepped back. He was in a square-cut white shirt and wearing long baggy shorts. He held a margarita in each hand, offering one to her as he sang, "Da-dah! Cheers, babe! Here's to you." Then he was off, padding barefoot across the tiles. "Come on. I'm poolside, you know? It's a perfect day for it. You up for a dip?"

"I didn't bring a suit." She stopped long enough to pour the margarita into a potted plant.

"Don't need one here, babe. No close neighbors—not that they'd mind anyway."

His house was nice—the sort of thing that, as a child outside of Nambe, New Mexico, she'd have once considered to be straight out of a fairy tale. She followed him out onto the terraced poolside. A tall stone formation spouted water that flowed down a cascading waterfall to a sparkling turquoise pool. He'd been right—from where she stood, none of the neighboring places were visible.

"So, Tony, did you read the screen treatment that your writers put together on the Genesis Athena thing?"

He turned, smiling in the golden sunlight. "Yeah, dynamite, I tell you. Soderbergh's flipped over it. I mean, like, Sheela's still feeling fidgety, but she'll give in the end. This thing's gonna blow the top right out of the box office. Do you understand? Babe, there ain't never been nothing like it before! Sheela playing herself, pulling up all that rich emotion." He glanced down at her empty glass. "Wow! Sucked it down already, huh? I'll get you another."

"No." She set the glass on one of the poolside tables. Smiling, she took off her jacket. "I'm here for something else, Tony." She let her voice soften, and raised an eyebrow as her coat slipped off her fingers. "Didn't you say it was a perfect day for it?"

Tony grinned, set his own drink down, and in one fluid movement, slipped his baggy shorts off. "Yeah, it is. You know, I've been thinking. It would be way cool if you played yourself." He crossed his arms, and started to pull his shirt over his head. "You've got chops! The part—"

Christal's booted foot caught him squarely in the dangling genitals. The force of the blow lifted him off the cement, spiking a pain up her leg in the process. He screamed, staggering, trying to grab himself through the folds of the confining shirt. She stepped in close and used an elbow to hammer the side of his head. As he shrieked and screamed, she went after him: kicking and punching. Then, grabbing his staggering form, she bodily threw him through the poolside window.

The shirt ripped, leaving him blinking and moaning in the midst of the broken shards of glass. He tucked his knees to his chest, arms up protectively as he gaped up from his lime green carpet. "*Don't hurt me!* Christal? What the fuck?"

She stood over him, hands knotting, as she glared down. "It wasn't until I read the script that I knew. It was you, asshole. All the time it was you! Shit, you had Sheela's schedule, knew her every move. I couldn't figure out how Hank and Neal found me. You gave them my address, you piece of shit! And you tipped them that Sheela was onto them—that *I* was onto them! The whole time, you were ratting us out."

"No!" He tried to stand, and she took the opportunity to land a kick under his jaw. At the impact, his head snapped back, and he collapsed onto the glass. She could see little dabs of blood sopping into the carpet.

"It's in the treatment, Tony! The details of how I was kidnapped, flown across the country, and carried aboard the *ZoeGen*. How I was locked in a tiny little cabin in the secure part of the ship! Nobody knows that outside of the FBI, asshole."

He raised his hands in a pleading gesture. His eyes were unfocused, and blood was leaking out of the corner of his mouth. "Don't," he whispered. "Don't hurt me anymore! I'm sorry! I'm fucking sorry!"

In bitter rage, she hauled off and kicked him again. "You're a piece of shit, Tony. A filthy piece of stinking shit."

She turned, walked back to her jacket, and picked it up from the cement. As she started for the door, she looked down. "Nice place you have here." She paused. "By the way, I'm pregnant."

She was out the door and in her Concorde before the shakes started. She made it halfway to the main road before she had to pull over and cry.

A lazy surf rolled itself against the pure white sand. Lymon glanced out at the turquoise water and squinted from behind his sunglasses. In the distance he could just see the green mound of St. Kitts floating at the edge of the blue. The warm salty breeze ruffled his too-colorful flower-pattern shirt and teased his legs below his white cutoffs. Beside him, Sid walked barefoot, trousers rolled, head down, with his coat thrown over his shoulder. His white shirt was unbuttoned at the collar to betray his black thatch of chest hair. Lymon could see the sunlight gleaming on the incipient bald spot at the back of Sid's head.

"They still haven't found April Hayes. The best guess is that she passed herself off as a patient. Wherever she is, she's gone to ground until the dust clears."

"What's the point of hiding?" Lymon reached down and picked up a seashell before flinging it into the light surf. "Hank and Neal are already out on bail. The Sheik's jetted off to Qatar, and they've almost refloated *ZoeGen* off the beach at Sandy Hook. Hayes could have just cooled her heels like the rest of them."

"That's what I came to tell you. It's been a fucking madhouse. I've been hauled into meetings with everyone from the White House to the attorney general and the secretary of state. I've been grilled up one side and down the other. If there was a way they could twist the story, they've tried it." He glanced at Lymon. "A lot of people are really pissed about this, Lymon."

"Good, their pal Abdulla shouldn't have been acting like a sultan. Slavery went out with the Ottoman Empire."

Sid's expression soured. "That's not why they're pissed."

"No?"

"Most of them are wishing it just hadn't happened. That Everly hadn't driven that ship aground. Sure, they're pissed at the Sheik for stealing his little clones, but they're more worried about what it will do to stability in the Gulf." He paused. "Lymon, I want you to prepare yourself. My superiors are telling me in not-so-subtle ways that they're going to, and I quote, 'Try to minimize the damage.'"

" 'Minimize the damage'?" Lymon growled. "You heard the reports! Abdulla has clones of over four hundred women in his palace back in Qatar."

"They want it to go away. It's politics. He's a powerful man. I've been told over and over what a great friend he is to the United States." Sid made a face. "You seen TV recently?"

"No."

"It's one Genesis Athena ad after another. Little angelic-looking children talking about how Genesis Athena's medical miracles saved their lives." Sid rubbed the back of his neck. "The whole world knows what Genesis Athena is, what they do, and how they sell it. Hits on their Web site topped forty million last week."

Lymon fixed his gaze on the turquoise water. "I heard yesterday that Neal Gray just sold book rights for two million, and Hank Abrams . . ."

Sid gave him a look from the corner of his eye. "He could

have pulled that trigger, boss. No matter what, you can't forget that."

"No, I suppose not. I just hated to hear he'd gone on *Larry King*." He reached down to pitch another shell.

"You talk to Brian Everly?"

"No. But his embassy just kicked him loose. I heard he flew to LA first thing." Lymon paused. "Christal had an abortion yesterday. Said she wasn't sure what that would do to her immortal soul. She wasn't happy about it."

"No, I suppose not." Sid stomped a wave. "What's it called when you abort your own clone? Suicide?"

"Well, just keep your mouth shut when we get back to the villa, huh?"

"How is Sheela? She coming to grips with it?"

"I guess. Felix has filed a civil suit against Genesis Athena. During our conference call last night, he said that they're already offering a five million out-of-court settlement tied up with a billion strings."

"She gonna take it?"

"I dunno."

Sid glanced around. "You sure I shouldn't just take the ferry back to Basseterre?"

"Yeah. The place is big enough you'll probably get lost in it as it is. We won't be disturbed unless we want to be."

Sid's lips tried to smile, but failed. "You know, the whole world's looking for you two."

"Yeah, and to date, they haven't found us." He chucked another shell. "We rode to Montana on the Beemer, then caught a charter from Billings to Miami to here."

"Word is that Sheela Marks is the most sought-after interview in the world." Sid kicked at the pristine sand. "Your boy, Tony, made sure of that. I hear he's having trouble eating."

"It'll be another couple of weeks before they take the wires out. He's declined to press charges."

"I also hear that the Sheik and his investors are very pleased with Sheela's profile right now, and the last thing they want to do is upset her. You might get more than that five million."

"I'll tell the Sheik what he can do with his profile." Lymon felt his jaw muscles tensing, and a slow anger burning around his heart.

"Don't, Lymon. Let it lie. Trust me on this. Just love the lady. Hold her, and support her any way she needs it."

"Yeah."

"One last thing before we head back. Claire hates DC."

"So, move her."

"Yeah, well, you still interested in having someone help you with the IRS paperwork? I've got to give them two weeks notice, but after that . . ."

"You might give June a call."

"Yeah, I know. I've heard from a reliable source at LBA that she runs the place."

It looked like the same world, but it wasn't. It never would be. Sheela sat in the shade beside the row of soft green plants on the villa balcony. Beside her, a lemonade sweated condensation in the tropical breeze. The droplets trickled down to soak the envelope on which the glass rested. The words GENESIS ATHENA were barely legible as the ink ran. Inside, absorbing the moisture, lay the Sheik's last insult: an invoice for the balance due on her procedure.

Down the tree-covered slope, she could see Lymon, walking tall and confidently across the sand beside Sid Harness. Every once in a while, Lymon would bend and toss something into the surf.

He's alive because of me. She took a deep breath, staring out over the turquoise Caribbean water.

Yes, he was alive.

She closed her eyes, remembering the easy and languid sex they'd shared that morning before Sid's arrival. She recalled how she'd run her fingers down his sides and felt him shudder at her touch.

She had to believe that everything balanced, that the life she had taken made her love Lymon with a greater intensity. That the part of herself that had died in that blast of automatic fire had been replaced by something more profound.

Each breath that Lymon took, each pulsing beat of his heart, had been bought and paid for by her sacrifice.

She placed a hand on the form-fitting white sundress and pressed her abdomen. How could she comprehend the eight million sperm he had shot inside her? All those copies of Lymon's DNA churning about in a frenzy of futility. Even as she sat there they exhausted themselves by the thousands, frantic flagellae ceasing to thrash in her warm fluid. Energy spent, they drifted, carried relentlessly away from their goal by her dark vaginal currents. Did they surrender themselves to oblivion knowing they were already too late? Did some subtle hormone warn them that her womb was already taken?

She closed her eyes, trying to imagine what it looked like: Round, slightly rough on the outside. She could imagine it resting there against the blood-rich lining of her uterus. It had already begun to siphon energy and nourishment from her body. The first pangs of nausea had made their presence known that morning.

She still had to tell Lymon. And what would he say? That she was crazy?

No, not Lymon. But perhaps she was crazy in her own curious and odd fashion.

After an agony of indecision, Christal had chosen abortion. *I can't blame her.*

She stared longingly at the two men as they turned and began retracing their tracks on the deserted beach. Lymon was on his way back to her. No matter what, she wouldn't face this alone. The knowledge warmed her soul in a way she couldn't describe.

She had met her devils, slain them, and come out stronger for it. The future would come with its own antagonistic choices, hard questions, and difficult explanations. One by one, she would face them, deal with them. She would do it with a steel conviction, and damn the critics. Perhaps now, finally, Father could be proud of his little runaway.

She took a deep breath and pressed on the softness above her uterus, carried away by the mystery of how they had managed to do it so quickly.

She wondered if she even cared.

I am the Madonna, brought to prominence through immaculate conception. Will my daughter be divine? Or just another life? Will she share my soul, or create her own? And, if she creates her own soul, does that mean that the spark of God glows in each of us?

So what was a person? A collection of proteins and molecules in which a discrete soul would eventually find a home? A piece of herself to replace the part that had died in that machine gun burst?

God must be laughing.